W9-BSK-387

PRAISE FOR STEPHEN KING AND
DREAMCATCHER

"Big, dynamic. . . . In this craftily phantasmagoric story about dreams, telepathy, and extraterrestrials, the emphasis is less on fear than on the shared will and capacity to survive. . . . [*DREAMCATCHER* is] a busy, vigorously told, increasingly trippy story . . . [with] some very neat tricks . . . [and written] with imaginative gusto. . . . King writes more fluently than ever, and at times with simple, unexpected grace."

—*The New York Times*

"Engrossing . . . exquisitely detailed. . . . Don't start this one on a school night, kids. You'll be up till dawn."

—*People*

"A horrifying thrill ride."

—*The Times Picayune* (New Orleans)

"A book that evokes King at his harrowing best. . . . [He] infuses a standard 'aliens are among us' story line with his own brew of terror."

—*Daily News* (New York)

"King knows how to weave a story. . . . *DREAMCATCHER* displays his talents and drive."

—*USA Today*

"*DREAMCATCHER* has a little something for everyone: aliens, scary dreams, boyhood friends . . . but most of all, it tells a compelling story. . . . [It] reaches into the reader's gut, grabs those deep-down hide-under-the-pillow fears and yanks them out into the open."

—*St. Louis Post-Dispatch*

"A breathless race leading up to a denouement designed to induce nail-biting. . . . His plotting is as expert and enjoyable as ever."

—*Chicago Sun-Times*

"King remains the master of fright. . . . Arguably, John le Carré does the best and truest spies; Anne Rice, the most spectacular vampires. But Stephen King owns the things that go bump in the night. . . . This novel is King at his story-telling best. . . . He's at the top of his really big-game game."

—*The Tampa Tribune*

"There's a raw and authentic psychological underpinning to King's best novels. . . . [DREAMCATCHER has a] rough and authentic narrative power."

—National Public Radio

"King keeps the story moving on a kinetic level . . . [and] perfectly fleshes out [the] characters and their middle-age fatigue and confusion, making them real even as he subtly insinuates the supernatural."

—*The Atlanta Journal-Constitution*

"An eclectic tale . . . DREAMCATCHER pounds home the truth of our mortality."

—*The Tennessean*

"King's characters are as wonderfully woven as ever. . . . The action grips the readers' attention to the full."

—*Birmingham Evening Mail*

"You'll take a shining to Stephen King's DREAMCATCHER. . . . Enjoyably escapist. . . . An engrossing long-past-midnight page-turner. . . . King continues to scare up those goosebumps and take you by surprise."

—*The San Diego Union-Tribune*

"Mr. King's writing is more self-assured, his main characters are solid creations, and his dry Maine humor is ever-present."

—*The Dallas Morning News*

"King is still King."

—*The Sunday Gazette Mail* (Charleston, SC)

"A terrifying piece of fiction. King is a storyteller without literary peer. Every gruesome horror is illuminated in graphic detail, and just turning the pages evokes visceral reactions from palpitations to palm sweat. . . . King remains a wonderfully inventive wordsmith whose imagination continues to haunt us."

—*Dayton Daily News* (OH)

"*DREAMCATCHER* marks his bracing return to all-out horror, complete with trademark grisly gross-outs, a panoramic cast of deftly drawn characters, and a climactic race against time."

—*The Miami Herald*

"A fabulously spooky tale. . . . An ace read. . . . King's dialogue delights. *DREAMCATCHER* is a reassuring sign that more great fiction is on the way."

—*The Providence Journal-Bulletin*

"King's writing is faultless. His characters and story line are complex and thoroughly intertwined. . . . [*DREAMCATCHER* is] definitely a good read."

—*The Evening Standard* (N.Z.)

STEPHEN KING

DREAMCATCHER

POCKET BOOKS
New York   London   Toronto   Sydney   Singapore

The sale of this book without its cover is unauthorized. If you purchased this book without a cover, you should be aware that it was reported to the publisher as "unsold and destroyed." Neither the author nor the publisher has received payment for the sale of this "stripped book."

This book is a work of fiction. Names, characters, places, and incidents are products of the author's imagination or are used fictitiously. Any resemblance to actual events or locales or persons, living or dead, is entirely coincidental.

POCKET BOOKS, a division of Simon & Schuster, Inc.
1230 Avenue of the Americas, New York, NY 10020

Copyright © 2001 by Stephen King
Cover art © 2002 Warner Bros. All Rights Reserved.

Originally published in hardcover in 2001 by Scribner

All rights reserved, including the right to reproduce
this book or portions thereof in any form whatsoever.
For information address Scribner, 1230 Avenue
of the Americas, New York, NY 10020

ISBN: 0-7434-6752-3

First Pocket Books printing December 2001

10 9 8 7 6 5 4 3 2 1

POCKET and colophon are registered trademarks of
Simon & Schuster, Inc.

For information regarding special discounts for bulk purchases,
please contact Simon & Schuster Special Sales at 1-800-456-6798
or business@simonandschuster.com

Printed in the U.S.A.

Permissions

"Dying Man," © 1956 by Atlantic Monthly Co. *The Waking,* © 1953 by Theodore Roethke from *Collected Poems of Theodore Roethke* by Theodore Roethke, used by permission of Doubleday, a division of Random House, Inc.

"Scooby Doo Where Are You" by David Mook and Ben Raleigh © 1969 (renewed) Mook Bros. West & Ben Raleigh Music Co. All rights reserved o/b/o Mook Bros. West in the United States, administered by Warner-Tamerlane Publishing Corp. All rights reserved o/b/o Ben Raleigh Music Co. in the United States, administered by Wise Brothers Music LLC. All rights for the world excluding the United States controlled by Unichappell Music, Inc. All rights reserved. Used by permission. Warner Brothers Publications U.S. Inc., Miami, FL 33014.

"Sympathy for the Devil," words and music by Mick Jagger and Keith Richards, © 1968, renewed 1996, ABKCO Music Inc.

McElligots Pool by Dr. Seuss™. Copyright by Dr. Seuss Enterprises L.P. 1947, renewed 1975, reprinted by permission of Random House, Inc.

"I Am the Walrus" by John Lennon and Paul McCartney © 1967 Sony/ATV Tunes, LLC. All rights administered by Sony/ATV Music Publishing, 8 Music Square West, Nashville, TN 37203.

"Yes We Can Can" words and music by Allen Toussaint ©1970 (Renewed 1998), 1973 SCREEN GEMS-EMI INC., All Rights Reserved. International Copyright Secured. Used by Permission.

The Man Who Wasn't There by Hughes Mearns © 1925, Doubleday & Co., used by permission of Petra Cabot.

This is for Susan Moldow and Nan Graham.

DREAMCATCHER

FIRST, THE NEWS

From the *East Oregonian*, June 25th, 1947

FIRE CONTROL OFFICER SPOTS
"FLYING SAUCERS"
Kenneth Arnold Reports 9 Disc-Shaped Objects
"Shiny, Silvery, Moved Incredibly Fast"

From the Roswell (N.M.) *Daily Record*, July 8th, 1947

AIR FORCE CAPTURES "FLYING SAUCER"
ON RANCH IN ROSWELL REGION
Intelligence Officers Recover Crashed Disc

From the Roswell (N.M.) *Daily Record*, July 9th, 1947

AIR FORCE DECLARES "SAUCER"
WEATHER BALLOON

From the Chicago *Daily Tribune,* August 1st, 1947

USAF SAYS "CANNOT EXPLAIN" ARNOLD SIGHTING
850 Additional Sightings Since Original Report

From the Roswell (N.M.) *Daily Record,* October 19th, 1947

SO-CALLED SPACE WHEAT A HOAX, ANGRY FARMER DECLARES
Andrew Hoxon Denies "Saucer Connection" Red-Tinged Wheat "Nothing but a Prank," He Insists

From the (Ky.) *Courier Journal,* January 8th, 1948

AIR FORCE CAPTAIN KILLED CHASING UFO
Mantell's Final Transmission: "Metallic, Tremendous in Size" Air Force Mum

From the Brazilian *Nacional*, March 8th, 1957

STRANGE RINGED CRAFT CRASHES IN MATO GROSSO!
2 WOMEN MENACED NEAR PONTO PORAN!
"We Heard Squealing Sounds from Within," They Declare

From the Brazilian *Nacional*, March 12th, 1957

MATO GROSSO HORROR!
Reports of Gray Men with Huge Black Eyes
Scientists Scoff! Reports Persist!
VILLAGES IN TERROR!

From the *Oklahoman*, May 12th, 1965

STATE POLICEMAN FIRES AT UFO
Claims Saucer Was 40 Feet Above Highway 9
Tinker AFB Radar Confirms Sightings

From the *Oklahoman,* June 2nd, 1965

"ALIEN GROWTH" A HOAX,
FARM BUREAU REP DECLARES
"Red Weeds" Said to Be Work
of Spray-Gun, Teenagers

From the Portland (Me.) *Press-Herald,* September 14th, 1965

NEW HAMPSHIRE UFO SIGHTINGS
MOUNT
Most Sightings in Exeter Area
Some Residents Express Fear of Alien Invasion

From the Manchester (N.H.) *Union-Leader,* September 19th, 1965

ENORMOUS OBJECT SIGHTED NEAR
EXETER WAS OPTICAL ILLUSION
Air Force Investigators Refute
State Police Sighting
Officer Cleland Adamant: "I Know What I Saw"

From the Manchester (N.H.) *Union-Leader,* September 30th, 1965

FOOD POISONING EPIDEMIC IN PLAISTOW STILL UNEXPLAINED
Over 300 Affected, Most Recovering
FDA Officer Says May Have Been Contaminated Wells

From the Michigan *Journal,* October 9th, 1965

GERALD FORD CALLS FOR UFO INVESTIGATION
Republican House Leader Says "Michigan Lights" May Be Extraterrestrial in Origin

From the *Los Angeles Times,* November 19th, 1978

CALTECH SCIENTISTS REPORT SIGHTING HUGE DISC-SHAPED OBJECT IN MOJAVE
Tickman: "Was Surrounded by Small Bright Lights"
Morales: "Saw Red Growth Like Angel Hair"

From the *Los Angeles Times,* November 24th, 1978

STATE POLICE, USAF INVESTIGATORS FIND NO "ANGEL HAIR" AT MOJAVE SITE
Tickman and Morales Take, Pass, Lie Tests
Possibility of Hoax Discounted

From the *New York Times,* August 16th, 1980

"ALIEN ABDUCTEES" REMAIN CONVINCED
Psychologists Question Drawings of So-Called Gray Men

From the *Wall Street Journal,* February 9th, 1985

CARL SAGAN: "NO, WE ARE NOT ALONE"
Prominent Scientist Reaffirms Belief in ETs
Says, "Odds of Intelligent Life Are Enormous"

From the Phoenix *Sun,* March 14th, 1997

HUGE UFO SIGHTED NEAR PRESCOTT
DOZENS DESCRIBE
"BOOMERANG-SHAPED" OBJECT
Switchboard at Luke AFB Deluged
with Reports

From the Phoenix *Sun,* March 20th, 1997

"PHOENIX LIGHTS" REMAIN
UNEXPLAINED
Photos Not Doctored, Expert Says
Air Force Investigators Mum

From the Paulden (Ariz.) *Weekly,* April 9th, 1997

FOOD POISONING OUTBREAK
UNEXPLAINED
REPORTS OF "RED GRASS" DISCOUNTED
AS HOAX

From the Derry (Me.) *Daily News,* May 15th, 2000

MYSTERY LIGHTS ONCE AGAIN REPORTED IN JEFFERSON TRACT
Kineo Town Manager: "I Don't Know What They Are, but They Keep Coming Back"

SSDD

It became their motto, and Jonesy couldn't for the life of him remember which of them started saying it first. *Payback's a bitch,* that was his. *Fuck me Freddy* and half a dozen even more colorful obscenities originated with Beaver. Henry was the one who taught them to say *What goes around comes around,* it was the kind of Zen shit Henry liked, even when they were kids. SSDD, though; what about SSDD? Whose brainstorm had that been?

Didn't matter. What mattered was that they believed the first half of it when they were a quartet and all of it when they were five and then the second half of it when they were a quartet again.

When it was just the four of them again, the days got darker. There were more fuck-me-Freddy days. They knew it, but not why. They knew something was wrong with them—different, at least—but not what. They knew they were caught, but not exactly how. And all this long before the lights in the sky. Before McCarthy and Becky Shue.

SSDD: Sometimes it's just what you say. And sometimes you believe in nothing but the darkness. And then how do you go along?

1988: Even Beaver Gets the Blues

To say that Beaver's marriage didn't work would be like saying that the launch of the *Challenger* space shuttle went a little bit wrong. Joe "Beaver" Clarendon and Laurie Sue Kenopensky make it through eight months and then *kapow,* there goes my baby, somebody help me pick up the fuckin pieces.

The Beav is basically a happy guy, any of his hangout buddies would tell you that, but this is his dark time. He doesn't see any of his old friends (the ones he thinks of as his *real* friends) except for the one week in November when they are together every year, and last November he and Laurie Sue had still been hanging on. By a thread, granted, but still hanging on. Now he spends a lot of his time—too much, he knows—in the bars of Portland's Old Port district, The Porthole and The Seaman's Club and The Free Street Pub. He is drinking too much and smoking too much of the old rope-a-dope and come most mornings he doesn't like to look at himself in the bathroom mirror; his red-rimmed eyes skitter away from his reflection and he thinks *I ought to quit the clubs. Pretty soon I'm gonna have a problem the way Pete's got one. Jesus-Christ-bananas.*

Quit the clubs, quit the partying, good fuckin idea, and then he's back again, kiss my bender and how ya doin. This Thursday it's The Free Street, and damned if there isn't a beer in his hand, a joint in his pocket, and some old instrumental, sounds a little bit like The Ventures, pouring from the juke. He can't quite remember the name of this one, which was popular before his time. Still, he knows it; he listens a lot to the Portland oldies station since he got divorced. Oldies are soothing. A lot of the new stuff . . . Laurie Sue knew and liked a lot of it, but Beaver doesn't get it.

The Free Street is mostly empty, maybe half a dozen guys at the bar and another half a dozen shooting eightball in the back, Beaver and three of his hang-out buddies in one of the booths, drinking draft Millers and cutting a greasy deck of cards to see who pays for each round. What *is* that instrumental with all the burbling guitars? "Out of Limits"? "Telstar"? Nah, there's a synthesizer in "Telstar" and no synth in this. And who gives a shit? The other guys are talking about Jackson Browne, who played the Civic Center last night and put on a kick-ass show, according to George Pelsen, who was there.

"I'll tell you something else that was kick-ass," George says, looking at them impressively. He raises his undershot chin, showing them all a red mark on the side of his neck. "You know what that is?"

"Hickey, ain't it?" Kent Astor asks, a bit timidly.

"You're fuckin-A," George says. "I was hangin around the stage door after the show, me and a bunch of other guys, hopin to get Jackson's autograph. Or maybe, I don't know, David Lindley. He's cool."

Kent and Sean Robideau agree that Lindley is cool—not a guitar god, by any means (Mark Knopfler of Dire Straits is a guitar god; and Angus Young of AC/DC; and—of course—Clapton), but very cool just the same. Lindley has great licks; he has awesome dreads, as well. All down to his shoulders.

Beaver doesn't join in the talk. All at once he wants to get out of here, out of this stale going-nowhere bar, and cop some fresh air. He knows where George is going with this, and it's all a lie.

Her name wasn't Chantay, you don't know what her name was, she blew right past you like you weren't there, what would you be to a girl like her anyway, just another working-class longhair in another working-class New England town, into the band bus she went and out of your life. Your fuckin uninteresting life. The Chantays is the name of the group we're listening to, not the Mar-Kets or the Bar-Kays but the Chantays, it's "Pipeline" by the Chantays and that thing on your neck isn't a hickey it's a razor burn.

He thinks this, then he hears crying. Not in The Free Street but in his mind. Long-gone crying. It goes right into your head, that crying, goes in like splinters of glass, and oh fuck, fuck me Freddy, somebody make him stop *crying.*

I was the one who made him stop, Beaver thinks. *That was me. I was the one who made him stop. I took him in my arms and sang to him.*

Meanwhile George Pelsen is telling them about how the stage door finally opened, but it wasn't Jackson Browne who came out, not David Lindley, either; it was the trio of chick singers, one named Randi, one named Susi, and one named Chantay. Yummy ladies, oh so tall and tasty.

"*Man,*" Sean says, rolling his eyes. He's a chubby little fellow whose sexual exploits consist of occasional field-trips to Boston, where he eyes the strippers at the Foxy Lady and the waitresses at Hooters. "Oh man, fuckin *Chantay*." He makes jacking-off gestures in the air. At that, at least, Beav thinks, he looks like a pro.

"So I started talkin to them . . . to her, mostly, Chantay, and I ast her if she'd like to see some of the Portland night-life. So we . . ."

The Beav takes a toothpick from his pocket and slides it into his mouth, tuning the rest out. All at once the toothpick is just what he wants. Not the beer in front of him, not the joint in his pocket, certainly not George Pelsen's empty kahoot about how he and the mythical Chantay got it on in the back of his pickup, thank God for that camper cap, when George's Ram is rockin, don't come knockin.

It's all puff and blow, Beaver thinks, and suddenly he is desperately depressed, more depressed than he has been since Laurie Sue packed her stuff and moved back to her mother's. This is utterly unlike him, and suddenly the only thing he wants is to get the fuck out of here, fill his lungs with the cool, salt-tanged seaside air, and find a phone. He wants to do that and then to call Jonesy or Henry, it doesn't matter which, either one will do; he wants to say *Hey man, what's going on* and have one of them say back *Oh, you know, Beav, SSDD. No bounce, no play.*

He gets up.

"Hey, man," George says. Beaver went to Westbrook Junior College with George, and then he seemed cool enough, but juco was many long beers ago. "Where you goin?"

"Take a leak," Beaver says, rolling his toothpick from one side of his mouth to the other.

"Well, you want to hurry your bad ass back, I'm just getting to the good part," George says, and Beaver thinks *crotchless panties*. Oh boy, today that old weird vibe is strong, maybe it's the barometer or something.

Lowering his voice, George says, "When I got her skirt up—"

"I know, she was wearin crotchless panties," Beaver says. He registers the look of surprise—almost shock— in George's eyes but pays no attention. "I sure want to hear that part."

He walks away, walks toward the men's room with its yellow-pink smell of piss and disinfectant, walks past it, walks past the women's, walks past the door with OFFICE on it, and escapes into the alley. The sky overhead is white and rainy, but the air is good. So good. He breathes it in deep and thinks again. *No bounce, no play.* He grins a little.

He walks for ten minutes, just chewing toothpicks and clearing his head. At some point, he can't remember exactly when, he tosses away the joint that has been in his pocket. And then he calls Henry from the pay phone in Joe's Smoke Shop, up by Monument Square. He's expecting the answering machine— Henry is still in school—but Henry is actually there, he picks up on the second ring.

"How you doing, man?" Beaver asks.

"Oh, you know," Henry says. "Same shit, different day. How about you, Beav?"

Beav closes his eyes. For a moment everything is all right again; as right as it can be in such a piss-ache world, anyway.

"About the same, buddy," he replies. "Just about the same."

1993: Pete Helps a Lady in Distress

Pete sits behind his desk just off the showroom of Macdonald Motors in Bridgton, twirling his key-chain. The fob consists of four enameled blue letters: NASA.

Dreams age faster than dreamers, that is a fact of life Pete has discovered as the years pass. Yet the last ones often die surprisingly hard, screaming in low, miserable voices at the back of the brain. It's been a long time since Pete slept in a bedroom papered with pictures of Apollo and Saturn rockets and astronauts and space-walks (EVAs, to those in the know) and space capsules with their shields smoked and fused by the fabulous heat of re-entry and LEMs and Voyagers and one photograph of a shiny disc over Interstate 80, people standing in the breakdown lane and looking up with their hands shielding their eyes, the photo's caption reading THIS OBJECT, PHOTOGRAPHED NEAR ARVADA, COLORADO, IN 1971, HAS NEVER BEEN EXPLAINED. IT IS A GENUINE UFO.

A long time.

Yet he still spent one of his two weeks of vacation this year in Washington, D.C., where he went to the Smithsonian's National Air and Space Museum every day and spent nearly all of his time wandering among the displays with a wondering grin on his face. And most of that time he spent looking at the moon rocks and thinking, *Those rocks came from a place where the skies are always black and the silence is everlasting. Neil Armstrong and Buzz Aldrin took twenty kilograms of another world and now here it is.*

And here *he* is, sitting behind his desk on a day when he hasn't sold a single car (people don't like to buy cars when it's raining, and it has been drizzling in Pete's part of the world ever since first light), twirling his NASA keychain and looking up at the clock. Time moves slowly in the afternoons, ever more slowly as the hour of five approaches. At five it will be time for that first beer. Not before five; no way. You drank during the day, maybe you had to look at how much you were drinking, because that's what alcoholics did. But if you could wait . . . just twirl your keychain and wait . . .

As well as that first beer of the day, Pete is waiting for November. Going to Washington in April had been good, and the moon rocks had been stunning (they *still* stun him, every time he thinks about them), but he had been alone. Being alone wasn't so good. In November, when he takes his other week, he'll be with Henry and Jonesy and the Beav. *Then* he'll allow himself to drink during the day. When you're off in the woods, hunting with your friends, it's all right to drink during the day. It's practically a tradition. It—

The door opens and a good-looking brunette

comes in. About five-ten (and Pete likes them tall), maybe thirty. She glances around at the showroom models (the new Thunderbird, in dark burgundy, is the pick of the litter, although the Explorer isn't bad), but not as if she has any interest in buying. Then she spots Pete and walks toward him.

Pete gets up, dropping his NASA keychain on his desk-blotter, and meets her at the door of his office. He's wearing his best professional smile by now—two hundred watts, baby, you better believe it—and has his hand outstretched. Her grip is cool and firm, but she's distracted, upset.

"This probably isn't going to work," she says.

"Now, you never want to start that way with a car salesman," Pete says. "We love a challenge. I'm Pete Moore."

"Hello," she says, but doesn't give her name, which is Trish. "I have an appointment in Fryeburg in just"—she glances at the clock which Pete watches so closely during the slow afternoon hours—"in just forty-five minutes. It's with a client who wants to buy a house, and I think I have the right one, there's a sizeable commission involved, and . . ." Her eyes are now brimming with tears and she has to swallow to get rid of the thickness creeping into her voice. ". . . and I've lost my goddam *keys*! My goddam *car* keys!"

She opens her purse and rummages in it.

"But I have my registration . . . plus some other papers . . . there are all sorts of numbers, and I thought maybe, just *maybe,* you could make me a new set and I could be on my way. This sale could make my year, Mr.——" She has forgotten. He isn't offended. Moore is almost as common as Smith or Jones. Besides, she's upset. Losing your keys will do that. He's seen it a hundred times.

"Moore. But I answer just as well to Pete."

"Can you help me, Mr. Moore? Or is there someone in the service department who can?"

Old Johnny Damon's back there and he'd be happy to help her, but she wouldn't make her appointment in Fryeburg, that's for sure.

"We can get you new car keys, but it's liable to take at least twenty-four hours and maybe more like forty-eight," he says.

She looks at him from her brimming eyes, which are a velvety brown, and lets out a dismayed cry. "Damn it! *Damn* it!"

An odd thought comes to Pete then: she looks like a girl he knew a long time ago. Not well, they hadn't known her well, but well enough to save her life. Josie Rinkenhauer, her name had been.

"I *knew* it!" Trish says, no longer trying to keep that husky thickness out of her voice. "Oh boy, I just *knew* it!" She turns away from him, now beginning to cry in earnest.

Pete walks after her and takes her gently by the shoulder. "Wait, Trish. Wait just a minute."

That's a slip, saying her name when she hasn't given it to him, but she's too upset to realize they haven't been properly introduced, so it's okay.

"Where did you come from?" he asks. "I mean, you're not from Bridgton, are you?"

"No," she says. "Our office is in Westbrook. Dennison Real Estate. We're the ones with the lighthouse?"

Pete nods as if this means something to him.

"I came from there. Only I stopped at the Bridgton Pharmacy for some aspirin because I always get a headache before a big presentation . . . it's the stress, and oh boy, it's pounding like a hammer now . . ."

Pete nods sympathetically. He knows about headaches. Of course most of his are caused by beer rather than stress, but he knows about them, all right.

"I had some time to kill, so I also went into the little store next to the pharmacy for a coffee . . . the caffeine, you know, when you have a headache the caffeine can help . . ."

Pete nods again. Henry's the headshrinker, but as Pete has told him more than once, you have to know a fair amount about how the human mind works in order to succeed at selling. Now he's pleased to see that his new friend is calming down a little. That's good. He has an idea he can help her, if she'll let him. He can feel that little click wanting to happen. He likes that little click. It's no big deal, it'll never make his fortune, but he likes it.

"And I also went across the street to Renny's. I bought a scarf . . . because of the rain, you know . . ." She touches her hair. "Then I went back to my car . . . and my son-of-a-damn-bitch keys were gone! I retraced my steps . . . went backward from Renny's to the store to the pharmacy, and they're not *any-*

where! And now I'm going to miss my appointment!"

Distress is creeping back into her voice. Her eyes go to the clock again. Creeping for him; racing for her. That's the difference between people, Pete reflects. One of them, anyway.

"Calm down," he says. "Calm down just a few seconds and listen to me. We're going to walk back to the drugstore, you and I, and look for your car keys."

"They're not there! I checked all the aisles, I looked on the shelf where I got the aspirin, I asked the girl at the counter—"

"It won't hurt to check again," he says. He's walking her toward the door now, his hand pressed lightly against the small of her back, getting her to walk with him. He likes the smell of her perfume and he likes her hair even more, yes he does. And if it looks this pretty on a rainy day, how might it look when the sun is out?

"My appointment—"

"You've still got forty minutes," he says. "With the summer tourists gone, it only takes twenty to drive up to Fryeburg. We'll take ten minutes to try and find your keys, and if we can't, I'll drive you myself."

She peers at him doubtfully.

He looks past her, into one of the other offices. "Dick!" he calls. "Hey, Dickie M.!"

Dick Macdonald looks up from a clutter of invoices.

"Tell this lady I'm safe to drive her up to Fryeburg, should it come to that."

"Oh, he's safe enough, ma'am," Dick says. "Not a

sex maniac or a fast driver. He'll just try to sell you a new car."

"I'm a tough sell," she says, smiling a little, "but I guess you're on."

"Cover my phone, would you, Dick?" Pete asks.

"Oh yeah, that'll be a hardship. Weather like this, I'll be beatin the customers off with a stick."

Pete and the brunette—Trish—go out, cross the alley, and walk the forty or so feet back to Main Street. The Bridgton Pharmacy is the second building on their left. The drizzle has thickened; now it's almost rain. The woman puts her new scarf up over her hair and glances at Pete, who's bare-headed. "You're getting all wet," she says.

"I'm from upstate," he says. "We grow em tough up there."

"You think you can find them, don't you?" she asks.

Pete shrugs. "Maybe. I'm good at finding things. Always have been."

"Do you know something I don't?" she asks.

No bounce, no play, he thinks. *I know that much, ma'am.*

"Nope," he says. "Not yet."

They walk into the pharmacy, and the bell over the door jingles. The girl behind the counter looks up from her magazine. At three-twenty on a rainy late-September afternoon, the pharmacy is deserted except for the three of them down here and Mr. Diller up behind the prescription counter.

"Hi, Pete," the counter-girl says.

"Yo, Cathy, how's it going?"

"Oh, you know—slow." She looks at the brunette. "I'm sorry, ma'am, I checked around again, but I didn't find them."

"That's all right," Trish says with a wan smile. "This gentleman has agreed to give me a ride to my appointment."

"Well," Cathy says, "Pete's okay, but I don't think I'd go so far as to call him a *gentleman*."

"You want to watch what you say, darlin," Pete tells her with a grin. "There's a Rexall just down 302 in Naples." Then he glances up at the clock. Time has sped up for him, too. That's okay, that makes a nice change.

Pete looks back at Trish. "You came here first. For the aspirin."

"That's right. I got a bottle of Anacin. Then I had some time to kill, so—"

"I know, you got a coffee next door at Christie's, then went across to Renny's."

"Yes."

"You didn't take your aspirin with hot coffee, did you?"

"No, I had a bottle of Poland water in my car." She points out the window at a green Taurus. "I took them with some of that. But I checked the seat, too, Mr.— Pete. I also checked the ignition." She gives him an impatient look which says, *I know what you're thinking: daffy woman.*

"Just one more question," he says. "If I find your car keys, would you go out to dinner with me? I could meet you at The West Wharf. It's on the road between here and—"

"I know The West Wharf," she says, looking amused in spite of her distress. At the counter, Cathy isn't even pretending to read her magazine. This is better than *Redbook,* by far. "How do *you* know I'm not married, or something?"

"No wedding ring," he replies promptly, although he hasn't even looked at her hands yet, not closely, anyway. "Besides, I was just talking about fried clams, cole slaw, and strawberry shortcake, not a lifetime commitment."

She looks at the clock. "Pete . . . Mr. Moore . . . I'm afraid that at this minute I have absolutely no interest in flirting. If you want to give me a ride, I would be very happy to have dinner with you. But—"

"That's good enough for me," he says. "But you'll be driving your own car, I think, so I'll meet you. Would five-thirty be okay?"

"Yes, fine, but—"

"Okay." Pete feels happy. That's good; happy is good. A lot of days these last couple of years he hasn't felt within a holler of happy, and he doesn't know why. Too many late and soggy nights cruising the bars along 302 between here and North Conway? Okay, but is that all? Maybe not, but this isn't the time to think about it. The lady has an appointment to keep. If she keeps it and sells the house, who knows how lucky Pete Moore might get? And even if he doesn't get lucky, he's going to be able to help her. He feels it.

"I'm going to do something a little weird now," he

says, "but don't let it worry you, okay? It's just a little trick, like putting your finger under your nose to stop a sneeze or thumping your forehead when you're trying to remember someone's name. Okay?"

"Sure, I guess," she says, totally mystified.

Pete closes his eyes, raises one loosely fisted hand in front of his face, then pops up his index finger. He begins to tick it back and forth in front of him.

Trish looks at Cathy, the counter-girl. Cathy shrugs as if to say *Who knows?*

"Mr. Moore?" Trish sounds uneasy now. "Mr. Moore, maybe I just ought to—"

Pete opens his eyes, takes a deep breath, and drops his hand. He looks past her, to the door.

"Okay," he says. "So you came in . . ." His eyes move as if watching her come in. "And you went to the counter . . ." His eyes go there. "You asked, probably, 'Which aisle's the aspirin in?' Something like that."

"Yes, I—"

"Only you got something, too." He can see it on the candy-rack, a bright yellow mark something like a handprint. "Snickers bar?"

"Mounds." Her brown eyes are wide. "How did you know that?"

"You got the candy, *then* you went up to get the aspirin . . ." He's looking up Aisle 2 now. "After that you paid and went out . . . let's go outside a minute. Seeya, Cathy."

Cathy only nods, looking at him with wide eyes.

Pete walks outside, ignoring the tinkle of the bell,

ignoring the rain, which now really *is* rain. The yellow is on the sidewalk, but fading. The rain's washing it away. Still, he can see it and it pleases him to see it. That feeling of *click*. Sweet. It's the line. It has been a long time since he's seen it so clearly.

"Back to your car," he says, talking to himself now. "Back to take a couple of your aspirin with your water . . ."

He crosses the sidewalk, slowly, to the Taurus. The woman walks behind him, eyes more worried than ever now. Almost frightened.

"You opened the door. You've got your purse . . . your keys . . . your aspirin . . . your candy . . . all this stuff . . . juggling it around from hand to hand . . . and that's when . . ."

He bends, fishes in the water flowing along the gutter, hand in it all the way up to the wrist, and brings something up. He gives it a magician's flourish. Keys flash silver in the dull day.

". . . you dropped your keys."

She doesn't take them at first. She only gapes at him, as if he has performed an act of witchcraft (warlock-craft, in his case, maybe) before her eyes.

"Go on," he says, smile fading a little. "Take them. It wasn't anything too spooky, you know. Mostly just deduction. I'm good at stuff like that. Hey, you should have me in the car sometime when you're lost. I'm great at getting unlost."

She takes the keys, then. Quickly, being careful not to touch his fingers, and he knows right then that she isn't going to meet him later. It doesn't take any special gift to figure that; he only has to look in her eyes, which are more frightened than grateful.

"Thank . . . thank you," she says. All at once she's measuring the space between them, not wanting him to use too much of it up.

"Not a problem. Now don't forget. The West Wharf, at five-thirty. Best fried clams in this part of the state." Keeping up the fiction. You have to keep it up, sometimes, no matter how you feel. And although some of the joy has gone out of the afternoon, some is still there; he has seen the line, and that always makes him feel good. It's a minor trick, but it's nice to know it's still there.

"Five-thirty," she echoes, but as she opens her car door, the glance she throws back over her shoulder is the kind you'd give to a dog that might bite if it got off its leash. She is very glad she won't be riding up to Fryeburg with him. Pete doesn't need to be a mind-reader to know that, either.

He stands there in the rain, watching her back out of the slant parking space, and when she drives away he tosses her a cheerful car-salesman's wave. She gives him a distracted little flip of the fingers in return, and of course when he shows up at The West Wharf (at five-fifteen, just to be Johnny on the spot, just in case) she isn't there and an hour later she's still not there. He stays for quite awhile just the same, sitting at the bar and drinking beer, watching the traffic out on 302. He thinks he sees her go by without slowing at about five-forty, a green Taurus busting past in a rain which has now become heavy, a green Taurus that might or might not be pulling a light yellow nimbus behind it that fades at once in the graying air.

Same shit, different day, he thinks, but now the joy is gone and the sadness is back, the sadness that feels like something deserved, the price of some not-quite-forgotten betrayal. He lights a cigarette—in the old days, as a kid, he used to pretend to smoke but now he doesn't have to pretend anymore—and orders another beer.

Milt brings it, but says, "You ought to lay some food on top of that, Peter."

So Pete orders a plate of fried clams and even eats a few dipped in tartar sauce while he drinks another couple of beers, and at some point, before moving on up the line to some other joint where he isn't so well-known, he tries to call Jonesy, down there in Massachusetts. But Jonesy and Carla are enjoying the rare night out, he only gets the baby-sitter, who asks him if he wants to leave a message.

Pete almost says no, then reconsiders. "Just tell him Pete called. Tell him Pete said SSDD."

"S . . . S . . . D . . . D." She is writing it down. "Will he know what—"

"Oh yeah," Pete says, "he'll know."

By midnight he's drunk in some New Hampshire dive, the Muddy Rudder or maybe it's the Ruddy Mother, he's trying to tell some chick who's as drunk as he is that once he really believed he was going to be the first man to set foot on Mars, and although she's nodding and saying yeah-yeah-yeah, he has an idea that all she understands is that she'd like to get outside of one more coffee brandy before closing. And that's okay. It doesn't matter. Tomorrow he'll wake up with a headache but he'll go in to work just the same and maybe he'll sell a car and maybe he won't but either way things will go on. Maybe he'll sell the burgundy Thunderbird, goodbye, sweetheart. Once things were different, but now they're the same. He reckons he can live with that; for a guy like him, the rule of thumb is just SSDD, and so fucking what. You grew up, became a man, had to adjust to taking less than you hoped for; you discovered the dream-machine had a big OUT OF ORDER sign on it.

In November he'll go hunting with his friends, and that's enough to look forward to . . . that, and maybe a big old sloppy-lipstick blowjob from this drunk chick out in his car. Wanting more is just a recipe for heartache.

Dreams are for kids.

1998: Henry Treats a Couch Man

The room is dim. Henry always keeps it that way when he's seeing patients. It's interesting to him how few seem to notice it. He thinks it's because their states of mind are so often dim to start with. Mostly he sees neurotics (*The woods are full of em,* as he once told Jonesy while they were in, ha-ha, the woods) and it is his assessment—completely unscientific—that their problems act as a kind of polarizing shield between them and the rest of the world. As the neurosis deepens, so does the interior darkness. Mostly what he feels for his patients is a kind of distanced sympathy. Sometimes pity. A very few of them make him impatient. Barry Newman is one of those.

Patients who enter Henry's office for the first time are presented with a choice they usually don't register as a choice. When they come in they see a pleasant (if rather dim) room, with a fireplace to the left. It's equipped with one of those everlasting logs, steel disguised as birch with four cunningly placed gas jets beneath. Beside the fireplace is a wing chair, where Henry always sits beneath an excellent reproduction of Van Gogh's *Marigolds*. (Henry sometimes tells colleagues that every psychiatrist should have at least one Van Gogh in his or her consulting space.) Across the room is an easy chair and a couch. Henry is always interested to see which one a new patient will choose. Certainly he has been plying the trade long enough to know that what a patient chooses the first time is what he or she will choose almost every time. There is a paper in this. Henry knows there is, but he cannot isolate the thesis. And in any case, he finds he has less interest these days in such things as papers and journals and conventions and colloquia. They used to matter, but now things have changed. He is sleeping less, eating less, laughing less, too. A darkness has come into his own life—that polarizing filter—and Henry finds he has no objection to this. Less glare.

Barry Newman was a couch man from the first, and Henry has never once made the mistake of believing this has anything to do with Barry's mental condition. The couch is simply more comfortable for

Barry, although Henry sometimes has to give him a hand to get Barry up from it when his fifty minutes have expired. Barry Newman stands five-seven and weighs four hundred and twenty pounds. This makes the couch his friend.

Barry Newman's sessions tend to be long, droning accounts of each week's adventures in gastronomy. Not that Barry is a discriminating eater, oh, no, Barry is the antithesis of that. Barry eats anything that happens to stray into his orbit. Barry is an eating machine. And his memory, on this subject, at least, is eidetic. He is to food what Henry's old friend Pete is to directions and geography.

Henry has almost given up trying to drag Barry away from the trees and make him examine the forest. Partly this is because of Barry's soft but implacable desire to discuss food in its specifics; partly it's because Henry doesn't like Barry and never has. Barry's parents are dead. Dad went when Barry was sixteen, Mom when he was twenty-two. They left a very large estate, but it is in trust until Barry is thirty. He can get the principal then . . . *if* he continues in therapy. If not, the principal will remain in trust until he is fifty.

Henry doubts Barry Newman will make fifty.

Barry's blood pressure (he has told Henry this with some pride) is one-ninety over one-forty.

Barry's whole-cholesterol number is two hundred and ninety; he is a lipid goldmine.

I'm a walking stroke, I'm a walking heart attack, he has told Henry, speaking with the gleeful solemnity of one who can state the hard, cold truth because he knows in his soul that such ends are not meant for him, not for him, no, not for him.

"I had two of those Burger King X-tras for lunch," he is saying now. "I love those, because the cheese is actually hot." His fleshy lips—oddly small lips for such a large man, the lips of a perch—tighten and tremble, as if tasting that exquisitely hot cheese. "I also had a shake, and on my way back home I had a couple of Mallomars. I took a nap, and when I got up I microwaved a whole package of those frozen waffles. 'Leggo my Eggo!' " he cries, then laughs. It is the laugh of a man in the grip of fond recall—the sight of a sunset, the firm feel of a woman's breast through a thin silk shirt (not that Barry has, in Henry's estimation, ever felt such a thing), or the packed warmth of beach sand.

"Most people use the toaster oven for their Eggo waffles," Barry continues, "but I find that makes them too crispy. The microwave just gets them hot and soft. Hot . . . and soft." He smacks his little perch lips. "I had a certain amount of guilt about eating the whole package." He throws this last in almost as an aside, as if remembering Henry has a job to do here. He throws out similar little treats four or five times in every session . . . and then it's back to the food.

Barry has now reached Tuesday evening. Since this is Friday, there are plenty of meals and snacks still to go. Henry lets his mind drift. Barry is his last appointment of the day. When Barry has finished taking caloric inventory, Henry is going back to his apartment to pack. He'll be up tomorrow at six A.M., and sometime between seven and eight, Jonesy will pull into his driveway. They will pack their stuff into Henry's old Scout, which he now keeps around solely for their autumn hunting trips, and by eight-thirty the two of them will be on their way north. Along the way they will pick up Pete in Bridgton, and then the Beav, who still lives close to Derry. By evening they will be at Hole in the Wall up in the Jefferson Tract, playing cards in the living room and listening to the wind hoot around the eaves. Their guns will be leaning in the corner of the kitchen, their hunting licenses hung over the hook on the back door.

He will be with his friends, and that always feels like coming home. For a week, that polarizing filter may lift a little bit. They will talk about old times, they will laugh at Beaver's outrageous profanities, and if one or more of them actually shoots a deer, that will be an extra added attraction. Together they are still good. Together they still defeat time.

Far in the background, Barry Newman drones on and on. Pork chops and mashed potatoes and corn on the cob dripping with butter and Pepperidge Farm chocolate cake and a bowl of Pepsi-Cola with four scoops of Ben and Jerry's Chunky Monkey ice cream floating in it and eggs fried eggs boiled eggs poached . . .

Henry nods in all the right places and hears it all without really listening. This is an old psychiatric skill.

God knows Henry and his old friends have their problems. Beaver is terrible when it comes to relationships, Pete drinks too much (*way* too much is what

Henry thinks), Jonesy and Carla have had a near-miss with divorce, and Henry is now struggling with a depression that seems to him every bit as seductive as it does unpleasant. So yes, they have their problems. But together they are still good, still able to light it up, and by tomorrow night they will be together. For eight days, this year. That's good.

"I know I shouldn't, but I just get this *compulsion* early in the morning. Maybe it's low blood sugar, I think it might be that. Anyway, I ate the rest of the pound-cake that was in the fridge, then I got in the car and drove down to Dunkin' Donuts and I got a dozen of the Dutch Apple and four of—"

Henry, still thinking about the annual hunting trip that starts tomorrow, isn't aware of what he is saying until it is out.

"Maybe this compulsive eating, Barry, maybe it has something to do with thinking you killed your mother. Do you think that's possible?"

Barry's words stop. Henry looks up and sees Barry Newman staring at him with eyes so wide they are actually visible. And although Henry knows he should stop—he has no business doing this at *all*, it has absolutely nothing to do with therapy—he doesn't *want* to stop. Some of this may have to do with thinking about his old friends, but most of it is just seeing that shocked look on Barry's face, and the pallor of his cheek. What really bugs Henry about Barry, he supposes, is Barry's complacency. His inner assurance that there is no need to change his self-destructive behavior, let alone search for its roots.

"You *do* think you killed her, don't you?" Henry asks. He speaks casually, almost lightly.

"I—I never—I resent—"

"She called and she called, said she was having chest-pains, but of course she said that often, didn't she? Every other week. Every other *day,* it sometimes seemed. Calling downstairs to you. 'Barry, phone Dr. Withers. Barry, call an ambulance. Barry, dial 911.'"

They have never talked about Barry's parents. In his soft, fat, implacable way, Barry will not allow it. He will begin to discuss them—or seem to—and then bingo, he'll be talking about roast lamb again, or roast chicken, or roast duck with orange sauce. Back to the inventory. Hence Henry knows nothing about Barry's parents, certainly not about the day Barry's mother died, falling out of bed and pissing on the carpet, still calling and calling, three hundred pounds and so disgustingly fat, calling and calling. He can know nothing about that because he hasn't been told, but he *does* know. And Barry was thinner then. A relatively svelte one-ninety.

This is Henry's version of the line. Seeing the line. Henry hasn't seen it for maybe five years now (unless he sometimes sees it in dreams), thought all that was over, and now here it is again.

"You sat there in front of the TV, listening to her yell," he says. "You sat there watching Ricki Lake and eating—what?—a Sara Lee cheesecake? A bowl of ice cream? I don't know. But you let her yell."

"Stop it!"

"You let her yell, and really, why not? *She'd been cry-*

ing wolf her whole life. You are not a stupid man and you know that's true. This sort of thing happens. I think you know that, too. You've cast yourself in your own little Tennessee Williams play simply because you like to eat. But guess what, Barry? *It's really going to kill you.* In your secret heart you don't believe that, but it's true. Your heart's already pounding like a premature burial victim beating his fists on the lid of a coffin. What's it going to be like eighty or a hundred pounds from now?"

"Shut—"

"When you fall, Barry, it's going to be like the fall of Babel in the desert. The people who see you go down will talk about it for *years.* Man, you'll shake the dishes right off the shelves—"

"Stop it!" Barry is sitting up now, he hasn't needed Henry to give him a hand this time, and he is deadly pale except for little wild roses, one growing in each cheek.

"—you'll splash the coffee right out of the cups, and you'll piss yourself just like she did—"

"STOP IT!" Barry Newman shrieks. *"STOP IT, YOU MONSTER!"*

But Henry can't. Henry can't. He sees the line and when you see it, you can't unsee it.

"—unless you wake up from this poisoned dream you're having. You see, Barry—"

But Barry doesn't want to see, absolutely will *not* see. Out the door he runs, vast buttocks jiggling, and he is gone.

At first Henry sits where he is, not moving, listening to the departing thunder of the one-man buffalo herd that is Barry Newman. The outer room is empty; he has no receptionist, and with Barry gone, the week is over. Just as well. That was a mess. He goes to the couch and lies down on it.

"Doctor," he says, "I just fucked up.

"How did you do that, Henry?

"I told a patient the truth.

"If we know the truth, Henry, does it not set us free?

"No," he replies to himself, looking up at the ceiling. "Not in the slightest.

"Close your eyes, Henry.

"All right, doctor."

He closes his eyes. The room is replaced by darkness, and that is good. Darkness has become his friend. Tomorrow he will see his other friends (three of them, anyway), and the light will once more seem good. But now . . . now . . .

"Doctor?

"Yes, Henry.

"This is a bona fide case of same shit, different day. Do you know that?

"What does that mean, Henry? What does that mean to you?

"Everything," he says, eyes closed, and then adds: "Nothing." But that's a lie. Not the first one that was ever told in here.

He lies on the couch, eyes closed and hands folded on his chest, and after a little while he sleeps.

The next day the four of them drive up to Hole in the Wall, and it is a great eight days. The great hunting trips are coming to an end, only a few left, although they of course do not know this. The real darkness is still a few years away, but it is coming.

The darkness is coming.

2001: Jonesy's Student-Teacher Conference

We don't know the days that will change our lives. Probably just as well. On the day that will change his, Jonesy is in his third-floor John Jay College office, looking out at his little slice of Boston and thinking how wrong T. S. Eliot had been to call April the cruelest month just because an itinerant carpenter from Nazareth supposedly got himself crucified then for fomenting rebellion. Anyone who lives in Boston knows that it's March that's the cruelest, holding out a few days of false hope and then gleefully hitting you with the shit. Today is one of the untrustworthy ones when it looks as if spring might really be coming, and he's thinking about taking a walk when the bit of impending nastiness just ahead is over. Of course at this point, Jonesy has no idea how nasty a day can get; no idea that he is going to finish this one in a hospital room, smashed up and fighting for his goddam life.

Same shit, different day, he thinks, but this will be different shit indeed.

That's when the phone rings, and he grabs it at once, filled with a hopeful premonition: it'll be the Defuniak kid, calling to cancel his eleven-o'clock. *He's gotten a whiff of what's in the wind,* Jonesy thinks, and that is very possible. Usually it's the students who make appointments to see the teacher. When a kid gets a message saying that one of his teachers wants to see *him* . . . well, you don't have to be a rocket-scientist, as the saying goes.

"Hello, it's Jones," he says.

"Hey, Jonesy, how's life treating you?"

He'd know that voice anywhere. "Henry! Hey! Good, life's good!"

Life does not, in fact, seem all that great, not with Defuniak due in a quarter of an hour, but it's all relative, isn't it? Compared to where he's going to be twelve hours from now, hooked up to all those beeping machines, one operation behind him and three more ahead of him, Jonesy is, as they say, farting through silk.

"Glad to hear it."

Jonesy might have heard the heaviness in Henry's voice, but more likely it's a thing he senses.

"Henry? What's wrong?"

Silence. Jonesy is about to ask again when Henry answers.

"A patient of mine died yesterday. I happened to see the obit in the paper. Barry Newman, his name was." Henry pauses. "He was a couch man."

Jonesy doesn't know what that means, but his old friend is hurting. He knows that.

"Suicide?"

"Heart attack. At the age of twenty-nine. Dug his grave with his own fork and spoon."

"I'm sorry."

"He hasn't been my patient for almost three years.

I scared him away. I had . . . one of those things. Do you know what I'm talking about?"

Jonesy thinks he does. "Was it the line?"

Henry sighs. It doesn't sound like regret to Jonesy. It sounds like relief. "Yeah. I kind of socked it to him. He took off like his ass was on fire."

"That doesn't make you responsible for his coronary."

"Maybe you're right. But that's not the way it feels." A pause. And then, with a shade of amusement: "Isn't that a line from a Jim Croce song? *Are you all right, Jonesy?*"

"Me? Yeah. Why do you ask?"

"I don't know," Henry says. "Only . . . I've been thinking about you ever since I opened the paper and saw Barry's picture on the obituary page. I want you to be careful."

Around his bones (many of which will soon be broken), Jonesy feels a slight coldness. "What exactly are you talking about?"

"I don't know," Henry says. "Maybe nothing. But . . ."

"Is it the line now?" Jonesy is alarmed. He swings around in his chair and looks out the window at the chancy spring sunlight. It crosses his mind that maybe the Defuniak kid is disturbed, maybe he's carrying a gun (*packing heat,* as they say in the mystery and suspense novels Jonesy likes to read in his spare time) and Henry has somehow picked this up.

"I don't know. The most likely thing is that I'm

just having a displaced reaction from seeing Barry's picture on the all-done page. But watch yourself the next little while, would you?"

"Well . . . yeah. I can do that."

"Good."

"And you're okay?"

"I'm fine."

But Jonesy doesn't think Henry is fine at all. He's about to say something else when someone clears his throat behind him and he realizes that Defuniak has probably arrived.

"Well, that's good," he says, and swivels around in his chair. Yep, there's his eleven-o'clock in the doorway, not looking dangerous at all: just a kid bundled into a big old duffel coat that's too heavy for the day, looking thin and underfed, wearing one earring and a punky haircut that spikes over his worried eyes. "Henry, I've got an appointment. I'll call you back—"

"No, that's not necessary. Really."

"You're sure?"

"I am. But there's one other thing. Got thirty more seconds?"

"Sure, you bet." He holds up a finger to Defuniak and Defuniak nods. But he just goes on standing there until Jonesy points to the one chair in the little office besides his own that isn't stacked with books. Defuniak goes to it reluctantly. Into the phone, Jonesy says, "Shoot."

"I think we ought to go back to Derry. Just a quick trip, just you and me. See our old friend."

"You mean—?" But he doesn't want to say that

name, that baby-sounding name, with a stranger in the room.

He doesn't have to; Henry says it for him. Once they were a quartet, then for a little while they were five, and then they were four again. But the fifth one has never exactly left them. Henry says that name, the name of a boy who is magically still a boy. About him, Henry's worries are more clear, more easily expressed. It isn't anything he knows, he tells Jonesy, just a feeling that their old pal might need a visit.

"Have you talked to his mother?" Jonesy asked.

"I think," Henry says, "it might be better if we just . . . you know, orbited on in there. How's your calendar look for this weekend? Or the one after?"

Jonesy doesn't need to check. The weekend starts day after tomorrow. There's a faculty thing Saturday afternoon, but he can easily get clear of that.

"I'm fine both days this weekend," he says. "If I was to come by Saturday? At ten?"

"That'd be fine." Henry sounds relieved, more like himself. Jonesy relaxes a little. "You're sure?"

"If you think we ought to go see . . ." Jonesy hesitates. ". . . see Douglas, then probably we should. It's been too long."

"Your appointment's there, isn't he?"

"Uh-huh."

"Okay. I'll look for you at ten on Saturday. Hey, maybe we'll take the Scout. Give it a run. How would that be?"

"That would be terrific."

Henry laughs. "Carla still makin your lunch, Jonesy?"

"She is." Jonesy looks toward his briefcase.

"What you got today? Tuna fish?"

"Egg salad."

"Mmm-mmm. Okay, I'm out of here. SSDD, right?"

"SSDD," Jonesy agrees. He can't call their old friend by his right name in front of a student, but SSDD is all right. "Talk to you l—"

"And take care of yourself. *I mean it.*" The emphasis in Henry's voice is unmistakable, and a little scary. But before Jonesy can respond (and what he would say with Defuniak sitting in the corner, watching and listening, he doesn't know), Henry is gone.

Jonesy looks at the phone thoughtfully for a moment, then hangs up. He flips a page on his desk calendar, and on Saturday he crosses out *Drinks at Dean Jacobson's house* and writes *Beg off—going to Derry with Henry to see D.* But this is an appointment he will not keep. By Saturday, Derry and his old friends will be the furthest things from his mind.

Jonesy pulls in a deep breath, lets it out, and transfers his attention to his troublesome eleven-o'clock. The kid shifts uncomfortably in his chair. He has a pretty good idea why he's been summoned here, Jonesy guesses.

"So, Mr. Defuniak," he says. "You're from Maine, according to your records."

"Uh, yeah. Pittsfield. I—"

"Your records also say that you're here on scholarship, and that you've done well."

The kid, he sees, is actually a lot more than worried. The kid is on the verge of tears. Christ, but this is hard. Jonesy has never had to accuse a student of cheating before, but he supposes this won't be the last time. He only hopes it doesn't happen too often. Because this is hard, what Beaver would call a fuckarow.

"Mr. Defuniak—David—do you know what happens to scholarships if the students holding them are caught cheating? On a mid-term exam, let us say?"

The kid jerks as if a hidden prankster under his chair has just triggered a low-voltage electrical charge into one of his skinny buttocks. Now his lips are trembling and the first tear, oh God, there it goes down his unshaven boy's cheek.

"I can tell you," Jonesy says. "Such scholarships evaporate. That's what happens to them. *Poof,* and gone into thin air."

"I—I—"

There is a folder on Jonesy's desk. He opens it and takes out a European History mid-term, one of those multiple-choice monstrosities upon which the Department, in its great unwisdom, insists. Written on top of this one, in the black strokes of an IBM pencil ("Make sure your marks are heavy and unbroken, and if you need to erase, erase completely"), is the name DAVID DEFUNIAK.

"I've reviewed your course-work, David; I've re-scanned your paper on feudalism in France during the

Middle Ages; I've even been through your transcripts. You haven't exhibited brilliance, but you've done okay. And I'm aware that you're simply satisfying a requirement here—your real interests don't lie in my field, do they?"

Defuniak shakes his head mutely. The tears gleam on his cheeks in that untrustworthy mid-March sunlight.

There's a box of Kleenex on the corner of Jonesy's desk, and he tosses it to the boy, who catches it easily even in his distress. Good reflexes. When you're nineteen, all your wiring is still nice and tight, all your connections nice and solid.

Wait a few years, Mr. Defuniak, he thinks. *I'm only thirty-seven and already some of my wires are getting loose.*

"Maybe you deserve another chance," Jonesy says.

Slowly and deliberately, he begins to crumple Defuniak's mid-term, which is suspiciously perfect, A-plus work, into a ball.

"Maybe what happened is you were sick the day of the mid-term, and you never took it at all."

"I *was* sick," David Defuniak says eagerly. "I think I had the flu."

"Then maybe I ought to give you a take-home essay instead of the multiple-choice test to which your colleagues have been subjected. If you want it. To make up for the test you missed. Would you want that?"

"Yeah," the kid says, wiping his eyes madly with a large swatch of tissues. At least he hasn't gone through all that small-time cheapshit stuff about how

Jonesy can't prove it, can't prove a thing, he'd take it to the Student Affairs Council, he'd call a protest, blah-blah-blah-de-blah. He's crying instead, which is uncomfortable to witness but probably a good sign—nineteen is young, but too many of them have lost most of their consciences by the time they get there. Defuniak has pretty much owned up, which suggests there might still be a man in there, waiting to come out. "Yeah, that'd be great."

"And you understand that if anything like this ever happens again—"

"It won't," the kid says fervently. "It won't, Professor Jones."

Although Jonesy is only an associate professor, he doesn't bother to correct him. Someday, after all, he *will* be Professor Jones. He better be; he and his wife have a houseful of kids, and if there aren't at least a few salary-bumps in his future, life is apt to be a pretty tough scramble. They've had some tough scrambles already.

"I hope not," he says. "Give me three thousand words on the short-term results of the Norman Conquest, David, all right? Cite sources but no need of footnotes. Keep it informal, but present a cogent thesis. I want it by next Monday. Understood?"

"Yes. Yes, sir."

"Then why don't you go on and get started." He points at Defuniak's tatty footwear. "And the next time you think of buying beer, buy some new sneakers instead. I wouldn't want you to catch the flu again."

Defuniak goes to the door, then turns. He is anxious to be gone before Mr. Jones changes his mind, but he is also nineteen. And curious. "How did you know? You weren't even there that day. Some grad student proctored the test."

"I knew, and that's enough," Jonesy says with some asperity. "Go on, son. Write a good paper. Hold onto your scholarship. I'm from Maine myself— Derry—and I know Pittsfield. It's a better place to be from than to go back to."

"You got *that* right," Defuniak says fervently. "Thank you. Thank you for giving me another chance."

"Close the door on your way out."

Defuniak—who will spend his sneaker-money not on beer but on a get-well bouquet for Jonesy—goes out, obediently closing the door behind him. Jonesy swings around and looks out the window again. The sunshine is untrustworthy but enticing. And because the Defuniak thing went better than he had expected, he thinks he wants to get out in that sunlight before more March clouds—and maybe snow—come rolling in. He has planned to eat in his office, but a new plan occurs to him. It is absolutely the worst plan of his life, but of course Jonesy doesn't know that. The plan is to grab his briefcase, pick up a copy of the Boston *Phoenix*, and walk across the river to Cambridge. He'll sit on a bench and eat his egg salad sandwich in the sun.

He gets up to put Defuniak's file in the cabinet marked D–F. *How did you know?* the boy had asked, and Jonesy supposes that was a good question. An *excellent* question, really. The answer is this: he knew because . . . sometimes he *does.* That's the truth, and there's no other. If someone put a gun to his head, he'd say he found out during the first class after the mid-term, that it was right there in the front of David Defuniak's mind, big and bright, flashing on and off in guilty red neon: CHEATER CHEATER CHEATER.

But man, that's dope—he *can't* read minds. He never could. Never-ever, never-ever, never-ever could. Sometimes things flash into his head, yes—he knew about his wife's problems with pills that way, and he supposes he might have known in that same way that Henry was depressed when he called (*No, it was in his voice, doofus, that's all it was*), but stuff like that hardly ever happens anymore. There has been nothing *really* odd since the business with Josie Rinkenhauer. Maybe there *was* something once, and maybe it trailed them out of their childhood and adolescence, but surely it is gone now. Or almost gone.

Almost.

He circles the words *going to Derry* on his desk calendar, then grabs his briefcase. As he does, a new thought comes to him, sudden and meaningless but very powerful: *Watch out for Mr. Gray.*

He stops with one hand on his doorknob. That was his own voice, no doubt about it.

"What?" he asks the empty room.

Nothing.

Jonesy steps out of his office, closes the door, and tests the lock. In the corner of his door's bulletin board is a blank white card. Jonesy unpins it and turns it over. On the flip side is the printed message BACK AT ONE—UNTIL THEN I'M HISTORY. He pins the message side to the bulletin board with perfect confidence, but it will be almost two months before Jonesy enters this room again and sees his desk calendar still turned to St. Patrick's Day.

Take care of yourself, Henry said, but Jonesy isn't thinking about taking care of himself. He is thinking about March sunlight. He's thinking about eating his sandwich. He's thinking he might watch a few girls over on the Cambridge side—skirts are short, and March winds are frisky. He's thinking about all sorts of things, but watching out for Mr. Gray isn't one of them. Neither is taking care of himself.

This is a mistake. This is also how lives change forever.

PART 1

CANCER

This shaking keeps me steady. I should know.
What falls away is always. And is near.
I wake to sleep, and take my waking slow.
I learn by going where I have to go.

THEODORE ROETHKE

CHAPTER ONE

MCCARTHY

1

Jonesy almost shot the guy when he came out of the woods. How close? Another pound on the Garand's trigger, maybe just a half. Later, hyped on the clarity that sometimes comes to the horrified mind, he wished he had shot before he saw the orange cap and the orange flagman's vest. Killing Richard McCarthy couldn't have hurt, and it might have helped. Killing McCarthy might have saved them all.

2

Pete and Henry had gone to Gosselin's Market, the closest store, to stock up on bread, canned goods, and beer—the real essential. They had plenty for another two days, but the radio said there might be snow coming. Henry had already gotten his deer, a good-sized doe, and Jonesy had an idea Pete cared a lot more about making sure of the beer supply than he did about getting his own deer—for Pete Moore, hunting was a hobby, beer a religion. The Beaver was out there someplace, but Jonesy hadn't heard the crack of a rifle any closer than five miles, so he guessed that the Beav, like him, was still waiting.

There was a stand in an old maple about seventy yards from the camp and that was where Jonesy was, sipping coffee and reading a Robert Parker mystery novel, when he heard something coming and put the book and the Thermos aside. In other years he might have spilled the coffee in his excitement, but not this time. This time he even took a few seconds to screw on the Thermos's bright red stopper.

The four of them had been coming up here to hunt in the first week of November for almost twenty-five years, if you counted in the times Beav's Dad had taken them, and Jonesy had never bothered with the tree-stand until now. None of them had; it was too confining. This year Jonesy had staked it out. The others thought they knew why, but they only knew half of it.

In mid-March of 2001, Jonesy had been struck by a car while crossing a street in Cambridge, not far from John Jay College, where he taught. He had fractured his skull, broken two ribs, and suffered a shattered hip, which had been replaced with some exotic combination of Teflon and metal. The man who'd struck him was a retired BU history professor who was—according to his lawyer, anyway—in the early stages of Alzheimer's, more to be pitied than punished. So often, Jonesy thought, there was no one to blame when the dust cleared. And even if there was, what good did it do? You still had to live with what was left, and console yourself with the fact that, as people told him every day (until they forgot the whole thing, that was), it could have been worse.

And it could have been. His head was hard, and the crack in it healed. He had no memory of the hour or so leading up to his accident near Harvard Square, but the rest of his mental equipment was fine. His ribs healed in a month. The hip was the worst, but he was off the crutches by October, and now his limp only became appreciable toward the end of the day.

Pete, Henry, and the Beav thought it was the hip and only the hip that had caused him to opt for the tree-stand instead of the damp, cold woods, and the hip was certainly a factor—just not the only one. What he had kept from them was that he now had little interest in shooting deer. It would have dismayed them. Hell, it dismayed Jonesy himself. But there it was, something new in his existence that he hadn't even suspected until they had actually gotten up here on November eleventh and he had uncased the Garand. He wasn't revolted by the idea of hunting, not at all—he just had no real urge to do it. Death had brushed by him on a sunny day in March, and Jonesy had no desire to call it back, even if he was dealing rather than receiving.

3

What surprised him was that he still liked being at camp—in some ways, better than ever. Talking at night—books, politics, the shit they'd gotten up to as kids, their plans for the future. They were in their thirties, still young enough to have plans, plenty of them, and the old bond was still strong.

And the days were good, too—the hours in the tree-stand, when he was alone. He took a sleeping-bag and skid into it up to his hips when he got cold, and a book, and a Walkman. After the first day, he stopped listening to the Walkman, discovering that he liked the music of the woods better—the silk of the wind in the pines, the rust of the crows. He would read a little, drink coffee, read a little more, sometimes work his way out of the sleeping-bag (it was as red as a stoplight) and piss off the edge of the platform. He was a man with a big family and a large circle of colleagues. A gregarious man who enjoyed all the various relationships the family and the colleagues entailed (and the students, of course, the endless stream of students) and balanced them well. It was only out here, *up* here, that he realized the attractions of silence were still real, still strong. It was like meeting an old friend after a long absence.

"You sure you want to be up there, man?" Henry had asked him yesterday morning. "I mean, you're welcome to come out with me. We won't overuse that leg of yours, I promise."

"Leave him alone," Pete said. "He likes it up there. Don't you, Jones-boy?"

"Sort of," he said, unwilling to say much more— how much he actually *did* like it, for instance. Some things you didn't feel safe telling even your closest friends. And sometimes your closest friends knew, anyway.

"Tell you something," the Beav said. He picked up a pencil and began to gnaw lightly at it—his oldest, dearest trick, going all the way back to first grade. "I like coming back and seeing you there—like a lookout in the crow's nest in one of those fuckin Hornblower books. Keepin an eye out, you know."

"Sail, ho," Jonesy had said, and they all laughed, but Jonesy knew what the Beav meant. He felt it. Keeping an eye out. Just thinking his thoughts and keeping an eye out for ships or sharks or who knew what. His hip hurt coming back down, the pack with his shit in it was heavy on his back, and he felt slow and clumsy on the wooden rungs nailed to the trunk of the maple, but that was okay. Good, in fact. Things changed, but only a fool believed they only changed for the worse.

That was what he thought then.

4

When he heard the whicker of moving brush and the soft snap of a twig—sounds he never questioned were those of an approaching deer—Jonesy thought of something his father said: *You can't make yourself be lucky.* Lindsay Jones was one of life's losers and had said few things worth committing to memory, but that was one, and here was the proof of it again: days after deciding he had finished with deer hunting, here came one, and a big one by the sound—a buck, almost surely, maybe one as big as a man.

That it *was* a man never so much as crossed Jonesy's mind. This was an unincorporated township fifty miles north of Rangely, and the nearest hunters were two hours' walk away. The nearest paved road, the one which eventually took you to Gosselin's Market (BEER BAIT OUT OF STATE LICS LOTTERY TIX), was at least sixteen miles away.

Well, he thought, *it isn't as if I took a vow, or anything.*

No, he hadn't taken a vow. Next November he might be up here with a Nikon instead of a Garand, but it wasn't next year yet, and the rifle was at hand. He had no intention of looking a gift deer in the mouth.

Jonesy screwed the red stopper into the Thermos of coffee and put it aside. Then he pushed the sleeping-bag off his lower body like a big quilted sock (wincing at the stiffness in his hip as he did it) and grabbed his gun. There was no need to chamber a round, producing that loud, deer-frightening click; old habits died hard, and the gun was ready to fire as soon as he thumbed off the safety. This he did when he was solidly on his feet. The old wild excitement was gone, but there was a residue—his pulse was up and he welcomed the rise. In the wake of his accident, he welcomed all such reactions—it was as if there were two of him now, the one before he had been knocked flat in the street and the warier, older fellow who had awakened in Mass General . . . if you could call that slow, drugged awareness being awake. Sometimes he still heard a voice—whose he didn't know, but not his—

calling out *Please stop, I can't stand it, give me a shot, where's Marcy, I want Marcy.* He thought of it as death's voice—death had missed him in the street and had then come to the hospital to finish the job, death masquerading as a man (or perhaps it had been a woman, it was hard to tell) in pain, someone who said Marcy but meant Jonesy.

The idea passed—all of the funny ideas he'd had in the hospital eventually passed—but it left a residue. Caution was the residue. He had no memory of Henry's calling and telling him to watch himself for the next little while (and Henry hadn't reminded him), but since then Jonesy *had* watched himself. He was careful. Because maybe death was out there, and maybe sometimes it called your name.

But the past was the past. He had survived his brush with death, and nothing was dying here this morning but a deer (a buck, he hoped) who had strolled in the wrong direction.

The sound of the rustling brush and snapping twigs was coming toward him from the southwest, which meant he wouldn't have to shoot around the trunk of the maple—good—and put him upwind. Even better. Most of the maple's leaves had fallen, and he had a good, if not perfect, sightline through the interlacing branches. Jonesy raised the Garand, settled the buttplate into the hollow of his shoulder, and prepared to shoot himself a conversation-piece.

What saved McCarthy—at least temporarily—was Jonesy's disenchantment with hunting. What almost got McCarthy killed was a phenomenon George Kilroy, a friend of his father's, had called "eye-fever." Eye-fever, Kilroy claimed, was a form of buck-fever, and was probably the second most common cause of hunting accidents. "First is drink," said George Kilroy . . . and like Jonesy's father, Kilroy knew a bit on that subject, as well. "First is always drink."

Kilroy said that victims of eye-fever were uniformly astounded to discover they had shot a fence-post, or a passing car, or the broad side of a barn, or their own hunting partner (in many cases the partner was a spouse, a sib, or a child). "But I *saw* it," they would protest, and most of them, according to Kilroy, could pass a lie-detector test on the subject. They had seen the deer or the bear or the wolf, or just the grouse flip-flapping through the high autumn grass. They had *seen* it.

What happened, according to Kilroy, was that these hunters were afflicted by an anxiety to make the shot, to get it over with, one way or the other. This anxiety became so strong that the brain persuaded the eye that it saw what was not yet visible, in order to end the tension. This was eye-fever. And although Jonesy was aware of no particular anxiety—his fingers had been perfectly steady as he screwed the red stopper back into the throat of the Thermos—he admitted later to himself that yes, he might have fallen prey to the malady.

For one moment he saw the buck clearly at the end of the tunnel made by the interlocking branches—as clearly as he had seen any of the previous sixteen deer (six bucks, ten does) he had brought down over the years at Hole in the Wall. He saw its brown head, one eye so dark it was almost the black of jeweler's velvet, even part of its rack.

Shoot now! part of him cried—it was the Jonesy from the other side of the accident, the whole Jonesy. That one had spoken more frequently in the last month or so, as he began to approach some mythical state which people who had never been hit by a car blithely referred to as "total recovery," but he had never spoken as loudly as he did now. This was a command, almost a shout.

And his finger *did* tighten on the trigger. It never put on that last pound of pressure (or perhaps it only would have taken another half, a paltry eight ounces), but it *did* tighten. The voice that stopped him was that second Jonesy, the one who had awakened in Mass General, doped and disoriented and in pain, not sure of anything anymore except that someone wanted something to stop, someone couldn't stand it—not without a shot, anyway—that someone wanted Marcy.

No, not yet—wait, watch, this new cautious Jonesy said, and that was the voice he listened to. He froze in place, most of his weight thrown forward on his good left leg, rifle raised, barrel angled down that interlacing tunnel of light at a cool thirty-five degrees.

The first flakes of snow came skating down out of the white sky just then, and as they did, Jonesy saw a bright vertical line of orange below the deer's head—it was as if the snow had somehow conjured it up. For a moment perception simply gave up and what he was seeing over the barrel of his gun became only an unconnected jumble, like paints swirled all together on an artist's palette. There was no deer and no man, not even any woods, just a puzzling and untidy jumble of black, brown, and orange.

Then there was more orange, and in a shape that made sense: it was a hat, the kind with flaps you could fold down to cover your ears. The out-of-staters bought them at L. L. Bean's for forty-four dollars, each with a little tag inside that said PROUDLY MADE IN THE USA BY UNION LABOR. Or you could pick one up at Gosselin's for seven bucks. The tag in a Gosselin's cap just said MADE IN BANGLADESH.

The hat brought everything into horrible oh-God focus: the brown he had mistaken for a buck's head was the front of a man's wool jacket, the black jeweler's velvet of the buck's eye was a button, and the antlers were only more branches—branches belonging to the very tree in which he was standing. The man was unwise (Jonesy could not quite bring himself to use the word *crazy*) to be wearing a brown coat in the woods, but Jonesy was still at a loss to understand how he himself could have made a mistake of such potentially horrifying consequence. Because the man was also wearing an orange cap, wasn't he? And a bright orange flagman's vest as well, over the admittedly unwise brown coat. The man was—

—was a pound of finger-pressure from death. Maybe less.

It came home to him in a visceral way then, knocking him clean out of his own body. For a terrible, brilliant moment he never forgot, he was neither Jonesy

Number One, the confident pre-accident Jonesy, nor Jonesy Number Two, the more tentative survivor who spent so much of his time in a tiresome state of physical discomfort and mental confusion. For that moment he was some other Jonesy, an invisible presence looking at a gunman standing on a platform in a tree. The gunman's hair was short and already graying, his face lined around the mouth, beard-speckled on the cheeks, and haggard. The gunman was on the verge of using his weapon. Snow had begun to dance around his head and light on his untucked brown flannel shirt, and he was on the verge of shooting a man in an orange cap and vest of the very sort he would have been wearing himself if he had elected to go into the woods with the Beaver instead of up into this tree.

He fell back into himself with a thud, exactly as one fell back into one's seat after taking a car over a bad bump at a high speed. To his horror, he realized he was still tracking the man below with the Garand, as if some stubborn alligator deep in his brain refused to let go of the idea that the man in the brown coat was prey. Worse, he couldn't seem to make his finger relax on the rifle's trigger. There was even an awful second or two when he thought he was actually still squeezing, inexorably eating up those last few ounces between him and the greatest mistake of his life. He later came to accept that that at least had been an illusion, something akin to the feeling you get of rolling backward in your stopped car when you glimpse a slowly moving car beside you, out of the corner of your eye.

No, he was just frozen, but that was bad enough,

that was hell. *Jonesy, you think too much,* Pete liked to say when he caught Jonesy staring out into the middle distance, no longer tracking the conversation, and what he probably meant was *Jonesy, you imagine too much,* and that was very likely true. Certainly he was imagining too much now as he stood up here in the middle of the tree and the season's first snow, hair leaping up in tufts, finger locked on the Garand's trigger—not tightening still, as he had for a moment feared, but not loosening, either, the man almost below him now, the Garand's gunsight on the top of the orange cap, the man's life on an invisible wire between the Garand's muzzle and that cap, the man maybe thinking about trading his car or cheating on his wife or buying his oldest daughter a pony (Jonesy later had reason to know McCarthy had been thinking about none of those things, but of course not then, not in the tree with his forefinger a frozen curl around the trigger of his rifle) and not knowing what Jonesy had not known as he stood on the curb in Cambridge with his briefcase in one hand and a copy of the Boston *Phoenix* under his arm, namely that death was in the neighborhood, or perhaps even Death, a hurrying figure like something escaped from an early Ingmar Bergman film, something carrying a concealed implement in the coarse folds of its robe. Scissors, perhaps. Or a scalpel.

And the worst of it was that the man would not die, or at least not at once. He would fall down and lie there screaming, as Jonesy had lain screaming in the street. He couldn't remember screaming, but of course he had; he had been told this and had no reason to disbelieve it.

Screamed his fucking head off, most likely. And what if the man in the brown coat and orange accessories started screaming for Marcy? Surely he would not—not *really*—but Jonesy's mind might *report* screams of Marcy. If there was eye-fever—if he could look at a man's brown coat and see it as a deer's head—then there was likely the auditory equivalent, as well. To hear a man screaming and know you were the reason—dear God, no. And still his finger would not loosen.

What broke his paralysis was both simple and unexpected: about ten paces from the base of Jonesy's tree, the man in the brown coat fell down. Jonesy heard the pained, surprised sound he made—*mrof!* was what it sounded like—and his finger released the trigger without his even thinking about it.

The man was down on his hands and knees, his brown-gloved fingers (brown gloves, another mistake, this guy almost could have gone out with a sign reading SHOOT ME taped to his back, Jonesy thought) spread on the ground, which had already begun to whiten. As the man got up again, he began to speak aloud in a fretful, wondering voice. Jonesy didn't realize at first that he was also weeping.

"Oh dear, oh dear," the man said as he worked his way back to a standing position. He swayed on his feet as if drunk. Jonesy knew that men in the woods, men away from their families for a week or a weekend, got up to all sorts of small wickedness—drinking at ten in the morning was one of the most common. But Jonesy didn't think this guy was drunk. No reason; just a vibe.

"Oh dear, oh dear, oh dear." And then, as he began

to walk again: "Snow. Now it's snow. Please God, oh God, now it's snow, oh dear."

His first couple of steps were lurching and unsure. Jonesy had about decided that his vibe was incorrect, the guy *was* loaded, and then the fellow's gait smoothed out and he began to walk a little more evenly. He was scratching at his right cheek.

He passed directly beneath the stand, for a moment he wasn't a man at all but only a round circle of orange cap with brown shoulders to either side of it. His voice drifted up, liquid and full of tears, mostly *Oh dear* with the occasional *Oh God* or *Now it's snow* thrown in for salt.

Jonesy stood where he was, watching as the guy first disappeared directly beneath the stand, then came out on the other side. He pivoted without being aware of it to keep the plodding man in view—nor was he aware that he had lowered his rifle to his side, even pausing long enough to put the safety back on.

Jonesy didn't call out, and he supposed he knew why: simple guilt. He was afraid that the man down there would take one look at him and see the truth in Jonesy's eyes—even through his tears and the thickening snow, the man would see that Jonesy had been up there with his gun pointed, that Jonesy had almost shot him.

Twenty paces beyond the tree, the man stopped and only stood there, his gloved right hand raised to his brow, shielding his eyes from the snow. Jonesy realized he had seen Hole in the Wall. Had probably realized he was on an actual path, too. *Oh dear* and *Oh God* stopped, and the guy began to run toward the sound of the generator, rocking from side to side like a man on the deck of a ship. Jonesy could hear the stranger's short, sharp gasps for breath as he pounded toward the roomy cabin with the lazy curl of smoke rising from the chimney and fading almost at once into the snow.

Jonesy began to work his way down the rungs nailed to the trunk of the maple with his gun slung over his shoulder (the thought that the man might present some sort of danger did not occur to him, not then; he simply didn't want to leave the Garand, which was a fine gun, out in the snow). His hip had stiffened, and by the time he got to the foot of the tree, the man he'd almost shot had made it nearly all the way to the cabin door . . . which was unlocked, of course. No one locked up, not way out here.

5

About ten feet from the granite slab that served as Hole in the Wall's front stoop, the man in the brown coat and orange hat fell down again. His hat tumbled off, revealing a sweaty clump of thinning brown hair. He stayed on one knee for a moment, head lowered. Jonesy could hear his harsh, fast breathing.

The man picked up his cap, and just as he set it back on his head, Jonesy hailed him.

The man staggered to his feet and turned tipsily. Jonesy's first impression was that the man's face was very long—that he was almost what people meant when they called someone "horsefaced." Then, as

Jonesy got closer, hitching a little but not really limping (and that was good, because the ground underfoot was getting slippery fast), he realized the guy's face wasn't particularly long at all—he was just very scared and very *very* pale. The red patch on his cheek where he had been scratching stood out brightly. The relief that came over him when he saw Jonesy hurrying toward him was large and immediate. Jonesy almost laughed at himself, standing up there on the platform in the tree and worrying about the guy reading his eyes. This man wasn't into reading faces, and he clearly had no interest in where Jonesy had come from or what he might have been doing. This man looked like he wanted to throw his arms around Jonesy's neck and cover him with big gooey kisses.

"Thank God!" the man cried. He held out one hand toward Jonesy and shuffled toward him through the thin icing of new snow. "Oh gee, thank God, I'm lost, I've been lost in the woods since yesterday, I thought I was going to die out here. I . . . I . . ."

His feet slipped and Jonesy grabbed his upper arms. He was a big man, taller than Jonesy, who stood six-two, and broader, as well. Nevertheless, Jonesy's first impression was of insubstantialness, as if the man's fear had somehow scooped him out and left him light as a milkweed pod.

"Easy, fella," Jonesy said. "Easy, you're all right now, you're okay. Let's just get you inside and get you warm, how would that be?"

As if the word *warm* had been his cue, the man's teeth began to chatter. "S-S-Sure." He tried to smile, without much success. Jonesy was again struck by his extreme pallor. It was cold out here this morning, upper twenties at best, but the guy's cheeks were all ashes and lead. The only color in his face, other than the red patch, was the brown crescents under his eyes.

Jonesy got an arm around the man's shoulders, suddenly swept by an absurd and sappy tenderness for this stranger, an emotion so strong it was like his first junior-high-school crush—Mary Jo Martineau in a sleeveless white blouse and straight knee-length denim skirt. He was now absolutely sure the man hadn't been drinking—it was fear (and maybe exhaustion) rather than booze that had made him unsteady on his feet. Yet there *was* a smell on his breath—something like bananas. It reminded Jonesy of the ether he'd sprayed into the carburetor of his first car, a Vietnam-era Ford, to get it to crank over on cold mornings.

"Get you inside, right?"

"Yeah. C-Cold. Thank God you came along. Is this—"

"My place? No, a friend's." Jonesy opened the varnished oak door and helped the man over the threshold. The stranger gasped at the feel of the warm air, and a flush began to rise in his cheeks. Jonesy was relieved to see there was some blood in him, after all.

6

Hole in the Wall was pretty grand by deep-woods standards. You came in on the single big downstairs room—kitchen, dining room, and living room, all in one—but there were two bedrooms behind it and another upstairs, under the single eave. The big room was filled with the scent of pine and its mellow, varnished glow. There was a Navajo rug on the floor and a Micmac hanging on one wall which depicted brave little stick-hunters surrounding an enormous bear. A plain oak table, long enough to accommodate eight places, defined the dining area. There was a woodstove in the kitchen and a fireplace in the living area; when both were going, the place made you feel stupid with the heat even if it was twenty below outside. The west wall was all window, giving a view of the long, steep slope which fell off to the west. There had been a fire there in the seventies, and the dead trees stood black and twisted in the thickening snow. Jonesy, Pete, Henry, and the Beav called this slope The Gulch, because that's what the Beav's Dad and *his* friends had called it.

"Oh God, thank God, and thank you, too," the man in the orange hat said to Jonesy, and when Jonesy grinned—that was a lot of thank-you's—the man laughed shrilly as if to say yes, he knew it, it was a funny thing to say but he couldn't help it. He began to take deep breaths, for a few moments looking like one of those exercise gurus you saw on high-number cable. On every exhale, he talked.

"God, I really thought I was done-for last night . . . it was so cold . . . and the damp air, I remember that . . . remember thinking Oh boy, oh dear, what if there's snow coming after all . . . I got coughing and couldn't stop . . . something came and I thought I have to stop coughing, if that's a bear or something I'll . . . you know

. . . provoke it or something . . . only I couldn't and after awhile it just . . . you know, went away on its own—"

"You saw a bear in the night?" Jonesy was both fascinated and appalled. He had heard there were bears up here—Old Man Gosselin and his pickle-barrel buddies at the store loved to tell bear stories, particularly to the out-of-staters—but the idea that this man, lost and on his own, had been menaced by one in the night was keenly horrible. It was like hearing a sailor talk about a sea monster.

"I don't know that it was," the man said, and suddenly shot Jonesy a sideward look of cunning that Jonesy didn't like and couldn't read. "I can't say for sure, by then there was no more lightning."

"Lightning, too? Man!" If not for the guy's obviously genuine distress, Jonesy would have wondered if he wasn't getting his leg pulled. In truth, he wondered it a little, anyway.

"Dry lightning, I guess," the man said. Jonesy could almost see him shrugging it off. He scratched at the red place on his cheek, which might have been a touch of frostbite. "See it in winter, it means there's a storm on the way."

"And you saw this? Last night?"

"I guess so." The man gave him another quick, sideways glance, but this time Jonesy saw no slyness in it, and guessed he had seen none before. He saw only exhaustion. "It's all mixed up in my mind . . . my stomach's been hurting ever since I got lost . . . it always hurts when I'm ascairt, ever since I was a little kid . . ."

And he was *like* a little kid, Jonesy thought, looking everywhere at once with perfect unselfconsciousness. Jonesy led the guy toward the couch in front of the fireplace and the guy let himself be led. *Ascairt. He even said ascairt instead of afraid, like a kid. A little kid.*

"Give me your coat," Jonesy said, and as the guy first unbuttoned the buttons and then reached for the zipper under them, Jonesy thought again of how he had thought he was looking at a deer, at a *buck* for Chrissake—he had mistaken one of those buttons for an eye and had damned near put a bullet through it.

The guy got the zipper halfway down and then it stuck, one side of the little gold mouth choking on the cloth. He looked at it—gawked at it, really—as if he had never seen such a thing before. And when Jonesy reached for the zipper, the man dropped his hands to his sides and simply let Jonesy reach, as a first-grader would stand and let the teacher put matters right when he got his galoshes on the wrong feet or his jacket on inside out.

Jonesy got the little gold mouth started again and pulled it the rest of the way down. Outside the window-wall, The Gulch was disappearing, although you could still see the black scrawled shapes of the trees. Almost twenty-five years they had come up here together for the hunting, almost twenty-five years without a single miss, and in none of that time had there been snow heavier than the occasional squall. It looked like all that was about to change, although how could you tell? These days the guys on radio and TV made four inches of fresh powder sound like the next Ice Age.

For a moment the guy only stood there with his jacket hanging open and snow melting around his boots on the polished wooden floor, looking up at the rafters with his mouth open, and yes, he was like a great big six-year-old—or like Duddits. You almost expected to see mittens dangling from the cuffs of his jacket on clips. He shrugged out of his coat in that perfectly recognizable child's way, simply slumping his shoulders once it was unzipped and letting it fall. If Jonesy hadn't been there to catch it, it would have gone on the floor and gotten right to work sopping up the puddles of melting snow.

"What's that?" he asked.

For a moment Jonesy had no idea what the guy was talking about, and then he traced the stranger's gaze to the bit of weaving which hung from the center rafter. It was colorful—red and green, with shoots of canary yellow, as well—and it looked like a spiderweb.

"It's a dreamcatcher," Jonesy said. "An Indian charm. Supposed to keep the nightmares away, I guess."

"Is it yours?"

Jonesy didn't know if he meant the whole place (perhaps the guy hadn't been listening before) or just the dreamcatcher, but in either case the answer was the same. "No, my friend's. We come up hunting every year."

"How many of you?" The man was shivering, holding his arms crisscrossed over his chest and cupping his elbows in his palms as he watched Jonesy hang his coat on the tree by the door.

"Four. Beaver—this is his camp—is out hunting now. I don't know if the snow'll bring him back in or not. Probably it will. Pete and Henry went to the store."

"Gosselin's? That one?"

"Uh-huh. Come on over here and sit down on the couch."

Jonesy led him to the couch, a ridiculously long sectional. Such things had gone out of style decades ago, but it didn't smell too bad and nothing had infested it. Style and taste didn't matter much at Hole in the Wall.

"Stay put now," he said, and left the man sitting there, shivering and shaking with his hands clasped between his knees. His jeans had the sausagey look they get when there are longjohns underneath, and still he shook and shivered. But the heat had brought on an absolute flood of color; instead of looking like a corpse, the stranger now looked like a diphtheria victim.

Pete and Henry were doubling in the bigger of the two downstairs bedrooms. Jonesy ducked in, opened the cedar chest to the left of the door, and pulled out one of the two down comforters folded up inside. As he recrossed the living room to where the man sat shivering on the couch, Jonesy realized he hadn't asked the most elementary question of all, the one even six-year-olds who couldn't get their own zippers down asked.

As he spread the comforter over the stranger on

the outsized camp couch, he said: "What's your name?" And realized he almost knew. McCoy? McCann?

The man Jonesy had almost shot looked up at him, at once pulling the comforter up around his neck. The brown patches under his eyes were filling in purple.

"McCarthy," he said. "Richard McCarthy." His hand, surprisingly plump and white without its glove, crept out from beneath the coverlet like a shy animal. "You are?"

"Gary Jones," he said, and took the hand with the one which had almost pulled the trigger. "Folks mostly call me Jonesy."

"Thanks, Jonesy." McCarthy looked at him earnestly. "I think you saved my life."

"Oh, I don't know about that," Jonesy said. He looked at that red patch again. Frostbite, just a small patch. Frostbite, had to be.

CHAPTER TWO

THE BEAV

1

"You know I can't call anyone, don't you?" Jonesy said. "The phone lines don't come anywhere near here. There's a genny for the electric, but that's all."

McCarthy, only his head showing above the comforter, nodded. "I was hearing the generator, but you know how it is when you're lost—noises are funny. Sometimes the sound seems to be coming from your left or your right, then you'd swear it's behind you and you better turn back."

Jonesy nodded, although he did not, in fact, know how it was. Unless you counted the week or so immediately after his accident, time he had spent wandering in a fog of drugs and pain, he had never been lost.

"I'm trying to think what'd be the best thing," Jonesy said. "I guess when Pete and Henry get back, we better take you out. How many in your party?"

It seemed McCarthy had to think. That, added to the unsteady way he had been walking, solidified Jonesy's impression that the man was in shock. He wondered that one night lost in the woods would do that; he wondered if it would do it to him.

"Four," McCarthy said, after that minute to think. "Just like you guys. We were hunting in pairs. I was with a friend of mine, Steve Otis. He's a lawyer like me, down in Skowhegan. We're all from Skowhegan, you know, and this week for us . . . it's a big deal."

Jonesy nodded, smiling. "Yeah. Same here."

"Anyway, I guess I just wandered off." He shook his head. "I don't know, I was hearing Steve over on my right, sometimes seeing his vest through the trees, and then I . . . I just don't know. I got thinking about stuff, I guess—one thing the woods are great for is thinking about stuff—and then I was on my own. I guess I tried to backtrack but then it got dark . . ." He shook his head yet again. "It's all mixed up in my mind, but yeah—there were four of us, I guess that's one thing I'm sure of. Me and Steve and Nat Roper and Nat's sister, Becky."

"They must be worried sick."

McCarthy looked first startled, then apprehensive. This was clearly a new idea for him. "Yeah, they must be. Of course they are. Oh dear, oh gee."

Jonesy had to restrain a smile at this. When he got going, McCarthy sounded a little like a character in that movie, *Fargo*.

"So we better take you out. If, that is—"

"I don't want to be a bother—"

"We'll take you out. If we can. I mean, this weather came in *fast*."

"It sure did," McCarthy said bitterly. "You'd think they could do better with all their darn satellites and doppler radar and gosh knows what else. So much for fair and seasonably cold, huh?"

Jonesy looked at the man under the comforter, just the flushed face and the thatch of thinning brown hair showing, with some perplexity. The forecasts *he* had heard—he, Pete, Henry, and the Beav—had been full of the prospect of snow for the last two days. Some of the prognosticators hedged their bets, saying the snow could change over to rain, but the fellow on the Castle Rock radio station that morning (WCAS was the only radio they could get up here, and even that was thin and jumbled with static) had been talking about a fast-moving Alberta Clipper, six or eight inches, and maybe a nor'easter to follow, if the temperatures stayed down and the low didn't go out to sea. Jonesy didn't know where McCarthy had gotten his weather forecasts, but it sure hadn't been WCAS. The guy was just mixed up, that was most likely it, and had every right to be.

"You know, I could put on some soup. How would that be, Mr. McCarthy?"

McCarthy smiled gratefully. "I think that would be pretty fine," he said. "My stomach hurt last night and something fierce this morning, but I feel better now."

"Stress," Jonesy said. "I would have been puking my guts. Probably filling my pants, as well."

"I didn't throw up," McCarthy said. "I'm pretty

sure I didn't. But . . ." Another shake of the head, it was like a nervous tic with him. "I don't know. The way things are jumbled, it's like a nightmare I had."

"The nightmare's over," Jonesy said. He felt a little foolish saying such a thing—a little auntie-ish—but it was clear the guy needed reassurance.

"Good," McCarthy said. "Thank you. And I *would* like some soup."

"There's tomato, chicken, and I think maybe a can of Chunky Sirloin. What do you fancy?"

"Chicken," McCarthy said. "My mother always said chicken soup was the thing when you're not feeling your best."

He grinned as he said it, and Jonesy tried to keep the shock off his face. McCarthy's teeth were white and even, really too even to be anything but capped, given the man's age, which had to be forty-five or thereabouts. But at least four of them were missing—the canines on top (what Jonesy's father had called "the vampire teeth") and two right in front on the bottom—Jonesy didn't know what those were called. He knew one thing, though: McCarthy wasn't aware they were gone. No one who knew about such gaps in the line of his teeth could expose them so unselfconsciously, even under circumstances like these. Or so Jonesy believed. He felt a sick little chill rush through his gut, a telephone call from nowhere. He turned toward the kitchen before McCarthy could see his face change and wonder what was wrong. Maybe *ask* what was wrong.

"One order chicken soup coming right up. How about a grilled cheese to go with it?"

"If it's no trouble. And call me Richard, will you? Or Rick, that's even better. When people save my life, I like to get on a first-name basis with them as soon as possible."

"Rick it is, for sure." *Better get those teeth fixed before you step in front of another jury, Rick.*

The feeling that something was wrong here was very strong. It was that click, just as almost guessing McCarthy's name had been. He was a long way from wishing he'd shot the man when he had the chance, but he was already starting to wish McCarthy had stayed the hell away from his tree and out of his life.

2

He had the soup on the stove and was making the cheese sandwiches when the first gust of wind arrived—a big whoop that made the cabin creak and raised the snow in a furious sheet. For a moment even the black scrawled shapes of the trees in The Gulch were erased, and there was nothing outside the big window but white: it was as if someone had set up a drive-in movie screen out there. For the first time, Jonesy felt a thread of unease not just about Pete and Henry, presumably on their way back from Gosselin's in Henry's Scout, but for the Beaver. You would have said that if anybody knew these woods it would have been the Beav, but nobody knew anything in a white-out—*all bets were off,* that was another of his ne'er-do-well father's sayings, probably not as good as *you can't make yourself be lucky,* but not bad. The sound of the genny might help Beav find his way, but as McCarthy had pointed out, sounds had a way of deceiving you. Especially if the wind started kicking up, as it had now apparently decided to do.

His Mom had taught him the dozen basic things he knew about cooking, and one of them had to do with the art of making grilled cheese sandwiches. *Lay in a little mouseturds first,* she said—*mouseturds* being Janet Jones for *mustard*—*and then butter the goddam bread, not the skillet. Butter the skillet and all's you got's fried bread with some cheese in it.* He had never understood how the difference between where you put the butter, on the bread or in the skillet, could change the ultimate result, but he always did it his mother's way, even though it was a pain in the ass buttering the tops of the sandwiches while the bottoms cooked. No more would he have left his rubber boots on once he was in the house . . . because, his mother had always said, "they draw your feet." He had no idea just what that meant, but even now, as a man going on forty, he took his boots off as soon as he was in the door, so they wouldn't draw his feet.

"I think I might have one of these babies myself," Jonesy said, and laid the sandwiches in the skillet, butter side down. The soup had begun to simmer, and it smelled fine—like comfort.

"Good idea. I certainly hope your friends are all right."

"Yeah," Jonesy said. He gave the soup a stir. "Where's your place?"

"Well, we used to hunt in Mars Hill, at a place Nat and Becky's uncle owned, but some god-bless'd idiot burned it down two summers ago. Drinking and then getting careless with the old smokes, that's what the Fire Marshal said, anyway."

Jonesy nodded. "Not an uncommon story."

"The insurance paid the value of the place, but we had nowhere to hunt. I thought probably that'd be the end of it, and then Steve found this nice place over in Kineo. I think it's probably an unincorporated township, just another part of the Jefferson Tract, but Kineo's what they call it, the few people who live there. Do you know where I mean?"

"I know it," Jonesy said, speaking through lips that felt oddly numb. He was getting another of those telephone calls from nowhere. Hole in the Wall was about twenty miles east of Gosselin's. Kineo was maybe thirty miles to the west of the market. That was fifty miles in all. Was he supposed to believe that the man sitting on the couch with just his head sticking out of the down comforter had wandered fifty miles since becoming lost the previous afternoon? It was absurd. It was impossible.

"Smells good," McCarthy said.

And it did, but Jonesy no longer felt hungry.

3

He was just bringing the chow over to the couch when he heard feet stamping on the stone outside the door. A moment later the door opened and Beaver

ame in. Snow swirled around his legs in a dancing
nist.

"Jesus-Christ-bananas," the Beav said. Pete had once
made a list of Beav-isms, and Jesus-Christ-bananas
was high on it, along with such standbys as *doodlyfuck*
and *Kiss my bender.* They were exclamations both Zen
and profane. "I thought I was gonna end up spendin the
night out there, then I saw the light." Beav raised his
hands roofward, fingers spread. "Seen de light, Lawd,
essir, praise Je—" His glasses started to unfog then,
and he saw the stranger on the couch. He lowered his
hands, slowly, then smiled. That was one of the reasons
Jonesy had loved him ever since grade school, although
the Beav could be tiresome and wasn't the brightest
bulb in the chandelier, by any means: his first reaction
to the unplanned and unexpected wasn't a frown but a
smile.

"Hi," he said. "I'm Joe Clarendon. Who're you?"

"Rick McCarthy," he said, and got to his feet. The
comforter tumbled off him and Jonesy saw he had a
pretty good potbelly pooching out the front of his
sweater. *Well,* he thought, *nothing strange about that, at
least, it's the middle-aged man's disease, and it's going to
kill us in our millions during the next twenty years or so.*

McCarthy stuck out his hand, started to step forward, and almost tripped over the fallen comforter. If
Jonesy hadn't reached out and grabbed his shoulder,
steadying him, McCarthy probably would have fallen
forward, very likely cleaning out the coffee-table on
which the food was now set. Again Jonesy was struck
by the man's queer ungainliness—it made him think of

himself a little that past spring, as he had learned t
walk all over again. He got a closer look at the patc
on the guy's cheek, and sort of wished he hadn't. I
wasn't frostbite at all. It looked like a skin-tumor c
some kind, or perhaps a portwine stain with stubbl
growing out of it.

"Who, whoa, shake it but don't break it," Beave
said, springing forward. He grabbed McCarthy's han
and pumped it until Jonesy thought McCarthy woul
end up swan-diving into the coffee-table after all. H
was glad when the Beav—all five-feet-six of him, wit
snow still melting into all that long black hippie hair—
stepped back. The Beav was still smiling, more broadl
than ever. With the shoulder-length hair and the thic
glasses, he looked like either a math genius or a seria
killer. In fact, he was a carpenter.

"Rick here's had a time of it," Jonesy said. "Go
lost yesterday and spent last night in the woods."

Beaver's smile stayed on but became concerned
Jonesy had an idea what was coming next and willec
Beaver not to say it—he had gotten the impression
that McCarthy was a fairly religious man who migh
not care much for profanity—but of course asking
Beaver to clean up his mouth was like asking the
wind not to blow.

"Bitch-in-a-buzzsaw!" he cried now. "That's fuckir
terrible! Sit down! Eat! You too, Jonesy."

"Nah," Jonesy said, "you go on and eat that
You're the one who just came in out of the snow."

"You sure?"

"I am. I'll just scramble myself some eggs. Rick

can catch you up on his story." *Maybe it'll make more sense to you than it does to me,* he thought.

"Okay." Beaver took off his jacket (red) and his vest (orange, of course). He started to toss them on the woodpile, then thought better of it. "Wait, wait, got something you might want." He stuck his hand deep into one of the pockets of his down jacket, rummaged, and came out with a paperback book, considerably bent but seemingly none the worse for wear otherwise. Little devils with pitchforks danced across the cover—*Small Vices,* by Robert Parker. It was the book Jonesy had been reading in the stand.

The Beav held it out to him, smiling. "I left your sleeping-bag, but I figured you wouldn't be able to sleep tonight unless you knew who the fuck done it."

"You shouldn't have gone up there," Jonesy said, but he was touched in a way only Beaver could touch him. The Beav had come back through the blowing snow and hadn't been able to make out if Jonesy was up in the tree-stand or not, not for sure. He could have called, but for the Beav, calling wasn't enough, only seeing was believing.

"Not a problem," Beaver said, and sat down next to McCarthy, who was looking at him as a person might look at a new and rather exotic kind of small animal.

"Well, thanks," Jonesy said. "You get around that sandwich. I'm going to do eggs." He started away, then stopped. "What about Pete and Henry? You think they'll make it back okay?"

The Beav opened his mouth, but before he could

answer the wind gasped around the cabin again, making the walls creak and rising to a grim whistle in the eaves.

"Aw, this is just a cap of snow," Beaver said when the gust died away. "They'll make it back. Getting out again if there comes a real norther, that might be a different story." He began to gobble the grilled cheese sandwich. Jonesy went over to the kitchen to scramble some eggs and heat up another can of soup. He felt better about McCarthy now that Beaver was here. The truth was he always felt better when the Beav was around. Crazy but true.

4

By the time he got the eggs scrambled and the soup hot, McCarthy was chatting away to Beaver as if the two of them had been friends for the last ten years. If McCarthy was offended by the Beav's litany of mostly comic profanity, that was outweighed by Beav's considerable charm. "There's no explaining it," Henry had once told Jonesy. "He's a tribble, that's all—you can't help liking him. It's why his bed is never empty—it sure isn't his looks women respond to."

Jonesy brought his eggs and soup into the living area, working not to limp—it was amazing how much more his hip hurt in bad weather; he had always thought that was an old wives' tale but apparently it was not—and sat in one of the chairs at the end of the couch. McCarthy had been doing more talking than eating, it seemed. He'd barely touched his soup, and had eaten only half of his grilled cheese.

"How you boys doin?" Jonesy asked. He shook pepper onto his eggs and fell to with a will—his appetite had made a complete comeback, it seemed.

"We're two happy whoremasters," Beaver said, but although he sounded as chipper as ever, Jonesy thought he looked worried, perhaps even alarmed. "Rick's been telling me about his adventures. It's as good as a story in one of those men's magazines they had in the barber shop when I was a kid." He turned back to McCarthy, still smiling—that was the Beav, always smiling—and flicked a hand through the heavy fall of his black hair. "Old Man Castonguay was the barber on our side of Derry when I was a kid, and he scared me so fuckin bad with those clippers of his that I been stayin away from em ever since."

McCarthy gave a weak little smile but made no reply. He picked up the other half of his cheese sandwich, looked at it, then put it back down again. The red mark on his cheek glowed like a brand. Beaver, meanwhile, rushed on, as if he was afraid of what McCarthy might say if given half a chance. Outside it was snowing harder than ever, blowing, too, and Jonesy thought of Henry and Pete out there, probably on the Deep Cut Road by now, in Henry's old Scout.

"Not only did Rick here just about get eaten up by something in the middle of the night—a bear, he thinks it was—he lost his rifle, too. A brand-new Remington .30-.30, fuckin A, you won't never see that again, not a chance in a hundred thousand."

"I know," McCarthy said. The color was fading out of his cheeks again, that leaden look coming back in. "I don't even remember when I put it down, or—"

There was a sudden low rasping noise, like a locust. Jonesy felt the hair on the back of his neck stiffen, thinking it was something caught in the fireplace chimney. Then he realized it was McCarthy. Jonesy had heard some loud farts in his time, some long ones, too, but nothing like this. It seemed to go on forever, although it couldn't have been more than a few seconds. Then the smell hit.

McCarthy had picked up his spoon; now he dropped it back into his barely touched soup and raised his right hand to his blemished cheek in an almost girlish gesture of embarrassment. "Oh gosh, I'm sorry," he said.

"Not a bit, more room out than there is in," Beaver said, but that was just instinct running his mouth, instinct and the habits of a lifetime—Jonesy could see he was as shocked by that smell as Jonesy was himself. It wasn't the sulfurous rotten-egg odor that made you laugh and roll your eyes and wave your hand in front of your face, yelling *Ah, Jesus, who cut the cheese?* Nor one of those methane swamp-gas farts, either. It was the smell Jonesy had detected on McCarthy's breath, only stronger—a mixture of ether and overripe bananas, like the starter fluid you shot into your carburetor on a subzero morning.

"Oh dear, that's *awful*," McCarthy said. "I am so darned sorry."

"It's all right, really," Jonesy said, but his stomach

had curled up into a ball, like something protecting itself from assault. He wouldn't be finishing his own early lunch; no way in hell could he finish it. He wasn't prissy about farts as a rule, but this one really reeked.

The Beav got up from the couch and opened a window, letting in a swirl of snow and a draft of blessedly fresh air. "Don't you worry about it, partner . . . but that is pretty ripe. What the hell you been eatin? Woodchuck turds?"

"Bushes and moss and other stuff, I don't know just what," McCarthy said. "I was just so hungry, you know, I had to eat *something,* but I don't know much about that sort of thing, never read any of those books by Euell Gibbons . . . and of course it was dark." He said this last almost as if struck by an inspiration, and Jonesy looked up at Beaver, catching his eye to see if the Beav knew what Jonesy did— McCarthy was lying. McCarthy didn't know what he'd eaten in the woods, or if he had eaten anything at all. He just wanted to explain that ghastly unexpected frog's croak. And the stench which had followed it.

The wind gusted again, a big, gaspy whoop that sent a fresh skein of snow in through the open window, but at least it was turning the air over, and thank God for that.

McCarthy leaned forward so suddenly he might have been propelled by a spring, and when he hung his head forward between his knees, Jonesy had a good idea of what was coming next; so long Navajo rug, it's been good to know ya. The Beav clearly thought the same; he pulled back his legs, which had been splayed out before him, to keep them from being splattered.

But instead of vomit, what came out of McCarthy was a long, low buzz—the sound of a factory machine which has been put under severe strain. McCarthy's eyes bulged from his face like glass marbles, and his cheeks were so taut that little crescents of shadow appeared under the corners of his eyes. It went on and on, a rumbling, rasping noise, and when it finally ceased, the genny out back seemed far too loud.

"I've heard some mighty belches, but that's the all-time blue-ribbon winner," Beav said. He spoke with quiet and sincere respect.

McCarthy leaned back against the couch, eyes closing, mouth downturned in what Jonesy took for embarrassment, pain, or both. And once again he could smell that aroma of bananas and ether, a fermenting *active* smell, like something which has just started to go over.

"Oh God, I am so sorry," McCarthy said without opening his eyes. "I've been doing that all day, ever since light. And my stomach hurts again."

Jonesy and the Beav shared a silent, concerned look.

"You know what I think?" Beaver asked. "I think you need to lie down and take you a little sleep. You were probably awake all night, listening to that pesky bear and God knows what else. You're tired out and stressed out and fuck-a-duck knows what else out. You just need some shuteye, a few hours and you'll be right as the goddam rain."

McCarthy looked at Beaver with such wretched gratitude that Jonesy felt a little ashamed to be seeing it. Although McCarthy's complexion was still leaden, he had begun to break a sweat—great big beads that formed on his brow and temples, and then ran down his cheeks like clear oil. This in spite of the cold air now circulating in the room.

"You know," he said, "I bet you're right. I'm tired, that's all it is. My stomach hurts, but that part's just stress. And I was eating all sorts of things, bushes and just . . . gosh, oh dear, I don't know . . . all sorts of things." He scratched his cheek. "Is this darn thing on my face bad? Is it bleeding?"

"No," Jonesy said. "Just red."

"It's a reaction," McCarthy said dolefully. "I get the same thing from peanuts. I'll lie down. That's the ticket, all right."

He got to his feet, then tottered. Beaver and Jonesy both reached for him, but McCarthy steadied on his feet before either of them could take hold. Jonesy could have sworn that what he had taken for a middle-aged potbelly was almost gone. Was it possible? Could the man have passed that much gas? He didn't know. All he knew for sure was that it had been a mighty fart and an even mightier belch, the sort of thing you could yarn on for twenty years or more, starting off *We used to go up to Beaver Clarendon's camp the first week of hunting season every year, and one*

November—it was '01, the year of the big fall storm—this fella wandered into camp . . . Yes, it would make a good story, people would laugh about the big fart and the big burp, people *always* laughed at stories about farts and burps. He wouldn't tell the part about how he had come within eight ounces of press on a Garand's trigger of taking McCarthy's life, though. No, he wouldn't want to tell that part. Would he.

Pete and Henry were doubling, and so Beaver led McCarthy to the other downstairs bedroom, the one Jonesy had been using. The Beav shot him a little apologetic look, and Jonesy shrugged. It was the logical place, after all. Jonesy could double in with Beav tonight—Christ knew they'd done it enough as kids—and in truth, he wasn't sure McCarthy could have managed the stairs, anyway. He liked the man's sweaty, leaden look less and less.

Jonesy was the sort of man who made his bed and then buried it—books, papers, clothes, bags, assorted toiletries. He swept all this off as quick as he could, then turned back the coverlet.

"You need to take a squirt, partner?" the Beav asked.

McCarthy shook his head. He seemed almost hypnotized by the clean blue sheet Jonesy had uncovered. Jonesy was once again struck by how glassy the man's eyes were. Like the eyes of a stuffed trophy head. Suddenly and unbidden, he saw his living room back in Brookline, that upscale municipality next door to Boston. Braided rugs, early American furniture . . . and McCarthy's head mounted over the fireplace. *Bagged that one up in Maine,* he would tell his guests at cocktail parties. *Big bastard, dressed out at one-seventy.*

He closed his eyes, and when he opened them, the Beav was looking at him with something like alarm.

"Twinge in the hip," he said. "Sorry. Mr. McCarthy—Rick—you'll want to take off your sweater and pants. Boots too, of course."

McCarthy looked around at him like a man roused from a dream. "Sure," he said. "You bet."

"Need help?" Beaver asked.

"No, gosh no." McCarthy looked alarmed or amused or both. "I'm not that far gone."

"Then I'll leave Jonesy to supervise."

Beaver slipped out and McCarthy began to undress, starting by pulling his sweater off over his head. Beneath it he wore a red-and-black hunter's shirt, and beneath that a thermal undershirt. And yes, there was less gut poking out the front of that shirt, Jonesy was sure of it.

Well—*almost* sure. Only an hour ago, he reminded himself, he had been sure McCarthy's coat was the head of a deer.

McCarthy sat down in the chair beside the window to take off his shoes, and when he did there was another fart—not as long as the first one, but just as loud and hoarse. Neither of them commented on it, or the resulting smell, which was strong enough in the little room to make Jonesy's eyes feel like watering.

McCarthy kicked his boots off—they made

clunking sounds on the wooden floor—then stood up and unbuckled his belt. As he pushed his blue jeans down, revealing the lower half of his thermal underwear, the Beav came back in with a ceramic pot from upstairs. He put it down by the head of the bed. "Just in case you have to, you know, urk. Or if you get one of those collect calls you just have to take right away."

McCarthy looked at him with a dullness Jonesy found alarming—a stranger in what had been his bedroom, somehow ghostly in his baggy long underwear. An *ill* stranger. The question was just *how* ill.

"In case you can't make the bathroom," the Beav explained. "Which, by the way, is close by. Just bang a left outside the bedroom door, but remember it's the *second* door as you go along the wall, okay? If you forget and go in the first one, you'll be taking a shit in the linen closet."

Jonesy was surprised into a laugh and didn't care for the sound of it in the slightest—high and slightly hysterical.

"I feel better now," McCarthy said, but Jonesy detected absolutely zero sincerity in the man's voice. And the guy just stood there in his underwear, like an android whose memory circuits have been about three-quarters erased. Before, he had shown some life, if not exactly vivacity; now that was gone, like the color in his cheeks.

"Go on, Rick," Beaver said quietly. "Lie down and catch some winks. Work on getting your strength back."

"Yes, okay." He sat down on the freshly opened bed and looked out the window. His eyes were wide and blank. Jonesy thought the smell in the room was dissipating, but perhaps he was just getting used to it, the way you got used to the smell of the monkey-house at the zoo if you stayed in there long enough. "Gosh, look at it snow."

"Yeah," Jonesy said. "How's your stomach now?"

"Better." McCarthy's eyes moved to Jonesy's face. They were the solemn eyes of a frightened child. "I'm sorry about passing gas that way—I never did anything like that before, not even in the Army when it seemed like we ate beans every day—but I feel better."

"Sure you don't need to take a leak before you turn in?" Jonesy had four children, and this question came almost automatically.

"No. I went in the woods just before you found me. Thank you for taking me in. Thank you both."

"Ah, hell," Beaver said, and shuffled his feet uncomfortably. "Anybody woulda."

"Maybe," McCarthy said. "And maybe not. In the Bible it says, 'Behold, I stand at the door and knock.' " Outside, the wind gusted more fiercely yet, making Hole in the Wall shake. Jonesy waited for McCarthy to finish—it sounded as if he had more to say—but the man just swung his feet into bed and pulled the covers up.

From somewhere deep in Jonesy's bed there came another of those long, rasping farts, and Jonesy decided that was enough for him. It was one thing to let in a wayfaring stranger when he came to your door just ahead of a storm; it was another to stand around while he laid a series of gas-bombs.

The Beaver followed him out and closed the door gently behind him.

5

When Jonesy started to talk, the Beav shook his head, raised his finger to his lips, and led Jonesy across the big room to the kitchen, which was as far as they could get from McCarthy without going into the shed out back.

"Man, that guy's in a world of hurt," Beaver said, and in the harsh glow of the kitchen's fluorescent strips, Jonesy could see just how worried his old friend was. The Beav rummaged into the wide front pocket of his overalls, found a toothpick, and began to nibble on it. In three minutes—the length of time it took a dedicated smoker to finish a cigarette—he would reduce it to a palmful of flax-fine splinters. Jonesy didn't know how the Beav's teeth stood up to it (or his stomach), but he had been doing it his whole life.

"I hope you're wrong, but . . ." Jonesy shook his head. "Did you ever smell anything like those farts?"

"Nope," Beaver said. "But there's a lot more going on with that guy than just a bad stomach."

"What do you mean?"

"Well, he thinks it's November eleventh, for one thing."

Jonesy had no idea what the Beav was talking

about. November eleventh was the day their own hunting party had arrived, bundled into Henry's Scout, as always.

"Beav, it's Wednesday. It's the *fourteenth*."

Beaver nodded, smiling a little in spite of himself. The toothpick, which had already picked up an appreciable warp, rolled from one side of his mouth to the other. "I know that. *You* know that. Rick, he don't know that. Rick thinks it's the Lord's Day."

"Beav, what exactly did he say to you?" Whatever it was, it couldn't have been much—it just didn't take that long to scramble a couple of eggs and heat a can of soup. That started a train of thought, and as Beaver talked, Jonesy ran water to do up the few dishes. He didn't mind camping out, but he was damned if he was going to live in squalor, as so many men seemed willing to do when they left their homes and went into the woods.

"What he said was they came up on Saturday so they could hunt a little, then spend Sunday working on the roof, which had a couple of leaks in it. He goes, 'At least I didn't have to break the commandment about working on the Sabbath. When you're lost in the woods, the only thing you have to work on is not going crazy.' "

"Huh," Jonesy said.

"I guess I couldn't swear in a court of law that he thinks this is the eleventh, but it's either that or go back a week further, to the fourth, because he sure does think it's Sunday. And I just can't believe he's been out there ten days."

Jonesy couldn't, either. But three? Yes. That he *could* believe. "It would explain something he told me," Jonesy said. "He—"

The floor creaked and they both jumped a little, looking toward the closed bedroom door on the other side of the big room, but there was nothing to see. And the floors and walls were always creaking out here, even when the wind wasn't blowing up high. They looked at each other, a little shamefaced.

"Yeah, I'm jumpy," Beaver said, perhaps reading Jonesy's face, perhaps picking the thought out of Jonesy's mind. "Man, you have to admit it's a little creepy, him turning up right out of the woods like that."

"Yeah, it is."

"That fart sounded like he had something crammed up his butt that was dying of smoke inhalation."

The Beav looked a little surprised at that, as he always did when he said something funny. They began laughing simultaneously, holding onto each other and doing it through open mouths, expelling the sounds as a series of harsh sighs, trying to keep it down, not wanting the poor guy to hear them if he was still awake, hear and know they were laughing at him. Jonesy had a particularly hard time keeping it quiet because the release was so necessary—it had a hysterical severity to it and he doubled over, gasping and snorting, water running out of his eyes.

At last Beaver grabbed him and yanked him out the door. There they stood coatless in the deepening snow, finally able to laugh out loud with the booming wind to cover the sounds they made.

6

When they went back in again, Jonesy's hands were so numb he barely felt the hot water when he plunged his hands into it, but he was laughed out and that was good. He wondered again about Pete and Henry—how they were doing and if they'd make it back okay.

"You said it explained some stuff," the Beav said. He had started another toothpick. "What stuff?"

"He didn't know snow was coming," Jonesy said. He spoke slowly, trying to recall McCarthy's exact words. " 'So much for fair and seasonably cold,' I think that's what he said. But that would make sense if the last forecast he heard was for the eleventh or twelfth. Because until late yesterday, it *was* fair, wasn't it?"

"Yeah, and seasonably fuckin cold," Beaver agreed. He pulled a dishtowel with a pattern of faded lady-bugs on it from the drawer by the sink and began to dry the dishes. He looked across at the closed bedroom door as he worked. "What else'd he say?"

"That their camp was in Kineo."

"*Kineo?* That's forty, fifty miles west of here. He—" Beaver took the toothpick out of his mouth, examined the bite-marks on it, and put the other end in his mouth. "Oh, I see."

"Yeah. He couldn't have done all that in a single

night, but if he was out there for three days—"

"—and four nights, if he got lost on Saturday afternoon that makes four nights—"

"Yeah, and four nights. So, supposing he kept pretty much headed dead east that whole time . . ." Jonesy calculated fifteen miles a day. "I'd say it's possible."

"But how come he didn't freeze?" Beaver had lowered his voice to a near-whisper, probably without being aware of it. "He's got a nice heavy coat and he's wearin longies, but nights have been in the twenties everywhere north of the county line since Halloween. So you tell me how he spends four nights out there and doesn't freeze. Doesn't even look like he's got any frostbite, just that mess on his cheek."

"I don't know. And there's something else," Jonesy said. "How come he doesn't have the start of a beard?"

"Huh?" Beaver's mouth opened. The toothpick hung from his lower lip. Then, very slowly, he nodded. "Yeah. All he's got is stubble."

"I'd say less than a day's growth."

"I guess he was shavin, huh?"

"Right," Jonesy said, picturing McCarthy lost in the woods, scared and cold and hungry (not that he looked like he'd missed many meals, that was another thing), but still kneeling by a stream every morning, breaking the ice with a booted foot so he could get to the water beneath, then taking his trusty Gillette from . . . where? His coat pocket?

"And then this morning he lost his razor, which is

why he's got the stubble," the Beav said. He was smiling again, but there didn't seem to be a lot of humor in it.

"Yeah. Same time he lost his gun. Did you see his teeth?"

Beaver made a what-now grimace.

"Four gone. Two on top, two on the bottom. He looks like the What-me-worry kid that's always on the front of *Mad* magazine."

"Not a big deal, buddy. I've got a couple of AWOL choppers myself." Beaver hooked back one corner of his mouth, baring his left gum in a one-sided grin Jonesy could have done without. "Eee? Ight ack ere."

Jonesy shook his head. It wasn't the same. "The guy's a lawyer, Beav—he's out in public all the time, his looks are part of his living. And these babies are right out in front. He didn't know they were gone. I'd swear to it."

"You don't suppose he got exposed to radiation or something, do you?" Beaver asked uneasily. "Your teeth fall out when you get fuckin radiation poisonin, I saw that in a movie one time. One of the ones *you're* always watching, those monster shows. You don't suppose it's that, do you? Maybe he got that red mark the same time."

"Yeah, he got a dose when the Mars Hill Nuclear Power Plant blew up," Jonesy said, and Beaver's puzzled expression made him immediately sorry for the crack. "Beav, when you get radiation poisoning, I think your hair falls out, too."

The Beaver's face cleared. "Yeah, that's right. The

guy in the movie ended up as bald as Telly what's-his-fuck, used to play that cop on TV." He paused. "Then the guy died. The one in the movie, I mean, not Telly, although now that I think of it—"

"This guy's got plenty of hair," Jonesy interrupted. Let Beaver get off on a tangent and they would likely never get back to the point. He noticed that, out of the stranger's presence, neither of them called him Rick, or even McCarthy. Just "the guy," as if they subconsciously wanted to turn him into something less important than a man—something generic, as if that would make it matter less if . . . well, if.

"Yeah," Beaver said. "He does, doesn't he? Plenty of hair."

"He must have amnesia."

"Maybe, but he remembers who he is, who he was with, shit like that. Man, that was some trumpet-blast he blew, wasn't it? And the *stink*! Like ether!"

"Yeah," Jonesy said. "I kept thinking of starter fluid. Diabetics get a smell when they're tipping over. I read that in a mystery novel, I think."

"Is it like starter fluid?"

"I can't remember."

They stood there looking at each other, listening to the wind. It crossed Jonesy's mind to tell Beaver about the lightning the guy claimed to have seen, but why bother? Enough was enough.

"I thought he was going to blow his cookies when he leaned forward like that," the Beav said. "Didn't you?"

Jonesy nodded.

"And he don't look well, not at all well."

"No."

Beaver sighed, tossed his toothpick in the trash, and looked out the window, where the snow was coming down harder and heavier than ever. He flicked his fingers through his hair. "Man, I wish Henry and Pete were here. Henry especially."

"Beav, Henry's a *psychiatrist*."

"I know, but he's the closest thing to a doctor we got—and I think that fellow needs doctoring."

Henry actually *was* a physician—had to be, in order to get his certificate of shrinkology—but he'd never practiced anything except psychiatry, as far as Jonesy knew. Still, he understood what Beaver meant.

"Do you still think they'll make it back, Beav?"

Beaver sighed. "Half an hour ago I would have said for sure, but it's really comin heavy. I think so." He looked at Jonesy somberly; there was not much of the usually happy-go-lucky Beaver Clarendon in that look. "I hope so," he said.

CHAPTER THREE

HENRY'S SCOUT

1

Now, as he followed the Scout's headlights through the thickening snow, burrowing as if through a tunnel along the Deep Cut Road toward Hole in the Wall, Henry was down to thinking about ways to do it.

There was the Hemingway Solution, of course— way back at Harvard, as an undergraduate, he had written a paper calling it that, so he might have been thinking about it—in a personal way, not just as another step toward fulfilling some twinky course requirement, that was—even then. The Hemingway Solution was a shotgun, and Henry had one of those now . . . not that he would do it here, with the others. The four of them had had a lot of fine times at Hole in the Wall, and it would be unfair to do it there. It would pollute the place for Pete and Jonesy—for Beaver too, maybe Beaver most of all, and that wouldn't be right. But it would be soon, he could feel it coming on, something like a sneeze. Funny to compare the ending of your life to a sneeze, but that was probably what it came to. Just *kerchoo,* and then hello darkness, my old friend.

When implementing the Hemingway Solution, you took off your shoe and your sock. Butt of the gun went on the floor. Barrel went into your mouth. Great toe went around the trigger. *Memo to myself,* Henry thought as the Scout fishtailed a little in the fresh snow and he corrected—the ruts helped, that was really all this road was, a couple of ruts dug by the skidders that used it in the summertime. *If you do it that way, take a laxative and don't do it until after that final dump, no need to make any extra mess for the people who find you.*

"Maybe you better slow down a little," Pete said. He had a beer between his legs and it was half gone, but one wouldn't be enough to mellow Pete out. Three or four more, though, and Henry could go barrel-assing down this road at sixty and Pete would just sit there in the passenger seat, singing along with one of those horrible fucking Pink Floyd discs. And he *could* go sixty, probably, without putting so much as another ding in the front bumper. Being in the ruts of the Deep Cut, even when they were filled with snow, was like being on rails. If it kept snowing that might change, but for now, all was well.

"Don't worry, Pete—everything's five-by-five."

"You want a beer?"

"Not while I'm driving."

"Not even out here in West Overshoe?"

"Later."

Pete subsided, leaving Henry to follow the bore of the headlights, to thread his way along this white lane between the trees. Leaving him with his thoughts, which was where he wanted to be. It was like returning to a bloody place inside your mouth, exploring it again and again with the tip of your tongue, but it was where he wanted to be.

There were pills. There was the old Baggie-over-the-head-in-the-bathtub trick. There was drowning. There was jumping from a high place. The handgun in the ear was too unsure—too much chance of waking up paralyzed—and so was slitting the wrists, that was for people who were only practicing, but the Japanese had a way of doing it that interested Henry very much. Tie a rope around your neck. Tie the other end to a large rock. Put the rock on the seat of a chair, then sit down with your back braced so you can't fall backward but have to keep sitting. Tip the chair over and the rock rolls off. Subject may live for three to five minutes in a deepening dream of asphyxiation. Gray fades to black; hello darkness, my old friend. He had read about that method in one of Jonesy's beloved Kinsey Milhone detective novels, of all places. Detective novels and horror movies: those were the things that floated Jonesy's boat.

On the whole, Henry leaned toward the Hemingway Solution.

Pete finished his first beer and popped the top on his second, looking considerably more content. "What'd you make of it?" Pete asked.

Henry felt called to from that other universe, the one where the living actually wanted to live. As always these days, that made him feel impatient. But it was important that none of them suspect, and he had an idea Jonesy already did, a little. Beaver might, too. They were the ones who could sometimes see inside. Pete didn't have a clue, but he might say the wrong thing to one of the others, about how preoccupied ole Henry had gotten, like there was something on his mind, something *heavy,* and Henry didn't want that. This was going to be the last trip to Hole in the Wall for the four of them, the old Kansas Street gang, the Crimson Pirates of the third and fourth grades, and he wanted it to be a good one. He wanted them to be shocked when they heard, even Jonesy, who saw into him the most often and always had. He wanted them to say they'd had no idea. Better that than the three of them sitting around with their heads hung, not able to make eye contact with one another except in fleeting glances, thinking that they should have known, they had seen the signs and should have done something. So he came back to that other universe, simulating interest smoothly and convincingly. Who could do that better than a headshrinker?

"What did I make of what?"

Pete rolled his eyes. "At *Gosselin's,* dimbulb! All that stuff Old Man Gosselin was talking about."

"Peter, they don't call him Old Man Gosselin for nothing. He's eighty if he's a day, and if there's one thing old women and old men are *not* short on, it's hysteria." The Scout—no spring chicken itself, fourteen years old and far into its second trip around the odometer—popped out of the ruts and immediately skidded, four-wheel drive or not. Henry steered into the skid, almost laughing when Pete dropped his beer onto the floor and yelled, "Whoa—fuck, watch out!"

Henry let off on the gas until he felt the Scout start to straighten out, then zapped the go-pedal again, deliberately too fast and too hard. The Scout went into another skid, this time widdershins to the first, and Pete yelled again. Henry let up once more and the Scout thumped back into the ruts and once again ran smoothly, as if on rails. One positive to deciding to end your life, it seemed, was no longer sweating the small stuff. The lights cut through the white and shifting day, full of a billion dancing snowflakes, not one of them the same, if you believed the conventional wisdom.

Pete picked up his beer (only a little had spilled), and patted his chest. "Aren't you going a little fast?"

"Not even close," Henry said, and then, as if the skid had never occurred (it had) or interrupted his train of thought (it hadn't), he went on, "Group hysteria is most common in the very old and the very young. It's a well-documented phenomenon in both my field and that of the sociology heathens who live next door."

Henry glanced down and saw he was doing thirty-five, which was, in fact, a little fast for these conditions. He slowed down. "Better?"

Pete nodded. "Don't get me wrong, you're a great

driver, but man, it's *snowing*. Also, we got the supplies." He jerked his thumb back over his shoulder at the two bags and two boxes in the back seat. "In addition to hot dogs, we got the last three boxes of Kraft Macaroni and Cheese. Beaver can't live without that stuff, you know."

"I know," Henry said. "I like it, too. Remember those stories about devil-worship in Washington State, the ones that made the press in the mid-nineties? They were traced back to several old people living with their children—grandchildren, in one case—in two small towns south of Seattle. The mass reports of sexual abuse in daycare centers apparently began with teenage girls working as part-time aides crying wolf at the same time in Delaware and California. Possibly coincidence, or possibly the time was simply ripe for such stories to gain credence and these girls caught a wave out of the air."

How smoothly the words rolled out of his mouth, almost as if they mattered. Henry talked, the man beside him listened with dumb admiration, and no one (certainly not Pete) could have surmised that he was thinking of the shotgun, the rope, the exhaust pipe, the pills. His head was full of tape-loops, that was all. And his tongue was the cassette player.

"In Salem," Henry went on, "the old men and the young girls combined their hysteria, and *voilà*, you have the Salem Witch Trials."

"I saw that movie with Jonesy," Pete said. "Vincent Price was in it. Scared the shit out of me."

"I'm sure," Henry said, and laughed. For one wild

moment he'd thought Pete was talking about *The Crucible.* "And when are hysterical ideas most likely to gain credence? Once the crops are in and the bad weather closes down, of course—then there's time for telling stories and making mischief. In Wenatchee, Washington, it's devil-worship and child sacrifices in the woods. In Salem it was witches. And in the Jefferson Tract, home of the one and only Gosselin's Market, it's strange lights in the sky, missing hunters, and troop maneuvers. Not to mention weird red stuff growing on the trees."

"I don't know about the helicopters and the soldiers, but enough people have seen those lights so they're having a special town meeting. Old Man Gosselin told me so while you were getting the canned stuff. Also, those folks over Kineo way are really missing. *That* ain't hysteria."

"Four quick points," Henry said. "First, you can't have a town meeting in the Jefferson Tract because there's no town—even Kineo's just an unincorporated township with a name. Second, the meeting will be held around Old Man Gosselin's Franklin stove and half those attending will be shot on peppermint schnapps or coffee brandy."

Pete snickered.

"Third, what else have they got to do? And fourth—this concerns the hunters—they probably either got tired of it and went home, or they all got drunk and decided to get rich at the rez casino up in Carrabassett."

"You think, huh?" Pete looked crestfallen, and

Henry felt a great wave of affection for him. He reached over and patted Pete's knee.

"Never fear," he said. "The world is full of strange things." If the world had really been full of strange things, Henry doubted he would have been so eager to leave it, but if there was one thing a psychiatrist knew how to do (other than write prescriptions for Prozac and Paxil and Ambien, that was), it was tell lies.

"Four hunters all disappearing at the same time seems pretty strange to me, all right."

"Not a bit," Henry said, and laughed. "*One* would be odd. *Two* would be strange. Four? They went off together, depend on it."

"How far are we from Hole in the Wall, Henry?" Which, when translated, meant *Do I have time for another beer?*

Henry had zeroed the Scout's tripmeter at Gosselin's, an old habit that went back to his days working for the State of Massachusetts, where the deal had been twelve cents a mile and all the psychotic geriatrics you could write up. The mileage between the store and the Hole was easy enough to remember: 22.2. The odometer currently read 12.7, which meant—

"*Look out!*" Pete shouted, and Henry snapped his gaze back to the windshield.

The Scout had just topped the steep rise of a tree-covered ridge. The snow here was thicker than ever, but Henry was running with the high beams on and clearly saw the person sitting in the road about a hundred feet ahead—a person wearing a duffel coat, an orange vest that blew backward like Superman's cape in the strengthening wind, and one of those Russian fur hats. Orange ribbons had been attached to the hat, and they also blew back in the wind, reminding Henry of the streamers you sometimes saw strung over used-car lots. The guy was sitting in the middle of the road like an Indian that wants to smoke-um peace pipe, and he did not move when the headlights struck him. For one moment Henry saw the sitting figure's eyes, wide open but still, so still and bright and blank, and he thought: *That's how my eyes would look if I didn't guard them so closely.*

There was no time to stop, not with the snow. Henry twisted the wheel to the right and felt the thump as the Scout came out of the ruts again. He caught another glimpse of the white, still face and had time to think, *Why, goddam! It's a woman.*

Once out of the ruts the Scout began to skid again at once. This time Henry turned against it, deliberately snowplowing the wheels to deepen the skid, knowing without even thinking about it (there was no time to think) that it was the road-sitter's only chance. And he didn't rate it much of one, at that.

Pete screamed, and from the corner of his eye, Henry saw him raise his hands in front of his face, palms out in a warding-off gesture. The Scout tried to go broadside and *now* Henry spun the wheel back, trying to control the skid just enough so that the rear end wouldn't smash the road-sitter's face backward into her skull. The wheel spun with greasy, giddy ease under his gloved hands. For perhaps three seconds the Scout shot down the snow-covered Deep Cut Road at a forty-five-degree angle, a thing belonging partly to Henry Devlin and partly to the storm. Snow flew up and around it in a fine spray; the headlights painted the snow-slumped pines on the left side of the road in a pair of moving spots. Three seconds, not long, but just long enough. He saw the figure pass by as if she were moving instead of them, except she never moved, not even when the rusty edge of the Scout's bumper flirted past her with perhaps no more than an inch of snowy air between it and her face.

Missed you! Henry exulted. *Missed you, you bitch!* Then the last thin thread of control broke and the Scout broached broadside. There was a juddering vibration as the wheels found the ruts again, only crosswise this time. It was still trying to turn all the way around, swapping ends—*Frontsies-backsies!* they used to cry when in line back in grammar school—and then it hit a buried rock or perhaps a small fallen tree with a terrific thud and rolled over, first on the passenger side, the windows over there disintegrating into glittering crumbs, then over onto the roof. One side of Henry's seatbelt broke, spilling him onto the roof on his left shoulder. His balls thumped against the steering column, producing instant leaden pain. The turnsignal stalk broke off against his thigh and he felt blood begin to run at once, soaking his jeans. *The claret,* as the old boxing radio announcers used to call it, as in *Look out, folks, the claret has begun to flow.* Pete was yelling or screaming or both.

For several seconds the overturned Scout's engine

continued to run, then gravity did its work and the motor died. Now it was just an overturned hulk in the road, wheels still spinning, lights shining at the snow-loaded trees on the left side of the road. One of them went out, but the other continued to shine.

2

Henry had talked with Jonesy a lot about his accident (listened, really; therapy was creative listening), and he knew that Jonesy had no memory of the actual collision. As far as Henry could tell, he himself never lost consciousness following the Scout's flip, and the chain of recollection remained intact. He remembered fumbling for the seatbelt clasp, wanting to be all the way free of the fucking thing, while Pete bellowed that his leg was broken, his cocksucking *leg* was broken. He remembered the steady *whick-thump, whick-thump* of the windshield wipers and the glow of the dashlights, which were now up instead of down. He found the seatbelt clasp, lost it, found it again, and pushed it. The seatbelt's lap-strap released him and he thumped awkwardly against the roof, shattering the domelight's plastic cover.

He flailed with his hand, found the doorhandle, couldn't move it.

"*My leg!* Oh man, my fucking *leg!*"

"Shut up about it," Henry said. "Your leg's okay." As if he knew. He found the doorhandle again, yanked, and there was nothing. Then he realized why—he was upside down and yanking the wrong way. He reversed

is grip and the domelight's uncovered bulb glared
otly in his eye as the door clicked open. He shoved the
oor with the back of his hand, sure there would be no
eal result; the frame was probably bent and he'd be
ıcky to get six inches.

But the door grated and suddenly he could feel
now swirling coldly around his face and neck. He
ushed harder on the door, getting his shoulder into it,
nd it wasn't until his legs came free of the steering col-
ımn that he realized they had been hung up. He did
ıalf a somersault and was suddenly regarding his own
lenim-covered crotch at close range, as if he had
lecided to try and kiss his throbbing balls, make them
ll well. His diaphragm folded in on itself and it was
ıard to breathe.

"Henry, help me! I'm caught! I'm fuckin *caught*!"

"Just a minute." His voice sounded squeezed and
ıigh, hardly his own voice at all. Now he could see the
ıpper left leg of his jeans darkening with blood. The
vind in the pines sounded like God's own Electrolux.

He grabbed the doorpost, grateful he'd left his
;loves on while he was driving, and gave a tremen-
lous yank—he had to get out, had to unfold his
liaphragm so he could breathe.

For a moment nothing happened, and then Henry
oopped out like a cork out of a bottle. He lay where he
was for a moment, panting and looking up into a sift-
ng, falling net of snow. There was nothing odd about
:he sky then; he would have sworn to it in court on a
.tack of Bibles. Just the low gray bellies of the clouds
ınd the psychedelic downrush of the snow.

Pete was calling his name again and again, wit increasing panic.

Henry rolled over, got to his knees, and when tha went all right he lurched to his feet. He only stood fo a moment, swaying in the wind and waiting to see his bleeding left leg would buckle and spill him int the snow again. It didn't, and he limped around th back of the overturned Scout to see what he could d about Pete. He spared one glance at the woman wh had caused all this fuckarow. She sat as she had, cross legged in the middle of the road, her thighs and th front of her parka frosted with snow. Her vest snappe and billowed. So did the ribbons attached to her cap She had not turned to look at them but stared back i the direction of Gosselin's Market just as she had whe they came over the rise and saw her. One swooping curving tire-track in the snow came within a foot of he cocked left leg, and he had no idea, absolutely none a all, how he could have missed her.

"Henry! *Henry, help me!*"

He hurried on, slipping in the new snow as h rounded the passenger side. Pete's door was stuck, bu when Henry got on his knees and yanked with bot hands, it came open about halfway. He reached in grabbed Pete's shoulder, and yanked. Nothing.

"Unbuckle your belt, Pete."

Pete fumbled but couldn't seem to find it even though it was right in front of him. Working care fully, with not the slightest feeling of impatience (he supposed he might be in shock), Henry unclipped the belt and Pete thumped to the roof, his head bending sideways. He screamed in mingled surprise and pain and then came floundering and yanking his way out of the half-open door. Henry grabbed him under his arms and pulled backward. They both went over in the snow and Henry was afflicted with *déjà vu* so strong and so sudden it was like swooning. Hadn't they played just this way as kids? Of course they had. The day they'd taught Duddits how to make snow angels, for one. Someone began to laugh, startling him badly. Then he realized it was him.

Pete sat up, wild-eyed and glowering, the back of him covered with snow. "The fuck are *you* laughing about? That asshole almost got us killed! I'm gonna strangle the son of a bitch!"

"Not her son but the bitch herself," Henry said. He was laughing harder than ever and thought it quite likely that Pete didn't understand what he was saying—especially with the wind thrown in—but he didn't care. Seldom had he felt so delicious.

Pete flailed to his feet much as Henry had done himself, and Henry was just about to say something wise, something about how Pete was moving pretty well for a guy with a broken leg, when Pete went back down with a cry of pain. Henry went to him and felt Pete's leg, thrust out in front of him. It seemed intact, but who could tell through two layers of clothing?

"It ain't broke after all," Pete said, but he was panting with pain. "Fucker's locked up is all, just like when I was playin football. Where is she? You sure it's a woman?"

"Yes."

Pete got up and hobbled around the front of the car holding his knee. The remaining headlight still shone bravely into the snow. "She better be crippled or blind, that's all I can say," he told Henry. "If she's not, I'm gonna kick her ass all the way back to Gosselin's."

Henry began to laugh again. It was the mental picture of Pete hopping . . . then *kicking*. Like some fucked-up Rockette. "Peter, don't you really hurt her!" he shouted, suspecting any severity he might have managed was negated by the fact that he was speaking between gusts of maniacal laughter.

"I won't unless she puts some sass on me," Pete said. The words, carried back to Henry on the wind, had an offended-old-lady quality to them that made him laugh harder than ever. He scooted down his jeans and long underwear and stood there in his Jockeys to see how badly the turnsignal stalk had wounded him.

It was a shallow gash about three inches long on the inside of his thigh. It had bled copiously—was still oozing—but Henry didn't think it was deep.

"What in the *hell* did you think you were doing?" Pete scolded from the other side of the overturned Scout, whose wipers were still *whick-thumping* back and forth. And although Pete's tirade was laced with profanity (much of it decidedly Beaverish), his friend still sounded to Henry like an offended old lady schoolteacher, and this got him laughing again as he hauled up his britches.

"Why you sittin out here in the middle of the

motherfuckin road in the middle of a motherfuckin snowstorm? You drunk? High on drugs? What kind of dumb doodlyfuck are you? Hey, talk to me! You almost got me n my buddy killed, the least you can do is . . . *oww, FUCK-ME-FREDDY!*"

Henry came around the wreck just in time to see Pete fall over beside Ms. Buddha. His leg must have locked up again. She never looked at him. The orange ribbons on her hat blew out behind her. Her face was raised into the storm, wide eyes not blinking as the snowflakes whirled into them to melt on their warm living lenses, and Henry felt, in spite of everything, his professional curiosity aroused. Just what had they found here?

3

"*Oww, fuck me sideways, shit-a-goddam, don't that fuckin HURT!*"

"Are you all right?" Henry asked, and that started him laughing again. What a foolish question.

"Do I *sound* all right, shrink-boy?" Pete asked waspishly, but when Henry bent toward him, he raised one hand and waved him away. "Nah, I got it, it's lettin go, check Princess Dipshit. She just *sits* there."

Henry dropped to his knees in front of the woman, wincing at the pain—his legs, yes, but his shoulder also hurt where he had banged it on the roof and his neck was stiffening rapidly—but still chuckling.

This was no dewy damsel in distress. She was forty at least, and heavyset. Although her parka was thick and she was wearing God knew how many layers beneath it, it swelled noticeably in front, indicating the sort of prodigious jugs for which breast-reduction surgery had been made. The hair whipping out from beneath and around the flaps of her cap was cut in no particular style. Like them, she was wearing jeans, but one of her thighs would have made two of Henry's. The first word to occur to him was *country-woman*—the kind of woman you saw hanging out her wash in the toy-littered yard beside her doublewide trailer while Garth or Shania blared from a radio stuck in an open window . . . or maybe buying a few groceries at Gosselin's. The orange gear suggested that she might have been hunting, but if so, where was her rifle? Already covered in snow? Her wide eyes were dark blue and utterly blank. Henry looked for her tracks and saw none. The wind had erased them, no doubt, but it was still eerie; she might have dropped from the sky.

Henry pulled his glove off and snapped his fingers in front of those staring eyes. They blinked. It wasn't much, but more than he had expected, given the fact that a multi-ton vehicle had just missed her by inches and never a twitch from her.

"Hey!" he shouted in her face. "Hey, come back! Come back!"

He snapped his fingers again and could hardly feel them—when had it turned so cold? *We're in a goddam situation here,* he thought.

The woman burped. The sound was startlingly loud even with the wind in the trees, and before it was snatched away by the moving air, he got a whiff of something both bitter and pungent—it smelled like medicinal alcohol. The woman shifted and grimaced, then broke wind—a long, purring fart that sounded like ripping cloth. *Maybe,* Henry thought, *it's how the locals say hello.* The idea got him laughing again.

"Holy shit," Pete said, almost in his ear. "Sounds like she ripped out the seat of her pants with that one. What you been drinkin, lady, Prestone?" And then, to Henry: "She's been drinkin *somethin,* by Christ, and if it ain't antifreeze, I'm a monkey."

Henry could smell it, too.

The woman's eyes suddenly shifted, met Henry's own. He was shocked by the pain he saw in them. "Where's Rick?" she asked. "I have to find Rick—he's the only one left." She grimaced, and when her lips peeled back, Henry saw that half her teeth were gone. Those remaining looked like stakes in a dilapidated fence. She belched again, and the smell was strong enough to make his eyes water.

"Aw, holy *Christ*!" Pete nearly screamed. "What's wrong with her?"

"I don't know," Henry said. The only things he knew for sure were that the woman's eyes had gone blank again and that they were in a goddam situation here. Had he been alone, he might have considered sitting down next to the woman and putting his arm around her—a much more interesting and unique answer to the final problem than the Hemingway Solution. But there was Pete to think about—Pete hadn't even been through his first alcohol rehab yet, although that was undoubtedly in the cards.

And besides, he was curious.

4

Pete was sitting in the snow, working at his knee again with his hands, looking at Henry, waiting for him to do something, which was fair enough, since so often he had been the idea man of their quartet. They hadn't had a leader, but Henry had been the closest thing to it. Even back in junior high school that had been true. The woman, meanwhile, was looking at no one, just staring off into the snow again.

Settle, Henry thought. *Just take a deep breath and settle.*

He took the breath, held it, and let it out. Better. A little better. All right, what was up with this lady? Never mind where she'd come from, what she was doing here, or why she smelled like diluted antifreeze when she burped. What was up with her right now?

Shock, obviously. Shock so deep it was like a form of catatonia—witness how she had not so much as stirred when the Scout went skidding by her at shaving distance. And yet she hadn't retreated so far inside that only a hypo of something excitable could reach her; she had responded to the snap of his fingers, and she had spoken. Had inquired about someone named Rick.

"Henry—"

"Quiet a minute."

He took off his gloves again, held his hands in

front of her face, and clapped them smartly. He thought the sound very small compared to the steady whoosh of the wind in the trees, but she blinked again.

"On your feet!"

Henry took her gloved hands and was encouraged when they closed reflexively around his. He leaned forward, getting into her face, smelling that ethery odor. No one who smelled like that could be very well.

"On your feet, get up! With me! On three! One, two, *three*!"

He stood, holding her hands. She rose, her knees popping, and burped again. She broke wind again as well. Her hat went askew, dipping over one eye. When she made no move to straighten it, Henry said, "Fix her hat."

"Huh?" Pete had also gotten up, although he didn't look very steady.

"I don't want to let go of her. Fix her hat, get it out of her eye."

Gingerly, Pete reached out and straightened her hat. The woman bent slightly, grimaced, farted.

"Thank you very much," Pete said sourly. "You've been a wonderful audience, good night."

Henry could feel her sagging and tightened his grip.

"Walk!" he shouted, getting into her face again. "Walk with me! On three! One, two, *three*!"

He began walking backward, toward the front of the Scout. She was looking at him now and he held her gaze. Without glancing at Pete—he didn't want to risk losing her—he said, "Take my belt. Lead me."

"Where?"

"Around the other side of the Scout."

"I'm not sure I can—"

"You have to, Pete, now do it."

For a moment there was nothing, and then he felt Pete's hand slip under his coat, fumble, and catch hold of his belt. They shuffled across the narrow string of road in an awkward conga-line, through the staring yellow spotlight of the Scout's remaining headlamp. On the far side of the overturned vehicle they were at least partly sheltered from the wind, and that was good.

The woman abruptly pulled her hands out of Henry's and leaned forward, mouth opening. Henry stepped back, not wanting to be splattered when she let go . . . but instead of vomiting she belched, the loudest one yet. Then, while still bent over, she broke wind again. The sound was like nothing Henry had ever heard before, and he would have sworn he'd heard everything on the wards in western Massachusetts. She kept her feet, though, breathing through her nose in big horselike snuffles of air.

"Henry," Pete said. His voice was hoarse with terror, awe, or both. "My God, *look.*"

He was staring up at the sky, jaw loose and mouth gaping. Henry followed his gaze and could hardly believe what he was seeing. Bright circles of light, nine or ten of them, cruised slowly across the low-hanging clouds. Henry had to squint to look at them. He thought briefly of spotlights stabbing the night sky at Hollywood film premieres, but of course there were no such lights out here in the woods, and if there had been he would have seen the beams themselves, rising in the snowy air. Whatever was projecting those lights was above or in the clouds, not below them. They ran back and forth, seemingly at random, and Henry felt a sudden atavistic terror invade him . . . except it actually seemed to rise up from inside, somewhere deep inside. All at once his spinal cord felt like a column of ice.

"What is it?" Pete asked, nearly whining. "Christ, Henry, what is it?"

"I don't—"

The woman looked up, saw the dancing lights, and began to shriek. They were amazingly loud, those shrieks, and so full of terror they made Henry feel like shrieking himself.

"They're back!" she screamed. *"They're back! They're back!"*

Then she covered her eyes and put her head against the front tire of the overturned Scout. She quit screaming and only moaned, like something caught in a trap with no hope of getting free.

5

For some unknown length of time (probably no more than five minutes, although it felt longer) they watched those brilliant lights run across the sky—circling, skidding, hanging lefts and rights, appearing to leapfrog each other. At some point Henry became aware there

were only five instead of nearly a dozen, and then there
were only three. Beside him the woman with her face
against the tire farted again, and Henry realized they
were standing out here in the middle of nowhere, gawp-
ing at some sort of storm-related celestial phenomenon which, while interesting, would contribute
absolutely nothing toward getting them into a place
that was dry and warm. He could remember the final
reading on the tripmeter with perfect clarity: 12.7.
They were nearly ten miles from Hole in the Wall, a
good hike under the best of circumstances, and here
they were in a storm only two steps below a blizzard.
Plus, he thought, *I'm the only one who can walk.*

"Pete."

"It's somethin, isn't it?" Pete breathed. "They're
fucking UFOs, just like on *The X-Files.* What d'you
suppose—"

"Pete." He took Pete's chin in his hand and turned
his face away from the sky, to his own. Overhead, the
last two lights were paling. "It's some sort of electrical phenomenon, that's all."

"You think?" Pete looked absurdly disappointed.

"Yeah—something related to the storm. But even
if it's the first wave of the Butterfly Aliens from
Planet Alnitak, it isn't going to make any difference
to us if we turn into Popsicles out here. Now I need
you to help me. I need you to do that trick of yours.
Can you?"

"I don't know," Pete said, venturing one final look
at the sky. There was only one light now, and so dim
you wouldn't have known it was there if you hadn't

been looking for it. "Ma'am? Ma'am, they're almost gone. Mellow out, okay?"

She made no reply, only stood with her face pressed against the tire. The streamers on her hat flapped and flew. Pete sighed and turned to Henry.

"What do you want?"

"You know the loggers' shelters along this road?" There were eight or nine of them, Henry thought, nothing but four posts each, with pieces of rusty corrugated tin on top for roofs. The pulpers stored cut logs or pieces of equipment beneath them until spring.

"Sure," Pete said.

"Where's the closest one? Can you tell me?"

Pete closed his eyes, raised one finger, and began moving it back and forth. At the same time he made a little ticking sound with the tip of his tongue against the roof of his mouth. This had been a part of Pete ever since high school. It didn't go back as far as Beaver's gnawed pencils and chewed toothpicks, or Jonesy's love of horror movies and murder stories, but it went back a long way. And it was usually reliable. Henry waited, hoping it would be reliable now.

The woman, her ears perhaps catching that small regular ticking sound beneath the boom of the wind, raised her head and looked around. There was a large dark smear across her forehead from the tire.

At last Pete opened his eyes. "Right up there," he said, pointing in the direction of Hole in the Wall. "Go around that curve and then there's a hill. Go down the other side of the hill and there's a straight stretch. At the end of the straight there's one of those shelters. It's on the left. Part of the roof's fallen in. A man named Stevenson had a nosebleed there once."

"Yeah?"

"Aw, man, I don't know." And Pete looked away, as if embarrassed.

Henry vaguely remembered the shelter . . . and the fact that the roof had partially fallen in was good, or could be; if it had fallen the right way, it would have turned the wall-less shelter into a lean-to.

"How far?"

"Half a mile. Maybe three-quarters."

"And you're sure."

"Yeah."

"Can you walk that far on your knee?"

"I think so—but will she?"

"She better," Henry said. He put his hands on the woman's shoulders, turned her wide-eyed face to his, and moved in until they were almost nose to nose. The smell of her breath was awful—antifreeze with something oily and organic beneath it—but he stayed close, and made no move to draw back.

"We need to walk!" he told her, not quite shouting but speaking loudly and in a tone of command. "Walk with me now, on three! One, two, *three*!"

He took her hand and led her back around the Scout and into the road. There was one moment of resistance and then she followed with perfect docility, not seeming to feel the push of the wind when it struck them. They walked for about five minutes,

Henry holding the woman's gloved right hand in his left one, and then Pete lurched.

"Wait," he said. "Bastardly knee's tryin to lock up on me again."

While he bent and massaged it, Henry looked up at the sky. There were no lights up there now. "Are you all right? Can you make it?"

"I'll make it," Pete said. "Come on, let's go."

6

They made it around the curve all right and halfway up the hill all right and then Pete dropped, groaning and cursing and clutching his knee. He saw the way Henry was looking at him and made a peculiar sound, something caught between a laugh and a snarl. "Don't you worry about me," he said. "Petie-bird's gonna make it."

"You sure?"

"Ayuh." And to Henry's alarm (although there was amusement, too, that dark amusement which never seemed to leave him now), Pete balled his gloved hands into fists and began pounding on his knee.

"Pete—"

"Let go, you hump, let *go*!" Pete cried, ignoring him completely. And during this the woman stood slump-shouldered with the wind now at her back and the orange hat-ribbons blowing out in front of her, as silent as a piece of equipment that has been turned off.

"Pete?"

"I'm all right now," Pete said. He looked up at Henry with exhausted eyes . . . but they, too, were not without amusement. "Is this a total fuckarow or not?"

"It is."

"I don't think I could walk all the way back to Derry, but I'll get to that shelter." He held out a hand. "Help me up, chief."

Henry took his old friend's hand and pulled. Pete came up stiff-legged, like a man rising from a formal bow, stood still for a moment, then said: "Let's go. I'm lookin forward to gettin out of this wind." He paused, then added: "We should have brought a few beers."

They got to the top of the hill and the wind was better on the other side. By the time they got to the straight stretch at the bottom, Henry had begun allowing himself to hope that this part of it, at least, was going to go all right. Then, halfway along the straight with a shape up ahead that just about had to be the loggers' shelter, the woman collapsed—first to her knees, then onto her front. She lay like that for a moment, head turned, only the breath rising from her open mouth to indicate she was still alive (*and how much simpler this would be if she weren't,* Henry thought). Then she rolled over on her side and let out another long bray of a belch.

"Oh you troublesome cunt," Pete said, sounding not angry but only tired. He looked at Henry. "What now?"

Henry knelt by her, told her in his loudest voice to

get up, snapped his fingers, clapped his hands, and counted to three several times. Nothing worked.

"Stay here with her. Maybe I can find something up there to drag her on."

"Good luck."

"You have a better idea?"

Pete sat down in the snow with a grimace, his bad leg stretched out in front of him. "Nosir," he said, "I do not. I'm fresh out of ideas."

7

It took Henry five minutes to walk up to the shelter. His own leg was stiffening where the turnsignal lever had gouged it, but he thought he was all right. If he could get Pete and the woman to shelter, and if the Arctic Cat back at Hole in the Wall would start, he thought this might still turn out okay. And damn, it was *interesting,* there was that. Those lights in the sky . . .

The shelter's corrugated top had fallen perfectly: the front, facing the road, was open, but the back was almost entirely closed off. And poking out of the thin scrim of snow that had drifted inside was a swatch of dirty gray tarpaulin with a coating of sawdust and ancient splinters clinging to it.

"Bingo," Henry said, and grabbed it. At first it stuck to the ground, but when he put his back to it, the tarp came loose with a hoarse ripping sound that made him think of the woman farting.

Dragging it behind him, he plodded back toward

where Pete, his leg still pointed out stiffly before him, sat in the snow next to the prone woman.

8

It was far easier than Henry had dared hope. In fact, once they got her on the tarpaulin, it was a breeze. She was a hefty woman, but she slid on the snow like grease. Henry was glad it wasn't five degrees warmer; sticky snow might have changed things considerably. And, of course, it helped being on a straight stretch.

The snow was now ankle deep and falling more thickly than ever, but the flakes had gotten bigger. *It's stopping,* they'd tell each other in tones of disappointment when they saw flakes like that as kids.

"Hey, Henry?" Pete sounded out of breath, but that was okay; the shelter was just up ahead. In the meantime Pete walked in a kind of stiff-legged strut to keep his knee from coming out of whack again.

"What?"

"I been thinkin about Duddits a lot just lately—how strange is that?"

"No bounce," Henry said at once, without even thinking about it.

"That's right." Pete gave a somehow nervous laugh. "No bounce, no play. You *do* think it's strange, don't you?"

"If it is," Henry said, "we're both strange."

"What do you mean?"

"I've been thinking of Duddits myself, and for

quite awhile. Since at least March. Jonesy and I were going to go see him——"

"You were?"

"Yeah. Then Jonesy had that accident——"

"Crazy old cocksucker that hit him never should have been driving," Pete said with a dark frown. "Jonesy's lucky to be alive."

"You got *that* right," Henry said. "His heart stopped in the ambulance. The EMTs had to give him the juice."

Pete halted, wide-eyed. "No shit? It was that bad? That *close?*"

It occurred to Henry that he had just been indiscreet. "Yes, but you ought to keep your mouth shut about it. Carla told me, but I don't think Jonesy knows. I never . . ." He waved his arm vaguely, and Pete nodded with perfect understanding. *I never sensed that he did* was what Henry meant.

"I'll keep it under my hat," Pete said.

"I think it's best you do."

"And you never got to see Duds."

Henry shook his head. "In all the excitement about Jonesy, I forgot. Then it was summer, and you know how things come up . . ."

Pete nodded.

"But you know what? I was thinking of him just a little while ago. Back in Gosselin's."

"Was it the kid in the Beavis and Butt-head shirt?" Pete asked. His words came out in little puffs of white vapor.

Henry nodded. "The kid" could have been twelve or

twenty-five, when it came to Down's syndrome you just couldn't tell. He had been red-haired, wandering along the middle aisle of the dark little market next to a man who just about had to be his father—same green-and-black-checked hunting jacket, more important the same carroty red hair, the man's now thin enough to show the scalp underneath, and he had given them a look, the kind that says *Don't you say nothing about my kid unless you want trouble,* and of course neither of them had said anything, they had come the twenty or so miles from Hole in the Wall for beer and bread and hot dogs, not trouble, and besides, they had once known Duddits, *still* knew Duddits in a way— sent him Christmas presents and birthday cards, anyway, Duddits who had once been, in his own peculiar fashion, one of them. What Henry could not very well confide to Pete was that he'd been thinking of Duds at odd moments ever since realizing, some sixteen months ago, that he meant to take his own life and that everything he did had become either a holding action against that event or a preparation for it. Sometimes he even dreamed of Duddits, and of the Beav saying *Let me fix that, man* and Duddits saying *Fit wha?*

"Nothing wrong with thinking about Duddits, Pete," he said as he hauled the makeshift sled with the woman on it into the shelter. He was out of breath himself. "Duddits was how we defined ourselves. He was our finest hour."

"You think so?"

"Yup." Henry plopped down to get his breath

before going on to the next thing. He looked at his watch. Almost noon. By now Jonesy and Beaver would be past the point of thinking the snow had just slowed them down; would be almost sure something had gone wrong. Perhaps one of them would fire up the snowmobile (*if it works,* he reminded himself again, *if the damn thing works*). Come out looking for them. That would simplify things a bit.

He looked at the woman lying on the tarp. Her hair had fallen over one eye, hiding it; the other looked at Henry—and through him—with chilly indifference.

Henry believed that all children were presented with self-defining moments in early adolescence, and that children in groups were apt to respond more decisively than children alone. Often they behaved badly, answering distress with cruelty. Henry and his friends had behaved well, for whatever reason. It meant no more than anything else in the end, but it did not hurt to remember, especially when your soul was dark, that once you had confounded the odds and behaved decently.

He told Pete what he was going to do and what Pete was going to do, then got to his feet to start doing it—he wanted them all safe behind the doors of Hole in the Wall before the light left the day. A clean, well-lighted place.

"Okay," Pete said, but he sounded nervous. "Just hope she doesn't die on me. And that those lights don't come back." He craned to look out at the sky, where now there were only dark, low-hanging clouds.

"What were they, do you think? Some kind of lightning?"

"Hey, you're the space expert." Henry got up. "Start picking up the little sticks—you don't even have to get up to do that."

"Kindling, right?"

"Right," Henry said, then stepped over the woman on the tarp and walked to the edge of the woods, where there was plenty of bigger stuff lying around in the snow. Roughly nine miles, that was the walk ahead of him. But first they were going to light a fire. A nice big one.

CHAPTER FOUR

McCarthy
Goes to the John

1

Jonesy and Beaver sat in the kitchen, playing cribbage, which they simply called the game. That was what Lamar, Beaver's father, had always called it, as though it were the only game. For Lamar Clarendon, whose life revolved around his central Maine construction company, it probably *was* the only game, the one most at home in logging camps, railroad sheds, and, of course, construction trailers. A board with a hundred and twenty holes, four pegs, and an old greasy deck of cards; if you had those things, you were in business. The game was mostly played when you were waiting to do something else—for the rain to let up, for a freight order to arrive, or for your friends to get back from the store so you could figure out what to do with the strange fellow now lying behind a closed bedroom door.

Except, Jonesy thought, *we're really waiting for Henry. Pete's just with him. Henry's the one who'll know what to do, Beaver was right. Henry's the one.*

But Henry and Pete were late back. It was too early to say something had happened to them, it could just be the snow slowing them down, but Jonesy was starting to wonder if that was all, and guessed the Beav was, too. Neither of them had said anything about it as yet—it was still on the morning side of noon and things might still turn out okay—but the idea was there, floating unspoken between them.

Jonesy would concentrate on the board and the cards for awhile, and then he'd look at the closed bedroom door behind which McCarthy lay, probably sleeping, but oh boy his color had looked bad. Two or three times he saw Beav's eyes flicking over there, too.

Jonesy shuffled the old Bikes, dealt, gave himself a couple of cards, then set aside the crib when Beaver slid a couple across to him. Beaver cut and then the preliminaries were done; it was time to peg. *You can peg and still lose the game,* Lamar told them, that Chesterfield always sticking out from the corner of his mouth, his Clarendon Construction cap always pulled down over his left eye like a man who knows a secret he will tell only if the price is right, Lamar Clarendon a no-play workadaddy dead of a heart attack at forty-eight, *but if you peg you won't never get skunked.*

No play, Jonesy thought now. *No bounce, no play.* And then, on the heels of that, the wavering damned voice that day in the hospital: *Please stop, I can't stand it, give me a shot, where's Marcy?* And oh man, why was the world so hard? Why were there so many spokes hungry for your fingers, so many gears eager to grab for your guts?

"Jonesy?"

"Huh?"

"You okay?"

"Yeah, why?"

"You shivered."

"Did I?" Sure he did, he knew he did.

"Yeah."

"Drafty, maybe. You smell anything?"

"You mean . . . like him?"

"I wasn't talking about Meg Ryan's armpits. Yeah, him."

"No," Beaver said. "A couple of times I thought . . . but it was just imagination. Because those farts, you know—"

"—smelled so bad."

"Yeah. They did. The burps, too. I thought he was gonna blow chunks, man. For sure."

Jonesy nodded. *I'm scared,* he thought. *Sitting here shit-scared in a snowstorm. I want Henry, goddammit. How about that.*

"Jonesy?"

"*What?* Are we ever gonna play this hand or not?"

"Sure, but . . . do you think Henry and Pete are okay?"

"How the hell do I know?"

"You don't . . . have a feeling? Maybe see—"

"I don't see anything but your face."

Beav sighed. "But do you think they're okay?"

"As a matter of fact, I do." Yet his eyes stole first to the clock—half past eleven, now—and then to the closed bedroom door with McCarthy behind it. In the middle of the room, the dreamcatcher danced and slowly turned in some breath of air. "Just going slow. They'll be right along. Come on, let's play."

"All right. Eight."

"Fifteen for two."

"Fuck." Beaver put a toothpick in his mouth. "Twenty-five."

"Thirty."

"Go."

"One for two."

"*Doodlyfuck!*" Beaver gave an exasperated little laugh as Jonesy turned the corner onto Third Street. "You peg my ass off every time you deal."

"I peg your ass when *you* deal, too," Jonesy said. "The truth hurts. Come on, play."

"Nine."

"Sixteen."

"And one for last card," the Beav said, as if he had won a moral victory. He stood up. "I'm gonna go out, take a leak."

"Why? We've got a perfectly good john, in case you didn't know it."

"I know it. I just want to see if I can write my name in the snow."

Jonesy laughed. "Are you ever gonna grow up?"

"Not if I can help it. And keep it down. Don't wake the guy up."

Jonesy swept the cards together and began to shuffle them as Beaver walked to the back door. He found himself thinking about a version of the game they had played when they were kids. They called it the Duddits Game, and they usually played in the Cavell rec room. It was the same as regular cribbage, except they let Duddits peg. *I got ten,* Henry would say, *peg me ten, Duddits.* And Duddits, grinning that loopy grin of his that never failed to make Jonesy feel happy, might peg four or six or ten or two fucking dozen. The rule when you played the Duddits Game was that you never complained, never said *Duddits, that's too many* or *Duddits, that's not enough.* And man, they'd laugh. Mr. and Mrs. Cavell, they'd laugh, too, if they happened to be in the room, and Jonesy remembered once, they must have been fifteen, sixteen, and Duddits of course was whatever he was, Duddits Cavell's age was never going to change, that was what was so beautiful and scary about him, and this one time Alfie Cavell had started crying, saying *Boys, if you only knew what this means, to me and to the missus, if you only knew what it means to Douglas—*

"Jonesy." Beaver's voice, oddly flat. Cold air came in through the open kitchen door, raising a rash of gooseflesh on Jonesy's arms.

"Close the door, Beav, was you born in a barn?"

"Come over here. You need to look at this."

Jonesy got up and went to the door. He opened his mouth to say something, then closed it again. The backyard was filled with enough animals to stock a petting zoo. Deer, mostly, a couple of dozen assorted does and bucks. But moving with them were raccoons, waddling woodchucks, and a contingent of squirrels that seemed to move effortlessly along the top of the snow. From around the side of the shed where the Arctic Cat and assorted tools and engine parts were stored came three large canines Jonesy at first mistook for wolves. Then he saw the old discolored length of clothesline hanging around the neck of one of them and realized they were dogs, probably gone feral. They were all moving east, up the slope from The Gulch. Jonesy saw a pair of good-sized wildcats moving between two little groups of deer and actually rubbed his eyes, as if to clear them of a mirage. The cats were still there. So were the deer, the woodchucks, the coons and squirrels. They moved steadily, barely giving the men in the doorway a glance, but without the panic of creatures running before a fire. Nor was there any smell of fire. The animals were simply moving east, vacating the area.

"Holy Christ, Beav," Jonesy said in a low, awed voice.

Beaver had been looking up. Now he gave the animals a quick, cursory glance and lifted his gaze to the sky again. "Yeah. Now look up there."

Jonesy looked up and saw a dozen glaring lights—some red, some blue-white—dancing around up there. They lit the clouds, and he suddenly understood that they were what McCarthy had seen when he was lost. They ran back and forth, dodging each other or sometimes briefly merging, making a glow so bright he couldn't look at it without squinting. "What *are* they?" he asked.

"I don't know," Beaver said, not looking away. On his pale face, the stubble stood out with almost eerie clarity. "But the animals don't like it. *That's* what they're trying to get away from."

2

They watched for ten, perhaps fifteen minutes, and Jonesy became aware of a low humming, like the sound of an electrical transformer. Jonesy asked Beaver if he heard it, and the Beav simply nodded, not taking his eyes off the dancing lights in the sky, which to Jonesy looked to be the size of manhole covers. He had an idea that it was the sound the animals wanted to escape, not the lights, but said nothing. Speech all at once seemed hard; he felt a debilitating fear grip him, something feverish and constant, like a low-grade flu.

At last the lights began to dim, and although Jonesy hadn't seen any of them wink out, there seemed to be fewer of them. Fewer animals, too, and that nagging hum was fading.

Beaver started, like a man awakening from a deep sleep. "Camera," he said. "I want to get some pictures before they're gone."

"I don't think you'll be able to—"

"I got to try!" Beaver almost shouted. Then, in a lower tone of voice: "I got to try. At least I can get some of the deers and such before they . . ." He was turning away, heading back across the kitchen, probably trying to remember what heap of dirty clothes he'd left his old battered camera under, when he stopped suddenly. In a flat and decidedly un-Beaverish voice, he said, "Oh, Jonesy. I think we got a problem."

Jonesy took a final look at the remaining lights, still fading (smaller, too), then turned around. Beaver was standing beside the sink, looking across the counter and the big central room.

"What? What now?" That nagging, shrewish voice with the little tremor in it . . . was that really his?

Beaver pointed. The door to the bedroom where they'd put Rick McCarthy—Jonesy's room—stood open. The door to the bathroom, which they had left open so McCarthy could not possibly miss his way if nature called, was now closed.

Beaver turned his somber, beard-speckled face to Jonesy's. "Do you smell it?"

Jonesy did, in spite of the cold fresh air coming in through the door. Ether or ethyl alcohol, yes, there was still that, but now it was mixed with other stuff. Feces for sure. Something that could have been blood. And something else, something like mine-gas trapped a million years and finally let free. Not the kind of fart-smells kids giggled over on camping trips, in other words. This was something richer and far more awful. You could only compare it to farts because there was nothing else even close. At bottom, Jonesy thought, it was the smell of something contaminated and dying badly.

"And look there."

Beaver pointed at the hardwood floor. There was blood on it, a trail of bright droplets running from

the open door to the closed one. As if McCarthy had
dashed with a nosebleed.

Only Jonesy didn't think it was his nose that had
been bleeding.

3

Of all the things in his life he hadn't wanted to do—
calling his brother Mike to tell him Ma had died of a
heart attack, telling Carla she had to do something
about the booze and all the prescriptions or he was
going to leave her, telling Big Lou, his cabin counselor
at Camp Agawam, that he had wet his bed—crossing
the big central room at Hole in the Wall to that closed
bathroom door was the hardest. It was like walking in
a nightmare where you seem to cover ground at the
same dreamy, underwater pace no matter how fast you
move your legs.

In bad dreams you never get to where you're
going, but they made it to the other side of the room
and so Jonesy supposed it wasn't a dream after all.
They stood looking down at the splatters of blood.
They weren't very big, the largest the size of a dime.

"He must have lost another tooth," Jonesy said,
still whispering. "That's probably it."

The Beav looked at him, one eyebrow raised. Then
he went to the bedroom door and looked in. After a
moment he turned to Jonesy and curled his finger in a
beckoning gesture. Jonesy went to where Beaver stood
in a kind of sidle, not wanting to lose sight of the
closed bathroom door.

In the bedroom the covers had been thrown all the way back onto the floor, as if McCarthy had risen suddenly, urgently. The shape of his head was still in the middle of the pillow and the shape of his body still lay printed on the sheet. Also printed on the sheet, about halfway down, was a large bloody blotch. Soaking into the blue sheet, it looked purple.

"Funny place to lose a tooth from," Beaver whispered. He bit down on the toothpick in his mouth and the ragged front half of it fell on the doorsill. "Maybe he was hoping for a quarter from the Ass Fairy."

Jonesy didn't respond. He pointed to the left of the doorway, instead. There, in a tangle, were the bottoms of McCarthy's longjohns and the Jockey briefs he'd been wearing beneath them. Both were matted with blood. The Jockeys had caught the worst of it; if not for the waistband and the cotton high up on the front, you might have thought they were a racy, jaunty red, the kind of shorts a devotee of the *Penthouse* Forum might put on if he was expecting to get laid when the date was over.

"Go look in the chamber pot," Beaver whispered.

"Why don't we just knock on the bathroom door and ask him how he is?"

"Because I want to know what to fucking *expect,*" Beaver replied in a vehement whisper. He patted his chest, then spit out the ragged remains of his latest toothpick. "Man, my ticker's goin nuts."

Jonesy's own heart was racing, and he could feel sweat running down his face. Nevertheless he stepped into the room. The cold fresh air coming in the back door had cleaned out the main room pretty well, but the stench in here was foul—shit and mine-gas and ether. Jonesy felt the little bit of food he'd eaten take an uneasy lurch in his stomach and willed it to stay where it was. He approached the chamber pot and at first couldn't make himself look in. Half a dozen horror-movie images of what he might see danced in his head. Organs floating in blood soup. Teeth. A severed head.

"Go *on*!" Beaver whispered.

Jonesy squeezed his eyes shut, bent his head, held his breath, then opened his eyes again. There was nothing but clean china gleaming in the glow thrown by the overhead light. The chamber pot was empty. He released his breath in a sigh through his clenched teeth, then walked back to the Beav, avoiding the splashes of blood on the floor.

"Nothing," he said. "Now come on, let's stop screwing around."

They walked past the closed door of the linen closet and regarded the closed pine-paneled door to the john. Beaver looked at Jonesy. Jonesy shook his head. "It's your turn," he whispered. "I looked in the thunderjug."

"You found him," Beaver whispered back. His jaw was set stubbornly. "*You* do it."

Now Jonesy was hearing something else—hearing it without hearing it, exactly, partly because this sound was more familiar, mostly because he was so fiercely fixed on McCarthy, the man he had almost shot. A *whup-whup-whup* sound, faint but growing louder. Coming this way.

"Well fuck this," Jonesy said, and although he spoke in a normal tone of voice, it was loud enough to make them both jump a little. He rapped a knuckle on the door. "Mr. McCarthy! Rick! Are you all right in there?"

He won't answer, Jonesy thought. *He won't answer because he's dead. Dead and sitting on the throne, just like Elvis.*

But McCarthy wasn't dead. He groaned, then said: "I'm a little sick, fellows. I need to move my bowels. If I can move my bowels, I'll be—" There was another groan, then another fart. This one was low, almost liquid. The sound made Jonesy grimace. "—I'll be all right," McCarthy finished. To Jonesy, the man didn't sound on the same continent with all right. He sounded out of breath and in pain. As if to underline this, McCarthy groaned again, louder. There was another of those liquid ripping sounds, and then McCarthy cried out.

"McCarthy!" Beaver tried the doorknob but it wouldn't turn. McCarthy, their little gift from the woods, had locked it from the inside. "Rick!" The Beav rattled the knob. "Open up, man!" Beaver was trying to sound lighthearted, as if the whole thing were a big joke, a camp prank, which only made him sound more scared.

"I'm okay," McCarthy said. He was panting now. "I just . . . fellows, I just need to make a little room." There came the sound of more flatulence. It was ridiculous to think of what they were hearing as "passing gas" or "breaking wind"—those were airy phrases, light as meringue. The sounds coming from behind the closed door were brutal and meaty, like ripping flesh.

"McCarthy!" Jonesy said. He knocked. "Let us in!" But did he want to go in? He did not. He wished McCarthy had stayed lost or been found by someone else. Worse, the amygdala in the base of his brain, that unapologetic reptile, wished he had shot McCarthy to begin with. "Keep it simple, stupid," as they said in Carla's Narcotics Anonymous program. "*McCarthy!*"

"Go away!" McCarthy called with weak vehemence. "Can't you go away and let a fellow . . . let a fellow make a little number two? Gosh!"

Whup-whup-whup: louder and closer now.

"Rick!" Now it was the Beav. Holding onto the light tone with a kind of desperation, like a climber in trouble holding onto his rope. "Where you bleedin from, buddy?"

"Bleeding?" McCarthy sounded honestly puzzled. "I'm not bleeding."

Jonesy and Beaver exchanged a scared glance.

WHUP-WHUP-WHUP!

The sound had finally gotten Jonesy's full attention, and what he felt was enormous relief. "That's a helicopter," he said. "Bet they're looking for him."

"You think so?" Beaver wore the expression of a man hearing something too good to be true.

"Yeah." Jonesy supposed the people in the chopper could be chasing the foo-lights in the sky or trying to figure out what the animals were up to, but he didn't want to think about those things, didn't *care* about those things. What he cared about was getting Rick

McCarthy off the hopper, off his hands, and into a hospital in Machias or Derry. "Go on out there and flag them down."

"What if—"

WHUP! WHUP! WHUP! And from behind the door there came more of those wrenching, liquid sounds, followed by another cry from McCarthy.

"Get out there!" Jonesy shouted. "Flag those fuckers down! I don't care if you have to drop trou and dance the hootchie-koo, *just get them to land*!"

"Okay—" Beaver had started to turn away. Now he jerked and screamed.

A number of things Jonesy had been quite successfully not thinking about suddenly leaped out of the closet and came running into the light, capering and leering. When he wheeled around, however, all he saw was a doe standing in the kitchen with its head extended over the counter, examining them with its mild brown eyes. Jonesy took a deep, gasping breath and slumped back against the wall.

"Eat snot and rot," Beaver breathed. Then he advanced on the doe, clapping his hands. "Bug out, Mabel! Don't you know what time of year this is? Go on! Put an egg in your shoe and beat it! Make like an amoeba and split!"

The deer stayed where she was for a moment, eyes widening in an expression of alarm that was almost human. Then she whirled around, her head skimming the line of pots and ladles and tongs hanging over the stove. They clanged together and some fell from their hooks, adding to the clangor.

Then she was out the door, little white tail flipping.

Beaver followed, pausing long enough to look at the cluster of droppings on the linoleum with a jaundiced eye.

4

The mixed migration of animals had pretty well dried up to stragglers. The doe Beav had scared out of their kitchen leaped over a limping fox that had apparently lost one paw to a trap, and then disappeared into the woods. Then, from above the low-hanging clouds just beyond the snowmobile shed, a lumbering helicopter the size of a city bus appeared. It was brown, with the letters ANG printed on the side in white.

Ang? Beaver thought. *What the hell is Ang?* Then he realized: Air National Guard, probably out of Bangor.

It dipped, nose-heavy. Beaver stepped into the backyard, waving his arms over his head. "Hey!" he shouted. "Hey, little help here! Little help, guys!"

The helicopter descended until it was no more than seventy-five feet off the ground, close enough to raise the fresh snow in a cyclone. Then it moved toward him, carrying the snow-cyclone with it.

"Hey! We got a hurt guy here! Hurt guy!" Jumping up and down now like one of those numbass bootscooters on The Nashville Network, feeling like a jerk but doing it anyway. The chopper drifted toward him, low but not coming any lower, not showing any sign of actually landing, and a horrid idea filled him. Beav didn't know if it was something he was getting from the guys in the chopper or just paranoia. All he could be sure of was that he suddenly felt like something pinned to the center ring of a target in a shooting gallery: hit the Beaver and win a clock-radio.

The chopper's side door slid back. A man holding a bullhorn and wearing the bulkiest parka Beaver had ever seen came tilting out toward him. The parka and the bullhorn didn't bother the Beav. What bothered him was the oxygen mask the guy was wearing over his mouth and nose. He'd never heard of fliers needing to wear oxygen masks at an altitude of seventy-five feet. Not, that was, if the air they were breathing was okay.

The man in the parka spoke into the bullhorn, the words coming out loud and clear over the *whup-whup-whup* of the helicopter's rotors but sounding strange anyway, partly because of the amplification but mostly, Beaver thought, because of the mask. It was like being addressed by some strange robot god.

"HOW MANY ARE YOU?" the god-voice called down. "SHOW ME ON YOUR FINGERS."

Beaver, confused and frightened, at first thought only of himself and Jonesy; Henry and Pete weren't back from the store, after all. He raised two fingers like a guy giving the peace sign.

"STAY WHERE YOU ARE!" the man leaning out of the helicopter boomed in his robot god's voice. "THIS AREA IS UNDER TEMPORARY QUARANTINE! SAY AGAIN, THIS AREA IS UNDER TEMPORARY QUARANTINE! YOU MUST NOT LEAVE!"

The snowfall was thinning, but now the wind kicked up and blew a sheet of the snow which had been sucked up by the copter's rotors into Beaver's face. He slitted his eyes against it and waved his arms. He sucked in freezing snow, spat out his toothpick to keep from yanking *that* down his throat, too (it was how he would die, his mother constantly predicted, by pulling a toothpick down his throat and choking on it), and then screamed: "What do you *mean*, quarantine? We got a sick guy down here, you got to come and get him!"

Knowing they couldn't hear him under the big *whup-whup-whup* of the rotor blades, *he* didn't have any fucking bullhorn to boost his voice, but yelling anyway. And as the words *sick guy* passed through his lips, he realized he'd given the guy in the chopper the wrong number of fingers—they were three, not two. He started to raise that number of fingers, then thought of Henry and Pete. They weren't here yet but unless something had happened to them, they *would* be—so how many *were* they? Two was the wrong answer, but was three the right one? Or was it five? As he usually did in such situations, Beaver went into mental doglock. When it happened in school, there'd been Henry sitting beside him or Jonesy behind him to give him the answers. Out here there was no one to help, only that big *whup-whup-whup* smacking into his ears and all that swirling snow going down his throat and into his lungs, making him cough.

"STAY WHERE YOU ARE! THIS SITUATION WILL BE RESOLVED IN TWENTY-FOUR TO FORTY-EIGHT HOURS! IF YOU NEED FOOD,

CROSS YOUR ARMS OVER YOUR HEAD!"

"There are more of us!" Beaver screamed at the man leaning out of the helicopter. He screamed so loudly red dots danced in front of his eyes. *"We got a hurt guy here! We . . . have got . . . A HURT GUY!"*

The idiot in the helicopter tossed his bullhorn back into the cabin behind him, then made a thumb-and-forefinger circle down at Beaver, as if to say, *Okay! Gotcha!* Beaver felt like dancing in frustration. Instead, he raised one open hand above his head—a finger each for him and his friends, plus the thumb for McCarthy. The man in the helicopter took this in, then grinned. For one truly wonderful moment, Beaver thought he had gotten through to the mask-wearing fuckwad. Then the fuckwad returned what he thought was Beaver's wave, said something to the pilot behind him, and the ANG helicopter began to rise. Beaver Clarendon was still standing there, frosted with swirling snow and screaming. *"There's five of us and we need help! There's five of us and we need some fucking HELP!"*

The copter vanished back into the clouds.

5

Jonesy heard some of this—certainly he heard the amplified voice from the Thunderbolt helicopter—but registered very little. He was too concerned with McCarthy, who had given a number of small and breathless screams, then fallen silent. The stench coming under the door continued to thicken.

"McCarthy!" he yelled as Beaver came back in.

"Open this door or we'll break it down!"

"Get away from me!" McCarthy screamed back in a thin, distracted voice. "I have to shit, that's all, *I HAVE TO SHIT!* If I can shit I'll be all right!"

Such straight talk, coming from a man who seemed to consider *oh gosh* and *oh dear* strong language, frightened Jonesy even more than the bloody sheet and underwear. He turned to Beaver, barely noticing that the Beav was powdered with snow and looking like Frosty. "Come on, help me break it down. We've got to try and help him."

Beaver looked scared and worried. Snow was melting on his cheeks. "I dunno. The guy in the helicopter said something about quarantine—what if he's infected or something? What if that red thing on his face—"

In spite of his own ungenerous feelings about McCarthy, Jonesy felt like striking his old friend. This previous March he himself had lain bleeding in a street in Cambridge. Suppose people had refused to touch him because he might have AIDS? Refused to help him? Just left him there to bleed because there were no rubber gloves handy?

"Beav, we were right down in his face—if he's got something really infectious, we've probably caught it already. Now what do you say?"

For a moment what Beaver said was nothing. Then Jonesy felt that click in his head. For just a moment he saw the Beaver he'd grown up with, a kid in an old beat-up motorcycle jacket who had cried *Hey, you guys, quit it! Just fucking QUIT it!* and knew it was going to be all right.

Beaver stepped forward. "Hey, Rick, how about opening up? We just want to help."

Nothing from behind the door. Not a cry, not a breath, not so much as the sound of shifting cloth. The only sounds were the steady rumble of the genny and the fading *whup* of the helicopter.

"Okay," Beaver said, then crossed himself. "Let's break the fucker down."

They stepped back together and turned their shoulders toward the door, half-consciously miming cops in half a hundred movies.

"On three," Jonesy said.

"Your leg up to this, man?"

In fact, Jonesy's leg and hip hurt badly, although he hadn't precisely realized this until Beaver brought it up. "I'm fine," he said.

"Yeah, and my ass is king of the world."

"On three. Ready?" And when Beaver nodded: "One . . . two . . . three."

They rushed forward together and hit the door together, almost four hundred pounds behind two dropped shoulders. It gave way with an absurd ease that spilled them, stumbling and grabbing at each other, into the bathroom. Their feet skidded in the blood on the tiles.

"Ah, *fuck*," Beaver said. His right hand crept to his mouth, which was for once without a toothpick, and covered it. Above his hand, his eyes were wide and wet. "Ah, *fuck*, man—*fuck*."

Jonesy found he could say nothing at all.

CHAPTER FIVE

DUDDITS,
PART ONE

1

"Lady," Pete said.

The woman in the duffel coat said nothing. Lay on the sawdusty piece of tarp and said nothing. Pete could see one eye, staring at him, or through him, or at the jellyroll center of the fucking universe, who knew. Creepy. The fire crackled between them, really starting to take hold and throw some heat now. Henry had been gone about fifteen minutes. It would be three hours before he made it back, Pete calculated, three hours at the very least, and that was a long time to spend under this lady's creepy jackalope eye.

"Lady," he said again. "You hear me?"

Nothing. But once she had yawned, and he'd seen that half her goddam teeth were gone. What the fuck was up with that? And did he really want to know?

The answer, Pete had discovered, was yes and no. He was curious—he supposed a man couldn't help being curious—but at the same time he didn't want to know. Not who she was, not who Rick was or what had happened to him, and not who "they" were. *They're back!* the woman had screamed when she saw the lights in the sky, *They're back!*

"Lady," he said for the third time.

Nothing.

She'd said that Rick was the only one left, and then she'd said *They're back,* presumably meaning the lights in the sky, and since then there had been nothing but those unpleasant burps and farts . . . the one yawn, exposing all those missing teeth . . . and the eye. The creepy jackalope eye. Henry had only been gone fifteen minutes—he'd left at five past twelve and it was now twelve-twenty by Pete's watch—and it felt like an hour and a half. This was going to be one long fucking day, and if he was going to get through it without cracking up (he kept thinking of some story they'd had to read in the eighth grade, he couldn't remember who wrote it, only that the guy in the story had killed this old man because he couldn't stand the old man's eye, and at the time Pete hadn't understood that but now he did, yessir), he needed something.

"Lady, do you hear me?"

Nada. Just the creepy jackalope eye.

"I have to go back to the car because I kind of forgot something. But you'll be all right. Won't you?"

No answer—and then she let loose with another of those long buzz-saw farts, her face wrinkling up as she let go, as if it hurt her . . . and probably it did, something that sounded like that just about *had* to hurt. And even though Pete had been careful to get upwind, some of the smell came to him—hot and rank but somehow not *human*. Nor did it smell like cow-farts. He had worked for Lionel Sylvester as a kid, he'd milked more than his share of cows, and sometimes they blew gas at you while you were on the stool, sure—a heavy green smell, a *marshy* smell. This wasn't like that, not a bit. This was like . . . well, like when you were a kid and got your first chemistry set, and after awhile you got tired of the faggy little experiments in the booklet and just went hogwild and mixed all that shit together, just to see if it would explode. And, he realized, that was part of what was troubling him, part of what was making him nervous. Except that was stupid. People didn't just *explode,* did they? Still, he had to get him a little help here. Because she was giving him the willies, bigtime.

He got two of the pieces of wood Henry had scrounged, added them to the fire, debated, and added a third. Sparks rose, whirling, and winked out against the sloping piece of corrugated tin. "I'll be back before that-all burns down, but if you want to add on another, be my guest. Okay?"

Nothing. He suddenly felt like shaking her, but he had a mile and a half to walk, up to the Scout and back here again, and he had to save his strength. Besides, she'd probably fart again. Or burp right in his face.

"Okay," he said. "Silence gives consent, that's what

Mrs. White always used to say back in the fourth grade."

He got to his feet, bracing his knee as he did so, grimacing and slipping, almost falling, but finally getting up because he needed that beer, goddammit, *needed* it, and there was no one to get it except for him. Probably he was an alcoholic. In fact, there was no probably about it, and he supposed eventually he'd have to do something about it, but for now he was on his own, wasn't he? Yes, because this bitch was gone, nothing left of her but some nasty gas and that creepy jackalope eye. If she needed to put some more wood on the fire she'd just have to do it, but she *wouldn't* need to, he'd be back long before then. It was only a mile and a half. Surely his leg would hold him that long.

"I'll be back," he said. He leaned over and massaged his knee. Stiff, but not too bad. Really not too bad. He'd just put the beer in a bag—maybe a box of Hi Ho crackers for the bitch while he was at it—and be right back. "You sure you're okay?"

Nothing. Just the eye.

"Silence gives consent," he repeated, and began walking back up the Deep Cut Road, following the wide drag-mark of the tarpaulin and their almost-filled-in tracks. He walked in little hitches, pausing to rest every ten or twelve steps . . . and to massage his knee. He stopped once to look back at the fire. It already looked small and insubstantial in the gray early-afternoon light. "This is fuckin crazy," he said once, but he kept on going.

2

He got to the end of the straight stretch all right, and
halfway up the hill all right. He was just starting to
walk a little faster, to trust the knee a little when—
ha-ha, asshole, fooled ya—it locked again, turning to
something that felt like pig-iron, and he went down,
yelling squeezed curses through his clenched teeth.

It was as he sat there cursing in the snow that he
realized something very odd was going on out here. A
large buck went walking past him on the left, with
no more than a quick glance at the human from
which it would have fled in great, springy bounds on
any other day. Running along almost under its feet
was a red squirrel.

Pete sat there in the lessening snow—huge flakes
falling in a shifting wave that looked like lace—with his
leg stuck out in front of him and his mouth open.
There were more deer coming along the road, other animals, too, walking and hopping like refugees fleeing
some disaster. There were even more of them in the
woods, a wave moving east.

"Where you guys going?" he asked a snowshoe
rabbit that went lolloping past him with its ears laid
along its back. "Big coverall game at the rez? Casting
call for a new Disney cartoon? Got a—"

He broke off, the spit in his mouth drying up to
something that felt like an electric mist. A black bear,
fat with its pre-hibernation stuffing, was ambling
through the screen of thin second-growth trees to his

left. It went with its head down and its rump switching from side to side, and although it never spared Pete so much as a look, Pete's illusions about his place here in the big North Woods were for the first time entirely stripped away. He was nothing but a heap of tasty white meat that happened to still be breathing. Without his rifle, he was more defenseless than the squirrel he'd seen scurrying around the buck's feet—if noticed by a bear, the squirrel could at least run up the nearest tree, all the way to the thin top branches where no bear could possibly follow. The fact that *this* bear never so much as looked at him didn't make Pete feel much better. Where there was one, there would be more, and the next one might not be so preoccupied.

Once he was sure the bear was gone, Pete struggled to his feet again, his heart hammering. He had left that foolish farting woman back there alone, but really, how much protection would he have been able to provide if a bear decided to attack? The thing was, he had to get his rifle. Henry's too, if he could carry it. For the next five minutes—until he got to the top of the hill— Pete thought about firepower first and beer second. By the time he began his cautious descent on the other side, however, he was back to beer. Put it in a bag and hang the bag over his shoulder. And no stopping to drink one on the way back. He'd have one when he was sitting in front of the campfire again. It would be a reward beer, and there was nothing better than a reward beer.

You're an alcoholic. You know that, don't you? Fucking alcoholic.

Yes, and what did that mean? That you couldn't

fuck up. Couldn't get caught leaving a semi-comatose woman alone in the woods, let's say, while you went off in search of the suds. And once he got back to the shelter, he had to remember to toss his empties deep into the woods. Although Henry might know anyway. The way they always seemed to know stuff about each other when they were together. And mental link or no mental link, you had to get up pretty goddam early in the morning to put one over on Henry Devlin.

Yet Pete thought Henry would probably let him alone about the beer. Unless, that was, Pete decided the time had come to talk about it. To maybe ask Henry for help. Which Pete might do, in time. Certainly he didn't like the way he felt about himself right now; leaving that woman alone back there said something about Peter Moore that wasn't so nice. But Henry . . . there was something wrong with Henry, too, this November. Pete didn't know if Beaver felt it, but he was pretty sure Jonesy did. Henry was kind of fucked up. He was maybe even—

From behind him there came a wet grunt. Pete screamed and whirled around. His knee locked up again, locked up savagely, but in his fright he barely noticed. It was the bear, the bear had circled back behind him, that bear or another one—

It wasn't a bear. It was a moose, and it walked past Pete with no more than a glance as he fell into the road again, cursing low in his throat and holding his leg, looking up into the lightly falling snow and cursing himself for a fool. An *alcoholic* fool.

He had a frightening few moments when it seemed that this time the knee wasn't going to let go—he'd torn something in it and here he would lie in the exodus of animals until Henry finally returned on the snowmobile, and Henry would say *What the fuck are you doing here? Why did you leave her alone? As if I didn't know.*

But at last he was able to get up again. The best he could do was a gimpy sidesaddle hobble, but it was better than lying in the snow a couple of yards from a fresh pile of steaming moose shit. He could now see the overturned Scout, its wheels and undercarriage covered with fresh snow. He told himself that if his latest fall had happened on the other side of the hill, he would have gone back to the woman and the fire, but that now, with the Scout actually in sight, it was better to go on. That the guns were his main objective, the bottles of Bud just an extra added attraction. And almost believed it. As far as getting back . . . well, he would make it somehow. He'd gotten this far, hadn't he?

Fifty yards or so from the Scout, he heard a rapidly approaching *whup-whup-whup*—the unmistakable sound of a helicopter. He looked skyward eagerly, preparing himself to stand upright long enough to wave—God, if anyone needed a little help from the sky, it was him—but the helicopter never quite broke through the low ceiling. For a moment he saw a dark shape running through the dreck almost directly above him, the bleary flash of its lights, as well—and then the sound of the copter was moving off to the east, in the direction the animals were running. He was dismayed to feel a nasty sense of relief lurking just below his disappointment: if the helicopter had landed, he never would've gotten to the beer, and he had come all this way, all this damn way.

3

Five minutes later he was down on his knees and climbing carefully into the overturned Scout. He quickly learned that his bad knee wouldn't support him for long (it was swelled against his jeans now like a big painful loaf of bread), and more or less swam into the snow-coated interior. He didn't like it; all the smells seemed too strong, all the dimensions too close. It was almost like crawling into a grave, one that smelled of Henry's cologne.

The groceries were sprayed all over the back, but Pete barely gave the bread and cans and mustard and the package of red hot dogs (red dogs were about all Old Man Gosselin carried for meat) a glance. It was the beer he was interested in, and it looked like only one bottle had broken when the Scout turned turtle. Drunk's luck. The smell was strong—of course the one he'd been drinking from had spilled as well—but beer was a smell he liked. Henry's cologne, on the other hand . . . phew, Jesus. In a way it was as bad as the smell of the crazy lady's gas. And he didn't know why the smell of cologne should make him think of coffins and graves and funeral flowers, but it did.

"Why would you want to wear cologne in the woods

anyway, old sport?" he asked, the words coming out in little puffs of white vapor. And the answer of course was that Henry hadn't been—the smell wasn't really here at all, just the smell of beer. For the first time in a long time Pete found himself thinking about the pretty real estate lady who had lost her keys outside the Bridgton Pharmacy, and how he had known she wasn't going to meet him for dinner, didn't want to be within ten miles of him. Was smelling nonexistent cologne like that? He didn't know, only that he didn't like the way the smell seemed all mixed up in his mind with the idea of death.

Forget it, numbnuts. You're spooking yourself, that's all. There's a big difference between really seeing the line and just spooking yourself. Forget about it and get what you came for.

"Good fuckin idea," Pete said.

The store-bags were plastic, not paper, the kind with handles; Old Man Gosselin had marched at least that far into the future. Pete snagged one, and as he did, felt a rip of pain on the pad of his right hand. Only one goddam broken bottle and so naturally he'd cut himself on it, and pretty deep, from the feel. Maybe this was his punishment for leaving the woman alone back there. If so, he'd take it like a man and count himself let off easy.

He gathered up eight bottles, started to work his way back out of the Scout, then thought again. Had he staggered all the way back here for a lousy eight beers? "I think not," he muttered, and then got the other seven, taking time to scrounge them all in spite of how creepy the Scout was making him feel. At last he backed out, fighting the panicky idea that something small, but with big teeth would soon spring at him, taking a great big chomp out of his balls. Pete's Punishment, Part Two.

He didn't exactly freak, but he wiggled back out faster than he'd wiggled in, and his knee locked up again just as he got entirely clear. He rolled over on his back, whimpering, looking up into the snow—the last of it, now coming down in great big flakes as lacy as a woman's best underwear—and massaging the knee, telling it to come on, now, honey, come on now, sweetie, let go, you fucking bitch. And just as he was starting to think that this time it wouldn't, it did. He hissed through his teeth, sat up, and looked at the bag with THANKS FOR SHOPPING AT OUR PLACE! printed on the side in red.

"Where else *would* I shop, you old bastard?" he asked. He decided to allow himself one beer after all before starting back to the woman. Hell, it would lighten the load.

Pete fished one out, twisted the cap, and poured the top half down his throat in four big gulps. It was cold and the snow he was sitting in was even colder, but he still felt better. That was the magic of beer. The magic of Scotch, vodka, and gin as well, but when it came to alcohol, he was with Tom T. Hall: he liked beer.

Looking at the bag, he thought again of the carrot-top back in the store—the mystified grin, the Chinese eyes that had originally earned such people the term *mongoloids,* as in mongoloid idiot. That led him to Duddits again, Douglas Cavell if you wanted to be formal about it. Why Duds had been on his mind so much lately Pete couldn't say, but he had, and Pete made himself a promise: when this was over, he was going to stop in Derry and see old Duddits. He'd make the others go with him, and somehow he didn't think he'd have to try very hard to convince them. Duddits was probably the reason they were still friends after so many years. Hell, most kids never so much as thought of their college or high-school buddies again, let alone those they'd chummed with in junior high . . . what was now known as middle school, although Pete had no doubt it was the same sad jungle of insecurities, confusion, smelly armpits, crazy fads, and half-baked ideas. They hadn't known Duddits from school, of course, because Duddits didn't go to Derry Junior High. Duds went to The Mary M. Snowe School for the Exceptional, which was known to the neighborhood kids as The Retard Academy or sometimes just The Dumb School. In the ordinary course of events their paths never would have crossed, but there was this vacant lot out on Kansas Street, and the abandoned brick building that went with it. Facing the street you could still read TRACKER BROTHERS SHIPPING TRUCKING AND STORAGE in fading white paint on the old red brick. And on the other side, in the big alcove where the trucks had once backed up to unload . . . something else was painted there.

Now, sitting in the snow but no longer feeling it melting to cold slush under his ass, drinking his second beer without even being aware he had opened it (the first empty he had cast into the woods where he could still see animals moving east), Pete remembered the day they had met Duds. He remembered Beaver's stupid jacket that the Beav had loved so much, and Beaver's voice, thin but somehow powerful, announcing the end of something and the beginning of something else, announcing in some ungraspable but perfectly real and knowable way that the course of their lives had changed one Tuesday afternoon when all they had been planning was some two-on-two in Jonesy's driveway and then maybe a game of Parcheesi in front of the TV; now, sitting here in the woods beside the overturned Scout, still smelling the cologne Henry hadn't been wearing, drinking his life's happy poison with a hand wearing a bloodstained glove, the car salesman remembered the boy who had not quite given up his dreams of being an astronaut in spite of his increasing problems with math (Jonesy had helped him, and then Henry had helped him and then, in tenth grade, he'd been beyond help), and he remembered the other boys as well, mostly the Beav, who had turned the world upside down with a high yell in his just-beginning-to-change voice: *Hey you guys, quit it! Just fucking QUIT it!*

"Beaver," Pete said, and toasted the dark afternoon as he sat with his back propped against the overturned Scout's hood. "You were beautiful, man." But hadn't they all been?

Hadn't they all been beautiful?

4

Because he is in the eighth grade and his last class of the day is music, on the ground floor, Pete is always out before his three best friends, who always finish the day on the second floor, Jonesy and Henry in American Fiction, which is a reading class for smart kids, and Beaver next door in Math for Living, which is actually Math for Stupid Boys and Girls. Pete is fighting hard not to have to take that one next year, but he thinks it's a fight he will ultimately lose. He can add, subtract, multiply, and divide; he can do fractions, too, although it takes him too much time. But now there is something new, now there is the x. Pete does not understand the x, and fears it.

He stands outside the gate by the chainlink fence as the rest of the eighth-graders and the babyass seventh-graders stream by, stands there kicking his boots and pretending to smoke, one hand cupped to his mouth and the other concealed beneath it—the concealed hand the one with the hypothetical hidden butt.

And now here come the ninth-graders from the second floor, and walking among them like royalty—like uncrowned kings, almost, although Pete would never say such a corny thing out loud—are his friends, Jonesy and Beaver and Henry. And if there is a king of kings it is Henry, whom all the girls love even if he *does* wear glasses. Pete is lucky to have such friends, and he knows it—is probably the luckiest eighth-grader in Derry, x or no x. The fact that having friends in the ninth grade keeps him from getting beaten up by any of the eighth-grade badasses is the very least of it.

"Hey, Pete!" Henry says as the three of them come sauntering out through the gate. As always, Henry seems surprised to see him there, but absolutely delighted. "What you up to, my man?"

"Nothin much," Pete replies as always. "What's up with you?"

"SSDD," Henry says, whipping off his glasses and giving them a polish. If they had been a club, SSDD likely would have been their motto; eventually they will even teach Duddits to say it—it came out *Say shih, iffa deh* in Duddits-ese, and is one of the few things Duddits says that his parents can't understand. This of course will delight Pete and his friends.

Now, however, with Duddits still half an hour in their future, Pete just echoes Henry: "Yeah, man, SSDD."

Same shit, different day. Except in their hearts, the boys only believe the first half, because in their hearts they believe it's the same day, day after day. It's Derry, it's 1978, and it will always be 1978. They say there will be a future, that they will live to see the twenty-first century—Henry will be a lawyer, Jonesy will be a writer, Beaver will be a long-haul truck-driver, Pete will be an astronaut with a NASA patch on his shoulder—but this is just what they *say,* as they chant the Apostle's Creed in church with no real idea of what's coming out of their mouths; what they're really interested in is Maureen Chessman's skirt, which was short to begin with and has ridden a pretty good way up her thighs as she shifted around. They believe in their hearts that one day Maureen's skirt will ride up high enough for them to see the color of her panties, and they similarly believe that Derry is forever and so are they. It will always be junior high school and quarter of three, they will always be walking up Kansas Street together to play basketball in Jonesy's driveway (Pete also has a hoop in his driveway but they like Jonesy's better because his father has posted it low enough so you can dunk), talking about the same old things: classes and teachers and which kid got into a fuckin pisser with which kid, or which kid is *going* to get into a fuckin pisser with which kid, whether or not so-and-so could take so-and-so if they got into a fuckin pisser (except they never will because so-and-so and so-and-so are tight), who did something gross lately (their favorite so far this year has to do with a seventh-grader named Norm Parmeleau, now known as Macaroni Parmeleau, a nickname that will pursue him for years, even into the new century of which these boys speak but do not in their hearts actually believe; to win a fifty-cent bet, Norm Parmeleau had one day in the cafeteria firmly plugged both nostrils with macaroni and cheese, then hawked it back like snot and swallowed it; Macaroni Parmeleau who, like so many junior-high-school kids, has mistaken notoriety for celebrity), who is going out with whom (if a girl and a guy are observed going home together after school, they are presumed to be *probably* going out; if they are observed hangin onto hands or suckin face it is a certainty), who is going to win the Super Bowl (fuckin Patriots, fuckin Boston

Patriots, only they never do, having to root for the Patriots is a fuckin pisser). All these topics are the same and yet endlessly fascinating as they walk from the same school (*I believe in God the father almighty*) on the same street (*maker of heaven and earth*) under the same white everlasting October sky (*world without end*) with the same friends (*amen*). Same shit, same day, that is the truth in their hearts, and they're down with K.C. and the Sunshine Band on this one, even though they will all tell you RIR-DS (rock is rolling, disco sucks): that's the way they like it. Change will come upon them sudden and unannounced, as it always does with children of this age; if change needed permission from junior-high-school students, it would cease to exist.

Today they also have hunting to talk about, because next month Mr. Clarendon is for the first time going to take them up to Hole in the Wall. They'll be gone for three days, two of them school-days (there is no problem getting permission for this trip from the school, and absolutely no need to lie about the trip's purpose; southern Maine may have gotten citified, but up here in God's country, hunting is still considered part of a young person's education, especially if the young person is a boy). The idea of creeping through the woods with loaded rifles while their friends are back at dear old DJHS, just droning away, strikes them as incredibly, delightfully boss, and they walk past The Retard Academy on the other side of the street without even seeing it. The retards get out at the same time as the kids at Derry Junior High, but most of them go home with their mothers on the special retard bus, which is blue instead of yellow and is reputed to have a bumper sticker on it that says SUPPORT MENTAL HEALTH OR I'LL KILL YOU. As Henry, Beaver, Jonesy, and Pete walk past Mary M. Snowe on the other side, a few high-functioning retards who are allowed to go home by themselves are still walking along, goggling around themselves with those weird expressions of perpetual wonder. Pete and his friends see them without seeing them, as always. They are just part of the world's wallpaper.

Henry, Jonesy, and Pete are listening closely to the Beav, who's telling them that when they get to Hole in the Wall they have to get down in The Gulch, because that's where the big ones always go, there's bushes down there that they like. "Me and my Dad have seen about a billion deer in there," he says. The zippers on his old motorcycle jacket jingle agreeably.

They argue about who's going to get the biggest deer and where is the best place to shoot one so you can bring it down with one shot and it won't suffer. ("Except my father says that animals don't suffer the way people do when they get hurt," Jonesy tells them. "He says God made them different that way so it would be okay for us to hunt them.") They laugh and squabble and argue over who is the most likely to blow lunch when it comes time to gut their kills, and The Retard Academy falls farther and farther behind. Ahead of them, on their side of the street, looms the square red brick building where Tracker Brothers used to do business.

"If anyone hurls, it won't be me," Beaver boasts. "I

seen deerguts a thousand times and they don't bother me at all. I remember once——"

"Hey you guys," Jonesy breaks in, suddenly excited. "You want to see Tina Jean Schlossinger's pussy?"

"Who's Tina Jean Sloppinger?" Pete asks, but he is already intrigued. Seeing *any* pussy seems like a great idea to him; he is always looking at his Dad's *Penthouse* and *Playboy* magazines, which his Dad keeps out in his workshop, behind the big Craftsman toolbox. Pussy is very interesting. It doesn't give him a boner and make him feel sexy the way bare tits do, but he guesses that's because he's still a kid.

And pussy *is* interesting.

"*Schlossinger,*" Jonesy says, laughing. "*Schlossinger,* Petesky. The Schlossingers live two blocks over from me, and——" He stops suddenly, struck by an important question which must be answered immediately. He turns to Henry. "Are the Schlossingers Jews or Republicans?"

Now it's Henry laughing at Jonesy, but without any malice. "Technically, I think it's possible to be both at the same time . . . or neither one." Henry pronounces the word *nyther* instead of *neether,* which impresses Pete. It sounds smart as a motherfucker, and he reminds himself to say it that way from now on—*nyther, nyther, nyther,* he tells himself . . . but knows somehow that he will forget, that he is one of those people condemned to say *neether* all his life.

"Never mind religion and politics," Henry says, still laughing. "If you've got a picture of Tina Jean

Schlossinger showing her pussy, I want to see it."

The Beav, meanwhile, has become visibly excited—cheeks flushed, eyes bright, and he goes to stick a fresh toothpick in his mouth before the old one is even half finished. The zippers on his jacket, the one Beaver's older brother wore during his four or five years of Fonzie-worship, jingle faster.

"Is she blonde?" the Beav asks. "Blonde, and in high school? Super good-looking? Got—" He holds his hands out in front of his chest, and when Jonesy nods, grinning, Beaver turns to Pete and blurts: "This year's Homecoming Queen up at the high school, ringmeat! Her picture was in the fuckin paper! Up on that float with Richie Grenadeau?"

"Yes, but the fucking Tigers lost the Homecoming game and Grenadeau ended up with a broken nose," Henry says. "First Derry High team ever to play a Class-A team from southern Maine and those fools—"

"Fuck the Tigers," Pete breaks in. He has more interest in high school football than he does in the dreaded *x,* but not much. Anyway, he's got the girl placed now, remembers the newspaper photo of her standing on the flower-decked bed of a pulp truck next to the Tiger quarterback, both of them wearing tinfoil crowns, smiling, and waving to the crowd. The girl's hair fell around her face in big blowy Farrah Fawcett waves, and her gown was strapless, showing the tops of her breasts.

For the first time in his life, Pete feels real lust—it is a meaty feeling, red and heavy, that stiffens his prick, dries up the spit in his mouth, and makes it hard for him to think. Pussy is interesting; the idea of seeing *local* pussy, *Homecoming Queen* pussy . . . that is a lot more than exciting. That is, as the Derry *News*'s film critic sometimes says about movies she especially likes, "a must-see."

"Where?" he asks Jonesy breathlessly. He is imagining seeing this girl, this Tina Jean Schlossinger, waiting on the corner for the school bus, just standing there giggling with her girlfriends, not having the slightest idea that the boy walking past has seen what is under her skirt or her jeans, that he knows if the hair on her pussy is the same color as the hair on her head. Pete is on fire. "Where is it?"

"There," Jonesy says, and points at the red brick box that is Tracker Brothers old freight and storage depot. There is ivy crawling up the sides, but this has been a cold fall and most of the leaves have already died and turned black. Some of the windows are broken and the rest are bleary. Looking at the place gives Pete a little chill. Partly because the big kids, the high-school kids and even some that are beyond high school, play baseball in the vacant lot behind the building, and big kids like to beat up little kids, who knows why, it relieved the monotony or something. But this isn't the big deal, because baseball is over for the year and the big kids have probably moved on to Strawford Park, where they will play two-hand touch football until the snow flies. (Once the snow flies, they will beat each others' brains in playing hockey with old friction-taped sticks.) No, the big deal is that kids sometimes disappear in

Derry, Derry is funny that way, and when they *do* disappear, they are often last seen in out-of-the-way places like the deserted Tracker Brothers depot. No one talks about this unpleasant fact, but everyone knows about it.

Yet a pussy . . . not some fictional *Penthouse* pussy but the actual muff of an actual girl from town . . . that would be something to see, all right. That would be a fuckin pisser.

"Tracker Brothers?" Henry says with frank disbelief. They have stopped now, are standing together in a little clump not far from the building while the last of the retards go moaning and goggling by on the other side of the street. "I think the world of you, Jonesy, don't get me wrong—the fucking *world*—but why would there be a picture of Tina Jean's pussy in there?"

"I don't know," Jonesy said, "but Davey Trask saw it and said it was her."

"I dunno about goin in there, man," Beaver says. "I mean, I'd love to see Tina Jean Slophanger's pussy—"

"Schlossinger—"

"—but that place has been empty at least since we were in the fifth grade—"

"Beav—"

"—and I bet it's full of rats."

"Beav—"

But Beav intends to have his entire say. "Rats get rabies," he says. "They get rabies up the old wazoo."

"We don't have to go in," Jonesy says, and all three look at him with renewed interest. This is, as the fellow said when he saw the black-haired Swede, a Norse of a different color.

Jonesy sees he has their full attention, nods, goes on. "Davey says all you have to do is go around on the driveway side and look in the third or fourth window. It used to be Phil and Tony Tracker's office. There's still a bulletin board on the wall. And Davey said the only two things on the bulletin board are a map of New England showing all the truck routes, and a picture of Tina Jean Schlossinger showing all of her pussy."

They look at him with breathless interest, and Pete asks the question which has occurred to all of them. "Is she bollocky?"

"No," Jonesy admits. "Davey says you can't even see her tits, but she's holding her skirt up and she isn't wearing pants and you can see *it,* just as clear as day."

Pete is disappointed that this year's Tiger Homecoming Queen isn't bollocky bare-ass, but the thing about how she's holding her skirt up inflames them all, feeding some primal, semi-secret notion of how sex really works. A girl *could* hold her skirt up, after all; any girl could.

Not even Henry asks any more questions. The only question comes from the Beav, who asks if Jonesy is *sure* they won't have to go inside in order to see. And they are already moving in the direction of the driveway running down the far side of the building toward the vacant lot, powerful as a spring tide in their nearly mindless motion.

5

Pete finished the second beer and heaved the bottle deep into the woods. Feeling better now, he got cautiously to his feet and dusted the snow from his ass. And was his knee a little bit looser? He thought maybe it was. Looked awful, of course—looked like he had a little model of the Minnesota goddam Metrodome under there—but felt a bit better. Still, he walked carefully, swinging his plastic sack of beer in short arcs beside him. Now that the small but powerful voice insisting that he *had* to have a beer, just goddam *had* to, had been silenced, he thought of the woman with new solicitude, hoping she hadn't noticed he was gone. He would walk slowly, he would stop to massage his knee every five minutes or so (and maybe talk to it, encourage it, a crazy idea, but he was out here on his own and it couldn't hurt), and he would get back to the woman. Then he would have another beer. He did not look back at the overturned Scout, did not see that he had written DUDDITS in the snow, over and over again, as he sat thinking of that day back in 1978.

Only Henry had asked why the Schlossinger girl's picture would be there in the empty office of an empty freight depot, and Pete thought now that Henry had only asked because he had to fulfill his role as Group Skeptic. Certainly he'd only asked once; as for the rest of them, they had simply *believed,* and why not? At thirteen, Pete had still spent half his life believing in Santa Claus. And besides—

Pete stopped near the top of the big hill, not because he was out of breath or because his leg was cramping up, but because he could suddenly feel a low humming sound in his head, sort of like an electrical transformer, only with a kind of cycling quality to it, a low *thud-thud-thud*. And no, it wasn't "suddenly" as in "suddenly started up"; he had an idea the sound had been there for awhile and he was just becoming aware of it. And he had started to think some funny stuff. All that about Henry's cologne, for instance . . . and Marcy. Someone named Marcy. He didn't think he knew anyone named Marcy but the name was suddenly in his head, as in *Marcy I need you* or *Marcy I want you* or maybe *Zounds, Marcy, bring the gasogene.*

He stood where he was, licking his dry lips, the bag of beer hanging straight down from his hand now, its pendulum motion stilled. He looked up in the sky, suddenly sure the lights would be there . . . and they *were* there, only just two of them now, and very faint.

"Tell Marcy to make them give me a shot," Pete said, enunciating each word carefully in the stillness, and knew they were exactly the right words. Right *why* or right *how* he couldn't say, but yes, those were the words in his head. Was it the click, or had the lights caused those thoughts? Pete couldn't say for sure.

"Maybe nyther," he said.

Pete realized the last of the snow had stopped. The world around him was only three colors: the deep gray of the sky, the deep green of the firs, and the perfect unblemished white of the new snow. And hushed.

Pete cocked his head first to one side and then to the other, listening. Yes, hushed. Nothing. No sound in the world and the humming noise had stopped as completely as the snow. When he looked up, he saw that the pale, mothlike glow of the lights was also gone.

"Marcy?" he said, as if calling someone. It occurred to him that Marcy might be the name of the woman who had caused them to wreck, but he dismissed the idea. That woman's name was Becky, he knew it as surely as he had known the name of the real estate woman that time. Marcy was just a word now, and nothing about it called to him. Probably he'd just had a brain-cramp. Wouldn't be the first time.

He finished climbing the hill and started down the other side, his thoughts returning to that day in the fall of 1978, the day they had met Duddits.

He was almost back to the place where the road leveled when his knee abruptly let go, not locking up this time but seeming to explode like a pine knot in a hot fire.

Pete pitched forward into the snow. He didn't hear the Bud bottles break inside the bag—all but two of them. He was screaming too loudly.

CHAPTER SIX

DUDDITS,
PART TWO

1

Henry started off in the direction of the camp at a quick walk, but as the snow subsided to isolated flurries and the wind began to die, he upped the walk to a steady, clocklike jog. He had been jogging for years, and the pace felt natural enough. He might have to pull up for awhile, walk or even rest, but he doubted it. He had run road-races longer than nine miles, although not for a couple of years and never with four inches of snow underfoot. Still, what was there to worry about? Falling down and busting a hip? Maybe having a heart attack? At thirty-seven a heart attack seemed unlikely, but even if he had been a prime candidate for one, worrying about it would have been ludicrous, wouldn't it? Considering what he was planning? So what was there to worry about?

Jonesy and Beaver, that was what. On the face of it that seemed as ludicrous as worrying about suffering a catastrophic cardiac outage here in the middle of nowhere—the trouble was behind him, with Pete and that strange, semi-comatose woman, not up ahead at Hole in the Wall . . . except there *was* trouble at Hole in the Wall, bad trouble. He didn't know how he knew that, but he did and he accepted the knowing. Even before he started encountering the animals, all hurrying by and none giving him more than the most cursory glance, he knew that.

Once or twice he glanced up into the sky, looking for more foo-lights, but there were none to be seen and after that he just looked straight ahead, sometimes having to zig or zag to keep out of the way of the animals. They weren't quite stampeding, but their eyes had an odd, spooky look that Henry had never seen before. Once he had to skip handily to keep from being upended by a pair of hurrying foxes.

Eight more miles, he told himself. It became a jogging mantra, different from the ones that usually went through his head when he was running (nursery rhymes were the most common), but not *that* different—same idea, really. *Eight more miles, eight more miles to Banbury Cross.* No Banbury Cross, though, just Mr. Clarendon's old camp—Beaver's camp, now—and no cock horse to get him there. What *was* a cock horse, anyway? Who knew? And what in Christ's name was happening out here—the lights, the slow-motion stampede (dear God, what was that in the woods off to his left, was that a fucking *bear*?), the woman in the road, just sitting there with most of her teeth and most of her brains missing? And those *farts,* dear God. The only thing he'd ever smelled even remotely like it was the breath of a patient he'd had once, a schizophrenic with intestinal cancer. *Always that smell,* an internist friend had told Henry when Henry tried to describe it. *They can brush their teeth a dozen times a day, use Lavoris every hour on the hour, and that smell still comes through. It's the smell of the body eating itself, because that's all cancer is when you take the diagnostic masks off: autocannibalism.*

Seven more miles, seven more miles, and all the animals are running, all the animals are headed for Disneyland. And when they get there they'll form a conga line and sing "It's a Small World After All."

The steady, muted thud of his booted feet. The feel of his glasses bouncing up and down on the bridge of his nose. His breath coming out in balloons of cold vapor. But he felt warm now, felt good, those endorphins kicking in. Whatever was wrong with him, it was no shortage of those; he was suicidal but by no means dysthymic.

That at least some of his problem—the physical and emotional emptiness that was like a near-white-out in a blizzard—*was* physical, hormonal, he had no doubt. That the problem could be addressed if not entirely corrected by pills he himself had prescribed by the bushel . . . he had no doubt of that, either. But like Pete, who undoubtedly knew there was a rehab and years of AA meetings in his most plausible future, Henry did not *want* to be fixed, was somehow convinced that the fix would be a lie, something that would lessen him.

He wondered if Pete had gone back for the beer, and knew the answer was probably yes. Henry would have suggested bringing it along if he'd thought of it, making such a risky return trip (risky for the woman as well as Pete himself) unnecessary, but he'd been pretty freaked out—and the beer hadn't even crossed his mind.

He bet it had crossed Pete's, though. Could Pete make it roundtrip on that sprung knee? It was possible, but Henry would not have bet on it.

They're back! the woman had screamed, looking up at the sky. *They're back! They're back!*

Henry put his head down and jogged a little faster.

2

Six more miles, six more to Banbury Cross. Was it down to six yet, or was he being optimistic? Giving those old endorphins a little too much free rein? Well, so what if he was? Optimism couldn't hurt at this point. The snow had almost stopped falling and the tide of animals had slackened, and that was also good. What wasn't so good was the thoughts in his head, some of which seemed less and less like his own. Becky, for instance, who was Becky? The name had begun to resonate in his head, had become another part of the mantra. He supposed it was the woman he'd just avoided killing. *Whose little girl are you? Becky, why I'm Becky, I'm pretty Becky Shue.*

Except she hadn't been pretty, not pretty at all. One heavyset smelly mama was what she'd been, and now she was in Pete Moore's less than reliable care.

Six. Six. Six more miles to Banbury Cross.

Jogging steadily—as steadily as was possible, given the footing—and hearing strange voices in his head. Except only one of them was really strange, and that one wasn't a voice at all but a kind of hum with a rhythmic beat

(whose little girl, whose little girl, pretty Becky Shue)

caught in it. The rest were voices he knew, or voices his friends knew. One was a voice Jonesy had told him about, a voice he'd heard after his accident and associated with all his pain: *Please stop, I can't stand it, give me a shot, where's Marcy.*

He heard Beaver's voice: *Go look in the chamber pot.*

Jonesy, answering: *Why don't we just knock on the bathroom door and ask him how he is?*

A stranger's voice saying that if he could just do a number two he'd be okay . . .

. . . only he was no stranger, he was Rick, pretty Becky's friend Rick. Rick what? McCarthy? McKinley? McKeen? Henry wasn't sure, but he leaned toward McCarthy, like Kevin McCarthy in that old horror movie about the pods from space that made themselves look like people. One of Jonesy's faves. Get a few drinks in him and mention that movie and Jonesy would respond with the key line at once: *"They're here! They're here!"*

The woman, looking up at the sky and screaming *They're back, they're back.*

Dear Christ, there'd been nothing like this since they were kids and this was *worse,* like picking up a power-line filled with voices instead of electricity.

All those patients over the years, complaining of voices in their heads. And Henry, the big psychiatrist (Young Mr. God, one state hospital patient called him back in the early days), had nodded as if he knew what they were talking about. Had in fact believed he *did* know what they were talking about. But maybe only now did he really know.

Voices. Listening to them so hard he missed the *whup-whup-whup* of the helicopter passing overhead, a dark rushing shark-shape barely obscured by the bottoms of the clouds. Then the voices began to fade as radio signals from faraway places do when daylight comes and the atmosphere once more begins to thicken. At last there was only the voice of his own thoughts, insisting that something terrible had happened or was about to happen at Hole in the Wall; that something equally terrible was about to happen or had happened back there at the Scout or the loggers' shelter.

Five more miles. Five more miles.

In an effort to turn his mind away from his friend behind and his friends ahead, or what might be happening all around him, he let his mind go to where he knew Pete's mind had already gone: to 1978, and Tracker Brothers, and to Duddits. How Duddits Cavell could have anything to do with this fuckarow Henry didn't understand, but they had all been thinking about him, and Henry didn't even need that old mental connection to know it. Pete had mentioned Duds while they were dragging the woman to the loggers' shelter on that piece of tarp, Beaver had been talking about Duddits just the other day when Henry and the Beav had been in the woods together—the day Henry had tagged his deer, that had been. The Beav reminiscing about how the four of them had taken Duddits Christmas shopping in Bangor one year. Just after Jonesy had gotten his license that was; Jonesy would have driven anyone anywhere that winter. The Beav laughing about how Duddits had worried Santa Claus wasn't real, and all four of them—big high-school galoots by then, thinking they had the world by the tail—working to reconvince Duddits that Santa was a true thing, the real deal. Which of course they'd done. And Jonesy had called Henry from Brookline just last month, drunk (drunkenness was much rarer for Jonesy, especially since his accident, than it was for Pete, and it was the only maudlin call Henry had *ever* gotten from the man), saying that he'd never done anything in his life that was as good, as plain and simple baldass *fine,* as what they had done for poor old Duddits Cavell back in 1978. *That was our finest hour,* Jonesy had said on the phone, and with a nasty jolt, Henry realized he had told Pete exactly the same thing. Duddits, man. Fucking Duds.

Five more miles . . . or maybe four. Five more miles . . . or maybe four.

They had been going to see a picture of a girl's pussy, the picture supposedly tacked up on the bulletin board of some deserted office. Henry couldn't remember the girl's name, not after all these years, only that she'd been that prick Grenadeau's girlfriend and the 1978 Homecoming Queen at Derry High. Those things had made the prospect of seeing her pussy especially interesting. And then, just as they got to the driveway, they had seen a discarded red-and-white Derry Tigers shirt. And a little way down the driveway there had been something else.

I hate that fuckin show, they never change their clothes, Pete had said, and Henry opened his mouth to reply, only before he could . . .

"The kiddo screamed," Henry said. He slipped in the snow, tottered for a moment, then ran on again, remembering that October day under that white sky. He ran on remembering Duddits. How Duddits had screamed and changed all their lives. For the better, they had always assumed, but now Henry wondered.

Right now he wondered very much.

3

When they get to the driveway—not much of a driveway, weeds are growing even in the gravelly wheelruts now—Beaver is in the lead. Beaver is, indeed, almost foaming at the jaws. Henry guesses that Pete is nearly as wrought-up, but Pete is holding it in better, even though he's a year younger. Beaver is . . . what's the word? *Agog.* Henry almost laughs at the aptness of it, and then the Beav stops so suddenly Pete almost runs into him.

"Hey!" Beaver says. "Fuck me Freddy! Some kid's shirt!"

It is indeed. Red and white, and not old and dirty, as if it had been there a thousand years. In fact, it looks almost new.

"Shirt, schmirt, who gives a shit?" Jonesy wants to know. "Let's just—"

"Hold your horses," the Beav says. "This is a good shirt."

Except when he picks it up, they see that it isn't. New, yes—a brand-new Derry Tigers shirt, with 19 on the back. Pete doesn't give a shit for football, but the rest of them recognize it as Richie Grenadeau's number. Good, no—not anymore. It's ripped deeply at the back collar, as if the person wearing it had tried to run away, then been grabbed and hauled back.

"Guess I was wrong," the Beav says sadly, and drops it again. "Come on."

But before they get very far, they come across something else—this time it's yellow instead of red, that bright yellow plastic only a kid could love. Henry trots ahead of the others and picks it up. It's a lunchbox with Scooby-Doo and his friends on it, all of them running from what appears to be a haunted house. Like the shirt it looks new, not anything that's been lying out here for any length of time, and all at once Henry is starting to have a bad feeling about this, starting to wish they hadn't detoured into this deserted driveway by this deserted building at all . . . or at least had saved it for another day. Which, even at fourteen, he realizes is stupid. When it comes to pussy, he thinks, you either go or you don't, there's no such thing as saving it for another day.

"I hate that fuckin show," Pete says, looking over Henry's shoulder at the lunchbox. "They never change their clothes, did you ever notice that? Wear the same fuckin thing, show in and show out."

Jonesy takes the Scooby-Doo lunchbox from Henry and turns it to look at something he's seen pasted on the end. The wild look has gone out of Jonesy's eyes, he's frowning slightly, and Henry has an idea Jonesy is also wishing they'd just gone on and played some two-on-two.

The sticker on the side reads: I BELONG TO DOUG-LAS CAVELL, 19 MAPLE LANE, DERRY, MAINE. IF THE BOY I BELONG TO IS LOST, CALL 949-1864. THANKS!

Henry opens his mouth to say the lunchbox and the shirt must belong to a kid who goes to The Retard Academy—he's sure of it just looking at the sticker, which is almost like the tag their fucking *dog* wears—but before he can, there is a scream from the far side of the building, over where the big kids play baseball in the summer. It's full of hurt, that scream, but what starts Henry running before he can even think about it is the *surprise* in it, the awful surprise of someone who has been hurt or scared (or both) for the very first time.

The others follow him. They run up the weedy right rut of the driveway, the one closest to the building, in single file: Henry, Jonesy, the Beav, and Pete.

There is hearty male laughter. "Go on and eat it," someone says. "Eat it and you can go. Duncan might even give you your pants back."

"Yeah, if you—" Another boy, probably Duncan,

begins and then he stops, staring at Henry and his friends.

"Hey you guys, quit it!" Beaver shouts. "Just fucking quit it!"

Duncan's friends—there are two of them, both wearing Derry High School jackets—realize they are no longer unobserved at their afternoon's entertainment, and turn. Kneeling on the gravel amid them, dressed only in underpants and one sneaker, his face smeared with blood and dirt and snot and tears, is a child of an age Henry cannot determine. He's not a little kid, not with that powdering of hair on his chest, but he has the look of a little kid just the same. His eyes have a Chinese tilt and are bright green, swimming with tears.

On the red brick wall behind this little group, printed in large white letters which are fading but still legible, is this message: NO BOUNCE, NO PLAY. Which probably means keep the games and the balls away from the building and out in the vacant lot where the deep ruts of the basepaths and the ragged hill of the pitcher's mound can still be seen, but who can say for sure? NO BOUNCE, NO PLAY. In the years to come they will say this often; it will become one of the private catch-phrases of their youth and has no exact meaning. *Who knows?* perhaps comes closest. Or *What can you do?* It is always best spoken with a shrug, a smile, and hands tipped up to the sky.

"Who the fuck're *you*?" one of the big boys asks the Beav. On his left hand he's wearing what looks like a batting glove or maybe a golf glove . . . something athletic, anyway. In it is the dried dog-turd he has been trying to make the mostly naked boy eat.

"What are you *doing?*" Jonesy asks, horrified. "You tryin to make him *eat* that? The fuck's *wrong* with you?"

The kid holding the dog-turd has a wide swatch of white tape across the bridge of his nose, and Henry utters a bark of recognition that is half surprise and half laughter. It's too perfect, isn't it? They're here to look at the pussy of the Homecoming Queen and here, by God, is the Homecoming King, whose football season has apparently been ended by nothing worse than a broken nose, and who is currently passing his time doing stuff like this while the rest of the team practices for this week's game.

Richie Grenadeau hasn't noticed Henry's look of recognition; he's staring at Jonesy. Because he has been startled and because Jonesy's tone of disgust is so completely unfeigned, Richie at first takes a step backward. Then he realizes that the kid who has dared to speak to him in such reproving tones is at least three years younger and a hundred pounds lighter than he is. The sagging hand straightens again.

"I'm gonna make him eat this piece of shit," he says. "Then he can go. You go now, snotball, unless you want half."

"Yeah, fuck off," the third boy says. Richie Grenadeau is big but this boy is even bigger, a six-foot-five hulk whose face flames with acne. "While you got the—"

"I know who you are," Henry says.

Richie's eyes switch to Henry. He looks suddenly wary . . . but he also looks pissed off. "Fuck off, sonny. I mean it."

"You're Richie Grenadeau. Your picture was in the paper. What do you think people will say if we tell em what we caught you doing?"

"You're not gonna tell anyone anything, because you'll be fuckin *dead*," the one named Duncan says. He has dirty-blond hair falling around his face and down to his shoulders. "Get outta here. Beat feet."

Henry pays no attention to him. He stares at Richie Grenadeau. He is aware of no fear, although there's no doubt these three boys could stomp them flat; he is burning with an outrage he has never felt before, never even suspected. The kid kneeling on the ground is undoubtedly retarded, but not so retarded he doesn't understand these three big boys intended to hurt him, tore off his *shirt,* and then—

Henry has never in his life been closer to getting good and beaten up, or been less concerned with it. He takes a step forward, fists clenching. The kid on the ground sobs, head now lowered, and the sound is a constant tone in Henry's head, feeding his fury.

"I'll tell," he says, and although it is a little kid's threat, he doesn't sound like a little kid to himself. Nor to Richie, apparently; Richie takes a step backward and the gloved hand with the dried turd in it sags again. For the first time he looks alarmed. "Three against one, a little retarded kid, fuck yeah, man, I'll tell. I'll tell and *I know who you are!*"

Duncan and the big boy—the only one not wearing a high-school jacket—step up on either side of Richie. The boy in the underpants is behind them now, but Henry can still hear the pulsing drone of his sobs, it's in his head, beating in his head and driving him fucking *crazy*.

"All right, okay, that's it," the biggest boy says. He grins, showing several holes where teeth once lived. "You're gonna die now."

"Pete, you run when they come," Henry says, never taking his eyes from Richie Grenadeau. "Run home and tell your mother." And, to Richie: "You'll never catch him, either. He runs like the fucking *wind*."

Pete's voice sounds thin but not scared. "You got it, Henry."

"And the worse you beat us up, the worse it's gonna be for you," Jonesy says. Henry has already seen this, but for Jonesy it is a revelation; he's almost laughing. "Even if you really *did* kill us, what good would it do you? Because Pete *does* run fast, and he'll tell."

"I run fast, too," Richie says coldly. "I'll catch him."

Henry turns first to Jonesy and then to the Beav. Both of them are standing firm. Beaver, in fact, is doing a little more than that. He bends swiftly, picks up a couple of stones—they are the size of eggs, only with jagged edges—and begins to chunk them together. Beav's narrowed eyes shift back and forth between Richie Grenadeau and the biggest boy, the galoot. The toothpick in his mouth jitters aggressively up and down.

"When they come, go for Grenadeau," Henry says. "The other two can't even get close to Pete." He switches his gaze to Pete, who is pale but unafraid—his eyes are shining and he is almost dancing on the balls of his feet, eager to be off. "Tell your ma. Tell her where we are, to send the cops. And don't forget this bully motherfucker's name, whatever you do." He shoots a district attorney's accusing finger at Grenadeau, who once more looks uncertain. No, more than uncertain. He looks afraid.

"Richie Grenadeau," Pete says, and now he *does* begin to dance. "I won't forget."

"Come on, you dickweed," Beaver says. One thing about the Beav, he knows a really excellent rank when he hears it. "I'm gonna break your nose again. What kind of chickenshit quits off the football team cause of a broken nose, anyhow?"

Grenadeau doesn't reply—no longer knows which of them to reply to, maybe—and something rather wonderful is happening: the other boy in the high-school jacket, Duncan, has also started to look uncertain. A flush is spreading on his cheeks and across his forehead. He wets his lips and looks uncertainly at Richie. Only the galoot still looks ready to fight, and Henry almost hopes they *will* fight, Henry and Jonesy and the Beav will give them a hell of a scrap if they do, *hell* of a scrap, because of that *crying,* that fucking awful *crying,* the way it gets in your head, the beat-beat-beat of that awful crying.

"Hey Rich, maybe we ought to—" Duncan begins.

"Kill em," the galoot rumbles. "Fuck em the fuck up."

This one takes a step forward and for a moment it almost goes down. Henry knows that if the galoot had been allowed to take even one more step he would have been out of Richie Grenadeau's control, like a mean old pitbull that breaks its leash and just goes flying at its prey, a meat arrow.

But Richie doesn't let him get that next step, the one which will turn into a clumsy charge. He grabs the galoot's forearm, which is thicker than Henry's bicep and bristling with reddish-gold hair. "No, Scotty," he says, "wait a minute."

"Yeah, wait," Duncan says, sounding almost panicky. He shoots Henry a look which Henry finds, even at the age of fourteen, grotesque. It is a *reproachful* look. As if Henry and his friends were the ones doing something wrong.

"What do you want?" Richie asks Henry. "You want us to get out of here, that it?"

Henry nods.

"If we go, what are you gonna do? Who are you going to tell?"

Henry discovers an amazing thing: he is as close to coming unglued as Scotty, the galoot. Part of him wants to actually *provoke* a fight, to scream *EVERYBODY! FUCKING EVERYBODY!* Knowing that his friends would back him up, would never say a word even if they got trashed and sent to the hospital.

But the kid. That poor little crying retarded kid.

Once the big boys finished with Henry, Beaver, and Jonesy (with Pete as well, if they could catch him), they would finish with the retarded kid, too, and it would likely go a lot further than making him eat a piece of dried dog-turd.

"No one," he says. "We won't tell anyone."

"Fuckin liar," Scotty says. "He's a fuckin liar, Richie, lookit him."

Scotty starts forward again, but Richie tightens his grip on the big galoot's forearm.

"If no one gets hurt," Jonesy says in a blessedly reasonable tone of voice, "no one's got a story to tell."

Grenadeau glances at him, then back at Henry. "Swear to God?"

"Swear to God," Henry agrees.

"All of you swear to God?" Grenadeau asks.

Jonesy, Beav, and Pete all dutifully swear to God.

Grenadeau thinks about it for a moment that seems very long, and then he nods. "Okay, fuck this. We're going."

"If they come, run around the building the other way," Henry says to Pete, speaking very rapidly because the big boys are already in motion. But Grenadeau still has his hand clamped firmly on Scotty's forearm, and Henry thinks this is a good sign.

"I wouldn't waste my time," Richie Grenadeau says in a lofty tone of voice that makes Henry feel like laughing . . . but with an effort he manages to keep a straight face. Laughing at this point would be a bad idea. Things are almost fixed up. There's a part of him that hates that, but the rest of him nearly trembles with relief.

"What's up with you, anyway?" Richie Grenadeau asks him. "What's the big deal?"

Henry wants to ask his own question—wants to ask Richie Grenadeau how he could do it, and it's no rhetorical question, either. That crying! My God! But he keeps silent, knowing anything he says might just provoke the asshole, get him going all over again.

There is a kind of dance going on here; it looks almost like the ones you learn in first and second grade. As Richie, Duncan, and Scott walk toward the driveway (sauntering, attempting to show they are going of their own free will and haven't been frightened off by a bunch of homo junior-high kids), Henry and his friends first move to face them and then step backward in a line toward the weeping kid kneeling there in his underpants, blocking him from them.

At the corner of the building Richie pauses and gives them a final look. "Gonna see you fellas again," he says. "One by one or all together."

"Yeah," Duncan agrees.

"You're gonna be lookin at the world through a *oxygen tent*!" Scott adds, and Henry comes perilously close to laughing again. He prays that none of his friends will say anything—let done be done—and none of them do. It's almost a miracle.

One final menacing look from Richie and they are gone around the corner. Henry, Jonesy, Beaver, and

Pete are left alone with the kid, who is rocking back and forth on his dirty knees, his dirty bloody tearstreaked uncomprehending face cocked to the white sky like the face of a broken clock, all of them wondering what to do next. Talk to him? Tell him it's okay, that the bad boys are gone and the danger has passed? He will never understand. And oh that crying is so *freaky*. How could those kids, mean and stupid as they were, go on in the face of that crying? Henry will understand later—sort of—but at that moment it's a complete mystery to him.

"I'm gonna try something," Beaver says abruptly.

"Yeah, sure, anything," Jonesy says. His voice is shaky.

The Beav starts forward, then looks at his friends. It is an odd look, part shame, part defiance, and—yes, Henry would swear it—part hope.

"If you tell anybody I did this," he says, "I'll never chum with you guys again."

"Never mind that crap," Pete says, and he also sounds shaky. "If you can shut him up, *do* it!"

Beaver stands for a moment where Richie was standing while he tried to get the kid to eat the dogturd, then drops to his knees. Henry sees the kid's underwear shorts are in fact Underoos, and that they feature the Scooby-Doo characters, plus Shaggy's Mystery Machine, just like the kid's lunchbox.

Then Beaver takes the wailing, nearly naked boy into his arms and begins to sing.

4

*Four more miles to Banbury Cross . . . or maybe only three.
Four more miles to Banbury Cross . . . or maybe only—*

Henry's feet skidded again, and this time he had no chance to get his balance back. He had been in a deep daze of memory, and before he could come out of it, he was flying through the air.

He landed heavily on his back, hitting hard enough to lose his wind in a loud and painful gasp— *"Uh!"* Snow rose in a dreamy sugarpuff, and he hit the back of his head hard enough to see stars.

He lay where he was for a moment, giving anything broken ample opportunity to announce itself. When nothing did, he reached around and prodded the small of his back. Pain, but no agony. When they were ten and eleven and spent what seemed like whole winters sledding in Strawford Park, he had taken worse hits than this and gotten up laughing. Once, with the idiotic Pete Moore piloting his Flexible Flyer and Henry riding behind him, they had gone head-on into the big pine at the foot of the hill, the one all the kids called the Death Tree, and survived with nothing more than a few bruises and a couple of loose teeth each. The trouble was, he hadn't been ten or eleven for a lot of years.

"Get up, ya baby, you're okay," he said, and carefully came to a sitting position. Twinges from his back, but nothing worse. Just shaken up. Nothing hurt but your fuckin pride, as they used to say. Still, he'd maybe sit here another minute or two. He was making great time and he deserved a rest. Besides, those memories had shaken him. Richie Grenadeau, fucking Richie Grenadeau, who had, it turned out, *flunked* off the football team—it hadn't been the broken nose at all. *Gonna see you fellas again,* he had told them, and Henry guessed he had meant it, but the threatened confrontation had never happened, no, never happened. Something else had happened instead.

And all that was a long time ago. Right now Banbury Cross awaited—Hole in the Wall, at least—and he had no cock horse to ride there, only that poor man's steed, shank's mare. Henry got to his feet, began to brush snow from his ass, and then someone screamed inside his head.

"Ow, ow, ow!" he cried. It was like something played through a Walkman you could turn up to concert-hall levels, like a shotgun blast that had gone off directly behind his eyes. He staggered backward, flailing for balance, and had he not run into the stiffly jutting branches of a pine growing at the left side of the road, he surely would have fallen down again.

He disengaged himself from the tree's clutch, ears still ringing—hell, his entire *head* was ringing—and stepped forward, hardly believing he was still alive. He raised one of his hands to his nose, and the palm of his hand came away wet with blood. There was something loose in his mouth, too. He held his hand under it, spat out a tooth, looked at it wonderingly, then tossed it aside, ignoring his first impulse, which had been to put it in his coat pocket. No one, as far as he knew, did surgical implants of teeth, and he strongly doubted that the Tooth Fairy came this far out in the boonies.

He couldn't say for sure whose scream that had been, but he had an idea Pete Moore had maybe just run into a big load of bad trouble.

Henry listened for other voices, other thoughts, and heard none. Excellent. Although he had to admit that, even without voices, this had certainly turned into the hunting trip of a lifetime.

"Go, big boy, on you huskies," he said, and started running toward Hole in the Wall again. His sense that something had gone wrong there was stronger than ever, and it was all he could do to hold himself to a fast jog.

Go look in the chamber pot.

Why don't we just knock on the bathroom door and ask him how he is?

Had he actually heard those voices? Yes, they were gone now, but he had heard them, just as he had heard that terrible agonal scream. Pete? Or had it been the woman? Pretty Becky Shue?

"Pete," he said, the word coming out in a puff of vapor. "It was Pete." Not entirely sure, even now, but *pretty* sure.

At first he was afraid he wouldn't be able to find his rhythm again, but then, while he was still worrying about it, it came back—the synchronicity of his hurrying breath and thudding feet, beautiful in its simplicity.

Three more miles to Banbury Cross, he thought. *Going home. Just like we took Duddits home that day.*

(if you tell anybody I did this I'll never chum with you guys again)

Henry returned to that October afternoon as to a deep dream. He dropped down the well of memory so far and so fast that at first he didn't sense the cloud rushing toward him, the cloud that was not words or thoughts or screams but only its redblack self, a thing with places to go and things to do.

5

Beaver steps forward, hesitates for a moment, then drops to his knees. The retard doesn't see him; he is still wailing, eyes squeezed shut and narrow chest heaving. Both the Underoos and Beaver's zipper-studded old motorcycle jacket are comical, but none of the other boys are laughing. Henry only wants the retard to stop crying. That crying is killing him.

Beaver shuffles forward a little bit on his knees, then takes the weeping boy into his arms.

"Baby's boat's a silver dream, sailing near and far . . ."

Henry has never heard Beaver sing before, except maybe along with the radio—the Clarendons are most certainly not churchgoers—and he is astounded by the clear tenor sweetness of his friend's voice. In another year or so the Beav's voice will change completely and become unremarkable, but now, in the weedy vacant lot behind the empty building, it pierces them all, astounds them. The retarded boy reacts as well; stops crying and looks at Beaver with wonder.

*"It sails from here in Baby's room and to the nearest star;
Sail, Baby, sail, sail on home to me, sail the seas and sail
the stars, sail on home to me . . ."*

The last note drifts on the air and for a moment nothing in the world breathes for beauty. Henry feels like crying. The retarded boy looks at Beaver, who has been rocking him back and forth in rhythm with the song. On his teary face is an expression of blissful astonishment. He has forgotten his split lip and bruised cheek, his missing clothes, his lost lunchbox. To Beaver he says *ooo or,* open syllables that could mean almost anything, but Henry understands them perfectly and sees Beaver does, too.

"I *can't* do more," the Beav says. He realizes his arm is still around the kid's shirtless shoulders and takes it away.

As soon as he does, the kid's face clouds over, not with fear this time, or with the petulance of one balked of getting his way, but in pure sorrow. Tears fill those amazingly green eyes of his and spill down the clean tracks on his dirty cheeks. He takes Beaver's hand and puts Beaver's arm back over his shoulders. *"Ooo or! Ooo or!"* he says.

Beaver looks at them, panicked. "That's all my mother ever sang me," he says. "I always went right to fuckin sleep."

Henry and Jonesy exchange a look and burst out laughing. Not a good idea, it'll probably scare the kid and he'll start that terrible bawling again, but neither of them can help it. And the kid *doesn't* cry. He smiles at Henry and Jonesy instead, a sunny smile that displays a mouthful of white crammed-together teeth, and then looks back at Beaver. He continues to hold Beaver's arm firmly around his shoulders.

"*Ooo or!*" he commands.

"Aw, fuck, sing it again," Pete says. "The part you know."

Beaver ends up singing it three more times before the kid will let him stop, will let the boys work him into his pants and his torn shirt, the one with Richie Grenadeau's number on it. Henry has never forgotten that haunting fragment and will sometimes recall it at the oddest times: after losing his virginity at a UNH fraternity party with "Smoke on the Water" pounding through the speakers downstairs; after opening his paper to the obituary page and seeing Barry Newman's rather charming smile above his multiple chins; feeding his father, who had come down with Alzheimer's at the ferociously unfair age of fifty-three, his father insisting that Henry was someone named Sam. "A real man pays off his debts, Sammy," his father had said, and when he accepted the next bite of cereal, milk ran down his chin. At these times what he thinks of as Beaver's Lullaby will come back to him, and he will feel transiently comforted. No bounce, no play.

Finally they've got the kid all dressed except for one red sneaker. He's trying to put it on himself, but he's got it pointing backward. He is one fucked-up young American, and Henry is at a loss to know how the three big boys could have bullied up on him. Even aside from the crying, which was like no crying

Henry had ever heard before, why would you want to be so mean?

"Let me fix that, man," Beaver says.

"Fit wha?" the kid asks, so comically perplexed that Henry, Jonesy, and Pete all burst out laughing again. Henry knows you're not supposed to laugh at retards, but he can't help it. The kid just has a naturally funny face, like a cartoon character.

Beaver only smiles. "Your sneaker, man."

"Fit neek?"

"Yeah, you can't put it on that way, fuckin imposseeblo, señor." Beaver takes the sneaker from him and the kid watches with close interest as the Beav slips his foot into it, draws the laces firmly against the tongue, and then ties the ends in a bow. When he's done, the kid looks at the bow for a moment longer, then at Beaver. Then he puts his arms around Beaver's neck and plants a big loud smack on Beaver's cheek.

"If you guys tell anybody he did that—" Beaver begins, but he's smiling, clearly pleased.

"Yeah, yeah, you'll never chum with us again, ya fuckin wank," Jonesy says, grinning. He has held onto the lunchbox and now squats in front of the kid, holding it out. "This yours, guy?"

The kid grins with the delight of someone encountering an old friend and snatches it. "Ooby-Ooby-Doo, where-are-oo?" he sings. "We gah-sum urk oo-do-now!"

"That's right," Jonesy agrees. "Got some work to do now. Gotta get you the fuck home is what we got to do. Douglas Cavell, that's your name, right?"

The boy is holding his lunchbox to his chest in both of his dirty hands. Now he gives it a loud smack, just like the one he put on Beaver's cheek. "I Duddits!" he cries.

"Good," Henry says. He takes one of the boy's hands, Jonesy takes the other, and they help him to his feet. Maple Lane is only three blocks away and they can be there in ten minutes, always assuming that Richie and his friends aren't hanging around and hoping to ambush them. "Let's get you home, Duddits. Bet your Mom's worried about you."

But first Henry sends Pete to the corner of the building to look up the driveway. When Pete comes back and reports the coast clear, Henry lets them go that far. Once they are on the sidewalk, where people can see them, they'll be safe. Until then, he will take no chances. He sends Pete out a second time, tells him to scout all the way to the street, then whistle if everything is cool.

"Dey gone," Duddits says.

"Maybe," Henry says, "but I'll feel better if Pete takes a look."

Duddits stands serenely among them, looking at the pictures on his lunchbox, while Pete goes out to look around. Henry feels okay about sending him. He hasn't exaggerated Pete's speed; if Richie and his friends try to jump him, Pete will turn on the jets and leave them in the dust.

"You like this show, man?" Beaver says, taking the lunchbox. He speaks quietly. Henry watches with some interest, curious to see if the retarded boy will cry for his lunchbox. He doesn't.

"Ey Ooby-Doos!" the retarded kid says. His hair is golden, curly. Henry still can't tell what age he is.

"I *know* they're Scooby-Doos," the Beav says patiently, "but they never change their clothes. Pete's right about that. I mean, fuck me Freddy, right?"

"Ite!" He holds out his hands for the lunchbox and Beaver gives it back. The retarded boy hugs it, then smiles at them. It is a beautiful smile, Henry thinks, smiling himself. It makes him think of how you are cold when you have been swimming in the ocean for awhile, but when you come out, you wrap a towel around your bony shoulders and goosepimply back and you're warm again.

Jonesy is also smiling. "Duddits," he says, "which one is the dog?"

The retarded boy looks at him, still smiling, but puzzled now, too.

"The *dog*," Henry says. "Which one's the *dog*?"

Now the boy looks at Henry, his puzzlement deepening.

"Which one's *Scooby*, Duddits?" Beaver asks, and Duddits's face clears. He points.

"Ooby! Ooby-Ooby-Doo! *Eee* a dog!"

They all burst out laughing, Duddits is laughing too, and then Pete whistles. They start moving and have gone about a quarter of the way up the driveway when Jonesy says, "Wait! Wait!"

He runs to one of the dirty office windows and peers in, cupping his hands to the sides of his face to cut the glare, and Henry suddenly remembers why they came. Tina Jean What's-Her-Face's pussy. All that seems about a thousand years ago.

After about ten seconds, Jonesy calls, "Henry! Beav! Come here! Leave the kid there!"

Beaver runs to Jonesy's side. Henry turns to the retarded boy and says, "Stand right there, Duddits. Right there with your lunchbox, okay?"

Duddits looks up at him, green eyes shining, lunchbox held to his chest. After a moment he nods, and Henry runs to join his friends at the window. They have to squeeze together, and Beaver grumbles that someone is steppin on his fuckin feet, but they manage. After a minute or so, puzzled by their failure to show up on the sidewalk, Pete joins them, poking his face in between Henry's and Jonesy's shoulders. Here are four boys at a dirty office window, three with their hands cupped to the sides of their faces to cut the glare, and a fifth boy standing behind them in the weedy driveway, holding his lunchbox against his narrow chest and looking up at the white sky, where the sun is trying to break through. Beyond the dirty glass (where they will leave clean crescents to mark the places where their foreheads rested) is an empty room. Scattered across the dusty floor are a number of deflated white tadpoles that Henry recognizes as jizzbags. On one wall, the one directly across from the window, is a bulletin board. Tacked to it is a map of northern New England and a Polaroid photograph of a woman holding her skirt up. You can't see her pussy, though, just some white panties. And she's no high-school girl. She's old. She must be at least thirty.

"Holy God," Pete says at last, giving Jonesy a disgusted look. "We came all the way down here for *that*?"

For a moment Jonesy looks defensive, then grins and jerks his thumb back over his shoulder. "No," he says. "We came for *him*."

6

Henry was pulled from recall by an amazing and totally unexpected realization: he was terrified, had been terrified for some time. Some new thing had been hovering just below the threshold of his consciousness, held down by the vivid memory of meeting Duddits. Now it had burst forward with a frightened yell, insisting on recognition.

He skidded to a stop in the middle of the road, flailing his arms to keep from falling down in the snow again, and then simply stood there panting, eyes wide. What now? He was only two and a half miles from Hole in the Wall, almost there, so what the Christ now?

There's a cloud, he thought. *Some kind of cloud, that's what. I can't tell what it is but I can feel it—I never felt anything so clearly in my life. My adult life, anyway. I have to get off the road. I have to get away from it. Get away from the movie. There's a movie in the cloud. The kind Jonesy likes. A scary one.*

"That's stupid," he muttered, knowing it wasn't.

He could hear the approaching wasp-whine of an engine. It was coming from the direction of Hole in the Wall and coming fast, a snowmobile engine, almost certainly the Arctic Cat stored at camp . . . but it was also the redblack cloud with the movie going on inside it, some terrible black *energy* rushing toward him.

For a moment Henry was frozen with a hundred childish horrors, things under beds and things in coffins, squirming bugs beneath overturned rocks and the furry jelly that was the remains of a long-dead baked rat the time Dad had moved the stove out from the wall to check the plug. And horrors that weren't childish at all: his father, lost in his own bedroom and bawling with fear; Barry Newman, running from Henry's office with that vast look of terror on his face, terror because he had been asked to look at something he wouldn't, perhaps couldn't, acknowledge; sitting awake at four in the morning with a glass of Scotch, all the world a dead socket, his own mind a dead socket and oh baby it was a thousand years till dawn and all lullabys had been cancelled. Those things were in the redblack cloud rushing down on him like that pale horse in the Bible, those things and more. Every bad thing he had ever suspected was now coming toward him, not on a pale horse but on an old snowmobile with a rusty cowling. Not death but worse than death. It was Mr. Gray.

Get off the road! his mind screamed. *Get off the road now! Hide!*

For a moment he couldn't move—his feet seemed to grow heavy. The gash on his thigh, the one the turnsignal had made, burned like a brand. Now he understood how a deer caught in the headlights felt, or a chipmunk hopping stupidly back and forth in front of an oncoming lawnmower. The cloud had robbed him of his ability to help himself. He was frozen in its rushing path.

What got him going, oddly enough, was all those thoughts of suicide. Had he agonized his way to that decision on five hundred sleepless nights only to be robbed of his option by a kind of buck-fever? No, by God, no, it wouldn't be. Suffering was bad enough; allowing his own terrified body to mock that suffering by locking up and just standing here while a demon ran him down . . . no, he would not allow that to happen.

And so he moved, but it was like moving in a nightmare, fighting his way through air which seemed to have grown as thick as taffy. His legs rose and fell with the slowness of an underwater ballet. Had he been running down this road? Actually *running*? The idea now seemed impossible, no matter how strong the memory.

Still, he kept moving while the whine of the approaching engine grew closer, deepening to a stuttery roar. And at last he was able to get into the trees on the south side of the road. He managed perhaps fifteen feet, far enough so there was no snow cover, only a dust of white on the aromatic orange-brown needles. There Henry fell on his knees, sobbing with terror and putting his gloved hands to his mouth to stifle the sound, because what if it heard? It was Mr. Gray, the cloud was Mr. Gray, and what if it heard?

He crawled behind the moss-girdled trunk of a

spruce tree, clutched it, then peered around it through the tumbled screen of his sweaty hair. He saw a spark of light in the dark afternoon. It jittered, wavered, and rounded. It became a headlight.

Henry began to moan helplessly as the blackness neared. It seemed to hover over his mind like an eclipse, obliterating thought, replacing it with terrible images: milk on his father's chin, panic in Barry Newman's eyes, scrawny bodies and staring eyes behind barbed wire, flayed women and hanged men. For a moment his understanding of the world seemed to turn inside out like a pocket and he realized that *everything* was infected . . . or could be. *Everything.* His reasons for contemplating suicide were paltry in the face of this oncoming thing.

He pressed his mouth against the tree to keep from screaming, felt his lips tattoo a kiss into the springy moss all the way down to where it was moist and tasted of bark. In that moment the Arctic Cat flashed past and Henry recognized the figure which straddled it, the person who was generating the red-black cloud which now filled Henry's head like a dry fever.

He bit into the moss, screamed against the tree, inhaled fragments of moss without being aware of it, and screamed again. Then he simply knelt there, holding onto the tree and shuddering, as the sound of the Arctic Cat began to diminish into the west. He was still there when it had died away to a troublesome whine again; still there when it faded away entirely.

Pete's back there somewhere, he thought. *It'll come to Pete, and to the woman.*

Henry stumbled back to the road, unaware that his nose had begun bleeding again, unaware that he was crying. He began moving toward Hole in the Wall once more, although now the best pace he could manage was a shambling limp. But maybe that was all right, because it was all over back at camp.

Whatever the horrible thing was that he had been sensing, it had happened. One of his friends was dead, one was dying, and one, God help him, had become a movie star.

CHAPTER SEVEN

JONESY

AND THE BEAV

1

Beaver said it again. No Beaver-isms now; just that bare Anglo-Saxon syllable you came to when you were up against the wall and had no other way to express the horror you saw. "Ah, *fuck*, man—*fuck*."

However much pain McCarthy had been in, he had taken time to snap on both of the switches just inside the bathroom door, lighting the fluorescent bars on either side of the medicine chest mirror and the overhead fluorescent ring. These threw a bright, even glare that gave the bathroom the feel of a crime-scene photograph . . . and yet there was a kind of stealthy surrealism, too, because the light wasn't quite steady; there was just enough flicker for you to know the power was coming from a genny and not through a line maintained by Derry and Bangor Hydroelectric.

The tile on the floor was baby blue. There were only spots and splatters of blood on it near the door, but as they approached the toilet next to the tub, the splotches ran together and became a red snake. Scarlet capillaries had spread off from this. The tiles were tattooed with the footprints of their boots, which neither Jonesy nor Beaver had taken off. On the blue vinyl shower curtain were four blurred fingerprints, and Jonesy thought: *He must have reached out and grabbed at the curtain to keep from falling when he turned to sit.*

Yes, but that wasn't the awful part. The awful part was what Jonesy saw in his mind's eye: McCarthy scuttling across the baby blue tiles with one hand behind him, clutching himself, trying to hold something in.

"Ah, *fuck!*" Beaver said again. Almost sobbing. "I don't want to see this, Jonesy—man, I *can't* see this."

"We've got to." He heard himself speaking as if from a great distance. "We can do this, Beav. If we could face up to Richie Grenadeau and his friends that time, we can face up to this."

"I dunno, man, I dunno . . ."

Jonesy didn't know, either—not really—but he reached out and took Beaver's hand. Beav's fingers closed over his with panicky tightness and together they went a step deeper into the bathroom. Jonesy tried to avoid the blood, but it was hard; there was blood everywhere. And not all of it was blood.

"Jonesy," Beaver said in a dry near-whisper. "Do you see that crud on the shower curtain?"

"Yeah." Growing in the blurred fingerprints were

little clumps of reddish golden mold, like mildew. There was more of it on the floor, not in the fat blood-snake, but in the narrow angles of the grout.

"What is it?"

"I don't know," Jonesy said. "Same shit he had on his face, I guess. Shut up a minute." Then: "Mr. McCarthy? . . . Rick?"

McCarthy, sitting there on the toilet, made no response. He had for some reason put his orange cap back on—the bill stuck off at a crooked, slightly drunken angle. He was otherwise naked. His chin was down on his breastbone, in a parody of deep thought (or maybe it *wasn't* a parody, who knew?). His eyes were mostly closed. His hands were clasped primly together over his pubic thatch. Blood ran down the side of the toilet in a big sloppy paintstroke, but there was no blood on McCarthy himself, at least not as far as Jonesy could see.

One thing he *could* see: the skin of McCarthy's stomach hung in two slack dewlaps. The look of it reminded Jonesy of something, and after a moment or two it came to him. It was how Carla's stomach had looked after she had delivered each of their four children. Above McCarthy's hip, where there was a little love-handle (and some give to the flesh), the skin was only red. Across the belly, however, it had split open in tiny weals. If McCarthy had been pregnant, it must have been with some sort of parasite, a tapeworm or a hookworm or something like that. Only there was stuff growing in his spilled blood, and what had he said as he lay there in Jonesy's bed with the blankets pulled up to his chin? *Behold, I stand at the door and knock.* This was one knock Jonesy wished he had never answered. In fact, he wished he had shot him. Yes. He saw more clearly now. He was hyped on the clarity that sometimes comes to the completely horrified mind, and in that state wished he had put a bullet in McCarthy before he saw the orange cap and the orange flagman's vest. It couldn't have hurt and it might have helped.

"Stand at the door and knock on my ass," Jonesy muttered.

"Jonesy? Is he still alive?"

"I don't know."

Jonesy took another step forward and felt Beaver's fingers slide out of his; the Beav had apparently come as close to McCarthy as he was able.

"Rick?" Jonesy asked in a hushed voice. A don't-wake-the-baby voice. A viewing-the-corpse voice. "Rick, are you—"

There was a loud, dank fart from beneath the man on the toilet, and the room immediately filled with an eyewatering aroma of excrement and airplane glue. Jonesy thought it a wonder that the shower curtain didn't melt.

From the bowl there came a splash. Not the plop of a turd dropping—at least Jonesy didn't think so. It sounded more like a fish jumping in a pond.

"Christ almighty, the *stink* of it!" Beaver cried. He had the heel of his hand over his mouth and nose and his words were muffled. "But if he can fart, he must be alive. Huh, Jonesy? He must still be—"

"Hush," Jonesy said in a quiet voice. He was astonished at its steadiness. "Just hush, okay?" And the Beav hushed.

Jonesy leaned in close. He could see everything: the small stipple of blood in McCarthy's right eyebrow, the red growth on his cheek, the blood on the blue plastic curtain, the joke sign—LAMAR'S THINKIN PLACE—that had hung in here when the toilet was still of the chemical variety and the shower had to be pumped up before it could be used. He saw the little gelid gleam from between McCarthy's eyelids and the cracks in his lips, which looked purple and liverish in this light. He could smell the noxious aroma of the passed gas and could almost see that, too, rising in filthy dark yellow streamers, like mustard gas.

"McCarthy? Rick? Can you hear me?"

He snapped his fingers in front of those nearly closed eyes. Nothing. He licked a spot on the back of his wrist and held it first in front of McCarthy's nostrils, then in front of his lips. Nothing.

"He's dead, Beav," he said, drawing back.

"Bullshit he is," Beaver replied. His voice was ragged, absurdly offended, as if McCarthy had violated all the rules of hospitality. "He just dropped a clinker, man, I heard it."

"I don't think that was—"

Beav stepped past him, bumping Jonesy's bad hip against the sink hard enough to hurt. "That's enough, fella!" Beaver cried. He grabbed McCarthy's round freckled unmuscled shoulder and shook it. "Snap out of it! Snap—"

McCarthy listed slowly tubward and Jonesy had a moment when he thought Beaver had been right after all, the guy was still alive, alive and trying to get up. Then McCarthy fell off the throne and into the tub, pushing the shower curtain ahead of him in a filmy blue billow. The orange hat fell off. There was a bony crack as his skull hit the porcelain and then Jonesy and Beaver were screaming and clutching each other, the sound of their horror deafening in the little tile-lined room. McCarthy's ass was a lopsided full moon with a giant bloody crater in its center, the site of some terrible impact, it seemed. Jonesy saw it for only a second before McCarthy collapsed facedown into the tub and the curtain floated back into place, hiding him, but in that second it seemed to Jonesy that the hole was a foot across. Could that be? A *foot*? Surely not.

In the toilet bowl, something splashed again, hard enough to spatter droplets of bloody water up onto the ring, which was also blue. Beaver started to lean forward to look in, and Jonesy slammed the lid down on the ring without even thinking about it. "No," he said.

"No?"

"No."

Beaver tried to get a toothpick out of the front pocket of his overalls, came up with half a dozen, and dropped them on the floor. They rolled across the bloody blue tiles like jackstraws. The Beav looked at them, then looked up at Jonesy. There were tears standing in his eyes. "Like Duddits, man," he said.

"What in God's name are you talking about?"

"Don't you remember? *He* was almost naked, too. Fuckers snatched off his shirt and his pants, didn't leave him nothing but his underpants. But we saved him." Beaver nodded vigorously, as if Jonesy—or some deep and doubtful part of himself—had scoffed at this idea.

Jonesy scoffed at nothing, although McCarthy didn't remind him in the slightest of Duddits. He kept seeing McCarthy going over sideways into the tub, his orange hat falling off, the fatty deposits on his chest (*the tits of easy living,* Henry called them whenever he saw a pair underneath some guy's polo shirt) wobbling. And then his ass turning up to the light—that harsh fluorescent light that kept no secrets but blabbed everything in a droning monotone. That perfect white man's ass, hairless, just starting to turn flabby and settle down on the backs of the thighs; he had seen a thousand like it in the various locker rooms where he had dressed and showered, was developing one himself (or had been until the guy had run him over, changing the physical configuration of his backside perhaps forever), only he had never seen one like McCarthy's was now, one that looked like something inside had fired a flare or a shotgun shell in order to—to what?

There was another hollow splash from the toilet. The lid bumped up. It was as good an answer as any. In order to get out, of course.

In order to get out.

"Sit on that," Jonesy told Beaver.

"Huh?"

"Sit on it!" Jonesy almost shouted it this time and

Beaver sat down on the closed lid in a hurry, looking startled. In the no-secrets, flat-toned light of the fluorescents, Beaver's skin looked as white as freshly turned clay and every fleck of black stubble was a mole. His lips were purple. Above his head was the old joke sign: LAMAR'S THINKIN PLACE. Beav's blue eyes were wide and terrified.

"I'm sittin, Jonesy—see?"

"Yeah. I'm sorry, Beav. But you just sit there, all right? Whatever he had inside him, it's trapped. Got nowhere to go but the septic tank. I'll be back—"

"Where you goin? Cause I don't want you to leave me sittin in the shithouse next to a dead man, Jonesy. If we both run—"

"We're not running," Jonesy said grimly. "This is our place, and we're not running." Which sounded noble but left out at least one aspect of the situation: he was mostly just afraid the thing that was now in the toilet might be able to run faster than they could. *Or squiggle* faster. Or something. Clips from a hundred horror films—*Parasite, Alien, They Came from Within*—ran through his mind at super-speed. Carla wouldn't go to the movies with him when one of those was playing, and she made him go downstairs and use the TV in his study when he brought them home on tape. But one of those movies—something he'd seen in one of them—just might save their lives. Jonesy glanced at the reddish-gold mildewy stuff growing on McCarthy's bloody handprint. Save their lives from the thing in the toilet, anyway. The mildewy stuff . . . who in God's name knew?

The thing in the bowl leaped again, thudding the

underside of the lid, but Beaver had no trouble holding the lid down. That was good. Maybe whatever it was would drown in there, although Jonesy didn't see how they could count on that; it had been living inside McCarthy, hadn't it? It had been living inside old Mr. Behold-I-stand-at-the-door-and-knock for quite some time, maybe the whole four days he'd been lost in the woods. It had slowed the growth of McCarthy's beard, it seemed, and caused a few of his teeth to fall out; it had also caused McCarthy to pass gas that probably couldn't have gone ignored even in the politest of polite society—farts like poison gas, to be perfectly blunt about it—but the thing itself had apparently been fine . . . lively . . . growing . . .

Jonesy had a sudden vivid image of a wriggling white tapeworm emerging from a pile of raw meat. His gorge rose with a liquid chugging sound.

"Jonesy?" Beaver started to get up. He looked more alarmed than ever.

"Beaver, sit back down!"

Beaver did, just in time. The thing in the toilet leaped and hit the underside of the lid with a hard, hollow rap. *Behold, I stand at the door and knock.*

"Remember that *Lethal Weapon* movie where Mel Gibson's partner didn't dare to get off the crapper?" Beaver said. He smiled, but his voice was dry and his eyes were terrified. "This is like that, isn't it?"

"No," Jonesy said, "because nothing's going to blow up. Besides, I'm not Mel Gibson and you're too fucking white to be Danny Glover. Listen, Beav. I'm going out to the shed—"

"Huh-uh, no way, don't leave me here all by myself—"

"Shut up and listen. There's friction tape out there, isn't there?"

"Yeah, hangin on a nail, at least I think—"

"Hanging on a nail, that's right. Near the paint-cans, I think. A big fat roll of it. I'm going to get that, then come back and tape the lid down. Then—"

It leaped again, furiously, as if it could hear and understand. *Well, how do we know it can't?* Jonesy thought. When it hit the bottom of the lid with a hard, vicious thud, the Beav winced.

"Then we're getting out of here," Jonesy finished.

"On the Cat?"

Jonesy nodded, although he had in fact forgotten all about the snowmobile. "Yeah, on the Cat. And we'll hook up with Henry and Pete—"

The Beav was shaking his head. "Quarantine, that's what the guy in the helicopter said. That must be why they haven't come back yet, don't you think? They musta got held out by the—"

Thud!

Beaver winced. So did Jonesy.

"—by the quarantine."

"That could be," Jonesy said. "But listen, Beav— I'd rather be quarantined with Pete and Henry than here with . . . than here, wouldn't you?"

"Let's just flush it down," Beaver said. "How about that?"

Jonesy shook his head.

"Why not?"

"Because I saw the hole it made getting out," Jonesy said, "and so did you. I don't know what it is, but we're not going to get rid of it just by pushing a handle. It's too big."

"Fuck." Beaver slammed the heel of his hand against his forehead.

Jonesy nodded.

"All right, Jonesy. Go get the tape."

In the doorway, Jonesy paused and looked back. "And Beaver . . . ?"

The Beav raised his eyebrows.

"Sit tight, buddy."

Beaver started to giggle. So did Jonesy. They looked at each other, Jonesy in the doorway and the Beav sitting on the closed toilet seat, snorting laughter. Then Jonesy hurried across the big central room (still giggling—sit tight, the more he thought about it the funnier it seemed) toward the kitchen door. He felt hot and feverish, both horrified and hilarious. Sit tight. Jesus-Christ-Bananas.

2

Beav could hear Jonesy giggling all the way across the room, still giggling when he went out the door. In spite of everything, Beav was glad to hear that sound. It had already been a bad year for Jonesy, getting run over the way he had—for awhile there at first they'd all thought he was going to step out, and that was awful, poor old Jonesy wasn't yet thirty-eight. Bad year for Pete, who'd been drinking too much, a bad year for Henry, who sometimes got a spooky absence about him that Beav didn't understand and didn't like . . . and now he guessed you could say it had been a bad year for Beaver Clarendon, as well. Of course this was only one day in three hundred and sixty-five, but you just didn't get up in the morning thinking that by afternoon there'd be a dead guy lying naked in the tub and you'd be sitting on a closed toilet seat in order to keep something you hadn't even *seen* from—

"Nope," Beaver said. "Not going there, okay? Just not going there."

And he didn't have to. Jonesy would be back with the friction tape in a minute or two, three minutes tops. The question was where *did* he want to go until Jonesy returned? Where could he go and feel good?

Duddits, that was where. Thinking about Duddits always made him feel good. And Roberta, thinking about her was good, too. Undoubtedly.

Beav smiled, remembering the little woman in the yellow dress who'd been standing at the end of her walk on Maple Lane that day. The smile widened as he remembered how she'd caught sight of them. She had called her boy that same thing. She had called him

3

"Duddits!" she cries, a little graying wren of a woman in a flowered print dress, then runs up the sidewalk toward them.

Duddits has been walking contentedly with his new friends, chattering away six licks to the minute, holding his Scooby-Doo lunchbox in his left hand and Jonesy's hand in his right, swinging it cheerfully back and forth. His gabble seems to consist almost entirely of open vowel-sounds. The thing which amazes Beaver the most about it is how much of it he understands.

Now, catching sight of the graying birdie-woman, Duddits lets go of Jonesy's hand and runs toward her, both of them running, and it reminds Beaver of some musical about a bunch of singers, the Von Cripps or Von Crapps or something like that. "Ah-mee, Ah-mee!" Duddits shouts exuberantly—*Mommy! Mommy!*

"Where have you been? Where have you been, you bad boy, you bad old Duddits!"

They come together and Duddits is so much bigger—two or three inches taller, too—that Beaver winces, expecting the birdie-woman to be flattened the way Coyote is always getting flattened in the Roadrunner cartoons. Instead, she picks him up and swings him around, his sneakered feet flying out behind him, his mouth stretched halfway up to his ears in an expression of joyful ecstasy.

"I was just about to go in and call the police, you bad old late thing, you bad old late D—"

She sees Beaver and his friends and sets her son down on his feet. Her smile of relief is gone; she is solemn as she steps toward them over some little girl's hopscotch grid—crude as it is, Beav thinks, even that will always be beyond Duddits. The tears on her cheeks gleam in the glow of the sun that has finally broken through.

"Uh-oh," Pete says. "We're gonna catch it."

"Be cool," Henry says, speaking low and fast. "Let her rant and then I'll explain."

But they have misjudged Roberta Cavell—have judged her by the standard of so many adults who seem to view boys their age as guilty until proven innocent. Roberta Cavell isn't that way, and neither is her husband, Alfie. The Cavells are different. Duddits has *made* them different.

"Boys," she says again. "Was he wandering? Was he lost? I've been so afraid to let him walk, but he wants to so much to be a real boy . . ."

She gives Beaver's fingers a strong squeeze with one hand and Pete's with the other. Then she drops them, takes Jonesy's and Henry's hands, and gives them the same treatment.

"Ma'am . . ." Henry begins.

Mrs. Cavell looks at Henry with fixed concentration, as if she is trying to read his mind. "Not just lost," she says. "Not just wandering."

"Ma'am . . ." Henry tries again, and then gives up any thought of dissembling. It is Duddits's green gaze looking up at him from her face, only intelligent and aware, keen and questioning. "No, ma'am." Henry sighs. "Not just wandering."

"Because usually he comes right home. He says he can't get lost because he sees the line. How many were there?"

"Oh, a few," Jonesy says, then shoots a swift look at Henry. Beside them, Duddits has found a last few gone-to-seed dandelions on the neighbors' lawn and is down on his belly, blowing the fluff off them and watching it float away on the breeze. "A few boys were teasing him, ma'am."

"Big boys," Pete says.

Again her eyes search them, from Jonesy to Pete, from Pete to Beaver, and then back to Henry again. "Come up to the house with us," she says. "I want to hear all about it. Duddits has a big glass of ZaRex every afternoon—it's his special drink—but I'll bet you guys would rather have iced tea. Wouldn't you?"

The three of them look at Henry, who considers and then nods. "Yes, ma'am, iced tea would be great."

So she leads them back to the house where they'll spend so much of their time in the following years— the house at 19 Maple Lane—only it is really Duddits who leads the way, prancing, skipping, sometimes lifting his yellow Scooby-Doo lunchbox over his head, but always, Beaver notices, keeping at almost exactly the same place on the sidewalk, about a foot from the grass margin between the walk and the street. Years later, after the thing with the Rinkenhauer girl, he will consider what Mrs. Cavell said. They all will. *He sees the line.*

4

"Jonesy?" Beaver called.

No answer. Christ, it seemed like Jonesy had been

gone a long time. Probably hadn't been, but there was no way Beaver could tell; he'd forgotten to put on his watch that morning. Stupid, but then, he'd always been stupid, he ought to be used to it by now. Next to Jonesy and Henry, both he and Pete had been stupid. Not that Jonesy or Henry had ever treated them that way—that was one of the great things about them.

"*Jonesy?*"

Still nothing. Probably he was having trouble finding the tape, that was all.

There was a vile little voice far back in Beaver's head telling him that the tape had nothing to do with it, that Jonesy had just gone Powder River, leaving him here to sit on the toilet like Danny Glover in that movie, but he wouldn't listen to that voice because Jonesy would never do anything like that. They were friends to the end, always had been.

That's right, the vile voice agreed. *You were friends. And this is the end.*

"Jonesy? You there, man?"

Still nothing. Maybe the tape had fallen off the nail it had been hung on.

Nothing from beneath him, either. And hey, it really wasn't possible that McCarthy had shit some kind of monster into the john, was it? That he'd given birth to—*Gasp!*—The Beast in the Bowl? It sounded like a horror-movie spoof on *Saturday Night Live*. And even if that *had* happened, The Beast in the Bowl had probably drowned by now, drowned or gone deep. A line from a story suddenly occurred to him, one they'd read to Duddits—taking turns, and it was good there were four of them because when Duddits liked some-thing he never got tired of it.

"Eee doool!" Duddits would shout, running to one of them with the book held high over his head, the way he'd carried his lunchbox home that first day. "Eee doool, eee doool!" Which in this case meant *Read* Pool! *Read* Pool! The book was *McElligot's Pool*, by Dr. Seuss, the first memorable couplet of which went, "Young man," laughed the farmer, / "You're sort of a fool! / You'll *never* catch fish / In McElligot's Pool." But there *had* been fish, at least in the imagi-nation of the little boy in the story. Plenty of fish. *Big* fish.

No splashes from beneath him, though. No bumps on the underside of the lid, either. Not for awhile now. He could maybe risk one quick look, just raise the lid a little and slam it back down if anything—

But *sit tight, buddy* was the last thing Jonesy had said to him, and that was what he'd better do.

Jonesy's most likely a mile down the road by now, the vile voice estimated. *A mile down the road and still pick-ing up speed.*

"No, he ain't," Beaver said. "Not Jonesy."

He shifted a little bit on the closed seat, waiting for the thing to jump, but it didn't. It might be sixty yards away by now and swimming with the turds in the septic tank. Jonesy had said it was too big to go down, but since neither of them had actually seen it, there was no way to tell for sure, was there? But in either case, Monsieur Beaver Clarendon was going to sit right here. Because he'd said he would. Because time always seemed slower when you were worried or scared. And because he trusted Jonesy. Jonesy and Henry had never hurt him or made fun, not of him and not of Pete. And none of them had ever hurt Duddits or made fun of him, either.

Beav snorted laughter. Duddits with his Scooby-Doo lunchbox. Duddits on his belly, blowing the fluff off dandelions. Duddits running around in his back-yard, happy as a bird in a tree, yeah, and people who called kids like him *special* didn't know the half of it. He had been special, all right, their present from a fucked-up world that usually didn't give you jack-shit. Duddits had been their own special thing, and they had loved him.

5

They sit in the sunny kitchen nook—the clouds have gone away as if by magic—drinking iced tea and watching Duddits, who drank his ZaRex (awful-look-ing orange stuff) in three or four huge splattering gulps and then ran out back to play.

Henry does most of the talking, telling Mrs. Cavell that the boys were just "kinda pushing him around." He says that they got a little bit rough and ripped his shirt, which scared Duddits and made him cry. There is no mention of how Richie Grenadeau and his friends took off his pants, no mention of the nasty after-school snack they wanted Duddits to eat, and when Mrs. Cavell asks them if they know who these big boys were, Henry hesitates briefly and then says no, just some big boys from the high school, he didn't know any of them, not by name. She looks at Beaver, Jonesy, and Pete; they all shake their heads. It may be wrong—dangerous to Duddits in the long run, as well—but they can't step that far outside the rules which govern their lives. Already Beaver cannot understand where they found the sack to intervene in the first place, and later the others will say the same. They marvel at their courage; they also marvel that they aren't in the fuckin hospital.

She looks at them sadly for a moment, and Beaver realizes she knows a lot of what they aren't telling, probably enough to keep her awake that night. Then she smiles. Right at Beaver she smiles, and it makes him tingle all the way down to his toes. "What a lot of zippers you have on your jacket!" she says.

Beaver smiles. "Yes, ma'am. It's my Fonzie jacket. It was my brother's first. These guys make fun of it, but I like it just the same."

"*Happy Days,*" she says. "We like it, too. Duddits likes it. Perhaps you'd like to come over some night and watch it with us. With him." Her smile grows wistful, as if she knows nothing like that will ever happen.

"Yeah, that'd be okay," Beav says.

"Actually it would," Pete agrees.

They sit for a little without talking, just watching him play in the backyard. There's a swing-set with two swings. Duddits runs behind them, pushing them, making the swings go by themselves. Sometimes he stops, crosses his arms over his chest, turns the clockless dial of his face up to the sky, and laughs.

"Seems all right now," Jonesy says, and drinks the last of his tea. "Guess he's forgotten all about it."

Mrs. Cavell has started to get up. Now she sits back down, giving him an almost startled look. "Oh no, not at all," she says. "He remembers. Not like you and I, perhaps, but he remembers things. He'll probably have nightmares tonight, and when we go into his room—his father and me—he won't be able to explain. That's the worst for him; he can't tell what it is he sees and thinks and feels. He doesn't have the vocabulary."

She sighs.

"In any case, those boys won't forget about him. What if they're laying for him now? What if they're laying for *you*?"

"We can take care of ourselves," Jonesy says, but although his voice is stout enough, his eyes are uneasy.

"Maybe," she says. "But what about Duddits? I can walk him to school—I used to, and I suppose I'll have to again, for awhile at least, anyway—but he loves to walk home on his own so much."

"It makes him feel like a big boy," Pete says.

She reaches across the table and touches Pete's hand, making him blush. "That's right, it makes him feel like a big boy."

"You know," Henry says, "*we* could walk him. We all go together to the junior high, and it would be easy enough to come down here from Kansas Street."

Roberta Cavell only sits there without saying anything, a little birdie-woman in a print dress, looking at Henry attentively, like someone waiting for the punchline of a joke.

"Would that be okay, Missus Cavell?" Beaver asks her. "Because we could do it, easy. Or maybe you don't want us to."

Something complicated happens to Mrs. Cavell's face—there are all those little twitches, mostly under the skin. One eye almost winks, and then the other one *does* wink. She takes a handkerchief from her pocket and blows her nose. Beaver thinks, *She's trying not to laugh at us.* When he tells Henry that as they are walking home, Jonesy and Pete already dropped off, Henry will look at him with utter astonishment. *Cry is what she was tryin not to do,* he will say . . . and then, affectionately, after a pause: *Dope.*

"You would do that?" she asks, and when Henry nods for all of them, she changes the question slightly. "*Why* would you do that?"

Henry looks around as if to say *Someone else take this one, willya?*

Pete says, "We *like* him, ma'am."

Jonesy is nodding. "I like the way he carries his lunchbox over his head—"

"Yeah, that's bitchin," Pete says. Henry kicks him under the table. Pete replays what he just said—you can see him doing it—and begins blushing furiously.

Mrs. Cavell appears not to notice. She's looking at Henry with fixed intensity. "He has to go by quarter of eight," she says.

"We're always near here by then," Henry replies. "Aren't we, you guys?"

And although seven forty-five is in fact a little early for them, they all nod and say yeah right sure yeah.

"You would do that?" she asks again, and this time Beaver has no trouble reading her tone; she is incredyouwhatsis, the word that means you can't fuckin believe it.

"Sure," Henry says. "Unless you think Duddits wouldn't . . . you know . . ."

"Wouldn't want us to," Jonesy finishes.

"Are you crazy?" she asks. Beaver thinks she is speaking to herself, trying to convince herself that these boys are really in her kitchen, that all of this is in fact happening. "Walking to school with the big boys? Boys who go to what Duddits calls 'real school'? He'd think he was in heaven."

"Okay," Henry says. "We'll come by quarter of eight, walk him to school. And we'll walk home with him, too."

"He gets out at—"

"Aw, we know what time The Retard Academy gets out," Beaver says cheerfully, and realizes a second before he sees the others' stricken faces that he's said something a lot worse than *bitchin*. He claps his hands over his mouth. Above them, his eyes are huge. Jonesy kicks his shin so hard under the table that Beav almost tumbles over backward.

"Don't mind him, ma'am," Henry says. He is talking rapidly, which he only does when he's embarrassed. "He just—"

"I don't mind," she says. "I know what people call it. Sometimes Alfie and I call it that ourselves." This topic, incredibly, hardly seems to interest her. "Why?" she says again.

And although it's Henry she's looking at, it's Beaver who answers, in spite of his blazing cheeks. "Because he's cool," he says. The others nod.

They will walk Duddits to school and back for the next five years or so, unless he is sick or they are at Hole in the Wall; by the end of it Duddits is no longer going to Mary M. Snowe, aka The Retard Academy, but to Derry Vocational, where he learns to bake cookies (*baitin tooties,* in Duddits-ese), replace car batteries, make change, and tie his own tie (the knot is always perfect, although it sometimes appears about halfway down his shirt). By then the Josie Rinkenhauer thing has come and gone, a little nine days' wonder forgotten by everyone except Josie's parents, who will never forget. In those years when they walk with him to and from his school, Duddits will sprout up until he's the tallest of all of them, a gangly teenager with a strangely beautiful child's face. By then they will have taught him how to play Parcheesi and a simplified version of Monopoly; by then they will have invented the Duddits Game and played it incessantly, sometimes laughing so hard that Alfie Cavell (he was the tall one of the pair, but he also had a birdie look about him) would come to the head of the stairs in the kitchen, the ones that led to the rec room, and yell down at them, wanting to know what was going on, what was so funny, and maybe they would try to explain that Duddits had pegged Henry fourteen on a two hand or that Duddits had pegged Pete fifteen *backward,* but Alfie never seemed to get it; he'd stand there at the head of the stairs with a section of the newspaper in his hand, smiling perplexedly, and at last he'd always say the same thing, *Keep it down to a dull roar, boys,* and close the door, leaving them to their own devices . . . and of all those devices the Duddits Game was the best, totally bitchin, as Pete would have said. There were times when Beaver thought he might actually laugh until he exploded, and Duddits sitting there all the time on the rug beside the big old Parkmunn cribbage board, feet folded under him and grinning like Buddha. What a fuckaree! All of that ahead of them but now just this kitchen, and the surprising sun, and Duddits outside, pushing the swings. Duddits who had done them such a favor by coming into their lives. Duddits who is—they know it from the first—not like anyone else they know.

"I don't see how they could have done it," Pete says suddenly. "The way he was crying. I don't see how they could have gone on teasing him."

Roberta Cavell looks at him sadly. "Older boys don't hear him the same way," she says. "I hope you never understand."

6

"Jonesy!" Beaver shouted. *"Hey, Jonesy!"*

This time there's a response, faint but unmistakable. The snowmobile shed was a kind of ground-level attic, and one of the things out there was an old-fashioned bulb horn, the kind a bicycle delivery-man back in the twenties or thirties might have had mounted on the handlebars of his bike. Now Beaver heard it: *Ooogah! How-oogah!* A noise that surely would have made Duddits laugh until he cried—a sucker for big, juicy noises, that had been ole Duds.

The filmy blue shower curtain rustled and the Beav's arms broke out in lush bundles of gooseflesh. For a moment he almost leaped up, thinking that it was McCarthy, then realized he'd brushed the curtain with his own elbow—it was close quarters in here, close quarters, no doubt—and settled back. Still nothing from beneath him, though; that thing, whatever it was, was either dead or gone. For certain.

Well . . . *almost* for certain.

The Beav reached behind him, fingered the flush lever for a moment, then let his hand fall away. *Sit tight,* Jonesy had said, and Beaver would, but why the fuck didn't Jonesy come back? If he couldn't find the tape, why didn't he just come back without it? It *had* to have been at least ten minutes now, didn't it? And felt like a fucking *hour.* Meantime, here he sat on the john with a dead man in the tub beside him, one who looked as if his ass had been blown open by dynamite, man, talk about having to take a shit—

"Beep the horn again, at least," Beaver muttered. "Honk that jeezly thing, let me know you're still there." But Jonesy didn't.

7

Jonesy couldn't find the tape.

He'd looked everywhere and couldn't find it anywhere. He knew it had to be here, but it wasn't hanging from any of the nails and it wasn't on the tool-littered worktable. It wasn't behind the paint-cans, or on the hook beneath the old painting masks that hung there by their yellowing elastics. He looked under the table, looked in the boxes stacked against the far wall, then in the compartment under the Arctic Cat's passenger seat. There was a spare headlight in there, still in its carton, and half a pack of ancient Lucky Strikes, but no goddam tape. He could feel the minutes ticking away. Once he was pretty sure he heard the Beav calling for him, but he didn't want to go back without the tape and so he blew the old horn that was lying on the floor, pumping its cracked black rubber horn and making an *oogah-oogah* sound that Duddits no doubt would have loved.

The more he looked for the tape and didn't find it, the more imperative it seemed. There was a ball of twine, but how would you tie down a toilet seat with *twine,* for Christ's sake? And there was Scotch tape in one of the kitchen drawers, he was almost sure of it, but the thing in the toilet had sounded pretty strong, like a good-sized fish or something. Scotch tape just wasn't good enough.

Jonesy stood beside the Arctic Cat, looking around with wide eyes, running his hands through his hair (he hadn't put his gloves back on and he'd been out here long enough to numb his fingers), breathing out big white puffs of vapor.

"Where the *fuck*?" he asked aloud, and slammed his fist down on the table. A stack of little boxes filled with nails and screws fell over when he did, and there was the friction tape behind them, a big fat roll of it. He must have looked right past it a dozen times.

He grabbed it, stuffed it in his coat pocket—he had remembered to put that on, at least, although he hadn't bothered to zip it up—and turned to go. And that was when Beaver began to scream. His calls had been barely there, but Jonesy had no trouble at all hearing the screams. They were big, lusty, filled with pain.

Jonesy sprinted for the door.

8

Beaver's Mom had always said the toothpicks would kill him, but she had never imagined anything like this.

Sitting there on the closed toilet seat, Beaver felt in the bib pocket of his overalls for a pick to chew on, but there weren't any—they were scattered all over the floor. Two or three had landed clear of the blood, but he'd have to rise up off the toilet seat a little to get them—rise up and lean forward.

Beaver debated. *Sit tight,* Jonesy had said, but surely the thing in the toilet was gone; *dive, dive, dive,* as they said in the submarine war movies. Even if it wasn't, he'd only be lifting his ass for a second or two. If the thing jumped, Beaver could bring his weight right back down again, maybe break its scaly little neck for it (always assuming it *had* one).

He looked longingly at the toothpicks. Three or

four were close enough so he could just reach down and pick them up, but he wasn't going to put bloody toothpicks in his mouth, especially considering where the blood had come from. There was something else, too. That funny furry stuff was growing on the blood, growing in the gutters of grout between the tiles, as well—he could see it more clearly than ever. It was on some of the toothpicks, too . . . but not on those which had fallen clear of the blood. Those were clean and white, and if he had ever in his life needed the comfort of something in his mouth, a little piece of wood to gnaw on, it was now.

"Fuck it," the Beav murmured, and leaned forward, reaching out. His stretching fingers came up just short of the nearest clean pick. He flexed the muscles of his thighs and his butt came up off the seat. His fingers closed on the toothpick—*ah, got it*—and something hit the closed lid of the toilet seat at just that moment, hit it with terrifying force, driving it up into his unprotected balls and knocking him forward. Beaver grabbed at the shower curtain in a last-ditch effort to maintain his balance, but it pulled free of the bar in a metallic clitter-clack of rings. His boots slipped in the blood and he went sprawling forward onto the floor like a man blown out of an ejection seat. Behind him he heard the toilet seat fly up hard enough to crack the porcelain tank.

Something wet and heavy landed on Beaver's back. Something that felt like a tail or a worm or a muscular segmented tentacle curled between his legs and seized his already aching balls in a contracting python's grip.

Beaver screamed, chin lifting from the bloody tiles (a red crisscross pattern tattooed faintly on his chin), eyes bulging. The thing lay wet and cold and heavy from the nape of his neck to the small of his back, like a rolled-up breathing rug, and now it began to utter a feverish high-pitched chittering noise, the sound of a rabid monkey.

Beaver screamed again, wriggled toward the door on his belly, then lurched up onto all fours, trying to shake the thing off. The muscular rope between his legs squeezed again, and there was a low popping sound from somewhere in the liquid haze of pain that was now his groin.

Oh Christ, the Beav thought. *Mighty Christ bananas, I think that was one of my balls.*

Squealing, sweating, tongue dancing in and out of his mouth like a demented party-favor, Beaver did the only thing he could think of: rolled over onto his back, trying to crush the whatever-it-was between his spine and the tiles. It chittered in his ear, almost deafening him, and began to wriggle frantically. Beaver seized the tail curled between his legs, smooth and hairless on top, thorny—as if plated with hooks made of clotted hair—underneath. And wet. Water? Blood? Both?

"Ahhh! Ahhh! Oh God let go! Fuckin thing, let go! Jesus! My fuckin sack! Jeesus!"

Before he could get either hand beneath the tail, a mouthful of needles sank into the side of his neck. He reared up, bellowing, and then the thing was gone. Beaver tried to get to his feet. He had to push with his hands because there was no strength in his legs, and his hands kept slipping. In addition to McCarthy's blood, the bathroom floor was now covered with murky water from the cracked toilet tank and the tiled surface was a skating rink.

As he finally got up, he saw something clinging to the doorway about halfway up. It looked like some kind of freak weasel—no legs but with a thick reddish-gold tail. There was no real head, only a kind of slippery-looking node from which two feverish black eyes stared.

The lower half of the node split open, revealing a nest of teeth. The thing struck at Beaver like a snake, the node lashing forward, the hairless tail curled around the doorjamb. Beaver screamed and raised a hand in front of his face. Three of the four fingers on it—all but the pinky—disappeared. There was no pain, either that or the pain from his ruptured testicle swallowed it whole. He tried to step away, but the backs of his knees struck the bowl of the battered toilet. There was nowhere to go.

That thing was in *him?* Beaver thought; there was time for that much. *It was* in *him?*

Then it uncoiled its tail or its tentacle or whatever it was and leaped at him, the top half of its rudimentary head full of its stupidly furious black eyes, the lower half a packet of bone needles. Far away, in some other universe where there still might be sane life, Jonesy was calling his name, but Jonesy was late, Jonesy was way late.

The thing that had been in McCarthy landed on the Beav's chest with a smack. It smelled like

McCarthy's wind—a heavy reek of oil and ether and methane gas. The muscular whip that was its lower body wrapped around Beaver's waist. Its head darted forward and its teeth closed on Beaver's nose.

Screaming, beating at it with his fists, Beaver fell backward onto the toilet. The ring and the lid had flown up against the tank when the thing came out. The lid had stayed up, but the ring had fallen back into place. Now the Beav landed on it, broke it, and dropped ass-first into the toilet with the weasel-thing clutching him around the waist and chewing his face.

"Beaver! Beav, what—"

Beaver felt the thing stiffen against him—it literally stiffened, like a dick getting hard. The grip of the tentacle around his waist tightened, then loosened. Its black-eyed idiotic face whipped around toward the sound of Jonesy's voice, and Beav saw his old friend through a haze of blood, and with dimming eyes: Jonesy standing slack-jawed in the doorway, a roll of friction tape (*won't need that now,* Beaver thought, *nah*) in one dangling hand. Jonesy standing there utterly defenseless in his shocked horror. This thing's next meal.

"Jonesy, get outta here!" Beaver shouted. His voice was wet, strained through a mouthful of blood. He sensed the thing getting ready to leap and wrapped his arms around its pulsing body as if it were his lover. "Get out! Shut the door! B—" *Burn it,* he wanted to say. *Lock it in, lock both of us in, burn it, burn it alive, I'm going to sit here ass-deep in this fucking toilet with my arms wrapped around it, and if I can die smelling it roast, I can die happy.*

But the thing was struggling too hard and fucking Jonesy was just standing there with that roll of friction tape in his hand and his jaw dropped, and goddam if he didn't look like Duddits, dumb as a stone boat and never going to improve. Then the thing turned back to Beaver, its earless noseless node of a head drawn back, and before that head darted forward and the world detonated for the last time, Beaver had a final, partial thought: *Those toothpicks, damn, Mamma always said—*

Then the exploding red and blooming black and somewhere far off the sound of his own screams, the final ones.

9

Jonesy saw Beaver sitting in the toilet with something that looked like a giant red-gold worm clinging to him. He called out and the thing turned toward him, no real head, just the black eyes of a shark and a mouthful of teeth. Something *in* the teeth, something that couldn't be the mangled remains of Beaver Clarendon's nose but probably was.

Run away! he screamed at himself, and then: *Save him! Save Beaver!*

Both imperatives had equal power, and the result kept him frozen in the doorway, feeling as if he weighed a thousand pounds. The thing in Beaver's arms was making a noise, a crazed chattering sound that got into his head and made him think of something, something from a long time ago, he didn't know just what.

Then Beaver was screaming at him from his awkward sprawl in the toilet, telling him to get out, to shut the door, and the thing turned back to the sound of his voice as if recalled to temporarily forgotten business, and it was Beaver's eyes it went for this time, his fucking *eyes,* Beaver writhing and screaming and trying to hold on as the thing chittered and chattered and bit, its tail or whatever it was flexing and tightening around Beaver's waist, pulling Beaver's shirt out of his overalls and then slithering inside against his bare skin, Beaver's feet jerking on the tiles, the heels of his boots spraying bloody water in thin sheets, his shadow flailing on the wall, and that mossy stuff was everywhere now, it grew so fucking *fast*—

Jonesy saw Beaver thrash backward in a final throe; saw the thing let go its grip and leap clear just as the Beav rolled off the toilet, his upper half falling into the tub on top of McCarthy, old Mr. Behold-I-Stand-at-the-Door-and-Knock. The thing hit the floor and slithered around—Christ, it was quick—and started toward him. Jonesy took a step backward and swept the bathroom door shut just before the thing hit it, making a thump almost exactly like the one it had made when it hit the underside of the toilet seat. It hit hard enough to shiver the door against the jamb. Light flickered in shutters from beneath the door as it moved restlessly on the tiles, and then it slammed into the door again. Jonesy's first thought was to run and get a chair, put it under the doorknob, but how dumb was that, as his kids said, how fucking brainless, the door opened *in,* not out. The real question was whether the thing understood the function of the doorknob, and if it could reach it.

As if it had read his mind—and who could say that was impossible?—there was a slithering sound on the other side of the door and he felt the doorknob trying to turn. Whatever the thing was, it was incredibly strong. Jonesy had been holding the knob with his right hand; now he added his left, as well. There was a bad moment when the pressure on the knob continued to mount, when he felt sure the thing in there would be able to turn the knob in spite of his doubled grip, and Jonesy almost panicked, almost turned and ran.

What stopped him was his memory of how quick it was. *It'd run me down before I could get halfway across the room,* he thought, wondering in the back of his mind why the room had to be so goddam big in the first place. *It'd run me down, go up my leg, and then right up my—*

Jonesy redoubled his grip on the doorknob, cords standing out on his forearms and on the sides of his neck, lips skinned back to show his teeth. His hip hurt, too. His goddam hip, if he *did* try to run his hip would slow him down even more thanks to the retired professor, fucking elderly asshole shouldn't have been driving in the first place, thanks a lot, prof, thanks a fucking pantload, and if he couldn't hold the door shut and he couldn't run, what then?

What had happened to Beaver, of course. It had had the Beav's nose stuck in its teeth like a shish kebab.

Moaning, Jonesy held the knob. For a moment the

pressure increased even more, and then it stopped. From behind the thin wood of the door, the thing yammered angrily. Jonesy could smell the ethery aroma of starter fluid.

How was it holding on in there? It had no limbs, not that Jonesy had been able to see, just that reddish tail-thing, so how—

He heard the minute *crackle-crunch-splinter* of wood on the other side of the door, directly in front of his own head by the sound, and knew. It was clinging by its teeth. The idea filled Jonesy with unreasoning horror. That thing had been inside McCarthy, he had absolutely no doubt of it. Inside McCarthy and growing like a giant tapeworm in a horror movie. Like a cancer, one with teeth. And when it had grown enough, when it was ready to go to bigger and better things, you might say, it had simply chewed its way out.

"No, man, no," Jonesy said in a watery, almost weeping voice.

The knob of the bathroom door began trying to turn the other way. Jonesy could see it in there, on its side of the bathroom door, battened to the wood like a leech with its teeth, its tail or single tentacle wrapped around the doorknob like a loop ending in a hangman's noose, pulling—

"No, no, *no*," Jonesy panted, hanging onto the knob with all of his strength. It was on the verge of slipping away from him. There was sweat on his face and on his palms, too, he could feel it.

In front of his bulging, frightened eyes, a constellation of bumps appeared in the wood. Those were where its teeth were planted and working deeper all the time. Soon the points would burst through (if he didn't lose his grip on the doorknob first, that was) and he'd actually have to *look* at the fangs that had torn his friend's nose off his face.

That brought it home to him: Beaver was dead. His old friend.

"You killed him!" Jonesy cried at the thing on the other side of the door. His voice quivered with sorrow and terror. "You killed the Beav!"

His cheeks were hot, the tears which now began to course down them even hotter. Beaver in his black leather jacket (*What a lot of zippers!* Duddits's Mom had said on the day they met her), Beaver next door to shitfaced at the Senior Prom and dancing like a Cossack, arms folded across his chest and his feet kicking, Beaver at Jonesy and Carla's wedding reception, hugging Jonesy and whispering fiercely in his ear, "You got to be happy, man. You got to be happy for all of us." And that had been the first he knew that Beaver wasn't—Henry and Peter, of course, about them there had never been a question, but the *Beav*? And now Beaver was dead, Beaver was lying half in and half out of the tub, lying noseless on top of Mr. Richard Fucking I-Stand-at-the-Door-and-Knock McCarthy.

"*You killed him, you fuck!*" he shouted at the bulges in the door—there had been six of them and now there were nine, hell, a dozen.

As if surprised by his rage, the widdershins pressure on the doorknob eased again. Jonesy looked around wildly for anything that might help him, saw nothing, then looked down. The roll of friction tape was there. He might be able to bend and snatch it up, but then what? He would need both hands to pull lengths of tape off it, both hands and his teeth to rip them, and even supposing the thing gave him time, what was the good of it, when he could barely hold the doorknob still against its pressure?

And now the knob began to turn again. Jonesy held it on his side, but he was getting tired now, the adrenaline in his muscles starting to decay and turn to lead, his palms more slippery than ever, and that smell—the ethery smell was clearer now and somehow *purer,* untainted by the wastes and gases of McCarthy's body, and how could it be so strong on this side of the door? How could it unless—

In the half-second or so before the rod connecting the doorknobs on the inside and outside of the bathroom door snapped, Jonesy became aware that it was darker now. Just a little. As if someone had crept up behind him, was standing between him and the light, him and the back door—

The rod snapped. The knob in Jonesy's hand pulled free and the bathroom door immediately swung in a little, pulled by the weight of the eelish thing clinging to it. Jonesy shrieked and dropped the knob. It hit the roll of tape and bounced askew.

He turned to run and there stood a gray man.

He—*it*—was a stranger, but in a way no stranger at all. Jonesy had seen representations of him on a hundred "weird mysteries" TV shows, on the front pages of a thousand tabloid newspapers (the kind that shouted their serio-comic horrors at you as you stood prisoner in the supermarket checkout lanes), in movies like *ET* and *Close Encounters* and *Fire in the Sky;* Mr. Gray who was an *X-Files* staple.

All the images had gotten the eyes right, at least, those huge black eyes that were just like the eyes of the thing that had chewed its way out of McCarthy's ass, and the mouth was close—a vestigial slit, no more than that—but its gray skin hung in loose folds and swags, like the skin of an elephant dying of old age. From the wrinkles there ran listless yellow-white streams of some pussy substance; the same stuff ran like tears from the corners of its expressionless eyes. Clots and smears of it puddled across the floor of the big room, across the Navajo rug beneath the dreamcatcher, back toward the kitchen door through which it had entered. How long had Mr. Gray been there? Had he been outside, watching Jonesy run from the snowmobile shed to the back door with the useless roll of friction tape in his hand?

He didn't know. He only knew that Mr. Gray was dying, and Jonesy had to get past him because the thing in the bathroom had just dropped onto the floor with a heavy thud. It would be coming for him.

Marcy, Mr. Gray said.

He spoke with perfect clarity, although the vestige of a mouth never moved. Jonesy heard the word in the middle of his head, in the same precise place where he had always heard Duddits's crying.

"What do you want?"

The thing in the bathroom slithered across his feet, but Jonesy barely noticed it. Barely noticed it curl between the bare, toeless feet of the gray man.

Please stop, Mr. Gray said inside Jonesy's head. It was the click. More; it was the line. Sometimes you saw the line; sometimes you heard it, as he had heard the run of Defuniak's guilty thoughts that time. *I can't stand it, give me a shot, where's Marcy?*

Death looking for me that day, Jonesy thought. *Missed me in the street, missed me in the hospital—if only by a room or two—been looking ever since. Finally found me.*

And then the thing's head exploded, tore wide open, releasing a red-orange cloud of ether-smelling particles.

Jonesy breathed them in.

CHAPTER EIGHT

ROBERTA

With her hair now all gray, a widow at fifty-eight (but still a birdie-woman who favored flowered print dresses, those things hadn't changed), Duddits's mother sat in front of the television of the ground-floor apartment in West Derry Acres which she and her son now shared. She had sold the house on Maple Lane after Alfie died. She could have afforded to keep it— Alfie had left plenty of money, the life insurance had paid out plenty more, and there was her share of the imported auto-parts company he'd started in 1975 on top of that—but it was too big and there were too many memories above and below the living room where she and Duddits spent most of their time. Above was the bedroom where she and Alfie had slept and talked, made plans and made love. Below was the rec room where Duddits and his friends had spent so many afternoons and evenings. In Roberta's view they had been friends sent from heaven, angels with kind hearts and dirty mouths who had actually expected her to believe that when Duddits started saying *fut,* he was trying to say Fudd, which, they explained earnestly, was the name of Pete's new puppy—Elmer Fudd, just Fudd for short. And of course she had pretended to believe this.

Too many memories, too many ghosts of happier times. And then, of course, Duddits had gotten sick. Two years now he'd been sick, and none of his old friends knew because they didn't come around anymore and she hadn't had the heart to pick up the phone and call Beaver, who would have called the others.

Now she sat in front of the TV, where the local-news folks had finally given up just breaking into her afternoon stories and had gone on the air full-time. Roberta listened, afraid of what might be happening up north but fascinated, too. The scariest part was that no one seemed to *know* exactly what was happening or just what the story was or how big it was. There were missing hunters, maybe as many as a dozen, in a remote area of Maine a hundred and fifty miles north of Derry. That part was clear enough. Roberta wasn't positive, but she was quite sure that the reporters were talking about Jefferson Tract, where the boys used to go hunting, coming back with bloody stories that both fascinated Duddits and frightened him.

Were those hunters just cut off by an Alberta Clipper storm that had passed through, dropping six or eight inches of snow on the area? Maybe. No one could say for sure, but one party of four that had been hunting in the Kineo area really did seem to be missing. Their pictures were flashed on the screen, their names recited solemnly: Otis, Roper, McCarthy, Shue. The last was a woman.

Missing hunters weren't big enough to warrant interrupting the afternoon soaps, but there was other stuff, too. People had glimpsed strange, varicolored lights in the sky. Two hunters from Millinocket who had been in the Kineo area two days previous claimed to have seen a cigar-shaped object hovering over a powerline-cut in the woods. There had been no rotors on the craft, they said, and no visible means of propulsion. It simply hung there about twenty feet above the powerlines, emitting a deep hum that buzzed in your bones. And in your teeth, it seemed. Both of the hunters claimed to have lost teeth, although when they opened their mouths to display the gaps, Roberta had thought the rest of their teeth looked ready to fall out, as well. The hunters had been in an old Chevy pickup, and when they tried to drive closer for a better look, their engine had died. One of the men had a battery-powered watch that had run backward for about three hours following the event and had then quit for good (the other's watch, the old-fashioned wind-up kind, had been fine). According to the reporter, a number of other hunters and area residents had been seeing unidentified flying objects—some cigar-shaped, some of the more traditional saucer shape—for the last week or so. The military slang for such an outbreak of sightings, the reporter said, was a "flap."

Missing hunters, UFOs. Juicy, and certainly good enough to lead with on *Live at Six* ("Local! Late-breaking! Your Town and Our State!"), but now there was more. There was *worse*. Still only rumors, to be sure, and Roberta prayed they would prove to be untrue, but creepy enough to have kept her here for almost two hours now, drinking too much coffee and growing more and more nervous.

The scariest rumors clustered around reports that something had crash-landed in the woods, not far from where the men had reported the cigar-shaped craft hovering over the powerlines. Almost as disquieting were reports that a fairly large area of Aroostook County, perhaps two hundred square miles mostly owned by the paper companies or the government, had been quarantined.

A tall, pale man with deep-set eyes spoke briefly to reporters at the Air National Guard base in Bangor (he stood in front of a sign which proclaimed HOME OF THE MANIACS) and said that none of the rumors were true, but that "a number of conflicting reports" were being checked. The super beneath him read simply ABRA-HAM KURTZ. Roberta couldn't tell what his rank was, or indeed if he was really a military man at all. He was dressed in a simple green coverall with nothing on it but a zipper. If he was cold—you would have thought so, wearing nothing but that coverall—he didn't show it. There was something in his eyes, which were very large and fringed with white lashes, that Roberta didn't much like. They looked to her like liar's eyes.

"Can you at least confirm that the downed aircraft is neither foreign nor . . . nor extraterrestrial in origin?" a reporter asked. He sounded young.

"ET phone home," Kurtz said, and laughed. There was laughter from most of the other reporters as well, and no one except Roberta, watching the clip here in her West Derry Acres apartment, seemed to realize that was not an answer at all.

"Can you confirm that there is no quarantine in the area of the Jefferson Tract?" another reporter asked.

"I can neither confirm nor deny that at this time," Kurtz said. "We're taking this matter quite seriously. Your government dollars are working very hard today, ladies and gentlemen." He then walked away toward a helicopter with slowly turning rotors and ANG printed on the side in big white letters.

That clip had been videotaped at 9:45 A.M., according to the news anchor. The next clip—shaky footage from a hand-held video camera—had been taken from a Cessna chartered by Channel 9 News to overfly the Jefferson Tract. The air had obviously been bumpy and there was a lot of snow, but not enough to obscure the two helicopters which had appeared and flanked the Cessna on either side like big brown dragonflies. There was a radio transmission, so blurry that Roberta needed to read the transcript printed in yellow at the bottom of the TV screen: *"This area is interdicted. You are ordered to turn back to your point of flight origination. Repeat, this area is interdicted. Turn back."*

Did interdicted mean the same as quarantined? Roberta Cavell thought it probably did, although she also thought fellows like that man Kurtz might quibble. The letters on the flanking helicopters were clearly visible: ANG. One of them might have been the very one that took Abraham Kurtz north.

Cessna pilot: *"Under whose orders is this operation being carried out?"*

Radio: *"Turn back, Cessna, or you will be forced to turn back."*

The Cessna had turned back. It had been low on fuel anyway, the news anchor reported, as if that explained everything. Since then they had just been rehashing the same stuff and calling it updates. The major networks supposedly had correspondents en route.

She was getting up to turn the TV off—watching had begun to make her nervous—when Duddits screamed. Roberta's heart stopped in her chest, then jackrabbited into doubletime. She whirled around, bumping the table by the La-Z-Boy which had been Alfie's and was now hers, overturning her coffee cup. It soaked the *TV Guide,* drowning the cast of *The Sopranos* in a puddle of brown.

The scream was followed by high, hysterical sobbing, the sobs of a child. But that was the thing about Duddits—he was in his thirties now, but he would die a child, and long before he turned forty.

For a moment all she could do was stand still. At last she got moving, wishing that Alfie were here . . . or even better, one of the boys. Not that any of them were boys now, of course; only Duddits was still a boy; Down's syndrome had turned him into Peter Pan, and soon he would die in Never-Never Land.

"I'm coming, Duddie!" she called, and so she was,

but she felt old to herself as she went hurrying down the hall to the back bedroom, her heart banging leakily against her ribs, arthritis pinging her hips. No Never Land for her.

"Coming, Mummy's coming!"

Sobbing and sobbing, as if his heart had broken. He had cried out the first time he realized his gums were bleeding after he brushed his teeth, but he had never screamed and it had been years since he'd cried like this, the kind of wild sobbing that got into your head and tore at your brains. Thump and hum, thump and hum, thump and hum.

"Duddie, what is it?"

She burst into his room and looked at him, wide-eyed, so convinced he must be hemorrhaging that at first she actually *saw* blood. But there was only Duddits, rocking back and forth in his crank-up hospital bed, cheeks wet with tears. His eyes were that same old brilliant green, but the rest of his color was gone. His hair was gone, too, his lovely blond hair that had reminded her of the young Art Garfunkel. The faint winterlight coming in through the window gleamed on his skull, gleamed on the bottles ranked on the bedside table (pills for infection, pills for pain, but no pills that would stop what was happening to him, or even slow it down), gleamed on the IV pole standing in front of the table.

But there was nothing wrong that she could see. Nothing that would account for the almost grotesque expression of pain on his face.

She sat down beside him, captured the restlessly

whipping head and held it to her bosom. Even now, in his agitation, his skin was cool; his exhausted, dying blood could bring no heat to his face. She remembered reading *Dracula* long ago, back in high school, the pleasurable terror that had been quite a bit less pleasurable once she was in bed, the lights out, her room filled with shadows. She remembered being very glad there were no real vampires, except now she knew different. There was at least one, and it was far more terrifying than any Transylvanian count; its name wasn't Dracula but leukemia, and there was no stake you could put through its heart.

"Duddits, Duddie, honey, what is it?"

And he screamed it out as he lay against her breast, making her forget all about what might or might not be happening up in the Jefferson Tract, freezing her scalp to her skull and making her skin crawl and horripilate. *"Eeyer-eh! Eeeyer-eh! Oh Amma, Eeeyer-eh!"* There was no need to ask him to say it again or to say it more clearly; she had been listening to him her whole life, and she knew well enough:

Beaver's dead! Beaver's dead! Oh, Mamma, Beaver's dead!

CHAPTER NINE

PETE AND BECKY

1

Pete lay screaming in the snow-covered rut where he had landed until he could scream no more and then just lay there for awhile, trying to cope with the pain, to find some way to compromise with it. He couldn't. This was no-compromise pain, blitzkrieg agony. He'd had no idea the world had such pain— had he known, surely he would have stayed with the woman. With Marcy, although Marcy wasn't her name. He almost *knew* her name, but what did it matter? He was the one who was in trouble here, the pain coming up from his knee in baked spasms, hot and terrible.

He lay shivering in the road with the plastic bag beside him. THANKS FOR SHOPPING AT OUR PLACE! on the side. Pete reached for it, wanting to see if there was a bottle or two in there that wasn't broken, and when his leg shifted, a bolt of agony flew up from the knee. It made the others feel like twinges. Pete screamed again, and passed out.

2

He didn't know how long he'd been out when he came to—the light suggested it hadn't been long, but his feet were numb and his hands were going as well, in spite of the gloves.

Pete lay partially turned on his side, the beer-bag lying beside him in a puddle of freezing amber slush. The pain in his knee had receded a little—probably that was numbing up, too—and he found he could think again. That was good, because this was a fuckin pisser he'd gotten himself into here. He had to get back to the lean-to and the fire, and he had to do it on his own. If he simply lay here waiting for Henry and the snowmobile, he was apt to be a Petesicle when Henry arrived—a Petesicle with a bag of busted beer-bottles beside him, thank you for shopping at our place, you fucking alcoholic, thanks a lot. And there was the woman to think of. She might die, too, and all because Pete Moore had to have his brewskis.

He looked at the bag with distaste. Couldn't throw it into the woods; couldn't risk waking his knee up again. So he covered it with snow, like a dog covering its own scat, and then he began to crawl.

The knee wasn't that numb after all, it seemed. Pete crawled on his elbows and pushed with his good foot, teeth clenched, hair hanging in his eyes. No animals now; the stampede had stopped and there was only him—the gaspy sound of his breathing and the stifled moans of pain each time his knee bumped. He could feel sweat running down his arms and back, but his feet remained numb and so did his hands.

He might have given up, but halfway along the straight stretch he caught sight of the fire he and Henry had made. It had burned down considerably, but it was there. Pete began to crawl toward it, and each time he bumped his leg and the bolts of agony came, he tried to project them into the orange spark of the fire. He wanted to get there. It hurt like pluperfect hell to move, but oh how he wanted to get there. He didn't want to die freezing to death in the snow.

"I'll make it, Becky," he muttered. "I'll make it, Becky." He spoke her name half a dozen times before he heard himself using it.

As he approached the fire he paused to glance at his watch and frowned. It said eleven-forty or thereabouts, and that was nuts—he remembered checking it before starting back to the Scout, and it had said twenty past twelve then. A slightly longer look revealed the source of the confusion. His watch was running backward, the second hand moving counterclockwise in irregular, spasmodic jerks. He looked at this without much surprise. His ability to appreciate anything so fine as mere peculiarity had passed. Even his leg was no longer his chief concern. He was very cold, and big shudders began to course his body as he elbowed his way and pushed with his rapidly tiring good leg, covering the last fifty yards to the dying fire.

The woman was no longer on the tarp. She now lay on the far side of the fire, as if she had crawled toward the remaining wood and then collapsed.

"Hi, honey, I'm home," he panted. "Had a little trouble with my knee, but now I'm back. Goddam knee's your fault anyway, Becky, so don't complain, all right? Becky, is that your name?"

Maybe, but she made no response. Just lay there staring. He could still see only one of her eyes, although whether it was the same one or the other he didn't know. Didn't seem so creepy now, but maybe that was because he had other things to worry about. Like the fire. It was guttering, but there was a good bed of coals and he thought he was in time. Get some wood on that sweetheart, really build her up, then lie here with his gal Becky (but upwind, please God—those bangers were *bad*). Wait for Henry to show up. Wouldn't be the first time Henry had pulled his nuts out of the fire.

Pete crawled toward the woman and the little stock-pile of wood beyond her, and as he got close—close enough to start picking up that ethery chemical smell again—he understood why her gaze no longer bothered him. That creepy jackalope look had gone out of it. Everything had. She'd crawled halfway around the fire and died. The crusting of snow around her waist and hips had gone a dark red.

Pete stopped for a moment, up on his aching arms and peering at her, but his interest in her, dead or alive, was not much more than the passing interest he'd felt in his back-turning watch. What he wanted to do was get some wood on the fire and get *warm.* He would consider the problem of the woman later. Next month, maybe, when he was sitting in his own living room with a cast on his knee and a cup of hot coffee in his hand.

He finally made it to the wood. Only four pieces were left, but they were *big* pieces. Henry might be back before they burned down, and Henry would pick up some more before going on to get help. Good old Henry. Still wearing his dorky horn-rims, even in this age of soft contacts and laser surgery, but you could count on him.

Pete's mind tried to return to the Scout, crawling into the Scout and smelling the cologne Henry had not, in fact, been wearing, and he wouldn't let it. *Let's not go there,* as the kids said. As if memory was a desti-nation. No more ghost-cologne, no more memories of Duddits. No more no bounce, no more no play. He had enough on his plate already.

He threw the wood onto the fire one branch at a time, sidearming the pieces awkwardly, wincing at the pain in his knee but enjoying the way the sparks rose in a cloud, whirling beneath the lean-to's canted tin ceiling like crazy fireflies before winking out.

Henry would be back soon. That was the thing to hold onto. Just watch the fire blaze up and hold that thought.

No, he won't. Because things have gone wrong back at Hole in the Wall. Something to do with—

"Rick," he said, watching the flames taste the new wood. Soon they would feed and grow tall.

He stripped off his gloves, using his teeth, and held his hands up to the warmth of the fire. The cut on the pad of his right hand, where the busted bottle had gotten him, was long and deep. Was going to leave a scar, but so what? What was a scar or two between friends? And they *were* friends, weren't they? Yeah. The old Kansas Street Gang, the Crimson Pirates with their plastic swords and battery-powered *Star Wars* ray-guns. Once they had done something heroic— twice, if you counted the Rinkenhauer girl. They had even gotten their pictures in the paper that time, and so what if he had a few scars? And so what if they had once maybe—just maybe—killed a guy? Because if ever there was a guy who deserved killing—

But he wasn't going to go there, either. No way, baby.

He saw the line, though. Like it or not, he saw the line, more clearly than he'd seen it in years. Primarily he saw Beaver . . . and heard him, too. Right in the center of his head.

Jonesy? You there, man?

"Don't get up, Beav," Pete said, watching the flames crackle and climb. The fire was hot now, beating warmth against his face, making him feel sleepy. "You stay right where you are. Just . . . you know, just sit tight."

What, exactly, was all this about? *What's all this jobba-nobba?* as the Beav himself had sometimes said when they were kids, a phrase that meant nothing but still cracked them up. Pete sensed he could know if he wanted to, the line was that bright. He got a glimpse of blue tiles, a filmy blue shower curtain, a bright orange cap—Rick's cap, McCarthy's cap, old Mr. I-Stand-at-the-Door's cap—and sensed he could have all the rest if he wanted it. He didn't know if this was the future, the past, or what was happening right this minute, but he could have it if he wanted it, if he—

"I don't," he said, and pushed the whole thing away.

There were a few sticks and twigs left on the ground. Pete fed them to the fire, then looked at the woman. Her open eye had no menace in it now. It was dusty, the way a deer's eyes got dusty after you shot it. All that blood around her . . . he supposed she'd hemorrhaged. Something inside had gone bust. Hell of a tough break. He supposed maybe she'd known it was coming and had sat down in the road because she wanted to be sure of being seen if someone came along. Someone had, but look how it had turned out. Poor bitch. Poor unlucky bitch.

Pete shifted to the left, slowly, until he could snag the tarp, then began to move forward again. It had been her makeshift sled; now it could be her makeshift shroud. "I'm sorry," he said. "Becky or whatever your name is, I'm really sorry. But I couldn't have helped you by staying, you know; I'm not a doctor, I'm a fucking car salesman. You were—"

—*fucked from the start* was how he'd meant to finish, but the words dried up in his throat as he saw the back of her. That part hadn't been visible until he got close, because she had died facing the fire. The seat of her jeans was blown out, as if she'd finally finished farting fumes and had gotten down to the dynamite. Torn rags of denim fluttered in the breeze. Also fluttering were fragments of the garments she had been wearing beneath, at least two pairs of longjohns— one heavy white cotton, the other pink silk. And something was growing on both the legs of the jeans and the back of her parka. It looked like mildew or some kind of fungus. Red-gold, or maybe that was just reflected firelight.

Something had come out of her. Something—

Yes. Something. And it's watching me right now.

Pete looked into the woods. Nothing. The flood of animals had dried up. He was alone.

Except I'm not.

No, he wasn't. Something was out there, something that didn't do well in the cold, something that preferred warm, wet places. Except—

Except it got too big. And it ran out of food.

"Are you out there?"

Pete thought that calling out like that would make him feel foolish, but it didn't. What it made him feel was more frightened than ever.

His eye fastened on a sketchy track of that mildewy stuff. It stretched away from Becky—yeah, she was a Becky, all right, as Becky as Becky could be—and around the corner of the lean-to. A moment later Pete heard a scaly scraping sound as something slithered on the tin roof. He craned up, following the sound with his eyes.

"Go away," he whispered. "Go away and leave me alone. I . . . I'm fucked up."

There was another brief slither as the thing moved farther up the tin. Yes, he was fucked up. Unfortunately, he was also food. The thing up there slithered again. Pete didn't think it would wait long, maybe *couldn't* wait long, not up there; it would be like a gecko in a refrigerator. What it was going to do was drop on him. And now he realized a terrible thing: he had gotten so fixated on the beer that he had forgotten the fucking guns.

His first impulse was to crawl deeper into the lean-to, but that might be a mistake, like running into a blind alley. He grabbed the jutting end of one of the fresh branches he'd just put on the fire instead. He didn't take it out, not yet, just made a loose fist around it. The other end was burning briskly. "Come on," he said to the tin roof. "You like it hot? I've got something hot for you. Come on and get it. Yum-fuckin-yum."

Nothing. Not from the roof, anyway. There was a soft *flump* of snow falling from one of the pines behind him as the lower branches shed their burden. Pete's hand tightened on his makeshift torch, half-lifting it from the fire. Then he let it settle back in a little swirl of sparks. "Come on, motherfucker. I'm hot, I'm tasty, and I'm waiting."

Nothing. But it was up there. It couldn't wait long, he was sure of it. Soon it would come.

3

Time passed. Pete wasn't sure how much; his watch had given up entirely. Sometimes his thoughts seemed to intensify, as they sometimes had when he and the others were hanging with Duddits (although as they grew older and Duddits stayed the same, there had been less of that—it was as though their changing brains and bodies had lost the knack of picking up Duddits's strange signals). This was like that, but not *exactly* like that. Something new, maybe. Maybe even something to do with the lights in the sky. He was aware that Beaver was dead and that something terrible might have happened to Jonesy, but he didn't know what.

Whatever had happened, Pete thought Henry knew about it, too, although not clearly; Henry was deep inside his own head and he thought *Banbury Cross, Banbury Cross, ride a cock horse to Banbury Cross.*

The stick burned down further, closer to his hand, and Pete wondered what he'd do if it burned down too far to be of use, if the thing up there could outwait him after all. And then a new thought came to him, bright as day and red with panic. It filled his head and he began to cry it aloud, masking the sound of the thing on the roof as it slithered quickly down the slope of the tin.

"Please don't hurt us! *Ne nous blessez pas!*"

But they would, they would, because . . . what?

Because they are not helpless little ETs, boys, waiting around for someone to give them a New England Telephone card so they can phone home, they are a disease. *They are cancer, praise Jesus, and boys, we're one big hot radioactive shot of chemotherapy. Do you hear me, boys?*

Pete didn't know if *they* did, the boys to whom

the voice spoke, but *he* did. They were coming, the boys were coming, the Crimson Pirates were coming and not all the begging in the world would stop them. And still they begged, and Pete begged with them.

"Please don't hurt us! Please! *S'il vous plaît! Ne nous blessez pas! Ne nous faites pas mal, nous sommes sans défense!*" Weeping now. "Please! *For the love of God, we're helpless!*"

In his mind he saw the hand, the dog-turd, the weeping nearly naked boy. And all the time the thing on the roof was slithering, dying but not helpless, stupid but not *entirely* stupid, getting behind Pete while he screamed, while he lay on his side by the dead woman, listening as some apocalyptic slaughter began.

Cancer, said the man with the white eyelashes.

"*Please!*" he screamed. "*Please, we're helpless!*"

But, lie or the truth, it was too late.

4

The snowmobile had passed Henry's hiding place without slowing, and the sound of it was now receding to the west. It was safe to come out, but Henry didn't come out. Couldn't come out. The intelligence which had replaced Jonesy hadn't sensed him, either because it was distracted or because Jonesy had somehow—might somehow still be—

But no. The idea that there could be *any* of Jonesy left inside that terrible cloud was so much dreamwork.

And now that the thing was gone—receding, at least—there were the voices. They filled Henry's head, making him feel half-mad with their babble, as Dud-dits's crying had always made him feel half-mad, at least until puberty had ended most of that crap. One of the voices belonged to a man who said something about a fungus

(dies easily unless it gets on a living host)

and then something about a New England Tel phone card and . . . chemotherapy? Yes, a big hot radioactive shot. It was the voice, Henry thought, of a lunatic. He had treated enough of them to judge, God knew.

The other voices were the ones which made him question his own sanity. He didn't know all of them, but he knew some: Walter Cronkite, Bugs Bunny, Jack Webb, Jimmy Carter, a woman he thought was Margaret Thatcher. Sometimes the voices spoke in English, sometimes in French.

"Il n'y a pas d'infection ici," Henry said, and then began to weep. He was astounded and exhilarated to find there were still tears in his heart, from which he thought all tears and all laughter—true laughter—had fled. Tears of horror, tears of pity, tears that opened the stony ground of self-regarding obsession and burst the rock inside. "There is no infection here, please, oh God *stop* it, don't, don't, *nous sommes sans défense, NOUS SOMMES SANS*—"

Then the human thunder began in the west and Henry put his hands to his head, thinking that the screams and the pain in there would tear it apart. The bastards were—

5

The bastards were slaughtering them.

Pete sat by the fire, unmindful of the bellows of pain from his separated knee, unaware that he was now holding the branch from the fire up beside his temple. The screams inside his head could not quite drown out the sound of the machine-guns in the west, big machine-guns, .50s. Now the cries—please don't hurt us, we are defenseless, there is no infection—began to fade into panic; it wasn't working, nothing *could* work, the deal was done.

Movement caught Pete's eye and he turned just as the thing that had been on the roof struck at him. He caught a blurred glimpse of a slender, weaselly body that seemed powered by a muscular tail rather than legs, and then its teeth sank into his ankle. He shrieked and yanked his good leg toward him so hard he almost clocked himself in the chin with his own knee. The thing came with it, clinging like a leech. Were these the things that were begging for mercy? Fuck them, if they were. Fuck them!

He reached for it with his right hand, the one he'd cut on the Bud bottle, without even thinking about it; the torch he continued to hold up at the side of his head with his uninjured left. He seized something that felt like cool, fur-covered jelly. The thing let go of his ankle at once, and Pete caught just a glimpse of expressionless black eyes—shark's eyes, eagle eyes—before it sank the needle-nest of its teeth into his clutching hand, tearing it wide open along the perforation of the previous cut.

The agony was like the end of the world. The thing's head—if it had one—was buried in the hand, ripping and tearing, digging deeper. Blood flew in splattery fans as Pete tried to shake it off, stippling the snow and the sawdusty tarp and the dead woman's parka. Droplets flew into the fire and hissed like fat in a hot skillet. Now the thing was making a ferocious chittering sound. Its tail, as thick as a moray eel's body, wrapped around Pete's thrashing arm, endeavoring to keep it still.

Pete made no conscious decision to use the torch, because he'd forgotten he had it; his only thought was to tear the terrible biting thing off his right hand with his left. At first, when it caught fire and flared up, as hot and bright as a roll of newspaper, he didn't understand what was happening. Then he screamed, partly in fresh pain and partly in triumph. He bolted to his feet—for the time being, at least, his bulging knee did not hurt at all—and swung his burdened right arm at one of the lean-to's support posts in a great sweeping roundhouse. There was a crunch and the chittering sound was replaced by muffled squealing. For one endless moment the knot of teeth planted in his hand burrowed in deeper than ever. Then they loosened and the burning creature fell free and landed on the frozen ground. Pete stamped on it, felt it writhe under his heel, and was filled with one moment of pure and savage triumph before his outraged knee gave way entirely and his leg bent inside out, the tendons torn loose.

He fell heavily on his side, face to face with Becky's lethal hitchhiker, unaware that the lean-to was beginning to shift, the pole he'd struck with his arm bowing slowly outward. For a moment the weasel-thing's rudiment of a face was three inches from Pete's own. Its burning body flapped against his jacket. Its black eyes boiled. It had nothing so sophisticated as a mouth, but when the bulge in the top of its body unhinged, revealing its teeth, Pete screamed at it—"*No! No! No!*"—and batted it into the fire, where it writhed and made its frantic, monkeylike chittering.

His left foot swung in a short arc as he shoved the thing farther into the fire. The tip of his boot struck the tilting pole, which had just decided to hold the lean-to up a little longer. This was one outrage too many and the pole snapped, dropping half of the tin roof. A second or two later, the other pole snapped as well. The rest of the roof fell into the fire, sending out a whirling squirt of sparks.

For a moment that was all. Then the fallen sheet of rusty tin began to heave itself up and down, as if it were breathing. A moment later, Pete crawled out from under. His eyes were glazed. His skin was pasty with shock. The left cuff of his jacket was on fire. He stared at this for a moment with his legs still under the fallen roof from the knees down, then raised his arm in front of his face, drew in a deep breath, and blew out the flames rising from his jacket like a giant birthday candle.

Approaching from the east was the buzz of a snowmobile engine. Jonesy . . . or whatever was left of him. The cloud. Pete didn't think it would show him any mercy. This was no day for mercy in the Jefferson Tract. He should hide. But the voice advising him of that was distant, unimportant. One thing was good: he had an idea he had finally quit drinking.

He raised his savaged right hand in front of his face. One finger was gone, presumably down the thing's gullet. Two others lay in a swoon of severed tendons. He saw that reddish-gold stuff already growing along the deepest slashes—the ones the monster had inflicted and the one he'd done himself, crawling back into the Scout after the beer. He could feel a kind of fizzy sensation as whatever that stuff was fed on his flesh and blood.

Pete suddenly felt that he couldn't die soon enough.

The sound of the machine-guns in the west had stopped, but it wasn't over there, not by a long shot. And as if the thought had summoned it, a huge explosion hammered the day, blotting out the wasp-whine of the oncoming snowmobile and everything else. Everything but the busy fizz in his hand, that was. In his hand, the crud was dining on him the way the cancer that had killed his father had dined on the old man's stomach and lungs.

Pete ran his tongue over his teeth, felt gaps where some of them had fallen out.

He closed his eyes and waited.

GRAYBOYS

A ghost comes out of the unconscious mind
To grope my sill: It moans to be reborn!
The figure at my back is not my friend;
The hand upon my shoulder turns to horn.

THEODORE ROETHKE

CHAPTER TEN

KURTZ

AND UNDERHILL

1

The only thing in the ops area was a little beer n deer store called Gosselin's Country Market. Kurtz's cleaners began arriving there shortly after the snow began to fall. By the time Kurtz himself got there, at ten-thirty, support was starting to appear. They were getting a grip on the situation.

The store was designated Blue Base. The barn, the adjacent stable (dilapidated but still standing), and the corral had been designated Blue Holding. The first detainees had already been deposited there.

Archie Perlmutter, Kurtz's new aide-de-camp (his old one, Calvert, had died of a heart attack not two weeks before—goddam bad timing), had a clipboard with a dozen names on it. Perlmutter had arrived with both a laptop computer and a PalmPilot only to discover that electronic gear was currently FUBAR in the Jefferson Tract: fucked up beyond recognition. The top two names on the clipboard were Gosselins: the old man who ran the store and his wife.

"More on the way," Perlmutter said.

Kurtz gave the names on Pearly's clipboard a cursory look, then handed it back. Big recreational vehicles were being parked behind them; semi trailers were being jacked and leveled; light poles were going up. When night came, this place would be as well-lighted as Yankee Stadium at World Series time.

"We missed two guys by this much," Perlmutter said, and held up his right hand with the thumb and forefinger a quarter of an inch apart. "They came in for supplies. Principally beer and hot dogs." Perlmutter's face was pale, with a wild pink rose blooming in each cheek. He had to raise his voice against the steadily increasing noise level. Helicopters were coming in two by two and landing on the blacktop lane that eventually made its way out to Interstate 95, where you could go north toward one dull town (Presque Isle) or south toward any number of other dull towns (Bangor and Derry, for starters). The helicopters were fine, as long as their pilots didn't have to depend on all the sophisticated navigational equipment, which was also FUBAR.

"Did those fellows go in or out?" Kurtz asked.

"Back in," Perlmutter said. He could not quite bring himself to meet Kurtz's eyes; he looked everywhere but. "There's a woods road, Gosselin says it's called the Deep Cut Road. It's not on the standard maps, but I have a Diamond International Paper survey map that shows—"

"That's fine. Either they'll come back out or stay in. Either way, it's fine."

More helicopters, some unshipping their .50s now that they were safely away from the wrong eyes. This could end up being as big as Desert Storm. Maybe bigger.

"You understand your mission here, Pearly, don't you?"

Perlmutter most definitely did. He was new, he wanted to make an impression, he was almost jumping up and down. *Like a spaniel that smells lunch,* Kurtz thought. And he did it all without making eye contact. "Sir, my job is triune in nature."

Triune, Kurtz thought. *Triune, how about that?*

"I am to a, intercept, b, turn intercepted persons over to medical, and c, contain and segregate pending further orders."

"Exactly. That's—"

"But sir, beg your pardon, sir, but we don't have any doctors here yet, only a few corpsmen, and—"

"Shut up," Kurtz said. He didn't speak loudly, but half a dozen men in unmarked green coveralls (they were all wearing unmarked green coveralls, including Kurtz himself) hesitated as they went double-timing on their various errands. They glanced toward where Kurtz and Perlmutter were standing, then got moving again. Triple-time. As for Perlmutter, the roses in his cheeks died at once. He stepped back, putting another foot between himself and Kurtz.

"If you ever interrupt me again, Pearly, I'll knock you down. Interrupt me a second time and I'll put you in the hospital. Do you understand?"

With what was clearly a tremendous effort, Perlmutter brought his gaze up to Kurtz's face. To Kurtz's eyes. He snapped off a salute so crisp it almost crackled with static electricity. "Sir, yes sir!"

"You can quit that too, you know better." And when Perlmutter's gaze began to drop: "Look at me when I'm talking to you, laddie."

Very reluctantly, Perlmutter did so. His complexion was now leaden. Although the noise of the helicopters lined up along the road was cacophonous, it somehow seemed very quiet right here, as if Kurtz traveled in his own weird air-pocket. Perlmutter was convinced that everyone was watching them and that they could all see how terrified he was. Some of it was his new boss's eyes—the cataclysmic absence in those eyes, as if there were really no brain behind them at all. Perlmutter had heard of the thousand-yard stare, but Kurtz's seemed to go on for a *million* yards, maybe light-years.

Yet somehow Perlmutter held Kurtz's gaze. Looked into the absence. He was not off to a good start here. It was important—it was *imperative*—that the slide be stopped before it could become an avalanche.

"All right, good. Better, anyway." Kurtz's voice was low but Perlmutter had no problem hearing him despite the overlapping chunter of the helicopters. "I'm going to say this to you just once, and only because you're new to my service and you clearly don't know your asshole from your piehole. I have been asked to run a phooka operation here. Do you know what a phooka is?"

"No," Perlmutter said. It caused him almost physical pain not to be able to say *No sir*.

"According to the Irish, who as a race have never entirely crawled from the bath of superstition in which their mothers gat them, a phooka is a phantom horse that kidnaps travelers and carries them away on its back. I use it to mean an operation which is both covert and wide open. A paradox, Perlmutter! The good news is that we've been developing contingency plans for just this sort of clusterfuck since 1947, when the Air Force first recovered the sort of extraterrestrial artifact now known as a flashlight. The bad news is that the future is now and I have to face it with guys like you in support. Do you understand me, buck?"

"Yes, s . . . yes."

"I hope so. What we've got to do here, Perlmutter, is go in fast and hard and utterly phooka. We're going to do as much dirtywork as we have to and come out as clean as we can . . . clean . . . yes, Lord, and *smilin* . . ."

Kurtz bared his teeth in a brief smile of such brutally satiric intensity that Perlmutter felt a little like screaming. Tall and stoop-shouldered, Kurtz had the build of a bureaucrat. Yet something about him was terrible. You saw some of it in his eyes, sensed some of it in the still, prim way he held his hands in front of him . . . but those weren't the things that made him scary, that made the men call him Old Creepy Kurtz. Perlmutter didn't know exactly what the really scary thing was, and didn't want to know. What he wanted right now—the *only* thing he wanted—was to get out of this conversation with his ass on straight. Who needed to go twenty or thirty miles west to make contact with an alien species? Perlmutter had one standing right here in front of him.

Kurtz's lips snapped shut over his teeth. "On the same page, are we?"

"Yes."

"Saluting the same flag? Pissing in the same latrine?"

"Yes."

"How are we going to come out of this, Pearly?"

"Clean?"

"Boffo! And how else?"

For one horrible second he didn't know. Then it came to him. "*Smiling,* sir."

"Call me sir again and I'll knock you down."

"I'm sorry," Perlmutter whispered. He was, too.

Here came a school bus rolling slowly up the road with its offside wheels in the ditch and canted almost to the tipover point so it could get past the helicopters. MILLINOCKET SCHOOL DEPT. was written up the side, big black letters against a yellow background. Commandeered bus. Owen Underhill and his men inside. The A-team. Perlmutter saw it and felt better. At different times both men had worked with Underhill.

"You'll have doctors by nightfall," Kurtz said. "All the doctors you need. Check?"

"Check."

As he walked toward the bus, which stopped in front of Gosselin's single gasoline pump, Kurtz looked at his pocket-watch. Almost eleven. Gosh, how the time flew when you were having fun. Perlmutter walked with him, but all the cocker spaniel spring had gone out of Perlmutter's step.

"For now, Archie, eyeball em, smell em, listen to their tall tales, and document any Ripley you see. You know about the Ripley, I assume?"

"Yes."

"Good. Don't touch it."

"God, no!" Perlmutter exclaimed, then flushed.

Kurtz smiled thinly. This one was no more real than his shark's grin. "Excellent idea, Perlmutter! You have breathing masks?"

"They just arrived. Twelve cartons of them, and more on the w—"

"Good. We want Polaroids of the Ripley. We need mucho documentation. Exhibit A, Exhibit B, so on and so forth. Got it?"

"Yes."

"And none of our . . . our guests get away, right?"

"Absolutely not." Perlmutter was shocked by the idea, and looked it.

Kurtz's lips stretched. The thin smile grew and once more became the shark's grin. Those empty eyes looked through Perlmutter—looked all the way to the center of the earth, for all Perlmutter knew. He found himself wondering if anyone would leave Blue Base when this was over. Except Kurtz, that was.

"Carry on, Citizen Perlmutter. In the name of the government, I order you to carry on."

Archie Perlmutter watched Kurtz continue on toward the bus, where Underhill—a squat jug of a man—was climbing off. Never in his life had he been so utterly delighted to see a man's back.

2

"Hello, boss," Underhill said. Like the rest, he wore a plain green coverall, but like Kurtz, he also wore a sidearm. Sitting in the bus were roughly two dozen men, most of them just finishing an early lunch.

"What have they got there, buck?" Kurtz asked. At six-foot-six he towered above Underhill, but Underhill probably outweighed him by seventy pounds.

"Burger King. We drove through. I didn't think the bus would fit, but Yoder said it would, and he was right. Want a Whopper? They're probably a little on the cold side by now, but there must be a microwave in there someplace." Underhill nodded toward the store.

"I'll pass. Cholesterol's not so good these days."

"Groin okay?" Six years before, Kurtz had suffered a serious groin-pull while playing racquetball. This had indirectly led to their only disagreement. Not a serious one, Owen Underhill judged, but with Kurtz, it was hard to tell. Behind the man's patented game-face, thoughts came and went at near light-speed, agendas were constantly being rewritten, and emotions were turning on a dime. There were people—quite a few of them, actually—who thought Kurtz was crazy. Owen Underhill didn't know if he was or not, but he knew you wanted to be careful around this one. Very.

"As the Irish might put it," Kurtz said, "me groin's foine." He reached between his legs, gave his balls a burlesque yank, and favored Owen with that teeth-baring grin.

"Good."

"And you? Been okay?"

"Me groin's foine," Owen said, and Kurtz laughed.

Now coming up the road, rolling slowly and carefully but having an easier time than the bus, was a brand-new Lincoln Navigator with three orange-clad hunters inside, hefty boys all three, gawking at the helicopters and the double-timing soldiers in their green coveralls. Gawking at the guns, mostly. Vietnam comes to northern Maine, praise God. Soon they would join the others in the Holding Area.

Half a dozen men approached as the Navigator pulled up behind the bus, with its stickers reading BLUE DEVIL PRIDE and THIS VEHICLE STOPS AT ALL RR CROSSINGS. Three lawyers or bankers with their own cholesterol problems and fat stock portfolios, lawyers or bankers pretending to be good old boys, under the impression (of which they would soon be disabused) that they were still in an America at peace. Soon they would be in the barn (or the corral, if they craved fresh air), where their Visa cards would not be honored. They would be allowed to keep their cell phones. They wouldn't work this far up in the willywags, but hitting REDIAL might keep them amused.

"You plugged in tight?" Kurtz asked.

"I think so, yes."

"Still a quick study?"

Owen shrugged.

"How many people in the Blue Zone altogether, Owen?"

"We estimate eight hundred. No more than a hundred in Zones Prime A and Prime B."

That was good, assuming no one slipped through. In terms of possible contamination, a few slips wouldn't matter—the news, at least so far, was good on that score. In terms of information management, however, it would not be good at all. It was hard to ride a phooka horse these days. Too many people with videocams. Too many TV station helicopters. Too many watching eyes.

Kurtz said, "Come inside the store. They're setting me up a 'Bago, but it's not here yet."

"*Un momento,*" Underhill said, and dashed up the steps of the bus. When he came back down, he had a grease-spotted Burger King sack in his hand and a tape recorder over his shoulder on a strap.

Kurtz nodded toward the bag. "That stuff'll kill you."

"We're starring in *The War of the Worlds* and you're worried about high cholesterol?"

Behind them, one of the newly arrived mighty hunters was saying he wanted to call his lawyer, which probably meant he was a banker. Kurtz led Underhill into the store. Above them, the flashlights were back, running their glow over the bottoms of the clouds, jumping and dancing like animated characters in a Disney cartoon.

3

Old Man Gosselin's office smelled of salami, cigars, beer, Musterole, and sulfur—either farts or boiled eggs, Kurtz reckoned. Maybe both. There was also a smell, faint but discernible, of ethyl alcohol. The smell of *them*. It was everywhere up here now. Another man might have been tempted to ascribe that smell to a combination of nerves and too much imagination, but Kurtz had never been overburdened with either. In any case, he did not believe the hundred or so square miles of forestland surrounding Gosselin's Country Market had much future as a viable ecosystem. Sometimes you just had to sand a piece of furniture down to the bare wood and start again.

Kurtz sat behind the desk and opened one of the drawers. A cardboard box with CHEM/U.S./10 UNITS stamped on it lay within. Good for Perlmutter. Kurtz took it out and opened it. Inside were a number of small plastic masks, the transparent sort that fitted over the mouth and nose. He tossed one to Underhill and then put one on himself, quickly adjusting the elastic straps.

"Are these necessary?" Owen asked.

"We don't know. And don't feel privileged; in another hour, everyone is going to be wearing them. Except for the John Q's in the Holding Area, that is."

Underhill donned his mask and adjusted the straps

without further comment. Kurtz sat behind the desk with his head leaning back against the latest piece of OSHA paperwork (post it or die) taped to the wall behind him.

"Do they work?" Underhill's voice was hardly muffled at all. The clear plastic did not fog with his breathing. It seemed to have no pores or filters, but he found he could breathe easily enough.

"They work on Ebola, they work on anthrax, they work on the new super-cholera. Do they work on Ripley? Probably. If not, we're fucked, soldier. In fact, we may be fucked already. But the clock is running and the game is on. Should I hear the tape you've doubtless got in that thing over your shoulder?"

"There's no need for you to hear all of it, but you ought to taste, I think."

Kurtz nodded, made a spinning motion in the air with his forefinger (like an ump signalling a home run, Owen thought), and leaned back further in Gosselin's chair.

Underhill unslung the tape recorder, set it on the desk facing Kurtz, and pushed PLAY. A toneless robot voice said: "NSA radio intercept. Multiband. 62914A44. This material is classified top secret. Time of intercept 0627, November fourteen, two-zero-zero-one. Intercept recording begins after the tone. If you are not rated Security Clearance One, please press STOP now."

"Please," Kurtz said, nodding. "Good. That'd stop most unauthorized personnel, don't you think?"

There was a pause, a two-second beep, then a young

woman's voice said: "One. Two. Three. Please don't hurt us. *Ne nous blessez pas.*" A two-second silence, and then a young man's voice said: "Five. Seven. Eleven. We are helpless. *Nous sommes sans défense.* Please don't hurt us, we are helpless. *Ne nous faites—*"

"By God, it's like a Berlitz language lesson from the Great Beyond," Kurtz said.

"Recognize the voices?" Underhill asked.

Kurtz shook his head and put a finger to his lips.

The next voice was Bill Clinton's. "Thirteen. Seventeen. Nineteen." In Clinton's Arkansas accent, the last one came out *Nahnteen.* "There is no infection here. *Il n'y a pas d'infection ici.*" Another two-second pause, and then Tom Brokaw spoke from the tape recorder. "Twenty-three. Twenty-nine. We are dying. *On se meurt, on crève.* We are dying."

Underhill pushed STOP. "In case you wondered, the first voice is Sarah Jessica Parker, an actress. The second is Brad Pitt."

"Who's he?"

"An actor."

"Uh-huh."

"Each pause is followed by another voice. All the voices are or would be recognizable to large segments of the people in this area. There's Alfred Hitchcock, Paul Harvey, Garth Brooks, Tim Sample—he's a Maine-style humorist, very popular—and hundreds of others, some of which we haven't identified."

"*Hundreds* of others? How long did this intercept last?"

"Strictly speaking, it's not an intercept at all but a

clear-band transmission which we have been jamming since 0800. Which means a bunch of it got out, but we doubt if anyone who picked it up will have understood much of it. And if they do—" Underhill gave a little *What can you do* shrug. "It's still going on. The voices appear to be real. The few voiceprint comparisons that were run are identical. Whatever else they are, these guys could put Rich Little out of business."

The *whup-whup-whup* of the helicopters came clearly through the walls. Kurtz could feel it as well as hear it. Through the boards, through the OSHA poster, and from there into the gray meat that was mostly water, telling him to come on come on come on, hurry up hurry up hurry up. His blood responded to it, but he sat quietly, looking at Owen Underhill. Thinking about Owen Underhill. Make haste slowly; that was a useful saying. Especially when dealing with folks like Owen. How's your groin, indeed.

You fucked with me once, buck, Kurtz thought. *Maybe didn't cross my line, but by God, you scuffed at it, didn't you? Yes, I think so. And I think you'll bear watching.*

"Same four messages over and over," Underhill said, and ticked them off on the fingers of his left hand. "Don't hurt us. We're helpless. There's no infection here. The last one—"

"No infection," Kurtz mused. "Huh. They've got their nerve, don't they?"

He had seen pictures of the reddish-gold fuzz growing on all the trees around Blue Boy. And on people. Corpses, mostly, at least so far. The techs had named it Ripley fungus, after the tough broad

Sigourney Weaver had played in those space movies. Most of them were too young to remember the other Ripley, who had done the "Believe It or Not" feature in the newspapers. "Believe It or Not" was pretty much gone, now; too freaky for the politically correct twenty-first century. But it fit this situation, Kurtz thought. Oh yes, like a glove. Made old Mr. Ripley's Siamese twins and two-headed cows look positively normal by comparison.

"The last one is *We're dying*," Underhill said. "That one's interesting because of the two different French versions accompanying the English. The first is straightforward. The second—*on crève*—is slangy. We might say 'Our goose is cooked.' " He looked directly at Kurtz, who wished Perlmutter were here to see that yes, it *could* be done. "*Are* they cooked? I mean, assuming we don't help them along?"

"Why French, Owen?"

Underhill shrugged. "It's still the other language up here."

"Ah. And the prime numbers? Just to show us we're dealing with intelligent beings? As if any other kind could travel here from another star system, or dimension, or wherever it is they come from?"

"I guess so. What about the flashlights, boss?"

"Most are now down in the woods. They disintegrate fairly rapidly, once they run out of juice. The ones we've been able to retrieve look like soup cans with the labels stripped off. Considering their size, they put on a hell of a show, don't they? Scared the living hell out of the locals."

When the flashlights disintegrated, they left patches of the fungus or ergot or whatever the hell it was behind. The same seemed true of the aliens themselves. The ones that were left were just up there standing around their ship like commuters standing around a broken-down bus, bawling that they weren't infectious, *il n'y a pas d'infection ici,* praise the Lord and pass the biscuits. And once the stuff was on you, you were most likely—what had Owen said? A cooked goose. They didn't know that for sure, of course, it was early yet, but they had to make the assumption.

"How many ETs still up there?" Owen asked.

"Maybe a hundred."

"How much don't we know? Does anybody have any idea?"

Kurtz waved this aside. He was not a knower; knowing was someone else's department, and none of those guys had been invited to this particular pre-Thanksgiving party.

"The survivors," Underhill persisted. "Are they crew?"

"Don't know, but probably not. Too many for crew; not enough to be colonists; nowhere *near* enough to be shock-troops."

"What else is going on up here, boss? *Something* is."

"Pretty sure of that, are you?"

"Yes."

"Why?"

Underhill shrugged. "Intuition?"

"It's not intuition," Kurtz said, almost gently. "It's telepathy."

"Say *what*?"

"Low-grade, but there's really not any question about it. The men sense something, but they haven't put a name on it yet. Give them a few hours and they will. Our gray friends are telepaths, and they seem to spread that just as they spread the fungus."

"Holy fucking shit," Owen Underhill whispered.

Kurtz sat calmly, watching him think. He liked watching people think, if they were any good at it, and now there was more: he was *hearing* Owen think, a faint sound like the ocean in a conch shell.

"The fungus isn't strong in the environment," Owen said. "Neither are they. What about the ESP?"

"Too soon to tell. If it lasts, though, and if it gets out of this pine-tree pisspot we're in, everything changes. You know that, don't you?"

Underhill knew. "I can't believe it," he said.

"I'm thinking of a car," Kurtz said. "What car am I thinking of?"

Owen looked at him, apparently trying to decide if Kurtz was serious. He saw that Kurtz was, then shook his head. "How should I . . ." He paused. "Fiat."

"Ferrari, actually. I'm thinking of an ice cream flavor. Which f—"

"Pistachio," Owen said.

"There you go."

Owen sat another moment, then asked Kurtz—hesitantly—if Kurtz could tell him his brother's name.

"Kellogg," Kurtz replied. "Jesus, Owen, what kind of name is that for a kid?"

"My mother's maiden name. Christ. *Telepathy.*"

"It's going to fuck with the ratings of *Jeopardy* and *Who Wants to Be a Millionaire,* I can tell you that," Kurtz said, then repeated, "*If* it gets loose."

From outside the building there came a gunshot and a scream. "You didn't have to *do* that!" someone cried in a voice filled with outrage and fear. "You didn't have to *do* that!"

They waited, but there was no more.

"The confirmed grayboy body-count is eighty-one," Kurtz said. "There are probably more. Once they go down, they decompose pretty fast. Nothing left but goo . . . and then the fungus."

"Throughout the Zone?"

Kurtz shook his head. "Think of a wedge pointing east. The thick end is Blue Boy. Where we are is about the middle of the wedge. There are a few more illegal immigrants of the gray persuasion wandering around east of here. The flashlights have mostly stayed over the wedge area. ET Highway Patrol."

"It's all toast, isn't it?" Owen asked. "Not just the grayboys and the ship and the flashlights—the whole fucking geography."

"I'm not prepared to speak to that just now," Kurtz said.

No, Owen thought, *of course you're not.* He wondered immediately if Kurtz could read his thought. There was no way of telling, certainly not from those pale eyes.

"We *are* going to take out the rest of the grayboys, I can tell you that much. Your men will crew the gunships and your men only. You are Blue Boy Leader. Got that?"

"Yes, sir."

Kurtz did not correct it. In this context, and given Underhill's obvious distaste for the mission, *sir* was probably good. "I am Blue One."

Owen nodded.

Kurtz got up and drew out his pocket-watch. It had gone noon.

"This is going to get out," Underhill said. "There are a lot of U.S. citizens in the Zone. There's simply no way to keep it quiet. How many have those . . . those implants?"

Kurtz almost smiled. The weasels, yes. A good many here, a few more over the years. Underhill didn't know, but Kurtz did. Nasty little fellows they were. And one good thing about being the boss: you didn't have to answer questions you didn't want to answer.

"What happens later is up to the spin doctors," he said. "Our job is to react to what certain people—the voice of one of them is probably on your tape—have determined is a clear and present danger to the people of the United States. Got it, buck?"

Underhill looked into that pale gaze and at last looked away.

"One other thing," Kurtz said. "Do you remember the phooka?"

"The Irish ghost-horse."

"Close enough. When it comes to nags, that one's

mine. Always has been. Some folks in Bosnia saw you riding my phooka. Didn't they?"

Owen chanced no reply. Kurtz didn't look put out by that, but he looked intent.

"I want no repeat, Owen. Silence is golden. When we ride the phooka horse, we must be invisible. Do you understand that?"

"Yes."

"Perfect understanding?"

"Yes," Owen said. He wondered again how much of his mind Kurtz could read. Certainly he could read the name currently in the front of Kurtz's mind, and supposed Kurtz wanted him to. Bosanski Novi.

4

They were on the verge of going, four gunship crews with Owen Underhill's men from the bus replacing the ANG guys who had brought the CH-47s this far, they were cranking up, filling the air with the thunder of the rotors, and then came Kurtz's order to stand down.

Owen passed it on, then flicked his chin to the left. He was now on Kurtz's private com channel.

"Beg pardon, but what the *fuck*?" Owen asked. If they were going to do this thing, he wanted to do it and get it behind him. It was worse than Bosanski Novi, worse by far. Writing it off by saying the grayboys weren't human beings just did not wash. Not for him, anyway. Beings that could build something like Blue Boy—or fly it, at least—were more than human.

"It's none of mine, lad," Kurtz said. "The weather

boys in Bangor say this shit is moving out fast. It's what they call an Alberta Clipper. Thirty minutes, forty-five, max, and we're on our way. With our nav gear all screwed up, it's better to wait if we can . . . and we can. You'll thank me at the other end."

Man, I doubt that.

"Roger, copy." He flicked his head to the right. "Conklin," he said. No rank designations to be used on this mission, especially not on the radio.

"I'm here, s . . . I'm here."

"Tell the men we're on hold thirty to forty-five. Say again, thirty to forty-five."

"Roger that. Thirty to forty-five."

"Let's have some jukebox rhythm."

"Okay. Requests?"

"Go with what you like. Just save the Squad Anthem."

"Roger, Squad Anthem is racked back." No smile in Conk's voice. There was one man, at least, who liked this as little as Owen did. Of course, Conklin had also been on the Bosanski Novi mission in '95. Pearl Jam started up in Owen's cans. He pulled them off and laid them around his neck like a horse-collar. He didn't care for Pearl Jam, but in this bunch he was a minority.

Archie Perlmutter and his men ran back and forth like chickens with their heads cut off. Salutes were snapped, then choked off, with many of the saluters sneaking did-he-see-that looks at the small green scout copter in which Kurtz sat with his own cans clamped firmly in place and a copy of the Derry *News* upraised.

Kurtz looked engrossed in the paper, but Owen had an idea that the man marked every half-salute, every soldier who forgot the situation and reverted to old beast habit. Beside Kurtz, in the left seat, was Freddy Johnson. Johnson had been with Kurtz roughly since Noah's ark grounded on Mount Ararat. He had also been at Bosanski, and had undoubtedly given Kurtz a full report when Kurtz himself had been forced to stay behind, unable to climb into the saddle of his beloved phooka horse because of his groin-pull.

In June of '95, the Air Force had lost a scout pilot in NATO's no-fly zone, near the Croat border. The Serbs had made a very big deal of Captain Tommy Callahan's plane, and would have made an even bigger one of Callahan himself, if they caught him; the brass, haunted by images of the North Vietnamese gleefully parading brainwashed pilots before the international press, made recovering Tommy Callahan a priority.

The searchers had been about to give up when Callahan contacted them on a low-frequency radio band. His high-school girlfriend gave them a good ID marker, and when the man on the ground was queried, he confirmed it, telling them his friends had started calling him The Pukester following a truly memorable night of drinking in his junior year.

Kurtz's boys went in to get Callahan in a couple of helicopters much smaller than any of the ones they were using today. Owen Underhill, already tabbed by most (including himself, Owen supposed) as Kurtz's successor, had been in charge. Callahan's job was to pop some smoke when he saw the birds, then stand by. Underhill's job—the phooka part of it—had been to yank Callahan without being seen. This was not strictly necessary, so far as Owen could see, but was simply the way Kurtz liked it: his men were invisible, his men rode the Irish horse.

The extraction had worked perfectly. There were some SAMs fired, but nothing even close—Milosevic had shit, for the most part. It was as they were taking Callahan on board that Owen had seen his only Bosnians: five or six children, the oldest no more than ten, watching them with solemn faces. The idea that Kurtz's directive to make sure there were no witnesses might apply to a group of dirtyface kids had never crossed Owen's mind. And Kurtz had never said anything about it.

Until today, that was.

That Kurtz was a terrible man Owen had no doubt. Yet there were many terrible men in the service, more devils than saints, most certainly, and many were in love with secrecy. What made Kurtz different Owen had no idea—Kurtz, that long and melancholy man with his white eyelashes and still eyes. Meeting those was hard because there was nothing in them—no love, no laughter, and absolutely no curiosity. That lack of curiosity was somehow the worst.

A battered Subaru pulled up at the store, and two old men got carefully out. One clutched a black cane in a weather-chapped hand. Both wore red-and-black-checked hunting overshirts. Both wore faded caps, one with CASE above the bill and the other with DEERE. They looked wonderingly at the contingent of soldiers that descended upon them. Soldiers at Gosselin's? What in the tarnal? They were in their eighties, by the look of them, but they had the curiosity Kurtz lacked. You could see it in the set of their bodies, the tilt of their heads.

All the questions Kurtz had not voiced. *What do they want? Do they really mean us harm? Will doing this bring the harm? Is it the wind we sow to bring the whirlwind? What was there in all the previous encounters—the flaps, the flashlights, the falls of angel hair and red dust, the abductions that began in the late sixties—that has made the powers that be so afraid? Has there been any real effort to communicate with these creatures?*

And the last question, the most important question: Were the grayboys like us? Were they by any definition human? Was this murder, pure and simple?

No question in Kurtz's eyes about that, either.

5

The snow lightened, the day brightened, and exactly thirty-three minutes after ordering the stand-down, Kurtz gave them a go. Owen relayed it to Conklin and the Chinnies revved hard again, pulling up gauzy veils of snow and turning themselves into momentary ghosts. Then they rose to treetop level, aligned themselves on Underhill—Blue Boy Leader—and flew west in the direction of Kineo. Kurtz's Kiowa 58 flew below them and slightly to starboard, and Owen thought briefly of a troop of soldiers in a John Wayne movie, bluelegs with a single Indian scout riding his pony bareback off to one side. He couldn't see, but guessed Kurtz would still be reading the paper. Maybe his horoscope. "Pisces, this is your day of infamy. Stay in bed."

The pines and spruces below appeared and disappeared in vapors of white. Snow flew against the Chinook's two front windows, danced, disappeared. The ride was extremely rough—like a ride in a washing machine—and Owen wouldn't have had it any other way. He clapped the cans back on his head. Some other group, maybe Matchbox Twenty. Not great, but better than Pearl Jam. What Owen dreaded was the Squad Anthem. But he would listen. Yes indeed, he would listen.

In and out of the low clouds, vapory glimpses of an apparently endless forest, west west west.

"Blue Boy Leader, this is Blue Two."

"Roger, Two."

"I have visual contact with Blue Boy. Confirm?"

For a moment Owen couldn't, and then he could. What he saw took his breath away. A photograph, an image inside a border, a thing you could hold in your hand, that was one thing. This was something else entirely.

"Confirm, Two. Blue Group, this is Blue Boy Leader. Hold your current positions. I say again, hold your current positions."

One by one the other copters rogered. Only Kurtz

did not, but he also stayed put. The Chinooks and the Kiowa hung in the air perhaps three quarters of a mile from the downed spacecraft. Leading up to it was an enormous swath of trees that had been whacked off in a slanted lane, as if by an enormous hedge-clipper. At the end of this lane was a swampy area. Dead trees clutched at the white sky, as if to snatch the clouds open. There were zig-zags of melting snow, some of it turning yellow where it was oozing into the damp ground. In other places there were veins and capillaries of open black water.

The ship, an enormous gray plate nearly a quarter of a mile across, had torn through the dead trees at the center of the swamp, exploding them and casting the splintery fragments in every direction. The Blue Boy (it was not blue at all, not a bit blue) had come to rest at the swamp's far end, where a rocky ridge rose at a steep angle. A long arc of its curved edge had disappeared into the watery, unstable earth. Dirt and bits of broken trees had sprayed up and littered the ship's smooth hull.

The surviving grayboys were standing around it, most on snow-covered hummocks under the upward-tilted end of their ship; if the sun had been shining, they would have been standing in the crashed ship's shadow. Well . . . clearly there was *someone* who thought it was more Trojan Horse than crashed ship, but the surviving grayboys, naked and unarmed, didn't look like much of a threat. *About a hundred*, Kurtz had said, but there were fewer than that now; Owen put the number at sixty. He saw at least a dozen corpses, in greater or lesser states of red-tinged decay, lying on the snow-covered hummocks. Some were facedown in the shallow black water. Here and there, startlingly bright against the snow, were reddish-gold patches of the so-called Ripley fungus . . . except not all of the patches *were* bright, Owen realized as he raised his binoculars and looked through them. Several had begun to gray out, victims of the cold or the atmosphere or both. No, they didn't survive well here—not the grayboys, not the fungus they had brought with them.

Could this stuff actually spread? He just didn't believe it.

"Blue Boy Leader?" Conk asked. "You there, boy?"

"I'm here, shut up a minute."

Owen leaned forward, reached under the pilot's elbow (Tony Edwards, a good man), and flicked the radio switch to the common channel. Kurtz's mention of Bosanski Novi never crossed his mind; the idea that he was making a terrible mistake never crossed his mind; the idea that he might have seriously under-estimated Kurtz's lunacy never crossed his mind. In fact, he did what he did with almost no conscious thought at all. So it seemed to him later, when he cast his mind back and re-examined the incident not just once but again and again. Only a flip of the switch. That was all it took to change the course of a man's life, it seemed.

And there it was, loud and clear, a voice none of Kurtz's laddie-bucks would recognize. They knew Eddie Vedder; Walter Cronkite was a different deal. "*—here. Il n'y a pas d'infection ici.*" Two seconds, and then a voice that might have belonged to Barbra Streisand: "One hundred and thirteen. One hundred and nineteen."

At some point, Owen realized, they had started over counting primes from one. On the way up to Gosselin's in the bus, the various voices had reached primes in the high four figures.

"We are dying," said the voice of Barbra Streisand. *"On se meurt, on crève."* A pause, then the voice of David Letterman: "One hundred—"

"Belay that!" Kurtz cried. For the only time in the years Owen had known him, Kurtz sounded really upset. Almost shocked. "Owen, why do you want to run that filth into the ears of my boys? You come back and tell me, and right *now.*"

"Just wanted to hear if any of it had changed, boss," Owen said. That was a lie, and of course Kurtz knew it and at some point would undoubtedly make him pay for it. It was failing to shoot the kids all over again, maybe even worse. Owen didn't care. Fuck the phooka horse. If they were going to do this, he wanted Kurtz's boys (Skyhook in Bosnia, Blue Group this time, some other name next time, but it always came back to the same hard young faces) to hear the grayboys one last time. Travellers from another star system, perhaps even another universe or time-stream, knowers of things their hosts would never know (not that Kurtz would care). Let them hear the grayboys one last time instead of Pearl Jam or Jar of Flies or Rage Against the Machine; the grayboys appealing to what they had foolishly hoped was some better nature.

"And has it changed?" Kurtz's voice crackled back. The green Kiowa was still down there, just below the hanging line of gunships, its rotors beating at the split top of a tall old pine just under it, making it ruffle and sway. "*Has* it, Owen?"

"No," he said. "Not at all, boss."

"Then belay that chatter. Daylight's wasting, praise Jesus."

Owen paused, then said, with careful deliberation: "Yes, *sir.*"

6

Kurtz sat bolt-upright in the Kiowa's right seat—"ramrod-straight" was how they always put it in the books and movies. He had donned his sunglasses in spite of the day's mild gray light, but Freddy, his pilot, still only dared to look at him from the corners of his eyes. The sunglasses were wraparounds, hipster-hodaddy shades, and now that they were on, you couldn't tell where the boss was looking. You certainly couldn't trust the way his head was pointing.

The Derry *News* lay on Kurtz's lap (MYSTERIOUS SKY-LIGHTS, MISSING HUNTERS SPARK PANIC IN JEFFERSON TRACT, read the headline). Now he picked up the paper and folded it carefully. He was good at this, and soon the Derry *News* would be folded into what Owen Underhill's career had just become: a cocked hat. Underhill no doubt thought he would face some sort of disciplinary action—Kurtz's own, since this was a black-ops deal, at least so far—followed by a second chance.

What he didn't seem to realize (and that was probably good; unwarned usually meant unarmed) was that this *had* been his second chance. Which was one more than Kurtz had ever given anyone else, and one he now regretted. *Bitterly* regretted. For Owen to go and pull a trick like that after their conversation in the office of the store . . . after he had been specifically warned . . .

"Who gives the order?" Underhill's voice crackled in Kurtz's private comlink.

Kurtz was surprised and a little dismayed by the depth of his rage. Most of it was caused by no more than surprise, the simplest emotion, the one babies registered before any other. Owen had zinged him a good one, putting the grayboys on the squad channel like that; just wanted to hear if any of it had changed indeed, that was one you could roll tight and stick up your ass. Owen was probably the best second Kurtz had ever had in a long and complicated career that stretched all the way back to Cambodia in the early seventies, but Kurtz was going to break him, just the same. For the trick with the radio; because Owen hadn't learned. It wasn't about kids in Bosanski Novi, or a bunch of babbling voices now. It wasn't about following orders, or even the principle of the matter. It was about the line. *His* line. The Kurtz Line.

Also, there was that *sir*.

That damned snotty *sir*.

"Boss?" Owen sounding just a tad nervous now, and he was right to sound nervous, Jesus love him. "Who gives—"

"Common channel, Freddy," Kurtz said. "Key me in."

The Kiowa, much lighter than the gunships, caught a gust of wind and took a giddy bounce. Kurtz and Freddy ignored it. Freddy keyed him wide.

"Listen up, boys," Kurtz said, looking at the four gunships hanging in a line, glass dragonflies above the trees and beneath the clouds. Just ahead of them was the swamp and the vast pearlescent tilted dish with its surviving crew—or whatever they were—standing beneath its aft lip.

"Listen now, boys, Daddy's gonna sermonize. Are you listening? Answer up."

Yes, yes, affirmative, affirm, roger that (with an occasional sir thrown in, but that was all right; there was a difference between forgetfulness and insolence).

"I'm not a talker, boys, talking's not what I do, but I want you to know that this is not repeat *not* a case of what you see is what you get. What you *see* is about six dozen gray, apparently unsexed humanoids standing around naked as a loving God made them and you say, *some* would say anyway, 'Why, those poor folks, all naked and unarmed, not a cock or a cunt to share among em, pleading for mercy there by their crashed intergalactic Trailways, and what kind of a *dog*, what kind of a *monster* could hear those pleading voices and go in just the same?' And I have to tell you, boys, that I am that dog, I am that monster, I am that post-industrial post-modern crypto-fascist politically incorrect male cocka-rocka warpig, praise Jesus, and for anyone listening in I am Abraham Peter Kurtz, USAF Retired, serial number 241771699, and I am leading this charge, I'm the Lieutenant Calley in charge of this particular Alice's Restaurant Massacree."

He took a deep breath, eyes fixed on the hovering helicopters.

"But fellows, I'm here to tell you that the grayboys have been messing with us since the late nineteen-forties, and I have been messing with them since the late nineteen-seventies, and I can tell you that just because a fellow comes walking toward you with his hands raised saying I surrender, that doesn't mean, praise Jesus, that he doesn't have a pint of nitroglycerine shoved up his ass. Now the big old smart goldfish who go swimming around in the think-tanks, most of those guys say the grayboys came when we started lighting off atomic and hydrogen bombs, that they came to that the way bugs come to a buglight. I don't know about that, I am not a thinker, I leave the thinking to others, leave it to the cabbage, cabbage got the head on him, as the saying goes, but there's nothing wrong with my eyes, fellows, and I tell you those grayboy sons of bitches are as harmless as a wolf in a henhouse. We have taken a good many of them over the years, but not one has lived. When they die, their corpses decompose rapidly and turn into exactly the sort of stuff you see down there, what you lads call Ripley fungus. Sometimes they explode. Got that? They *explode*. The fungus they carry—or maybe it's the fungus that's in charge, some of the think-tank goldfish believe that might be the case—dies easily enough unless it gets on a living host, I say again *living host,* and the host it

seems to like the best, fellows, praise Jesus, is good old
homo sap. Once you've got it so much as under the nail
of your little finger, it's Katie bar the door and Homer
run for home."

This was not precisely the truth—not precisely
anywhere near the truth, as a matter of fact—but
nobody fought for you as ferociously as a scared soldier. This Kurtz knew from experience.

"Boys, our little gray buddies are telepathic, and
they seem to pass this ability on to us through the air.
We catch it even when we don't catch the fungus, and
while you might think a little mind-reading could be
fun, the sort of thing that would make you the life of
the party, I can tell you what lies a little farther down
that road: *schizophrenia, paranoia,* separation from *reality,* and total I say again *TOTAL FUCKING INSAN-
ITY.* The think-tank boys, God bless em, believe that
this telepathy is relatively short-acting right now, but I
don't have to tell you what could happen in that regard
if the grayboys are allowed to settle in and be comfortable. I want you fellows to listen to what I'm going
to say now very carefully. I want you to listen as if your
lives depended on it, all right? When *they* take *us,*
boys—say again, when *they* take *us*—and you all know
there have been abductions, most people who claim to
have been abducted by aliens are lying through their
asshole neurotic teeth, but not all—those who are let
go have often undergone implants. Some are nothing
but instruments—transmitters, perhaps, or monitors of
some sort—but some are living things which eat their
hosts, grow fat, and then tear them apart. These

implants have been put in place by the very creatures you see down there, milling around all naked and innocent. They claim there's no infection among them even though we know they are infected right up the ying-yang and the old wazoo and everywhere else. I have seen these things at work for twenty-five years or more, and I tell you this is *it,* this is the invasion, this is the Super Bowl of Super Bowls, and you fellows are on defense. They are *not* helpless little ETs, boys, waiting around for someone to give them a New England Tel phone card so they can phone home, they are a *disease.* They are cancer, praise Jesus, and boys, we're one big hot radioactive shot of chemotherapy. Do you hear me, boys?"

No affirmatives this time. No rogers, no I-copy-thats. Raw cheers, nervous and neurotic, jigging with eagerness. The comlink bulged with them.

"Cancer, boys. *They are cancer.* That's the best I can put it, although as you know, I'm no talker. Owen, do you copy?"

"Copy, boss." Flat. Flat and calm, damn him. Well, let him be cool. Let him be cool while he still could. Owen Underhill was all finished. Kurtz raised the paper hat and looked at it admiringly. Owen Underhill was *over.*

"What is it down there, Owen? What is it shuffling around that ship? What is it forgot to put on their pants and their shoes before they left the house this morning?"

"Cancer, boss."

"That's right. Now you give the order and in we go.

Sing it out, Owen." And, with great deliberation, knowing that the men in the gunships would be watching him (never had he given such a sermon, never, and not a word of it preplanned, unless in his dreams), he turned his own hat around backward.

7

Owen watched Tony Edwards turn his Mets cap around so that the bill pointed down the nape of his neck, heard Bryson and Bertinelli racking the .50s, and understood this was really happening. They were going hot. He could get in the car and ride or stand in the road and get run down. Those were the only choices Kurtz had left him.

And there was something more, something bad he remembered from long ago, when he had been—what? Eight? Seven? Maybe even younger. He had been out on the lawn of his house, the one in Paducah, his father still at work, his mother off somewhere, probably at the Grace Baptist, getting ready for one of her endless bake sales (unlike Kurtz, when Randi Underhill said praise Jesus, she meant it), and an ambulance had pulled up next door, at the Rapeloews'. No siren, but lots of flashing lights. Two men in jumpsuits very much like the coverall Owen now wore had gone running up the Rapeloews' walk, unfolding a gleaming stretcher. Never even breaking stride. It was like a magic trick.

Less than ten minutes later they were back out with Mrs. Rapeloew on the stretcher. Her eyes had been closed. Mr. Rapeloew came along behind her, not even bothering to close the door. Mr. Rapeloew, who was Owen's Daddy's age, looked suddenly as old as a grampy. It was another magic trick. Mr. Rapeloew glanced to his right as the men loaded his wife into the ambulance and saw Owen kneeling on his lawn in his short pants and playing with his ball. *They say it was a stroke!* Mr. Rapeloew called. *St. Mary's Memorial! Tell your mother, Owen!* And then he climbed into the back of the ambulance and the ambulance drove away. For the next five minutes or so Owen continued to play with his ball, throwing it up and catching it, but in between throws and catches he kept looking at the door Mr. Rapeloew had left open and thinking he ought to close it. That closing it would be what his mother called a Christian Act of Charity.

Finally he got up and crossed to the Rapeloews' lawn. The Rapeloews had been good to him. Nothing really special ("Nothing to get up in the night and write home about," his mother would have said), but Mrs. Rapeloew made lots of cookies and always remembered to save him some; many were the bowls of frosting and cookie-dough he had scraped clean in chubby, cheery Mrs. Rapeloew's kitchen. And Mr. Rapeloew had shown him how to make paper airplanes that really flew. Three different kinds. So the Rapeloews deserved charity, Christian charity, but when he stepped through the open door of the Rapeloews' house, he had known perfectly well that Christian charity wasn't the reason he was there. Doing Christian charity did not make your dingus hard.

For five minutes—or maybe it was fifteen minutes or half an hour, the time passed like time in a dream—Owen had just walked around in the Rapeloews' house, doing nothing, but all the time his dingus had been just as hard as a rock, so hard it throbbed like a second heartbeat, and you would think something like that would hurt, but it hadn't, it had felt *good,* and all these years later he recognized that silent wandering for what it had been: foreplay. The fact that he had nothing against the Rapeloews, that he in fact *liked* the Rapeloews, somehow made it even better. If he was caught (he never was), he could say *I dunno* if asked why he did it, and be telling the God's honest.

Not that he did so much. In the downstairs bathroom he found a toothbrush with DICK printed on it. Dick was Mr. Rapeloew's name. Owen tried to piss on the bristles of Mr. Rapeloew's toothbrush, that was what he wanted to do, but his dingus was too hard and no piss would come out, not a single drop. So he spat on the bristles instead, then rubbed the spit in and put the brush back in the toothbrush holder. In the kitchen, he poured a glass of water over the electric stove-burners. Then he took a large china serving platter from the sideboard. "They said it was the stork," Owen said, holding the platter over his head. "It must be a baby, because he said it was a stork." And then he heaved the platter into the corner, where it shattered into a thousand pieces. Once that was done he had fled from the house. Whatever had been inside him, the thing that had made his dingus hard and his eyeballs feel too big for their sockets, the shattering sound of the plate had broken it, popped it like a pimple, and if his parents hadn't been so worried about Mrs. Rapeloew, they almost certainly would have seen something wrong with him. As it was, they probably just assumed that he was worried about Mrs. R., too. For the next week he had slept little, and what sleep he did get had been haunted by bad dreams. In one of these, Mrs. Rapeloew came home from the hospital with the baby the stork had brought her, only the baby was black and dead. Owen had been all but consumed with guilt and shame (never to the point of confessing, however; what in God's name would he have said when his Baptist mother asked him what had possessed him), and yet he never forgot the blind pleasure of standing in the bathroom with his shorts down around his knees, trying to piss on Mr. Rapeloew's toothbrush, or the thrill that had gusted through him when the serving platter shattered. If he had been older, he would have come in his pants, he supposed. The purity was in the senselessness; the joy was in the sound of the shatter; the afterglow was the slow and pleasurable wallow in remorse for having done it and the fear of being caught. Mr. Rapeloew had said it was a stork, but when Owen's father came in that night, he told him it was a stroke. That a blood-vessel in Mrs. Rapeloew's brain had sprung a leak and that was a stroke.

And now here it was again, all of that.

Maybe this time I will *come,* he thought. *It'll certainly be a lot goddam grander than trying to piss on Mr. Rapeloew's toothbrush.* And then, as he turned his own hat around: *Same basic concept, though.*

"Owen?" Kurtz's voice, "Are you there, son? If you

don't roger me right now, I'm going to assume you either can't or won't—"

"Boss, I'm here." Voice steady. In his mind's eye he saw a sweaty little boy holding a china serving platter over his head. "Boys, are you ready to kick a little interstellar ass?"

A roar of affirmation that included one *goddam right* and one *let's tear em up*.

"What do you want first, boys?"

Squad Anthem and *Anthem* and *Fucking Stones, right now!*

"Anyone want out, sing out."

Radio silence. On some other frequency where Owen would never go again, the grayboys were pleading in famous voices. Starboard and below was the little Kiowa OH-58. Owen didn't need binoculars to see Kurtz with his own hat now turned around, Kurtz watching him. The newspaper was still on his lap, now for some reason folded into a triangle. For six years Owen Underhill had needed no second chances, which was good because Kurtz didn't give them—in his heart Owen supposed he had always known that. He would think about that later, however. If he had to. One final coherent thought flared in his mind—*You're the cancer, Kurtz, you*—and then died. Here was a fine and perfect darkness in its place.

"Blue Group, this is Blue Boy Leader. Come in on me. Commence firing at two hundred yards. Avoid hitting the Blue Boy if possible, but we are going to sweep those motherfuckers clean. Conk, play the Anthem."

Gene Conklin flicked a switch and racked a CD in the Discman sitting on the floor of Blue Boy Two. Owen, no longer inside himself, leaned forward in Blue Boy Leader and cranked the volume.

Mick Jagger, the voice of the Rolling Stones, filled his earphones. Owen raised his hand, saw Kurtz snap him a salute—whether sarcastic or sincere Owen neither knew nor cared—and then Owen brought his arm down. As Jagger sang it out, sang the Anthem, the one they always played when they went in hot, the helicopters dropped, tightened, and flew to target.

8

The grayboys—the ones that were left—stood beneath the shadow of their ship which lay in turn at the end of the shattered aisle of trees it had destroyed in its final descent. They made no initial effort to run or hide; in fact half of them actually stepped forward on their naked toeless feet, squelching in the melted snow, the muck, and the scattered fuzz of reddish-gold moss. These faced the oncoming line of gunships, long-fingered hands raised, showing that they were empty. Their huge black eyes gleamed in the dull daylight.

The gunships did not slow, although all of them heard the final transmissions briefly in their heads: *Please don't hurt us, we are helpless, we are dying.* With that, twining through it like a pigtail, came the voice of Mick Jagger: *"Please allow me to introduce myself, I'm a man of wealth and taste; I've been around for many a long year, stolen many man's soul and faith . . ."*

The gunships heeled around as briskly as a marching band doing a square turn on the fifty-yard line of the Rose Bowl, and the .50s opened up. The bullets plowed into the snow, struck dead branches from already wounded trees, struck pallid little sparks from the edge of the great ship. They ripped into the bunched gray-boys standing with their arms upraised and tore them apart. Arms spun free of rudimentary bodies, spouting a kind of pink sap. Heads exploded like gourds, raining a reddish backsplash on their ship and their ship-mates—not blood but that mossy stuff, as if their heads were full of it, not really heads at all but grisly produce baskets. Several of them were cut in two at the mid-section and went down with their hands still raised in surrender. As they fell, the gray bodies went a dirty white and seemed to boil.

Mick Jagger confided: *"I was around when Jesus Christ had His moment of doubt and pain . . ."*

A few grays, still standing under the lip of the ship, turned as if to run, but there was nowhere to go. Most of them were shot down immediately. The last few survivors—maybe four in all—retreated into the scant shadows. They seemed to be doing something, fid-dling with something, and Owen had a horrible pre-monition.

"I can get them!" came crackling over the radio. That was Deforest in Blue Boy Four, almost panting with eagerness. And, anticipating Owen's order to go for it, the Chinook dropped almost to ground-level, its rotors kicking up snow and muddy water in a filthy blizzard, battering the underbrush flat.

"No, negative, belay that, back off, resume station plus fifty!" Owen shouted, and whacked Tony's shoulder. Tony, looking only slightly odd in the transparent mask over his mouth and nose, yanked back on the yoke and Blue Boy Leader rose in the unsteady air. Even over the music—the mad bongos, the chorus going *Hoo-hoo,* "Sympathy for the Devil" hadn't played through to its conclusion even a single time, at least not yet—Owen could hear his crew grumbling. The Kiowa, he saw, was already small with distance. Whatever his mental peculiarities might be, Kurtz was no fool. And his instincts were exquisite.

"Ah, boss—" Deforest, sounding not just disappointed but on fire.

"Say again, say again, return to station, Blue Group, *return—*"

The explosion hammered him back in his seat and tossed the Chinook upward like a toy. Beneath the roar, he heard Tony Edwards cursing and wrestling with the yoke. There were screams from behind them, but while most of the crew was injured, they lost only Pinky Bryson, who had been leaning out the bay for a better look and fell when the shockwave hit.

"Got it, got it, got it," Tony yammered, but Owen thought it was at least thirty seconds before Tony actually did, seconds that felt like hours. On the sound systems, the Anthem had cut off, a fact that did not bode well for Conk and the boys in Blue Boy Two.

Tony swung Blue Boy Leader around, and Owen saw the windscreen Perspex was cracked in two

places. Behind them someone was still screaming—
Mac Cavanaugh, it turned out, had somehow managed to lose two fingers.

"Holy shit," Tony muttered, and then: "You saved
our bacon, boss. Thanks."

Owen barely heard him. He was looking back at the
remains of the ship, which now lay in at least three
pieces. It was hard to tell because the shit was flying
and the air had turned a hazy reddish-orange. It was a
little easier to see the remains of Deforest's gunship. It
lay canted on its side in the muck with bubbles bursting all around it. On its port side, a long piece of
busted rotor floated in the water like a giant's canoe-
paddle. About fifty yards away, more rotors protruded,
black and crooked, from a furious ball of yellow-white
fire. That was Conklin and Blue Boy Two.

Graggle and bleep from the radio. Blakey in Blue
Boy Three. "Boss, hey boss, I see—"

"Three, this is Leader. I want you to—"

"Leader, this is Three, I see survivors, repeat, *I see
Blue Boy Four survivors,* at least three . . . no, four . . . I
am going down to—"

"Negative, Blue Boy Three, not at all. Resume station plus fifty—belay that, station plus *one*-fifty, one-
five-oh, and do it now!"

"Ah, but sir . . . boss, I mean . . . I can see Friedman, he's on fucking *fire*—"

"Joe Blakey, listen up."

No mistaking Kurtz's rasp, Kurtz who had gotten
clear of the red crap in plenty of time. *Almost,* Owen
thought, *as if he knew what was going to happen.*

"Get your ass out of there now, or I guarantee that by next week you'll be shovelling camel-shit in a hot climate where booze is illegal. *Out.*"

Nothing more from Blue Boy Three. The two surviving gunships pulled back to their original rally-point plus a hundred and fifty yards. Owen sat watching the furious upward spiral of the Ripley fungus, wondering if Kurtz *had* known or just intuited, wondering if he and Blakey had cleared the area in time. Because they *were* infectious, of course; whatever the grayboys said, they *were* infectious. Owen didn't know if that justified what they had just done, but he thought the survivors of Ray Deforest's Blue Boy Four were most likely dead men walking. Or worse: live men changing. Turning into God knew what.

"Owen." The radio.

Tony looked at him, eyebrows raised.

"Owen."

Sighing, Owen flicked the toggle over to Kurtz's closed channel with his chin. "I'm here, boss."

9

Kurtz sat in the Kiowa with the newspaper hat still in his lap. He and Freddy were wearing their masks; so were the rest of boys in the attack group. Likely even the poor fellows now on the ground were still wearing them. The masks were probably unnecessary, but Kurtz, who had no intention of contracting Ripley if he could avoid it, was the big cheese. Among other things, he was supposed to set an example. Besides, he played the odds. As for Freddy Johnson . . . well, he had plans for Freddy.

"I'm here, boss," Underhill said in his phones.

"That was good shooting, better flying, and superlative thinking. You saved some lives. You and I are back where we were. Right back to Square One. Got that?"

"I do, boss. Got it and appreciate it."

And if you believe it, Kurtz thought, *you're even stupider than you look.*

10

Behind Owen, Cavanaugh was still making noises, but the volume was decreasing now. Nothing from Joe Blakey, who was maybe coming to understand the implications of that gauzy red-gold whirlwind, which they might or might not have managed to avoid.

"Everything okay, buck?" Kurtz asked.

"We have some injuries," Owen replied, "but basically five-by. Work for the sweepers, though; it's a mess back there."

Kurtz's crowlike laughter came back, loud in Owen's headphones.

11

"Freddy."

"Yes, boss."

"We need to keep an eye on Owen Underhill."

"Okay."

"If we need to leave suddenly—Imperial Valley—Underhill stays here."

Freddy Johnson said nothing, just nodded and flew the helicopter. Good lad. Knew which side of the line he belonged on, unlike some.

Kurtz again turned to him.

"Freddy, get us back to that godforsaken little store and don't spare the horses. I want to be there at least fifteen minutes before Owen and Joe Blakey. Twenty, if possible."

"Yes, boss."

"And I want a secure satellite uplink to Cheyenne Mountain."

"You got it. Take about five."

"Make it three, buck. Make it three."

Kurtz settled back and watched the pine forest flow under them. So much forest, so much wildlife, and not a few human beings—most of them at this time of year wearing orange. And a week from now—maybe in seventy-two hours—it would all be as dead as the mountains of the moon. A shame, but if there was one thing of which there was no shortage in Maine, it was woods.

Kurtz spun the cocked hat on the end of his finger. If possible, he intended to see Owen Underhill wearing it after he had ceased breathing.

"He just wanted to hear if any of it had changed," Kurtz said softly.

Freddy Johnson, who knew which side his bread was buttered on, said nothing.

12

Halfway back to Gosselin's and Kurtz's speedy little Kiowa already a speck that might or might not still be there, Owen's eyes fixed on Tony Edwards's right hand, which was gripping one branch of the Chinook's Y-shaped steering yoke. At the base of the right thumbnail, fine as a spill of sand, was a curving line of reddish-gold. Owen looked down at his own hands, inspecting them as closely as Mrs. Jankowski had during Personal Hygiene, back in those long-ago days when the Rapeloews had been their neighbors. He could see nothing yet, not on his, but Tony had his mark, and Owen guessed his own would come in time.

Baptists the Underhills had been, and Owen was familiar with the story of Cain and Abel. *The voice of thy brother's blood crieth unto me from the ground,* God had said, and he had sent Cain out to live in the land of Nod, to the east of Eden. With the low men, according to his mother. But before Cain was set loose to wander, God had put a mark upon him, so even the low men of Nod would know him for what he was. And now, seeing that red-gold thread on the nail of Eddie's thumb and looking for it on his own hands and wrists, Owen guessed he knew what color Cain's mark had been.

CHAPTER ELEVEN

THE EGGMAN'S JOURNEY

1

Suicide, Henry had discovered, had a voice. It wanted to explain itself. The problem was that it didn't speak much English; mostly it lapsed into its own fractured pidgin. But it didn't matter; just the talking seemed to be enough. Once Henry allowed suicide its voice, his life had improved enormously. He even had nights when he slept again (not a lot of them, but enough), and he had never had a really bad day.

Until today.

It had been Jonesy's body on the Arctic Cat, but the thing now inside his old friend was full of alien images and alien purpose. Jonesy might also still be inside—Henry rather thought he was—but if so, he was now too deep, too small and powerless, to be of any use. Soon Jonesy would be gone completely, and that would likely be a mercy.

Henry had been afraid the thing now running

Jonesy would sense him, but it went by without slow-ing. Toward Pete. And then what? Then where? Henry didn't want to think, didn't want to care.

At last he started back to camp again, not because there was anything left at Hole in the Wall but because there was no place else to go. As he reached the gate with its one-word sign—CLARENDON—he spat another tooth into his gloved hand, looked at it, then tossed it away. The snow was over, but the sky was still dark and he thought the wind was picking up again. Had the radio said something about a storm with a one-two punch? He couldn't remember, wasn't sure it mat-tered.

Somewhere to the west of him, a huge explosion hammered the day. Henry looked dully in that direc-tion, but could see nothing. Something had either crashed or exploded, and at least some of the nagging voices in his head had stopped. He had no idea if those things were related or not, no idea if he should care. He stepped through the open gate, walking on the packed snow marked with the tread of the departing Arctic Cat, and approached Hole in the Wall.

The generator brayed steadily, and above the granite slab that served as their welcome mat, the door stood open. Henry paused outside for a moment, examining the slab. At first he thought there was blood on it, but blood, either fresh or dried, did not have that unique red-gold sheen. No, he was looking at some sort of organic growth. Moss or maybe fungus. And something else . . .

Henry tipped his head back, flared his nostrils, and

sniffed gently—he had a memory, both clear and absurd, of being in Maurice's a month ago with his ex-wife, smelling the wine the *sommelier* had just poured, seeing Rhonda there across the table and thinking, *We sniff the wine, dogs sniff each other's assholes, and it all comes to about the same.* Then, in a flash, the memory of the milk running down his father's chin had come. He had smiled at Rhonda, she had smiled back, and he had thought what a relief the end would be, and if it were done, then 'twere well it were done quickly.

What he smelled now wasn't wine but a marshy, sulfurous odor. For a moment he couldn't place it, then it came: the woman who had wrecked them. The smell of her wrong innards was here, too.

Henry stepped onto the granite slab, aware that he had come to this place for the last time, feeling the weight of all the years—the laughs, the talks, the beers, the occasional lid of pot, a food-fight in '96 (or maybe it had been '97), the gunshots, that bitter mixed smell of powder and blood that meant deer season, the smell of death and friendship and child-hood's brilliance.

As he stood there, he sniffed again. Much stronger, and now more chemical than organic, perhaps because there was so much of it. He looked inside. There was more of that fuzzy, mildewy stuff on the floor, but you could see the hardwood. On the Navajo rug, however, it had already grown so thick that it was hard to make out the pattern. No doubt whatever it was did better in the heat, but still, the rate of growth was scary.

Henry started to step in, then thought better of it.

He backed two or three paces away from the doorway instead and only stood there in the snow, very aware of his bleeding nose and the holes in his gums where there had been teeth when he woke up this morning. If that mossy stuff was producing some sort of airborne virus, like Ebola or Hanta, he was probably cooked already, and anything he did would amount to no more than locking the barn door after the horse had been stolen. But there was no sense taking unnecessary risks, was there?

He turned and walked around Hole in the Wall to the Gulch side, still walking in the packed tread of the departed Arctic Cat to keep from sinking into the new snow.

2

The door to the shed was open, too. And Henry could see Jonesy, yes, clear as day, Jonesy pausing in the doorway before going in to get the snowmobile, Jonesy holding to the side of the doorway with a casual hand, Jonesy listening to . . . to the what?

To the nothing. No crows cawing, no jays scolding, no woodpeckers pecking, no squirrels scuttering. There was only the wind and an occasional padded *plop* as a clot of snow slid off a pine or spruce and hit the new snow beneath. The local wildlife was gone, had moved on like goofy animals in a Gary Larson cartoon.

He stood where he was for a moment, calling up his memory of the shed's interior. Pete would have done better—Pete would have stood here with his eyes closed and his forefinger ticking back and forth, then told you where everything was, right down to the smallest jar of screws—but in this case Henry thought he could do without Pete's special skill. He'd been out here just yesterday, looking for something to help him open a kitchen cabinet door that was swelled shut. He had seen then what he wanted now.

Henry inhaled and exhaled rapidly several times, hyperventilating his lungs clean, then pressed his gloved hand tight over his mouth and nose and stepped in. He stood still for a moment, waiting for his eyes to adjust to the dim. He didn't want to be surprised by anything if he could help it.

When he could see well again, Henry stepped across the empty place where the snowmobile had been. There was nothing on the floor now but an overlaid pattern of oil stains, but there were more patches of that reddish-gold crud growing on the green tarp which had covered the Cat and was now cast aside in the corner.

The worktable was a mess—a jar of nails and one of screws overturned so that what had been kept carefully separate was now mixed together, an old pipe-holder that had belonged to Lamar Clarendon knocked to the floor and broken, all the drawers built into the table's thickness yanked open and left that way. One of them, Beaver or Jonesy, had gone through this place like a whirlwind, looking for something.

It was Jonesy.

Yeah. Henry might never know what it was, but it

had been Jonesy, he *knew* that, and it had clearly been almighty important to him or to both of them. Henry wondered if Jonesy had found it. He would probably never know that, either. Meanwhile, what *he* wanted was clearly visible in the far corner of the room, hung on a nail above a pile of paint-cans and sprayguns.

Still holding his hand over his mouth and nose, breath held, Henry crossed the interior of the shed. There were at least four of the little nose-and-mouth painters' masks hanging from elastics which had lost most of their snap. He took them all and turned in time to see something move behind the door. He kept himself from gasping, but his heartbeat jumped, and all at once the double lungful of air that had gotten him this far seemed too hot and heavy. Nothing there, either, it had just been his imagination. Then he saw that yeah, there *was* something. Light came in through the open door; a little more came in through the single dirty window over the table, and Henry had literally jumped at his own shadow.

He left the shed in four big steps, the painters' masks swinging from his right hand. He held onto his lungful of decayed air until he'd made four more steps along the packed track of the snowmobile, then let it out in an explosive rush. He bent over, hands planted on his thighs above his knees, small black dots flocking before his eyes and then dissolving.

From the east came a distant crackle of gunfire. Not rifles; it was too loud and fast for that. Those were automatic weapons. In Henry's mind there came a vision as clear as the memory of milk running down his father's chin or Barry Newman fleeing his office with rockets on his heels. He saw the deer and the coons and the chucks and the feral dogs and the rabbits being cut down in their dozens and their hundreds as they tried to escape what was now pretty clearly a plague zone; he could see the snow turning red with their innocent (but possibly contaminated) blood. This vision hurt him in a way he had not expected, piercing through to a place that wasn't dead but only dozing. It was the place that had resonated so strongly to Duddits's weeping, setting up a harmonic tone that made you feel as if your head were going to explode.

Henry straightened up, saw fresh blood on the palm of his left glove, and cried "Ah, *shit!*" at the sky in a voice that was both furious and amused. He had covered his mouth and nose, he had gotten the masks and was planning on wearing at least two when he went inside Hole in the Wall, but he had completely forgotten the gash in his thigh, the one he'd gotten when the Scout rolled over. If there had been a contaminant out there in the shed, something given off by the fungus, the chances were excellent that it was in him now. Not that the precautions he *had* taken were any such of a much. Henry imagined a sign, big red letters reading BIOHAZARD AREA! PLEASE HOLD BREATH AND COVER ANY SCRATCHES YOU MAY HAVE WITH YOUR HAND!

He grunted laughter and started back toward the cabin. Well, good God, Maude, it wasn't as if he had planned to live forever, anyway.

Off to the east, the gunfire crackled on and on.

3

Once again standing outside Hole in the Wall's open door, Henry felt in his back pocket for a handkerchief without much hope of finding one . . . and didn't. Two of the unadvertised attractions of spending time in the woods were urinating where you wanted and just leaning over and giving a honk when your nose felt in need of a blow. There was something primally satisfying about letting the piss and the snot fly . . . to men, at least. When you thought about it, it was sort of a blue-eyed wonder that women could love the best of them, let alone the rest of them.

He took off his coat, the shirt under it, and the thermal undershirt beneath that. The final layer was a faded Boston Red Sox tee-shirt with GARCIAPARRA 5 on the back. Henry took this off, spun it into a bandage, and wrapped it around the blood-caked tear in the left leg of his jeans, thinking again that he was locking the barn door after the horse had been stolen. Still, you filled in the blanks, didn't you? Yes, you filled in the blanks and you printed neatly and legibly. These were the concepts upon which life ran. Even when life was running out, it seemed.

He put the rest of his outerwear back on over his goosepimply top half, then donned two of the teardrop-shaped painters' masks. He considered fixing two of the others over his ears, imagined those narrow bands of elastic crisscrossing the back of his head like the straps of a shoulder holster, and burst out laughing. What else? Use the last mask to cover one eye?

"If it gets me, it gets me," he said, at the same time reminding himself that it wouldn't hurt to be careful; a little dose of careful never hurt a man, old Lamar used to say.

Inside Hole in the Wall, the fungus (or mildew, or whatever it was) had gone forward appreciably even during the short time Henry had been in the shed. The Navajo rug was now covered side to side, with not even the slightest pattern showing through. There were patches on the couch, the counter between the kitchen and the dining area, and on the seats of two of the three stools which stood on the living-room side of the counter. A crooked capillary of red-gold fuzz ran up one leg of the dining-room table, as if following the line of a spill, and Henry was reminded of how ants will congregate on even the thinnest track of spilled sugar. Perhaps the most distressing thing of all was the red-gold fuzz of cobweb hanging high over the Navajo rug. Henry looked at it fixedly for several seconds before realizing what it really was: Lamar Clarendon's dreamcatcher. Henry didn't think he would ever know exactly what had happened here, but of one thing he was sure: the dreamcatcher had snared a real nightmare this time.

You aren't really going any farther in here, are you? Now that you've seen how fast it grows? Jonesy looked all right when he went by, but he wasn't all right, and you know it. You felt it. So . . . you aren't really going on, are you?

Henry glanced at his watch and saw that it

"I think so," Henry said. The doubled thickness of masks bobbed on his face when he spoke. "If it gets hold of me . . . why, I'll just have to kill myself."

Laughing like Stubb in *Moby-Dick,* Henry moved farther into the cabin.

4

With one exception, the fungus grew in thin mats and clumps. The exception was in front of the bathroom door, where there was an actual hill of fungus, all of it matted together and growing upward in the doorway, bearding both jambs to a height of at least four feet. This hill-like clump of growth seemed to be lying over some grayish, spongy growth medium. On the side facing the living room, the gray stuff split in two, making a V-shape that reminded Henry unpleasantly of splayed legs. As if someone had died in the doorway and the fungus had overgrown the corpse. Henry recalled an off-print from med school, some article quickly scanned in the search for something else. It had contained pho-tographs, one of them a gruesome medical examiner's shot he had never quite forgotten. It showed a murder victim dumped in the woods, the nude body discovered after approximately four days. There had been toad-stools growing from the nape of the neck, the creases at the backs of the knees, and from the cleft of the but-tocks.

Four days, all right. But this place had been clean this morning, only . . .

Henry glanced at his watch and saw that it had

stopped at twenty till twelve. It was now Eastern Standard No Time At All.

He turned and peeked behind the door, suddenly convinced that something was lurking there.

Nah. Nothing but Jonesy's Garand, leaning against the wall.

Henry started to turn away, then turned back again. The Garand looked clear of the goo, and Henry picked it up. Loaded, safety on, one in the chamber. Good. Henry slung it over his shoulder and turned back toward the unpleasant red lump growing outside the bathroom door. The smell of ether, mingled with something sulfurous and even more unpleasant, was strong in here. He walked slowly across the room toward the bathroom, forcing himself forward a step at a time, afraid (and increasingly certain) that the red hump with the leglike extrusions was all that remained of his friend Beaver. In a moment he would see the straggly remains of the Beav's long black hair or his Doc Martens, which Beaver called his "lesbian solidarity statement." The Beav had gotten the idea that Doc Martens were a secret sign by which lesbians recognized each other, and no one could talk him out of this. He was likewise convinced that people named Rothschild and Goldfarb ran the world, possibly from a bedrock-deep bunker in Colorado. Beaver, whose preferred expression of surprise was fuck me Freddy.

But there was absolutely no way of telling if the lump in the doorway had once been the Beav, or indeed if it had once been anyone at all. There was only that suggestive shape. Something glinted in the spongy mass of growth and Henry leaned a little closer, wondering even as he did it if microscopic bits of the fungus were already growing on the wet, unprotected surfaces of his eyes. The thing he spotted turned out to be the bathroom doorknob. Off to one side, sporting its own fuzz of growth, was a roll of friction tape. He remembered the mess scattered across the surface of the worktable out back, the yanked-open drawers. Had this been what Jonesy had been out there looking for? A goddam roll of tape? Something in his head—maybe the click, maybe not—said it was. But why? In God's name, why?

In the last five months or so, as the suicidal thoughts came more frequently and visited for longer and longer periods of time, chatting in their pidgin language, Henry's curiosity had pretty much deserted him. Now it was raging, as if it had awakened hungry. He had nothing to feed it. Had Jonesy wanted to tape the door shut? Yeah? Against what? Surely he and the Beav must have known it wouldn't work against the fungus, which would just send its fingers creeping under the door.

Henry looked into the bathroom and made a low grunting sound. Whatever obscene craziness had gone on, it had started and ended in there—he had no doubt of it. The room was a red cave, the blue tiles almost completely hidden under drifts of the stuff. It had grown up the base of the sink and the toilet, as well. The seat's lid was back against the tank, and although he couldn't be positive—there was too much overgrowth to be positive—he thought that the ring itself had been broken inward. The shower curtain was now a solid red-gold instead of filmy blue; most of it had been torn off the rings (which had grown their own vegetable beards) and lay in the tub.

Jutting from the edge of the tub, also overgrown with fungus, was a boot-clad foot. The boot was a Doc Marten, Henry was sure of it. He had found Beaver after all, it seemed. Memories of the day they had rescued Duddits suddenly filled him, so bright and clear it might have been yesterday. Beaver wearing his goofy old leather jacket, Beaver taking Duddits's lunchbox and saying *You like this show? But they never change their clothes!* And then saying—

"Fuck me Freddy," Henry told the overgrown cabin. "That's what he said, what he *always* said." Tears running from his eyes and down his cheeks. If it was just wetness the fungus wanted—and judging by the jungle growing out of the toilet-bowl, it liked wetness just fine—it could land on him and have a feast.

Henry didn't much care. He had Jonesy's rifle. The fungus could start on him, but he could make sure that he was long gone before it ever got to the dessert course. If it came to that.

It probably would.

5

He was sure he'd seen a few rug-remnants heaped up in one corner of the shed. Henry debated going out and getting them. He could lay them down on the bathroom floor, walk over them, and get a better look into the tub. But to what purpose? He knew that was Beaver, and he had no real desire to see his old friend, author of such witticisms as *Kiss my bender,* being overgrown by red fungus as the pallid corpse in that long-ago medical offprint had been growing its own colony of toadstools. If it might have answered some of his questions about what had happened, yes, perhaps. But Henry didn't think that likely.

Mostly what he wanted was to get out of here. The fungus was creepy, but there was something else. An even creepier sensation that he was not alone.

Henry backed away from the bathroom door. There was a paperback on the dining table, a pattern of dancing devils with pitchforks on its cover. One of Jonesy's, no doubt, already growing its own little colony of crud.

He became aware of a whickering noise from the west, one that quickly rose to a thunder. Helicopters, and not just one, this time. A lot. Big ones. They sounded as if they were coming in at rooftop level, and Henry ducked without even being aware of it. Images from a dozen Vietnam War movies filled his head and he was momentarily sure that they would open up with their machine-guns, spraying the house. Or maybe they'd hose it down with napalm.

They passed over without doing either, but came close enough to rattle the cups and dishes on the kitchen shelves. Henry straightened up as the thunder began to fade, becoming first a chatter and then a harmless drone. Perhaps they had gone off to join the animal slaughter at the east end of Jefferson Tract. Let them. He was going to get the fuck out of here and—

And what? Exactly what?

While he was thinking this question over, there was a sound from one of the two downstairs bedrooms. A rustling sound. This was followed by a moment of silence, just long enough for Henry to decide it was his imagination pulling a little more overtime. Then there came a series of low clicks and chitters, almost the sound of a mechanical toy—a tin monkey or parrot, maybe—on the verge of running down. Gooseflesh broke out all over Henry's body. The spit dried up in his mouth. The hairs on the back of his neck began to straighten in bunches.

Get out of here, run!

Before he could listen to that voice and let it get a hold on him, he crossed to the bedroom door in big steps, unshouldering the Garand as he went. The adrenaline dumped into his blood, and the world stood forth brightly. Selective perception, that unacknowledged gift to the safe and cozy, fell away and he saw every detail: the trail of blood which ran from bedroom to bathroom, a discarded slipper, that weird red mold growing on the wall in the shape of a handprint. Then he went through the door.

It was on the bed, whatever it was; to Henry it looked like a weasel or a woodchuck with its legs amputated and a long, bloody tail strung out behind it like an afterbirth. Only no animal he'd ever seen—with the possible exception of the moray eel at the Boston Seaquarium—had such disproportionately large black eyes. And another similarity: when it yawned open the rudimentary line that was its mouth, it revealed a nest of shocking fangs, as long and thin as hatpins.

Behind it, pulsing on the blood-soaked sheet, were a hundred or more orange-and-brown eggs. They were the size of large marbles and coated with a murky, snotlike slime. Within each Henry could see a moving, hairlike shadow.

The weasel-thing rose up like a snake emerging from a snake-charmer's basket and chittered at him. It lurched on the bed—Jonesy's bed—but seemed unable to move much. Its glossy black eyes glared. Its tail (except Henry thought it might actually be some sort of gripping tentacle) lashed back and forth, then laid itself over as many of the eggs as it could reach, as if protecting them.

Henry realized he was saying the same word, *no*, over and over in a monotonous drone, like a helpless neurotic who has been loaded up on Thorazine. He shouldered the rifle, aimed, and tracked the thing's repulsive wedge of a head as it twitched and dodged. *It knows what this is, it knows at least that much,* Henry thought coldly, and then he squeezed the trigger.

It was close range and the creature wasn't up to much in the way of evasion; either laying its eggs had exhausted it or it wasn't doing well in the cold—with the main door open, Hole in the Wall had gotten quite cold indeed. The report was very loud in the closed room, and the thing's upraised head disintegrated in a liquid splatter that blew back against the wall in strings and clots. Its blood was the same red-gold as the fungus.

The decapitated body tumbled off the bed and onto a litter of clothes Henry didn't recognize: a brown coat, an orange flagman's vest, a pair of jeans with cuffs (none of them had ever worn cuffed jeans; in junior high school, those who did had been branded shitkickers). Several of the eggs tumbled off with the body. Most landed on either the clothes or the litter of Jonesy's books and remained whole, but a couple hit the floor and broke open. Cloudy stuff like spoiled eggwhite oozed out, about a tablespoonful from each egg. Within it were those hairs, writhing and twisting and seeming to glare at Henry with black eyes the size of pinheads. Looking at them made him feel like screaming.

He turned and walked jerkily out of the room on legs with no more feeling in them than the legs of a table. He felt like a puppet being manipulated by someone who means well but has just begun to learn his craft. He had no real idea where he was going until he reached the kitchen and bent over the cabinet under the sink.

"I am the eggman, I am the eggman, I am the walrus! Goo-goo-joob!"

He didn't sing this but declaimed it in a loud, hortatory voice he hadn't realized was in his repertoire. It was the voice of a ham actor from the nineteenth century. That idea called up an image—God knew why—of Edwin Booth dressed as d'Artagnan, plumed hat and all, quoting from the lyrics of John Lennon, and Henry uttered two loud laugh-syllables—*Ha! Ha!*

I'm going insane, he thought . . . but it was okay. Better d'Artagnan reciting "I Am the Walrus" than the image of that thing's blood splattering onto the wall, or the mold-covered Doc Marten sticking out of the bathtub, or, worst of all, those eggs splitting open and releasing a load of twitching hairs with eyes. All those eyes looking at him.

He moved aside the dish detergent and the floor-bucket, and there it was, the yellow can of Sparx barbecue lighter fluid. The inept puppeteer who had taken him over advanced Henry's arm in a series of jerks, then clamped his right hand on the Sparx can. He carried it back across the living room, pausing long enough to take the box of wooden matches from the mantel.

"I am he and you are me and we are all together!" he declaimed, and stepped briskly back into Jonesy's bedroom before the terrified person inside his head could seize the controls, turn him, and make him run away. That person wanted to make him run until he fell down unconscious. Or dead.

The eggs on the bed were also splitting open. Two dozen or more of those hairs were crawling around on the blood-soaked sheet or squirming on Jonesy's pillow. One raised its nub of a head and chittered at Henry, a sound almost too thin and high-pitched to be heard.

Still not allowing himself any pause, if he paused he would never get started again (in any direction save doorward, that was), Henry took two steps to the foot of the bed. One of the hairs came sliding across the floor toward him, propelling itself with its tail like a spermatozoon under a microscope.

Henry stepped on it, thumbing the red plastic cap off the spout of the can as he did. He aimed the spout at the bed and squeezed, flicking his wrist back and forth, making sure he got plenty on the floor as well. When the lighter fluid hit the hairlike things, they made high, mewling cries like kittens which had just been born.

"Eggman . . . eggman . . . *walrus!*"

He stepped on another of the hairs and saw that a third was clinging to the leg of his jeans, holding on with its wisp of a tail and trying to bite through the cloth with its still soft teeth.

"Eggman," Henry muttered, and scraped it off with the side of his other boot. When it tried to squirm away he stepped on it. He was suddenly aware that he was drenched with sweat, sopping from head to toe, if he went out into the cold like this (and he would have to; he couldn't stay here), he'd probably catch his death.

"Can't stay here, can't take no *rest!*" Henry cried in his new hortatory voice.

He opened the matchbox, but his hands were shaking so badly he spilled half of them on the floor. More of the threadlike worms were crawling toward him. They might not know much, but they knew he was the enemy, all right; they knew that.

Henry got hold of a match, held it up, put his thumb against the tip. A trick Pete had taught him in the way back when. It was your friends who always taught you the finer things, wasn't it? Like how to give your old pal Beaver a Viking funeral and get rid of these noisome little snakelets at the same time.

"*Eggman!*"

He scratched the tip of the match and it popped fire. The smell of the burning sulfur was like the smell that had greeted him when he stepped into the cabin, like the smell of the burly woman's farts.

"*Walrus!*"

He flung the match at the foot of the bed, where there was a crumpled duvet now soaked with lighter fluid. For a moment the flame guttered down blue around the little stick, and Henry thought it would go out. Then there was a soft *flump* sound, and the duvet grew a modest crown of yellow flames.

"*Goo-goo-joob!*"

The flames crawled up the sheet, turning the blood soaked into it black. It reached the mass of jelly-coated eggs, tasted them, and found them good. There was a series of thick popping sounds as the eggs began to burst. More of those mewling cries as the worms burned. Sizzling noises as fluid ran out of the burst eggs.

Henry backed out of the room, squirting lighter fluid as he went. He got halfway across the Navajo rug before the can ran empty. He tossed it aside, scratched another match, and tossed it. This time the *flump!* was immediate, and the flames sprang up orange. The heat baked against his sweat-shiny face, and he felt a sudden urge—it was both strong and joyful—to cast the painters' masks aside and simply stride into the fire. Hello heat, hello summer, hello darkness my old friend.

What stopped him was as simple as it was powerful. If he pulled the pin now, he would have suffered the unpleasant awakening of all his quiescent emotions to no purpose. He would never be clear on the details of what had happened here, but he might get at least some answers from whoever was flying the helicopters and shooting the animals. If they didn't just shoot him, too, that was.

At the door, Henry was struck by a memory so clear that his heart cried out inside him: Beaver kneeling in front of Duddits, who is trying to put on his sneaker backward. *Let me fix that, man,* Beaver says, and Duddits, looking at him with a wide-eyed perplexity that you could only love, replies: *Fit neek?*

Henry was crying again. "So long, Beav," he said. "Love you, man—and that's straight from the heart."

Then he stepped out into the cold.

6

He walked to the far end of Hole in the Wall, where the woodpile was. Beside it was another tarp, this one ancient, black fading to gray. It was frost-frozen to the ground, and Henry had to yank hard with both hands in order to pull it free. Under it was a tangle of snowshoes, skates, and skis. There was an antediluvian ice-auger, as well.

As he looked at this unprepossessing pile of long-dormant winter gear, Henry suddenly realized how tired he was . . . except *tired* was really too mild a word. He had just come ten miles on foot, much of it at a fast trot. He had also been in a car accident and discovered the body of a childhood friend. He believed both his other two childhood friends were likewise lost to him.

If I hadn't been suicidal to begin with, I'd be stark-raving crazy by now, he thought, and then laughed. It felt good to laugh, but it didn't make him feel any less tired. Still, he had to get out of here. Had to find someone in authority and tell them what had happened. They might already know—based on the sounds, they sure as shit knew something, although their methods of dealing with it made Henry feel uneasy—but they might not know about the weasels. And the eggs. He, Henry Devlin, would tell them— who better? He was the eggman, after all.

The rawhide lacings of the snowshoes had been chewed by so many mice that the shoes were little more than empty frames. After some sorting, however, he found a stubby pair of cross-country skis that looked as if they might have been state-of-the-art around 1954 or so. The clamps were rusty, but when he pushed them with both thumbs, he was able to move them enough to take a reluctant grip on his boots.

There was a steady crackling sound coming from inside the cabin now. Henry laid one hand on the wood and felt the heat. There was a clutch of assorted ski- poles leaning under the eave, their handgrips buried in a dirty cobweb caul. Henry didn't like to touch that stuff—the memory of the eggs and the weasel-thing's wriggling spawn was still too fresh—but at least he had his gloves on. He brushed the cobwebs aside and sorted through the poles, moving quickly. He could now see sparks dancing inside the window beside his head.

He found a pair of poles that were only a little short for his lanky height and skied clumsily to the corner of the building. He felt like a Nazi snow-trooper in an Alistair MacLean film, with the old skis on his feet and Jonesy's rifle slung over his shoulder. As he turned around, the window beside which he had been standing blew out with a surprisingly loud report—as if someone had dropped a large glass bowl from a second-story window. Henry hunched his shoulders and felt pieces of glass spatter against his coat. A few landed in his hair. It occurred to him that if he had spent another twenty or thirty seconds sorting through the skis and poles, that exploding glass would have erased most of his face.

He looked up at the sky, spread his hands palms-out beside his cheeks like Al Jolson, and said, "Somebody up there likes me! Hotcha!"

Flames were shooting through the window now, licking up under the eaves, and he could hear more stuff breaking inside as the heat-gradient zoomed. Lamar Clarendon's father's camp, originally built just after World War Two, now burning merry hell. It was a dream, surely.

Henry skied around the house, giving it a wide berth, watching as gouts of sparks rose from the chimney and swirled toward the low-bellied clouds. There was still a steady crackle of gunfire off to the east. Someone was bagging their limit, all right. Their limit and more. Then there was that explosion in the west—what in God's name had that been? No way of telling. If he got back to other people in one piece, perhaps they would tell him.

"If they don't just decide to bag me, too," he said. His voice came out in a dry croak, and he realized he was all but dying of thirst. He bent down carefully (he hadn't been on skis of any type in ten years or more), scooped up a double handful of snow, and took a big mouthful. He let it melt and trickle down his throat. The feeling was heavenly. Henry Devlin, psychiatrist and onetime author of a paper about the Hemingway Solution, a man who had once been a virgin boy and who was now a tall and geeky fellow whose glasses always slid down to the tip of his nose, whose hair was going gray, whose friends were either dead, fled, or changed, this man stood in the open gate of a place to which he would never come again, stood on skis, stood eating snow like a kid eating a Sno-Cone at the Shrine Circus, stood and watched the last really good place in his life burn. The flames came through the cedar shingles. Melting snow turned to steaming water and ran hissing down the rusting gutters. Arms of fire popped in and out of the open door like enthusiastic hosts encouraging the newly arrived guests to hurry up, hurry up, dammit, get your asses in here before the whole place burns down. The mat of red-gold fuzz growing on the granite slab had crisped, lost its color, turned gray. "Good," Henry muttered under his breath. He was clenching his fists rhythmically on the grips of his ski-poles without being aware of it. "Good, that's good."

He stood that way for another fifteen minutes, and when he could bear it no more, he set his back to the flames and started back the way he had come.

7

There was no hustle left in him. He had twenty miles to go (*22.2 to be exact,* he told himself), and if he didn't pace himself he'd never make it. He stayed in the packed track of the snowmobile, and stopped to rest more frequently than he had going the other way.

Ah, but I was younger then, he thought with only slight irony.

Twice he checked his watch, forgetting that it was now Eastern Standard No Time At All in the Jefferson Tract. With the mat of clouds firmly in place overhead, all he knew for sure was that it was daytime. Afternoon, of course, but whether mid or late he couldn't tell. On another afternoon his appetite might have served as a gauge, but not today. Not after the thing on Jonesy's bed, and the eggs, and the hairs with their protuberant black eyes. Not after the foot sticking out of the bath-tub. He felt that he would never eat again . . . and if he did, he would never eat anything with even a slight tinge of red. And mushrooms? No thanks.

Skiing, at least on cross-country stubs like these, was sort of like riding a bike, he discovered: you never for-got how to do it. He fell once going up the first hill, the skis slipping out from under him, but glided giddily down the other side with only a couple of wobbles and no spills. He guessed that the skis hadn't been waxed since the peanut-farmer was President, but if he stayed in the crimped and flattened track of the snowmobile, he should be all right. He marvelled at the stippling of animal tracks on the Deep Cut Road—he had never seen a tenth as many. A few critters had gone walking along it, but most of the tracks only crossed it, west to east. The Deep Cut took a lazy northwest course, and west was clearly a point of the compass the local animal population wanted to avoid.

I'm on a journey, he told himself. *Maybe someday someone will write an epic poem about it: "Henry's Journey."*

"Yeah," he said. " 'Time slowed and reality bent; on and on the eggman went.' " He laughed at that, and in his dry throat the laughter turned to hacking coughs. He skied to the side of the snowmobile track, got another double handful of snow, and ate it down.

"Tasty . . . and good for you!" he proclaimed. "Snow! Not just for breakfast anymore!"

He looked up at the sky, and that was a mistake. For a moment he was overwhelmed with dizziness and thought he might go right over on his back. Then the vertigo retreated. The clouds overhead looked a little darker. Snow coming? Night coming? Both coming at the same time? His knees and ankles hurt from the steady shuffle-shuffle of the skis, and his arms hurt even worse from wielding the poles. The pads of muscle on his chest were the worst. He had already accepted as certainty that he wouldn't make it to Gosselin's before dark; now, standing here and eating more snow, it occurred to him that he might not make it at all.

He loosened the Red Sox tee-shirt he'd tied around his leg, and terror leaped in him when he saw a brilliant thread of scarlet against his blue jeans. His heart beat so hard that white dots appeared in his field of vision, flocking and pumping. He reached down to the red with shaking fingers.

What do you think you're going to do? he jeered at himself. *Pick it off like it was a thread or a piece of lint?*

Which was exactly what he *did* do, because it *was* a thread: a red one from the shirt's printed logo. He dropped it and watched it float down to the snow. Then he retied the shirt around the tear in his jeans. For a man who had been considering all sorts of final options not four hours ago—the rope and the noose, the tub and the plastic bag, the bridge abutment and the ever-popular Hemingway Solution, known in some quarters as The Policeman's Farewell—he had been pretty goddamned scared there for a second or two.

Because I don't want to go like that, he told himself. *Not eaten alive by . . .*

"By toadstools from Planet X," he said.

The eggman got moving again.

8

The world shrank, as it always does when we approach exhaustion with our work not done, or even close to done. Henry's life was reduced to four simple, repetitive motions: the pump of his arms on the poles and the push of the skis in the snow. His aches and pains faded, at least for the time being, as he entered some other zone. He only remembered anything remotely like this happening once before, in high school, when he'd been the starting center on the Derry Tigers basketball team. During a crucial pre-playoff game, three of their four best players had somehow fouled out before three minutes of the third quarter were gone. Coach had left Henry in for the rest of the game—he didn't get a single blow except for time-outs and trips to the foul line. He made it, but by the time the final buzzer honked and put an end to the affair (the Tigers had lost gaudily), he had been floating in a kind of happy dream. Halfway down the corridor to the boys' locker room, his legs had given out and down he had gone, with a silly smile still on his face, while his teammates, clad in their red traveling unis, laughed and cheered and clapped and whistled.

No one to clap or whistle here; only the steady crackle-and-stutter of gunfire off to the east. Slowing a little bit now, maybe, but still heavy.

More ominous were the occasional gunshots from up ahead. Maybe from Gosselin's? It was impossible to tell.

He heard himself singing his least favorite Rolling Stones song, "Sympathy for the Devil" (*Made damn sure that Pilate washed his hands and sealed His fate,* thank you very much, you've been a wonderful audience, good night), and made himself stop when he realized the song had gotten all mixed up with memories of Jonesy in the hospital, Jonesy as he had looked last

March, not just gaunt but somehow reduced, as if his essence had pulled itself in to form a protective shield around his surprised and outraged body. Jonesy had looked to Henry like someone who was probably going to die, and although he *hadn't* died, Henry realized now that it was around that time that his own thoughts of suicide had become really serious. To the rogue's gallery of images that haunted him in the middle of the night—blue-white milk running down his father's chin, Barry Newman's giant economy-sized buttocks jiggling as he flew from the office, Richie Grenadeau holding out a dog-turd to the weeping and nearly naked Duddits Cavell, telling him to eat it, he had to eat it—there was now the image of Jonesy's too-thin face and addled eyes, Jonesy who had been swopped into the street without a single rhyme or reason, Jonesy who looked all too ready to put on his boogie shoes and get out of town. They said he was in stable condition, but Henry had read critical in his old friend's eyes. Sympathy for the devil? Please. There was no god, no devil, no sympathy. And once you realized that, you were in trouble. Your days as a viable, paying customer in the great funhouse that was Kulture Amerika were numbered.

He heard himself singing it again—*But what's puzzling you is the nature of my game*—and made himself stop it. What, then? Something really mindless. Mindless and pointless and tasty, something just oozing Kulture Amerika. How about that one by the Pointer Sisters? That was a good one.

Looking down at his shuffling skis and the horizontal crimps left by the snowmobile treads, he began to sing it. Soon he was droning it over and over in a whispery, tuneless monotone while the sweat soaked through his shirts and clear mucus ran from his nose to freeze on his upper lip: *"I know we can make it, I know we can, we can work it out, yes we can-can yes we can yes we can . . ."*

Better. Much better. All those *yes we can-cans* were as Amerikan Kulture as a Ford pickup in a bowling alley parking lot, a lingerie sale at JCPenney, or a dead rock star in a bathtub.

9

And so he eventually returned to the shelter where he had left Pete and the woman. Pete was gone. No sign of him at all.

The rusty tin roof of the lean-to had fallen, and Henry lifted it, peeking under it like a metal bedsheet to make sure Pete wasn't there. He wasn't, but the woman was. She had crawled or been moved from where she'd been when Henry set out for Hole in the Wall, and somewhere along the line she'd come down with a bad case of dead. Her clothes and face were covered with the rust-colored mold that had choked the cabin, but Henry noticed an interesting thing: while the growth on her was doing pretty well (especially in her nostrils and her visible eye, which had sprouted a jungle), the stuff which had spread out from her, outlining her body in a ragged sunburst, was in trouble. The fungus behind her, on the side blocked from the fire, had turned gray and stopped spreading. The stuff in front of her was doing a little better—it had had warmth, and ground to grow on which had been melted clear of snow—but the tips of the tendrils were turning the powdery gray of volcanic ash.

Henry was pretty sure it was dying.

So was the daylight—no question of that now. Henry dropped the rusty piece of corrugated tin back on the body of Becky Shue and on the embery remains of the fire. Then he looked at the track of the Cat again, wishing as he had back at the cabin that he had Natty Bumppo with him to explain what he was seeing. Or maybe Jonesy's good friend Hercule Poirot, he of the little gray cells.

The track swerved in toward the collapsed roof of the lean-to before continuing on northwest toward Gosselin's. There was a pressed-down area in the snow that almost made the shape of a human body. To either side, there were round divots in the snow.

"What do you say, Hercule?" Henry asked. "What means this, *mon ami*?" But Hercule said nothing.

Henry began to sing under his breath again and leaned closer to one of the round divots, unaware that he had left the Pointer Sisters behind and switched back to the Rolling Stones.

There was enough light for him to see a pattern in the three dimples to the left of the body shape, and he recalled the patch on the right elbow of Pete's duffel coat. Pete had told him with an odd sort of pride that his girlfriend had sewed that on there, declaring he had no business going off hunting with a ripped jacket.

Henry remembered thinking it was sad and funny at the same time, how Pete had built up a wistful fantasy of a happy future from that single act of kindness . . . an act which probably had more to do, in the end, with how the lady in question had been raised than with any feelings she might have for her beer-soaked boyfriend.

Not that it mattered. What mattered was that Henry felt he could draw a *bona fide* deduction at last. Pete had crawled out from under the collapsed roof. Jonesy—or whatever was now running Jonesy, the cloud—had come along, swerved over to the remains of the lean-to, and picked Pete up.

Why?

Henry didn't know.

Not all of the splotches in the flattened shape of his thrashing friend, who had crawled out from under the piece of tin by hooking himself along on his elbows, were that mold stuff. Some of it was dried blood. Pete had been hurt. Cut when the roof fell in? Was that all?

Henry spotted a wavering trail leading away from the depression which had held Pete's body. At the end of it was what he first took to be a fire-charred stick. Closer examination changed his mind. It was another of the weasel things, this one burned and dead, now turning gray where it wasn't seared. Henry flipped it aside with the toe of his boot. Beneath it was a small frozen mass. More eggs. It must have been laying them even as it died.

Henry kicked snow over both the eggs and the little monster's corpse, shuddering. He unwrapped the makeshift bandage for another look at the wound on his leg, and as he did it he realized what song was coming out of his mouth. He quit singing. New snow, just a scattering of light flakes, began to skirl down.

"*Why* do I keep singing that?" he asked. "Why does that fucking song keep coming back?"

He expected no answer; these were questions uttered aloud mostly for the comfort of hearing his own voice (this was a death place, perhaps even a haunted place), but one came anyway.

"Because it's *our* song. It's the Squad Anthem, the one we play when we go in hot. We're Cruise's boys." Cruise? Was that right? As in Tom Cruise? Maybe not quite.

The gunfire from the east was much lighter now. The slaughter of the animals was almost done. But there were men, a long skirmish line of hunters who were wearing green or black instead of orange, and they were listening to that song over and over again as they did their work, adding up the numbers of an incredible butcher's bill: *I rode a tank, held a general's rank, when the blitzkrieg raged and the bodies stank . . . Pleased to meet you, hope you guess my name.*

What exactly was going on here? Not in the wild, wonderful, wacky Outside World, but inside his own head? He'd had flashes of understanding his whole life—his life since Duddits, anyway—but nothing like this. What *was* this? Was it time to examine this new and powerful way of seeing the line?

No. No, no, no.

And, as if mocking him, the song in his head: *general's rank, bodies stank.*

"Duddits!" he exclaimed in the graying, dying afternoon; lazy flakes falling like feathers from a split pillow. Some thought struggled to be born but it was too big, too big.

"Duddits!" he cried again in his hortatory eggman's voice, and one thing he did understand: the luxury of suicide had been denied him. Which was the most horrible thing of all, because these weird thoughts—*I shouted out who killed the Kennedys*—were tearing him apart. He began to weep again, bewildered and afraid, alone in the woods. All his friends except Jonesy were dead, and Jonesy was in the hospital. A movie star in the hospital with Mr. Gray.

"What does that *mean*?" Henry groaned. He clapped his hands to his temples (he felt as though his head were bulging, bulging) and his rusty old ski-poles flapped aimlessly at the ends of their wrist-loops like broken propeller blades. *"Oh Christ, what does that MEAN?"*

Only the song came in answer: *Pleased to meet you! Hope you guess my name!*

Only the snow: red with the blood of slaughtered animals and they lay everywhere, a Dachau of deer and raccoon and rabbit and weasel and bear and groundhog and—

Henry screamed, held his head and screamed so loud and so hard that he felt sure for a moment that he was going to pass out. Then his lightheadedness passed and his mind seemed to clear, at least for the time being. He was left with a brilliant image of Duddits as he had been when they first met him, Duddits not under the light of a blitzkrieg winter as in that Stones song but under the sane light of a cloudy October afternoon, Duddits looking up at them with his tilted, somehow wise Chinese eyes. Duddits was our finest hour, he had told Pete.

"Fit wha?" Henry said now. "Fit neek?"

Yeah, fit neek. Turn it around, put it on the right way, fit neek.

Smiling a little now (although his cheeks were still wet with tears that were beginning to freeze), Henry began to ski along the crimped track of the snowmobile again.

10

Ten minutes later he came to the overturned wreck of the Scout. He suddenly realized two things: that he was ragingly hungry after all and that there was food in there. He had seen the tracks both going and coming and hadn't needed Natty Bumppo to know that Pete had left the woman and returned to the Scout. Nor did he need Hercule Poirot to tell him that the food they'd bought at the store—most of it, at least—would still be in there. He knew what Pete had come back for.

He skied around to the passenger side, following Pete's tracks, then froze in the act of loosening the ski bindings. This side was away from the wind, and what Pete had written in the snow as he sat drinking his two beers was mostly still here: DUDDITS, printed over and over again. As he looked at the name in the snow, Henry began to shiver. It was like coming to the grave of a loved one and hearing a voice speak out of the ground.

11

There was broken glass inside the Scout. Blood, as well. Because most of the blood was on the back seat, Henry felt sure it hadn't been spilled in the original accident; Pete had cut himself on his return trip. To Henry, the interesting thing was that there was none of the red-gold fuzz. It grew rapidly, and so the logical conclusion was that Pete hadn't been infected when he'd come for the beer. Later, maybe, but not then.

He grabbed the bread, the peanut butter, the milk, and the carton of orange juice. Then he backed out of the Scout and sat with his shoulders against the overturned rear end, watching the fresh snow sift down and gobbling bread and peanut butter as fast as he could, using his index finger as a knife and licking it clean between spreads. The peanut butter was good and the orange juice went down in two long drafts, but it wasn't enough.

"What you're thinking of," he announced to the darkening afternoon, "is grotesque. Not to mention *red*. Red food."

Red or not, he *was* thinking of it, and surely it wasn't all *that* grotesque; he was, after all, a man who had spent long nights thinking about guns and ropes and plastic bags. All of that seemed a little childish just now, but it *was* him, all right. And so—

"And so let me close, ladies and gentlemen of the American Psychiatric Association, by quoting the late Joseph 'Beaver' Clarendon: 'Said fuck it and put a dime in the Salvation Army bucket. And if you don't like it, grab my cock and suck it.' Thank you very much."

Having thus discoursed to the American Psychiatric Association, Henry crawled back into the Scout, once more successfully avoiding the broken glass, and got the package wrapped in butcher's paper ($2.79 printed on it in Old Man Gosselin's shaky hand). He backed out again with the package in his pocket, then took it out and snapped the twine. Inside were nine plump hot dogs. The red kind.

For a moment his mind tried to show him the legless reptilian thing squirming on Jonesy's bed and looking at him with its empty black eyes, but he banished it with the speed and ease of one whose survival instincts have never wavered.

The hot dogs were fully cooked, but he warmed them up just the same, running the flame of his butane lighter back and forth beneath each one until it was at least warm, then wrapping it in Wonder Bread and gobbling it down. He smiled as he did it, knowing how ridiculous he would look to an observer. Well, didn't they say that psychiatrists eventually ended up as loony as their patients, if not more so?

The important thing was that he was finally full. Even more important, all the disconnected thoughts and fragmented images had drained out of his mind. Also the song. He hoped none of that crap would come back. Ever, please God.

He swallowed more milk, belched, then leaned his head against the side of the Scout and closed his eyes. No going to sleep, though; these woods were lovely, dark and deep, and he had twelve-point-seven miles to go before he could sleep.

He remembered Pete talking about the gossip in Gosselin's—missing hunters, lights in the sky—and how blithely The Great American Psychiatrist had dismissed it, gassing about the Satanism hysteria in Washington State, the abuse hysteria in Delaware. Playing Mr. Smartass Shrink-Boy with his mouth and the front of his mind while the back of his mind went on playing with suicide like a baby who's just discovered his toes in the bathtub. He had sounded entirely plausible, ready for any TV panel show that wanted to spend sixty minutes on the interface between the unconscious and the unknown, but things had changed. Now *he* had become one of the missing hunters. Also, he had seen things you couldn't find on the Internet no matter how big your search engine was.

He sat there, head back, eyes closed, belly full. Jonesy's Garand was propped against one of the Scout's tires. The snow lit on his cheeks and forehead like the light touch of a kitten's paws. "This is it, what all the geeks have been waiting for," he said. "Close encounters of the third kind. Hell, maybe the fourth or fifth kind. Sorry I made fun of you, Pete. You were right and I was wrong. Hell, it's worse than that. *Old Man Gos-*

selin was right and I was wrong. So much for a Harvard education."

And once he'd said that much out loud, things began to make sense. Something had either landed or crashed. There had been an armed response from the United States government. Were they telling the outside world what had happened? Probably not, that wasn't their style, but Henry had an idea they would have to before much longer. You couldn't put the entire Jefferson Tract in Hangar 57.

Did he know anything else? Maybe, and maybe it was a little more than the men in charge of the helicopters and the firing parties knew. They clearly believed they were dealing with a contagion, but Henry didn't think it was as dangerous as they seemed to. The stuff caught, bloomed . . . but then it died. Even the parasite that had been inside the woman had died. This was a bad time of year and a bad place to culture interstellar athlete's foot, if that was what it was. All that argued strongly for the possibility of a crash landing . . . but what about the lights in the sky? What about the implants? For years people who claimed they'd been abducted by ETs had also claimed they had been stripped . . . examined . . . forced to undergo implants . . . all ideas so Freudian they were almost laughable . . .

Henry realized he was drifting and snapped awake so strongly that the unwrapped package of hot dogs tumbled off his lap and into the snow. No, not just drifting; dozing. A good deal more light had seeped out of the day, and the world had gone a dull slate color. His pants were speckled with the fresh snow. If he'd gone any deeper, he'd've been snoring.

He brushed himself off and stood up, wincing as his muscles screamed in protest. He regarded the hot dogs lying there in the snow with something like revulsion, then bent down, rewrapped them, and tucked them into one of his coat pockets. They might start looking good to him again later on. He sincerely hoped not, but you never knew.

"Jonesy's in the hospital," he said abruptly. No idea what he meant. "Jonesy's in the hospital with Mr. Gray. Got to stay there. ICU."

Madness. Prattling madness. He clamped the skis to his boots again, praying that his back wouldn't lock up while he was bent over, and then pushed off along the track once more, the snow starting to thicken around him now, the day darkening.

By the time he realized that he had remembered the hot dogs but forgotten Jonesy's rifle (not to mention his own), he'd gone too far to turn around.

12

He stopped what might have been three quarters of an hour later, peering stupidly down at the Arctic Cat's print. There was little more than a glimmer of light left in the day now, but enough to see that the track—what was left of it—veered abruptly to the right and went into the woods.

Into the fucking *woods*. Why had Jonesy (and Pete, if Pete was with him) gone into the woods? What sense did that make when the Deep Cut ran straight and clear, a white lane between the darkening trees?

"Deep Cut goes northwest," he said, standing there with his skis toeing in toward each other and the loosely wrapped package of hot dogs poking out of his coat pocket. "The road to Gosselin's—the blacktop—can't be more than three miles from here. Jonesy knows that. *Pete* knows that. Still . . . snowmobile goes . . ." He held up his arms like the hands of a clock, estimating. "Snowmobile goes almost dead *north*. Why?"

Maybe he knew. The sky was brighter in the direction of Gosselin's, as if banks of lights had been set up there. He could hear the chatter of helicopters, waxing and waning but always tending in that same direction. As he drew closer, he expected to hear other heavy machinery as well: supply vehicles, maybe generators. To the east there was still the isolated crackle of gunfire, but the big action was clearly in the direction he was going.

"They've set up a base camp at Gosselin's," Henry said. "And Jonesy didn't want any part of it."

That felt like a bingo to Henry. Only . . . there *was* no more Jonesy, was there? Just the redblack cloud.

"Not true," he said. "Jonesy's still there. Jonesy's in the hospital with Mr. Gray. That's what the cloud is—Mr. Gray." And then, apropos of nothing (at least that he could tell): "Fit wha? Fit neek?"

Henry looked up into the sifting snow (it was much less urgent than the earlier snowfall, at least so far, but it was starting to accumulate) as if he

believed there was a God above it somewhere, studying him with all the genuine if detached interest of a
scientist looking at a wriggling paramecium. "What
the fuck am I talking about? Any idea?"

No answer, but an odd memory came. He, Pete,
Beaver, and Jonesy's wife had kept a secret among
them last March. Carla had felt Jonesy could do without knowing that his heart had stopped twice, once just
after the EMTs put him in the back of their ambulance,
and again shortly after he had arrived at Mass General.
Jonesy knew he'd come close to stepping out, but not
(at least as far as Henry knew) just *how* close. And if
Jonesy had had any Kübler-Ross step-into-the-light
experiences, he had either kept them to himself or forgotten thanks to repeated doses of anesthetic and lots of
pain-killers.

A roar built out of the south with terrifying speed
and Henry ducked, putting his hands to his ears as
what sounded like a full squadron of jet fighters
passed in the clouds overhead. He saw nothing, but
when the roar of the jets faded as fast as it had come,
he straightened with his heart beating hard and fast.
Yow! Christ! It occurred to him that this was what
the airbases surrounding Iraq must have sounded like
during the days leading up to Operation Desert
Storm.

That big boom. Did it mean the United States of
America had just gone to war against beings from
another world? Was he now living in an H. G. Wells
novel? Henry felt a hard, squeezing flutter under his
breastbone. If so, this enemy might have more than a

few hundred rusty Soviet Scuds to throw back at Uncle Sammy.

Let it go. You can't do anything about any of that. What's next for you, that's the question. What's next for you?

The rave of the jets had already faded to a mutter. He guessed that they would be back, though. Maybe with friends.

"Two paths diverged in a snowy wood, is that how it goes? Something like that, anyway."

But following the snowmobile's track any farther was really not an option. He'd lose it in the dark half an hour from now, and this new snowfall would wipe it out in any case. He would end up wandering and lost . . . as Jonesy very likely was now.

Sighing, Henry turned away from the snowmobile track and continued along the road.

13

By the time he neared the place where the Deep Cut joined up with the two-lane blacktop known as the Swanny Pond Road, Henry was almost too tired to stand, let alone ski. The muscles in his thighs felt like old wet teabags. Not even the lights on the northwestern horizon, now much brighter, or the sound of the motors and helicopters could offer him much comfort. Ahead of him was a final long, steep hill. On the other side, Deep Cut ended and Swanny Pond began. There he might actually encounter traffic, especially if there were troops being moved in.

"Come on," he said. "Come on, come on, come on."
Yet he stood where he was awhile longer. He didn't
want to go over that hill. "Better underhill than overhill," he said. That seemed to mean something but it
was probably just another idiotic *non sequitur.* Besides,
there was nowhere else to go.

He bent, scooped up more snow—in the dark the
double handful looked like a small pillowcase. He
nibbled some, not because he wanted it but because
he really *didn't* want to start moving again. The lights
coming from Gosselin's were more understandable
than the lights he and Pete had seen playing in the
sky (*They're back!* Becky had screamed, like the little
girl sitting in front of the TV in that old Steven Spielberg movie), but Henry liked them even less, somehow. All those motors and generators sounded
somehow . . . hungry.

"That's right, rabbit," he said. And then, because
there really *were* no other options, he started up the
last hill between him and a real road.

14

He paused at the top, gasping for breath and bent
over his ski-poles. The wind was stronger up here, and
it seemed to go right through his clothing. His left leg
throbbed where it had been gored by the turnsignal
stalk, and he wondered again if he was incubating a little red-gold colony under the makeshift bandage. Too
dark to see, and when the only possible good news
would be no news, maybe that was just as well.

"Time slowed, reality bent, on and on the eggman went." No yuks left in that one, so he started down the hill toward the T-junction where the Deep Cut Road ended.

This side of the hill was steeper and soon he was skiing rather than walking. He picked up speed, not knowing if what he felt was terror, exhilaration, or some unhealthy mix of the two. Certainly he was going too fast for the visibility, which was almost nil, and his abilities, which were as rusty as the clamps holding the skis to his boots. The trees blurred past on either side, and it suddenly occurred to him that all his problems might be solved at a stroke. Not the Hemingway Solution after all. Call this way out the Bono Solution.

His hat blew off his head. He reached for it automatically, one of his poles flailing out ahead of him, half-seen in the dark, and all at once his balance was gone. He was going to take a tumble. And maybe that was good, as long as he didn't break his goddam leg. Falling would stop him, at least. He would just pick himself up, and—

Lights blazed out, big truck-mounted spotlights, and before his vision disappeared into dazzle, Henry glimpsed what might have been a flatbed pulp-truck pulled across the end of the Deep Cut Road. The lights were undoubtedly motion-sensitive, and there was a line of men standing in front of them.

"HALT!" a terrifying, amplified voice commanded. It could have been the voice of God. "HALT OR WE'LL FIRE!"

Henry went down hard and awkwardly. His skis

shot off his feet. One ankle bent painfully enough to make him cry out. He lost one ski-pole; the other snapped off halfway up its shaft. The wind was knocked out of him in a large frosty whoop of breath. He slid, snowplowing with his wide-open crotch, then came to rest, bent limbs forming a shape something like a swastika.

His vision began to come back, and he heard feet crunching in the snow. He flailed and managed to sit up, not able to tell if anything was broken or not.

Six men were standing about ten feet down the hill from him, their shadows impossibly long and crisp on the diamond-dusted new snow. They were all wearing parkas. They all had clear plastic masks over their mouths and noses—these looked more efficient than the painters' masks Henry had found in the snowmobile shed, but Henry had an idea that the basic purpose was the same.

The men also had automatic weapons, all of them pointed at him. It now seemed rather lucky to Henry that he had left Jonesy's Garand and his own Winchester back at the Scout. If he'd had a gun, he might have a dozen or more holes in him by now.

"I don't think I've got it," he croaked. "Whatever it is you're worried about, I don't think—"

"ON YOUR FEET!" God's voice again. Coming from the truck. The men standing in front of him blocked out at least some of the glare and Henry could see more men at the foot of the hill where the roads met. All of them had weapons, too, except for the one holding the bullhorn.

"I don't know if I can g—"

"ON YOUR FEET *NOW!*" God commanded, and one of the men in front of him made an expressive little jerking motion with the barrel of his gun.

Henry got shakily to his feet. His legs were trembling and the ankle he'd bent was outraged, but everything was holding together, at least for the time being. *Thus ends the eggman's journey,* he thought, and began to laugh. The men in front of him looked at each other uneasily, and although they pointed their rifles at him again, he was comforted to see even that small demonstration of human emotion.

In the brilliant glow of the lights mounted on the pulper's flatbed, Henry saw something lying in the snow—it had fallen from his pocket when he wiped out. Slowly, knowing they might shoot him anyway, he bent down.

"DON'T TOUCH THAT!" God cried from His loudspeaker atop the cab of the pulp-truck, and now the men down there also raised their weapons, a little hello darkness my old friend peeping from the muzzle of each.

"Bite shit and die," Henry said—one of the Beav's better efforts—and picked up the package. He held it out to the armed and masked men in front of him, smiling. "I come in peace for all mankind," he said. "Who wants a hot dog?"

CHAPTER TWELVE

JONESY

IN THE HOSPITAL

1

This was a dream.

It didn't feel like one, but it had to be. For one thing, he'd already been through March fifteenth once, and it seemed monstrously unfair to have to go through it again. For another, he could remember all sorts of things from the eight months between mid-March and mid-November—helping the kids with their home-work, Carla on the phone with her friends (many from the Narcotics Anonymous program), giving a lecture at Harvard . . . and the months of physical rehab, of course. All the endless bends, all the tiresome scream-ing as his joints stretched themselves out again, oh so reluctantly. He telling Jeannie Morin, his therapist, that he couldn't. She telling him that he could. Tears on his face, big smile on hers (that hateful undentable junior-miss smile), and in the end she had turned out to be right. He could, he was the little engine that could, but what a price the little engine had paid.

He could remember all those things and more: getting out of bed for the first time, wiping his ass for the first time, the night in early May when he'd gone to bed thinking *I'm going to get through this* for the first time, the night in late May when he and Carla had made love for the first time since the accident, and afterward he'd told her an old joke: *How do porcupines fuck? Very carefully.* He could remember watching fireworks on Memorial Day, his hip and upper thigh aching like a bastard; he could remember eating watermelon on the Fourth of July, spitting seeds into the grass and watching Carla and her sisters play badminton, his hip and upper leg still aching but not so fiercely; he could remember Henry calling in September—"Just to check in," he'd said—and talking about all sorts of things, including the annual hunting trip to Hole in the Wall come November. "Sure I'm coming," Jonesy had said, not knowing then how little he would like the feel of the Garand in his hands. They had talked about their work (Jonesy had taught the final three weeks of summer session, hopping around pretty spryly on one crutch by then), about their families, about the books they had read and the movies they had seen; Henry had mentioned again, as he had in January, that Pete was drinking too much. Jonesy, having already been through one substance-abuse war with his wife, hadn't wanted to talk about that, but when Henry passed along Beaver's suggestion that they stop in Derry and see Duddits Cavell when their week of hunting was over, Jonesy had agreed enthusiastically. It had been too long, and there was nothing like a shot of Duddits to cheer a person up. Also . . .

"Henry?" he had asked. "We made plans to go see Duddits, didn't we? We were going on St. Patrick's Day. I don't remember it, but it's written on my office calendar."

"Yeah," Henry had replied. "As a matter of fact, we did."

"So much for the luck of the Irish, huh?"

As a result of such memories, Jonesy was positive March fifteenth had already happened. There were all sorts of evidence supporting the thesis, his office calendar being Exhibit A. Yet here they were again, those troublesome Ides . . . and now, oh goddam, how was *this* for unfair, now there seemed to be more of the fifteenth than ever.

Previously, his memory of that day faded out at around ten A.M. He'd been in his office, drinking coffee and making a stack of books to take down to the History Department office, where there was a FREE WITH STUDENT ID table. He hadn't been happy, but he couldn't for the life of him remember why. According to the same office calendar on which he had spied the unkept March seventeenth appointment to go see Duddits, he'd had a March fifteenth appointment with a student named David Defuniak. Jonesy couldn't remember what it had been about, but he later found a notation from one of his grad assistants about a make-up essay from Defuniak—short-term results of the Norman

Conquest—so he supposed it had been that. Still, what was there in a make-up assignment that could possibly have made Associate Professor Gary Jones feel unhappy?

Unhappy or not, he had been humming something, humming and then scatting the words, which were close to nonsense: *Yes we can, yes we can-can, great gosh a'mighty yes we can-can.* There were a few little shreds after that—wishing Colleen, the Department secretary, a nice St. Paddy's Day, grabbing a Boston *Phoenix* from the newspaper box outside the building, dropping a quarter into the saxophone case of a skinhead just over the bridge on the Cambridge side, feeling sorry for the guy because he was wearing a light sweater and the wind coming off the Charles was sharp—but mostly what he remembered after making that stack of give-away books was darkness. Consciousness had returned in the hospital, with that droning voice from a nearby room: *Please stop, I can't stand it, give me a shot, where's Marcy, I want Marcy.* Or maybe it had been *where's Jonesy, I want Jonesy.* Old creeping death. Death pretending to be a patient. Death had lost track of him— sure, it was possible, it was a big hospital stuffed full of pain, sweating agony out its very seams—and now old creeping death was trying to find him again. Trying to trick him. Trying to make him give himself away.

This time around, though, all that merciful darkness in the middle is gone. This time around he not only wishes Colleen a happy St. Paddy's Day, he tells her a joke: *What do you call a Jamaican proctologist? A Pokémon.* He goes out, his future self—his *November* self—riding in his March head like a stowaway. His future self hears his March self think *What a beautiful day it turned out to be* as he starts walking toward his appointment with destiny in Cambridge. He tries to tell his March self that this is a bad idea, a *grotesquely* bad idea, that he can save himself months of agony just by hailing a Red Top or taking the T, but he can't get through. Perhaps all the science-fiction stories he read about time travel when he was a teenager had it right: you can't change the past, no matter how you try.

He walks across the bridge, and although the wind is a little cold, he still enjoys the sun on his face and the way it breaks into a million bright splinters on the Charles. He sings a snatch of "Here Comes the Sun," then reverts to the Pointer Sisters: *Yes we can-can, great gosh a'mighty.* Swinging his briefcase in rhythm. His sandwich is inside. Egg salad. Mmm-mmmm, Henry said. SSDD, Henry said.

Here is the saxophonist, and surprise: he's not on the end of the Mass Ave Bridge but farther up, by the MIT campus, outside one of those funky little Indian restaurants. He's shivering in the cold, bald, with nicks on his scalp suggesting he wasn't cut out to be a barber. The way he's playing "These Foolish Things" suggests he wasn't cut out to be a horn-player, either, and Jonesy wants to tell him to be a carpenter, an actor, a terrorist, anything but a musician. Instead, Jonesy actually encourages him, not dropping the quarter he previously remembered into the guy's case (it's lined with scuffed purple velvet), but a whole fistful of change—these foolish things, indeed. He blames it on the first warm sun after a long cold winter; he blames it on how well things turned out with Defuniak.

The sax-man rolls his eyes to Jonesy, thanking him but still blowing. Jonesy thinks of another joke: *What do you call a sax-player with a credit card? An optimist.*

He walks on, swinging his case, not listening to the Jonesy inside, the one who has swum upstream from November like some time-traveling salmon. *"Hey Jonesy, stop. Just a few seconds should be enough. Tie your shoe or something.* (No good, he's wearing loafers. Soon he will be wearing a cast, as well.) *That intersection up there is where it happens, the one where the Red Line stops, Mass Ave and Prospect. There's an old guy coming, a wonked-out history professor in a dark blue Lincoln Town Car and he's going to clean you like a house."*

But it's no good. No matter how hard he yells, it's no good. The phone lines are down. You can't go back, can't kill your own grandfather, can't shoot Lee Harvey Oswald as he kneels at a sixth-floor window of the Texas School Book Depository, congealing fried chicken on a paper plate beside him and his mail-order rifle aimed, can't stop yourself walking across the intersection of Mass Ave and Prospect Street with your briefcase in your hand and your copy of the Boston *Phoenix*—which you will never read—under your arm. *Sorry, sir, the lines are down somewhere in the Jefferson Tract, it's a real fuckarow up there, your call cannot go through—*

And then, oh God, this is new—the message *does* go through! As he reaches the corner, as he stands there on the curb, just about to step down into the crosswalk, it *does* go through!

"What?" he says, and the man who has stopped beside him, the first one to bend over him in a past which now may be blessedly cancelled, looks at him suspiciously and says "*I* didn't say anything," as though there might be a third with them. Jonesy barely hears him because there *is* a third, there is a voice inside him, one which sounds suspiciously like his own, and it's screaming at him to stay on the curb, to stay out of the street—

Then he hears someone crying. He looks across to the far side of Prospect and oh God, *Duddits* is there, Duddits Cavell naked except for his Underoos, and there is brown stuff smeared all around his mouth. It looks like chocolate, but Jonesy knows better. It's *dogshit,* that bastard Richie made him eat it after all, and people over there are walking back and forth regardless, ignoring him, as if Duddits wasn't there.

"Duddits!" Jonesy calls. "Duddits, hang on, man, I'm coming!"

And he plunges into the street without looking, the passenger inside helpless to do anything but ride along, understanding at last that this was exactly how and why the accident happened—the old man, yes, the old man with early-stage Alzheimer's who had no business behind the wheel of a car in the first place, but that had only been part of it. The other part, concealed in the blackness surrounding the crash until now, was this: he had seen Duddits and had simply bolted, forgetting to look.

He glimpses something more, as well: some huge pattern, something like a dreamcatcher that binds all the years since they first met Duddits Cavell in 1978, something that binds the future as well.

Sunlight twinkles on a windshield; he sees this in the corner of his left eye. A car coming, and too fast. The man who was beside him on the curb, old Mr. *I-Didn't-Say-Anything*, cries out: "Watch it, guy, watch it!" but Jonesy barely hears him. Because there is a deer on the sidewalk behind Duddits, a fine big buck, almost as big as a man. Then, just before the Town Car strikes him, Jonesy sees the deer *is* a man, a man in an orange cap and an orange flagman's vest. On his shoulder, like a hideous mascot, is a legless weasel-thing with enormous black eyes. Its tail—or maybe it's a tentacle—is curled around the man's neck. *How in God's name could I have thought he was a deer?* Jonesy thinks, and then the Lincoln strikes him and he is knocked into the street. He hears a bitter, muffled snap as his hip breaks.

2

There is no darkness, not this time; for better or worse, arc-sodiums have been installed on Memory Lane. Yet the film is confused, as if the editor took a few too many drinks at lunch and forgot just how the story was supposed to go. Part of this has to do with the strange way time has been twisted out of shape: he seems to be living in the past, present, and future all at the same time.

This is how we travel, a voice says, and Jonesy realizes it is the voice he heard weeping for Marcy, for a shot. *Once acceleration passes a certain point, all travel becomes time travel. Memory is the basis of every journey.*

The man on the corner, old Mr. I-Didn't-Say-Any-thing, bends over him, asks if he's all right, sees that he isn't, then looks up and says, "Who's got a cell phone? This guy needs an ambulance." When he raises his head, Jonesy sees there's a little cut under the guy's chin, old Mr. I-Didn't-Say-Anything probably did it that morning without even realizing it. *That's sweet,* Jonesy thinks, then the film jumps and here's an old dude in a rusty black topcoat and a fedora hat—call this elderly dickweed old Mr. What'd-I-Do. He's wandering around asking people that. He says he looked away for a moment and felt a thump—what'd I do? He says he has never liked a big car—what'd I do? He says he can't remember the name of the insurance company, but they call themselves the Good Hands People—what'd I do? There is a stain on the crotch of his trousers, and as Jonesy lies there in the street he can't help feeling a kind of exasperated pity for the old geezer—wishes he could tell him *You want to know what you did, take a look at your pants. You did Number One, Q-E-fuckin-D.*

The film jumps again. Now there are even more people gathered around him. They look very tall and Jonesy thinks it's like having a coffin's-eye view of a funeral. That makes him remember a Ray Bradbury story, he thinks it's called "The Crowd," where the people who gather at accident sites—always the same ones—determine your fate by what they say. If they stand around you murmuring that it isn't so bad, he's lucky the car swerved at the last second, you'll be okay. If, on the other hand, the people who make up the crowd start saying things like *He looks bad* or *I don't think he's going to make it,* you'll die. Always the same people. Always the same empty, avid faces. The lookie-loos who just have to see the blood and hear the groans of the injured.

In the cluster surrounding him, just behind old Mr. I-Didn't-Say-Anything, Jonesy sees Duddits Cavell, now fully dressed and looking okay—no dogshit mustache, in other words. McCarthy is there, too. *Call him old Mr. I-Stand-at-the-Door-and-Knock,* Jonesy thinks. And someone else, as well. A gray man. Only he's not a man at all, not really; he's the alien that was standing behind him while Jonesy was at the bathroom door. Huge black eyes dominate a face which is otherwise almost featureless. The saggy dewlapping elephant's skin is tighter here; old Mr. ET-Phone-Home hasn't started to succumb to the environment yet. But he will. In the end, this world will dissolve him like acid.

Your head exploded, Jonesy tries to tell the gray man, but no words come out; his mouth won't even open. And yet old Mr. ET-Phone-Home seems to hear him, because that gray head inclines slightly.

He's passing out, someone says, and before the film jumps again he hears old Mr. What'd-I-Do, the guy who hit him and smashed his hip like a china plate in a shooting gallery, telling someone *People used to say I look like Lawrence Welk.*

3

He's unconscious in the back of an ambulance but watching himself, having an actual out-of-body experience, and here is something else new, something no one bothers to tell him about later: he goes into V-tach while they are cutting his pants off, exposing a hip that looks as if someone had sewn two large and badly made doorknobs under it. V-tach, he knows exactly what that is because he and Carla never miss an episode of *ER,* they even watch the reruns on TNT, and here come the paddles, here comes the goo, and one of the EMTs is wearing a gold crucifix around his neck, it brushes Jonesy's nose as old Mr. EMT bends over what is essentially a dead body, and holy fuck *he died in the ambulance!* Why did no one ever tell him that he died in the fucking ambulance? Did they think that maybe he wouldn't be interested, that maybe he'd just go Ho-hum, been there, done that, got the tee-shirt?

"Clear!" shouts the other EMT, and just before they hit him the driver looks back and he sees it's Duddits's Mom. Then they whack him with the juice and his body jumps, all that white meat shakin on the bone, as Pete would say, and although the Jonesy watching *has* no body, he feels the electricity just the same, a great big *pow* that lights up the tree of his nerves like a skyrocket. Praise Jesus and get-down hallelujah.

The part of him on the stretcher jumps like a fish pulled from the water, then lies still. The EMT crouched behind Roberta Cavell looks down at his console and says, "Ah, man, no, flatline, hit him again." And when the other guy does, the film jumps and Jonesy's in an operating room.

No, wait, that's not quite right. *Part* of him's in the OR, but the rest of him is behind a piece of glass and looking in. Two other doctors are here, but they show no interest in the surgical team's efforts to put Jonesy-Dumpty back together again. They are playing cards. Above their heads, wavering in the airflow from a heating-vent, is the dreamcatcher from Hole in the Wall.

Jonesy has no urge to watch what's going on behind the glass—he doesn't like the bloody crater where his hip was, or the bleary gleam of shattered bone nosing out of it. Although he has no stomach to be sick to in his disembodied state, he feels sick to it just the same.

Behind him, one of the card-playing docs says, *Duddits was how we defined ourselves. Duddits was our finest hour.* To which the other replies, *You think so?* And Jonesy realizes the docs are Henry and Pete.

He turns toward them, and it seems he's not disembodied after all, because he catches a ghost of his reflection in the window looking into the operating room. He is not Jonesy anymore. Not *human* anymore. His skin is gray and his eyes are black bulbs staring out of his noseless face. He has become one of *them,* one of the—

One of the grayboys, he thinks. *That's what they call us, the grayboys. Some of them call us the space-niggers.*

He opens his mouth to say some of this, or perhaps to ask his old friends to help him—they have always helped each other, if they could—but then the film jumps again (goddam that editor, drinking on the job) and he's in bed, a hospital bed in a hospital room, and someone is calling *Where's Jonesy, I want Jonesy.*

There, he thinks with wretched satisfaction, *I always knew it was Jonesy, not Marcy. That's death calling, or maybe Death, and I must be very quiet if I'm to avoid him, he missed me in the crowd, made a grab for me in the ambulance and missed again, and now here he is in the hospital, masquerading as a patient.*

Please stop, crafty old Mr. Death groans in that hideous coaxing monotone, *I can't stand it, give me a shot, where's Jonesy, I want Jonesy.*

I'll just lie here until he stops, Jonesy thinks, *I can't get up anyway, I just had two pounds of metal put in my hip and it'll be days until I'm able to get up, maybe a week.*

But to his horror he realizes he *is* getting up, throwing the covers aside and getting out of bed, and although he can feel the sutures in his hip and across his belly straining and breaking open, spilling what is undoubtedly donated blood down his leg and into his pubic hair, soaking it, he walks across the room without a limp, through a patch of sunlight that casts a brief but very human shadow on the floor (not a grayboy now, there is that to be grateful for, at least, because the grayboys are toast), and to the door. He strolls unseen down a corridor, past a parked gurney with a bedpan on it, past a pair of laughing, talking nurses who are looking at photographs, passing them from hand to hand, and toward that droning voice. He is helpless to stop and understands that he is in the cloud. Not a redblack cloud, as both Pete and Henry sensed it, however; the cloud is gray and he floats within it, a unique particle that is not changed by the cloud, and Jonesy thinks: *I'm what they were looking for. I don't know how it can be, but I am just what they were looking for. Because . . . the cloud doesn't change me?*

Yes, sort of.

He passes three open doors. The fourth is closed. On it is a sign which reads COME IN, THERE IS NO INFECTION HERE, IL N'Y A PAS D'INFECTION ICI.

You lie, Jonesy thinks. *Cruise or Curtis or whatever his name is may be a madman, but he's right about one thing: there* is *infection.*

Blood is pouring down his legs, the bottom half of his johnny is now a bright scarlet (*the claret has really begun to flow,* the old boxing announcers used to say), but he feels no pain. Nor does he fear infection. He is unique and the cloud can only carry him, not change him. He opens the door and goes inside.

4

Is he surprised to see the gray man with the big black eyes lying in the hospital bed? Not even a little bit. When Jonesy turned and discovered this guy standing behind him back at Hole in the Wall, the sucker's head exploded. That was, all things considered, one hell of an Excedrin headache. It would put anyone in the hospital. The guy's head looks okay now, though; modern medicine is wonderful.

The room is crepitant with fungus, florid with red-gold growth. It's growing on the floor, the windowsill, the slats of the venetian blinds; it has bleared its way across the surface of the overhead light fixture and the glucose bottle (Jonesy assumes it's glucose) on the stand by the bed; little reddish-gold beards dangle from the bathroom doorknob and the crank at the foot of the bed.

As Jonesy approaches the gray thing with the sheet pulled up to its narrow hairless chest, he sees there is a single get-well card on the bedtable. FEEL BETTER SOON! is printed above a cartoon picture of a sad-looking turtle with a Band-Aid on its shell. And below the picture: FROM STEVEN SPIELBERG AND ALL YOUR PALS IN HOLLYWOOD.

This is a dream, full of a dream's tropes and in-jokes, Jonesy thinks, but he knows better. His mind is mixing things, pureeing them, making them easier to swallow, and that is the way of dreams; past, present, and future have all been stirred together, which is also like dreams, but he knows that he'd be wrong to dismiss this as nothing but a fractured fairy-tale from his subconscious. At least some of it is happening.

The bulbous black eyes are watching him. And now the sheet stirs and humps up beside the thing in the bed. What emerges from beneath it is the reddish weasel-thing that got the Beav. It is staring at him with those same glassy black eyes as it propels itself with its tail up the pillow, where it curls itself next to that narrow gray head. It was no wonder McCarthy felt a little indisposed, Jonesy thinks.

Blood continues to pour down Jonesy's legs, sticky as honey and hot as fever. It patters onto the floor and you'd think it would soon be sprouting its own colony of that reddish mold or fungus or whatever it is, a regular jungle of it, but Jonesy knows better. He is unique. The cloud can carry him, but it cannot change him.

No bounce, no play, he thinks, and then, immediately: *Shhh, shhh, keep that to yourself.*

The gray creature raises its hand in a kind of weary greeting. On it are three long fingers ending in rosy-pink nails. Thick yellow pus is oozing from beneath them. More of this stuff gleams loosely in the folds of the guy's skin, and from the corners of his—its?—eyes.

You're right, you do need a shot, Jonesy says. *Maybe a little Drāno or Lysol, something like that. Put you out of your mi—*

A terrible thought occurs to him then; for a moment it's so strong he is unable to resist the force moving him toward the bed. Then his feet begin to move again, leaving big red tracks behind him.

You're not going to drink my blood, are you? Like a vampire?

The thing in the bed smiles without smiling. *We are, so far as I can express it in your terms, vegetarians.*

Yeah, but what about Bowser there? Jonesy points to the legless weasel, and it bares a mouthful of needle teeth in a grotesque grin. *Is Bowser a vegetarian?*

You know he's not, the gray thing says, its slit of a

mouth not moving—this guy is one hell of a ventril-
oquist, you had to give him that; they'd love him in
the Catskills. *But you know you have nothing to fear from
him.*

Why? How am I different?

The dying gray thing (of course it's dying, its body
is breaking down, decaying from the inside out) does-
n't reply, and Jonesy once again thinks *No bounce, no
play.* He has an idea this is one thought the gray fellow would dearly love to read, but no chance of that;
the ability to shield his thoughts is another part of
what makes him different, unique, and *vive la dif-
férence* is all Jonesy can say (not that he *does* say it).

How am I different?

Who is Duddits? the gray thing asks, and when
Jonesy doesn't answer, the thing once more smiles
without moving its mouth. *There,* the gray thing says.
*We both have questions the other will not answer. Let's put
them aside, shall we? Facedown. They are . . . what do you
call it? What do you call it in the game?*

The crib, Jonesy says. Now he can smell the
thing's decay. It's the smell McCarthy brought into
camp with him, the smell of ether-spray. He thinks
again that he should have shot the oh-gosh oh-dear
son of a bitch, shot him before he could get in where
it was warm. Left the colony inside him to die
beneath the deer-stand in the old maple as the body
grew cold.

The crib, yes, the gray thing says. The dreamcatcher
is now in here, suspended from the ceiling and spinning slowly above the gray thing's head. *These things*

we each don't want the other to know, we'll set them aside to count later. We'll put them in the crib.

What do you want from me?

The gray creature gazes at Jonesy unblinkingly. So far as Jonesy can tell, it *can't* blink; it has neither lids nor lashes.

Nyther lids nor lashes, it says, only it's Pete's voice Jonesy hears. *Always nyther, never neether. Who's Duddits?*

And Jonesy is so surprised to hear Pete's voice that he almost by-God tells him . . . which, of course, was the intention: to surprise it out of him. This thing is crafty, dying or not. He would do well to be on his guard. He sends the gray fellow a picture of a big brown cow with a sign around its neck. The sign reads DUDDITS THE COW.

Again the gray fellow smiles without smiling, smiles inside Jonesy's head. *Duddits the cow,* it says. *I think not.*

Where are you from? Jonesy asks.

Planet X. We come from a dying planet to eat Domino's Pizza, buy on easy credit terms, and learn Italian the easy Berlitz way. Henry's voice this time. Then Mr. ET-Phone-Home reverts to its own voice . . . except, Jonesy realizes with a weary lack of surprise, its voice is *his* voice, Jonesy's voice. And he knows what Henry would say: that he's having one whopper of a hallucination in the wake of Beaver's death.

Not anymore, he wouldn't, Jonesy thinks. *Not anymore. Now he's the eggman, and the eggman knows better.*

Henry? He'll be dead soon, the gray fellow says indifferently. Its hand steals across the counterpane; the trio of long gray fingers enfolds Jonesy's hand. Its skin is warm and dry.

What do you mean? Jonesy asks, afraid for Henry . . . but the dying thing in the bed doesn't answer. It's another card for the crib, so Jonesy plays another one from his hand: *Why did you call me here?*

The gray creature expresses surprise, although its face still doesn't move. *No one wants to die alone,* it says. *I just want someone to be with. I know, we'll watch television.*

I don't want—

There's a movie I particularly want to see. You'll enjoy it, too. It's called Sympathy for the Grayboys. *Bowser! The remote!*

Bowser favors Jonesy with what seems a particularly ill-natured look, then slithers off the pillow, its flexing tail making a dry rasp like a snake crawling over a rock. On the table is a TV remote, also overgrown with fungus. Bowser seizes it, turns, and slithers back to the gray creature with the remote held in its teeth. The gray thing releases Jonesy's hand (its touch is not repulsive, but the release is still something of a relief), takes the controller, points it at the TV, and pushes the ON button. The picture that appears—blurred slightly but not hidden by the light fuzz growing on the glass—is of the shed behind the cabin. In the center of the screen is a shape hidden by a green tarp. And even before the door opens and he sees himself come in, Jonesy understands that this has already happened. The star of *Sympathy for the Grayboys* is Gary Jones.

Well, the dying creature in the bed says from its comfortable spot in the center of his brain, *we missed the credits, but really, the movie's just starting.*

That's what Jonesy's afraid of.

5

The shed door opens and Jonesy comes in. Quite the motley fellow he is, dressed in his own coat, Beaver's gloves, and one of Lamar's old orange hats. For a moment the Jonesy watching in the hospital room (he has pulled up the visitor's chair and is sitting by Mr. Gray's bed) thinks that the Jonesy in the snowmobile shed at Hole in the Wall has been infected after all, and that red moss is growing all over him. Then he remembers that Mr. Gray exploded right in front of him—his head did, anyway—and Jonesy is wearing the remains.

Only you didn't explode, he says. *You . . . you what? Went to seed?*

Shhh! says Mr. Gray, and Bowser bares its formidable headful of teeth, as if to tell Jonesy to stop being so impolite. *I love this song, don't you?*

The soundtrack is the Rolling Stones' "Sympathy for the Devil," fitting enough since this is almost the name of the movie (*my screen debut,* Jonesy thinks, *wait'll Carla and the kids see it*), but in fact Jonesy doesn't love it, it makes him sad for some reason.

How can you love it? he asks, ignoring Bowser's bared teeth—Bowser is no danger to him, and both of them know it. *How can you? It's what they were playing when they slaughtered you.*

They always slaughter us, Mr. Gray says. *Now be quiet, watch the movie, this part is slow but it gets a lot better.*

Jonesy folds his hands in his red lap—the bleeding seems to have stopped, at least—and watches *Sympathy for the Grayboys,* starring the one and only Gary Jones.

6

The one and only Gary Jones pulls the tarp off the snowmobile, spots the battery sitting on the work-table in a cardboard box, and puts it in, being careful to clamp the cables to the correct terminals. This pretty well exhausts his store of mechanical knowledge—he's a history teacher, not a mechanic, and his idea of home improvement is making the kids watch the History Channel once in a while instead of *Xena.* The key is in the ignition, and the dashboard lights come on when he turns the key—got the battery right, anyway—but the engine doesn't start. Doesn't even crank. The starter makes a *tut-tutting* sound and that's all.

"Oh dear oh gosh dadrattit number two," he says, running them all together in a monotone. He isn't sure he could manifest much in the way of emotion now even if he really wanted to. He's a horror-movie fan, has seen *Invasion of the Body Snatchers* two dozen times (he has even seen the wretched remake, the one with Donald Sutherland in it), and he knows what's going on here. His body has been snatched, most righteously and completely snatched. Although there will be no army of zombies, not even a townful. He is unique. He senses that Pete, Henry, and the Beav are also unique (*was* unique, in the Beav's case), but he is the most unique of all. You're not supposed to be able to say that—like the cheese belonging to the Farmer in the Dell, unique supposedly stands alone—but this is a rare case where that rule doesn't apply. Pete and Beaver were unique, Henry is uniquer, and he, Jonesy, is uniquest. Look, he's even starring in his own movie! How unique is *that,* as his oldest son would say.

The gray fellow in the hospital bed looks from the TV where Jonesy I is sitting astride the Arctic Cat to the chair where Jonesy II sits in his blood-sodden johnny.

What are you hiding? Mr. Gray asks.

Nothing.

Why do you keep seeing a brick wall? What is 19, besides a prime number? Who said "Fuck the Tigers"? What does that mean? What is the brick wall? When is the brick wall? What does it mean, why do you keep seeing it?

He can feel Mr. Gray prying at him, but for the time being that one kernel is safe. He can be carried, but not changed. Not entirely opened, either, it seems. Not yet, at least.

Jonesy puts his finger to his lips and gives the gray fellow's own words back to him: *Be quiet, watch the movie.*

It studies him with the black bulbs of its eyes (they are insectile, Jonesy thinks, the eyes of a praying mantis), and Jonesy can feel it prying for a moment or two longer. Then the sensation fades. There is no hurry; sooner or later it will dissolve the shell over that last kernel of pure uninvaded Jonesy, and then it will know everything it wants to know.

In the meantime, they watch the movie. And when Bowser crawls into Jonesy's lap—Bowser with his sharp teeth and his ethery antifreeze smell—Jonesy barely notices.

Jonesy I, Shed Jonesy (only that one's now actually Mr. Gray), reaches out. There are many minds to reach out to, they are hopping all over each other like late-night radio transmissions, and he finds one with the information he needs easily enough. It's like opening a file on your personal computer and finding a wonderfully detailed 3-D movie instead of words.

Mr. Gray's source is Emil "Dawg" Brodsky, from Menlo Park, New Jersey. Brodsky is an Army Tech Sergeant, a motor-pool munchkin. Only here, as part of Kurtz's Tactical Response Team, Tech Sergeant Brodsky has no rank. No one else does, either. He calls his superiors boss and those who rank below him (there are not many of those at this particular barbecue) hey you. If he doesn't know which is which, pal or buddy will do.

There are jets overflying the area, but not many (they'll be able to get all the pix they need from low earth orbit if the clouds ever clear), and they are not Brodsky's job, anyway. The jets fly out of the Air National Guard base in Bangor, and he is here in Jefferson Tract. Brodsky's job is the choppers and the trucks in the rapidly growing motor-pool (since noon, all the roads in this part of the state have been closed and the only traffic is olive-green trucks with their insignia masked). He's also in charge of setting up at least four generators to provide the electricity needed to serve the compound growing around Gosselin's Market. These needs include motion sensors, pole lights, perimeter lights, and the makeshift operating theater which is being hastily equipped in a Windstar motor home.

Kurtz has made it clear that the lights are a big deal—he wants this place as bright as day all night long. The greatest number of pole lights is going up around the barn and what used to be a horse corral and paddock behind the barn. In the field where old Reggie Gosselin's forty milkers once grazed away their days, two tents have been erected. The larger has a sign on its green roof: COMMISSARY. The other tent is white and unmarked. There are no kerosene heaters in it, as there are in the larger tent, and no need of them. This is the temporary morgue, Jonesy understands. There are only three bodies in there now (one is a banker who tried to run away, foolish man), but soon there may be lots more. Unless there's an accident that makes collecting bodies difficult or impossible. For Kurtz, the boss, such an accident would solve all sorts of problems.

And all that is by the way. Jonesy I's job is Emil Brodsky of Menlo Park.

Brodsky is striding rapidly across the snowy, muddy, churned-up ground between the helicopter landing zone and the paddock where the Ripley-positives are to be kept (there are already a good number of them in there, walking around with the bewildered expressions of freshly interned prisoners the world over, calling out to the guards, asking for cigarettes and information and making vain threats). Emil Brodsky is squat and crewcut, with a bulldog face that looks made for cheap cigars (in fact, Jonesy knows, Brodsky is a devout Catholic who has never smoked). He's as busy as a one-armed paperhanger just now. He's got earphones on and a receptionist's mike hung in front of his lips. He is in radio contact with the fuel-supply convoy coming up I-95—those guys are critical, because the helicopters out on mission are going to come back low—but he's also talking to Cambry, who is walking next to him, about the control-and-surveillance center Kurtz wants set up by nine P.M., midnight at the latest. This mission is going to be over in forty-eight hours at the outside, that's the scuttlebutt, but who the fuck knows for sure? According to the scuttlebutt, their prime target, Blue Boy, has already been taken out, but Brodsky doesn't know how anyone can be sure of that, since the big assault choppers haven't come back yet. And anyhow, their job here is simple: turn the whole works up to eleven and then yank the knobs off.

And ye gods, all at once there are *three* Jonesys: the one watching TV in the fungus-crawling hospital room, the one in the snowmobile shed . . . and Jonesy III, who suddenly appears in Emil Brodsky's crewcut Catholic head. Brodsky stops walking and simply looks up into the white sky.

Cambry walks on three or four steps by himself before realizing that Dawg has stopped cold, is just standing there in the middle of the muddy cow pasture. In the midst of all this frantic bustle—running men, hovering helicopters, revving engines—he's standing there like a robot with a dead battery.

"Boss?" Cambry asks. "Everything all right?"

Brodsky makes no reply . . . at least not to Cambry, he doesn't. To Jonesy I—Shed Jonesy—he says: *Open the engine cowling and show me the plugs.*

Jonesy has some trouble finding the catch that opens the cowling, but Brodsky directs him. Then Jonesy leans over the small engine, not looking for himself but turning his eyes into a pair of high-res cameras and sending the picture back to Brodsky.

"Boss?" Cambry asks with increasing concern. "Boss, what is it? What's wrong?"

"Nothing wrong," Brodsky says, slowly and distinctly. He pulls the headphones down around his neck; the chatter in them is a distraction. "Just let me think a minute."

And to Jonesy: *Someone yanked the plugs. Look around . . . yeah, there they are. End of the table.*

On the end of the worktable is a mayonnaise jar half filled with gasoline. The jartop has been vented—two punches with the tip of a screwdriver—to keep the fumes from building up. Sunk in it like exhibits preserved in formaldehyde are two Champion sparkplugs.

Aloud, Brodsky says "Dry them off good," and when Cambry asks, "Dry *what* off good?" Brodsky tells him absently to put a sock in it.

Jonesy fishes the plugs out, dries them off, then

seats and connects them as Brodsky directs. *Try it now,* Brodsky says, this time without moving his lips, and the snowmobile starts up with a roar. *Check the gas, too.*

Jonesy does, and says thank you.

"No problem, boss," Brodsky says, and starts walking briskly again. Cambry has to trot a little to catch up. He sees the faintly bewildered look on Dawg's face when Dawg discovers his headphones are now around his neck.

"What the hell was that all about?" Cambry asks.

"Nothing," Brodsky says, but it was something, all right; it sure as shit was something. Talking. A conversation. A . . . consultation? Yeah, that. He just can't remember exactly what the subject was. What he *can* remember is the briefing they got this morning, before daylight, when the team went hot. One of the directives, straight from Kurtz, had been to report anything unusual. Was this unusual? What, exactly, had it been?

"Had a brain-cramp, I guess," Brodsky says. "Too many things to do and not enough time to do them in. Come on, son, keep up with me."

Cambry keeps up. Brodsky resumes his divided conversation—convoy there, Cambry here—but remembers something else, some third conversation, one that is now over. Unusual or not? Probably not, Brodsky decides. Certainly nothing he could talk about to that incompetent bastard Perlmutter—as far as Pearly's concerned, if it isn't on his ever-present clipboard, it doesn't exist. Kurtz? Never. He respects the old buzzard, but fears him even more. They all do. Kurtz is smart, Kurtz is brave, but Kurtz is also the craziest ape in the jungle. Brodsky doesn't even like to walk where Kurtz's shadow has run across the ground.

Underhill? Could he talk to Owen Underhill?

Maybe . . . but maybe not. A deal like this, you could get into hack without even knowing why. He'd heard voices there for a minute or two—*a* voice, anyway—but he feels okay now. Still . . .

At Hole in the Wall, Jonesy roars out of the shed and heads up the Deep Cut Road. He senses Henry when he passes him—Henry hiding behind a tree, actually biting into the moss to keep from screaming—but successfully hides what he knows from the cloud which surrounds that last kernel of his awareness. It is almost certainly the last time he will be near his old friend, who will never make it out of these woods alive.

Jonesy wishes he could have said goodbye.

7

I don't know who made this movie, Jonesy says, *but I don't think they have to bother pressing their tuxes for the Academy Awards. In fact—*

He looks around and sees only snow-covered trees. Eyes front again and nothing but the Deep Cut Road unrolling in front of him and the snowmobile vibrating between his thighs. There was never any hospital, never any Mr. Gray. That was all a dream.

But it wasn't. And there *is* a room. Not a hospital

room, though. No bed, no TV, no IV pole. Not much of anything, actually; just a bulletin board. Two things are tacked to it: a map of northern New England with certain routes mapped—the Tracker Brothers routes—and a Polaroid photo of a teenage girl with her skirt raised to reveal a golden tuft of hair. He is looking out at the Deep Cut Road from the window. It is, Jonesy feels quite sure, the window that used to be in the hospital room. But the hospital room was no good. He had to get out of that room, because—

The hospital room wasn't safe, Jonesy thinks . . . as if this one is, as if anyplace is. And yet . . . this one's safe-*er,* maybe. This is his final refuge, and he has decorated it with the picture he supposed they all hoped to see when they went up that driveway back in 1978. Tina Jean Sloppinger, or whatever her name had been.

Some of what I saw was real . . . valid recovered memories, Henry might say. I really did think I saw Duddits that day. That's why I went into the street without looking. As for Mr. Gray . . . that's who I am now. Isn't it? Except for the part of me in this dusty, empty, uninteresting room with the used rubbers on the floor and the picture of the girl on the bulletin board, I'm all Mr. Gray. Isn't that the truth?

No answer. Which is all the answer he needs, really.

But how did it happen? How did I get here? And why? What's it for?

Still no answers, and to these questions he can supply none of his own. He's only glad he has a place where he can still be himself, and dismayed at how easily the rest of his life has been hijacked. He wishes again, with complete and bitter sincerity, that he had shot McCarthy.

8

A huge explosion ripped through the day, and although the source had to be miles away, it was still strong enough to send snow sliding off the trees. The figure on the snowmobile didn't even look around. It was the ship. The soldiers had blown it up. The byrum were gone.

A few minutes later, the collapsed lean-to hove into view on his right. Lying in front of it in the snow, one boot still caught beneath the tin roof, was Pete. He looked dead but wasn't. Playing dead wasn't an option, not in this game; he could hear Pete thinking. And as he pulled up on the snowmobile and shifted into neutral, Pete raised his head and bared his remaining teeth in a humorless grin. The left arm of his parka was blackened and melted. There seemed to be only one working finger remaining on his right hand. All of his visible skin was stippled with the byrus.

"You're not Jonesy," Pete said. "What have you done with Jonesy?"

"Get on, Pete," Mr. Gray said.

"I don't want to go anywhere with you." Pete raised his right hand—the swooning fingers, the red-gold clumps of byrus—and used it to wipe his forehead. "The fuck out of here. Get on your pony and ride."

Mr. Gray lowered the head that had once belonged to Jonesy (Jonesy watching it all from the window of his bolt-hole in the abandoned Tracker Brothers depot, unable to help or to change anything) and stared at Pete. Pete began to scream as the byrus growing all over his body tightened, the roots of the stuff digging into his muscles and nerves. The boot caught under the collapsed tin roof jerked free and Pete, still screaming, pulled himself up into a fetal position. Fresh blood burst from his mouth and nose. When he screamed again, two more teeth popped out of his mouth.

"Get on, Pete."

Weeping, holding his savaged right hand to his chest, Pete tried to get to his feet. The first effort was a failure; he sprawled in the snow again. Mr. Gray made no comment, simply sat astride the idling Arctic Cat and watched.

Jonesy felt Pete's pain and despair and wretched fear. The fear was by far the worst, and he decided to take a risk.

Pete.

Only a whisper, but Pete heard. He looked up, his face haggard and speckled with fungus—what Mr. Gray called byrus. When Pete licked his lips, Jonesy saw it was growing on his tongue, too. Outer-space thrush. Once Pete Moore had wanted to be an astronaut. Once he had stood up to some bigger boys on behalf of someone who was smaller and weaker. He deserved better than this.

No bounce, no play.

Pete almost smiled. It was both beautiful and heartbreaking. This time he made it to his feet and plodded slowly toward the snowmobile.

In the deserted office to which he had been exiled, Jonesy saw the doorknob begin to twist back and forth. *What does that mean?* Mr. Gray asked. *What is no bounce, no play? What are you doing in there? Come back to to the hospital and watch TV with me, why don't you? How did you get in there to begin with?*

It was Jonesy's turn not to answer, and he did so with great pleasure.

I'll get in, Mr. Gray said. *When I'm ready, I'll come in. You may think you can lock the door against me, but you're wrong.*

Jonesy kept silent—there was no need to provoke the creature currently in charge of his body—but he didn't think he *was* wrong. On the other hand, he didn't dare leave; he would be swallowed up if he tried. He was just a kernel in a cloud, a bit of undigested food in an alien gut.

Best to keep a low profile.

9

Pete got on behind Mr. Gray and put his arms around Jonesy's waist. Ten minutes later they motored past the overturned Scout, and Jonesy understood what had made Pete and Henry so late back from the store.

It was a wonder either of them had lived through it. He would have liked a longer look, but Mr. Gray didn't slow, just went on with the Cat's skis bouncing up and down, riding the crown of the road between the two snow-filled ruts.

Three miles or so beyond the Scout, they topped a rise and Jonesy saw a brilliant ball of yellow-white light hanging less than a foot above the road, waiting for them. It looked as hot as the flame of a welder's torch, but obviously wasn't; the snow just inches below it hadn't melted. It was almost certainly one of the lights he and Beaver had seen playing in the clouds, above the fleeing animals coming out of The Gulch.

That's right, Mr. Gray said. *What your people call a flashlight. This is one of the last. Perhaps the very last.*

Jonesy said nothing, only stared out the window of his office cell. He could feel Pete's arms around his waist, holding on mostly by instinct now, the way a nearly beaten fighter clinches with his opponent to keep from hitting the canvas. The head lying against his back was as heavy as a stone. Pete was a culture-medium for the byrus now, and the byrus liked him fine; the world was cold and Pete was warm. Mr. Gray apparently wanted him for something—what, Jonesy had no idea.

The flashlight led them another half a mile or so up the road, then veered into the woods. It slipped in between two big pines and then waited for them, spinning just above the snow. Jonesy heard Mr. Gray instruct Pete to hold on as tight as he could.

The Arctic Cat bounced and growled its way up a slight incline, its skis digging into the snow, then splashing it aside. Once they were actually under the forest canopy there was less of it, in some places none at all. In those spots the snowmobile's tread clattered angrily on the frozen ground, which was mostly rock beneath a thin cover of soil and fallen needles. They were headed north now.

Ten minutes later they bounced hard over a jut of granite and Pete went tumbling off the back with a low cry. Mr. Gray let go of the snowmobile's throttle. The flashlight also stopped, spinning above the snow. Jonesy thought it looked dimmer now.

"Get up," Mr. Gray said. He was turned around on the saddle, looking back at Pete.

"I can't," Pete said. "I'm done, fella. I—"

Then Pete began to howl and thrash on the ground again, feet kicking, his hands—one burned, the other mangled—jerking.

Stop it! Jonesy yelled. *You're killing him!*

Mr. Gray paid him no attention whatever, just remained as he was, swung around at the waist and watching Pete with deadly, emotionless patience as the byrus tightened and pulled at Pete's flesh. At last Jonesy felt Mr. Gray let up. Pete got groggily to his feet. There was a fresh cut on one cheek, and already it was swarming with byrus. His eyes were dazed and exhausted and swimming with tears. He got back on the snowmobile and his hands crept around Jonesy's waist once more.

Hold onto my coat, Jonesy whispered, and as Mr.

Gray turned forward and clapped the snowmobile back into gear, he felt Pete take hold. *No bounce, no play, right?*

No play, Pete agreed, but faintly.

Mr. Gray paid no attention this time. The flashlight, less bright but still speedy, started north again . . . or at least in a direction Jonesy assumed was north. As the snowmobile wove its way around trees, thick clumps of bushes, and knobs of rock, his sense of direction pretty much gave up. From behind them came a steady crackle of gunfire. It sounded as though someone was having a turkey-shoot.

10

About an hour later, Jonesy finally discovered why Mr. Gray had bothered with Pete. That was when the flashlight, which had dimmed to an anemic shadow of its original self, finally went out. It disappeared with a soft plosive sound—as if someone had popped a paper sack. Some leftover bit of detritus fell to the ground.

They were on a tree-lined ridge spang in the middle of the God-only-knows. Ahead of them was a snowy, forested valley; on its far side were eroded hills and brush-tangled brakes where not a single light shone. And to finish things off, the day was fading toward dusk.

Another fine mess you've gotten us into, Jonesy thought, but he sensed no dismay on Mr. Gray's part. Mr. Gray stopped the snowmobile by releasing the throttle, and then simply sat there.

North, Mr. Gray said. Not to Jonesy.

Pete answered out loud, his voice weary and slow. "How am I supposed to know? I can't even see where the sun's going down, for Christ's sake. One of my eyes is all fucked up, too."

Mr. Gray turned Jonesy's head and Jonesy saw that Pete's left eye was gone. The lid had been shoved up high, giving him a half-assed look of surprise. Growing out of the socket was a small jungle of byrus. The longest strands hung down, tickling against Pete's stubbly cheek. More strands twined through his thinning hair in lush red-gold streaks.

You know.

"Maybe I do," Pete said. "And maybe I don't want to point you there."

Why not?

"Because I doubt if what you want is healthy for the rest of us, fuckface," Pete said, and Jonesy felt an absurd sense of pride.

Jonesy saw the growth in Pete's eyesocket twitch. Pete screamed and clutched at his face. For a moment—brief but far too long—Jonesy fully imagined the reddish-gold tendrils reaching from that defunct eye into Pete's brain, where they spread like strong fingers clutching a gray sponge.

Go on, Pete, tell him! Jonesy cried. *For Christ's sake, tell him!*

The byrus grew still again. Pete's hand dropped from his face, which was now deathly pale where it wasn't reddish-gold. "Where are you, Jonesy?" he asked. "Is there room for two?"

The short answer, of course, was no. Jonesy didn't understand what had happened to him, but knew that his continued survival—that last kernel of autonomy—somehow depended on his staying right where he was. If he so much as opened the door, he would be gone for good.

Pete nodded. "Didn't think so," he said, and then spoke to the other. "Just don't hurt me anymore, fella."

Mr. Gray only sat, looking at Pete with Jonesy's eyes and making no promises.

Pete sighed, then raised his scorched left hand and extended one finger. He closed his eyes and began to tick his finger back and forth, back and forth. And as he did it, Jonesy came close to understanding everything. What had that little girl's name been? Rinkenhauer, wasn't it? Yes. He couldn't remember the first name, but a clumsy handle like Rinkenhauer was hard to forget. She had also gone to Mary M. Snowe, aka The Retard Academy, although by then Duddits had gone on to Vocational. And Pete? Pete had always had a funny trick of remembering things, but after Duddits—

The words came back to Jonesy as he crouched in his dirty little cell, looking out at the world which had been stolen from him . . . only they weren't really words at all, only those open vowel sounds, so strangely beautiful:

Ooo eee a yine, Ete? Do you see the line, Pete?

Pete, his face full of dreamy, surprised wonder, had said yes, he saw it. And he had been doing the thing with his finger then, that tick-tock thing, just as he was now.

The finger stopped, the tip still trembling minutely, like a dowsing rod at the edge of an aquifer. Then Pete pointed at the ridge on a line slightly to starboard of the snowmobile's current heading.

"There," he said, and dropped his hand. "Due north. Sight on that rock-face. The one with the pine growing out of the middle. Do you see it?"

Yes, I see it. Mr. Gray turned forward and put the snowmobile back into gear. Jonesy wondered fleetingly how much gas was left in the tank.

"Can I get off now?" Meaning, of course, could he die now.

No.

And they were off again, with Pete clinging weakly to Jonesy's coat.

11

They skirted the rock-face, climbed to the top of the highest hill beyond it, and here Mr. Gray paused again so his substitute flashlight could rehead them. Pete did so and they continued on, now moving on a path that was a little bit west of true north. Daylight continued to fade. Once they heard helicopters—at least two, maybe as many as four—coming toward them. Mr. Gray bulled the snowmobile into a thick stand of underbrush, heedless of the branches that slapped at Jonesy's face, drawing blood from his cheeks and brow. Pete tumbled off the back again. Mr. Gray killed the

Cat's engine, then dragged Pete, who was moaning and semi-conscious, under the thickest growth of bushes. There they waited until the helicopters passed over. Jonesy felt Mr. Gray reach up to one of the crew and quickly scan him, perhaps cross-checking what the man knew with what Pete had been telling him. When the choppers had passed off to the southeast, apparently heading back to their base, Mr. Gray re-started the snowmobile and they went on. It had begun to snow again.

An hour later they stopped on another rise and Pete fell off the Cat again, this time tumbling to the side. He raised his face, but most of his face was gone, buried under a beard of vegetation. He tried to speak aloud and couldn't; his mouth was stuffed, his tongue buried under a lush mat of byrus.

I can't, man. I can't, no more, please, let me be.

"Yes," Mr. Gray said. "I think you've served your purpose."

Pete! Jonesy cried. Then, to Mr. Gray: *No, No, don't!*

Mr. Gray paid no attention, of course. For a moment Jonesy saw silent understanding in Pete's remaining eye. And relief. For that moment he was still able to touch Pete's mind—his boyhood friend, the one who always stood outside the gate at DJHS, one hand cupped over his mouth, hiding a cigarette that wasn't really there, the one who was going to be an astronaut and see the world entire from earth orbit, one of the four who had helped save Duddits from the big boys.

For one moment. Then he felt something leap

from Mr. Gray's mind and the stuff growing on Pete did not just twitch but *clenched*. There was a tenebrous creaking sound as Pete's skull cracked in a dozen places. His face—what remained of it—pulled inward in a kind of yank, making him old at a stroke. Then he fell forward and snow began to fleck the back of his parka.

You bastard.

Mr. Gray, indifferent to Jonesy's curse and Jonesy's anger, made no reply. He faced forward again. The building wind dropped momentarily when he did, and a hole opened in the curtain of snow. About five miles northwest of their current position, Jonesy saw moving lights—not flashlights but headlights. Lots of them. Trucks moving in convoy along the turnpike. Trucks and nothing else, he supposed. This part of Maine belonged to the military now.

And they're all looking for you, asshole, he spat as the snowmobile began to roll again. The snow closed back around them, cutting off their momentary view of the trucks, but Jonesy knew that Mr. Gray would have no trouble finding the turnpike. Pete had gotten him this far, to a part of the quarantine zone where Jonesy supposed little trouble was expected. He was counting on Jonesy to take him the rest of the way, because Jonesy was different. For one thing, he was clear of the byrus. The byrus didn't like him for some reason.

You'll never get out of here, Jonesy said.

I will, Mr. Gray said. *We always die and we always live. We always lose and we always win. Like it or not, Jonesy, we're the future.*

If that's true, it's the best reason I ever heard for living in the past, Jonesy replied, but from Mr. Gray there was no answer. Mr. Gray as an entity, a consciousness, was gone, merged back into the cloud. There was only enough of him left to run Jonesy's motor skills and keep the snowmobile pointed toward the turnpike. And Jonesy, carried helplessly forward on whatever mission this thing had, took slender comfort from two things. One was that Mr. Gray didn't know how to get at the last piece of him, the tiny part that existed in his memory of the Tracker Brothers office. The other was that Mr. Gray didn't know about Duddits—about no bounce, no play.

Jonesy intended to make sure Mr. Gray didn't find out.

At least not yet.

CHAPTER THIRTEEN

AT GOSSELIN'S

1

To Archie Perlmutter, high-school valedictorian (speech topic: "The Joys and the Responsibilities of Democracy"), onetime Eagle Scout, faithful Presbyterian, and West Point grad, Gosselin's Country Market no longer looked real. Now spotlighted by enough candlepower to illuminate a small city, it looked like a set in a movie. Not just any movie, either, but the sort of James Cameron extravaganza where the catering costs alone would amount to enough to feed the people of Haiti for two years. Even the steadily increasing snow did not cut into the glare of the lights very much, or change the illusion that the whole works, from the crappy siding to the pair of tin woodstove stacks sticking acrooked out of the roof to the single rusty gaspump out front, was simply set-dressing.

This would be Act One, Pearly thought as he strode briskly along with his clipboard tucked under his arm

(Archie Perlmutter had always felt he was a man of considerable artistic nature . . . commercial, too). *We fade in on an isolated country store. The oldtimers are sitting around the woodstove—not the little one in Gosselin's office but the big one in the store itself—while the snow pelts down outside. They're talking about lights in the sky . . . missing hunters . . . sightings of little gray men skulking around in the woods. The store owner—call him Old Man Rossiter—scoffs. "Oh gosh 'n fishes, you're all a buncha old wimmin!" he says, and just then the whole place is bathed in these brilliant lights (think* Close Encounters of the Third Kind) *as a UFO settles down to the ground! Bloodthirsty aliens come piling out, firing their deathrays! It's like* Independence Day, *only, here's the hook, in the woods!*

Beside him, Melrose, the cook's third (which was about as close as anyone got to an official rating on this little adventure), struggled to keep up. He was wearing sneakers on his feet instead of shoes or boots—Perlmutter had dragged him out of Spago's, which was what the men called the cook-tent—and he kept slipping. Men (and a few women) passed everywhere around them, mostly at the double. Many were talking into lavalier mikes or walkie-talkies. The sense that this was a movie-set instead of a real place was enhanced by the trailers, the semis, the idling helicopters (the worsening weather had brought them all back in), and the endless conflicting roar of motors and generators.

"Why does he want to see me?" Melrose asked again. Out of breath and whinier than ever. They were passing the paddock and corral to one side of Gosselin's barn, now. The old and dilapidated fence (it had been ten years or more since there'd been an actual horse in the corral or exercised in the paddock) had been reinforced by alternating strands of barbwire and smoothwire. There was an electrical charge running through the smoothwire, probably not lethal but high enough to lay you out on the ground, convulsing . . . and the charge could be jacked up to lethal levels if the natives became restless. Behind this wire, watching them, were twenty or thirty men, Old Man Gosselin among them (in the James Cameron version, Gosselin would be played by some craggy oldtimer like Bruce Dern). Earlier, the men behind the wire would have called out, issuing threats and angry demands, but since they'd seen what happened to that banker from Massachusetts who tried to run, their peckers had wilted considerably, poor fellows. Seeing someone shot in the head took a lot of the fuck-you out of a man. And then there was the fact that all the ops guys were now wearing nose-and-mouth masks. That had to take whatever fuck-you was left.

"Boss?" *Almost* whining had given way to *actual* whining. The sight of American citizens standing behind barbed wire had apparently added to Melrose's unease. "Boss, come on—why does the big boy want to see me? Big boy shouldn't know a cook's third even exists."

"I don't know," Pearly replied. It was the truth.

Up ahead, standing at the head of what had been dubbed Eggbeater Alley, was Owen Underhill and some guy from the motor-pool. The motor-pool guy was almost shouting into Underhill's ear in order to make himself heard over the racket of the idling helicopters. Surely, Perlmutter thought, they'd shut the choppers down soon; nothing was going to fly in this shit, an early-season blizzard that Kurtz called "our gift from God." When he said stuff like that, you couldn't tell if Kurtz really meant it or was just being ironic. He always *sounded* like he meant it . . . but then sometimes he would laugh. The kind of laugh that made Archie Perlmutter nervous. In the movie, Kurtz would be played by James Woods. Or maybe Christopher Walken. Neither one of them looked like Kurtz, but had George C. Scott looked like Patton? Case closed.

Perlmutter abruptly detoured toward Underhill. Melrose tried to follow and went on his ass, cursing. Perlmutter tapped Underhill on his shoulder, then hoped his mask would at least partially conceal his expression of surprise when the other man turned. Owen Underhill looked as if he had aged ten years since stepping off the Millinocket School Department bus.

Leaning forward, Pearly shouted over the wind: "Kurtz in fifteen! Don't forget!"

Underhill gave him an impatient wave to say he wouldn't, and turned back to the motor-pool guy. Perlmutter had him placed now; Brodsky, his name was. The men called him Dawg.

Kurtz's command post, a humongous Winnebago (if this were a movie-set, it would be the star's home away from home, or perhaps Jimmy Cameron's), was just ahead. Pearly picked up the pace, facing boldly forward into the *flick-flick-flick* of the snow. Melrose scurried to catch up, brushing snow off his coverall.

"C'mon, Skipper," he pleaded. "Don'tcha have any idea?"

"No," Perlmutter said. He had no clue as to why Kurtz would want to see a cook's third with everything up and running in high gear. But he thought both of them knew it couldn't be anything good.

2

Owen turned Emil Brodsky's head, placed the bulb of his mask against the man's ear, and said: "Tell me again. Not all of it, just about the part you called the mind-fuck."

Brodsky didn't argue but took ten seconds or so to arrange his thoughts. Owen gave it to him. There was his appointment with Kurtz, and debriefing after that—plenty of crew, reams of paperwork—and God alone knew what gruesome tasks to follow, but he sensed this was important.

Whether or not he would tell Kurtz remained to be seen.

At last Brodsky turned Owen's head, placed the bulb of his own mask against Owen's ear, and began to talk. The story was a little more detailed this time, but essentially the same. He had been walking across the field next to the store, talking to Cambry beside him and to an approaching fuel-supply convoy at the same time, when all at once he felt as if his mind had been hijacked. He had been in a cluttery old shed with someone he couldn't quite see. The man wanted to get a snowmobile going, and couldn't. He needed the Dawg to tell him what was wrong with it.

"I asked him to open the cowling!" Brodsky shouted into Owen's ear. "He did, and then it seemed like I was looking through his eyes . . . but with my *mind*, do you see?"

Owen nodded.

"I could see right away what was wrong, someone had taken the plugs out. So I told the guy to look around, which he did. Which we both did. And there they were, in a jar of gasoline on the table. My Dad used to do the same thing with the plugs from his Lawnboy and his rototiller when the cold weather came."

Brodsky paused, clearly embarrassed either by what he was saying or how he imagined it must sound. Owen, who was fascinated, gestured for him to go on.

"There ain't much more. I told him to fish em out, dry em off, and pop em in. It was like a billion times I've helped some guy work on somethin . . . except I wasn't *there*—I was *here*. None of it was happening."

Owen said: "What next?" Bellowing to be heard over the engines, but the two of them still as private as a priest and his customer in a church confessional.

"Started up first crank. I told him to check the gas while he was at it, and there was a full tank. He said thanks." Brodsky shook his head wonderingly. "And *I* said, No problem, boss. Then I kind of thumped back into my own head and I was just walking along. You think I'm crazy?"

"No. But I want you to keep this to yourself for the time being."

Under his mask, Brodsky's lips spread in a grin. "Oh man, no problem there, either. I just . . . well, we're supposed to report anything unusual, that's the directive, and I thought—"

Quickly, not giving Brodsky time to think, Owen rapped: "What was his name?"

"Jonesy Three," Dawg replied, and then his eyes widened in surprise. "Holy shit! I didn't know I knew that."

"Is that some sort of Indian name, do you think? Like Sonny Sixkiller or Ron Nine Moons?"

"Coulda been, but . . ." Brodsky paused, thinking, then burst out: "It was awful! Not when it was happening, but later on . . . thinking about it . . . it was like being . . ." He dropped his voice. "Like being raped, sir."

"Let it go," Owen said. "You must have a few things to do?"

Brodsky smiled. "Only a few thousand."

"Then get started."

"Okay." Brodsky took a step away, then turned back. Owen was looking toward the corral, which had once held horses and now held men. Most of the detainees were in the barn, and all but one of the two dozen or so out here were huddled up together, as if for comfort. The one who stood apart was a tall, skinny drink of water wearing big glasses that made him look sort of like an owl. Brodsky looked from the doomed owl to Underhill. "You're not gonna get me in hack over this, are you? Send me to see the shrink?" Unaware, of course, both of them unaware that the skinny guy in the old-fashioned horn-rims *was* a shrink.

"Not a ch—" Owen began. Before he could finish, there was a gunshot from Kurtz's Winnebago and someone began to scream.

"Boss?" Brodsky whispered. Owen couldn't hear him over the contending motors; he read the word off Brodsky's lips. And: "Ohh, fuck."

"Go on, Dawg," Owen said. "Not your business."

Brodsky looked at him a moment longer, wetting his lips inside his mask. Owen gave him a nod, trying to project an air of confidence, of command, of everything's-under-control. Maybe it worked, because Brodsky returned the nod and started away.

From the Winnebago with the hand-lettered sign on the door (THE BUCK STOPS HERE), the screaming continued. As Owen started that way, the man standing by himself in the compound spoke to him. "Hey! Hey, you! Stop a minute, I need to talk to you!"

I'll bet, Underhill thought, not slowing his pace. *I bet you've got a whale of a tale to tell and a thousand reasons why you should be let out of here right now.*

"Overhill? No, *Underhill.* That's your name, isn't it? Sure it is. I have to talk to you—it's important to both of us!"

Owen stopped in spite of the screaming from the Winnebago, which was breaking up into hurt sobs now. Not good, but at least it seemed that no one had been killed. He took a closer look at the man in the spectacles. Skinny as a rail and shivering in spite of the down parka he was wearing.

"It's important to Rita," the skinny man called over the contending roar of the engines. "To Katrina, too." Speaking the names seemed to sap the geeky guy, as if he had drawn them up like stones from some deep well, but in his shock at hearing the names of his wife and daughter from this stranger's lips, Owen barely noticed. The urge to go to the man and ask him how he knew those names was strong, but he was currently out of time . . . he had an appointment. And just because no one had been killed yet didn't mean no one *would* be killed.

Owen gave the man behind the wire a final look, marking his face, and then hurried on toward the Winnebago with the sign on the door.

3

Perlmutter had read *Heart of Darkness,* had seen *Apocalypse Now,* and had on many occasions thought that the name Kurtz was simply a little too convenient. He would have bet a hundred dollars (a great sum for a non-wagering artistic fellow such as himself) that it wasn't the boss's real name—that the boss's real name was Arthur Holsapple or Dagwood Elgart, maybe even Paddy Maloney. Kurtz? Unlikely. It was almost surely an affectation, as much a prop as George Patton's pearl-handled .45. The men, some of whom had been with Kurtz since Desert Storm (Archie Perlmutter didn't go back nearly that far), thought he was one crazy motherfucker, and so did Perlmutter . . . crazy like Patton had been crazy. Crazy like a fox, in other words. Probably when he was shaving in the morning he looked at his reflection and practiced saying "The horror, the horror" in just the right Marlon Brando whisper.

So Pearly felt disquiet but no *unusual* disquiet as he escorted Cook's Third Melrose into the over-warm command trailer. And Kurtz looked pretty much okay. The skipper was sitting in a cane rocking chair in the living-room area. He had removed his coverall—it hung on the door through which Perlmutter and Melrose had entered—and received them in his longjohns. From one post of the rocking chair his pistol hung by its belt, not a pearl-handled .45 but a nine-millimeter automatic.

All the electronic gear was rebounding. On Kurtz's desk the fax hummed constantly, piling up paper. Every fifteen seconds or so, Kurtz's iMac cried "You've got mail!" in its cheery robot voice. Three radios, all turned low, crackled and hopped with transmissions. Mounted on the fake pine behind the desk were two framed photographs. Like the sign on the door, the photos went with Kurtz everywhere. The one on the left, titled INVESTMENT, showed an angelic young fellow in a Boy Scout uniform, right hand raised in the three-fingered Boy Scout salute. The one on the right, labelled DIVIDEND, was an aerial photograph of Berlin taken in the spring of 1945. Two or three buildings still stood, but mostly what the camera showed was witless brick-strewn rubble.

Kurtz waved his hand at the desk. "Don't mind all

that, boys—it's just noise. I've got Freddy Johnson to deal with it, but I sent him over to the commissary to grab some chow. Told him to take his time, go through the whole four courses, soup to nuts, *poisson* to sorbet, because this situation here . . . boys, this situation here is near-bout . . . *STABILIZED!*" He gave them a ferocious FDR grin and began to rock in his chair. Beside him, the pistol swung in the holster at the end of its belt like a pendulum.

Melrose returned Kurtz's smile tentatively, Perlmutter with less reserve. He had Kurtz's number, all right; the boss was an existential wannabe . . . and you wanted to believe that was a good call. A *brilliant* call. A liberal arts education didn't have many benefits in the career military, but there were a few. Phrase-making was one of them.

"My only order to Lieutenant Johnson—whoops, no rank on this one, to my *good pal* Freddy Johnson is what I meant to say—was that he say grace before chowing in. Do you pray, boys?"

Melrose nodded as tentatively as he had smiled; Perlmutter did so indulgently. He felt sure that, like his name, Kurtz's oft-professed belief in God was plumage.

Kurtz rocked, looking happily at the two men with the snow melting from their footgear and puddling on the floor. "The best prayers are the child's prayers," Kurtz said. "The simplicity, you know. 'God is great, God is good, let us thank Him for our food.' Isn't that simple? Isn't it beautiful?"

"Yes, b—" Pearly began.

"Shut the fuck up, you hound," Kurtz said cheerfully. Still rocking. The gun still swinging back and forth at the end of its belt. He looked from Pearly to Melrose. "What do *you* think, laddie-buck? Is that a beautiful little prayer, or is that a beautiful little prayer?"

"Yes, s—"

"Or *Allah akhbar,* as our Arab friends say; 'there is no God but God.' What could be more simple than that? It cuts the pizza directly down the middle, if you see what I mean."

They didn't reply. Kurtz was rocking faster now, and the pistol was swinging faster, and Perlmutter began to feel a little antsy, as he had earlier in the day, before Underhill arrived and sort of cooled Kurtz out. This was probably just more plumage, but—

"Or Moses at the burning bush!" Kurtz cried. His lean and rather horsey face lit with a daffy smile. " 'Who'm I talking to?' Moses asks, and God gives him the old 'I yam what I yam and that's all that I yam, uck-uck-uck.' What a kidder, that God, eh, Mr. Melrose, did you *really* refer to our emissaries from the Great Beyond as 'space-niggers'?"

Melrose's mouth dropped open.

"Answer me, buck."

"Sir, I—"

"Call me sir again while the group is hot, Mr. Melrose, and you will celebrate your next two birthdays in the stockade, do you understand that? Catch my old drift-ola?"

"Yes, boss." Melrose had snapped to attention, his face dead white except for the patches of cold-induced red on his cheeks, patches that were cut neatly in two by the straps of his mask.

"Now *did* you or did you not refer to our visitors as 'space-niggers'?"

"Sir, I may have just in passing said something—"

Moving with a speed Perlmutter could scarcely credit (it was like a special effect in a James Cameron movie, almost), Kurtz snatched the nine-millimeter from the swinging holster, pointed it without seeming to aim, and fired. The top half of the sneaker on Melrose's left foot exploded. Fragments of canvas flew. Blood and flecks of flesh splattered Perlmutter's pantsleg.

I didn't see that, Pearly thought. *That didn't happen.*

But Melrose was screaming, looking down at his ruined left foot with agonized disbelief and howling his head off. Perlmutter could see bone in there, and felt his stomach turn over.

Kurtz didn't get himself out of his rocker as quickly as he'd gotten his gun out of his holster—Perlmutter could at least see this happening—but it was still fast. *Spookily* fast.

He grabbed Melrose by the shoulder and peered into the cook third's contorted face with great intensity. "Stop that blatting, laddie-buck."

Melrose carried on blatting. His foot was *gushing,* and the part with the toes on it looked to Pearly as if it might be severed from the part with the heel on it. Pearly's world went gray and started to lose focus. With all the force of his will, he forced that grayness away. If he passed out now, Christ alone knew what

Kurtz might do to him. Perlmutter had heard stories and had dismissed ninety percent of them out of hand, thinking they were either exaggerations or Kurtz-planted propaganda designed to enhance his loony-crafty image.

Now I know better, Perlmutter thought. *This isn't myth-making; this is the myth.*

Kurtz, moving with a finicky, almost surgical precision, placed the barrel of his pistol against the center of Melrose's cheese-white forehead.

"Squelch that womanish bawling, buck, or I'll squelch it for you. These are hollow-points, as I think even a dimly lit American like yourself must now surely know."

Melrose somehow choked the screams off, turned them into low, in-the-throat sobs. This seemed to satisfy Kurtz.

"Just so you can hear me, buck. You *have* to hear me, because you have to spread the word. I believe, praise God, that your foot, what's left of it, will articulate the basic *concept,* but it's your own sacred mouth that must share the details. So are you listening, bucko? Are you listening for the details?"

Still sobbing, his eyes starting from his face like blue glass balls, Melrose managed a nod.

Quick as a striking snake, Kurtz's head turned and Perlmutter clearly saw the man's face. The madness there was stamped into the features as clearly as a warrior's tattoos. At that moment everything Perlmutter had ever believed about his OIC fell down.

"What about you, bucko? Listening? Because

you're a messenger, too. All of us are messengers."

Pearly nodded. The door opened and he saw, with unutterable relief, that the newcomer was Owen Underhill. Kurtz's eyes flew to him.

"Owen! Me foine bucko! Another witness! Another, praise God, another messenger! Are you listening? Will you carry the word hence from this happy place?"

Expressionless as a poker-player in a high-stakes game, Underhill nodded.

"Good! Good!"

Kurtz returned his attention to Melrose.

"I quote from the *Manual of Affairs,* Cook's Third Melrose, Part 16, Section 4, Paragraph 3—'Use of inappropriate epithets, whether racial, ethnic, or gender-based, are counterproductive to morale and run counter to armed service protocol. When use is proven, the user will be punished immediately by court-martial or in the field by appropriate command personnel,' end quote. Appropriate command personnel, that's me, user of inappropriate epithets, that's you. Do you understand, Melrose? Do you get the drift-ola?"

Melrose, blubbering, tried to speak, but Kurtz cut him off. In the doorway Owen Underhill continued to stand completely still as the snow melted on his shoulders and ran down the transparent bulb of his mask like sweat. His eyes remained fixed on Kurtz.

"Now, Cook's Third Melrose, what I have quoted to you in the presence of these, these praise God witnesses, is called 'an order of conduct,' and it means no spicktalk, no mockietalk, no krauttalk or redskin talk. It also means as is most applicable in the current situation no space-niggertalk, do you understand *that*?"

Melrose tried to nod, then reeled, on the verge of passing out. Perlmutter grabbed him by the shoulder and got him straight again, praying that Melrose wouldn't conk before this was over. God only knew what Kurtz might do to Melrose if Melrose had the temerity to turn out the lights before Kurtz was done reading him the riot act.

"We are going to wipe these invading assholes out, my friend, and if they ever come back to Terra Firma, we are going to rip off their collective gray head and shit down their collective gray neck; if they persist we will use their own technology, which we are already well on our way to grasping, against them, returning to their place of origin in their own ships or ships like them built by General Electric and DuPont and praise God Microsoft and once there we will burn their cities or hives or goddam anthills, whatever they live in, we'll napalm their amber waves of grain and nuke their purple mountains' majesty, praise God, *Allah akhbar*, we will pour the fiery piss of America into their lakes and oceans . . . but we will do it in a way that is *proper* and *appropriate* and without regard to *race* or *gender* or *ethnicity* or *religious preference*. We're going to do it because they came to the wrong neighborhood and knocked on the wrong fucking door. This is not Germany in 1938 or Oxford Mississippi in 1963. Now, Mr. Melrose, do you think you can spread that message?"

Melrose's eyes rolled up to the wet whites and his knees unhinged. Perlmutter once more grabbed his shoulder in an effort to hold him up, but it was a lost cause this time; down Melrose went.

"Pearly," Kurtz whispered, and when those burning blue eyes fell on him, Perlmutter thought he had never been so frightened in his life. His bladder was a hot and heavy bag inside him, wanting only to squirt its contents into his coverall. He felt that if Kurtz saw a dark patch spreading on his adjutant's crotch, Kurtz might shoot him out of hand, in his present mood . . . but that didn't seem to help the situation. In fact, it made it worse.

"Yes, s . . . boss?"

"Will he spread the word? Will he be a good messenger? Do you reckon he took enough in to do that, or was he too concerned with his damned old *foot*?"

"I . . . I . . ." In the doorway, he saw Underhill nod at him almost imperceptibly, and Pearly took heart. "Yes, boss—I think he heard you five-by."

Kurtz seemed first surprised by Perlmutter's vehemence, then gratified. He turned to Underhill. "What about you, Owen? Do you think he'll spread the word?"

"Uh-huh," Underhill said. "If you get him to the infirmary before he bleeds to death on your rug."

Kurtz's mouth turned up at the corners and he barked, "See to that, Pearly, will you?"

"Right now," Perlmutter said, starting toward the door. Once past Kurtz, he gave Underhill a look of fervent gratitude which Underhill either missed or chose not to acknowledge.

"Double-time, Mr. Perlmutter. Owen, I want to

talk to you *mano a mano,* as the Irish say." He stepped over Melrose's body without looking down at it and walked briskly into the kitchenette. "Coffee? Freddy made it, so I can't swear it's drinkable . . . no, I can't *swear,* but . . ."

"Coffee would be good," Owen Underhill said. "You pour and I'll try to stop this fellow's bleeding."

Kurtz stood by the Mr. Coffee on the counter and gave Underhill a look of darkly brilliant doubt. "Do you really think that's necessary?"

That was where Perlmutter went out. Never before in his life had stepping into a storm felt so much like an escape.

4

Henry stood at the fence (not touching the wire; he had seen what happened when you did that), waiting for Underhill—that was his name, all right—to come back out of what had to be the command post, but when the door opened, one of the other fellows he'd seen go in came hustling out. Once down the steps, the guy started running. The guy was tall, and possessed one of those earnest faces Henry associated with middle management. Now the face looked terrified, and the man almost fell before he got fully into stride. Henry was rooting for that.

The middle manager managed to keep his balance after the first slip, but halfway to a couple of semi trailers that had been pushed together, his feet flew out from beneath him and he went on his ass. The clipboard he'd been carrying went sliding like a toboggan for leprechauns.

Henry held his hands out and clapped as loudly as he could. Probably not loud enough to be heard over all the motors, so he cupped them around his mouth and yelled: *"Way to go shitheels! Let's look at the videotape!"*

The middle manager got up without looking at him, retrieved his clipboard, and ran on toward the two semi trailers.

There was a group of eight or nine guys standing by the fence about twenty yards from Henry. Now one of them, a portly fellow in an orange down-filled parka that made him look like the Pillsbury Dough Boy, walked over.

"I don't think you should do that, fella." He paused, then lowered his voice. "They shot my brother-in-law."

Yes. Henry saw it in the man's head. The portly man's brother-in-law, also portly, talking about his lawyer, his rights, his job with some investment company in Boston. The soldiers nodding, telling him it was just temporary, the situation was normalizing and would be straightened out by dawn, all the time hustling the two overweight mighty hunters toward the barn, which already held a pretty good trawl, and all at once the brother-in-law had broken away, running toward the motor-pool, and boom-boom, out go the lights.

The portly man was telling Henry some of this, his pale face earnest in the newly erected lights, and Henry interrupted him.

"What do you think they're going to do to the rest of us?"

The portly man looked at Henry, shocked, then backed off a step, as if he thought Henry might have something contagious. Quite funny, when you thought about it, because they *all* had something contagious, or at least this team of government-funded cleaners *thought* they did, and in the end it would come to the same.

"You can't be serious," the portly man said. Then, almost indulgently: "This is America, you know."

"Is it? You seeing a lot of due process, are you?"

"They're just . . . I'm sure they're just . . ." Henry waited, interested, but there was no more, at least not in this vein. "That was a gunshot, wasn't it?" the portly man asked. "And I think I heard some screaming."

From the two pushed-together trailers there emerged two hurrying men with a stretcher between them. Following them with marked reluctance came the middle manager, his clipboard once more tucked firmly beneath his arm.

"I'd say you got that right." Henry and the portly man watched as the stretcher-bearers hurried up the steps of the Winnebago. As Mr. Middle Management made his closest approach to the fence, Henry called out to him, "How's it going, shitheels? Having any fun yet?"

The portly man winced. The guy with the clipboard gave Henry a single dour look and then trudged on toward the Winnebago.

"This is just . . . it's just some sort of emergency situation," the portly man said. "It'll be straightened out by tomorrow morning, I'm sure."

"Not for your brother-in-law," Henry said.

The portly man looked at him, mouth tucked in and trembling slightly. Then he returned to the other men, whose views no doubt more closely corresponded to his own. Henry turned back to the Winnebago and resumed waiting for Underhill to come out. He had an idea that Underhill was his only hope . . . but whatever Underhill's doubts about this operation might be, the hope was a thin one. And Henry had only one card to play. The card was Jonesy. They didn't know about Jonesy.

The question was whether or not he should tell Underhill. Henry was terribly afraid that telling the man would do no good.

5

About five minutes after Mr. Middle Management followed the stretcher-bearers into the 'Bago, the three of them came out again, this time with a fourth on the stretcher. Under the brilliant overhead lights, the wounded man's face was so pale it looked purple. Henry was relieved to see that it wasn't Underhill, because Underhill was different from the rest of these maniacs.

Ten minutes passed. Underhill still hadn't come out of the command post. Henry waited in the thickening snow. There were soldiers watching the inmates (that was what they were, inmates, and it was best not to gild the lily), and eventually one of them strolled over. The men who had been stationed at the T-junction of the Deep Cut and Swanny Pond Roads had pretty well blinded Henry with their lights, and he didn't recognize this man by his face. Henry was both delighted and deeply unsettled to realize that minds also had features, every bit as distinctive as a pretty mouth, a broken nose, or a crooked eye. This was one of the guys who had been out there, the one who had hit him in the ass with the stock of his rifle when he decided Henry wasn't moving toward the truck fast enough. Whatever had happened to Henry's mind was skitzy; he couldn't pick out this guy's name, but he knew that the man's brother's name was Frankie, and that in high school Frankie had been tried and acquitted on a rape charge. There was more, as well—unconnected jumbles of stuff, like the contents of a wastebasket. Henry realized that he was looking at an actual river of consciousness, and at the flotsam and jetsam the river was carrying along. The humbling thing was how prosaic most of it was.

"Hey there," the soldier said, amiably enough. "It's the smartass. Want a hot dog, smartass?" He laughed.

"Already got one," Henry said, smiling himself. And Beaver popped out of his mouth, as Beaver had a way of doing. "Fuck off Freddy."

The soldier stopped laughing. "Let's see how smart your ass is twelve hours from now," he said. The image that went floating by, borne on the river between this man's ears, was of a truck filled with bodies, white limbs all tangled together. "You growing the Ripley yet, smartass?"

Henry thought: *the byrus. That's what he means. The byrus is what it's really called. Jonesy knows.*

Henry didn't reply and the soldier started away, wearing the comfortable look of a man who has won on points. Curious, Henry summoned all his concentration and visualized a rifle—Jonesy's Garand, as a matter of fact. He thought: *I have a gun. I'm going to kill you with it the second you turn your back on me, asshole.*

The soldier swung around again, the comfortable look going the way of the grin and the laughter. What replaced it was a look of doubt and suspicion. "What'd you say, smartass? You say something?"

"Just wondering if you got your share of that girl—you know, the one Frankie broke in. Did he give you sloppy seconds?"

For a moment, the soldier's face was idiotic with surprise. Then it filled in with black Italian rage. He raised his rifle. To Henry, its muzzle looked like a smile. He unzipped his jacket and held it open in the thickening snow. "Go on," he said, and laughed. "Go on, Rambo, do your thing."

Frankie's brother held the gun on Henry a moment longer, and then Henry felt the man's rage pass. It had been close—he had seen the soldier trying to think of what he would say, some plausible story—but he had taken a moment too long and his forebrain had pulled the red beast back to heel. It was all so familiar. The Richie Grenadeaus never died, not really. They were the world's dragon's teeth.

"Tomorrow," the soldier said. "Tomorrow's time enough for you, smartass."

This time Henry let him go—no more teasing the red beast, although God knew it would have been easy enough. He had learned something, too . . . or confirmed what he'd already suspected. The soldier had heard his thought, but not clearly. If he'd heard it clearly he would have turned around a lot faster. Nor had he asked Henry how Henry knew about his brother Frankie. Because on some level the soldier knew what Henry did: they had been infected with telepathy, the whole walking bunch of them—they had caught it like an annoying low-grade virus.

"Only I got it worse," he said, zipping his coat back up again. So had Pete and Beaver and Jonesy. But Pete and the Beav were both dead now, and Jonesy . . . Jonesy . . .

"Jonesy got it worst of all," Henry said. And where was Jonesy now?

South . . . Jonesy had hooked back south. These guys' precious quarantine had been breached. Henry guessed they had foreseen that that might happen. It didn't worry them. They thought one or two breaches wouldn't matter.

Henry thought they were wrong.

6

Owen stood with a mug of coffee in his hand, waiting until the guys from the infirmary were gone with their burden, Melrose's sobs mercifully reduced to mutters and moans by a shot of morphine. Pearly followed them out and then Owen was alone with Kurtz.

Kurtz sat in his rocker, looking up at Owen Underhill with curious, head-cocked amusement. The raving crazyman was gone again, put away like a Halloween mask.

"I'm thinking of a number," Kurtz said. "What is it?"

"Seventeen," Owen said. "You see it in red. Like on the side of a fire engine."

Kurtz nodded, pleased. "You try sending one to me."

Owen visualized a speed limit sign: 60 MPH.

"Six," Kurtz said after a moment. "Black on white."

"Close enough, boss."

Kurtz drank some coffee. His was in a mug with I LUV MY GRANDPA printed on the side. Owen sipped with honest pleasure. It was a dirty night and a dirty job, and Freddy's coffee wasn't bad.

Kurtz had found time to put on his coverall. Now he reached into the inner pocket and brought out a large bandanna. He regarded it for a moment, then got to his knees with a grimace (it was no secret that the old man had arthritis) and began to wipe up the splatters of Melrose's blood. Owen, who thought himself surely unshockable at this point, was shocked.

"Sir . . ." Oh, fuck. "Boss . . ."

"Stow it," Kurtz said without looking up. He

moved from spot to spot, as assiduous as any washer-woman. "My father always said that you should clean up your own messes. Might make you stop and think a little bit the next time. What was my father's name, buck?"

Owen looked for it and caught just a glimpse, like a glimpse of slip under a woman's dress. "Paul?"

"Patrick, actually . . . but close. Anderson believes it's a wave, and it's expending its force now. A tele-pathic wave. Do you find that an awesome concept, Owen?"

"Yes."

Kurtz nodded without looking up, wiping and cleaning. "More awesome in concept than in fact, however—do you also find that?"

Owen laughed. The old man had lost none of his capacity to surprise. *Not playing with a full deck,* people sometimes said of unstable individuals. The trouble with Kurtz, Owen reckoned, was that he was playing with *more* than a full deck. A few extra aces in there. Also a few extra deuces, and everyone knew that deuces were wild.

"Sit down, Owen. Drink your coffee on your ass like a normal person and let me do this. I need to."

Owen thought maybe he did. He sat down and drank the coffee. Five minutes passed in this fashion, then Kurtz got painfully back to his feet. Holding the bandanna fastidiously by one corner, he carried it to the kitchen, dropped it into the trash, and returned to his rocker. He took a sip of his coffee, grimaced, and put it aside. "Cold."

Owen rose. "I'll get you a fresh—"

"No. Sit down. We need to talk."

Owen sat.

"We had a little confrontation out there at the ship, you and I, didn't we?"

"I wouldn't say—"

"No, I know you wouldn't, but I know what went on and so do you. When the situation's hot, tempers also get hot. But we're past that now. We *have* to be past it because I'm the OIC and you're my second and we've still got this job to finish. Can we work together to do that?"

"Yes, sir." Fuck, there it was again. "Boss, I mean."

Kurtz favored him with a wintry smile.

"I lost control just now." Charming, frank, open-eyed and honest. This had fooled Owen for a lot of years. It did not fool him now. "I was going along, drawing the usual caricature—two parts Patton, one part Rasputin, add water, stir and serve—and I just . . . whew! I just lost it. You think I'm crazy, don't you?"

Careful, careful. There was telepathy in this room, honest-to-God telepathy, and Owen had no idea how deeply Kurtz might be able to see into him.

"Yes, sir. A little, sir."

Kurtz nodded matter-of-factly. "Yes. A little. That pretty well describes it. I've been doing this for a long time—men like me are necessary but hard to find, and you have to be a little crazy to do the job and not just high-side it completely. It's a thin line, that famous thin line the armchair psychologists love to talk about, and never in the history of the world has there been a cleanup job like this one . . . assuming, that is, the story of Hercules neatening up the Augean Stables is just a myth. I am not asking for your sympathy but for your understanding. If we understand each other, we'll get through this, the hardest job we've ever had, all right. If we don't . . ." Kurtz shrugged. "If we don't, I'll have to get through it without you. Are you following me?"

Owen doubted if he was, but he saw where Kurtz wanted him to go and nodded. He had read that there was a certain kind of bird that lived in the crocodile's mouth, at the croc's sufferance. He supposed that now he must be that kind of bird. Kurtz wanted him to believe he was forgiven for putting the alien broadcast on the common channel—heat of the moment, just as Kurtz had blown off Melrose's foot in the heat of the moment. And what had happened six years ago in Bosnia? Not a factor now. Maybe it was true. And maybe the crocodile had tired of the bird's tiresome pecking and was preparing to close its jaws. Owen got no sense of the truth from Kurtz's mind, and either way it behooved him to be very careful. Careful and ready to fly.

Kurtz reached into his coverall again and brought out a tarnished pocket-watch. "This was my grandfather's and it works just fine," he said. "Because it winds up, I think—no electricity. My wristwatch, on the other hand, is still FUBAR."

"Mine too."

Kurtz's lips twitched in a smile. "See Perlmutter when you have a chance, and feel you have the stomach for him. Among his many other chores and activities, he found time to take delivery of three hundred wind-up Timexes this afternoon. Just before the snow shut down our air-ops, this was. Pearly's damned efficient. I just wish to Christ he'd get over the idea that he's living in a movie."

"He may have made strides in that direction tonight, boss."

"Perhaps he has at that."

Kurtz meditated. Underhill waited.

"Laddie-buck, we should be drinking the whiskey. It's a bit of an Irish deathwatch we're having tonight."

"Is it?"

"Aye. Me beloved phooka is about to keel over dead."

Owen raised his eyebrows.

"Yes. At which point its magical cloak of invisibility will be whisked away. Then it will become just another dead horse for folks to beat. Primarily politicians, who are best at that sort of thing."

"I don't follow you."

Kurtz took another look at the tarnished pocketwatch, which he'd probably picked up in a pawnshop . . . or looted off a corpse. Underhill wouldn't have doubted either.

"It's seven o'clock. In just about forty hours, the President is going to speak before the UN General Assembly. More people are going to see and hear that speech than any previous speech in the history of the human race. It's going to be part of the biggest *story* in the history of the human race . . . and the biggest spin-job since God the Father Almighty created the cosmos and set the planets going round and round with the tip of his finger."

"What's the spin?"

"It's a beautiful tale, Owen. Like the best lies, it incorporates large swatches of the truth. The President will tell a fascinated world, a world hanging on every word with its breath caught in its throat, praise Jesus, that a ship crewed by beings from another world crashed in northern Maine on either November sixth or November seventh of this year. That's true. He will say that we were not completely surprised, as we and the heads of the other countries which constitute the UN Security Council have known for at least ten years that ET has been scoping us out. Also true, only some of us here in America have known about our pals from the void since the late nineteen-forties. We also know that Russian fighters destroyed a grayboy ship over Siberia in 1974 . . . although to this day the Russkies don't know we know. That one was probably a drone, a test-shot. There have been a lot of those. The grays have handled their early contacts with a care which strongly suggests that we scare them quite a lot."

Owen listened with a sick fascination he hoped didn't show on his face or at the top level of his thoughts, where Kurtz might still have access.

From his inner pocket, Kurtz now brought out a dented box of Marlboro cigarettes. He offered the pack to Owen, who first shook his head, then took one of the remaining four fags. Kurtz took another, then lit them up.

"I'm getting the truth and the spin mixed in together," Kurtz said after he'd taken a deep drag and exhaled. "That may not be the most profitable way to get on. Let's stick to the spin, shall we?"

Owen said nothing. He smoked rarely these days and the first drag made him feel light-headed, but the taste was wonderful.

"The President will say that the United States government quarantined the crash site and the area around it for three reasons. The first was purely logistical: because of the Jefferson Tract's remote location and low population, we *could* quarantine it. If the grayboys had come down in Brooklyn, or even on Long Island, that would not have been the case. The second reason is that we are not clear on the aliens' intentions. The third reason, and ultimately the most persuasive, is that the aliens carry with them an infectious substance which the on-scene personnel calls 'Ripley fungus.' While the alien visitors have assured us passionately that they are not infectious, they have brought a *highly* infectious substance with them. The President will also tell a horrified world that the *fungus* may in fact be the controlling intelligence, the grayboys just a growth medium. He will show videotape of a grayboy literally exploding *into* the Ripley fungus. The footage has been slightly doctored to improve visibility, but is basically true."

You're lying, Owen thought. *The footage is entirely fake from beginning to end, as fake as that* Alien Autopsy *shit.*

And why are you lying? Because you can. It's as simple as that, isn't it? Because to you, a lie comes more naturally than the truth.

"Okay, I'm lying," Kurtz said, never missing a beat. He gave Owen a quick gleaming look before dropping his gaze to his cigarette again. "But the facts are true and verifiable. Some of them *do* explode and turn into red dandelion fluff. The fluff is Ripley. You inhale enough of it and in a period of time we can't yet predict—it could be an hour or two days—your lungs and brain are Ripley salad. You look like a walking patch of poison sumac. And then you die.

"There will be no mention of our little venture earlier today. According to the President's version, the ship, which had apparently been badly damaged in the crash, was either blown up by its crew or blew up on its own. All the grayboys were killed. The Ripley, after some initial spread, is also dying, apparently because it does very poorly in the cold. The Russians corroborate that, by the way. There has been a fairly large kill-off of animals, which also carry the infection."

"And the human population of Jefferson Tract?"

"POTUS is going to say that about three hundred people—seventy or so locals and about two hundred and thirty hunters—are currently being monitored for the Ripley fungus. He will say that while some appear to have been infected, they also appear to be beating the infection with the help of such standard antibiotics as Ceftin and Augmentin."

"And now this word from our sponsor," Owen said. Kurtz laughed, delighted.

"At a later time, it's going to be announced that the Ripley seems a little more antibiotic-resistant than was first believed, and that a number of patients have died. The names we give out will be those of people who have in fact *already* died, either as a result of the Ripley or those gruesome fucking implants. Do you know what the men are calling the implants?"

"Yeah, shit-weasels. Will the President mention them?"

"No way. The guys in charge believe the shit-weasels are just a little too upsetting for John Q. Public. As would be, of course, the facts concerning our solution to the problem here at Gosselin's Store, that rustic beauty-spot."

"The *final* solution, you could call it," Owen said. He had smoked his cigarette all the way down to the filter, and now crushed it out on the rim of his empty coffee cup.

Kurtz's eyes rose to Owen's and met them unflinchingly. "Yes, you could call it that. We're going to wipe out approximately three hundred and fifty people—mostly men, there's that, but I can't say the cleansing won't include at least a few women and children. The upside, of course, is that we will be insuring the human race against a pandemic and, very possibly, subjugation. Not an inconsiderable upside."

Owen's thought—*I'm sure Hitler would like the spin*—was unstoppable, but he covered it as well as he could and got no sense that Kurtz had heard it or sensed it. Impossible to tell for sure, of course; Kurtz was sly.

"How many are we holding now?" Kurtz asked.

"About seventy. And twice that number on the way from Kineo; they'll be here around nine, if the weather doesn't get any worse." It was supposed to, but not until after midnight.

Kurtz was nodding. "Uh-huh. Plus I'm going to say fifty more from up north, seventy or so from St. Cap's and those little places down south . . . and our guys. Don't forget them. The masks seem to work, but we've already picked up four cases of Ripley in the medical debriefings. The men, of course, don't know."

"Don't they?"

"Let me rephrase that," Kurtz said. "Based on their behavior, I have no *reason* to believe the men know. All right?"

Owen shrugged.

"The *story*," Kurtz resumed, "will be that the detainees are being flown to a top-secret medical installation, a kind of Area 51, where they will undergo further examination, and, if necessary, long-term treatment. There will never be another official statement concerning them—not if all goes according to plan—but there will be time-release leaks over the next two years: encroaching infection despite best medical efforts to stop it . . . madness . . . grotesque physical changes better left undescribed . . . and finally, death comes as a mercy. Far from being outraged, the public will be relieved."

"While in reality . . . ?"

He wanted to hear Kurtz say it, but he should

have known better. There were no bugs here (except, maybe, for the ones hiding between Kurtz's ears), but the boss's caution was ingrained. He raised one hand, made a gun of his thumb and forefinger, and dropped his thumb three times. His eyes never left Owen's as he did this. *Crocodile's eyes,* Owen thought.

"All of them?" Owen asked. "The ones who aren't showing Ripley-Positive as well as those who are? And where does that leave us? The soldiers who also show Negative?"

"The laddies who are okay now are going to stay okay," Kurtz said. "Those showing Ripley were all careless. One of them . . . well, there's a little girl out there, about four years old, cute as the devil. You almost expect her to start tap-dancing across the barn floor and singing 'On the Good Ship *Lollipop.*' "

Kurtz obviously thought he was being witty, and Owen supposed that in a way he was, but Owen himself was overcome by a wave of intense horror. *There's a four-year-old out there,* he thought. *Just four years old, how about that.*

"She's cute, and she's hot," Kurtz was saying. "Visible Ripley on the inside of one wrist, growing at her hairline, growing in the corner of one eye. Classic spots. Anyway, this soldier gave her a candybar, just like she was some starving Kosovar rug-muncher, and she gave him a kiss. Sweet as pie, a real Kodak moment, only now he's got a lipstick print that ain't lipstick growing on his cheek." Kurtz grimaced. "He had himself a little tiny shaving cut, barely visible, but there goes your ballgame. Similar stuff with the others. The rules don't change, Owen; carelessness gets you killed. You may go along lucky for awhile, but in the end it never fails. Carelessness gets you killed. Most of our guys, I'm delighted to say, will walk away from this. We're going to face scheduled medical exams for the rest of our lives, not to mention the occasional surprise exam, but look at the upside—they're gonna catch your ass-cancer *wicked* early."

"The civilians who appear clean? What about them?"

Kurtz leaned forward, now at his most charming, his most persuasively sane. You were supposed to be flattered by this, to feel yourself one of the fortunate few to see Kurtz with his mask ("two parts Patton, one part Rasputin, add water, stir and serve") laid aside. It had worked on Owen before, but not now. Rasputin wasn't the mask; *this* was the mask.

Yet even now—here was the hell of it—he wasn't completely sure.

"Owen, Owen, Owen! Use your brain—that good brain God gave you! We can monitor our own without raising suspicions or opening the door to a worldwide panic—and there's going to be enough panic anyway, after our narrowly elected President slays the phooka horse. We couldn't do that with three hundred civilians. And if we really flew them out to New Mexico, put them up in some model village for fifty or seventy years at the taxpayers' expense? What if one or more of them escaped? Or what if—and I think this is what the smart boys are really afraid of—given time, the Ripley mutates? That instead of dying off, it turns into something a lot more infectious and a lot less vulnerable to the environmental factors that are killing it here in Maine? If the Ripley's intelligent, it's dangerous. Even if it isn't, what if it serves the grayboys as a kind of beacon, an interstellar road-flare marking our world out— yum-yum, come and get it, these guys are tasty . . . and there's plenty of them?"

"You're saying better safe than sorry."

Kurtz leaned back in his chair and beamed. "That's it. That's it in a nutshell."

Well, Owen thought, *it might be the nut, but the shell is something we're not talking about. We watch out for our own. We're merciless if we have to be, but even Kurtz watches out for his laddie-bucks. Civilians, on the other hand, are just civilians. If you need to burn em, they go up pretty easy.*

"If you doubt there's a God and that He spends at least some of His time looking out for good old *Homo sap,* you might look at the way we're coming out of this," Kurtz said. "The flashlights arrived early and were reported—one of the reports came from the store owner, Reginald Gosselin, himself. Then the grayboys arrive at the only time of year when there are actually *people* in these godforsaken woods, and two of them saw the ship go down."

"That *was* lucky."

"God's grace is what it was. Their ship crashes, their presence is known, the cold kills both them and the galactic dandruff they brought along." He ticked the points off rapidly on his long fingers, his white eyelashes blinking. "But that's not all. They do some implants and the goddam things don't work—far from establishing a harmonious relationship with their hosts, they turn cannibal and kill them.

"The animal kill-off went well—we've censused something like a hundred thousand critters, and there's already one hell of a barbecue going on over by the Castle County line. In the spring or summer we would've needed to worry about bugs carrying the Ripley out of the zone, but not now. Not in November."

"Some animals must have gotten through."

"Animals and people both, likely. But the Ripley spreads slowly. We're going to be all right on this because we netted the vast majority of infected hosts, because the ship has been destroyed, and because what they brought us smolders rather than blazes. We've sent them a simple message: come in peace or come with your rayguns blazing, but don't try it this way again, because it doesn't work. We don't think they will come again, or at least not for awhile. They played fiddly-fuck for half a century before getting this far. Our only regret is that we didn't secure the ship for the science-boffins . . . but it might've been too Ripley-infected, anyway. Do you know what our great fear has been? That either the grayboys or the Ripley would find a Typhoid Mary, someone who could carry it and spread it without catching it him- or herself."

"Are you sure there isn't such a person?"

"Almost sure. If there is . . . well, that's what the cordon's for." Kurtz smiled. "We lucked out, soldier. The odds are against a Typhoid Mary, the grayboys are dead, and all the Ripley is confined to the Jefferson Tract. Luck or God. Take your choice."

Kurtz lowered his head and pinched the bridge of his nose high up, like a man suffering a sinus infection. When he looked up again, his eyes were swimming. *Crocodile tears,* Owen thought, but in truth he wasn't sure. And he had no access to Kurtz's mind. Either the telepathic wave had receded too far for that, or Kurtz had found a way to slam the door. Yet when Kurtz spoke again, Owen was almost positive he was hearing the real Kurtz, a human being and not Tick-Tock the Croc.

"This is it for me, Owen. Once this job is finished, I'm going to punch my time. There'll be work here for another four days, I'd guess—maybe a week, if this storm's as bad as they say—and it'll be nasty, but the real nightmare's tomorrow morning. I can hold up my end, I guess, but after that . . . well, I'm eligible for full retirement, and I'm going to give them their choice: pay me or kill me. I think they'll pay, because I know where too many of the bodies are buried—that's a lesson I learned from J. Edgar Hoover—but I've almost reached the point of not caring. This won't be the worst one I've ever been involved in, in Haiti we did eight hundred in a single hour—1989, that was, and I still dream about it—but this is worse. By far. Because those poor schmucks out there in the barn and the paddock and the corral . . . they're *Americans.* Folks who drive Chevvies, shop at Kmart, and never miss *ER.* The thought of shooting Americans, *massacring* Americans . . . that turns my stomach. I'll do it only because it needs to be done in order to bring closure to this business, and because most of them would die anyway, and much more horribly. *Capish?*"

Owen Underhill said nothing. He thought he was keeping his face properly expressionless, but anything he said would likely give away his sinking horror. He had *known* this was coming, but to actually *hear* it . . .

In his mind's eye he saw the soldiers drifting toward the fence through the snow, heard the loudspeakers summoning the detainees in the barn. He had never been part of an operation like this, he'd missed Haiti, but he knew how it was supposed to go. How it *would* go.

Kurtz was watching him closely.

"I won't say all is forgiven for that foolish stunt you pulled this afternoon, that water's under the bridge, but you owe me one, buck. I don't need ESP to know how you feel about what I'm telling you, and I'm not going to waste my breath telling you to grow up and face reality. All I can tell you is that I need you. You have to help me this one time."

The swimming eyes. The infirm twitch, barely perceptible, at the corner of his mouth. It was easy to forget that Kurtz had blown a man's foot off not ten minutes ago.

Owen thought: *If I help him do this, it doesn't matter if I actually pull a trigger or not, I'm as damned as the men who herded the Jews into the showers at Bergen-Belsen.*

"If we start at eleven, we can be done at eleven-thirty," Kurtz said. "Noon at the very worst. Then it's behind us."

"Except for the dreams."

"Yes. Except for them. Will you help me, Owen?"

Owen nodded. He had come this far, and wouldn't let go of the rope now, damned or not. At the very least he could help make it merciful . . . as merciful as any mass murder could be. Later he would be struck by the lethal absurdity of this idea, but when you were with Kurtz, up close and with his eyes holding yours, perspective was a joke. His madness was probably much more infectious than the Ripley, in the end.

"Good." Kurtz slumped back in his rocker, looking relieved and drained. He took out his cigarettes again, peered in, then held the pack out. "Two left. Join me?"

Owen shook his head. "Not this time, boss."

"Then get on out of here. If necessary, shag ass over to the infirmary and get some Sonata."

"I don't think I'll need that," Owen said. He would, of course—he needed it already—but he wouldn't take it. Better to lie awake.

"All right, then. Off you go." Kurtz let him get as far as the door. "And Owen?"

Owen turned back, zipping his parka. He could hear the wind out there now. Building, starting to blow seriously, as it had not during the relatively harmless Alberta Clipper that had come through that morning.

"Thanks," Kurtz said. One large and absurd tear overspilled his left eye and ran down his cheek. Kurtz seemed unaware. In that moment Owen loved and pitied him. In spite of everything, which included knowing better. "Thank you, buck."

7

Henry stood in the thickening snow, turned away from the worst of the wind and looking over his left shoulder at the Winnebago, waiting for Underhill to come back out. He was alone now—the storm had driven the rest of them back into the barn, where there was a heater. Rumors would already be growing tall in the warmth, Henry supposed. Better the rumors than the truth that was right in front of them.

He scratched at his leg, realized what he was doing, and looked around, turning in a complete circle. No prisoners; no guards. Even in the thickening snow the compound was almost as bright as noonday, and he could see well in every direction. For the time being, at least, he was alone.

Henry bent and untied the shirt knotted around the place where the turnsignal stalk had cut his skin. He then spread the slit in his bluejeans. The men who had taken him into custody had made this same examination in the back of the truck where they had already stored five other refugees (on the way back to Gosselin's they had picked up three more). At that point he had been clean.

He wasn't clean now. A delicate thread of red lace grew down the scabbed center of the wound. If he hadn't known what he was looking for, he might have mistaken it for a fresh seep of blood.

Byrus, he thought. *Ah, fuck. Goodnight, Mrs. Calabash, wherever you are.*

A flash of light winked at the top of his vision. Henry straightened and saw Underhill just pulling the door of the Winnebago shut. Quickly, Henry retied the shirt around the hole in his jeans and then approached the fence. A voice in his head asked what he'd do if he called to Underhill and the man just kept on going. That voice also wanted to know if Henry really intended to give Jonesy up.

He watched Underhill trudge toward him in the glare of the security lights, his head bent against the snow and the intensifying wind.

8

The door closed. Kurtz sat looking at it, smoking and slowly rocking. How much of his pitch had Owen bought? Owen was bright, Owen was a survivor, Owen was not without idealism . . . and Kurtz thought Owen had bought it all, with hardly a single dicker. Because in the end most people believed what they wanted to believe. John Dillinger had also been a survivor, the wiliest of the thirties desperadoes, but he had gone to the Biograph Theater with Anna Sage just the same. *Manhattan Melodrama* had been the show, and when it was over, the feds had shot Dillinger down in the alley beside the theater like the dog he was. Anna Sage had also believed what she wanted to believe, but they deported her ass back to Poland just the same.

No one was going to leave Gosselin's Market tomorrow except for his picked cadre—the twelve men and two women who made up Imperial Valley.

Owen Underhill would not be among them, although he could have been. Until Owen had put the grayboys on the common channel, Kurtz had been sure he would be. But things changed. So Buddha had said, and on that one, at least, the old chink heathen had spoken true.

"You let me down, buck," Kurtz said. He had lowered his mask to smoke, and it bobbed against his grizzled throat as he spoke. "You let me down." Kurtz had let Owen Underhill get away with letting him down once. But twice?

"Never," Kurtz said. "Never in life."

CHAPTER FOURTEEN

GOING SOUTH

1

Mr. Gray ran the snowmobile down into a ravine which held a small frozen creek. He drove north along this for the remaining mile to I-95. Two or three hundred yards from the lights of the army vehicles (there were only a few now, moving slowly in the thickening snow), he stopped long enough to consult the part of Jonesy's mind that he—*it*—could get at. There were files and files of stuff that wouldn't fit into Jonesy's little office stronghold, and Mr. Gray found what he was looking for easily enough. There was no switch to turn off the Arctic Cat's headlight. Mr. Gray swung Jonesy's legs off the snowmobile, looked for a rock, picked it up with Jonesy's right hand, and smashed the headlight dark. Then he remounted and drove on. The Cat's fuel was almost gone, but that was all right; the vehicle had served its purpose.

The pipe which carried the creek beneath the turnpike was big enough for the snowmobile, but not for the snowmobile and its rider. Mr. Gray dismounted again. Standing beside the snowmobile, he revved the throttle and sent the machine bumping and yawing into the pipe. It went no more than ten feet before stopping, but that was far enough to keep it from being seen from the air if the snow lightened, allowing low-level recon.

Mr. Gray set Jonesy to climbing up the turnpike embankment. He stopped just shy of the guardrails and lay down on his back. Here he was temporarily protected from the worst of the wind. The climb had released a last little cache of endorphins, and Jonesy felt his kidnapper sampling them, enjoying them the way Jonesy himself might have enjoyed a cocktail, or a hot drink after watching a football game on a brisk October afternoon.

He realized, with no surprise, that he hated Mr. Gray.

Then Mr. Gray as an entity—something that could actually be hated—was gone again, replaced by the cloud Jonesy had first experienced back in the cabin when the creature's head had exploded. It was going out, as it had gone out in search of Emil Dawg. It had needed Brodsky because the information about how to get the snowmobile started hadn't been in Jonesy's files. Now it needed something else. A ride was the logical assumption.

And what was left here? What was left guarding the office where the last shred of Jonesy cowered— Jonesy who had been turned out of his own body like lint out of a pocket? The cloud, of course; the stuff Jonesy had breathed in. Stuff that should have killed him but had for some reason not done so.

The cloud couldn't think, not the way Mr. Gray could. The man of the house (who was now Mr. Gray instead of Mr. Jones) had departed, leaving the place under the control of the thermostats, the refrigerator, the stove. And, in case of trouble, the smoke detector and the burglar alarm, which automatically dialed the police.

Still, with Mr. Gray gone, he might be able to get out of the office. Not to regain control; if he tried that, the redblack cloud would report him and Mr. Gray would return from his scouting expedition at once. Jonesy would almost certainly be seized before he could retreat to the safety of the Tracker Brothers office with its bulletin board and its dusty floor and its one dirt-crusted window on the world . . . only there were four crescent-shaped clean patches in that dirt, weren't there? Patches where four boys had once leaned their foreheads, hoping to see the picture that was pinned to the bulletin board now: Tina Jean Schlossinger with her skirt up.

No, seizing control was far beyond his ability and he'd better accept that, bitter as it was.

But he might be able to get to his files.

Was there any reason to risk it? Any advantage? There might be, if he knew what Mr. Gray wanted. Beyond a ride, that was. And speaking of that, a ride where?

The answer was unexpected because it came in Duddits's voice: *Ow. Ih-her Ay onna oh ow.*

Mr. Gray wanna go south.

Jonesy stepped back from his dirty window on the world. There wasn't much to be seen out there just now, anyway; snow and dark and shadowy trees. This morning's snow had been the appetizer; here was the main course.

Mr. Gray wanna go south.

How far? And why? What was the big picture?

On these subjects Duddits was silent.

Jonesy turned and was surprised to see that the route-map and the picture of the girl were no longer on the bulletin board. Where they had been were four color snapshots of four boys. Each had the same background, Derry Junior High, and the same caption beneath: SCHOOL DAYS, 1978. Jonesy himself on the far left, face split in a trusting ear-to-ear grin that now broke his heart. Beav next to him, the Beav's grin revealing the missing tooth in front, victim of a skating fall, which had been replaced by a false one a year or so later . . . before high school, anyway. Pete, with his broad, olive-tinted face and his shamefully short hair, mandated by his father, who said he hadn't fought in Korea so his kid could look like a hippie. And Henry on the end, Henry in his thick glasses that made Jonesy think of Danny Dunn, Boy Detective, star of the mysteries Jonesy had read as a kid.

Beaver, Pete, Henry. How he had loved them, and how unfairly sudden the severing of their long friendship had been. No, it wasn't a bit fair—

All at once the picture of Beaver Clarendon came alive, scaring the hell out of Jonesy. Beav's eyes widened and he spoke in a low voice. "His head was off, remember? It was laying in the ditch and his eyes were full of mud. What a fuckarow! I mean, Jesus-Christ-bananas."

Oh my God, Jonesy thought, as it came back to him—the one thing about that first hunting trip to Hole in the Wall that he had forgotten . . . or suppressed. Had all of them suppressed it? Maybe so. *Probably* so. Because over the years since, they had talked about everything in their childhoods, all those shared memories . . . except that one.

His head was off . . . his eyes were full of mud.

Something had happened to them then, something that had to do with what was happening to him now.

If only I knew what it was, Jonesy thought. *If I only knew.*

2

Andy Janas had lost the other three trucks in his little squadron—had gotten ahead of them because they weren't used to driving in shit like this and he was. He had grown up in northern Minnesota, and you better *believe* he was used to it. He was by himself in one of Chevrolet's finer Army vehicles, a modified four-wheel-drive pickup, and he had the four-wheel drive engaged tonight. His father hadn't raised any fools.

Still, the turnpike was mostly clear; a couple of Army plows had gone by an hour or so ago (he would be catching up to them soon, he guessed, and when he did he would cut speed and fall in behind them like a good boy), and no more than two or three inches had piled up on the concrete since then. The real problem was the wind, which lifted the fluff and turned the road into a ghost. You had the reflectors to guide you, though. Keeping the reflectors in sight was the trick those other gomers didn't understand . . . or maybe with the convoy trucks and the Humvees, the head-lights were set too high to pick the reflectors up prop-erly. And when the wind really gusted, even the reflectors disappeared; the goddam world went totally white and you had to take your foot off the go-pedal until the air stilled again and just try to stay on course in the meantime. He would be all right, and if any-thing happened, he was in radio contact and more plows would be coming up behind, keeping the south-bound barrel of the turnpike open all the way from Presque Isle to Millinocket.

In the back of his truck were two triple-wrapped packages. In one were the bodies of two deer which had been killed by the Ripley. In the other—this Janas found moderately to seriously gruesome—was the body of a grayboy turning slowly to a kind of reddish-orange soup. Both were bound for the docs at Blue Base, which had been set up at a place called . . .

Janas looked up at the driver's visor. There, held in place by a rubber band, was a piece of notepaper and a ballpoint pen. Scrawled on the paper was GOSSELIN'S STO, TAKE EX 16, TURN L.

He'd be there in an hour. Maybe less. The docs would undoubtedly tell him they had all the animal samples they needed and the deer-carcasses would be burned, but they might want the grayboy, if the little fella hadn't turned entirely to mush. The cold might retard that process a little bit, but whether it did or didn't was really none of Andy Janas's nevermind. His concern was to get there, turn over his samples, and then await debriefing from whoever was in charge of asking questions about the q-zone's northern—and most quiet—perimeter. While he was awaiting, he would grab some hot coffee and a great big plate of scrambled eggs. If the right someone was around, he might even be able to promote something to spike his coffee with. That would be good. Get a little buzz going, then just hunker down and

pull over

Janas frowned, shook his head, scratched his ear as if something—a flea, perhaps—had bitten him there. The goddam wind gusted hard enough to shake the truck. The turnpike disappeared and so did the reflectors. He was encased in total white again and he had no doubt that this scared the everloving bejabbers out of the other guys, but not him, he was Mr. Minnesota-Twins-Taking-Care-of-Business, just pull the old foot off the gas (and never mind the brake, when you were driving in a snowstorm the brake was the best way he knew to turn a good ride bad), just coast and wait for

pull over

"Huh?" He looked at the radio, but there was

nothing there, just static and dim background chatter.

pull over

"Ow!" Janas cried, and grabbed at his head, which suddenly hurt like a motherfucker. The olive-green pickup swerved, skidded, then came back under control as his hands automatically steered into the skid. His foot was still off the gas and the Chevy's speedometer needle unwound rapidly.

The plows had made a narrow path down the center of the two southbound lanes. Now Janas steered into the thicker snow to the right of this path, the truck's wheels spuming up a haze of snow which the wind quickly whipped away. The guardrail reflectors were very bright, glaring in the dark like cat's eyes.

pull over here

Janas screamed with pain. From a great distance he heard himself shouting, "Okay, okay, I am! Just stop it! Quit *yanking* me!" Through watering eyes he saw a dark form rear up on the far side of the guardrails not fifty feet ahead. As the headlights struck the shape fully, he saw it was a man wearing a parka.

Andy Janas's hands no longer felt like his own. They felt like gloves with someone else's hands inside them. This was an odd and entirely unpleasant sensation. They turned the steering wheel farther to the left entirely without his help, and the pickup truck coasted to a stop in front of the man in the parka.

3

This was his chance, with Mr. Gray's attention entirely diverted. Jonesy sensed that if he thought about it he would lose his courage, so he didn't think. He simply acted, knocking back the bolt on the office door with the heel of his hand and yanking the door open.

He had never been inside Tracker Brothers as a kid (and it had been gone since the big storm of '85), but he was pretty sure that it had never looked like what he saw now. Outside the dingy office was a room so vast Jonesy couldn't see the end of it. Overhead were endless acres of fluorescent bars. Beneath them, stacked in enormous columns, were millions of cardboard boxes.

No, Jonesy thought. *Not millions. Trillions.*

Yes, probably trillions was closer. Thousands of narrow aisles ran between them. He was standing at one edge of eternity's own warehouse, and the idea of finding anything in it was ludicrous. If he ventured away from the door into his office hideout, he would become lost in no time. Mr. Gray wouldn't need to bother with him; Jonesy would wander until he died, lost in a mind-boggling wasteland of stored boxes.

That's not true. I could no more get lost in there than I could in my own bedroom. Nor will I have to hunt for what I want. This is my place. Welcome to your own head, big boy.

The concept was so huge that it made him feel weak . . . only he couldn't afford to be weak right now, or to hesitate. Mr. Gray, everyone's favorite invader from the Great Beyond, wouldn't be occupied with the truck-driver for long. If Jonesy meant to move some of these files to safety, he had to do it right now. The question was, which ones?

Duddits, his mind whispered. *This has something to do with Duddits. You know it does. He's been on your mind a lot lately. The other guys were thinking of him, too. Duddits is what held you and Henry and Pete and Beaver together—you've always known that, but now you know something else, as well. Don't you?*

Yes. He knew that his accident in March had been caused by thinking he'd seen Duddits once again being teased by Richie Grenadeau and his friends. Only "teased" was a ludicrously inapt word for what had been going on behind Tracker Brothers that day, wasn't it? *Tortured* was the word. And when he'd seen that torture being reenacted, he had plunged into the street without looking, and—

His head was off, Beaver suddenly said from the storeroom's overhead speakers, his voice so loud and sudden it made Jonesy cringe. *It was laying in the ditch and his eyes were full of mud. And sooner or later every murderer pays the price. What a fuckaroo!*

Richie's head. Richie Grenadeau's head. And Jonesy had no time for this. He was a trespasser in his *own* head now, and he'd do well to move quickly.

When he had first looked out at this enormous storeroom, all the boxes had been plain and unmarked. Now he saw that those at the head of the row closest to him were labeled in black grease-pencil: DUDDITS. Was that surprising? Fortuitous? Not at all. They were *his* memories, after all, stored flat and neatly folded in each of the trillions of boxes, and when it came to memory, the healthy mind was able to access them pretty much at will.

Need something to move them with, Jonesy thought, and when he looked around he was not exactly amazed to see a bright red hand-dolly. This was a magic place, a make-it-up-as-you-go-along place, and the most marvelous thing about it, Jonesy supposed, was that everybody had one.

Moving quickly, he stacked some of the boxes marked DUDDITS on the dolly and ran them into the Tracker Brothers office at a trot. He dumped them by tipping the dolly forward, spilling them across the floor. Untidy, but he could worry about the Good Housekeeping Seal of Approval later.

He ran back out, feeling for Mr. Gray, but Mr. Gray was still with the truck-driver . . . Janas, his name was. There was the cloud, but the cloud didn't sense him. It was as dumb as . . . well, as dumb as fungus.

Jonesy got the rest of the DUDDITS boxes, and saw that the next stack had also acquired scribbled grease-pencil labels. These latter said DERRY, and there were too many to take. The question was whether or not he needed to take any of them.

He pondered this as he pushed the second load of memory-boxes into the office. Of course the Derry boxes would be stacked near the Duddits boxes; memory was both the act and the art of association. The question remained whether or not his Derry memories mattered. How was he supposed to know that when he didn't know what Mr. Gray wanted?

But he *did* know.

Mr. Gray wanna go south.

Derry was south.

Jonesy sprinted back into the memory storehouse, pushing the dolly ahead of him. He'd take as many of the boxes marked DERRY as he could, and hope they were the right ones. He would also hope that he sensed Mr. Gray's return in time. Because if he was caught out here, he would be swatted like a fly.

4

Janas watched, horrified, as his left hand reached out and opened the driver's-side door of his truck, letting in the cold, the snow, and the relentless wind. "Don't hurt me anymore, mister, please don't, you can have a ride if you want a ride, just don't hurt me anymore, my *head*—"

Something suddenly rushed through Andy Janas's mind. It was like a whirlwind with eyes. He felt it prying into his current orders, his expected arrival time at Blue Base . . . and what he knew of Derry, which was nothing. His orders had taken him through Bangor, he'd never been to Derry in his life.

He felt the whirlwind pull back and had one moment of delirious relief—*I don't have what it needs, it's going to let me go*—and then understood that the thing in his mind had no intention of letting him go. It needed the truck, for one thing. It needed to shut his mouth, for another.

Janas put up a brief but bitterly energetic struggle.
It was this unexpected resistance that allowed Jonesy
time to remove at least one stack of the boxes marked
DERRY. Then Mr. Gray once more resumed his place
at Janas's motor controls.

Janas saw his hand shoot out and up to the driver's-side visor. His hand gripped the ballpoint pen
and yanked it free, snapping the rubber band which
held it.

No! Janas shouted, but it was too late. He caught a
shiny zipping glitter as his hand, which was gripping
the ballpoint like a dagger, plunged the pen into his
staring eye. There was a popping sound and he jittered
back and forth behind the wheel like a badly managed
puppet, his fist digging the pen in deeper and deeper, up
to the halfway mark, then to the three-quarter mark, his
split eyeball now running down the side of his face like
a freakish tear. The tip struck something that felt like
thin gristle, bound up for a moment, then passed
through into the meat of his brain.

You bastard, he thought, *what are you, you bas—*

There was a final brilliant flash of light inside his
head and then everything went dark. Janas slumped
forward over the wheel. The pickup's horn began to
blow.

5

Mr. Gray hadn't gotten much from Janas—mostly
that unexpected struggle for control at the end—but
one thing which came through clearly was that Janas

wasn't on his own. The transport column of which he had been a part had strung out because of the storm, but they were all headed to the same place, which Janas had identified in his mind as both Blue Base and Gosselin's. There was a man there that Janas had been afraid of, the man in charge, but Mr. Gray could not have cared less about Creepy Kurtz/the boss/Crazy Abe. Nor did he have to care, since he had no intention of going anywhere near Gosselin's store. This place was different and this species, although only semi-sentient, composed mostly of emotions, was different, too. They *fought*. Mr. Gray had no idea why, but they did.

Best to finish it quickly. And to that end, he had discovered an excellent delivery system.

Using Jonesy's hands, Mr. Gray pulled Janas from behind the wheel and carried him to the guardrails. He threw the body over the side, not bothering to watch as it tumbled down the slope to the frozen streambed. He went back to the truck, looked fixedly at the two plastic-wrapped bundles in the back, and nodded. The animal corpses were good for nothing. The other, though . . . that would be useful. It was rich with what he needed.

He looked up suddenly, Jonesy's eyes widening in the blowing snow. The owner of this body was out of its hiding place. Vulnerable. Good, because that consciousness was starting to annoy him, a constant muttering (sometimes rising to a panicky squeal) on the lower level of his thought-process.

Mr. Gray paused a moment longer, trying to make

his mind blank, not wanting Jonesy to have the slightest warning . . . and then he pounced.

He didn't know what he had expected, but not this.

Not this dazzling white light.

6

Jonesy was nearly caught out. *Would* have been caught out if not for the fluorescents with which he had lit his mental storeroom. This place might not actually exist, but it was real enough to him, and that made it real enough to Mr. Gray when Mr. Gray arrived.

Jonesy, who was pushing the dolly filled with boxes marked DERRY, saw Mr. Gray appear like magic at the head of a corridor of high-stacked cartons. It was the rudimentary humanoid that had been standing behind him at Hole in the Wall, the thing he had visited in the hospital. The dull black eyes were finally alive, *hungry.* It had crept up, caught him outside his office refuge, and it meant to have him.

But then its bulge of a head recoiled, and before its three-fingered hand shielded its eyes (it had no lids, not even any lashes), Jonesy saw an expression on its gray sketch of a face that had to be bewilderment. Maybe even pain. It had been out there, in the snowy dark, disposing of the driver's body. It had come in here unprepared for the discount-mart glare. He saw something else, too: The invader had borrowed its expression of surprise from the host. For a moment, Mr. Gray was a horrible caricature of Jonesy himself.

Its surprise gave Jonesy just enough time. Pushing the dolly ahead of him almost without realizing it and feeling like the imprisoned princess in some fucked-up fairy-tale, he ran into the office. He sensed rather than saw Mr. Gray reaching out for him with his three-fingered hands (the gray skin was raw-looking, like very old uncooked meat), and slammed the office door just ahead of their clutch. He bumped the dolly with his bad hip as he spun around—he accepted that he was inside his own head, but all of this was nevertheless completely real—and just managed to run the bolt before Mr. Gray could turn the knob and force his way in. Jonesy engaged the thumb-lock in the center of the doorknob for good measure. Had the thumb-lock been there before, or had he added it? He couldn't remember.

Jonesy stepped back, sweating, and this time ran his butt into the handle of the dolly. In front of him, the doorknob turned back and forth, back and forth. Mr. Gray was out there, in charge of the rest of his mind—and his body, as well—but he couldn't get in here. Couldn't force the door, didn't have the heft to break it down, didn't have the wit to pick the lock.

Why? How could that be?

"Duddits," he whispered. "No bounce, no play."

The doorknob rattled. "Let me in!" Mr. Gray snarled, and to Jonesy he didn't sound like an emissary from another galaxy but like anyone who has been denied what he wants and is pissed off about it. Was that because he was interpreting Mr. Gray's behavior in terms which he, Jonesy, understood? Humanizing the alien? *Translating* him?

"*Let . . . me . . . IN!*"

Jonesy responded without thinking: "Not by the hair of my chinny-chin-chin." And thought: *To which you say, "Then I'll huff . . . and I'll PUFF . . . and I'll BLOWWW your house in!"*

But Mr. Gray only rattled the knob harder than ever. He was not used to being balked in this manner (or in any manner, Jonesy guessed) and was very pissed. Janas's momentary resistance had startled him, but this was resistance on a whole other level.

"Where are you?" Mr. Gray called angrily. "How can you be in there? Come out!"

Jonesy didn't reply, only stood among the tumbled boxes, listening. He was almost positive Mr. Gray couldn't get in, but it would be just as well not to provoke him.

And after a little more knob-rattling, he sensed Mr. Gray leaving him.

Jonesy went to the window, stepping over the tumbled boxes marked DUDDITS and DERRY to get there, and stared out into the snowy night.

7

Mr. Gray climbed Jonesy's body back behind the wheel of the truck, slammed the door, and pushed the accelerator. The truck bolted forward, then lost purchase. All four wheels spun, and the truck skidded into the guardrails with a jarring bang.

"*Fuck!*" Mr. Gray cried, accessing Jonesy's profanity almost without being aware of it. "Jesus-Christ-bananas! Kiss my bender! Doodly-fuck! Bite my bag!"

Then he stopped and accessed Jonesy's driving skills again. Jonesy had some information on driving in weather like this, but nowhere near as much as Janas had possessed. Janas was gone, however, his files erased. What Jonesy knew would have to do. The important thing was to get beyond what Janas had thought of as the "q-zone." Beyond the q-zone he would be safe. Janas had been clear about that.

Jonesy's foot pressed down on the gas pedal again, much more gently this time. The truck started to move. Jonesy's hands steered the Chevrolet back into the fading path left by the plow.

Under the dash, the radio crackled to life. "Tubby One, this is Tubby Four. I got a rig off the road and turned over on the median. Do you copy?"

Mr. Gray consulted the files. What Jonesy knew about military communication was skimpy, mostly gleaned from books and something called *the movies,* but it might do. He took the mike, felt for the button Jonesy seemed to think would be on the side, found it, pushed it. "I copy," he said. Would Tubby Four be able to tell that Tubby One was no longer Andy Janas? Based on Jonesy's files, Mr. Gray doubted it.

"A bunch of us are going to get him up, see if we can get him back on the road. He's got the goddam *food,* you copy?"

Mr. Gray pushed the button. "Got the goddam food, copy."

A longer pause, long enough for him to wonder if

he'd said something wrong, stepped in some kind of a trap, and then the radio said: "We'll have to wait for the next bunch of plows, I guess. You might as well keep rolling, over?" Tubby Four sounded disgusted. Jonesy's files suggested that might be because Janas, with his superior driving skills, had gotten too far ahead to help. All this was good. He would've kept moving in any case, but it was good to have Tubby Four's official sanction, if that's what it was.

He checked Jonesy's files (which he now saw as *Jonesy* saw them—boxes in a vast room) and said, "Copy. Tubby One, over and out." And, as an after-thought: "Have a nice night."

The white stuff was horrible. Treacherous. None-theless, Mr. Gray risked driving a little faster. As long as he was in the area controlled by Creepy Kurtz's armed force, he might be vulnerable. Once out of the net, however, he would be able to complete his busi-ness very quickly.

What he needed had to do with a place called Derry, and when Mr. Gray went into the big store-room again, he discovered an amazing thing: his unwilling host had either known that or sensed it, because it was the Derry files Jonesy had been mov-ing when Mr. Gray had returned and almost caught him.

Mr. Gray searched the boxes that were left with sudden anxiety, and then relaxed.

What he needed was still here.

Lying on its side near the box which contained the most important information was another box, very small and very dusty. Written on the side in black pencil was the word DUDDITS. If there were other Duddits-boxes, they had been removed. Only this one had been overlooked.

More out of curiosity than anything else (his curiosity also borrowed from Jonesy's store of emotions), Mr. Gray opened it. Inside was a bright yellow container made of plastic. Outlandish figures capered upon it, figures Jonesy's files identified as both *cartoons* and *the Scooby-Doos*. On one end was a sticker reading I BELONG TO DUDDITS CAVELL, 19 MAPLE LANE, DERRY, MAINE. IF THE BOY I BELONG TO IS LOST, CALL

This was followed by numbers too faint and illegible to read, probably a communication-code Jonesy no longer remembered. Mr. Gray tossed the yellow plastic container, probably meant for carrying food, aside. It could mean nothing . . . although if that was really the case, why had Jonesy risked his existence getting the other DUDDITS-boxes (as well as some of those marked DERRY) to safety?

DUDDITS = CHILDHOOD FRIEND. Mr. Gray knew this from his initial encounter with Jonesy in "the hospital" . . . and if he had known what an annoyance Jonesy would turn out to be, he would have erased his host's consciousness right then. Neither the term CHILDHOOD nor the term FRIEND had any emotional resonance for Mr. Gray, but he understood what they meant. What he didn't understand was how Jonesy's childhood friend could have anything to do with what was happening tonight.

One possibility occurred to him: his host had gone

mad. Being turned out of his own body had driven him insane, and he'd simply taken the boxes closest to the door of his perplexing stronghold, assigning them in his madness an importance they did not actually have.

"Jonesy," Mr. Gray said, speaking the name with Jonesy's vocal cords. These creatures were mechanical geniuses (of course they would have to be, to survive in such a cold world), but their thought-processes were odd and crippled: rusty mentation sunk in corrosive pools of emotion. Their telepathic abilities were minus; the transient telepathy they were now experiencing thanks to the byrus and the kim ("flashlights," they called them) bewildered and frightened them. It was difficult for Mr. Gray to believe they hadn't murdered their entire species yet. Creatures incapable of real thought were maniacs—this was surely beyond argument.

Meanwhile, no answer from the creature in that strange, impregnable room.

"Jonesy."

Nothing. But Jonesy was listening. Mr. Gray was sure of it.

"There is no necessity for this suffering, Jonesy. See us for what we are—not invaders but saviors. Buddies."

Mr. Gray considered the various boxes. For a creature that couldn't actually think much, Jonesy had an enormous amount of storage capacity. Question for another day: why would beings who thought so poorly have so much retrieval capability? Did it have to do with their overblown emotional makeup? And the emotions were disturbing. He found Jonesy's emotions *very* disturbing. Always there. Always on call. And so *much* of them.

"War . . . famine . . . ethnic cleansing . . . killing for peace . . . massacring the heathen for Jesus . . . homosexual people beaten to death . . . bugs in bottles, the bottles sitting on top of missiles aimed at every city in the world . . . come on, Jonesy, compared to type-four anthrax, what's a little byrus between friends? Jesus-Christ-bananas, you'll all be dead in fifty years, anyway! This is *good*! Relax and enjoy it!"

"You made that guy stick a pen in his eye."

Grumpy, but better than nothing. The wind gusted, the pickup skidded, and Mr. Gray rode with it, using Jonesy's skills. The visibility was almost nil; he had dropped to twenty miles an hour and might do well to pull over completely for awhile once he cleared Kurtz's net. Meanwhile, he could chat with his host. Mr. Gray doubted that he could talk Jonesy out of his room, but chatting at least passed the time.

"I had to, buddy. I needed the truck. I'm the last one."

"And you never lose."

"Right," Mr. Gray agreed.

"But you've never had a situation like this, have you? You've never had someone you can't get at."

Was Jonesy taunting him? Mr. Gray felt a ripple of anger. And then he said something Mr. Gray had already thought of himself.

"Maybe you should have killed me in the hospital. Or was that only a dream?"

Mr. Gray, unsure what a *dream* was, didn't bother responding. Having this barricaded mutineer in what by now should have been Mr. Gray's mind and his alone was increasingly annoying. For one thing, he didn't like thinking of himself as "Mr. Gray"—that was not his concept of himself or the species-mind of which he was a part; he did not even like to think of himself as "he," for he was both sexes and neither. Yet now he was imprisoned by these concepts, and would be as long as the core being of Jonesy remained unabsorbed. A terrible thought occurred to Mr. Gray: what if it was *his* concepts that had no meaning?

He *hated* being in this position.

"Who's Duddits, Jonesy?"

No answer.

"Who is Richie? Why was he a shit? Why did you kill him?"

"We *didn't*!"

A little tremble in the mental voice. Ah, that shot had gone home. And something interesting: Mr. Gray had meant "you" in the singular, but Jonesy had taken it in the plural.

"You did, though. Or you think you did."

"That's a lie."

"How silly of you to say so. I have the memories, right here in one of your boxes. There's snow in the box. Snow and a moccasin. Brown suede. Come out and look."

For one giddy second he thought Jonesy might do just that. If he did, Mr. Gray would sweep him back to the hospital at once. Jonesy could see himself die on television. A happy ending to the movie they had been watching. And then, no more Mr. Gray. Just what Jonesy thought of as "the cloud."

Mr. Gray looked eagerly at the doorknob, willing it to turn. It didn't.

"Come out."

Nothing.

"You killed Richie, you coward! You and your friends. You . . . you *dreamed* him to death." And although Mr. Gray didn't know what dreams were, he knew that was true. Or that Jonesy believed it was.

Nothing.

"Come out! Come out and . . ." He searched Jonesy's memories. Many of them were in boxes called MOVIES, Jonesy seemed to love movies above all things, and Mr. Gray plucked what he thought a particularly potent line from one of these: ". . . and fight like a man!"

Nothing.

You bastard, Mr. Gray thought, once more dipping into the enticing pool of his host's emotions. *You son of a bitch. You stubborn asshole. Kiss my bender, you stubborn asshole.*

Back in the days when Jonesy had been Jonesy, he had often expressed anger by slamming his fist down on something. Mr. Gray did it now, bringing Jonesy's fist down on the center of the truck's wheel hard enough to honk the horn. "Tell me! Not about Richie, not about Duddits, about *you*! Something makes you different. I want to know what it is."

No answer.

"It's in the crib—is that it?"

Still no answer, but Mr. Gray heard Jonesy's feet shuffle behind the door. And perhaps a low intake of breath. Mr. Gray smiled with Jonesy's mouth.

"Talk to me, Jonesy—we'll play the game, we'll pass the time. Who was Richie, besides Number 19? Why were you angry with him? Because he was a Tiger? A Derry Tiger? What were they? Who's Duddits?"

Nothing.

The truck crept more slowly than ever through the storm, the headlights almost helpless against the swirling wall of white. Mr. Gray's voice was low, coaxing.

"You missed one of the Duddits-boxes, buddy, did you know that? There's a box inside the box, as it happens—it's yellow. There are Scooby-Doos on it. What are Scooby-Doos? They're not real people, are they? Are they movies? Are they televisions? Do you want the box? Come out, Jonesy. Come out and I'll give you the box."

Mr. Gray removed his foot from the gas pedal and let the truck coast slowly to the left, over into the thicker snow. Something was happening here, and he wanted to turn all his attention to it. Force had not dislodged Jonesy from his stronghold . . . but force wasn't the only way to win a battle, or a war.

The truck stood idling by the guardrails in what was now a full-fledged blizzard. Mr. Gray closed his eyes. Immediately he was in Jonesy's brightly lit memory storehouse. Behind him were miles of stacked boxes, marching away under the fluorescent tubes. In front of him was the closed door, shabby and dirty and for some reason very, very strong. Mr. Gray placed his three-fingered hands on it and began to speak in a low voice that was both intimate and urgent.

"Who is Duddits? Why did you call him after you killed Richie? Let me in, we need to talk. Why did you take some of the Derry boxes? What did you not want me to see? It doesn't matter, I have what I need, let me in, Jonesy, better now than later."

It was going to work. He sensed Jonesy's blank eyes, could see Jonesy's hand moving toward the knob and the lock.

"We always win," Mr. Gray said. He sat behind the wheel with Jonesy's eyes closed, and in another universe the wind screamed and rocked the truck on its springs. "Open the door, Jonesy, open it now."

Silence. And then, from less than three inches away and as surprising as a basinful of cold water dashed on warm skin: "Eat shit and die."

Mr. Gray recoiled so violently that the back of Jonesy's head connected with the truck's rear window. The pain was sudden and shocking, a second unpleasant surprise.

He slammed a fist down again, then the other, then the first once more; he was hammering on the wheel, the horn beating out a Morse code of rage. A largely emotionless creature and part of a largely emotionless species, he had been hijacked by his host's emotional juices—not just dipping in them this time but bathing. And again he sensed this was only happening because Jonesy was still there, an unquiet tumor in what should have been a serene and focused consciousness.

Mr. Gray hammered on the wheel, hating this emotional ejaculation—what Jonesy's mind identified as a *tantrum*—but loving it, too. Loving the sound of the horn when he hit it with Jonesy's fists, loving the beat of Jonesy's blood in Jonesy's temples, loving the way Jonesy's heart sped up and the sound of Jonesy's hoarse voice crying "You fuckhead! You fuckhead!" over and over and over.

And even in the midst of this rage, a cold part of him realized what the true danger was. They always came, they always made the worlds they visited over in their image. It was the way things had always been, and the way they were meant to be.

But now . . .

Something's happening to me, Mr. Gray thought, aware even as the thought came that it was essentially a "Jonesy" thought. *I'm starting to be human.*

The fact that the idea was not without its attractions filled Mr. Gray with horror.

8

Jonesy came out of a doze where the only sound was the soothing, lulling rhythm of Mr. Gray's voice, and saw that his hands were resting on the locks of the office door, ready to turn the lower and draw the bolt on the upper. The son of a bitch was trying to hypnotize him, and doing a pretty good job of it.

"We always win," said the voice on the other side of the door. It was soothing, which was nice after such a stressful day, but it was also vilely complacent. The usurper who would not rest until he had it all . . . who took getting it all as a given. "Open the door, Jonesy, open it now."

For a moment he almost did it. He was awake again, but he almost did it anyway. Then he remembered two sounds: the tenebrous creak of Pete's skull as the red stuff tightened on it, and the wet squittering Janas's eye had made when the tip of the pen pierced it.

Jonesy realized he hadn't been awake at all, not really. But now he was.

Now he was.

Dropping his hands away from the lock and putting his lips to the door, he said "Eat shit and die" in his clearest voice. He felt Mr. Gray recoil. He even felt the pain when Mr. Gray thumped back against the window, and why not? They were his nerves, after all. Not to mention his head. Few things in his life gave him so much pleasure as Mr. Gray's outraged surprise, and he vaguely realized what Mr. Gray already knew: the alien presence in his head was more human now.

If you could come back as a physical entity, would you still be Mr. Gray? Jonesy wondered. He didn't think so. Mr. Pink, maybe, but not Mr. Gray.

He didn't know if the guy would try his Monsieur Mesmer routine again, but Jonesy decided to take no chances. He turned and went to the office window, tripping over one of the boxes and stepping over the rest. Christ, but his hip hurt. It was crazy to feel such pain when you were imprisoned in your own head (which, Henry had once assured him, had no nerves anyway, at least not once you got into the old gray matter), but the pain was there, all right. He had read that amputees sometimes felt horrible agonies and unscratchable itches in limbs that no longer existed; probably this was the same deal.

The window had returned to a tiresome view of the weedy, double-rutted driveway which had run alongside the Tracker Brothers depot back in 1978. The sky was white and overcast; apparently when his window looked into the past, time was frozen at midafternoon. The only thing the view had to recommend it was that, as he stood here taking it in, Jonesy was as far from Mr. Gray as he could possibly get.

He guessed that he *could* change the view, if he really wanted to; could look out and see what Mr. Gray was currently seeing with the eyes of Gary Jones. He had no urge to do that, however. There was nothing to look at but the snowstorm, nothing to feel but Mr. Gray's stolen rage.

Think of something else, he told himself.

What?

I don't know—anything. Why not—

On the desk the telephone rang, and that was odd on an *Alice in Wonderland* scale, because a few minutes ago there had been no telephone in this room, and no desk for it to sit on. The litter of old used rubbers had disappeared. The floor was still dirty, but the dust on the tiles was gone. Apparently there was some sort of janitor inside his head, a neatnik who had decided Jonesy was going to be here for awhile and so the place ought to be at least tolerably clean. He found the concept awesome, the implications depressing.

On the desk, the phone shrilled again. Jonesy picked up the receiver and said, "Hello?"

Beaver's voice sent a sick and horrible chill down his back. A telephone call from a dead man—it was the stuff of the movies he liked. *Had* liked, anyway.

"His head was off, Jonesy. It was laying in the ditch and his eyes were full of mud."

There was a click, then dead silence. Jonesy hung up the phone and walked back to the window. The driveway was gone. *Derry* was gone. He was looking at Hole in the Wall under a pale clear early-morning sky. The roof was black instead of green, which meant this was Hole in the Wall as it had been before 1982, when the four of them, then strapping high-school boys (well, Henry had never been what you'd call strapping), had helped Beav's Dad put up the green shingles the camp still wore.

Only Jonesy needed no such landmark to know what time it was. No more than he needed someone to tell him the green shingles were no more, Hole in the Wall was no more, Henry had burned it to the ground. In a moment the door would open and Beaver would run out. It was 1978, the year all this had really started, and in a moment Beaver would run out, wearing only his boxer shorts and his many-zippered motorcycle jacket, the orange bandannas fluttering. It was 1978, they were young . . . and they had changed. No more same shit, different day. This was the day when they began to realize just how *much* they had changed.

Jonesy stared out the window, fascinated.

The door opened.

Beaver Clarendon, age fourteen, ran out.

CHAPTER FIFTEEN

HENRY AND OWEN

1

Henry watched Underhill trudge toward him in the glare of the security lights. Underhill's head was bent against the snow and the intensifying wind. Henry opened his mouth to call out, but before he could, he was overwhelmed, nearly *flattened*, by a sense of Jonesy. And then a memory came, blotting out Underhill and this brightly lit, snowy world completely. All at once it was 1978 again, not October but November and there was *blood*, blood on cattails, broken glass in marshy water, and then the bang of the door.

2

Henry awakes from a terrible confused dream—blood, broken glass, the rich smells of gasoline and burning rubber—to the sound of a banging door and a blast of cold air. He sits up and sees Pete sitting up beside him, Pete's hairless chest covered with goosebumps. Henry and Pete are on the floor in their sleeping-bags because they lost the four-way toss. Beav and Jonesy got the bed (later there will be a third bedroom at Hole in the Wall, but now there are only two and Lamar has one all to himself, by the divine right of adulthood), only now Jonesy is alone in the bed, also sitting up, also looking confused and frightened.

Scooby-ooby-Doo, where are you, Henry thinks for no appreciable reason as he gropes for his glasses on the windowsill. In his nose he can still smell gas and burning tires. *We got some work to do now—*

"Crashed," Jonesy says thickly, and throws back the covers. His chest is bare, but like Henry and Pete, he wore his socks and longjohn bottoms to bed.

"Yeah, went in the water," Pete says, his face suggesting he doesn't have the slightest idea what he's talking about. "Henry, you got his shoe—"

"Moccasin—" Henry says, but he hasn't any idea what *he's* talking about either. Nor wants to.

"Beav," Jonesy says, and gets out of bed in a clumsy lunge. One of his stocking-clad feet comes down on Pete's hand.

"Ow!" Pete cries. "Ya stepped on me, ya fuckin gomer, watch where *you're*—"

"Shut up, shut up," Henry says, grabbing Pete's shoulder and giving it a shake. "Don't wake up Mr. Clarendon!"

Which would be easy, because the door of the boys' bedroom is open. So is the door on the far side of the big central room, the one to the outside. No wonder they're cold, there's a hell of a draft. Now that Henry has his eyes back on (that is how he thinks of it), he can see the dreamcatcher out there dancing in the cold November breeze coming in through the open door.

"Where's Duddits?" Jonesy asks in a dazed, I'm-still-dreaming voice. "Did he go out with Beaver?"

"He's back in Derry, foolish," Henry says, getting up and pulling on his thermal undershirt. And he doesn't feel that Jonesy is foolish, not really; he also has a sense that Duddits was just here with them.

It was the dream, he thinks. *Duddits was in the dream. He was sitting on the bank. He was crying. He was sorry. He didn't mean to. If anyone meant to, it was us.*

And there is still crying. He can hear it, coming in through the front door, carried on the breeze. It's not Duddits, though; it's the Beav.

They leave the room in a line, pulling on scraps of clothes as they go, not bothering with their shoes, which would take too long.

One good thing—judging from the tin city of beer-cans on the kitchen table (plus a suburb of same on the coffee-table), it'll take more than a couple of open doors and some whispering kids to wake up Beaver's Dad.

The big granite doorstep is freezing under Henry's stocking feet, cold in the deep thoughtless way death must be cold, but he barely notices.

He sees the Beaver right away. He's at the foot of the maple tree with the deer-stand in it, on his knees as if praying. His legs and feet are bare, Henry sees. He's wearing his motorcycle jacket, and tied up and down its arms, fluttering like pirate's finery, are the orange bandannas his father made his son wear when Beaver insisted on wearing such a damned foolish unhunterly thing in the woods. The outfit looks pretty funny, but there's nothing funny about that agonized face tilted up toward the maple's nearly bare branches. The Beav's cheeks are streaming with tears.

Henry breaks into a run. Pete and Jonesy follow suit, their breath puffing white in the chill morning air. The needle-strewn ground under Henry's feet is almost as hard and cold as the granite doorstep.

He drops to his knees beside Beaver, scared and somehow awed by those tears. Because the Beav isn't just misting up, like the hero of a movie who may be allowed to shed a manly drop or two when his dog or his girlfriend dies; Beav is running like Niagara Falls. From his nose hang two ropes of clear glistening snot. You never saw stuff like *that* in the movies.

"Gross," Pete says.

Henry looks at him impatiently, but then he sees Pete isn't looking at Beaver but past him, at a steaming puddle of vomit. In it are kernels of last night's corn (Lamar Clarendon believes passionately in the virtues of canned food when it comes to camp cooking) and strings of last night's fried chicken. Henry's stomach takes a big unhappy lurch. And just as it starts to settle, Jonesy yarks. The sound is like a big liquid belch. The puke is brown.

"*Gross!*" Pete almost screams it this time.

Beaver doesn't seem to even notice. "Henry!" he

says. His eyes, submerged beneath twin lenses of tears, are huge and spooky. They seem to peer past Henry's face and into the supposedly private rooms behind his forehead.

"Beav, it's okay. You had a bad dream."

"Sure, a bad dream." Jonesy's voice is thick, his throat still plated with puke. He tries to clear it with a thick *ratching* noise that is somehow worse than what just came out of him, then bends over and spits. His hands are planted on the legs of his longhandles, and his bare back is covered with bumps.

Beav takes no notice of Jonesy, nor of Pete as Pete kneels down on his other side and puts a clumsy, tentative arm around Beav's shoulders. Beav continues to look only at Henry.

"His head was off," Beaver whispers.

Jonesy also drops to his knees, and now all three of them are surrounding the Beav, Henry and Pete to either side, Jonesy in front. There is vomit on Jonesy's chin. He reaches to wipe it away, but Beaver takes his hand before he can. The boys kneel beneath the maple, and suddenly they are all one. It is brief, this sense of union, but as vivid as their dream. It *is* the dream, but now they are all awake, the sensation is rational, and they cannot disbelieve.

Now it is Jonesy the Beav is looking at with his spooky swimming eyes. Clutching Jonesy's hand.

"It was laying in the ditch and his eyes were full of mud."

"Yeah," Jonesy whispers in an awed and shaky voice. "Oh Jeez, it was."

"Said he'd see us again, remember?" Pete asks. "One at a time or all together. He *said* that."

Henry hears these things from a great distance, because he's back in the dream. Back at the scene of the accident. At the bottom of a trash-littered embankment where there is a soggy piece of marsh, created by a blocked drainage culvert. He knows the place, it's on Route 7, the old Derry-Newport Road. Lying overturned in the muck and the murk is a burning car. The air stinks of gas and burning tires. Duddits is crying. Duddits is sitting halfway down the trashy slope and holding his yellow Scooby-Doo lunchbox against his chest and crying his eyes out.

A hand protrudes from one of the windows of the overturned car. It's slim, the nails painted candy-apple red. The car's other two occupants have been thrown clear, one of them almost thirty damn feet. This one's facedown, but Henry still recognizes him by the masses of soaked blond hair. *It's Duncan, the one who said you're not gonna tell anyone anything, because you'll be fuckin dead.* Only Duncan's the one who wound up dead.

Something floats against Henry's shin. "Don't pick that up!" Pete says urgently, but Henry does. It's a brown suede moccasin. He has just time to register this, and then Beaver and Jonesy shriek in terrible childish harmony. They are standing together, ankle-deep in the muck, both of them wearing their hunting clothes: Jonesy in his new bright orange parka, bought special from Sears for this trip (and Mrs. Jones still tearfully, unpersuadably convinced that her son will be killed in the woods by a hunter's bullet, cut down in his prime), Beaver in his tattered motorcycle jacket (*What a lot of zippers!* Duddie's Mom had said admiringly, thus winning Beaver's love and admiration forever) with the orange bandannas tied up and down the arms. They aren't looking at the third body, the one lying just outside the driver's door, but Henry does, just for a moment (still holding the moccasin, like a small water-logged canoe, in his hands), because something is terribly, fundamentally wrong with it, so wrong that for a moment he cannot tell what it might be. Then he realizes that there's nothing above the collar of the corpse's high-school jacket. Beaver and Jonesy are screaming because they have seen what *should* have been above it. They have seen Richie Grenadeau's head lying faceup, glaring at the sky from a blood-spattered stand of cattails. Henry knows it's Richie at once. Even though the swatch of tape no longer rides the bridge of his nose, there is no mistaking the guy who was trying to feed Duddits a piece of shit that day behind Tracker's.

Duds is up there on the bank, crying and crying, that crying that gets into your head like a sinus headache, and if it goes on it will drive Henry mad. He drops the moc and slogs around the back of the burning car to where Beaver and Jonesy stand with their arms around each other.

"Beaver! *Beav!*" Henry shouts, but until he reaches out and gives Beaver a hard shake, Beaver just continues to stare at the severed head, as if hypnotized.

Finally, though, Beaver looks at him. "His head's

off," he says, as if this were not evident. "Henry, his *head's*—"

"Never mind his head, take care of Duddits! Make him stop that goddam crying!"

"Yeah," Pete says. He looks at Richie's head, that final dead glare, then looks away, mouth twitching. "It's drivin me fuckin bugshit."

"Like chalk on a chalkboard," Jonesy mutters. Above his new orange parka, his skin is the color of old cheese. "Make him stop, Beav."

"H-H-H—"

"Don't be a dweeb, sing him the fuckin *song!*" Henry shouts. He can feel mucky water oozing up between his toes. "The lullaby, the goddam *lullaby!*"

For a moment the Beav looks as though he still doesn't understand, but then his eyes clear a little and he says "Oh!" He goes slogging toward the embankment where Duddits sits, clutching his bright yellow lunchbox and howling as he did on the day they met him. Henry sees something that he barely has time to notice: there is blood caked around Duddits's nostrils, and there's a bandage on his left shoulder. Something is poking out of it, something that looks like white plastic.

"Duddits," the Beav says, climbing the embankment. "Duddie, honey, don't. Don't cry no more, don't look at it no more, it's not for you to look at, it's so fuckin gross . . ."

At first Duddits takes no notice, just goes on howling. Henry thinks, *He cried himself into a nosebleed and that's the blood part, but what's that white thing sticking out of his shoulder?*

Jonesy has actually raised his hands to cover his ears. Pete has got one of his on top of his head, as if to keep it from blowing off. Then Beaver takes Duddits in his arms, just as he did a few weeks earlier, and begins to sing in that high clear voice that you'd never think could come out of a scrub like the Beav.

"Baby's boat's a silver dream, sailing near and far . . ."

And oh miracle of blessed miracles, Duddits begins to quiet.

Speaking from the corner of his mouth, Pete says: "Where are we, Henry? Where the fuck *are* we?"

"In a dream," Henry says, and all at once the four of them are back under the maple tree at Hole in the Wall, kneeling together in their underwear and shivering in the cold.

"What?" Jonesy says. He pulls free to wipe at his mouth, and when the contact among them breaks, reality comes all the way back. "What did you say, Henry?"

Henry feels the withdrawal of their minds, actually feels it, and he thinks, *We weren't meant to be like this, none of us. Sometimes being alone is better.*

Yes, alone. Alone with your thoughts.

"I had a bad dream," Beaver says. He seems to be explaining this to himself rather than to the rest of them. Slowly, as if he were *still* dreaming, he unzips one of his jacket pockets, rummages around inside, and comes out with a Tootsie Pop. Instead of unwrapping it, Beaver puts the stick end in his mouth and begins to roll it back and forth, nipping and gnawing lightly. "I dreamed that—"

"Never mind," Henry says, and pushes his glasses up on his nose. "We all know what you dreamed." *We ought to, we were there* trembles on his lips, but he keeps it inside. He's only fourteen, but wise enough to know that what is said cannot be unsaid. *When it's laid, it's played* they say when they're playing rummy or Crazy Eights and someone makes a goofy-ass discard. If he says it, they'll have to deal with it. If he doesn't, then maybe . . . just maybe it'll go away.

"I don't think it was your dream, anyhow," Pete says. "I think it was Duddits's dream and we all—"

"I don't give a shit *what* you think," Jonesy says, his voice so harsh that it startles them all. "It was a *dream,* and I'm going to forget it. We're *all* going to forget it, aren't we, Henry?"

Henry nods at once.

"Let's go back in," Pete says. He looks vastly relieved. "My feet're free—"

"One thing, though," Henry says, and they all look at him nervously. Because when they need a leader, Henry is it. *And if you don't like the way I do it,* he thinks resentfully, *someone else can do it. Because this is no tit job, believe me.*

"What?" Beaver asks, meaning *What now?*

"When we go into Gosselin's later on, someone's got to call Duds. In case he's upset."

No one replies to this, all of them awed to silence by the idea of calling their new retardo friend on the phone. It occurs to Henry that Duddits has likely never received a phone call in his life; this will be his first.

"You know, that's probably right," Pete agrees . . .

and then slaps his hand over his mouth like someone who has said something incriminating.

Beaver, naked except for his dopey boxers and his even dopier jacket, is now shivering violently. The Tootsie Pop jitters at the end of its gnawed stick.

"Someday you'll choke on one of those things," Henry tells him.

"Yeah, that's what my Mom says. Can we go in? I'm freezing."

They start back toward Hole in the Wall, where their friendship will end twenty-three years from this very day.

"Is Richie Grenadeau really dead, do you think?" Beaver asks.

"I don't know and I don't care," Jonesy says. He looks at Henry. "We'll call Duddits, okay—I've got a phone and we can bill the charges to my number."

"Your own phone," Pete says. "You lucky duck. Your folks spoil you fuckin rotten, Gary."

Calling him Gary usually gets under his skin, but not this morning—Jonesy is too preoccupied. "It was for my birthday and *I* have to pay the long-distance out of my allowance, so let's keep it short. And after that, this never happened—*never happened,* you got that?"

And they all nod. Never happened. Never fucking hap—

3

A gust of wind pushed Henry forward, almost into the electrified compound fence. He came back to himself, shaking off the memory like a heavy coat. It couldn't have come at a more inconvenient time (of course, the time for some memories was *never* convenient). He had been waiting for Underhill, freezing his katookis off and waiting for his only chance to get out of here, and Underhill could have walked right by him while he stood daydreaming, leaving him up shit creek without a paddle.

Only Underhill hadn't gone past. He was standing on the other side of the fence, hands in his pockets, looking at Henry. Snowflakes landed on the transparent, buglike bulb of the mask he wore, were melted by the warmth of his breath, and ran down its surface like . . .

Like Beaver's tears that day, Henry thought.

"You ought to go in the barn with the rest of them," Underhill said. "You'll turn into a snowman out here."

Henry's tongue was stuck to the roof of his mouth. His life quite literally depended on what he said to this man, and he could think of no way to get started. Couldn't even loosen his tongue.

And why bother? the voice inside inquired—the voice of darkness, his old friend. *Really and truly, why bother? Why not just let them do what you were going to do to yourself, anyway?*

Because it wasn't just him anymore. Yet he still couldn't speak.

Underhill stood where he was a moment longer, looking at him. Hands in pockets. Hood thrown back to expose his short dark-blond hair. Snow melting on the mask the soldiers wore and the detainees did not, because the detainees would not be needing them; for the detainees, as for the grayboys, there was a final solution.

Henry struggled to speak and could not, could not. Ah God, it should have been Jonesy here, not him; Jonesy had always been better with his mouth. Underhill was going to walk away, leaving him with a lot of could-have-beens and might-have-beens.

But Underhill stayed a moment longer.

"I'm not surprised you knew my name, Mr. . . . Henreid? Is your name Henreid?"

"Devlin. It's my first name you're picking up. I'm Henry Devlin." Moving very carefully, Henry thrust his hand through the gap between a strand of barbed wire and one of electrified smoothwire. After Underhill did nothing but look at it expressionlessly for five seconds or so, Henry pulled his hand back to his part of the newly drawn world, feeling foolish and telling himself not to be such an idiot, it wasn't as if he'd been snubbed at a cocktail party.

Once that was done, Underhill nodded pleasantly, as if they *were* at a cocktail party instead of out here in a shrieking storm, illuminated by the newly installed security lights.

"You knew my name because the alien presence in Jefferson Tract has caused a low-level telepathic effect." Underhill smiled. "Sounds silly when you say it right out, doesn't it? But it's true. The effect is transient, harmless, and too shallow to be good for much except party games, and we're a little too busy tonight for those."

Henry's tongue came finally, blessedly, unstuck.

"You didn't come over here in a snowstorm because I knew *your* name," Henry said. "You came over because I knew your *wife's* name. And your daughter's."

Underhill's smile didn't falter. "Maybe I did," he said. "In any case, I think it's time we both got under cover and got some rest—it's been a long day."

Underhill began walking, but his way took him alongside the fence, toward the other parked trailers and campers. Henry kept pace, although he had to work in order to do it; there was nearly a foot of snow on the ground now, it was drifting, and no one had tramped it down over here on the dead man's side.

"Mr. Underhill. Owen. Stop a minute and listen to me. I've got something important to tell you."

Underhill kept walking along the path on his side of the fence (which was *also* the dead man's side; did Underhill not know that?), head down against the wind, still wearing that faintly pleasant smile. And the awful thing, Henry knew, was that Underhill *wanted* to stop. It was just that Henry had not, so far, given him a reason to do so.

"Kurtz is crazy," Henry said. He was still keeping pace but he was panting audibly now, his exhausted legs screaming. "But he's crazy like a fox."

Underhill kept walking, head down and little smile in place under the idiotic mask. If anything, he walked faster. Soon Henry would have to run in order to keep up on his side of the fence. If running was still possible for him.

"You'll turn the machine-guns on us," Henry panted. "Bodies go in the barn . . . barn gets doused with gasoline . . . probably from Old Man Gosselin's own pump, why waste government issue . . . and then *ploof,* up in smoke . . . two hundred . . . four hundred . . . it'll smell like a VFW pig-roast in hell . . ."

Underhill's smile was gone and he walked faster still. Henry somehow found the strength to trot, gasping for air and fighting his way through knee-high snowdunes. The wind was keen against his throbbing face. Like a blade.

"But Owen . . . that's you, right? . . . Owen? . . . you remember that old rhyme . . . the one that goes 'Big fleas . . . got little fleas . . . to bite em . . . and so on and so on . . . and so on *ad infinitum?*' . . . that's here and that's you . . . because Kurtz has got his own cadre . . . the man under him, I think his name is Johnson . . ."

Underhill gave him a single sharp look, then walked faster than ever. Henry somehow managed to keep up, but he didn't think he would be able to much longer. He had a stitch in his side. It was hot and getting hotter. "That was supposed . . . to be your job . . . the second part of the clean-up . . . Imperial Valley, that's the . . . code name . . . mean anything to you?"

Henry saw it didn't. Kurtz must never have told Underhill about the operation that would wipe out most of Blue Group. Imperial Valley meant exactly squat to Owen Underhill, and now, in addition to the stitch, Henry had what felt like an iron band around his chest, squeezing and squeezing.

"Stop . . . Jesus, Underhill . . . can't you . . . ?"

Underhill just kept striding along. Underhill wanted to keep his last few illusions. Who could blame him?

"Johnson . . . a few others . . . at least one's a woman . . . could have been you too if you hadn't fucked up . . . you crossed the line, that's what he thinks . . . not the first time, either . . . you did it before, at some place like Bossa Nova . . ."

That earned Henry a sudden sharp look. Progress? Maybe.

"In the end I think . . . even Johnson goes . . . only Kurtz leaves here alive . . . the rest . . . nothing but a pile of ashes and bones . . . your fucking telepathy doesn't . . . tell you *that,* does it . . . your little parlor-trick mind-reading . . . won't even . . . fucking touch . . . *that* . . ."

The stitch in his side deepened and sank into his right armpit like a claw. At the same time his feet slipped and he went flailing headfirst into a snowdrift. His lungs tore furiously for air and instead got a great gasp of powdery snow.

Henry flailed to his knees, coughing and choking, and saw Underhill's back just disappearing into the wall of blowing snow. Not knowing what he was going to say, knowing only that it was his last chance, he screamed: "You tried to piss on Mr. Rapeloew's toothbrush and when you couldn't do that you broke their plate! Broke their plate and ran away! *Just like you're running away now, you fucking coward!*"

Ahead of him, barely visible in the snow, Owen Underhill stopped.

4

For a moment he only stood there, his back to Henry, who knelt panting like a dog in the snow with melting, icy water running down his burning face. Henry was aware in a way that was both distant and immediate that the scratch on his leg where the byrus was growing had begun to itch.

At last Underhill turned around and came back. "How do you know about the Rapeloews? The telepathy is fading. You shouldn't be able to get that deep."

"I know a lot," Henry said. He got to his feet and then stood there, gasping and coughing. "Because it runs deep in me. I'm different. My friends and I, we were all different. There were four of us. Two are dead. I'm in here. The fourth one . . . Mr. Underhill, the fourth one is your problem. Not me, not the people you've got in the barn or the ones you're still bringing in, not your Blue Group or Kurtz's Imperial Valley cadre. Only him." He struggled, not wanting to say the name—Jonesy was the one to whom he had been the closest, Beaver and Pete were great, but only Jonesy could run with him mind for mind, book for book, idea for idea; only Jonesy also had the knack of dreaming outside the lines as well as seeing the line. But Jonesy was gone, wasn't he? Henry was quite sure of that. He had been there, a tiny bit of him *had* been there when the redblack cloud passed Henry, but by now his old friend would have been eaten alive. His heart might still beat and his eyes might still see, but the essential Jonesy was as dead as Pete and the Beav.

"Jonesy's your problem, Mr. Underhill. Gary Jones, of Brookline, Massachusetts."

"Kurtz is a problem, too." Underhill spoke too softly to be heard over the howling wind, but Henry heard him, anyway—heard him in his mind.

Underhill looked around. Henry followed the shift of his head and saw a few men running down the makeshift avenue between the campers and trailer boxes—no one close. Yet the entire area around the store and the barn was mercilessly bright, and even with the wind he could hear revving engines, the stuttery roar of generators, and men yelling. Someone was giving orders through a bullhorn. The overall effect was eerie, as if the two of them had been trapped by the storm in a place filled with ghosts. The running men even *looked* like ghosts as they faded into the dancing sheets of snow.

"We can't talk here," Underhill said. "Listen to me, and don't make me repeat a single word, buck."

And in Henry's head, where there was now so much input that most of it was tangled into an incomprehensible stew, a thought from Owen Underhill's mind suddenly rose clear and plain: *Buck. His word. I can't believe I used his word.*

"I'm listening," Henry said.

5

The shed was on the far side of the compound, as far from the barn as it was possible to get, and although the outside was as brilliantly lit as the rest of this hell-ish concentration camp, the inside was dark and smelled sweetly of old hay. And something else, something a little more acrid.

There were four men and a woman sitting with their backs against the shed's far wall. They were all dressed in orange hunting togs, and they were passing a joint. There were only two windows in the shed, one facing in toward the corral, the other facing out toward the perimeter fence and the woods beyond. The glass was dirty, and cut the merciless white glare of the sodium lights a little. In the dimness, the faces of the pot-smoking prisoners looked gray, dead already.

"You want a hit?" the one with the joint asked. He spoke in a strained, miserly voice, holding the smoke in, but he held the joint out willingly enough. It was a bomber, Henry saw, big as a panatela.

"No. I want you all to get out of here."

They looked at him, uncomprehending. The woman was married to the man currently holding the joint. The guy on her left was her brother-in-law. The other two were just along for the ride.

"Go back to the barn," Henry said.

"No way," one of the other men said. "Too crowded in there. We prefer to be more exclusive. And since we were here first, I suggest that if you don't want to be sociable, *you* should be the one to—"

"I've got it," Henry said. He put a hand on the tee-shirt knotted around his leg. "Byrus. What *they* call Ripley. Some of you may have it . . . I think you do, Charles——" He pointed at the fifth man, burly in his parka and balding.

"No!" Charles cried, but the others were already scrambling away from him, the one with the Cambodian cigar (his name was Darren Chiles and he was from Newton, Massachusetts) being careful to hold onto his smoke.

"Yeah, you do," Henry said. "Major league. So do you, Mona. Mona? No, Marsha. It's Marsha."

"I don't!" she said. She got up, pressing her back against the shed wall and looking at Henry with large, terrified eyes. Doe's eyes. Soon all the does up here would be dead, and Marsha would be dead, as well. Henry hoped she could not see that thought in his mind. "I'm clean, mister, we're all clean in here except *you*!"

She looked at her husband, who was not big, but bigger than Henry. They all were, actually. Not taller, maybe, but bigger.

"Throw him out, Dare."

"There are two types of Ripley," Henry said, stating as fact what he only believed . . . but the more he thought about it, the more sense it made. "Call them Ripley Prime and Ripley Secondary. I'm pretty sure that if you didn't get a hot dose—in something you ate or inhaled or something that went live into an open wound—you can get better. You can beat it."

Now they were all looking at him with those big doe eyes, and Henry felt a moment of surpassing despair. Why couldn't he just have had a nice quiet suicide?

"I've got Ripley Prime," he said. He unknotted the tee-shirt. None of them would do more than glance at the rip in Henry's snow-powdered jeans, but Henry took a good big look for all of them. The wound made by the turnsignal stalk had now filled up with byrus. Some of the strands were three inches long, their tips wavering like kelp in a tidal current. He could feel the roots of the stuff working in steadily, deeper and deeper, itching and foaming and fizzing. Trying to think. That was the worst of it—*it was trying to think.*

Now they were moving toward the shed door, and Henry expected them to bolt as soon as they caught a clear whiff of the cold air. Instead they paused.

"Mister, can you help us?" Marsha asked in a trembling child's voice. Darren, her husband, put his arm around her.

"I don't know," Henry said. "Probably not . . . but maybe. Go on, now. I'll be out of here in half an hour, maybe less, but probably it's best if you stay in the barn with the others."

"Why?" asked Darren Chiles from Newton.

And Henry, who had only a ghost of an idea— nothing resembling a plan—said, "I don't know. I just think it is."

They went out, leaving Henry in possession of the shed.

6

Beneath the window facing the perimeter fence was an ancient bale of hay. Darren Chiles had been sitting on it when Henry came in (as the one with the dope, Chiles had rated the most comfortable seat), and now Henry took his place. He sat with his hands on his knees, feeling immediately sleepy in spite of the voices tumbling around in his head and the deep, spreading itch in his left leg (it was starting in his mouth, as well, where he had lost one of his teeth).

He heard Underhill coming before Underhill actually spoke from outside the window; heard the approach of his mind.

"I'm in the lee of the wind and mostly in the shadow of the building," Underhill said. "I'm having a smoke. If someone comes along, you're not in there."

"Okay."

"Lie to me, I'll walk away and you'll never in your short life speak to me again, out loud or . . . otherwise."

"Okay."

"How did you get rid of the people in there?"

"Why?" Henry would have said he was too tired to be angry, but that seemed not to be the case. "Was it some kind of goddam test?"

"Don't be a jerk."

"I told them I've got Ripley Prime, which is the truth. They scatted in a hurry." Henry paused. "You've got it too, don't you?"

"What makes you think so?" Henry could detect no strain in Underhill's voice, and as a psychiatrist, he was familiar with the signs. Whatever else Underhill might be, Henry had an idea that he was a man with a tremendously cool head, and that was a step in the right direction. *Also,* he thought, *it can't hurt if he understands he really has nothing to lose.*

"It's around your fingernails, isn't it? And a little in one ear."

"You'd wow em in Vegas, buddy." Henry saw Underhill's hand go up, with a cigarette between the gloved fingers. He guessed the wind would end up smoking most of that one.

"You get Primary direct from the source. I'm pretty sure Secondary comes from touching something that's growing it—tree, moss, deer, dog, another person. You catch that kind like you catch poison ivy. This isn't anything your own medical technicians don't know. For all I can tell, I got the information from them. My head's like a goddam satellite dish with everything beaming in on Free Preview and nothing blocked out. I can't tell where half of this stuff's coming from and it doesn't matter. Now here's some stuff your med-techs don't know. The grays call the red growth *byrus,* a word that means 'the stuff of life.' Under some circumstances, the Prime version of it can grow the implants."

"The shit-weasels, you mean."

"Shit-weasels, that's good. I like that. They spring from the byrus, then reproduce by laying eggs. They spread, lay more eggs, spread again. That's the way it's supposed to work, anyway. Here, most of the eggs go dead. I have no idea if it's the cold weather, the atmosphere, or something else. But in our environment, Underhill, it's all about the byrus. It's all they've got that works."

"The stuff of life."

"Uh-huh, but listen: the grays are having big problems here, which is probably why they hung around so long—half a century—before making their move. The weasels, for instance. They're supposed to be saprophytes . . . do you know what that means?"

"Henry . . . that's you, right? Henry? . . . Henry, does this have any bearing on our present—"

"It has *plenty* of bearing on our present situation. And unless you want to own a large part of the responsibility for the end of all life on Spaceship Earth—except for a lot of interstellar kudzu, that is—I advise you to shut up and listen."

A pause. Then: "I'm listening."

"Saprophytes are beneficial parasites. We have them living in our guts, and we deliberately swallow more in some dairy products. Sweet acidophilus milk, for instance, and yogurt. We give the bugs a place to live and they give us something in return. In the case of dairy bacteria, improved digestion. The weasels, under normal circumstances—normal on some other world, I guess, where the ecology differs in ways I can't even guess at—grow to a size maybe no bigger than the bowl of a teaspoon. I think that in females they may interfere with reproduction, but they don't kill. Not normally. They just live in the bowel. We give them food, they give us telepathy. That's supposed to be the trade. Only they also turn us into televisions. We are Grayboy TV."

"And you know all this because you have one living inside you?" There was no revulsion in Underhill's voice, but Henry felt it clearly in the man's mind, pulsing like a tentacle. "One of the quote-unquote normal weasels?"

"No." *At least,* he thought, *I don't think so.*

"Then how do you know what you know? Or are you maybe just making it up as you go along? Trying to write yourself a pass out of here?"

"How I know is the least important thing of all, Owen—but you know I'm not lying. You can read me."

"I know you *think* you're not lying. How much more of this mind-reading shit can I expect to get?"

"I don't know. More if the byrus spreads, probably, but not in my league."

"Because you're different." Skepticism, both in Underhill's voice and in Underhill's thoughts.

"Pal, I didn't know how different until today. But never mind that for a minute. For now, I just want you to understand that the grays are in a shitpull here. For maybe the first time in their history, they're in an actual battle for control. First, because when they get inside people, the weasels aren't saprophytic but violently parasitic. They don't stop eating and *they* don't stop growing. They're cancer, Underhill.

"Second, the byrus. It grows well on other worlds but poorly on ours, at least so far. The scientists and the medical experts who are running this rodeo think the cold is slowing it down, but I don't think that's it, or not all of it. I can't be positive because *they* don't know, but—"

"Whoa, whoa." There was a brief cupped flame as

Underhill lit another cigarette for the wind to smoke. "You're not talking about the medical guys, are you?"

"No."

"You think you're in touch with the grayboys. Telepathically in touch."

"I think . . . with one of them. Through a link."

"This Jonesy you spoke of?"

"Owen, I don't know. Not for sure. The point is, *they're losing*. Me, you, the men who went out there to the Blue Boy with you today, we might not be around to celebrate Christmas. I won't kid you about that. We got high, concentrated doses. But—"

"I've got it, all right," Underhill said. "Edwards, too—it showed up on him like magic."

"But even if it really takes hold on you, I don't think you can spread it very far. *It's not just that catchable.* There are people in that barn who'll never get it, no matter how many byrus-infected people they mingle with. And the people who do catch it like a cold come down with Byrus Secondary . . . or Ripley, if you like that better."

"Let's stick to byrus."

"Okay. They *might* be able to pass it on to a few people, who would have a very weak version we could call Byrus Three. It might even be communicable beyond that, but I think once you got to Byrus Four you'd need a microscope or a blood-test to pick it up. Then it's gone.

"Here's the instant replay, so pay attention.

"Point one. The grays—probably no more than delivery-systems for the byrus—are gone already. The ones the environment didn't kill, like the microbes finally killed the Martians in *War of the Worlds,* were wiped out by your gunships. All but one, that is, the one—yeah, must be—that I got my information from. And in a physical sense, he's gone, too.

"Point two. The weasels don't work. Like all cancers, they ultimately eat themselves to death. The weasels that escape from the lower intestine or the bowel quickly die in an environment they find hostile.

"Point three. The byrus doesn't work, either, not very well, but given a chance, given time to hide and grow, it could mutate. Learn to fit in. Maybe to rule."

"We're going to wipe it out," Underhill said. "We're going to turn the entire Jefferson Tract into a burn-scar."

Henry could have screamed with frustration, and some of that must have gotten through. There was a thud as Underhill jerked, striking the flimsy shed wall with his back.

"What you do up here doesn't matter," Henry said. "The people you've got interned can't spread it, the weasels can't spread it, and the byrus can't spread itself. If your guys folded their tents and just walked away right now, the environment would take care of itself and erase all this nonsense like a bad equation. I think the grays showed up the way they did because they just can't fucking believe it. I think it was a suicide mission with some gray version of your Mistuh Kurtz in charge. They simply cannot conceptualize failure. 'We always win,' they think."

"How do you—"

"Then, at the last minute, Underhill—maybe at the last *second*—one of them found a man who was remarkably different from all the others with whom the grays, the weasels, and the byrus had come in contact. He's your Typhoid Mary. And he's already out of the q-zone, rendering anything you do here meaningless."

"Gary Jones."

"Jonesy, right."

"What makes him different?"

Little as he wanted to go into this part of it, Henry realized he had to give Underhill something.

"He and I and our two other friends—the ones who are dead—once knew someone who was *very* different. A natural telepath, no byrus needed. He did something to us. If we'd gotten to know him when we were a little older, I don't think that would have been possible, but we met him when we were particularly . . . vulnerable, I suppose you'd say . . . to what he had. And then, years later, something else happened to Jonesy, something that had nothing to do with . . . with this remarkable boy."

But that wasn't the truth, Henry suspected; although Jonesy had been hit and almost killed in Cambridge and Duddits had never to Henry's knowledge been south of Derry in his life, Duds had somehow been a part of Jonesy's final, crucial change. A part of that, too. He *knew* it.

"And I'm supposed to . . . what? Just believe all this? Swallow it like cough-syrup?"

In the sweet-smelling darkness of the shed, Henry's lips spread in a humorless grin. "Owen," he said, "you *do* believe it. I'm a telepath, remember? The baddest one in the jungle. The question, though . . . the question is . . ."

Henry asked the question with his mind.

7

Standing outside the compound fence by the back wall of the old storage shed, freezing his balls off, filter-mask pulled down around his neck so he could smoke a series of cigarettes he did not want (he'd gotten a fresh pack in the PX), Owen would have said he never felt less like laughing in his life . . . but when the man in the shed responded to his eminently reasonable question with such impatient directness—*you do believe it . . . I'm a telepath, remember?*—a laugh was surprised out of him, nevertheless. Kurtz had said that if the telepathy became permanent and were to spread, society as they knew it would fall down. Owen had grasped the concept, but now he understood it on a gut level, too.

"The question, though . . . the question is . . ."

What are we going to do about it?

Tired as he was, Owen could see only one answer to that question. "We have to go after Jones, I suppose. Will it do any good? Do we have time?"

"I think we might. Just."

Owen tried to read what was behind Henry's response with his own lesser powers and could not. Yet he was positive that most of what the man had told him was true. *Either that or he believes it's true,* Owen thought. *God knows I want to believe it's true. Any excuse to get out of here before the butchery starts.*

"No," Henry said, and for the first time Owen thought he sounded upset, not entirely sure of himself. "No butchery. Kurtz isn't going to kill somewhere between two hundred and eight hundred people. People who ultimately can't influence this business one way or the other. They're just—Christ, they're just innocent bystanders!"

Owen wasn't entirely surprised to find himself rather enjoying his new friend's discomfort; God knew Henry had discomfited *him.* "What do you suggest? Bearing in mind that you yourself said that only your pal Jonesy matters."

"Yes, but . . ."

Floundering. Henry's mental voice was a little surer, but only a little. *I didn't mean we'd walk away and let them die.*

"We won't be walking anywhere," Owen said. "We'll be running like a couple of rats in a corncrib." He dropped his third cigarette after a final token puff and watched the wind carry it away. Beyond the shed, curtains of snow rippled across the empty corral, building up huge drifts against the side of the barn. Trying to go anywhere in this would be madness. *It'll have to be a Sno-Cat, at least to start with,* Owen thought. *By midnight, even a four-wheel drive might not be much good. Not in this.*

"Kill Kurtz," Henry said. "That's the answer. It'll make it easier for us to get away with no one to give orders, and it'll put the . . . the biological cleansing on hold."

Owen laughed dryly. "You make it sound so easy," he said. "Double-oh-Underhill, license to kill."

He lit a fourth cigarette, cupping his hands around the lighter and the end of the smoke. In spite of his gloves, his fingers were numb. *We better come to some conclusions pretty quick,* he thought. *Before I freeze to death.*

"What's the big deal about it?" Henry asked, but he knew what the big deal was, all right; Owen could sense (and half-hear) him trying not to see it, not wanting things to be worse than they already were. "Just walk in there and pop him."

"Wouldn't work." Owen sent Henry a brief image: Freddy Johnson (and other members of the so-called Imperial Valley cadre) keeping an eye on Kurtz's Winnebago. "Also, he's got the place wired for sound. If anything happens, the hard boys come running. Maybe I *could* get him. Probably not, because he covers himself as thoroughly as any Colombian cocaine *jefe,* especially when he's on active duty, but maybe. I like to think I'm not bad myself. But it would be a suicide mission. If he's recruited Freddy Johnson, then he's probably got Kate Gallagher and Marvell Richardson . . . Carl Friedman . . . Jocelyn McAvoy. Tough boys and tough girls, Henry. I kill Kurtz, they kill me, the brass running this show from under Cheyenne Mountain send out a new cleaner, some Kurtz clone that'll pick up where Kurtz left off. Or maybe they just elect Kate to the job. God knows she's crazy enough. The people in the barn might get twelve additional hours to stew in their own juice, but in the end they'll still burn. The only difference is that, instead of getting a chance to go charging gaily through the snowstorm with me, handsome, you'll burn with the rest of them. Your pal, meanwhile—this guy Jonesy—he'll be off to . . . to where?"

"That's something it might be prudent for me to keep to myself, for the time being."

Owen nonetheless probed for it with such telepathy as he possessed. For a moment he caught a blurred and perplexing vision—a tall white building in the snow, cylindrical, like a barn silo—and then it was gone, replaced by the image of a white horse that looked almost like a unicorn running past a sign. On the sign were red letters reading BANBURY CROSS under a pointing arrow.

He grunted in amusement and exasperation. "You're jamming me."

"You can think of it that way. Or you can think of it as teaching you a technique you better learn if you'd like to keep our conversation a secret."

"Uh-huh." Owen wasn't entirely displeased with what had just happened. For one thing, a jamming technique would be a very good thing to have. For another, Henry *did* know where his infected friend— call him Typhoid Jonesy—was going. Owen had seen a brief picture of it in Henry's head.

"Henry, I want you to listen to me now."

"All right."

"Here's the simplest, safest thing we can do, you and I. First, if time isn't an utterly crucial factor, we both need to get some sleep."

"I can buy that. I'm next door to dead."

"Then, around three o'clock, I can start to move and shake. This installation is going to be on high alert till the time when there isn't an installation here any longer, but if Big Brother's eyeball ever glazes over a little, it's apt to be between four and six A.M. I'll make a diversion, and I can short out the fence—that's the easiest part, actually. I can be here with a Sno-Cat five minutes after the shit hits the fan—"

Telepathy had certain shorthand advantages to verbal communication, Owen was discovering. He sent Henry the image of a burning MH-6 Little Bird helicopter and soldiers running toward it even as he continued to speak.

"—and off we go."

"Leaving Kurtz with a barnful of innocent civilians he plans to turn into crispy critters. Not to mention Blue Group. What's that, a couple-three hundred more?"

Owen, who had been full-time military since the age of nineteen and one of Kurtz's eraserheads for the last eight years, sent two hard words along the mental conduit the two of them had established: *Acceptable losses.*

Behind the dirty glass, the vague shape that was Henry Devlin stirred, then stood.

No, he sent back.

8

No? What do you mean, no?

No. That's what I mean.

Do you have a better idea?

And Owen realized, to his extreme horror, that Henry thought he did. Fragments of that idea—it would be far too generous to call it a plan—shot through Owen's mind like the brightly fragmented tail of a comet. It took his breath away. The cigarette dropped unnoticed from between his fingers and zipped away on the wind.

You're nuts.

No, I'm not. We need a diversion in order to get away, you already know that. This is a diversion.

They'll be killed anyway!

Some will. Maybe even most of them. But it's a chance. What chance will they have in a burning barn?

Out loud, Henry said: "And there's Kurtz. If he's got a couple of hundred escapees to worry about— most of whom who'd be happy to tell the first reporters they came across that the panic-stricken U.S. government had sanctioned a My Lai massacre right here on American soil—he's going to be a lot less concerned about us."

You don't know Abe Kurtz, Owen thought. *You don't know about the Kurtz Line.* Of course, neither had he. Not really. Not until today.

Yet Henry's proposal made a lunatic kind of sense. And it contained at least a measure of atonement. As this endless November fourteenth marched toward midnight and as odds of living until the end of the week grew longer, Owen was not surprised to find that the idea of atonement had its attractions.

"Henry."

"Yes, Owen. I'm here."

"I've always felt badly about what I did in the Rapeloews' house that day."

"I know."

"And yet I've done it again and again. How fucked up is that?"

Henry, an excellent psychiatrist even after his thoughts had turned to suicide, said nothing. Fucked up was normal human behavior. Sad but true.

"All right," Owen said at last. "You can buy the house, but I'm going to furnish it. Deal?"

"Deal," Henry replied at once.

"Can you really teach me that jamming technique? Because I think I may need it."

"I'm pretty sure I can."

"All right. Listen." Owen talked for the next three minutes, sometimes out loud, sometimes mind to mind. The two men had reached a point where they no longer differentiated between the modes of communication; thoughts and words had become one.

CHAPTER SIXTEEN

DERRY

1

It's hot in Gosselin's—it's so hot! The sweat pops out on Jonesy's face almost immediately, and by the time the four of them get to the pay phone (which is near the woodstove, wouldn't you know it), it's rolling down his cheeks, and his armpits feel like jungle growth after a heavy rain . . . not that he has all that much growth there yet, not at fourteen. *Don't you wish,* as Pete likes to say.

So it's hot, and he's still partly in the grip of the dream, which hasn't faded the way bad dreams usually do (he can still smell gasoline and burning rubber, can still see Henry holding that moccasin . . . and the head, he can still see Richie Grenadeau's awful severed head), and then the operator makes things worse by being a bitch. When Jonesy gives her the Cavells' number, which they call frequently to ask if they can come over (Roberta and Alfie always say yes, but it is only polite to ask permission, they have all been taught that at home), the operator asks: "Do your parents know you're calling long-distance?" The words come out not in a Yankee drawl but in the slightly Frenchified tones of someone who grew up in this part of the world, where Letourneau and Bissonette are more common than Smith or Jones. The tightwad French, Pete's Dad calls them. And now he's got one on the telephone, God help him.

"They let me make toll calls if I pay the charges," Jonesy says. And boy, he should have known that *he* would end up being the one to actually make it. He takes down the zipper of his jacket. God, but it's boiling in here! How those old geezers can sit around the stove like they're doing is more than Jonesy can understand. His own friends are pressing in close around him, which is probably understandable—they want to know how things go—but still, Jonesy wishes they would step back a little. Having them so close makes him feel even hotter.

"And if I were to call them, *mon fils,* your *mère et père,* d'ey say the same?"

"Sure," Jonesy says. Sweat runs into one of his eyes, stinging, and he wipes it away like a tear. "My father's at work, but my Mom should be home. Nine-four-nine, six-six-five-eight. Only I wish you'd make it quick, because—"

"I'll jus' ring on your party," she says, sounding disappointed. Jonesy slips out of his coat, switching the phone from one ear to the other in order to accomplish this, and lets it puddle around his feet. The others are still wearing theirs; Beav, in fact, hasn't even unzipped his Fonzie jacket. How they can stand it is beyond Jonesy. Even the *smells* are getting to him: Musterole and beans and floor-oil and coffee and brine from the pickle-barrel. Usually he likes the smells in Gosselin's, but today they make Jonesy feel like blowing chunks.

Connections click in his ear. So *slow.* His friends pushing in too close to the pay phone on the back wall, crowding him. Two or three aisles over, Lamar is looking fixedly at the cereal shelf and rubbing his forehead like a man with a severe headache. Considering how much beer he put away last night, Jonesy thinks, a headache would be natural. He's coming down with a headache himself, one that beer has nothing to do with, it's just so gosh-damn *hot* in h—

He straightens up a little. "Ringing," he says to his friends, and immediately wishes he'd kept his mouth shut, because they lean in closer than ever. Pete's breath is fuckin *awful,* and Jonesy thinks, *What do you do, Petesky? Brush em once a year, whether they need it or not?*

The phone is picked up on the third ring. "Yes, hello?" It's Roberta, but sounding distracted and upset rather than cheery, as she usually does. Not that it's very hard to figure out why; in the background he can hear Duddits bawling. Jonesy knows that Alfie and Roberta don't feel that crying the way Jonesy and his friends do—they are grownups. But they are also his parents, they feel *some* of it, and he doubts if this has exactly been Mrs. Cavell's favorite morning.

Christ, how can it be so *hot* in here? What did they load that fuckin woodstove up with this morning, anyway? Plutonium?

"Come on, who is it?" Impatient, which is also completely unlike Mrs. Cavell. If being the mother of a special person like Duddits teaches you anything, she has told the boys on many occasions, it's patience. Not this morning, though. This morning she sounds almost pissed off, which is unthinkable. "If you're selling something, I can't talk to you. I'm busy right now, and . . ."

Duddits in the background, trumpeting and wailing. *You're busy, all right,* Jonesy thinks. *He's been going on like that since dawn, and by now you must be just about out of your sneaker.*

Henry throws an elbow into Jonesy's side and flicks a hand at him—*Go on! Hurry up!*—and although it hurts, the elbow is still a good thing. If she hangs up on him, Jonesy will have to deal with that bitch of an operator again.

"Miz Cavell—Roberta? It's me, Jonesy."

"Jonesy?" He senses her deep relief; she has wanted so badly for Duddie's friends to call that she half-believes she is imagining this. "Is it really you?"

"Yeah," he said. "Me and the other guys." He holds out the telephone.

"Hi, Mrs. Cavell," Henry says.

"Hey, what's up?" is Pete's contribution.

"Hi, beautiful," Beaver says with a goony grin. He has been more or less in love with Roberta from the day they met her.

Lamar Clarendon looks over at the sound of his son's voice, winces, then goes back to his contemplation of the Cheerios and Shredded Wheat. *Go right ahead,* Lamar told the Beav when Beaver said they wanted to call Duddits. *Dunno why you'd want to talk to that meringue-head, but it's your buffalo nickel.*

When Jonesy puts the phone back to his ear, Roberta Cavell is saying: "—get back to Derry? I thought you were hunting up in Kineo or someplace."

"We're still up here," Jonesy says. He looks around at his friends and is astounded to see they are hardly sweating at all—a slight sheen on Henry's forehead, a few beads on Pete's upper lip, and that's all. Totally Weirdsville. "We just thought . . . um . . . that we better call."

"You knew." Her voice was flat—not unfriendly but unquestioning.

"Um . . ." He pulls at his flannel shirt, fanning it against his chest. "Yeah."

There are a thousand questions most people would ask at this point, probably starting with *How did you know?* or *What in God's name is wrong with him?* but Roberta isn't most people, and she has already had the best part of a month to see how they are with her son. What she says is, "Hold on, Jonesy. I'll get him."

Jonesy waits. Far off he can still hear Duddits wailing and Roberta, softer. Talking to him. Cajoling him to the phone. Using what are now magic words in the Cavell household: *Jonesy, Beaver, Pete, Henry.* The blatting moves closer, and even over the phone Jonesy can feel it working its way into his head, a blunt knife that digs and gouges instead of cutting. Yowch. Duddits's crying makes Henry's elbow seem like a love-tap. Meanwhile, the old jungle-juice is rolling down his neck in rivers. His eyes fix on the two signs above the phone. PLEASE LIMIT ALL CALLS TO 5 MINS, reads one. PROFAINITY NOT TOLERIDED, reads the other. Beneath this someone has gouged Who the fuck says so. Then Duddits is on, those awful bellowing cries right there in his ear. Jonesy winces against them, but in spite of the pain it is impossible to be mad at Duds. Up here they are four, all together. Down there he is one, all alone, and what a strange one he is. God has hurt him and blessed him at the same time, it makes Jonesy giddy just to think of it.

"Duddits," he says. "Duddits, it's us. Jonesy . . ."

He hands the phone to Henry. "Hi, Duddits, it's Henry . . ."

Henry hands the phone to Pete. "Hi, Duds, it's Pete, stop crying now, it's all right . . ."

Pete hands the phone to Beaver, who looks around, then stretches the phone as far toward the corner as the cord will allow. Cupping his hand over the mouthpiece so the old men by the stove (not to mention his own old man, of course) won't hear him, he sings the first two lines of the lullaby. Then he falls quiet, listening. After a moment he flashes the rest of them a thumb-and-forefinger circle. Then he hands the phone back to Henry.

"Duds? Henry again. It was just a dream, Duddits. It wasn't real. Okay? It wasn't real and *it's over.* Just . . ." Henry listens. Jonesy takes the opportunity to strip off his flannel shirt. The tee-shirt beneath is soaked right through.

There are a billion things in the world Jonesy

doesn't know—what kind of link he and his friends share with Duddits, for one—but he knows he can't stay in here in Gosselin's much longer. He feels like he's *in* the goddam stove, not just looking at it. Those old farts around the checkerboard must have ice in their bones.

Henry is nodding. "That's right, like a scary movie." He listens, frowning. "No, you didn't. None of us did. We didn't hurt him. We didn't hurt any of them."

And just like that—bingo—Jonesy knows they did. They didn't mean to, exactly, but they did. They were scared Richie would make good on his threat to get them . . . and so they got him first.

Pete is holding out his hand and Henry says, "Pete wants to talk to you, Dud."

He hands the phone to Pete and Pete is telling Duddits to just forget it, be chilly, Willy, they'll be home soon and they'll all play the game, they'll have fun, they'll have a fuckin *roll,* but in the meantime—

Jonesy raises his eyes and sees one of the signs over the phone has changed. The one on the left still says PLEASE LIMIT ALL CALLS TO 5 MINS, but the one on the right now says WHY NOT GO OUTSIDE IT'S COOLER. And that's a good idea, *such* a good idea. No reason not to, either—the Duddits situation is clearly under control.

But before he can make his move, Pete is holding the phone out to him and saying, "He wants to talk to you, Jonesy."

For a moment he almost bolts anyway, thinking to

hell with Duddits, to hell with all of them. But these are his friends, together they all caught the same terrible dream, did something they didn't mean to do

(liar fuckin liar you meant it you did)

and their eyes hold him where he is in spite of the heat, which is now clamped around his chest like a suffocating pad. Their eyes insist that he's a part of this and mustn't leave while Duddits is still on the phone. It's not how you play the game.

It's our dream and it's not over yet, their eyes insist— Henry's most of all. *It's been going on since the day we found him there behind Tracker Brothers, down on his knees and all but naked. He sees the line and now we see it, too. And although we may perceive it in different ways, part of us will always see the line. We'll see it until the day we die.*

There's something else in their eyes, too, something that will haunt them, all unacknowledged, until the day they die, and cast its shadow over even their happiest days. The fear of what they did. What they did in the unremembered part of their shared dream.

That's what keeps him where he is and makes him take the telephone even though he is sweltering, roasting, fucking *melting.*

"Duddits," he says, and even his *voice* sounds hot. "It's really okay. I'm gonna let you talk to Henry again, it's super-hot in here and I have to get a breath of fresh—"

Duddits interrupts him, his voice strong and urgent. *"Oh-oh-ow! Ohee, oh-oh-ow! Ay! Ay! Isser AY!"*

They have always understood his gabble from the

very first, and Jonesy understands it now: *Don't go out! Jonesy, don't go out! Gray! Gray! Mister GRAY!*

Jonesy's mouth drops open. He looks past the heat-shimmering stove, down the aisle where Beaver's hung-over father is now making a listless examination of the canned beans, past Mrs. Gosselin at the old scrolled cash register, and out the front window. That window is dirty, and it's filled with signs advertising every-thing from Winston cigarettes and Moosehead Ale to church suppers and Fourth of July picnics that hap-pened back when the peanut-farmer was still President . . . but there's still enough glass for him to look through and see the thing that's waiting for him out-side. It's the thing that came up behind him while he was trying to hold the bathroom door closed, the thing that has snatched his body. A naked gray figure stand-ing beside the Citgo pump on its toeless feet, staring at him with its black eyes. And Jonesy thinks: *It's not how they really are, it's just the way we see them.*

As if to emphasize this, Mr. Gray raises one of his hands and brings it down. From the tips of his three fingers, little specks of reddish-gold float upward like thistle.

Byrus, Jonesy thinks.

As if it were a magic word in a fairy-tale, everything freezes. Gosselin's Market becomes a still-life. Then the color drains out of it and it becomes a sepia-toned photograph. His friends are growing transparent and fading before his eyes. Only two things still seem real: the heavy black receiver of the pay phone, and the heat. The stifling heat.

"Ay UH!" Duddits cries into his ear. Jonesy hears a long, choking intake of breath which he remembers so well; it is Duddits readying himself to speak as clearly as he possibly can. *"Ownzy! Ownzy, ake UH! Ake UH! Ake*

2

up! Wake up! Jonesy, wake up!

Jonesy raised his head and for a moment could see nothing. His hair, heavy and sweat-clotted, hung in his eyes. He brushed it away, hoping for his own bedroom—either the one at Hole in the Wall, or, even better, the one back home in Brookline—but no such luck. He was still in the office at Tracker Brothers. He'd fallen asleep at the desk and had dreamed of how they'd called Duddits all those years ago. That had been real enough, but not the stuporous heat. If anything, Old Man Gosselin had always kept his place cold; he was chintzy that way. The heat had crept into his dream because it was hot in here, Christ, it had to be a hundred degrees, maybe a hundred and ten.

Furnace has gone nuts, he thought, and got up. *Or maybe the place is on fire. Either way, I have to get out. Before I roast.*

Jonesy went around the desk, barely registering the fact that the desk had changed, barely registering the feel of something brushing the top of his head as he hurried toward the door. He was reaching for the knob with one hand and the lock with the other when he remembered Duddits in the dream, telling him not to go out, Mr. Gray was out there waiting.

And he was. Right outside this door. Waiting in the storehouse of memories, to which he now had total access.

Jonesy spread his sweaty fingers on the wood of the door. His hair fell down over his eyes again, but he barely noticed. "Mr. Gray," he whispered. "Are you out there? You are, aren't you?"

No response, but Mr. Gray was, all right. He was standing with his hairless rudiment of a head cocked and his glass-black eyes fixed on the doorknob, waiting for it to turn. Waiting for Jonesy to come bursting out. And then—?

Goodbye annoying human thoughts. Goodbye distracting and disturbing human emotions.

Goodbye Jonesy.

"Mr. Gray, are you trying to smoke me out?"

Still no answer. Jonesy didn't need one. Mr. Gray had access to all the controls, didn't he? Including the ones that controlled his temperature. How high had he pushed it? Jonesy didn't know, but he knew it was still going up. The band around his chest was hotter and heavier than ever, and he could hardly breathe. His temples were pounding.

The window. What about the window?

Feeling a burst of hope, Jonesy turned in that direction, putting his back to the door. The window was dark now—so much for the eternal afternoon in October of 1978—and the driveway which ran up the side of Tracker Brothers was buried under shifting drifts of snow. Never, even as a child, had snow looked so inviting to Jonesy. He saw himself bursting through the window like Errol Flynn in some old pirate movie, saw himself charging into the snow and then throwing himself into it, bathing his burning face in its blessed white chill—

Yes, and then the feel of Mr. Gray's hands closing around his neck. Those hands had only three digits each, but they would be strong; they would choke the life out of him in no time. If he even cracked the window, tried to let in some of the cold night air, Mr. Gray would be in and battening on him like a vampire. Because that part of JonesyWorld wasn't safe. That part was conquered territory.

Hobson's choice. Fucked either way.

"Come out." Mr. Gray at last spoke through the door, and in Jonesy's own voice. "I'll make it quick. You don't want to roast in there . . . or do you?"

Jonesy suddenly saw the desk standing in front of the window, the desk that hadn't even been here when he first found himself in this room. Before he'd fallen asleep it had just been a plain wooden thing, the sort of bottom-of-the-line model you might buy at Office Depot if you were on a budget. At some point—he couldn't remember exactly when—it had gained a phone. Just a plain black phone, as utilitarian and undecorative as the desk itself.

Now, he saw, the desk was an oak rolltop, the twin of the one in his Brookline study. And the phone was a blue Trimline, like the one in his office at Jay. He wiped a palmful of piss-warm sweat off his forehead, and as he did it he saw what he had brushed with the top of his head.

It was the dreamcatcher.

The dreamcatcher from Hole in the Wall.

"Holy shit," he whispered. "I'm *decorating* the place."

Of course he was, why not? Didn't even prisoners on Death Row decorate their cells? And if he could add a desk and a dreamcatcher and a Trimline phone in his sleep, then maybe—

Jonesy closed his eyes and concentrated. He tried to call up an image of his study in Brookline. For a moment this gave him trouble, because a question intruded: if his memories were out there, how could he still have them in here? The answer, he realized, was probably simple. His memories were still in his head, where they had always been. The cartons in the storeroom were what Henry might call an externalization, his way of visualizing all the stuff to which Mr. Gray had access.

Never mind. Pay attention to what needs doing. The study in Brookline. See the study in Brookline.

"What are you doing?" Mr. Gray demanded. The smarmy self-confidence had left his voice. "What the doodlyfuck are you doing?"

Jonesy smiled a little at that—he couldn't help it—but he held onto his image. Not just the study, but one wall of the study . . . there by the door leading into the little half-bath . . . yes, there it was. The Honeywell thermostat. And what was he supposed to say? Was there a magic word, something like alakazam?

Yeah.

With his eyes still closed and a trace of a smile still on his sweat-streaming face, Jonesy whispered: "Duddits."

He opened his eyes and looked at the dusty, non-descript wall.

The thermostat was there.

3

"Stop it!" Mr. Gray shouted, and even as Jonesy crossed the room he was amazed by the familiarity of that voice; it was like listening to one of his own infrequent tantrums (the wild disorder of the kids' rooms was a likely flashpoint) on a tape recorder. "You just stop it! *This has got to stop!*"

"Kiss my bender, beautiful," Jonesy replied, and grinned. How many times had his kids wished they could say something like that to him, when he started quacking? Then a nasty thought occurred to him. He'd probably never see the inside of his Brookline duplex again, but if he did, it would be through eyes which now belonged to Mr. Gray. The cheek the kids kissed ("Eeu, scratchy, Daddy!" Misha would say) would now be Mr. Gray's cheek. The lips Carla kissed would like-wise be Mr. Gray's. And in bed, when she gripped him and guided him into her—

Jonesy shivered, then reached for the thermostat . . . which, he saw, was set to 120. The only one in the world that went so high, no doubt. He backed it half a turn to the left, not knowing what to expect, and was delighted to feel an immediate waft of cool air on his cheeks and brow. He turned his face gratefully up to catch the breeze more fully, and saw a heating/cooling grate set high in one wall. One more fresh touch.

"How are you doing that?" Mr. Gray shouted through the door. "Why doesn't your body incorporate the byrus? How can you be there at all?"

Jonesy burst out laughing. There was simply no way to hold it in.

"Stop that," Mr. Gray said, and now his voice was chilly. This was the voice Jonesy had used when he had given Carla his ultimatum: rehab or divorce, hon, you choose. "I can do more than just turn up the heat, you know. I can burn you out. Or make you blind yourself."

Jonesy remembered the pen going into Andy Janas's eye—that terrible thick popping sound—and winced. Yet he recognized a bluff when he heard one. *You're the last and I'm your delivery-system,* Jonesy thought. *You won't beat the machinery up too much. Not until your mission's accomplished, anyhow.*

He walked slowly back to the door, reminding himself to be wary . . . because, as Gollum had said of Bilbo Baggins, it was tricksy, precious, aye, very tricksy.

"Mr. Gray?" he asked softly.

No answer.

"Mr. Gray, what do you look like now? What do you look like when you're yourself? A little less gray and a little more pink? A couple more fingers on your hands? Little bit of hair on your head? Starting to get some toesies and some testes?"

No answer.

"Starting to look like me, Mr. Gray? To *think* like me? You don't like that, right? Or do you?"

Still no answer, and Jonesy realized Mr. Gray was gone. He turned and hurried across to the window, aware of even more changes: a Currier and Ives wood-cut on one wall, a Van Gogh print on another—*Marigolds,* a Christmas gift from Henry—and on this desk the Magic 8-Ball he kept on his desk at home. Jonesy barely noticed these things. He wanted to see what Mr. Gray was up to, what had engaged his attention now.

4

For one thing, the interior of the truck had changed. Instead of the olive-drab plainness of Andy Janas's government-issue pickup (clipboard of papers and forms on the passenger side, squawking radio beneath the dash), he was now in a luxy Dodge Ram with a club cab, gray velour seats, and roughly as many controls as a Lear jet. On the glove compartment was a sticker reading I ♥ MY BORDER COLLIE. The border collie in question was still pre-sent and accounted for, asleep in the passenger-side footwell with its tail curled neatly around it. It was a male named Lad. Jonesy sensed that he could access the name and the fate of Lad's master, but why would he want to? Somewhere north of their present position, Janas's army truck was now off the road, and the driver of this one would be lying nearby. Jonesy had no idea why the dog had been spared.

Then Lad lifted his tail and farted, and Jonesy did.

5

He discovered that by looking out the Tracker Brothers' office window and concentrating, he could look out through his own eyes. The snow was coming down more heavily than ever, but like the Army truck, the Dodge was equipped with four-wheel drive, and it poked along steadily enough. Going the other way, north toward Jefferson Tract, was a chain of headlights set high off the road: Army convoy trucks. Then, on this side, a reflectorized sign—white letters, green background—loomed out of the flying snow. DERRY NEXT 5 EXITS.

The city plows had been out, and although there was hardly any traffic (there wouldn't have been much at this hour even on a clear night), the turnpike was in passable shape. Mr. Gray increased the Ram's speed to forty miles an hour. They passed three exits Jonesy knew well from his childhood (KANSAS STREET, AIRPORT, UPMILE HILL/STRAWFORD PARK) then slowed.

Suddenly Jonesy thought he understood.

He looked at the boxes he'd dragged in here, most marked DUDDITS, a few marked DERRY. The latter ones he'd taken as an afterthought. Mr. Gray thought he still had the memories he needed—the *information* he needed—but if Jonesy was right about where they were going (and it made perfect sense), Mr. Gray was in for a surprise. Jonesy didn't know whether to be glad or afraid, and found he was both.

Here was a green sign reading EXIT 25—WITCHAM STREET. His hand flicked on the Ram's turnsignal.

At the top of the ramp, he turned left onto Witcham, then left again, half a mile later, onto Carter Street. Carter went up at a steep angle, heading back toward Upmile Hill and Kansas Street on the other side of what had once been a high wooded ridge and the site of a thriving Micmac Indian village. The street hadn't been plowed in several hours, but the four-wheel drive was up to the task. The Ram threaded its way among the snow-covered humps on either side—cars that had been street-parked in defiance of municipal snow emergency regulations.

Halfway up Mr. Gray turned again, this time onto an even narrower track called Carter Lookout. The Ram skidded, its rear end fishtailing. Lad looked up briefly, whined, then put his nose back down on the floormat as the tires took hold, biting into the snow and pulling the Ram the rest of the way up.

Jonesy stood at his window on the world, fascinated, waiting for Mr. Gray to discover . . . well, to discover.

At first Mr. Gray wasn't dismayed when the Ram's high beams showed nothing at the crest but more swirling snow. He was confident he'd see it in a few seconds, of course he would . . . just a few more seconds and he'd see the big white tower which stood here overlooking the drop to Kansas Street, the tower with the windows marching around it in a rising spiral. In just a few more seconds . . .

Except now there *were* no more seconds. The Ram had chewed its way to the top of what had once been called Standpipe Hill. Here Carter Lookout—and three or four other similar little lanes—ended in a large open circle. They had come to the highest, most open spot in Derry. The wind howled like a banshee, a steady fifty miles an hour with gusts up to seventy and even eighty. In the Ram's high beams, the snow flew horizontally, a storm of daggers.

Mr. Gray sat motionless. Jonesy's hands slid off the wheel and clumped to either side of Jonesy's body like birds shot out of the sky. At last he muttered, "Where is it?"

His left hand rose, fumbled at the doorhandle, and at last pulled it up. He swung a leg out, then fell to Jonesy's knees in a snowdrift as the howling wind snatched the door out of his hand. He got up again and floundered around to the front of the truck, his jacket rippling around him and the legs of his jeans snapping like sails in a gale. The wind-chill was well below zero (in the Tracker Brothers' office, the temperature went from cool to cold in the space of a few seconds), but the redblack cloud which now inhabited most of Jonesy's brain and drove Jonesy's body could not have cared less.

"Where is *it?"* Mr. Gray screamed into the howling mouth of the storm. *"Where's the fucking STAND-PIPE?"*

There was no need for Jonesy to shout; storm or no storm, Mr. Gray would hear even a whisper.

"Ha-ha, Mr. Gray," he said. "Hardy-fucking-har.

Looks like the joke's on you. The Standpipe's been gone since 1985."

6

Jonesy thought that if Mr. Gray had remained still, he would have done a full-fledged pre-schooler's tantrum, perhaps right down to the rolling around in the snow and the kicking of the feet; in spite of his best efforts not to, Mr. Gray was bingeing on Jonesy's emotional chemistry set, as helpless to stop now that he had started as an alcoholic with a key to McDougal's Bar.

Instead of throwing a fit or having a snit, he thrust Jonesy's body across the bald top of the hill and toward the squat stone pedestal that stood where he had expected to find the storage facility for the city's drinking water: seven hundred thousand gallons of it. He fell in the snow, floundered back up, limped forward on Jonesy's bad hip, fell again and got up again, all the time spitting Beaver's litany of childish curses into the gale: doodlyfuck, kiss my bender, munch my meat, bite my bag, shit in your fuckin hat and wear it backward, Bruce. Coming from Beaver (or Henry, or Pete), these had always been amusing. Here, on this deserted hill, screamed into the teeth of the storm by this lunging, falling monster that looked like a human being, they were awful.

He, it, whatever Mr. Gray was, at last reached the pedestal, which stood out clearly enough in the glow cast by the Ram's headlights. It had been built to a child's height, about five feet, and of the plain rock which had shaped so many New England stone walls. On top were two figures cast in bronze, a boy and a girl with their hands linked and their heads lowered, as if in prayer or in grief.

The pedestal was drifted to most of its height in snow, but the top of the plaque screwed to the front was visible. Mr. Gray fell to Jonesy's knees, scraped snow away, and read this:

TO THOSE LOST IN THE STORM
MAY 31, 1985
AND TO THE CHILDREN
ALL THE CHILDREN
LOVE FROM BILL, BEN, BEV, EDDIE, RICHIE,
STAN, MIKE
THE LOSERS' CLUB

Spray-painted across it in jagged red letters, also perfectly visible in the truck's headlights, was this further message:

PENNYWISE LIVES

7

Mr. Gray knelt looking at this for nearly five minutes, ignoring the creeping numbness in Jonesy's extremities. (And why would he take care? Jonesy was just your basic rental job, drive it as hard as you want and butt out your cigarettes on the floormat.) He was trying to make sense of it. Storm? Children? Losers? Who or what was Pennywise? Most of all, *where was the Standpipe,* which Jonesy's memories had insisted was here?

At last he got up, limped back to the truck, got in, and turned up the heater. In the blast of hot air, Jonesy's body began to shake. Soon enough, Mr. Gray was back at the locked door of the office, demanding an explanation.

"Why do you sound so angry?" Jonesy asked mildly, but he was smiling. Could Mr. Gray sense that? "Did you expect me to help you? Come on, pal—I don't know the specifics, but I have a pretty good idea what the overall plan is: twenty years from now and the whole planet is one big redheaded ball, right? No more hole in the ozone layer, but no more people, either."

"Don't you smartass me! Don't you dare!"

Jonesy fought back the temptation to taunt Mr. Gray into another tantrum. He didn't believe his unwelcome guest would be capable of huffing down the door between them no matter how angry he became, but what sense was there in putting that idea to the test? And besides, Jonesy was emotionally exhausted, his nerves jumping and his mouth full of a burnt-copper taste.

"How can it not be here?"

Mr. Gray brought one hand down on the center of the steering wheel. The horn honked. Lad the border collie raised his head and looked at the man behind the wheel with large, nervous eyes. "You can't lie to me! I have your memories!"

"Well . . . I *did* get a few. Remember?"

"Which ones? Tell me."

"Why should I?" Jonesy asked. "What'll you do for me?"

Mr. Gray fell silent. Jonesy felt him accessing various files. Then, suddenly, smells began to waft into the room from under the door and through the heating and cooling vent. They were his favorite aromas: popcorn, coffee, his mother's fish chowder. His stomach immediately began to roar.

"Of course I can't promise you your mother's chowder," Mr. Gray said. "But I'll feed you. And you're hungry, aren't you?"

"With you driving my body and pigging out on my emotions, it'd be a wonder if I wasn't," Jonesy replied.

"There's a place south of here—Dysart's. According to you, it's open twenty-four hours a day, which is a way of saying all the time. Or are you lying about that, too?"

"I never lied," Jonesy replied. "As you said, I can't. You've got the controls, you've got the memory banks, you've got everything but what's in here."

"Where *is* there? How can there *be* a there?"

"I don't know," Jonesy said truthfully. "How do I know you'll feed me?"

"Because I *have* to," Mr. Gray said from his side of the door, and Jonesy realized Mr. Gray was also being truthful. If you didn't pour gas into the machine from time to time, the machine stopped running. "But if you satisfy my curiosity, I'll feed you the things you like. If you don't . . ."

The smells from under the door changed, became the greenly assaultive odor of broccoli and brussels sprouts.

"All right," Jonesy said. "I'll tell you what I can, and you feed me pancakes and bacon at Dysart's. Breakfast twenty-four hours a day, you know. Deal?"

"Deal. Open the door and we'll shake on it."

Jonesy was surprised into a smile—it was Mr. Gray's first attempt at humor, and really not such a bad one. He glanced into the rearview mirror and saw an identical smile on the mouth which was no longer his. *That* was a little creepy.

"Maybe we'll skip the handshake part," he said.

"Tell me."

"Yes, but a word of warning—break a promise to me, and you'll never get to make another one."

"I'll keep it in mind."

The truck sat at the top of Standpipe Hill, rocking slightly on its springs, its headlamps blazing out cylinders of snow-filled light, and Jonesy told Mr. Gray what he knew. It was, he thought, the perfect place for a scary story.

8

The years of 1984 and '85 were bad ones in Derry. In the summer of 1984, three local teenagers had thrown a gay man into the Canal, killing him. In the ten months which followed, half a dozen children had been murdered, apparently by a psychotic who sometimes masqueraded as a clown.

"Who is this John Wayne Gacey?" Mr. Gray asked. "Was he the one who killed the children?"

"No, just someone from the midwest who had a similar *modus operandi*," Jonesy said. "You don't understand many of the cross-connections my mind makes, do you? Bet there aren't many poets out where you come from."

Mr. Gray made no reply to this. Jonesy doubted if he knew what a poet was. Or cared.

"In any case," Jonesy said, "the last bad thing to happen was a kind of freak hurricane. It hit on May thirty-first, 1985. Over sixty people died. The Standpipe blew over. It rolled down that hill and into Kansas Street." He pointed to the right of the truck, where the land sloped sharply away into the dark.

"Almost three quarters of a million gallons of water ran down Upmile Hill, then into downtown, which more or less collapsed. I was in college by then. The storm happened during my Finals Week. My Dad called and told me about it, but of course I knew—it was national news."

Jonesy paused, thinking, looking around the office which was no longer bare and dirty but nicely furnished (his subconscious had added both a couch that he had at home and an Eames chair he'd seen in the Museum of Modern Art catalogue, lovely but out of his financial reach) and really quite pleasant . . . certainly nicer than the blizzardy world his body's usurper was currently having to deal with.

"Henry was in school, too. Harvard. Pete was bumming around the West Coast, doing his hippie thing. Beaver was trying a junior college downstate. Majoring in hashish and video games, is what he said later." Only Duddits had been here in Derry when the big storm blew through . . . but Jonesy discovered he didn't want to speak Duddits's name.

Mr. Gray said nothing, but Jonesy got a clear sense of his impatience. Mr. Gray cared only about the Standpipe. And how Jonesy had fooled him.

"Listen, Mr. Gray—if there was any fooling going on, you did it to yourself. I got a few of the DERRY boxes, that's all, and brought them in here while you were busy killing that poor soldier."

"The poor soldiers came in ships from the sky and massacred all of my kind that they could find."

"Spare me. You guys didn't come here to welcome us into the Galactic Book Circle."

"Would things have been any different if we had?"

"You can also spare me the hypotheticals," Jonesy said. "After what you did to Pete and the Army guy, I could care less about having an intellectual discussion with you."

"We do what we have to do."

"That might be, but if you expect me to help you, you're mad."

The dog was looking at Jonesy with even more unease, apparently not used to masters who held animated conversations with themselves.

"The Standpipe fell over in 1985—sixteen years ago—but you stole this memory?"

"Basically, yeah, although I don't think you'd have

much luck with that in a court of law, since the memories were mine to begin with."

"What else have you stolen?"

"That's for me to know and you to think about."

There was a hard and ill-tempered thump at the door. Jonesy was once more reminded of the story about The Three Little Pigs. Huff and puff, Mr. Gray; enjoy the dubious pleasures of rage.

But Mr. Gray had apparently left the door.

"Mr. Gray?" Jonesy called. "Hey, don't go 'way mad, okay?"

Jonesy guessed that Mr. Gray might be off on another information search. The Standpipe was gone but Derry was still here; ergo, the town's water had to be coming from *somewhere*. Did Jonesy know the location of that somewhere?

Jonesy didn't. He had a vague memory of drinking a lot of bottled water after coming back from college for the summer, but that was all. Eventually water had started coming out of their taps again, but what was that to a twenty-one-year-old whose biggest concern had been getting into Mary Shratt's pants? The water came, you drank it. You didn't worry about where it came from as long as it didn't give you the heaves or the squitters.

A sense of frustration from Mr. Gray? Or was that just his imagination? Jonesy most sincerely hoped not.

This had been a good one . . . what the four of them, in the days of their misspent youth, would undoubtedly have called "a fuckin pisser."

9

Roberta Cavell woke up from some unpleasant dream and looked to her right, half-expecting to see only darkness. But the comforting blue numbers were still glowing from the clock by her bed, so the power hadn't gone out. That was pretty amazing, considering the way the wind was howling.

1:04 A.M., the blue numbers said. Roberta turned on the bedside lamp—might as well use it while she could—and drank some water from her glass. Was it the wind that had awakened her? The bad dream? It had been bad, all right, something about aliens with deathrays and everyone running, but she didn't think that was it, either.

Then the wind dropped, and she heard what had waked her: Duddits's voice from downstairs. Duddits . . . *singing?* Was that possible? She didn't see how, considering the terrible afternoon and evening the two of them had put in.

"Eeeyer-eh!" for most of the hours between two and five—*Beaver's dead!* Duddits seemingly inconsolable, finally bringing on a nosebleed. She feared these. When Duddits started bleeding, it was sometimes impossible to get him stopped without taking him to the hospital. This time she *had* been able to stop it by pushing cotton-wads into his nostrils and then pinching his nose high up, between the eyes. She had called Dr. Briscoe to ask if she could give Duddits one of his yellow Valium tablets, but Dr. Briscoe was off in Nas-

sau, if you please. Some other doctor was on call, some whitecoat johnny who had never seen Duddits in his life, and Roberta didn't even bother to call him. She just gave Duddits the Valium, painted his poor dry lips and the inside of his mouth with one of the lemon-flavored glycerine swabs that he liked—the inside of his mouth was always developing cankers and ulcers. Even when the chemo was over, these persisted. And the chemo *was* over. None of the doctors—not Briscoe, not any of them—would admit it, and so the plastic catheter stayed in, but it was over. Roberta would not let them put her boy through that hell again.

Once he'd taken his pill, she got in bed with him, held him (being careful of his left side, where the indwelling catheter hid under a bandage), and sang to him. Not Beaver's lullaby, though. Not today.

At last he had begun to quiet, and when she thought he was asleep, she had gently pulled the cotton-wads from his nostrils. The second one stuck a little, and Duddits's eyes had opened—that beautiful flash of green. His eyes were his true gift, she sometimes thought, and not that other business . . . seeing the line and all that went with it.

"Umma?"

"Yes, Duddie."

"Eeeyer in hen?"

She felt such sorrow at that, and at the thought of Beaver's absurd leather jacket, which he had loved so much and finally worn to tatters. If it had been someone else, *anyone* else but one of his four childhood friends, she would have doubted Duddie's premonition. But if Duddits said Beaver was dead, then Beaver almost certainly was.

"Yes, honey, I'm sure he's in heaven. Now go to sleep."

For another long moment those green eyes had looked into hers, and she had thought he would start crying again—indeed, one tear, large and perfect, *did* roll down his stubbly cheek. It was so hard for him to shave now, sometimes even the Norelco started little cuts that dribbled for hours. Then his eyes had closed again and she had tiptoed out.

After dark, while she was making him oatmeal (all but the blandest foods were now apt to set off vomiting, another sign that the end was nearing), the whole nightmare started again. Terrified already by the increasingly strange news coming out of the Jefferson Tract, she had raced back to his room with her heart hammering. Duddits was sitting upright again, whipping his head from side to side in a child's gesture of negation. The nosebleed had re-started, and at each jerk of his head, scarlet drops flew. They spattered his pillowcase, his signed photograph of Austin Powers (*"Groovy, baby!"* was written across the bottom), and the bottles on the table: mouthwash, Compazine, Percocet, the multi-vitamins that seemed to do absolutely no good, the tall jar of lemon swabs.

This time it was Pete he claimed was dead, sweet (and not terribly bright) Peter Moore. Dear God, could it be true? Any of it? All of it?

The second bout of hysterical grief hadn't gone on as

long, probably because Duddits was already exhausted from the first. She had gotten the nosebleed stanched again—lucky her—and had changed his bed, first helping him to his chair by the window. There he'd sat, looking out into the renewing storm, occasionally sobbing, sometimes heaving great, watery sighs that hurt her inside. Just *looking* at him hurt her: how thin he was, how pale he was, how *bald* he was. She gave him his Red Sox hat, signed across the visor by the great Pedro Martinez (*you get so many nice things when you're dying,* she sometimes mused), thinking his head would be cold there, so close to the glass, but for once Duddits wouldn't put it on. He only held it on his lap and looked out into the dark, his eyes big and unhappy.

At last she had gotten him back into bed, where once again her son's green eyes looked up at her with all their terrible dying brilliance.

"Eeet in hen, ooo?"

"I'm sure he is." She hadn't wanted to cry, desperately hadn't wanted to—it might set him off again—but she could feel the tears brimming. Her head was pregnant with them, and the inside of her nose tasted of the sea each time she pulled in breath.

"In hen wif Eeeyer?"

"Yes, honey."

"I eee Eeeyer n Eeet in hen?"

"Yes, you will. Of course you will. But not for a long while."

His eyes had closed. Roberta had sat beside him on the bed, looking down at her hands, feeling sadder than sad, more alone than lonely.

Now she hurried downstairs and yes, it was singing, all right. Because she spoke such fluent Duddits (and why not? it had been her second language for over thirty years), she translated the rolling syllables without even thinking much about them: *Scooby-Dooby-Doo, where are you? We got some work to do now. I've been telling you, Scooby-Doo, we need a helping hand, now.*

She went into his room, not knowing what to expect. Certainly not what she found: every light blazing, Duddits fully dressed for the first time since his last (and very likely final, according to Dr. Briscoe) remission. He had put on his favorite corduroy pants, his down vest over his Grinch tee-shirt, and his Red Sox hat. He was sitting in his chair by the window and looking out into the night. No frown now; no tears, either. He looked out into the storm with a bright-eyed eagerness that took her back to long before the disease, which had announced itself with such stealthy, easy-to-overlook symptoms: how tired and out of breath he got after just a short game of Frisbee in the backyard, how big the bruises were from even little thumps and bumps, and how slowly they faded. This was the way he used to look when . . .

But she couldn't think. She was too flustered to think.

"Duddits! Duddie, what—"

"Umma! Ere I unnox?"

Mumma! Where's my lunchbox?

"In the kitchen, but Duddie, it's the middle of the night. It's snowing! You aren't . . ."

Going anywhere was the way that one ended, of

course, but the words wouldn't cross her tongue. His eyes were so brilliant, so alive. Perhaps she should have been glad to see that light so strongly in his eyes, that energy, but instead she was terrified.

"I eed I unnox! I eed I unch!"

I need my lunchbox, I need my lunch.

"No, Duddits." Trying to be firm. "You need to take off your clothes and get back into bed. That's what you need and *all* you need. Here. I'll help you."

But when she approached, he raised his arms and crossed them over his narrow chest, the palm of his right hand pressed against his left cheek, the palm of his left against the right cheek. From earliest childhood, it was all he could muster in the way of defiance. It was usually enough, and it was now. She didn't want to upset him again, perhaps start another nosebleed. But she wasn't going to put up a lunch for him in his Scooby lunchbox at one-fifteen in the morning. Absolutely not.

She retreated to the side of his bed and sat down on it. The room was warm, but she was cold, even in her heavy flannel nightgown. Duddits slowly lowered his arms, watching her warily.

"You can sit up if you want," she said, "but why? Did you have a dream, Duddie? A bad dream?"

Maybe a dream but not a bad one. Not with that eager look on his face, and *now* she recognized it well enough: it was the way he had looked so often back in the eighties, in the good years before Henry, Pete, Beaver, and Jonesy had all gone their separate ways, calling less frequently and coming by to see him less frequently still as they raced toward their grownup lives and forgot the one who had to stay behind.

It was the look he got when his special sense told him that his friends were coming by to play. Sometimes they'd all go off together to Strawford Park or the Barrens (they weren't supposed to go there but they did, both she and Alfie had known that they did, and one of their trips there had gotten them all on the front page of the newspaper). Sometimes Alfie or one of their moms or dads would take them to Airport Minigolf or to Fun Town in Newport, and on those days she would always pack Duddits sandwiches and cookies and a Thermos of milk in his Scooby-Doo lunchbox.

He thinks his friends are coming. It must be Henry and Jonesy he's thinking of, because he says Pete and Beav—

Suddenly a terrible image came to her as she sat on Duddits's bed with her hands folded in her lap. She saw herself opening the door to a knock that came at the empty hour of three in the morning, not wanting to open it but helpless to stop herself. And the dead ones were there instead of the living ones. Beaver and Pete were there, returned to the childhood in which they had been living on the day she had first met them, the day they had saved Duddie from God knew what nasty trick and then brought him home safe. In her mind's eye Beaver was wearing his many-zippered motorcycle jacket and Pete was wearing the crewneck sweater of which he had been so proud, the one with NASA on the left breast. She saw them cold and pale, their eyes the lusterless grape-black glaze of corpses. She saw Beaver step forward—no smile for her now, no recognition of her now; when Joe "Beaver" Clarendon put out his pallid starfish hands, he was all business. *We've come for Duddits, Missus Cavell. We're dead, and now he is, too.*

She clasped her hands tighter as a shudder twisted through her body. Duddits didn't see; he was looking out the window again, his face eager and expectant. And very softly, he began to sing again.

"Ooby-Ooby-Ooo, eh ah ooo? Eee aht-sum urk-ooo ooo ow . . ."

10

"Mr. Gray?"

No answer. Jonesy stood at the door of what was now most definitely *his* office, not a trace of Tracker Brothers left except for the dirt on the windows (the matter-of-fact pornography of the girl with her skirt raised had been replaced by Van Gogh's *Marigolds*), feeling more and more uneasy. What was the bastard looking for?

"Mr. Gray, where are you?"

No answer this time either, but there was a sense of Mr. Gray returning . . . and he was happy. The son of a bitch was *happy*.

Jonesy didn't like that at all.

"Listen," Jonesy said. Hands still pressed to the door of his sanctuary; forehead now pressed to it, as well. "I've got a proposal for you, my friend—you're halfway human already; why not just go native? We can coexist, I guess, and I'll show you around. Ice cream's good, beer's even better. What do you say?"

He suspected Mr. Gray was tempted, as only an essentially formless creature could be tempted when offered form—a trade right out of a fairy-tale.

Not tempted enough, however.

There was the spin of the starter, the roar of the truck's motor.

"Where are we going, chum? Always assuming we can get off Standpipe Hill, that is?"

No answer, only that disquieting sense that Mr. Gray had been looking for something . . . and found it.

Jonesy hurried across to the window and looked out in time to see the truck's headlights sweep across the pillar erected to memorialize the lost. The plaque had drifted in again, which meant they must have been here awhile.

Slowly, carefully, now pushing its way through bumper-high drifts, the Dodge Ram started back down the hill.

Twenty minutes later they were on the turnpike again, once more headed south.

CHAPTER SEVENTEEN

HEROES

1

Owen couldn't raise Henry by calling out loud, the man was too deep in exhausted sleep, and so he called with his mind. He found this was easier as the byrus continued to spread. It was growing on three of the fingers on his right hand now, and had all but plugged the cup of his left ear with its spongy, itching growth. He had also lost a couple of teeth, although nothing seemed to be growing in the sockets, at least not yet.

Kurtz and Freddy had stayed clean, thanks to Kurtz's finely honed instincts, but the crews of the two surviving Blue Boy gunships, Owen's and Joe Blakey's, were lousy with byrus. Ever since talking to Henry in the shed, Owen had heard the voices of his compatriots, calling to each other across a previously unsuspected void. They were covering up the infection for now, as he himself was; lots of heavy winter clothing helped. But that wouldn't be possible for much longer, and they didn't know what to do.

In that regard, Owen supposed he was lucky. He at least had a wheel to which he could put his shoulder.

Standing outside the back of the shed and beyond the electrified wire, smoking another cigarette he didn't want, Owen went in search of Henry and found him working his way down a steep, brushy slope. Above him was the sound of kids playing baseball or softball. Henry was a boy, a teenager, and he was calling someone's name—Janey? Jolie? It didn't matter. He was dreaming, and Owen needed him in the real world. He had let Henry sleep as long as he could (almost an hour longer than he had really wanted to), but if they were going to get this show on the road, now was the time.

Henry, he called.

The teenager looked around, startled. There were other boys with him; three—no four of them, one peering into some kind of pipe. They were indistinct, hard to see, and Owen didn't care about them, anyway. Henry was the one he wanted, and not this pimply, startled version of him, either. Owen wanted the man.

Henry, wake up.

No, she's in there. We have to get her out. We—

I don't give a rat's ass about her, whoever she is. Wake up.

No, I—

It's time, Henry, wake up. Wake up. Wake

2

the fuck up!

Henry sat up with a gasp, not sure who or where he was. That was bad, but there was worse: he didn't know *when* he was. Was he eighteen or almost thirty-eight or somewhere in between? He could smell grass, hear the crack of a bat on a ball (a softball bat; it had been girls playing, girls in yellow shirts), and he could still hear Pete screaming *She's in here! Guys, I think she's in here!*

"Pete saw it, he saw the line," Henry murmured. He didn't know exactly what he was talking about. The dream was already fading, its bright images being replaced by something dark. Something he had to do, or try to do. He smelled hay and, more faintly, the sweet-sour aroma of pot.

Mister, can you help us?

Big doe eyes. Marsha, her name had been. Things coming into focus now. *Probably not,* he'd answered her, then added *but maybe.*

Wake up, Henry! It's quarter of four, time to drop your cock and grab your socks.

That voice was stronger and more immediate than the others, overwhelming them and damping them out; it was like a voice from a Walkman when the batteries were fresh and the volume was turned all the way up to ten. Owen Underhill's voice. He was Henry Devlin. And if they were going to try this, the time was now.

Henry got up, wincing at the pain in his legs, his back, his shoulders, his neck. Where his muscles weren't screaming, the advancing byrus was itching abominably. He felt a hundred years old until he took his first step toward the dirty window, then decided it was more like a hundred and ten.

3

Owen saw the man's shape come into view inside the window and nodded, relieved. Henry was moving like Methuselah on a bad day, but Owen had something that would fix that, at least temporarily. He had stolen it from the brand-new infirmary, which was so busy no one had noticed him coming or going. And all the time he had protected the front of his mind with the two blocking mantras Henry had taught him: *Ride a cock horse to Banbury Cross* and *Yes we can-can, yes we can, yes we can-can, great gosh a'mighty.* So far they seemed to be working—he'd gotten a few strange looks but no questions. Even the weather continued in their favor, the storm roaring on unabated.

Now he could see Henry's face at the window, a pale oval blur looking out at him.

I don't know about this, Henry sent. *Man, I can hardly walk.*

I can help with that. Stand clear of the window.

Henry moved back with no questions.

In one pocket of his parka, Owen had the small metal box (USMC stamped on the steel top) in which he kept his various IDs when he was on active duty—

the box had been a present from Kurtz himself after the Santo Domingo mission last year, a fine irony. In his other pocket were three rocks which he had picked up from beneath his own helicopter, where the fall of snow was thin.

He took one of them—a good-sized chunk of Maine granite—then paused, appalled, as a bright image filled his mind. Mac Cavanaugh, the fellow from Blue Boy Leader who had lost two of his fingers on the op, was sitting inside one of the semi trailer–boxes in the compound. With him was Frank Bellson from Blakey's Blue Boy Three, the other gunship that had made it back to base. One of them had turned on a powerful eight-cell flashlight and set it on its base like an electric candle. Its bright glow sprayed up into the gloom. This was happening right now, not five hundred feet from where Owen stood with a rock in one hand and his steel box in the other. Cavanaugh and Bellson sat side by side on the floor of the trailer. Both wore what looked like heavy red beards. Luxuriant growth had burst apart the bandages over the stumps of Cavanaugh's fingers. They had service automatics, the muzzles in their mouths. Their eyes were linked. So were their minds. Bellson was counting down: *Five . . . four . . . three . . .*

"Boys, no!" Owen cried, but got no sense they heard him; their link was too strong, forged with the resolve of men who have made up their minds. They would be the first of Kurtz's command to do this tonight; Owen did not think they would be the last.

Owen? That was Henry. *Owen, what's—*

Then he tapped into what Owen was seeing and fell silent, horrified.

. . . two . . . one.

Two pistol-shots, muffled by the roar of the wind and four Zimmer electrical generators. Two fans of blood and brain-tissue appearing like magic over the heads of Cavanaugh and Bellson in the dim light. Owen and Henry saw Bellson's right foot give a final dying jump. It struck the barrel of the flashlight, and for a moment they could see Cavanaugh's and Bellson's distorted, byrus-speckled faces. Then, as the flashlight went rolling across the bed of the box, casting cartwheels of light on the aluminum side, the picture went dark, like the picture on a TV when the plug has been pulled.

"Christ," Owen whispered. "Good Christ."

Henry had appeared behind the window again. Owen motioned him back, then threw the rock. The range was short, but his first shot missed anyway, bouncing harmlessly off the weathered boards to the left of the target. He took the second, pulled in a deep, settling breath, and threw. This one shattered the glass.

Got mail for you, Henry. Coming through.

He tossed the steel box through the hole where the glass had been.

4

It bounced across the shed floor. Henry picked the box up and undid the clasp. Inside were four foil-wrapped packets.

What are these?

Pocket rockets, Owen returned. *How's your heart?*

Okay, as far as I know.

Good, because that shit makes cocaine feel like Valium. There are two in each pack. Take three. Save the rest.

I don't have any water.

Owen sent a clear picture—south end of a north-bound horse. *Chew them, beautiful—you've got a few teeth left, don't you?* There was real anger in this, and at first Henry didn't understand it, but then of course he did. If there was anything he should be able to understand this early morning, it was the sudden loss of friends.

The pills were white, unmarked by the name of any pharmaceutical company, and terribly bitter in his mouth as they crumbled. Even his throat tried to pucker as he swallowed.

The effect was almost instantaneous. By the time he had tucked Owen's USMC box into his pants pocket, Henry's heartbeat had doubled. By the time he stepped back to the window, it had tripled. His eyes seemed to pulse from their sockets with each quick rap in his chest. This wasn't distressing, however; he actually found it quite pleasant. No more sleepiness, and his aches seemed to have flown away.

"Yow!" he called. "Popeye should try a few cans of *this* shit!" And laughed, both because speaking now seemed so odd—archaic, almost—and because he felt so fine.

Keep it down, what do you say?

Okay! OKAY!

Even his *thoughts* seemed to have acquired a new, crystalline force, and Henry didn't think this was just his imagination. Although the light behind the old feed shed was a little less than in the rest of the compound, it was still strong enough for him to see Owen wince and raise a hand to the side of his head, as if someone had shouted directly into his ear.

Sorry, he sent.

It's all right. It's just that you're so strong. You must be covered *with that shit.*

Actually, I'm not, Henry returned. A wink of his dream came back to him: the four of them on that grassy slope. No, the *five* of them, because Duddits had been there, too.

Henry—do you remember where I said I'd be?

Southwest corner of the compound. All the way across from the barn, on the diagonal. But—

No buts. That's where I'll be. If you want a ride out of here, it's where you better be, too. It's . . . A pause as Owen checked his watch. If it was still working, it must be the kind you wind up, Henry thought . . . *two minutes to four. I'll give you half an hour, then if the folks in the barn haven't started to move, I'm going to short the fence.*

Half an hour may not be long enough, Henry protested. Although he was standing still, looking out at Owen's form in the blowing snow, he was breathing fast, like a man in a race. His heart felt as if it *was* in a race.

It'll have to be, Owen sent. *The fence is alarmed. There'll be sirens. Even more lights. A general alert. I'll give you five minutes after the shit starts hitting the fan—that's a three hundred count—and if you haven't shown up, I'm on my merry way.*

You'll never find Jonesy without me.

That doesn't mean I have to stay here and die with you, Henry. Patient. As if talking to a small child. *If you don't make it to where I am in five minutes, there'll be no chance for either of us, anyway.*

Those two men who just committed suicide . . . they're not the only ones who are fucked up.

I know.

Henry caught a brief mental glimpse of a yellow school bus with MILLINOCKET SCHOOL DEPT. printed up the side. Looking out the windows were two score of grinning skulls. They were Owen Underhill's mates, Henry realized. The ones he'd arrived with yesterday morning. Men who were now either dying or already dead.

Never mind them, Owen replied. *It's Kurtz's ground support we have to worry about now. Especially the Imperial Valleys. If they exist, you better believe they'll follow orders and that they're well-trained. And training wins out over confusion every time—that's what training is for. If you stick around, they'll roast you and toast you. Five minutes is what you have once the alarms go. A three hundred count.*

Owen's logic was hard to like and impossible to refute.

All right, Henry said. *Five minutes.*

You have no business doing this in the first place, Owen told him. The thought came to Henry encrusted with a complex filigree of emotion: frustration, guilt, the inevitable fear—in Owen Underhill's case, not of dying but of failure. *If what you say is true, everything depends on whether or not we get out of here clean. For you to maybe put the entire world at risk because of a few hundred schmoes in a barn . . .*

It's not the way your boss would do it, right?

Owen reacted with surprise—no words, but a kind of comic-book ! in Henry's mind. Then, even over the ceaseless howl and hoot of the wind, he heard Owen laugh.

You got me there, beautiful.

Anyway, I'll get them moving. I'm a motivational master.

I know you'll try. Henry couldn't see Owen's face, but felt him smiling. Then Owen spoke aloud. "And after that? Tell me again."

Why?

"Maybe because soldiers need motivation, too, especially when they're derailing. And belay the telepathy—I want you to say it out loud. I want to hear the word."

Henry looked at the man shivering on the other side of the fence and said, "After that we're going to be heroes. Not because we want to, but because there are no other options."

Out in the snow and the wind, Owen was nodding. Nodding and still smiling. "Why not?" he said. "Just why the fuck not?"

In his mind, glimmering, Henry saw the image of a little boy with a plate raised over his head. What the man wanted was for the little boy to put the plate back—that plate that had haunted him so over the years and would forever stay broken.

5

Dreamless since childhood and thus unsane, Kurtz woke as he always did: at one moment nowhere, at the next completely awake and cognizant of his surroundings. Alive, hallelujah, oh yes, still in the big time. He turned his head and looked at the clock, but the goddam thing had gone off again in spite of its fancy antimagnetic casing, flashing 12-12-12, like a stutterer caught on one word. He turned on the lamp beside the bed and picked up the pocket-watch on the bedtable. Four-oh-eight.

Kurtz put it down again, swung his bare feet out onto the floor, and stood up. The first thing he became aware of was the wind, still howling like a woe-dog. The second was that the faraway mutter of voices in his head had disappeared entirely. The telepathy was gone and Kurtz was glad. It had offended him in an elemental, down-deep way, as certain sexual practices offended him. The idea that someone might be able to come into his very *head,* to be able to visit the upper levels of his mind . . . that had been horrible. The grayboys deserved to be wiped out for that alone, for bringing that disgustingly peculiar gift. Thank God it had proved ephemeral.

Kurtz shucked his gray workout shorts and stood naked in front of the mirror on the bedroom door, letting his eyes go up from his feet (where the first snarls of purple veins were beginning to show) to the crown of his head, where his graying hair stood up in a sleep-tousle. He was sixty, but not looking too bad; those busted veins on the sides of his feet were the worst of it. Had a hell of a good crank on him, too, although he had never made much use of it; women were, for the most part, vile creatures incapable of loyalty. They drained a man. In his secret unsane heart, where even his madness was starched and pressed and fundamentally not very interesting, Kurtz believed all sex was FUBAR. Even when it was done for procreation, the result was usually a brain-equipped tumor not much different from the shit-weasels.

From the crown of his head, Kurtz let his eyes descend again, slowly, looking for the least patch of red, the tiniest roseola blush. There was nothing. He turned around, looked at as much as he could see by craning back over his shoulder, and still saw nothing. He spread his buttocks, probed between them, slid a finger two knuckles deep into his anus, and felt nothing but flesh.

"I'm clean," he said in a low voice as he washed his hands briskly in the Winnebago's little bathroom. "Clean as a whistle."

He stepped into his shorts again, then sat on his rack to slip into his socks. Clean, praise God, clean. A good word *Clean.* The unpleasant feel of the telepathy—like sweaty skin pressed against sweaty skin—was gone. He wasn't supporting a single strand of Ripley; he had even checked his tongue and gums.

So what had awakened him? Why were there alarm bells clanging in his head?

Because telepathy wasn't the *only* form of extrasensory perception. Because long before the grayboys knew there was such a place as Earth tucked away in this dusty and seldom-visited carrel of the great interstellar library, there had been a little thing called instinct, the specialty of uniform-wearing *Homo saps* such as himself.

"The hunch," Kurtz said. "The good old all-American hunch-ola."

He put on his pants. Then, still bare-chested, he picked up the walkie which lay on the bedtable beside the pocket-watch (four-sixteen now, and how the time seemed to be *rushing,* like a brakeless car plunging down a hill toward a busy intersection). The walkie was a special digital job, encrypted and supposedly unjammable . . . but one look at his supposedly impervious digital clock made him realize none of the gear was un-anything.

He clicked the SEND/SQUEAL button twice. Freddy Johnson came back quickly and not sounding *too* sleepy . . . oh, but now that crunch time was here, how Kurtz (who had been born Robert Coonts, name, name, what's in a name) longed for Underhill. *Owen, Owen,* he thought, *why did you have to skid just when I needed you the most, son?*

"Boss?"

"I'm moving Imperial Valley up to six. That's Imperial Valley at oh-six hundred, come back and acknowledge me."

He had to listen to why it was impossible, crap Owen would not have spouted in his weakest dream.

He gave Freddy roughly forty seconds to vent before saying, "Close your clam, you son of a bitch."

Shocked silence from Freddy's end.

"We've got something brewing here. I don't know what, but it woke me up out of a sound sleep with the alarm bells ringing. Now I put all you fellows and girls together for a reason, and if you expect to be still drawing breath come suppertime, you want to get them moving. Tell Gallagher she may wind up on point. Acknowledge me, Freddy."

"Boss, I acknowledge. One thing you should know—we've had four suicides that I know of. There may have been more."

Kurtz was neither surprised nor displeased. Under certain circumstances, suicide wasn't just acceptable, but noble—the true gentleman's final act.

"From the choppers?"

"Affirmative."

"No Imperial Valleys."

"No, boss, no Valleys."

"All right. Floor it, buck. We got trouble. I don't know what it is, but I know it's coming. Big thunder."

Kurtz tossed the walkie back on the table and continued dressing. He wanted another cigarette, but they were all gone.

6

A pretty good herd of milkers had once been stabled in Old Man Gosselin's barn, and while the interior might not have passed USDA standards as it now stood, the building was still in okay shape. The soldiers had strung some high-wattage bulbs that cast a brilliant glare over the stalls, the milking stations in the parlor, and the upper and lower lofts. They had also put in a number of heaters, and the barn glowed with a pulsing, almost feverish warmth. Henry unzipped his coat as soon as he stepped in, but still felt the sweat break out on his face. He supposed Owen's pills had something to do with that—he'd taken another outside the barn.

His first thought as he looked around was how similar the barn was to the various refugee camps he had seen: Bosnian Serbs in Macedonia, Haitian rebels after Uncle Sugar's Marines had landed in Port-au-Prince, the African exiles who had left their home countries because of disease, famine, civil war, or a combination of all three. You got used to seeing such things on the TV news, but the pictures always came from far away; the horror with which one viewed them was almost clinical. But this wasn't a place you needed a passport to visit. This was a cowbarn in New England. The people packed into it weren't wearing rags and dirty dashikis but parkas from Bean's, cargo pants (so perfect for those extra shotgun shells) from Banana Republic, underwear from Fruit of the Loom. The look was the same, though. The only difference he could discern was how surprised they all still seemed. This wasn't supposed to be happening in the land of Sprint Nickel Nights.

The internees pretty well covered the main floor, where hay had been spread (jackets on top of that).

They were sleeping in little clumps or family groups. There were more of them in the lofts, and three or four to each of the forty stalls. The room was full of snores and gurgles and the groans of people dreaming badly. Somewhere a child was weeping. And there was piped-in Muzak: to Henry, this was the final bizarre touch. Right now the dozing doomed in Old Man Gosselin's barn were listening to the Fred Waring Orchestra float through a violin-heavy version of "Some Enchanted Evening."

Hyped as he was, everything stood out with brilliant, exclamatory clarity. *All the orange jackets and hats!* he thought. *Man! It's Halloween in hell!*

There was also a fair amount of the red-gold stuff. Henry saw patches growing on cheeks, in ears, between fingers; he also saw patches growing on beams and on the electrical cords of several dangling lights. The predominant smell in here was hay, but Henry had no trouble picking up the smell of sulfur-tinged ethyl alcohol under it. As well as the snores, there was a lot of farting going on—it sounded like six or seven seriously untalented musicians tootling away on tubas and saxophones. Under other circumstances it would have been funny . . . or perhaps even in these, to a person who hadn't seen that weasel-thing wriggling and snarling on Jonesy's bloody bed.

How many of them are incubating those things? Henry wondered. The answer didn't matter, he supposed, because the weasels were ultimately harmless. They might be able to live outside their hosts in this barn, but outside in the storm, where the wind was blowing a gale and the chill-factor was below zero, they wouldn't have a chance.

He needed to talk to these people—

No, that wasn't right. What he needed to do was scare the living hell out of them. Had to get them moving in spite of the warmth in here and the cold outside. There had been cows in here before; there were cows here again. He had to change them back into people—scared, pissed-off people. He could do it, but not alone. And the clock was ticking. Owen Underhill had given him half an hour. Henry estimated that a third of that was already gone.

Got to have a megaphone, he thought. *That's step one.*

He looked around, spotted a burly, balding man sleeping on his side to the left of the door leading to the milking parlor, and walked over to take a closer look. He *thought* it was one of the guys he'd kicked out of the shed, but he wasn't sure. When it came to hunters, burly, balding men were a dime a peck.

But it was Charles, and the byrus was re-thatching what old Charlie no doubt referred to as his "solar sex-panel." *Who needs Rogaine when you've got this shit going for you?* Henry thought, then grinned.

Charles was good; better yet, Marsha was sleeping nearby, holding hands with Darren, Mr. Bomber-Joint-from-Newton. Byrus was now growing down one of Marsha's smooth cheeks. Her husband was still clean, but his brother-in-law—Bill, had that been his name?—was lousy with the stuff. *Best-in-show,* Henry thought.

He knelt by Bill, took his byrus-speckled hand, and

spoke down into the tangled jungle of his bad dreams. *Wake up, Bill. Wakey-wakey. We have to get out of here. And if you help me, we can. Wake up, Bill.*

Wake up and be a hero.

7

It happened with a speed that was exhilarating.

Henry felt Bill's mind rising toward his, floundering out of the nightmares that had entangled it, reaching for Henry the way a drowning man will reach for the lifeguard who has swum out to save him. Their minds connected like couplers on a pair of freight-cars.

Don't talk, don't try to talk, Henry told him. *Just hold on. We need Marsha and Charles. The four of us should be enough.*

What—

No time, Billy. Let's go.

Bill took his sister-in-law's hand. Marsha's eyes flashed open at once, almost as if she had been waiting for this, and Henry felt all the dials inside his head turn up another notch. She wasn't supporting as much growth as Bill, but perhaps had more natural talent. She took Charles's hand without a single question. Henry had an idea she had already grasped what was going on here, and what needed to be done. Thankfully, she also grasped the necessity of speed. They were going to bomb these people, then swing them like a club.

Charles sat with a jerk, eyes wide and bulging from their fatty sockets. He got up as if someone had goosed him. Now all four of them were on their feet, hands joined like participants in a séance . . . which, Henry reflected, this almost was.

Give it to me, he told them, and they did. The feeling was like having a magic wand placed in his hand.

Listen to me, he called.

Heads rose; some people sat up out of sound sleeps as if they had been electrified.

Listen to me and boost me . . . boost me up! Do you understand? Boost me up! This is your only chance, so BOOST ME UP!

They did it as instinctively as people whistling a tune or clapping to a beat. If he'd given them time to think about it, it probably would have been harder, perhaps even impossible, but he didn't. Most of them had been sleeping, and he caught the infected ones, the telepaths, with their minds wide open.

Operating on instinct himself, Henry sent a series of images: soldiers wearing masks surrounding the barn, most with guns, some with backpacks connected to long wands. He made the faces of the soldiers into editorial-page caricatures of cruelty. At an amplified order, the wands unleashed streams of liquid fire: napalm. The sides of the barn and roof caught at once.

Henry shifted to the inside, sending pictures of screaming, milling people. Liquid fire dripped through holes in the blazing roof and ignited the hay in the lofts. Here was a man with his hair on fire; there a woman in a burning ski-parka still decorated with lift-tickets from Sugarloaf and Ragged Mountain.

They were all looking at Henry now—Henry and his linked friends. Only the telepaths were receiving the images, but perhaps as many as sixty percent of the people in the barn were infected, and even those who weren't caught the sense of panic; a rising tide lifts all boats.

Clamping Bill's hand tightly with one of his own and Marsha's with the other, Henry switched the images back to the outside perspective again. Fire; encircling soldiers; an amplified voice shouting for the soldiers to be sure no one got clear.

The detainees were on their feet now, speaking in a rising babble of frightened voices (except for the deep telepaths; they only stared at him, haunted eyes in byrus-speckled faces). He showed them the barn burning like a torch in the snow-driven night, the wind turning an inferno into an explosion, a firestorm, and still the napalm hoses poured it on and still the amplified voice exhorted: *"THAT'S RIGHT, MEN, GET THEM ALL, DON'T LET ANY OF THEM GET AWAY, THEY'RE THE CANCER AND WE'RE THE CURE!"*

Imagination fully pumped up now, feeding on itself in a kind of frenzy, Henry sent images of the few people who managed to find the exits or to wriggle out through the windows. Many of these were in flames. One was a woman with a child cradled in her arms. The soldiers machine-gunned all of them but the woman and the child, who were turned into napalm candles as they ran.

"No!" several women screamed in unison, and

Henry realized with a species of sick wonder that all of them, even those without children, had put their own faces on the burning woman.

They were up now, milling around like cattle in a thunderstorm. He had to move them before they had a chance to think once, let alone twice.

Gathering the force of the minds linked to his, Henry sent them an image of the store.

THERE! he called to them. *IT'S YOUR ONLY CHANCE! THROUGH THE STORE IF YOU CAN, BREAK DOWN THE FENCE IF THE DOOR'S BLOCKED! DON'T STOP, DON'T HESITATE! GET INTO THE WOODS! HIDE IN THE WOODS! THEY'RE COMING TO BURN THIS PLACE DOWN, THE BARN AND EVERYONE IN IT, AND THE WOODS ARE YOUR ONLY CHANCE! NOW, NOW!*

Deep in the well of his own imagination, flying on the pills Owen had given him and sending with all his strength—images of possible safety there, of certain death here, images as simple as those in a child's picture-book—he was only distantly aware that he had begun chanting aloud: *"Now, now, now."*

Marsha Chiles picked it up, then her brother-in-law, then Charles, the man with the overgrown solar sex-panel.

"Now! Now! Now!"

Although immune to the byrus and thus no more telepathic than the average bear, Darren was not immune to the growing vibe, and he also joined in.

"Now! Now! Now!"

It jumped from person to person and group to group, a panic-induced infection more catching than the byrus: *"Now! Now! Now!"*

The barn shook with it. Fists were pumping in unison, like fists at a rock concert.

"NOW! NOW! NOW!"

Henry let them take it over and build it, pumping his own fist without even realizing it, flinging his hand into the air to the farthest reach of his aching arm even as he reminded himself not to be caught up in the cyclone of the mass mind he had created: when *they* went north, he was going south. He was waiting for some point of no return to be reached—the point of ignition and spontaneous combustion.

It came.

"Now," he whispered.

He gathered Marsha's mind, Bill's, Charlie's . . . and then the others that were close and particularly locked in. He merged them, compressed them, and then flung that single word like a silver bullet into the heads of the three hundred and seventeen people in Old Man Gosselin's barn:

NOW.

There was a moment of utter silence before hell's door flew open.

8

Just before dusk, a dozen two-man sentry huts (they were actually Porta-Potties with the urinals and toilet-seats yanked out) had been set up at intervals along the security fence. These came equipped with heaters that threw a stuporous glow in the small spaces, and the guards had no interest in going outside them. Every now and then one of them would open a door to allow in a snowy swirl of fresh air, but that was the extent of the guards' exposure to the outside world. Most of them were peacetime soldiers with no gut understanding of how high the current stakes were, and so they swapped stories about sex, cars, postings, sex, their families, their future, sex, drinking and drugging expeditions, and sex. They had missed Owen Underhill's two visits to the shed (he would have been clearly visible from both Post 9 and Post 10) and they were the last to be aware that they had a full-scale revolt on their hands.

Seven other soldiers, boys who had been with Kurtz a little longer and thus had a little more salt on their skins, were in the back of the store near the woodstove, playing five-card stud in the same office where Owen had played Kurtz the *ne nous blessez pas* tapes roughly two centuries ago. Six of the card-players were sentries. The seventh was Dawg Brodsky's colleague Gene Cambry. Cambry hadn't been able to sleep. The reason was concealed by a stretchy cotton wristlet. He didn't know how long the wristlet would serve, however, because the red stuff under it was spreading. If he wasn't careful, someone would see it . . . and then, instead of playing cards in the office, he might be out there in the barn with the John Q's.

And would he be the only one? Ray Parsons had a big wad of cotton in one ear. He said it was an earache, but who knew for sure? Ted Trezewski had a bandage on one meaty forearm and claimed he'd gouged himself stringing compound barbed wire much earlier in the day. Maybe it was true. George Udall, the Dawg's immediate superior in more normal times, was wearing a knitted cap over his bald head; damn thing made him look like some kind of elderly white rapper. Maybe there was nothing under there but skin, but it was warm in here for a cap, wasn't it? Especially a knitted one.

"Kick a buck," Howie Everett said.

"Call," said Danny O'Brian.

Parsons called; so did Udall. Cambry barely heard. In his mind there rose an image of a woman with a child cradled in her arms. As she struggled across the drifted-in paddock, a soldier turned her into a napalm road-flare. Cambry winced, horrified, thinking this image had been served up by his own guilty conscience.

"Gene?" Al Coleman asked. "Are you going to call, or—"

"What's that?" Howie asked, frowning.

"What's what?" Ted Trezewski said.

"If you listen, you'll hear it," Howie replied. *Dumb Polack:* Cambry heard this unspoken corollary in his head, but paid it no mind. Once it had been called to their attention, the chant was clear enough, rising above the wind, quickly taking on strength and urgency.

"Now! Now! Now! Now! NOW!"

It was coming from the barn, directly behind them.

"What in the blue *hell*?" Udall asked in a musing

voice, blinking over the folding table with its scatter of cards, ashtrays, chips, and money. Gene Cambry suddenly understood that there was nothing under the stupid woolen cap but skin, after all. Udall was nominally in charge of this little group, but he didn't have a clue. He couldn't see the pumping fists, couldn't hear the strong thought-voice that was leading the chant.

Cambry saw alarm on Parsons's face, on Everett's, on Coleman's. They were seeing it, too. Understanding leaped among them while the uninfected ones only looked puzzled.

"Fuckers're gonna break out," Cambry said.

"Don't be stupid, Gene," George Udall said. "They don't know what's coming down. Besides, they're *civilians*. They're just letting off a little st—"

Cambry lost the rest as a single word—*NOW*—ripped through his brain like a buzzsaw. Ray Parsons and Al Coleman winced. Howie Everett cried out in pain, his hands going to his temples, his knees connecting with the underside of the table and sending chips and cards everywhere. A dollar bill landed atop the hot stove and began to burn.

"Aw, fuck a duck, look what you d—" Ted began.

"They're coming," Cambry said. "They're coming at *us*."

Parsons, Everett, and Coleman lunged for the M-4 carbines leaning beside Old Man Gosselin's coatrack. The others looked at them, surprised, still three steps behind . . . and then there was a vast thud as sixty or more of the internees struck the barn doors. Those doors had been locked from the outside—big steel locks, Army issue. They held, but the old wood gave with a splintering crack.

The prisoners charged through the gap, yelling *"Now! Now!"* into the snowy mouth of the wind and trampling several of their number underfoot.

Cambry also lunged, got one of the compact assault rifles, then had it snatched out of his hands. "That's mine, muhfuh," Ted Trezewski snarled.

There was less than twenty yards between the shattered barn doors and the back of the store. The mob swept across the gap, shouting *"NOW! NOW! NOW!"*

The poker-table went over with a crash, spilling crap everywhere. The perimeter alarm went off as the first internees struck the double-strung fence and were either fried or hooked like fish on the oversized bundles of barbs. Moments later the alarm's honking, pulsing bray was joined by a whooping siren, the General Quarters alert which was sometimes referred to as Situation Triple Six, the end of the world. In the plastic Porta-Potty sentry huts, surprised and frightened faces peered out dazedly.

"The barn!" someone shouted. "Collapse in on the barn! It's an escape!"

The sentries trotted out into the snow, many of them bootless, moving along the outside of the fence, unaware that it had been shorted out by the weight of more than eighty kamikaze deer-hunters, all screaming *"NOW"* at the top of their lungs, even as they jittered and fried and died.

No one noticed the single man—tall, skinny, wearing a pair of old-fashioned horn-rim specs—who left from the back of the barn and set out diagonally across the drifts filling the paddock. Although Henry could neither see nor sense anyone paying attention to him, he began to run. He felt horribly exposed under the brilliant lights, and the cacophony of the siren and the perimeter alarm made him feel panicky and half-crazy . . . made him feel the way Duddits's crying had, that day behind Tracker Brothers.

He hoped to God Underhill was waiting for him. He couldn't tell, the snow was too thick to see the far end of the paddock, but he would be there soon enough and then he would know.

9

Kurtz had everything on but one boot when the alarm went off and the emergency lights went on, flooding this godforsaken piece of ground with even more glare. He felt no surprise, no dismay, only a mixture of relief and chagrin. Relief that whatever had been chewing on his nerve-endings was now out in the open. Chagrin that this fucking mess hadn't held off for another two hours. Another two hours and he could have balanced the books on the whole deal.

He jerked open the door of the Winnebago with his right hand, still holding his other boot in his left. A savage roaring came from the barn, the sort of warrior's cry to which his heart responded in spite of everything. The gale-force wind thinned it a little, but not much; they were all in it together, it seemed. From somewhere in their well-fed, timorous, it-can't-happen-here ranks, a Spartacus had arisen—who would have thunk it?

It's the goddam telepathy, he thought. His instincts, always superb, told him this was serious trouble, that he was watching an operation go tits-up on a truly grand scale, but he was smiling in spite of that. *Got to be the goddam telepathy. They smelled out what was coming . . . and someone decided to do something about it.*

As he watched, a motley mob of men, most in parkas and orange hats, came moiling through the sagging, shattered barn doors. One fell on a splintered board and was impaled like a vampire. Some stumbled in the snow and were trampled under. All the lights were on now. Kurtz felt like a man with a ringside seat at a prizefight. He could see everything.

Wings of escapees, fifty or sixty in each complement, peeled off as neatly as squads in a drill-team and charged at the fence on either side of the ratty little store. Either they didn't know there was a lethal dose of electricity coursing through the smoothwire or they didn't care. The rest of them, the main body, charged directly at the back of the store. That was the weakest point in the perimeter, but it didn't matter. Kurtz thought it was all going to go.

Never in any of his contingency plans had he so much as considered this scenario: two or three hundred overweight November warriors mounting a no-guts-no-glory banzai charge. He had never expected them to do anything but stay put, clamoring for due process right up to the point where they were barbecued.

"Not bad, boys," Kurtz said. He smelled something else starting to burn—probably his goddam career—but the end had been coming anyway, and he'd picked one hell of an operation to go out on, hadn't he? As far as Kurtz was concerned, the little gray men from space were strictly secondary. If he ran the news, the headline above the fold would read: SURPRISE! NEW-AGE AMERICANS SHOW SOME BACKBONE! Outstanding. It was almost a shame to cut them down.

The General Quarters siren rose and fell in the snowy night. The first wave of men hit the back of the store. Kurtz could almost see the whole place shudder.

"That goddam telepathy," Kurtz said, grinning. He could see his guys responding, the first wave from the sentry huts, more coming from the motor-pool, the commissary, and the semi trailer–boxes that were serving as makeshift barracks. Then the smile on Kurtz's face began to fade, replaced by an expression of puzzlement. "Shoot them," he said. "Why don't you shoot them?"

Some *were* firing, but not enough—nowhere near enough. Kurtz thought he smelled panic. His men weren't shooting because they had gone chickenshit. Or because they knew they were next.

"The goddam telepathy," he said again, and suddenly automatic-rifle fire began inside the store. The windows of the office where he and Owen Underhill had had their original conference lit up in brilliant stutterflashes of light. Two of them blew out. A man attempted to exit the second of these, and Kurtz had time to recognize George Udall before George was seized by the legs and jerked back inside.

The guys in the office were fighting, at least, but of course they would; in there they were fighting for their lives. The laddie-bucks who had come running were, for the most part, still running. Kurtz thought about dropping his boot and grabbing his nine-millimeter. Shooting a few skedaddlers. Bagging his limit, in fact. It was falling down all around him, why not?

Underhill, that was why not. Owen Underhill had played a part in this snafu. Kurtz knew that as well as he knew his own name. This stank of line-crossing, and crossing the line was an Owen Underhill specialty.

More shooting from Gosselin's office . . . screams of pain . . . then triumphant howls. The computer-savvy, Evian-drinking, salad-eating Goths had taken their objective. Kurtz slammed the Winnebago's door on the scene and hurried back to the bedroom to call Freddy Johnson. He was still carrying his boot.

10

Cambry was on his knees behind Old Man Gosselin's desk when the first wave of prisoners smashed its way in. He was opening drawers, looking frantically for a gun. The fact that he didn't find one very likely saved his life.

"NOW! NOW! NOW!" the oncoming prisoners screamed. There was a monstrous thud against the back of the store, as if a truck had driven into it. From outside, Cambry could hear a juicy crackling sound as the first detainees hit the fence. The lights in the office began to flicker.

"Stand together, men!" Danny O'Brian cried. "For the love of Christ, stand toge—"

The rear door came off its hinges with so much force that it actually skittered backward across the room, shielding the first of the screaming men who clogged the doorway. Cambry ducked, hands laced over the back of his head, as the door fell on the desk at an angle with him beneath it, in the kneehole.

The sound of rifles on full auto was deafening in the tiny room, drowning out even the screams of the wounded, but Cambry understood that not all of them were firing. Trezewski, Udall, and O'Brian were, but Coleman, Everett, and Ray Parsons were only standing there with their weapons held to their chests and dazed expressions on their faces.

From his accidental shelter, Gene Cambry saw the prisoners charge across the room, saw the first of them caught by the bullets and thrown like scarecrows; saw their blood splash across the walls and the bean-supper posters and the OSHA notices. He saw George Udall throw his gun at two beefy young men in orange, then whirl and lunge at one of the windows. George got halfway out and was then yanked back; a man with Ripley growing on his cheek like a birthmark sank his teeth into George's calf as if it were a turkey drumstick while another man silenced the screaming head at the other end of George's body by jerking it briskly to the left. The room was blue with powder-smoke, but he saw Al Coleman throw his gun down and pick up the chant—*"Now! Now! Now!"* And he saw Ray Parsons, normally the most pacific of men, turn his rifle on Danny O'Brian and blow his brains out.

Now the matter was simple. Now it was just the infected versus the immune.

The desk was hit and slammed against the wall. The door fell on top of Cambry, and before he could get up, people were running over the door, squashing him. He felt like a cowboy who has fallen off his horse during a stampede. *I'm going to die under here,* he thought, and then for a moment the murderous pressure was gone. He lunged to his knees, driving with adrenaline-loaded muscles, and the door slid off him to the left, saying goodbye with a vicious dig of the doorknob into his hip. Someone dealt him a passing kick in the ribcage, another boot scraped by his right ear, and then he was up. The room was thick with smoke, crazy with shouts and screams. Four or five bulky hunters were propelled into the woodstove, which tore free of its pipe and went crashing over on its side, spilling flaming chunks of maple onto the floor. Money and playing cards caught fire. There was the rancid smell of melting plastic poker chips. *Those were Ray's,* Cambry thought incoherently. *He had them in the Gulf. Bosnia, too.*

He stood ignored in the confusion. There was no need for the escaping internees to use the door between the office and the store; the entire wall—no more than a flimsy partition, really—had been smashed flat. Pieces of this stuff were also catching fire from the overturned stove.

"Now," Gene Cambry muttered. "Now." He saw Ray Parsons running with the others toward the front of the store, Howie Everett at his heels. Howie snatched a loaf of bread as he ran down the center aisle.

A scrawny old party in a tassled cap and an overcoat was pushed forward onto the overturned stove, then stomped flat. Cambry heard his high-pitched, squealing screams as his face bonded to the metal and then began to boil.

Heard it and *felt it*.

"*Now!*" Cambry shouted, giving in and joining the others. "*Now!*"

He broad-jumped the growing flames from the stove and ran, losing his little mind in the big one.

For all practical purposes, Operation Blue Boy was over.

11

Three quarters of the way across the paddock, Henry paused, gasping for breath and clutching at his hammering chest. Behind him was the pocket armageddon he had unleashed; ahead of him he could see nothing but darkness. Fucking Underhill had run out on him, had—

Easy, beautiful—easy.

Lights flashed out twice. Henry had been looking in the wrong place, that was all; Owen was parked a little to the left of the paddock's southwest corner. Now Henry could see the Sno-Cat's boxy outline clearly. From behind him came screams, shouts, orders, shooting. Not as much shooting as he would have expected, but this was no time to wonder why.

Hurry up! Owen cried. *We have to get out of here!*

I'm coming as fast as I can—hold on.

Henry got moving again. Whatever had been in Owen's kickstart pills was already wearing off, and his feet felt heavy. His thigh itched maddeningly, and so did his mouth. He could feel the stuff creeping over his tongue. It was like a soft-drink fizz that wouldn't go away.

Owen had cut the fence—both the barbed wire and the smooth. Now he stood in front of the Sno-Cat (it was white to match the snow, and it was really no wonder Henry hadn't seen it) with an automatic rifle propped against his hip, attempting to look everywhere at once. The multiple lights gave him half a dozen shadows; they radiated out from his boots like crazy clock-hands.

Owen grabbed Henry around the shoulders. *You okay?*

Henry nodded. As Owen began to pull him toward the Sno-Cat, there was a loud, high-pitched explosion, as if someone had just fired the world's largest carbine. Henry ducked, stumbled over his own feet, and would have fallen if Owen hadn't held him up.

What—?

LP gas. Gasoline, too, maybe. Look.

Owen took him by the shoulders and turned him around. Henry saw a vast pillar of fire in the snowy night. Bits of the store—boards, shingles, flaming boxes of Cheerios, burning rolls of toilet paper—rose into the sky. Some of the soldiers were watching this, mesmerized. Others were running for the woods. In pursuit of the prisoners, Henry assumed, although he was hearing their panic in his head—*Run! Run! Now! Now!*—and simply could not credit it. Later, when he had time to think, he would understand that many of the soldiers were also fleeing. Now he understood nothing. Things were happening too fast.

Owen turned him around again and boosted him into the Sno-Cat's passenger seat, pushing him past a hanging canvas flap that smelled strongly of motor oil. It was blessedly warm in the 'Cat's cab. A radio bolted to the rudimentary dashboard chattered and squawked. The only thing Henry could make out clearly was the panic in the voices. It made him savagely happy—happier than he'd been since the afternoon the four of them had put the fear of God into Richie Grenadeau and his bullyrag buddies. And that's who was running this operation, as far as Henry could see: a bunch of grownup Richie Grenadeaus, armed with guns instead of dried-up pieces of dogshit.

There was something between the seats, a box with two blinking amber lights. As Henry bent over it, curious, Owen Underhill snatched back the tarp hanging beside the driver's seat and flung himself into the

'Cat. He was breathing hard and smiling as he looked at the burning store.

"Be careful of that, brother," he said. "Mind the buttons."

Henry lifted the box, which was about the size of Duddits's beloved Scooby-Doo lunchbox. The buttons of which Owen had spoken were under the blinking lights. "What are they?"

Owen turned the ignition key and the Sno-Cat's hot engine rumbled into immediate life. The transmission ran off a high stick, which Owen jammed into gear. Owen was still smiling. In the bright light falling through the Sno-Cat's windshield, Henry could now see a reddish-orange thread of byrus growing beneath each of the man's eyes, like mascara. There was more in his brows.

"Too much light in this place," he said. "We're gonna dial em down a little." He turned the 'Cat in a surprisingly smooth circle; it was like being on a motorboat. Henry collapsed back against the seat, holding the box with the blinking lights on his lap. He felt that if he didn't walk again for five years, that would be about right.

Owen glanced at him as he drove the Sno-Cat on a diagonal toward the snowbank-enclosed ditch that was the Swanny Pond Road. "You did it," he said. "I doubted that you could, I freely admit it, but you pulled the fucker off."

"I told you—I'm a motivational master." *Besides,* he sent, *most of them really are going to die anyway.*

Doesn't matter. You gave them a chance. And now—

There was more shooting, but it wasn't until a bullet whined off the metal just above their heads that Henry realized it was aimed at them. There was a brisk clank as another slug ricocheted off one of the Sno-Cat's treads and Henry ducked . . . as if *that* would do any good.

Still smiling, Owen pointed a gloved hand off to his right. Henry peered in that direction as two more slugs ricocheted off the 'Cat's squat pillbox body. Henry cringed both times; Owen seemed not even to notice.

Henry saw a cluster of trailer-boxes, some with brand names like Sysco and Scott Paper on them. In front of the trailers was a colony of motor homes, and in front of the biggest, a Winnebago that looked to Henry like a mansion on wheels, were six or seven men, all firing at the Sno-Cat. Although the range was long, the wind high, and the snow still heavy, too many were hitting. Other men, some only partially dressed (one bruiser came sprinting through the snow displaying a bare chest that would have looked at home on a comic-book superhero) were joining the group. At its center stood a tall man with gray hair. Beside him was a stockier guy. As Henry watched, the skinny man raised his rifle and fired, seemingly without bothering to aim. There was a *spanng* sound and Henry sensed something pass right in front of his nose, a small wicked droning thing.

Owen actually laughed. "The skinny one with the gray hair is Kurtz. He's in charge, and can that fucker shoot."

More bullets spanged off the 'Cat's treads, its body.

Henry sensed another of those buzzing, hustling presences in the cab, and suddenly the radio was silent. The distance between them and the shooters clustered around the Winnebago was getting longer, but it didn't seem to matter. As far as Henry was concerned, *all* those fuckers could shoot. It was only a matter of time before one of them took a hit . . . and yet Owen looked *happy*. It occurred to Henry that he had hooked up with someone even more suicidal than himself.

"The guy beside Kurtz is Freddy Johnson. Those Mouseketeers are all Kurtz's boys, the ones who were supposed to—whoops, look out!"

Another spang, another whining steel bee— between them, this time—and suddenly the knob on the transmission stick was gone. Owen burst out laughing. "Kurtz!" he shouted. "Bet you a nickel! Two years from mandatory retirement age and he still shoots like Annie Oakley!" He hammered a fist on the steering yoke. "But that's enough. Fun is fun and done is done. Turn out their lights, beautiful."

"Huh?"

Still grinning, Owen jerked a thumb at the box with the blinking amber bulbs. The curved streaks of byrus under his eyes now looked like warpaint to Henry. "Push the buttons, bub. Push the buttons and yank down the shades."

12

Suddenly—it was always sudden, always magical—the world fell away and Kurtz was in the zone. The scream of the blizzard wind, the pelt of the snow, the howl of the siren, the beat of the buzzer—all gone. Kurtz lost his awareness of Freddy Johnson next to him and the other Imperial Valleys gathering around. He fixed on the departing Sno-Cat and nothing else. He could see Owen Underhill in the left seat, right through the steel shell of the cab he could see him, as if he, Abe Kurtz, were all at once equipped with Superman's X-ray vision. The distance was incredibly long, but it didn't matter. The next round he fired was going right into the back of Owen Underhill's treacherous, line-crossing head. He raised the rifle, sighted down—

Two explosions ripped the night, one of them close enough to hammer Kurtz and his men with the shockwave. A trailer-box with the words INTEL INSIDE printed on it rose into the air, turned over, and came down on Spago's, the cook-tent. "Holy Christ!" one of the men shouted.

Not all of the lights went out—a half hour wasn't long and Owen had had time to equip only two of the gennies with thermite charges (all the time muttering "Banbury Cross, Banbury Cross, ride a cock horse to Banbury Cross" under his breath), but suddenly the fleeing Sno-Cat was swallowed in moving fire-flecked shadows, and Kurtz dropped his rifle into the snow without discharging it.

"Fuck a duck," he said tonelessly. "Cease firing. Cease firing, you humps. Quit it, praise Jesus. Inside. Every one of you but Freddy. Join hands and pray for God the Father Almighty to get our asses out of the sling they're in. Come here, Freddy. Step lively."

The others, nearly a dozen, trooped up the steps to the Winnebago, looking uneasily at the burning generators, the blazing cook-tent (already the commissary-tent next door was catching; the infirmary and the morgue would be next). Half the pole lights in the compound were out.

Kurtz put his arm around Freddy Johnson's shoulders and walked him twenty paces into the blowing snow, which the wind was now lifting and carrying in veils that looked like mystic steam. Directly ahead of the two men, Gosselin's—what was left of it—was burning merry hell. The barn had already caught. Its shattered doors gaped.

"Freddy, do you love Jesus? Tell me the truth."

Freddy had been through this before. It was a mantra. The boss was clearing his head.

"I love Him, boss."

"Do you swear that's true?" Kurtz looking keenly. Looking through him, more than likely. Planning ahead, if such creatures of instinct could be said to plan. "As you face the eternal pit of hell for a lie?"

"I swear it's true."

"You love Him a lot, do you?"

"Lots, boss."

"More than the group? More than going in hot and getting the job done?" A pause. "More than you love me?"

Not questions you wanted to answer wrong if you wanted to go on living. Fortunately, not hard ones, either. "No, boss."

"Telepathy gone, Freddy?"

"I had a touch of something, I don't know if it was telepathy, exactly, voices in my head—"

Kurtz was nodding. Red-gold flames the color of the Ripley fungus burst through the roof of the barn.

"—but that's gone."

"Other men in the group?"

"Imperial Valley, you mean?" Freddy nodded toward the Winnebago.

"Who else would I mean, The Firehouse Five Plus Two? Yes, them!"

"They're clean, boss."

"That's good, but it's also bad. Freddy, we need a couple of infected Americans. And when I say *we*, I mean you and I. I want Americans who are *crawling* with that red shit, understand me?"

"I do." What Freddy didn't understand was why, but at the moment the why didn't matter. He could see Kurtz taking hold, visibly taking hold, and that was a relief. When Freddy needed to know, Kurtz would tell him. Freddy looked uneasily at the blazing store, the blazing barn, the blazing cook-tent. This situation was FUBAR.

Or maybe not. Not if Kurtz was taking hold.

"Goddam telepathy's responsible for most of this," Kurtz mused, "but it wasn't telepathy that *triggered* it. That was pure human fuckery, praise Jesus. Who betrayed Jesus, Freddy? Who gave Him that traitor's kiss?"

Freddy had read his Bible, mostly because Kurtz had given it to him. "Judas Iscariot, boss."

Kurtz was nodding rapidly. His eyes were moving

everywhere, tabulating the destruction, calculating the response, which would be severely limited by the storm. "That's right, buck. Judas betrayed Jesus and Owen Philip Underhill betrayed us. Judas got thirty pieces of silver. Not much of a payday, do you think?"

"No, boss." He delivered this reply partially turned away from Kurtz because something in the commissary had exploded. A steel hand clutched his shoulder and turned him back. Kurtz's eyes were wide and burning. The white lashes made them look like ghost-eyes.

"Look at me when I talk to you," Kurtz said. "Listen to me when I speak to you." Kurtz put his free hand on the nine-millimeter's grip. "Or I'll blow your guts out on the snow. I have had a hard night here and *don't you make it any worse, you hound, do you understand me? Catch the old drift-ola?*"

Johnson was a man of good physical courage, but now he felt something turn over in his stomach and try to crawl away. "Yes, boss, I'm sorry."

"Accepted. God loves and forgives, we must do the same. I don't know how many pieces of silver Owen got, but I can tell you this: we're going to catch him, we're going to spread his cheeks, and we are going to tear that boy a splendid new asshole. Are you with me?"

"Yes." There was nothing Freddy wanted more than to find the person who had turned his previously ordered world upside down and fuck that person over. "How much of this do you reckon Owen's responsible for, boss?"

"Enough for me," Kurtz said serenely. "I have an idea I'm finally going down, Freddy—"

"No, boss."

"—but I won't go down alone." Arm still around Freddy's shoulders, Kurtz began to lead his new second back toward the 'Bago. Squat, dying pillars of fire marked the burning gennies. Underhill had done that; one of Kurtz's own boys. Freddy still found it difficult to believe, but he had begun to get steamed, just the same. *How many pieces of silver, Owen? How many did you get, you traitor?*

Kurtz stopped at the foot of the steps.

"Which one of those fellows do you like to command a search-and-destroy mission, Freddy?"

"Gallagher, boss."

"Kate?"

"That's right."

"Is she a cannibal, Freddy? The person we leave in charge has to be a cannibal."

"She eats em raw with slaw, boss."

"Okay," Kurtz said. "Because this is going to be dirty. I need two Ripley Positives, hopefully Blue Boy guys. The rest of them . . . like the animals, Freddy. Imperial Valley is now a search-and-destroy mission. Gallagher and the rest are to hunt down as many as they can. Soldiers and civilians alike. From now until 1200 hours tomorrow, it's feeding time. After that, it's every man for himself. Except for us, Freddy." The firelight painted Kurtz's face with byrus, turned his eyes into weasel's eyes. "We're going to hunt down Owen Underhill and teach him to love the Lord."

Kurtz bounded up the Winnebago's steps, sure as a mountain-goat on the packed and slippery snow. Freddy Johnson followed him.

13

The Sno-Cat plunged down the embankment to the Swanny Pond Road fast enough to make Henry's stomach roll over. It slued, then turned south. Owen worked the clutch and mangled the stick-shift, working the 'Cat up through the gears and into high. With the galaxies of snow flying at the windshield, Henry felt as if they were traveling at approximately mach one. He guessed it might actually be thirty-five miles an hour. That would get them away from Gosselin's, but he had an idea Jonesy was moving much faster.

Turnpike ahead? Owen asked. *It is, isn't it?*

Yes. About four miles.

We'll need to switch vehicles when we get there.

No one gets hurt if we can help it. And no one gets killed.

Henry . . . I don't know how to break it to you, but this isn't high-school basketball.

"No one gets hurt. No one gets killed. At least not when we're swapping vehicles. Agree to that or I'm rolling out this door right now."

Owen glanced at him. "You would, too, wouldn't you? And goddam what your friend's got planned for the world."

"My friend isn't responsible for any of this. He's been kidnapped."

"All right. No one gets hurt when we swap over. If we can help it. And no one gets killed. Except maybe us. Now where are we going?"

Derry.

That's where he is? This last surviving alien?

I think so. In any case, I have a friend in Derry who can help us. He sees the line.

What line?

"Never mind," Henry said, and thought: *It's complicated.*

"What do you mean, complicated? And no bounce, no play—what's that?"

I'll tell you while we're driving south. If I can.

The Sno-Cat rolled toward the Interstate, a capsule preceded by the glare of its lights.

"Tell me again what we're going to do," Owen said.

"Save the world."

"And tell me what that makes us—I need to hear it."

"It makes us heroes," Henry said. Then he put his head back and closed his eyes. In seconds he was asleep.

PART 3

QUABBIN

As I was going up the stair
I met a man who wasn't there;
He wasn't there again today!
I wish, I *wish* he'd stay away.

HUGHES MEARNS

CHAPTER EIGHTEEN

THE CHASE BEGINS

1

Jonesy had no idea what time it was when the green
DYSART'S sign twinkled out of the snowy gloom—the
Ram's dashboard clock was bitched up, just flashing
12:00 A.M. over and over—but it was still dark and still
snowing hard. Outside of Derry, the plows were losing
their battle with the storm. The stolen Ram was "a
pretty good goer," as Jonesy's Pop would have said, but
it too was losing its battle, slipping and slueing more
frequently in the deepening snow, fighting its way
through the drifts with increasing difficulty. Jonesy
had no idea where Mr. Gray thought he was going, but
Jonesy didn't believe he would get there. Not in this
storm, not in this truck.

The radio worked, but not very well; so far everything that came through was faint, blurred with static. He heard no time-checks, but picked up a
weather report. The storm had switched over to rain

from Portland south, but from Augusta to Brunswick, the radio said, the precipitation was a wicked mix of sleet and freezing rain. Most communities were without power, and nothing without chains on its wheels was moving.

Jonesy liked this news just fine.

2

When Mr. Gray turned the steering wheel to head up the ramp toward the beckoning green sign, the Ram pickup slid broadside, spraying up great clouds of snow. Jonesy knew he likely would have gone off the exit ramp and into the ditch if he'd been in control, but he wasn't. And although he was no longer immune to Jonesy's emotions, Mr. Gray seemed much less prone to panic in a stress situation. Instead of wrenching blindly against the skid, Mr. Gray turned into it, held the wheel over until the slide stopped, then straightened the truck out again. The dog sleeping in the passenger footwell never woke up, and Jonesy's pulse barely rose. If he had been in control, Jonesy knew, his heart would have been hammering like hell. But, of course, his idea of what to do with the car when it stormed like this was to put it in the garage.

Mr. Gray obeyed the stop-sign at the top of the ramp, although Route 9 was a drifted wasteland in either direction. Across from the ramp was a huge parking lot brilliantly lit by arc-sodiums; beneath their glare, the wind-driven snow seemed to move like the frozen respiration of an enormous, unseen beast. On an ordinary night, Jonesy knew, that yard would have been full of rumbling diesel semis, Kenworths and Macks and Jimmy-Petes with their green and amber cab-lights glimmering. Tonight the area was almost deserted, except for the area marked LONG-TERM SEE YARD MANAGER   MUST HAVE TICKET. In there were a dozen or more freight-haulers, their edges softened by the drifts. Inside, their drivers would be eating, playing pinball, watching Spank-O-Vision in the truckers' lounge, or trying to sleep in the grim dormitory out back, where ten dollars got you a cot, a clean blanket, and a scenic view of a cinderblock wall. All of them no doubt thinking the same two thoughts: *When can I roll?* And *How much is this going to cost me?*

Mr. Gray stepped down on the gas, and although he did it gently, as Jonesy's file concerning winter driving suggested, all four of the pickup's wheels spun, and the truck began to jitter sideways, digging itself in.

Go on! Jonesy cheered from his position at the office window. *Go on, stick it! Stick it right up to the rocker-panels! Because when you're stuck in a four-wheel drive, you're* really *stuck!*

Then the wheels caught—first the front ones, where the weight of the motor gave the Ram a little more traction—then the back ones. The Ram trundled across Route 9 and toward the sign marked ENTRANCE. Beyond it was another: WELCOME TO THE BEST TRUCK STOP IN NEW ENGLAND. Then the truck's headlights picked out a third, snowcaked but readable: HELL, WELCOME TO THE BEST TRUCK STOP ON EARTH.

Is this the best truck stop on earth? Mr. Gray asked.

Of course, Jonesy said. And then—he couldn't help it—he burst out laughing.

Why do you do that? Why do you make that sound?

Jonesy realized an amazing thing, both touching and terrifying: Mr. Gray was smiling with Jonesy's mouth. Not much, just a little, but it was a smile. *He doesn't really know what laughter is,* Jonesy thought. Of course he hadn't known what anger was, either, but he had proved to be a remarkably fast learner; he could now tantrum with the best of them.

What you said struck me funny.

What exactly is funny?

Jonesy had no idea how to answer the question. He wanted Mr. Gray to experience the entire gamut of human emotions, suspecting that humanizing his usurper might ultimately be his only chance of survival—we have met the enemy and he is us, Pogo had once said. But how did you explain funny to a collection of spores from another world? And what *was* funny about Dysart's proclaiming itself the best truck stop on earth?

Now they were passing yet another sign, one with arrows pointing left and right. BIGUNS it said beneath the left arrow. And LITTLEUNS under the right.

Which are we? Mr. Gray asked, stopping at the sign.

Jonesy could have made him retrieve the information, but what would have been the point? *We're a littleun,* he said, and Mr. Gray turned the Ram to the right. The tires spun a little and the truck lurched. Lad raised his head, let fly another long and fragrant fart, then whined. His lower midsection had swelled and distended; anyone who didn't know better would no doubt have mistaken him for a bitch about to give birth to a good-sized litter.

There were perhaps two dozen cars and pickups parked in the littleuns' lot, the ones most deeply buried in snow belonging to the help—mechanics (always one or two on duty), waitresses, short-order cooks. The cleanest vehicle there, Jonesy saw with sharp interest, was a powder-blue State Police car with packed snow around the roof-lights. Being arrested would certainly put a spike in Mr. Gray's plans; on the other hand, Jonesy had already been present at three murder-sites, if you counted the cab of the pickup. No witnesses at the first two crime scenes, and probably no Gary Jones fingerprints, either, but here? Sure. Plenty of them. He could see himself standing in a courtroom somewhere and saying, *But Judge, it was the alien inside me who committed those murders. It was Mr. Gray.* Another joke that Mr. Gray wouldn't get.

That worthy, meanwhile, had been rummaging again. *Dry Farts,* he said. *Why do you call this place Dry Farts when the sign says Dysart's?*

It's what Lamar used to call it, Jonesy said, remembering long, hilarious breakfasts here, usually going or coming back from Hole in the Wall. And this fit right into the tradition, didn't it? *My Dad called it that, too.*

Is it funny?

Moderately, I guess. It's a pun based on similar sounds. Puns are what we call the lowest form of humor.

Mr. Gray parked in the rank closest to the lighted island of the restaurant, but all the way down from the State Police cruiser. Jonesy had no idea if Mr. Gray understood the significance of the lightbars on top or not. He reached for the Ram's headlight knob and pushed it in. He reached for the ignition, then stopped and issued several hard barks of laughter: "Ha! Ha! Ha! Ha!"

How'd that feel? Jonesy asked, more than a little curious. A little apprehensive, too.

"Like nothing," Mr. Gray said flatly, and turned off the ignition. But then, sitting there in the dark with the wind howling around the cab of the truck, he did it again, and with a little more conviction: *"Ha! Ha, ha, ha!"* In his office refuge, Jonesy shivered. It was a creepy sound, like a ghost trying to remember how to be human.

Lad didn't like it either. He whined again, looking uneasily at the man behind the steering wheel of his master's truck.

3

Owen was shaking Henry awake, and Henry responded reluctantly. He felt as if he had gone to sleep only seconds ago. His limbs all seemed to have been dipped in cement.

"Henry."

"I'm here." Left leg itching. Mouth itching even worse; the goddam byrus was growing on his lips now, too. He rubbed it off with his forefinger, surprised at how easily it broke free. Like a crust.

"Listen up. And look. Can you look?"

Henry looked up the road, which was now dim and snow-ghostly—Owen had pulled the Sno-Cat over and turned off the lights. Farther along, there were mental voices in the dark, the auditory equivalent of a campfire. Henry went to them. There were four of them, young men with no seniority in . . . in . . .

Blue Group, Owen whispered. *This time we're Blue Group.*

Four young men with no seniority in Blue Group, trying not to be scared . . . trying to be tough . . . voices in the dark . . . a little campfire of voices in the dark . . .

By its light, Henry discovered he could see dimly: snow, of course, and a few flashing yellow lights illuminating a turnpike entrance ramp. There was also the lid of a pizza carton seen in the light of an instrument panel. It had been turned into a tray. On it were Saltines, several blocks of cheese, and a Swiss Army knife. The Swiss Army knife belonged to the one named Smitty, and they were all using it to cut the cheese. The longer Henry looked, the better he saw. It was like having your eyes adjust to the dark, but it was more than that too: what he saw had a creepy-giddy depth, as if all at once the physical world consisted not of three dimensions but of four or five. It was easy enough to understand why: he was seeing through four sets of eyes, all at the same time. They were huddled together in the . . .

Humvee, Owen said, delighted. *It's a fucking*

Humvee, Henry! Custom-equipped for snow, too! Bet you anything it is!

The young men were sitting close together, yes, but still in four different places, looking at the world from four different points of view, and with four different qualities of eyesight, ranging from eagle-eye sharp (Dana from Maybrook, New York) to the merely adequate. Yet somehow Henry's brain was processing them, just as it turned multiple still images on a reel of film into a moving picture. This wasn't like a movie, though, nor like some tricky 3-D image. It was an entirely new way of seeing, the kind that could produce a whole new way of thinking.

If this shit spreads, Henry thought, both terrified and wildly excited, *if it spreads . . .*

Owen's elbow thumped into his side. "Maybe you could save the seminar for another day," he said. "Look across the road."

Henry did so, employing his unique quadruple vision and realizing only belatedly that he had done more than look; he had moved their eyeballs so he could peer over to the far side of the turnpike. Where he saw more blinking lights in the storm.

"It's a choke-point," Owen muttered. "One of Kurtz's insurance policies. Both exits blocked, no movement onto the turnpike without authorization. I want the Humvee, it's the best thing we could have in a shitstorm like this, but I don't want to alert the guys on the other side. Can we do that?"

Henry experimented with their eyes again, moving them. He discovered that as soon as they weren't all looking at the same thing, his sense of godlike four or five-dimensional vision evaporated, leaving him with a nauseating, shattered perspective his processing equipment couldn't cope with. But he *was* moving them. Not much, just their eyeballs, but . . .

I think we can if we work together, Henry told him. *Get closer. And stop talking out loud. Get in my head. Link up.*

Suddenly Henry's head was fuller. His vision clarified again, but this time the perspective wasn't quite as deep. Only two sets of eyes instead of four: his and Owen's.

Owen put the Sno-Cat into first gear and crept forward with the lights off. The engine's low growl was lost beneath the constant shriek of the wind, and as they closed the distance, Henry felt his hold on those minds ahead tightening.

Holy shit, Owen said, half-laughing and half-gasping.

What? What is it?

It's you, man—it's like being on a magic carpet. Christ, but you're strong.

You think I'm *strong, wait'll you meet Jonesy.*

Owen stopped the Sno-Cat below the brow of a little hill. Beyond it was the turnpike. Not to mention Bernie, Dana, Tommy, and Smitty, sitting in their Humvee at the top of the southbound ramp, eating cheese and crackers off their makeshift tray. He and Owen were safe enough from discovery. The four young men in the Humvee were clean of the byrus and had no idea they were being scoped.

Ready? Henry asked.

I guess. The other person in Henry's head, cool as that storied cucumber when Kurtz and the others had been shooting at them, was now nervous. *You take the lead, Henry. I'm just flying support this mission.*

Here we go.

What Henry did next he did instinctively, binding the four men in the Humvee together not with images of death and destruction, but by impersonating Kurtz. To do this he drew on both Owen Underhill's energy— much greater than his own, at this point—and Owen Underhill's vivid knowledge of his OIC. The act of binding gave him a brilliant stab of satisfaction. Relief, as well. Moving their eyes was one thing; taking them over completely was another. And they were free of the byrus. That could have made them immune. Thank God it had not.

There's a Sno-Cat over that rise east of you, laddies, Kurtz said. *Want you to take it back to base. Right now, if you please—no questions, no comments, just get moving. You'll find the quarters a little tight compared to your current accommodations, but I think you can all fit in, praise Jesus. Now move your humps, God love you.*

Henry saw them getting out, their faces calm and blank around the eyes. He started to get out himself, then saw Owen was still sitting in the Sno-Cat's driver's seat, his own eyes wide. His lips moved, forming the words in his head: *Move your humps, God love you.*

Owen! Come on!

Owen looked around, startled, then nodded and

pushed out through the canvas hanging over his side
of the 'Cat.

4

Henry stumbled to his knees, picked himself up, and
looked wearily into the streaming dark. Not far to
go, God knew it wasn't, but he didn't think he could
slog through another twenty feet of drifted snow, let
alone a hundred and fifty yards. *On and on the eggman
went,* he thought, and then: *I did it. That's the answer,
of course. I offed myself and now I'm in hell. This is the
eggman in h—*

Owen's arm went around him . . . but it was more
than his arm. He was feeding Henry his strength.

Thank y—

*Thank me later. Sleep later, too. For now, keep your eye
on the ball.*

There *was* no ball. There were only Bernie, Dana,
Tommy, and Smitty trooping through the snow, a line
of silent somnambulists in coveralls and hooded parkas.
They trooped east on the Swanny Pond Road toward
the Sno-Cat while Owen and Henry struggled on west,
toward the abandoned Humvee. The cheese and
Saltines had also been abandoned, Henry realized, and
his stomach rumbled.

Then the Humvee was dead ahead. They'd drive it
away, no headlights at first, low gear and quiet-quiet-
quiet, skirting the yellow flashers at the base of the
ramp, and if they were lucky, the fellows guarding the
northbound ramp would never know they were gone.

If they do see us, could we make them forget? Owen asked. *Give them—oh, I don't know—give them amnesia?*

Henry realized they probably could.

Owen?

What?

If this ever got out, it would change everything. Everything.

A pause as Owen considered this. Henry wasn't talking about knowledge, the usual coin of Kurtz's bosses up the food-chain; he was talking about abilities that apparently went well beyond a little mind-reading.

I know, he replied at last.

5

They headed south in the Humvee, south into the storm. Henry Devlin was still gobbling crackers and cheese when exhaustion turned out the lights in his overstimulated head.

He slept with crumbs on his lips.

And dreamed of Josie Rinkenhauer.

6

Half an hour after it caught fire, old Reggie Gosselin's barn was no more than a dying dragon's eye in the booming night, waxing and waning in a black socket of melted snow. From the woods east of the Swanny Pond Road came the *pop-pop-pop* of rifle fire, heavy at first, then diminishing a little in both frequency and volume as the Imperial Valleys (Kate Gallagher's Imperial Valleys now) pursued the escaped detainees. It was a turkey shoot, and not many of the turkeys were going to get away. Enough of them to tell the tale, maybe, enough to rat them all out, but that was tomorrow's worry.

While this was going on—also while the traitorous Owen Underhill was getting farther and farther ahead of them—Kurtz and Freddy Johnson stood in the command post (except, Freddy supposed, it was now nothing but a Winnebago again; that feeling of power and importance had gone), flipping playing-cards into a hat.

No longer telepathic in the slightest, but as sensitive to the men under him as ever—that his command had been reduced to a single soldier really made no difference—Kurtz looked at Freddy and said, "Make haste slowly, buck—that's one saw that's still sharp."

"Yes, boss," Freddy said without much enthusiasm.

Kurtz flipped the two of spades. It fluttered down through the air and landed in the hat. Kurtz crowed like a child and prepared to flip again. There was a knock at the 'Bago's door. Freddy turned in that direction, and Kurtz fixed him with a forbidding look. Freddy turned back and watched Kurtz flip another card. This one started out well, then went long and landed on the cap's bill. Kurtz muttered something under his breath, then nodded at the door. Freddy, with a mental prayer of thanks, went to open it.

Standing on the top step was Jocelyn McAvoy, one of the two female Imperial Valleys. Her accent was soft country Tennessee; the face under the boy-cropped blond hair was hard as stone. She was holding a spectacularly non-reg Israeli burp-gun by the strap. Freddy wondered where she had gotten such a thing, then decided it didn't matter. A lot of things had ceased to matter, most of them in the last hour or so.

"Joss," Freddy said. "What's up with your bad self?"

"Delivering two Ripley Positives as ordered." More shooting from the woods, and Freddy saw the woman's eyes shift minutely in that direction. She wanted to get back over there across the road, wanted to bag her limit before the game was gone. Freddy knew how she felt.

"Send them in, lassie," Kurtz said. He was still standing over the cap on the floor (the floor that was still faintly stained with Cook's Third Melrose's blood), still holding the deck of cards in his hand, but his eyes were bright and interested. "Let's see who you found."

Jocelyn gestured with her gun. A male voice at the foot of the stairs growled, "The fuck up there. Don't make me say it twice."

The first man to step past Jocelyn was tall and very black. There was a cut down one of his cheeks and another on his neck. Both cuts had been clogged with Ripley. More was growing in the creases in his brow. Freddy knew the face but not the name. The old man, of course, knew both. Freddy supposed he remembered the names of all the men he had commanded, both the quick and the dead.

"Cambry!" Kurtz said, eyes lighting even more brightly. He dropped the playing-cards into the hat, approached Cambry, seemed about to shake hands, thought better of it, and snapped off a salute instead. Gene Cambry did not return it. He looked sullen and disoriented. "Welcome to the Justice League of America."

"Spotted him running through the woods along with the detainees he was supposed to be guarding," Jocelyn McAvoy said. Her face was expressionless; all her contempt was in her voice.

"Why not?" Cambry asked. He looked at Kurtz. "You were going to kill me, anyway. Kill all of us. Don't bother lying about it, either. I can see it in your mind."

Kurtz wasn't discomfited by this in the slightest. He rubbed his hands together and smiled at Cambry in a friendly way. "Do a good job and p'raps you'll *change* my mind, buck. Hearts were made to be broken and minds were made to be changed, that's a big praise God. Who else have you got for me, Joss?"

Freddy regarded the second figure with amazement. Also with pleasure. The Ripley could not have found a better home, in his humble opinion. Nobody liked the son of a bitch much in the first place.

"Sir . . . boss . . . I don't know why I'm here . . . I was in proper pursuit of the escapees when this . . . this . . . I'm sorry, I have to say it, when this officious *bitch* pulled me out of the sweep area and . . ."

"He was running with them," McAvoy said in a

bored voice. "Running with them and infected up the old wazoo."

"A lie!" said the man in the doorway. "A total lie! I'm perfectly clean! One hundred percent—"

McAvoy snatched off the watchcap her second prisoner was wearing. The man's thinning blond hair was much thicker now, and appeared to have been dyed red.

"I can explain, sir," Archie Perlmutter said, his voice fading even as he spoke. "There is . . . you see . . ." Then it died away entirely.

Kurtz was beaming at him, but he had donned his filter-mask again—they all had—and it gave his reassuring smile an oddly sinister look, the expression of a child molester inviting a little kid in for a piece of pie.

"Pearly, it's going to be all right," Kurtz said. "We're going for a ride, that's all. There's someone we need to find, someone you know—"

"Owen Underhill," Perlmutter whispered.

"That's right, buck," Kurtz said. He turned to McAvoy. "Bring this soldier his clipboard, McAvoy. I'm sure he'll feel better once he has his clipboard. Then you can carry on hunting, which I feel quite sure you're eager to do."

"Yes, boss."

"But first, watch this—a little trick I learned back in Kansas."

Kurtz sprayed the cards. In the crazy blizzard-wind coming through the door, they flew every whichway. Only one landed faceup in the hat, but it was the ace of spades.

7

Mr. Gray held the menu, looking at the lists of stuff—meatloaf, sliced beets, roast chicken, chocolate silk pie—with interest and an almost total lack of understanding. Jonesy realized it wasn't just not knowing how food tasted; Mr. Gray didn't know what taste *was*. How could he? When you cut to the chase, he was nothing but a mushroom with a high IQ.

Here came a waitress, moving under a vast tableland of frozen ash-blond hair. The badge on her not inconsiderable bosom read WELCOME TO DYSART'S, I AM YOUR WAITRESS DARLENE.

"Hi, hon, what can I get you?"

"I'd like scrambled eggs and bacon. Crisp, not limp."

"Toast?"

"How about canpakes?"

She raised her eyebrows and looked at him over her pad. Beyond her, at the counter, the State Trooper was eating some kind of drippy sandwich and talking with the short-order cook.

"Sorry—cakepans, I meant to say."

The eyebrows went higher. Her question was plain, blinking at the front of her mind like a neon sign in a saloon window: was this guy a mushmouth, or was he making fun of her?

Standing at his office window, smiling, Jonesy relented.

"*Pancakes,*" Mr. Gray said.

"Uh-huh. I sort of figured. Coffee with that?"

"Please."

She snapped her pad closed and started away. Mr. Gray was back at the locked door of Jonesy's office at once, and furious all over again.

How could you do that? he asked. *How could you do that from in there?* An ill-natured thump as Mr. Gray hit the door. And he was more than angry, Jonesy realized. He was frightened, as well. Because if Jonesy could interfere, everything was in jeopardy.

I don't know, Jonesy said, and truthfully enough. *But don't take it so hard. Enjoy your breakfast. I was just fucking with you a little.*

Why? Still furious. Still drinking from the well of Jonesy's emotions, and liking it in spite of himself. *Why would you do that?*

Call it payback for trying to roast me in my office while I was sleeping, Jonesy said.

With the restaurant section of the truck stop almost deserted, Darlene was back with the food in no time. Jonesy considered seeing if he could gain control of his mouth long enough to say something outrageous (*Darlene, can I bite your hair?* was what came to mind), and thought better of it.

She set his plate down, gave him a dubious look, then started away. Mr. Gray, looking at the bright yellow lump of eggs and the dark twigs of bacon (not just crispy but almost incinerated, in the great Dysart's tradition) through Jonesy's eyes, was feeling the same dubiety.

Go on, Jonesy said. He was standing at his office window, watching and waiting with amusement and curiosity. Was it possible that the bacon and eggs would kill Mr. Gray? Probably not, but it might at least make the hijacking motherfucker good and sick. *Go on, Mr. Gray, eat up. Bon-fuckin-appétit.*

Mr. Gray consulted Jonesy's files on the proper use of the silverware, then picked up a tiny clot of scrambled eggs on the tines of his fork, and put them in Jonesy's mouth.

What followed was both amazing and hilarious. Mr. Gray gobbled everything in huge bites, pausing only to drown the pancakes in fake maple syrup. He loved it all, but most particularly the bacon.

Flesh! Jonesy heard him exulting—it was almost the voice of the creature in one of those corny old monster movies from the thirties. *Flesh! Flesh! This is the taste of flesh!*

Funny . . . but maybe not all *that* funny, either. Maybe sort of horrible. The cry of a new-made vampire.

Mr. Gray looked around, ascertained that he wasn't being watched (the State Bear was now addressing a large piece of cherry pie), then picked up the plate and licked the grease from it with big swipes of Jonesy's tongue. He finished by licking the sticky syrup from the ends of his fingers.

Darlene returned, poured more coffee, looked at the empty dishes. "Why, you get a gold star," she said. "Anything else?"

"More bacon," Mr. Gray said. He consulted

Jonesy's files for the correct terminology, and added: "A double order."

And may you choke on it, Jonesy thought, but now without much hope.

"Gotta stoke the stove," Darlene said, a comment Mr. Gray didn't understand and didn't bother hunting down in Jonesy's files. He put two sugars in his coffee, looked around to make sure he wasn't observed, then poured the contents of a third packet down his throat. Jonesy's eyes half-closed for a few seconds as Mr. Gray drowned happily in the bliss of sweet.

You can have that any time you want it, Jonesy said through the door. Now he supposed he knew how Satan felt when he took Jesus up on the mountaintop and tempted him with all the cities of the earth. Not good; not really bad; just doing the job, selling the product.

Except . . . check that. It *did* feel good, because he knew he was getting through. He wasn't opening stab-wounds exactly, but he was at least pricking Mr. Gray. Making him sweat little blood-beads of desire.

Give it up, Jonesy coaxed. *Go native. You can spend years exploring my senses. They're pretty sharp; I'm still under forty.*

No reply from Mr. Gray. He looked around, saw no one looking his way, poured fake maple syrup into his coffee, slurped it, and looked around again for his supplemental bacon. Jonesy sighed. This was like being with a strict Muslim who has somehow wound up on a Las Vegas holiday.

On the far side of the restaurant was an arch with a

sign reading TRUCKERS' LOUNGE & SHOWERS above it. In the short hallway beyond, there was a bank of pay telephones. Several drivers stood there, no doubt explaining to spouses and bosses that they wouldn't be back on time, they'd been shut down by a surprise storm in Maine, they were at Dysart's Truck Stop (*known to the cognoscenti as Dry Farts,* Jonesy thought) south of Derry and here they would likely remain until at least noon tomorrow.

Jonesy turned from the office window with its view of the truck stop and looked at his desk, now covered with all his old and comforting clutter. There was his phone, the blue Trimline. Would it be possible to call Henry on it? Was Henry even still alive? Jonesy thought he was. He thought that if Henry were dead, he would have felt the moment of his passing—more shadows in the room, perhaps. *Elvis has left the building,* Beaver had often said when he spotted a name he knew in the obits. *What a fuckin pisser.* Jonesy didn't think Henry had left the building just yet. It was even possible that Henry had an encore in mind.

8

Mr. Gray didn't choke on his second order of bacon, but when his lower belly suddenly cramped up, he let out a dismayed roar. *You poisoned me!*

Relax, Jonesy said. *You just need to make a little room, my friend.*

Room? What do you—

He broke off as another cramp gripped his gut.

I mean that we had better hurry along to the little boys' room, Jonesy said. *Good God, didn't all those abductions you guys did in the sixties teach you* anything *about the human anatomy?*

Darlene had left the check, and Mr. Gray picked it up.

Leave her fifteen percent on the table, Jonesy said. *It's a tip.*

How much is fifteen percent?

Jonesy sighed. These were the masters of the universe that the movies had taught us to fear? Merciless, star-faring conquerors who didn't know how to take a shit or figure a tip?

Another cramp, plus a fairly silent fart. It smelled, but not of ether. *Thank God for small favors,* Jonesy thought. Then, to Mr. Gray: *Show me the check.*

Jonesy looked at the green slip of paper through his office window.

Leave her a buck and a half. And when Mr. Gray seemed dubious: *This is good advice I'm giving you, my friend. More and she remembers you as the night's big tipper. Less, and she remembers you as a chintz.*

He sensed Mr. Gray checking for the meaning of *chintz* in Jonesy's files. Then, without further argument, he left a dollar and two quarters on the table. With that taken care of, he headed for the cash register, which was on the way to the men's room.

The cop was working his pie—with slightly suspicious slowness, Jonesy thought—and as they passed him, Jonesy felt Mr. Gray as an entity (an ever more human entity) dissolve, going out to peek inside the cop's head. Nothing out there now but the redblack cloud, running Jonesy's various maintenance systems.

Quick as a flash, Jonesy grabbed the phone on his desk. For a moment he hesitated, unsure.

Just dial 1-800-HENRY, Jonesy thought.

For a moment there was nothing . . . and then, in some other somewhere, a phone began to ring.

9

"Pete's idea," Henry muttered.

Owen, at the wheel of the Humvee (it was huge and it was loud, but it was equipped with oversized snow tires and rode the storm like the *QE2*), looked over. Henry was asleep. His glasses had slid down to the end of his nose. His eyelids, now delicately fuzzed with byrus, rippled as the eyeballs beneath them moved. Henry was dreaming. *About what?* Owen wondered. He supposed he could dip into his new partner's head and have a look, but that seemed perverse.

"Pete's idea," Henry repeated. "Pete saw her first." And he sighed, a sound so tired that Owen felt bad for him. No, he decided, he didn't want any part of what was going on in Henry's head. Another hour to Derry, more if the wind stayed high. Better to just let him sleep.

10

Behind Derry High School is the football field where Richie Grenadeau once strutted his stuff, but Richie is five years in his teenage hero's grave, just another small-town car-crash James Dean. Other heroes have risen, thrown their passes, and moved on. It's not football season now, anyway. It's spring, and on the field there is a gathering of what look like birds—huge red ones with black heads. These mutant crows are laughing and talking as they sit in their folding chairs, but Mr. Trask, the principal, has no problem being heard; he's at the podium on the makeshift stage, and he's got the mike.

"One last thing before I dismiss you!" he booms. *"I won't tell you not to throw your mortarboards at the end of the ceremony, I know from years of experience I might as well be talking to myself on that score—"*

Laughter, cheers, applause.

"—but I'm telling you to PICK THEM UP AND TURN THEM IN OR YOU WILL BE CHARGED FOR THEM!"

There are a few boos and some raspberries, Beaver Clarendon's the loudest.

Mr. Trask gives them a final surveying look. *"Young men and women, members of the Class of '82, I think I speak for the entire faculty when I say I'm proud of you. This concludes rehearsal, so . . ."*

The rest is lost, amplification or no amplification; the red crows rise in a gusty flap of nylon, and they fly. Tomorrow at noon they will fly for good; although the three crows laughing and grabassing their way toward the parking lot where Henry's car is parked do not realize it, the childhood phase of their friendship is now only hours from the end. They don't realize it, and that is probably just as well.

Jonesy snatches Henry's mortarboard, slaps it on top of his own, and books for the parking lot.

"Hey, asshole, give that back!" Henry yells, and then he snatches Beaver's. Beav squawks like a chicken and runs after Henry, laughing. So the three of them swoop across the grass and behind the bleachers, graduation robes billowing around their jeans. Jonesy has two hats on his head, the tassels swinging in opposite directions, Henry has one (far too big; it's sitting on his ears), and Beaver runs bareheaded, his long black hair flowing out behind him and a toothpick jutting from his mouth.

Jonesy is looking back as he runs, taunting Henry ("Come on, Mr. Basketball, ya run like a girl"), and almost piles into Pete, who is looking at DERRY DOIN'S, the glassed-in notice-board by the north entrance to the parking lot. Pete, who is graduating from nothing but the junior class this year, grabs Jonesy, bends him backward like a guy doing a tango with some beautiful chick, and kisses him square on the mouth. Both mortarboards tumble off Jonesy's head, and he screams in surprise.

"Queerboy!" Jonesy yells, rubbing frantically at his mouth . . . but he's starting to laugh, too. Pete's an oddity—he'll go along quietly for weeks at a time, Norman Normal, and then he'll break out and do something nutso. Usually the nutso comes out after a couple of beers, but not this afternoon.

"I've always wanted to do that, Gariella," Pete says sentimentally. "Now you know how I really feel."

"Fuckin queerboy, if you gave me the syph, I'll kill you!"

Henry arrives, snatches his mortarboard off the grass, and swats Jonesy with it. "There's grass-stains on this," Henry says. "If I have to pay for it, I'll do a lot more than just kiss you, Gariella."

"Don't make promises you can't keep, fuckwad," Jonesy says.

"Beautiful Gariella," Henry says solemnly.

The Beav comes steaming up, puffing around his toothpick. He takes Jonesy's mortarboard, peers into it, and says, "There's a come-stain in this one. Ain't I seen enough on my own sheets to know?" He draws in a deep breath and bugles to the departing seniors in their Derry-red graduation gowns: *"Gary Jones beats off in his graduation hat! Hey, everybody, listen up, Gary Jones beats off—"*

Jonesy grabs him, pulls him to the ground, and the two of them roll over and over in billows of red nylon. Both mortarboards are cast off to one side and Henry grabs them to keep them from getting crushed.

"Get off me!" Beaver cries. "You're crushin me! Jesus-Christ-bananas! For God's sake—"

"Duddits knew her," Pete says. He has lost interest in their foolery, doesn't feel much of their high spirits anyway (Pete is perhaps the only one of them who senses the big changes that are coming). He's looking at the notice-board again. "We knew her, too. She was the one who always stood outside The Retard Academy. 'Hi, Duddie,' she'd go." When he says *Hi, Duddie,* Pete's voice goes up high, becomes momentarily girlish in a way that is sweet rather than mocking. And although Pete isn't a particularly good mimic, Henry knows that voice at once. He remembers the girl, who had fluffy blond hair and great brown eyes and scabbed knees and a white plastic purse which contained her lunch and her BarbieKen. That's what she always called them, BarbieKen, as if they were a single entity.

Jonesy and Beav also know who Pete's imitating, and Henry knows, too. There is that bond among them; it's been among them for years now. Them and Duddits. Jonesy and the Beav can't remember the little blond girl's name any more than Henry can—only that her last one was something impossibly long and clunky. And she had a crush on the Dudster, which was why she always waited for him outside The Retard Academy.

The three of them in their graduation gowns gather around Pete and look at the DERRY DOIN'S board.

As always, the board is crammed with notices—bake sales and car washes, tryouts for the Community Players version of *The Fantastiks,* summer classes at Fenster, the local junior college, plus plenty of hand-printed student ads—buy this, sell that, need ride to Boston after graduation, looking for roommate in Providence.

And, way up in the corner, a photo of a smiling girl with acres of blond hair (frizzy rather than fluffy now) and wide, slightly puzzled eyes. She's no longer a little girl—Henry is surprised again and again by how the children he grew up with (including himself) have disappeared—but he would know those dark and puzzled eyes anywhere.

MISSING, says the single block-capital word under the photo. And below that, in slightly smaller type: JOSETTE RINKENHAUER, LAST SEEN STRAWFORD PARK SOFT-BALL FIELD, JUNE 7, 1982. Below this there is more copy, but Henry doesn't bother reading it. Instead he reflects on how odd Derry is about missing children—not like other towns at all. This is June eighth, which means the Rinkenhauer girl has only been gone a day, and yet this poster has been tacked way up in the corner of the notice-board (or moved there), like somebody's after-thought. Nor is that all. There was nothing in the paper this morning—Henry knows, because he read it. Skimmed through it, anyway, while he was slurping up his cereal. *Maybe it was buried way back in the Local section,* he thinks, and knows at once that's it. The key word is *buried.* Lots of things are buried in Derry. Talk of missing children, for instance. There have been a lot of child dis-appearances here over the years—these boys know it, it certainly crossed their minds on the day they met Dud-dits Cavell, but nobody talks much about it. It's as if the occasional missing kid is the price of living in such a nice, quiet place. At this idea Henry feels a dawning indig-nation stealing in first to mix with and then replace his former goofy happiness. *She was sweet, too, with her Bar-bieKen. Sweet like Duddits.* He remembers how the four of them would deliver Duddits to school—all those walks—and how often she'd be outside, Josie Rinken-hauer with her scabby knees and her great big plastic purse: *"Hi, Duddie."* She was sweet.

And still is, Henry thinks. *She's—*

"She's alive," Beaver says flatly. He takes the chewed-up toothpick out of his mouth, looks at it, and drops it to the grass. "Alive and still around. Isn't she?"

"Yeah," Pete says. He's still looking at the picture, fascinated, and Henry knows what Pete is thinking, almost the same thing as he is: she grew up. Even Josie, who in a fairer life might have been Doug Cavell's girlfriend. "But I think she's . . . you know . . ."

"She's in deep shit," Jonesy says. He has stepped out of his gown and now folds it over his arm.

"She's stuck," Pete says dreamily, still looking at the picture. His finger has begun to go back and forth, tick-tock, tick-tock.

"Where?" Henry asks, but Pete shakes his head. So does Jonesy.

"Let's ask Duddits," Beaver says suddenly. And they all know why. There is no need of discussion. Because Duddits sees the line. Duddits

11

"—sees the line!" Henry shouted suddenly, and jerked upright in the passenger seat of the Humvee. It scared the hell out of Owen, who was deep in some private place where there was only him and the storm and the endless line of reflectors to tell him he was still on the road. "Duddits sees the line!"

The Humvee swerved, skidded, came back under control. "Jesus, man!" Owen said. "Give me a little warning next time before you blow your top, would you?"

Henry ran a hand down his face, drew in a deep breath, and let it out. "I know where we're going and what we have to do—"

"Well, good—"

"—but I have to tell you a story so you'll understand."

Owen glanced at him. "Do *you* understand?"

"Not everything, but more than I did."

"Go ahead. We've got an hour before Derry. Is that time enough?"

Henry thought it would be more than enough, especially talking mind to mind. He started at the beginning—what he now understood the beginning to be. Not the coming of the grays, not the byrus or the weasels, but four boys who had been hoping to see a picture of the Homecoming Queen with her skirt pulled up, no more than that. As Owen drove, his mind filled with a series of connected images, more like a dream than a movie. Henry told him about Duddits, about their first trip to Hole in the Wall, and Beaver puking in the snow. He told Owen about all those walks to school, and about the Duddits version of the game: they played and Duddits pegged. About the time they had taken Duddits to see Santa Claus—what a fuckin pisser that had been. And about how they had seen Josie Rinkenhauer's picture on the DERRY DOIN'S board the day before the three older boys graduated. Owen saw them going to Dudditses' house on Maple Lane in Henry's car, the gowns and mortarboard caps piled in back; saw them saying hi to Mr. and Mrs. Cavell, who were in the living room with an ashy-pale man in a Derry Gas coverall and a weeping woman—Roberta Cavell has her arm around Ellen Rinkenhauer's shoulders and is telling her it will be all right, she knows that God won't let anything happen to dear little Josie.

It's strong, Owen thought dreamily. *Man, what this guy's got is so strong. How can that be?*

The Cavells barely look at the boys, because the boys are such frequent visitors here at 19 Maple Lane, and the Rinkenhauers are too deep in their terror to even notice them. They have not touched the coffee Roberta has served. *He's in his room, guys,* Alfie Cavell says, giving them a wan smile. And Duddits, looking up at them from his GI Joe figures—he has all of them—gets up as soon as he sees them in the doorway. Duddits never wears his shoes in his room, always his bunny slippers that Henry gave him for his last birthday—he loves the bunny slippers, will wear them until they are nothing but pink rags held together with strapping tape—but his shoes are on now. He has been waiting for them, and although his smile is as sunny as ever, his eyes are serious. *Eh ee own?* Duddits asks— *Where we goin?* And—

"You were *all* that way?" Owen whispered. He supposed Henry had already told him that, but until now he hadn't understood what Henry meant. "Even before this?" He touched the side of his face, where a thin fuzz of byrus was now growing down his cheek.

"Yes. No. I don't know. Just be quiet, Owen. Listen."

And Owen's head once more filled up with those images from 1982.

12

By the time they get to Strawford Park it's four-thirty and a bunch of girls in yellow DERRY HARDWARE shirts are on the softball field, all of them with their hair in near-identical ponytails that have been threaded through the backs of their caps. Most have braces on their teeth. "My, my—they flubbin and dubbin," Pete says, and maybe they are, but they sure look like they're having fun. Henry is having no fun at all, his stomach is full of butterflies, and he's glad to see Jonesy at least looks the same, solemn and scared. Pete and Beaver don't have a whole lot of imagination between them; he and old Gariella have too much. To Pete and the Beav, this is just Frank and Joe Hardy stuff, Danny Dunn stuff. But to Henry it's different. To not find Josie Rinkenhauer would be bad (because they could, he knows they could), but to find her dead . . .

"Beav," he says.

Beaver has been watching the girls. Now he turns to Henry. "What?"

"Do you still think she's alive?"

"I . . ." Beav's smile fades, and he looks troubled. "I dunno, man. Pete?"

But Pete shakes his head. "I thought she was, back at school—shit, that picture almost talked to me— but now . . ." He shrugs.

Henry looks at Jonesy, who also shrugs, then spreads his hands: *Dunno.* So Henry turns to Duddits.

Duddits is looking at everything from behind what he calls his *ooo ays,* Duddits-ese for cool shades—wraparounds with silver mirrored surfaces. Henry thinks the ooo ays make Duddits look like Ray Walston in *My Favorite Martian,* but he'd never say such a thing to Duds, or think it at him. Duds is also wearing Beaver's mortarboard hat; he particularly likes to blow the tassel.

Duddits has no selective perception; to him the wino looking for returnables over by the trash barrels, the girls playing softball, and the squirrels running around on the branches of the trees are equally fascinating. It is part of what makes him special. "Duddits," Henry says. "There's this girl you went to school with at the Academy, her name was Josie? Josie Rinkenhauer?"

Duddits looks politely interested because his friend Henry is talking to him, but there is no recognition of the name, and why would there be? Duds can't remember what he had for breakfast, so why would he remember a little girl he went to school with three or four years ago? Henry feels a wave of hopelessness, which is strangely mixed with amusement. What were they thinking about?

"Josie," Pete says, but he doesn't look very hopeful, either. "We used to tease you about how she was your girlfriend, remember? She had brown eyes . . . all this blond hair sticking out from her head . . . and . . ." He sighs disgustedly. *"Fuck."*

"Ay ih, iffun-nay," Duddits says, because this usually makes them smile: *same shit, different day*. It doesn't work, so Duddits tries another one: "No-wounce, no-lay."

"Yeah," Jonesy said. "No bounce, no play, that's right. We might as well take him home, guys, this isn't gonna—"

"No," Beaver says, and they all look at him. Beaver's eyes are both bright and troubled. He's chewing on the toothpick in his mouth so fast and hard that it jitters up and down between his lips like a piston. "Dreamcatcher," he says.

13

"Dreamcatcher?" Owen asked. His voice seemed to come from far away, even to his own ears. The Humvee's headlights conned the endless snowy wasteland ahead, which resembled a road only because of the marching yellow reflectors. *Dreamcatcher,* he thought, and once more his head filled up with Henry's past, almost drowning him in the sights and sounds and smells of that day on the edge of summer:

Dreamcatcher.

14

"Dreamcatcher," Beav says, and they understand each other as they sometimes do, as they think (mistakenly, Henry will later realize) all friends do. Although they have never spoken directly of the dream they all shared on their first hunting trip to Hole in the Wall, they know Beaver believed that it had somehow been caused by Lamar's dreamcatcher. None of the others have tried to tell him differently, partly because they don't want to challenge Beaver's superstition about that harmless little string spiderweb and mostly because they don't want to talk about that day at all. But now they understand that Beaver has latched onto at least half a truth. A dreamcatcher has indeed bound them, but not Lamar's.

Duddits is their dreamcatcher.

"Come on," Beaver says quietly. "Come on, you guys, don't be afraid. Grab hold of him."

And so they do, although they *are* afraid—a little anyway; Beaver, too.

Jonesy takes Duddits's right hand, which has become so clever with machinery out there at Voke. Duddits looks surprised, then smiles and closes his fingers over Jonesy's. Pete takes Duddits's left hand. Beaver and Henry crowd in and slip their arms around Duddits's waist.

And so the five of them stand beneath one of Strawford Park's vast old oaks, with a lace of Junelight and shadows dappling their faces. They are like boys in a huddle before some big game. The softball girls in their bright yellow shirts ignore them; so do the squirrels; so does the industrious wino, who is putting together a bottle of dinner one empty soda-can at a time.

Henry feels the light steal into him and understands

that the light is his friends and himself; they make it together, that lovely lace of light and green shadow, and of them all, Duddits shines brightest. He is their ball; without him there is no bounce, there is no play. He is their dreamcatcher, he makes them one. Henry's heart fills up as it never will again (and the void of that lack will grow and darken as the years pile up around him), and he thinks: *Is it to find one lost retarded girl who probably matters to no one but her parents? Was it to kill one brainless bully-boy, joining together to somehow make him drive off the road, doing it, oh for God's sake doing it in our sleep? Can that be all? Something so great, something so wondrous, for such tiny matters? Can that be all?*

Because if it is—he thinks this even in the ecstasy of their joining—then what is the use? What can anything possibly *mean*?

Then that and all thought is swept away by the force of the experience. The face of Josie Rinkenhauer rises in front of them, a shifting image that is composed first of four perceptions and memories . . . then a fifth, as Duddits understands who it is they're making all this fuss about.

When Duddits weighs in, the image grows a hundred times brighter, a hundred times sharper. Henry hears someone—Jonesy—gasp, and he would gasp himself, if he had the breath to do so. Because Duddits may be retarded in some ways, but not in *this* way; in this way, they are the poor stumbling enfeebled idiots and Duddits is the genius.

"Oh my *God*," Henry hears Beaver cry, and in his voice there are equal parts ecstasy and dismay.

Because Josie is standing here with them. Their differing perceptions of her age have turned her into a child of about twelve, older than she was when they first encountered her waiting outside The Retard Academy, surely younger than she must be now. They have settled on a sailor dress with an unsteady color that cycles from blue to pink to red to pink to blue again. She is holding the great big plastic purse with BarbieKen peeking out the top and her knees are splendidly scabby. Ladybug earrings appear and disappear below her lobes and Henry thinks *Oh yeah, I remember those* and then they steady into the mix.

She opens her mouth and says, *Hi, Duddie*. Looks around and says, *Hi, you guys*.

Then, just like that, she's gone. Just like that they are five instead of six, five big boys standing under the old oak with June's ancient light printing their faces and the excited cries of the softball girls in their ears. Pete is crying. So is Jonesy. The wino is gone—he's apparently collected enough for his bottle—but another man has come, a solemn man dressed in a winter parka in spite of the day's warmth. His left cheek is covered with red stuff that could be a birthmark, except Henry knows it isn't. It's byrus. Owen Underhill has joined them in Strawford Park, is watching them, but that's all right; no one sees this visitor from the far side of the dreamcatcher except for Henry himself.

Duddits is smiling, but he looks puzzled at the tears on two of his friends' cheeks. "Eye-ooo ine?" he asks Jonesy—*why you cryin?*

"It doesn't matter," Jonesy says. When he slips his hand out of Duddits's, the last of the connection breaks. Jonesy wipes at his face and so does Pete. Beav utters a sobbing little laugh.

"I think I swallowed my toothpick," he says.

"Nah, there it is, ya fag," Henry says, and points to the grass, where the chewed-up pick is lying.

"Fine Osie?" Duddits asks.

"Can you, Duds?" Henry asks.

Duddits walks toward the softball field, and they follow him in a respectful little cluster. Duds walks right past Owen but of course doesn't see him; to Duds, Owen Underhill doesn't exist, at least not yet. He walks past the bleachers, past third base, past the little snackbar. Then he stops.

Beside him, Pete gasps.

Duddits turns and looks at him, bright-eyed and interested, almost laughing. Pete is holding out one finger, ticking it back and forth, looking past the moving finger at the ground. Henry follows his gaze and for a moment *thinks* he sees something—a bright flash of yellow on the grass, like paint—and then it's gone. There's only Pete, doing what he does when he's using his special remembering gift.

"Ooo you eee-a yine, Eete?" Duddits inquires in a fatherly way that almost makes Henry laugh—*Do you see the line, Pete?*

"Yeah," Pete says, bug-eyed. "Fuck, yeah." He looks up at the others. "She was *here,* you guys! She was *right here*!"

They walk across Strawford Park, following a line

only Duddits and Pete can see while a man only Henry can see follows along behind them. At the north end of the park is a rickety board fence with a sign on it: D.B.&A. R.R. PROPERTY *KEEP OUT!* Kids have been ignoring this sign for years, and it's been years since the Derry, Bangor, and Aroostook actually ran freights along the spur through The Barrens, anyway. But they see the train-tracks when they push through a break in the fence; they are down at the bottom of the slope, gleaming rustily in the sun.

The slope is steep, a-riot with poison sumac and poison ivy, and halfway down they find Josie Rinkenhauer's big plastic purse. It is old now and sadly battered—mended in several places with friction tape—but Henry would know that purse anywhere.

Duddits pounces on it happily, yanks it open, peers inside. "ArbyEN!" he announces, and pulls them out. Pete, meanwhile, has foraged on, bent over at the waist, grim as Sherlock Holmes on the trail of Professor Moriarty. And it is Pete Moore who actually finds her, looking wildly around at the others from a filthy concrete drainpipe that pokes out of the slope and tangled foliage: *"She's in here!"* Pete screams deliriously. Except for two flaring patches of color on his cheeks, his face is as pale as paper. *"Guys, I think she's in here!"*

There is an ancient and incredibly complex system of drains and sewers beneath Derry, a town which exists in what was once swampland shunned even by the Micmac Indians who lived all around it. Most of the sewer-system was built in the thirties, with New Deal money, and most of it will collapse in 1985, during the big storm that will flood the town and destroy the Derry Standpipe. Now the pipes still exist. This one slopes downward as it bores into the hill. Josie Rinkenhauer ventured in, fell, then slid on fifty years' worth of dead leaves. She went down like a kid on a slide and lies at the bottom. She has exhausted herself in her efforts to climb back up the greasy, crumbling incline; she has eaten the two or three cookies she had in the pocket of her pants and for the last series of endless hours—twelve, perhaps fourteen—has only lain in the reeking darkness, listening to the faint hum of the outside world she cannot reach and waiting to die.

Now at the sound of Pete's voice, she raises her head and calls with all of her remaining strength: *"Help mee! I can't get out! Pleeease, help meee!"*

It never occurs to them that they should go for an adult—perhaps for Officer Nell, who patrols this neighborhood. They are crazy to get her out; she has become their responsibility. They won't let Duddits in, they maintain at least that much sanity, but the rest of them create a chain into the dark without so much as thirty seconds' discussion: Pete first, then the Beav, then Henry, then Jonesy, the heaviest, as their anchor.

In this fashion they crawl into the sewage-smelling dark (there's the stench of something else, too, something old and nasty beyond belief), and before he's gotten ten feet Henry finds one of Josie's sneakers in the muck. He puts it in a back pocket of his jeans without even thinking about it.

A few seconds later, Pete calls back over his shoulder: "Whoa, stop."

The girl's weeping and pleas for help are very loud now, and Pete can actually see her sitting at the bottom of the leaf-lined slope. She's peering up at them, her face a smudged white circle in the gloom.

They stretch their chain farther, being as careful as they can despite their excitement. Jonesy has got his feet braced against a huge chunk of fallen concrete. Josie reaches up . . . gropes . . . cannot quite touch Pete's outstretched hand. At last, when it seems they must admit defeat, she scrambles a little way up. Pete grabs her scratched and filthy wrist.

"Yeah!" he screams triumphantly. *"Gotcha!"*

They pull her carefully back up the pipe toward where Duddits is waiting, holding up her purse in one hand and the two dolls in the other, shouting in to Josie not to worry, not to worry because he's got BarbieKen. There's sunlight, fresh air, and as they help her out of the pipe—

15

There was no telephone in the Humvee—two different radios but no telephone. Nevertheless, a phone rang loudly, shattering the vivid memory Henry had spun between them and scaring the hell out of both of them.

Owen jerked like a man coming out of a deep sleep and the Humvee lost its tenuous hold on the road, first skidding and then going into a slow and ponderous spin, like a dinosaur dancing.

"Holy fuck—"

He tried to turn into the skid. The wheel only spun, turning with sick ease, like the wheel of a sloop that has lost its rudder. The Humvee went backward down the single treacherous lane that was left on the southbound side of I-95, and at last fetched up askew in the snowbank on the median side, headlights opening a cone of snowy light back in the direction they had come.

Brring! Brring! Brring! Out of thin air.

It's in my head, Owen thought. *I'm projecting it, but I think it's actually in my head, more goddam telep—*

There was a pistol on the seat between them, a Glock. Henry picked it up, and when he did, the ringing stopped. He put the muzzle against his ear with his entire fist wrapped around the gunbutt.

Of course, Owen thought. *Makes perfect sense. He got a call on the Glock, that's all. Happens all the time.*

"Hello," Henry said. Owen couldn't hear the reply, but his companion's tired face lit in a grin. "Jonesy! I *knew* it was you!"

Who else would it be? Owen wondered. *Oprah Winfrey?*

"Where—"

Listening.

"Did he want Duddits, Jonesy? Is that why . . ."
Listening again. Then: "The *Standpipe?* Why . . . Jonesy? *Jonesy?*"

Henry held the pistol against the side of his head a moment longer, then looked at it without seeming to realize what it was. He laid it on the seat again. The smile had gone.

"He hung up. I think the other one was coming back. Mr. Gray, he calls him."

"He's alive, your buddy, but you don't look happy about it." It was Henry's *thoughts* that weren't happy about it, but there was no longer any need to say this. Happy at first, the way you were always happy when someone you liked gave you a little ringy-dingy on the old Glock, but not happy now. Why?

"He—*they*—are south of Derry. They stopped to eat at a truck stop called Dysart's . . . only Jonesy called it Dry Farts, like when we were kids. I don't think he even knew it. He sounded scared."

"For himself? For us?"

Henry gave Owen a bleak look. "He says he's afraid Mr. Gray means to kill a State Trooper and take his cruiser. I think that was mostly it. *Fuck.*" Henry struck his leg with his fist.

"But he's alive."

"Yeah," Henry said with a marked lack of enthusiasm. "He's immune. Duddits . . . you understand about Duddits now?"

No. I doubt if you do, either, Henry . . . but maybe I understand enough.

Henry lapsed into thoughtspeak—it was easier. *Duddits changed us—being* with *Duddits changed us. When Jonesy got hit by that car in Cambridge, it changed him again. The brainwaves of people who undergo near-death experiences often change, I saw a* Lancet *article on that just last year. For Jonesy it must mean this Mr. Gray can use him without infecting him or wearing him out. And it's also enabled him to keep from being subsumed, at least so far.*

"Subsumed?"

Co-opted. Gobbled up. Then aloud: "Can you get us out of this snowbank?"

I think so.

"That's what I was afraid of," Henry said glumly.

Owen turned to him, face greenish in the glow of the dashboard instruments. "What the fuck is *wrong* with you?"

Christ, don't you understand? How many ways do I have to tell you this? "He's still *in* there! Jonesy!"

For the third or fourth time since his and Henry's run had started, Owen was forced to leap over the gap between what his head knew and what his heart knew. "Oh. I see." He paused. "He's alive. Thinking and alive. Making *phone calls,* even." He paused again. "Christ."

Owen tried the Hummer in low forward and got about six inches before all four wheels began to spin. He geared reverse and drove them backward into the snowbank—*crunch.* But the Hummer's rear end came up a little on the packed snow, and that was what Owen wanted. When he went back to low, they'd come out of the snowbank like a cork out of a bottle. But he paused a moment with the brake pressed under the sole of his boot. The Hummer had a rough, powerful idle that shook the whole frame. Outside, the wind snarled and howled, sending snow-devils skating down the deserted turnpike.

"You know we have to do it, don't you?" Owen said. "Always assuming we're able to catch him in the first place. Because whatever the specifics might be, the general plan is almost certainly general contamination. And the math—"

"I can do the math," Henry said. "Six billion people on Spaceship Earth, versus one Jonesy."

"Yep, those are the numbers."

"Numbers can lie," Henry said, but he spoke bleakly. Once the numbers got big enough, they didn't, *couldn't* lie. Six billion was a very big number.

Owen let off the brake and laid on the accelerator. The Humvee rolled forward—a couple of feet, this time—started to spin, then caught hold and came roaring out of the snowbank like a dinosaur. Owen turned it south.

Tell me what happened after you pulled the kid out of the drainpipe.

Before Henry could do so, one of the radios under the dash crackled. The voice that followed came through loud and clear—its owner might have been sitting there in the Hummer with them.

"Owen? You there, buck?"

Kurtz.

16

It took them almost an hour to get the first sixteen miles south of Blue Base (the *former* Blue Base), but Kurtz wasn't worried. God would take care of them, he was quite sure of that.

Freddy Johnson was driving them (the happy quartet was packed into another snow-equipped Humvee). Perlmutter was in the passenger seat, handcuffed to the doorhandle. Cambry was likewise cuffed in back. Kurtz sat behind Freddy, Cambry behind Pearly. Kurtz wondered if his two press-ganged laddie-bucks were conspiring in telepathic fashion. Much good it would do them, if they were. Kurtz and Freddy both had their windows rolled down, although it rendered the Humvee colder than old Dad's outhouse in January; the heater was on high but simply couldn't keep up. The open windows were a necessity, however. Without them, the atmosphere of the Hummer would quickly become uninhabitable, as sulfurous as a poisoned coalmine. Only the smell on top wasn't sulfur but ether. Most of it seemed to be coming from Perlmutter. The man kept shifting in his seat, sometimes groaning softly under his breath. Cambry was hot with Ripley and growing like a wheat field after a spring rain, and he had that smell—Kurtz was getting it even with his mask on. But Pearly was the chief offender, shifting in his seat, trying to fart noiselessly (the one-cheek sneak, they had called such a maneuver back in the dim days of Kurtz's childhood), trying to pretend that suffocating smell wasn't coming from him. Gene Cambry was growing Ripley; Kurtz had an idea that Pearly, God love him, was growing something else.

To the best of his ability, Kurtz concealed these thoughts behind a mantra of his own: *Davis and Roberts, Davis and Roberts, Davis and Roberts.*

"Would you please stop that?" Cambry asked from Kurtz's right. "You're driving me crazy."

"Me too," Perlmutter said. He shifted in his seat

and a low *pffft* sound escaped him. The sound of a deflating rubber toy, perhaps.

"Oh, man, Pearly!" Freddy cried. He unrolled his window further, letting in a swirl of snow and cold air. The Humvee skated and Kurtz braced himself, but then it steadied again. "Would you *please* quit with the fuckin anal perfume?"

"I beg your pardon," Perlmutter said stiffly. "If you're insinuating that I broke wind, then I have to tell you—"

"I'm not insinuatin *anything,*" Freddy said. "I'm telling you to quit stinkin the place up or—"

Since there was no satisfactory way in which Freddy could complete this threat—for the time being they needed two telepaths, a primary and a backup—Kurtz broke in smoothly. "The story of Edward Davis and Franklin Roberts is an instructive one, because it shows there's really nothing new under the sun. This was in Kansas, back when Kansas really *was* Kansas . . ."

Kurtz, a pretty decent storyteller, took them back to Kansas during the Korean conflict. Ed Davis and Franklin Roberts had owned similar smallhold farms not far from Emporia, and not far from the farm owned by Kurtz's family (which had not quite been named Kurtz). Davis, never bolted together tightly in the first place, grew increasingly certain that his neighbor, the offensive Roberts, was out to steal his farm. Roberts was spreading tales about him in town, Ed Davis claimed. Roberts was poisoning his crops, Roberts was putting pressure on the Bank of Emporia to foreclose the Davis farm.

What Ed Davis had done, Kurtz said, was to catch him a rabid raccoon and put it in the henhouse—*his own* henhouse. The coon had slaughtered those chickens right and left, and when he was plumb wore out with killing, praise God, Farmer Davis had blown Mr. Coon's black-and-gray-striped head off.

They were silent in the rolling, chilly Humvee, listening.

Ed Davis had loaded all those dead chickens—and the dead raccoon—into the back of his International Harvester and had driven over onto his neighbor's property with them and by the dark of the moon had chucked his truckload of corpses down both of Franklin Roberts's wells—the stock-well and the house-well. Then, the next night, high on whiskey and laughing like hell, Davis had called his enemy on the phone and told him what he had done. *Been pretty hot today, ain't it?* the lunatic had inquired, laughing so hard Franklin Roberts could barely make him out. *Which did you and them girls of yours get, Roberts? The coon-water or the chicken-water? I can't tell you, because I don't remember which ones I chucked down which well! Ain't that a shame?*

Gene Cambry's mouth was trembling at the left corner, like the mouth of a man who has suffered a serious stroke. The Ripley growing along the crease of his brow was now so advanced that Mr. Cambry looked like a man whose forehead had been split open.

"What are you saying?" he asked. "Are you saying me and Pearly are no better than a couple of rabid chickens?"

"Watch how you talk to the boss, Cambry," Freddy said. His mask bobbed up and down on his face.

"Hey man, *fuck* the boss. This mission is *over*!"

Freddy raised a hand as if to swat Cambry over the back of the seat. Cambry jutted his truculent, frightened face forward to shorten the range. "Go on, Bubba. Or maybe you want to check your hand first, make sure there aren't no cuts on it. Cause one little cut is all it takes."

Freddy's hand wavered in the air for a moment, then returned to the wheel.

"And while you're at it, Freddy, you want to watch your back. You think *the boss* is going to leave witnesses, you're crazy."

"Crazy, yes." Kurtz said warmly, and chuckled. "Lots of farmers go crazy, or they did then before Willie Nelson and Farm Aid, God bless his heart. Stress of the life, I suppose. Poor old Ed Davis wound up in the VA—he was in Big Two, you know—and not long after the thing with the wells, Frank Roberts sold out, moved to Wichita, got work as a rep for Allis-Chalmers. And neither well was actually polluted, either. He had a state water inspector out to do some tests, and the inspector said the water was good. Rabies doesn't spread like that, anyway, he said. I wonder if the Ripley does?"

"At least call it by its right name," Cambry nearly spat. "It's *byrus.*"

"Byrus or Ripley, it's all the same," Kurtz said. "These fellows are trying to poison our wells. To pollute our precious fluids, as somebody or other once said."

"You don't care a damn about any of that!" Pearly spat—Freddy actually jumped at the venom in Perlmutter's voice. "All you care about is catching Underhill." He paused, then added in a mournful voice: "You *are* crazy, boss."

"Owen!" Kurtz cried, chipper as a chipmunk. "Almost forgot about him! Where is he, fellows?"

"Up ahead," Cambry said sullenly. "Stuck in a fucking snowbank."

"Outstanding!" Kurtz shouted. "Closing in!"

"Don't get your face fixed. He's pulling it out. Got a Hummer, just like us. You can drive one of those things straight through downtown hell if you know what you're doing. And he seems to."

"Shame. Did we make up any ground?"

"Not much," Pearly said, then shifted, grimaced, and passed more gas.

"Fuuck," Freddy said, low.

"Give me the mike, Freddy. Common channel. Our friend Owen likes the common channel."

Freddy handed the mike back on its kinked cord, made an adjustment to the transmitter bolted to the dash, then said, "Give it a try, boss."

Kurtz depressed the button on the side of the mike. "Owen? You there, buck?"

Silence, static, and the monotonous howl of the wind. Kurtz was about to depress the SEND button and try again when Owen came back—clear and crisp, moderate static but no distortion. Kurtz's face didn't change—it held the same look of pleasant interest— but his heartbeat kicked up several notches.

"I'm here."

"Lovely to hear you, bucko! Lovely! I estimate you are our location plus about fifty. We just passed Exit 39, so I'd say that's about right, wouldn't you?" They had actually just passed Exit 36, and Kurtz thought they were quite a bit closer than fifty miles. Half that, maybe.

Silence from the other end.

"Pull over, buck," Kurtz advised Owen in his kindliest, sanest voice. "It's not too late to save something out of this mess. Our careers are shot, no question about that, I guess—dead chickens down a poisoned well—but if you've got a mission, let me share it. I'm an old man, son, and all I want is to salvage something a little decent from—"

"Cut the shit, Kurtz." Loud and clear from all six of the Hummer's speakers, and Cambry actually had the nerve to *laugh*. Kurtz marked him with a vile look. Under other circumstances that look would have turned Cambry's black skin gray with terror, but this was not other circumstances, other circumstances had been cancelled, and Kurtz felt an uncharacteristic bolt of fear. It was one thing to know intellectually that things had gone tits-up; it was another when the truth landed in your gut like a heavy sack of meal.

"Owen . . . laddie-buck—"

"Listen to me, Kurtz. I don't know if there's a sane brain-cell left in your head, but if there is, I hope it's paying attention. I'm with a man named Henry Devlin. Ahead of us—probably a hundred miles ahead of us now—is a friend of his named Gary Jones. Only it's not really him anymore. He's been taken over by an alien intelligence he calls Mr. Gray."

Gary . . . Gray, Kurtz thought. *By their anagrams shall ye know em.*

"Nothing that happened in the Jefferson Tract matters," came the voice from the speakers. "The slaughter you planned is redundant, Kurtz—kill em or let em die on their own, they're not a threat."

"You hear that?" Perlmutter asked hysterically. "No threat! No—"

"Shut up," Freddy said, and backhanded him. Kurtz hardly noticed. He was sitting bolt-upright in the back seat, eyes glaring. Redundant? Was Owen Underhill telling him that the most important mission of his life had been *redundant*?

"—environment, do you understand? They can't live in this ecosystem. *Except for Gray.* Because he happened to find a host who is fundamentally different. So here it is. If you ever stood for anything, Kurtz—if you can stand for anything now—*you'll stop chasing us and let us take care of business.* Let us take care of Mr. Jones and Mr. Gray. You may be able to catch us, but it's extremely doubtful that you can catch them. They're too far south. And we think Gray has a plan. Something that *will* work."

"Owen, you're overwrought," Kurtz said. "Pull over. Whatever needs to be done, we'll do it together. We'll—"

"If you care, you'll quit," Owen said. His voice was flat. "That's it. Bottom line. I'm over and out."

"Don't do that, buck!" Kurtz shouted. "Don't do that, I forbid you to do that!"

There was a click, very loud, and then hissy silence from the speaker. "He's gone," Perlmutter said. "Pulled the mike out. Turned off the receiver. Gone."

"But you heard him, didn't you?" Cambry asked. "There's no sense in this. Call it off."

A pulse beat in the center of Kurtz's forehead. "As though I'd take his word for *anything,* after what he participated in back there."

"But he was telling the truth!" Cambry brayed. He turned fully to Kurtz for the first time, his eyes wide, the corners clogged with dabs of the Ripley, or the byrus, or whatever you wanted to call it. His spittle sprayed Kurtz's cheeks, his forehead, the surface of his breathing mask. *"I heard his thoughts! So did Pearly! HE WAS TELLING THE STONE TRUTH! HE—"*

Once again moving with a speed that was eerie, Kurtz drew the nine-millimeter from the holster on his belt and fired. The report inside the Humvee was deafening. Freddy shouted in surprise and jerked the wheel again, sending the Humvee into a diagonal skid through the snow. Perlmutter screamed, turning his horrified, red-speckled face to look into the back seat. For Cambry it was merciful—his brains were out the back of his head, through the broken window, and blowing in the storm in the time it might have taken him to raise a protesting hand.

Didn't see that coming at all, did you, buck? Kurtz thought. *Telepathy didn't help you one damn bit there, did it?*

"No," Pearly said dolorously. "You can't do much with someone who doesn't know what he's going to do until it's done. You can't do much with a crazyman."

The skid was back under control. Freddy was a superior motorman, even when he had been startled out of his wits.

Kurtz pointed the nine at Perlmutter. "Call me crazy again. Let me hear you."

"Crazy," Pearly said immediately. His lips stretched in a smile, opening over a line of teeth in which there were now several vacancies. "Crazy-crazy-crazy. But you won't shoot me for it. You shot your backup, and that's all you can afford." His voice was rising dangerously, Cambry's corpse lolled back against the door, tufts of hair blowing around his misshapen head in the cold wind coming through the window.

"Hush, Pearly," Kurtz said. He felt better now, back in control again. Cambry had been worth that much, at least. "Get a grip on your clipboard and just hush. Freddy?"

"Yes, boss."

"Are you still with me?"

"All the way, boss."

"Owen Underhill is a traitor, Freddy, can you give me a big praise God on that?"

"Praise God." Freddy sat ramrod-straight behind the wheel, staring into the snow and the cones of the Humvee's headlights.

"Owen Underhill has betrayed his country and his fellow-men. He—"

"He betrayed *you*," Perlmutter said, almost in a whisper.

"That's right, Pearly, and you don't want to over-estimate your own importance, son, that's one thing you don't want to do, because you never know what a crazyman is going to do next, you said so yourself."

Kurtz looked at the back of Freddy's broad neck.

We're going to take Owen Underhill down—him and this Devlin fellow, too, if Devlin's still with him. Understood?"

"Understood, boss."

"Meanwhile, let's lighten the load, shall we?" Kurtz produced the handcuff key from his pocket. He reached behind Cambry, wriggled his hand into the cooling goo that hadn't exited through the window, and at last found the doorhandle. He unlocked the cuff and five seconds or so later Mr. Cambry, praise God, rejoined the food-chain.

Freddy, meanwhile, had dropped one hand into his crotch, which itched like hell. His armpits, too, actually, and—

He turned his head slightly and saw Perlmutter staring at him—big dark eyes in a pallid, red-spotted face.

"What are *you* looking at?" Freddy asked.

Perlmutter turned away without saying anything more. He looked out into the night.

CHAPTER NINETEEN

THE CHASE
CONTINUES

1

Mr. Gray enjoyed bingeing on human emotions, Mr. Gray enjoyed human food, but Mr. Gray most definitely did *not* enjoy evacuating Jonesy's bowels. He refused to look at what he'd produced, simply snatched up his pants and buttoned them with hands that trembled slightly.

Jesus, aren't you going to wipe? Jonesy asked. *At least flush the damned toilet!*

But Mr. Gray only wanted to get out of the stall. He paused long enough to run his hands beneath the water in one of the basins then turned toward the exit.

Jonesy was not exactly surprised to see the State Trooper push in through the door.

"Forgot to zip your fly, my friend," the Trooper said.

"Oh. So I did. Thank you, officer."

"Come from up north, did you? Big doins up there, the radio says. When you can hear it, that is. Space aliens, maybe."

"I only came from Derry," Mr. Gray said. "I wouldn't know."

"What brings you out on a night like this, could I ask?"

Tell him a sick friend, Jonesy thought, but felt a prickle of despair. He didn't want to see this, let alone be a part of it.

"A sick friend," Mr. Gray said.

"Really. Well, sir, I'd like to see your license and regis—"

Then the Trooper's eyes came up double zeros. He walked in stilted strides toward the wall with the sign on it reading SHOWERS ARE FOR TRUCKERS ONLY. He stood there for a moment, trembling, trying to fight back . . . and then began to beat his head against the tile in big, sweeping jerks. The first strike knocked his Stetson off. On the third the claret began to flow, first beading on the beige tiles, then splattering them in dark ropes.

And because he could do nothing to stop it, Jonesy scrambled for the phone on his desk.

There was nothing. Either while he had been eating his second order of bacon or taking his first shit as a human being, Mr. Gray had cut the line. Jonesy was on his own.

2

In spite of his horror—or perhaps because of it—Jonesy burst out laughing as his hands wiped the blood from the tiled wall with a Dysart's towel. Mr. Gray had accessed Jonesy's knowledge concerning body concealment and/or disposal, and had found the motherlode. As a lifelong connoisseur of horror movies, suspense novels, and mysteries, Jonesy was, in a manner of speaking, quite the expert. Even now, as Mr. Gray dropped the bloody towel on the chest of the Trooper's sodden uniform (the Trooper's jacket had been used to wrap the badly bludgeoned head), a part of Jonesy's mind was running the disposal of Freddy Miles's corpse in *The Talented Mr. Ripley*, both the film version and Patricia Highsmith's novel. Other tapes were running, as well, so many overlays that looking too deeply made Jonesy dizzy, the way he felt when looking down a long drop. Nor was that the worst part. With Jonesy's help, the talented Mr. Gray had discovered something he liked more than crispy bacon, even more than bingeing on Jonesy's well of rage.

Mr. Gray had discovered murder.

3

Beyond the showers was a locker room. Beyond the lockers was a hallway leading to the truckers' dorm. The hall was deserted. On the far side of it was a door which opened on the rear of the building, where there was a snow-swirling cul-de-sac, now deeply drifted. Two large green Dumpsters emerged from the drifts. One hooded light cast a pallid glow and tall, lunging shadows. Mr. Gray, who learned fast, searched the Trooper's body for his car keys and found them. He also took the Trooper's gun and put it in one of the zippered pockets of Jonesy's parka. Mr. Gray used the bloodstained towel to keep the door to the cul-de-sac from latching shut, then dragged the body behind one of the Dumpsters.

All of it, from the Trooper's gruesome induced suicide to Jonesy's re-entry to the back hall, took less than ten minutes. Jonesy's body felt light and agile, all weariness gone, at least for the time being: he and Mr. Gray were enjoying another burst of endorphin euphoria. And at least some of this wetwork was the responsibility of Gary Ambrose Jones. Not just the body-disposal knowledge, but the bloodthirsty urges of the id under the thin candy frosting of "it's just make-believe." Mr. Gray was in the driver's seat—Jonesy was at least not burdened with the idea that he was the primary murderer—but he was the engine.

Maybe we deserve to be erased, Jonesy thought as Mr. Gray walked back through the shower-room (looking for blood-splatters with Jonesy's eyes and bouncing the Trooper's keys in one of Jonesy's palms as he went). *Maybe we deserve to be turned into nothing but a bunch of red spores blowing in the wind. That might be the best thing, God help us.*

4

The tired-looking woman working the cash-register asked him if he'd seen the Trooper.

"Sure did," Jonesy said. "Showed him my driver's license and registration, as a matter of fact."

"Been a bunch of mounties in ever since late afternoon," the cashier said. "Storm or no storm. They're all nervous as hell. So's everyone else. If I wanted to see folks from some other planet, I'd rent me a video. You heard anything new?"

"On the radio they're saying it's all a false alarm," he replied, zipping his jacket. He looked at the windows between the restaurant and the parking lot, verifying what he had already seen: with the combination of frost on the glass and the snow outside, the view was nil. No one in here was going to see what he drove away in.

"Yeah? Really?" Relief made her look less tired. Younger.

"Yeah. Don't be looking for your friend too soon, darlin. He said he had to lay a serious loaf."

A frown creased the skin between her eyebrows. "He said that?"

"Goodnight. Happy Thanksgiving. Merry Christmas. Happy New Year."

Some of that, Jonesy hoped, was him. Trying to get through. To be noticed.

Before he could see if it *was* noticed, the view before his office window revolved as Mr. Gray turned him away from the cash-register. Five minutes later he was heading south on the turnpike again, the chains on the Trooper's cruiser thrupping and zinging, allowing him to maintain a steady forty miles an hour.

Jonesy felt Mr. Gray reaching out, reaching back. Mr. Gray could touch Henry's mind but not get inside it—like Jonesy, Henry was to some degree different. No matter; there was the man with Henry, Overhill or Underhill. From him, Mr. Gray was able to get a good fix. They were seventy miles behind, maybe more . . . and pulling off the turnpike? Yes, pulling off in Derry.

Mr. Gray cast back farther yet, and discovered more pursuers. Three of them . . . but Jonesy felt this group's main focus was not Mr. Gray, but Overhill/Underhill. He found that both incredible and inexplicable, but it seemed to be true. And Mr. Gray liked that just fine. He didn't even bother to look for the reason why Overhill/Underhill and Henry might be stopping.

Mr. Gray's main concern was switching to another vehicle, a snowplow, if Jonesy's driving skills would allow him to operate it. It would mean another murder, but that was all right with the increasingly human Mr. Gray.

Mr. Gray was just getting warmed up.

5

Owen Underhill is standing on the slope very near to the pipe which juts out of the foliage, and he sees them help the muddy, wild-eyed girl—Josie—out of the pipe. He sees Duddits (a large young man with shoulders like a football player's and the improbable blond hair of a movie idol) sweep her into a hug, kissing her dirty face in big smacks. He hears her first words: "I want to see my mommy."

It's good enough for the boys; there's no call to the police, no call for an ambulance. They simply help her up the slope, through the break in the board fence, across Strawford Park (the girls in yellow have been replaced by girls in green; neither they nor their coach pay any attention to the boys or their filthy, dragglehaired prize), and then down Kansas Street to Maple Lane. They know where Josie's mommy is. Her Daddy, too.

Not just the Rinkenhauers, either. When the boys get back, there are cars parked the length of the block on both sides of the Cavell house. Roberta was the one who proposed calling the parents of Josie's friends and classmates. They will search on their own, and they will paper the town with the MISSING posters, she says. Not in shadowy, out-of-the-way places (which is where missing-children posters in Derry tend to wind up) either, but where people *must* see them. Roberta's enthusiasm is enough to light some faint hope in the eyes of Ellen and Hector Rinkenhauer.

The other parents respond, too—it is as if they have just been waiting to be asked. The calls started shortly after Duddits and his friends trooped out the door (to play, Roberta assumed, and someplace close by, because Henry's old jalopy is still parked in the driveway), and by the time the boys return, there are almost two dozen people crammed into the Cavells' living room, drinking coffee and smoking cigarettes. The man currently addressing them is a guy Henry has seen before, a lawyer named Dave Bocklin. His son, Kendall, sometimes plays with Duddits. Ken Bocklin also has Down's, and he's a good enough guy, but he's not like Duds. Get serious, though—who is?

The boys stand at the entrance to the living room, Josie among them. She is once more carrying her great big purse, with BarbieKen tucked away inside. Even her face is almost clean, because Beaver, seeing all the cars, has done a little work on it with his handkerchief out in the driveway. ("Tell you what, it made me feel funny," the Beav confides later, after all the hoopdedoo and fuckaree has died down. "Here I'm cleanin up this girl, she's got the bod of a Playboy Bunny and the brain, roughly speaking, of a lawn-sprinkler.") At first no one sees them but Mr. Bocklin, and Mr. Bocklin doesn't seem to realize what he's looking at, because he goes right on talking.

"So what we need to do, folks, is divide up into a number of teams, let's say three couples to each . . . each team . . . and we'll . . . we . . . we." Mr. Bocklin slows like one of those toys you need to wind up and then just stands there in front of the Cavells' TV, staring. There's a nervous rustle among the hastily assembled parents, who don't understand what can be wrong with him—he was going along so confidently.

"Josie," he says in a flat, uninflected voice utterly unlike his usual confident courthouse boom.

"Yes," says Hector Rinkenhauer, "that's her name. What's up, Dave? Are you all r—"

"Josie," Dave says again, and raises a trembling hand. To Henry (and hence to Owen, who is seeing this through Henry's eyes) he looks like the Ghost of Christmas Yet to Come pointing at Ebeneezer Scrooge's grave.

One face turns . . . two . . . four . . . Alfie Cavell's eyes, huge and unbelieving behind his specs . . . and finally, Mrs. Rinkenhauer's.

"Hi, Mom," Josie says nonchalantly. She holds up her purse. "Duddie found my BarbieKen. I was stuck in a—"

The rest is blotted out by the woman's shriek of joy. Henry has never heard such a cry in his life, and although it is wonderful, it is also somehow terrible.

"Fuck me Freddy," Beaver says . . . low, under his breath.

Jonesy is holding Duddits, who has been frightened by the scream.

Pete looks at Henry and gives a little nod: *We did okay.*

And Henry nods back. *Yeah, we did.*

It may not have been their finest hour, but surely it is a close second. And as Mrs. Rinkenhauer sweeps her daughter into her arms, now sobbing, Henry taps Duddits on the arm. When Duddits turns to look at him, Henry kisses him softly on the cheek. *Good old Duddits,* Henry thinks. *Good old—*

6

"This is it, Owen," Henry said quietly. "Exit 27."

Owen's vision of the Cavell living room popped like a soap bubble and he looked at the looming sign: KEEP RIGHT FOR EXIT 27—KANSAS STREET. He could still hear the woman's happy, unbelieving cries echoing in his ears.

"You okay?" Henry asked.

"Yeah. At least I guess so." He turned up the exit ramp, the Humvee shouldering its way through the snow. The clock built into the dashboard had gone as dead as Henry's wristwatch, but he thought he could see the faintest lightening in the air. "Right or left at the top of the ramp? Tell me now, because I don't want to risk stopping."

"Left, left."

Owen swung the Hummer left under a dancing blinker-light, rode it through another skid, and then moved south on Kansas Street. It had been plowed, and not that long ago, but it was drifting in again already.

"Snow's letting up," Henry said.

"Yeah, but the wind's a bitch. You're looking forward to seeing him, aren't you? Duddits."

Henry grinned. "A little nervous about it, but yeah." He shook his head. "Duddits, man . . . Duddits just makes you feel good. He's a tribble. You'll see for yourself. I just wish we weren't busting in like this at the crack of dawn."

Owen shrugged. *Can't do anything about it,* the gesture said.

"They've been over here on the west side for four years, I guess, and I've never even been to the new place." And, without even realizing, went on in mindspeak: *They moved after Alfie died.*

Did you—And then, instead of words, a picture: people in black under black umbrellas. A graveyard in the rain. A coffin on trestles with R.I.P. ALFIE carved on top.

No, Henry said, feeling ashamed. *None of us did.*
?

But Henry didn't know why they hadn't gone, although a phrase occurred to him: *The moving finger writes; and having writ, moves on.* Duddits had been an important (he guessed the word he actually wanted was *vital*) part of their childhood. And once that link was broken, going back would have been painful. Painful was one thing, *uselessly* painful another. He understood something now. The images he associated with his depression and his growing certainty of suicide—the trickle of milk on his father's chin, Barry Newman hustling his doublewide butt out of the office—had been hiding another, more potent, image all along: the dreamcatcher. Hadn't that been the real source of his despair? The grandiosity of the dreamcatcher concept coupled to the banality of the uses to which the concept had been put? Using Duddits to find Josie Rinkenhauer had been like discovering quantum physics and then using it to build a video game. Worse, discovering that was really all quantum physics was good for. Of course they had done a good thing—without them, Josie Rinkenhauer would have died in that pipe like a rat in a rainbarrel. But—come on—it wasn't as if they'd rescued a future Nobel Peace Prize winner—

I can't follow everything that just went through your head, Owen said, suddenly deep in Henry's mind, *but it sounds pretty goddam arrogant. Which street?*

Stung, Henry glared at him. "We haven't been back to see him lately, okay? Could we just leave it at that?"

"Yes," Owen said.

"But we all sent him Christmas cards, okay? Every year, which is how I know they moved to Dearborn Street, 41 Dearborn Street, West Side Derry, make your right three streets up."

"Okay. Calm down."

"Fuck your mother and die."

"Henry—"

"We just fell out of touch. It happens. Probably never happened to a Mr. Perfection like your honored self, but to the rest of us . . . the rest of us . . ." Henry looked down, saw that his fists were clenched, and forced them to roll open.

"Okay, I said."

"Probably Mr. Perfection stays in touch with *all* his junior-high-school friends, right? You guys probably get together once a year to snap bras, play your Mötley Crüe records, and eat Tuna Surprise just like they used to serve in the cafeteria."

"I'm sorry if I upset you."

"Oh, bite me. You act like we fucking *abandoned* him." Which, of course, was pretty much what they had done.

Owen said nothing. He was squinting through the swirling snow, looking for the Dearborn Street sign in the pallid gray light of early morning . . . and there it was, just up ahead. A plow passing along Kansas Street had plugged the end of Dearborn, but Owen thought the Humvee could beat its way past.

"It's not like I stopped thinking about him," Henry said. He started to continue by thought, then switched back to words again. Thinking about Dud-dits was too revealing. "We all thought about him. In fact, Jonesy and I were going to go see him this spring. Then Jonesy had his accident, and I forgot all about it. Is that so surprising?"

"Not at all," Owen said mildly. He swung the wheel hard to the right, flicked it back the other way to control the skid, then floored the accelerator. The Hummer hit the packed and crusty wall of snow hard enough to throw both of them forward against their seatbelts. Then they were through, Owen jockeying the wheel to keep from hitting the drifted-in cars parked on either side of the street.

"I don't need a guilt-trip from someone who was planning to barbecue a few hundred civilians," Henry grumbled.

Owen stamped on the brake with both feet, throwing them forward into their harnesses again, this time hard enough to lock them. The Humvee skidded to a diagonal stop in the street.

"Shut the fuck up."

Don't be talking shit you don't understand.

"I'm likely going to be a"

dead man because of

"you, so why don't you just keep all your fucking"

self-indulgent

(picture of a spoiled-looking kid with his lower lip stuck out)

"rationalizing bullshit"

to yourself.

Henry stared at him, shocked and stunned. When was the last time someone had talked to him that way? The answer was probably never.

"I only care about one thing," Owen said. His face was pale and strained and exhausted. "I want to find your Typhoid Jonesy and stop him. All right? Fuck your precious tender feelings, fuck how tired you are, and fuck you. I'm here."

"All right," Henry said.

"I don't need lessons in morality from a guy planning to blow his overeducated, self-indulgent brains out."

"Okay."

"So fuck *your* mother and die."

Silence inside the Humvee. Nothing from outside but the monotonous vacuum-cleaner shriek of the wind.

At last Henry said, "Here's what we'll do. I'll fuck *your* mother, then die; you fuck *my* mother, then die. At least we'll avoid the incest taboo."

Owen began to smile. Henry smiled back.

What're Jonesy and Mr. Gray doing? Owen asked Henry. *Can you tell?*

Henry licked at his lips. The itching in his leg had largely stopped, but his tongue tasted like an old piece of shag rug. "No. They're cut off. Gray's responsible for that, probably. And your fearless leader? Kurtz? He's getting closer, isn't he?"

"Yeah. If we're going to maintain any kind of lead on him at all, we better make this quick."

"Then we will." Owen scratched the red stuff on the side of his face, looked at the bits of red that came off on his fingers, then got moving again.

Number 41, you said?

Yeah. Owen?

What?

I'm scared.

Of Duddits?

Sort of, yeah.

Why?

I don't know.

Henry looked at Owen bleakly.

I feel like there's something wrong with him.

7

It was her after-midnight fantasy made real, and when the knock came at the door, Roberta was unable to get up. Her legs felt like water. The night was gone, but it had been replaced by a pallid, creepy morning light that wasn't much better, and they were out there, Pete and Beav, the dead ones had come for her son.

The fist fell again, booming, rattling the pictures on the walls. One of them was a framed front page of the Derry *News,* the photo showing Duddits, his friends, and Josie Rinkenhauer, all of them with their arms around each other, all of them grinning like mad (how well Duddits had looked in that picture, how strong and normal) below a headline reading HIGH-SCHOOL CHUMS PLAY DETECTIVE, FIND MISSING GIRL.

Wham! Wham! Wham!

No, she thought, *I'll just sit here and eventually they'll go away, they'll have to go away, because with dead people you have to invite them in and if I just sit tight—*

But then Duddits was running past her rocker— *running,* when these days just walking wore him out, and his eyes were full of their old blazing brightness, such good boys they had been and such happiness they had brought him, but now they were *dead,* they had come to him through the storm and they were *dead—*

"Duddie, *no!*" she screamed, but he paid her no attention. He rushed past that old framed picture— Duddits Cavell on the front page, Duddits Cavell a hero, would wonders never cease—and she heard what he was shouting just as he opened the door on the dying storm:

"Ennie! Ennie! ENNIE!"

8

Henry opened his mouth—to say what he never knew, because nothing came out. He was thunderstruck, dumbstruck. This wasn't Duddits, couldn't be—it was some sickly uncle or older brother, pale and apparently bald beneath his pushed-back Red Sox cap. There was stubble on his cheeks, crusts of blood around his nostrils, and deep dark circles beneath his eyes. And yet—

"Ennie! Ennie! Ennie!"

The tall, pale stranger in the doorway threw himself into Henry's arms with all of Duddie's old extravagance, knocking him backward on the snowy step not by force of his weight—he was as light as milkweed fluff—but simply because Henry was unprepared for the assault. If Owen hadn't steadied him, he and Duddits would have gone tumbling into the snow.

"Ennie! Ennie!"

Laughing. Crying. Covering him with those big old Duddits smackeroos. Deep in the storehouse of his memory, Beaver Clarendon whispered, *If you guys tell anybody he did that* . . . And Jonesy: *Yeah, yeah, you'll never chum with us again, ya fuckin wank.* It was Duddits, all right, kissing Henry's byrus-speckled cheeks . . . but the pallor on Duddits's cheeks, what was that? He was so thin—no, beyond thin, *gaunt*— and what was that? The blood in his nostrils, the smell drifting off his skin . . . not the smell that had been coming from Becky Shue, not the smell of the overgrown cabin, but a deathly smell just the same.

And here was Roberta, standing in the hall beside a photograph of Duddits and Alfie at the Derry Days carnival, riding the carousel, dwarfing their wild-eyed plastic horses and laughing.

Didn't go to Alfie's funeral, but sent a card, Henry thought, and loathed himself.

She was wringing her hands together, her eyes full of tears, and although she had put on weight at breast and hip, although her hair was now almost entirely gray, it was her, she was still she, but Duddits . . . oh boy, *Duddits* . . .

Henry looked at her, his arms wrapped around the old friend who was still crying his name. He patted at Duddits's shoulder blade. It felt insubstantial beneath his palm, as fragile as the bone in a bird's wing.

"Roberta," he said. "Roberta, my God! What's wrong with him?"

"ALL," she said, and managed a wan smile. "Sounds like a laundry detergent, doesn't it? It stands for acute lymphocytic leukemia. He was diagnosed nine months ago, and by then curing him was no longer an option. All we've been doing since then is fighting the clock."

"Ennie!" Duddits exclaimed. The old goofy smile illuminated his gray and tired face. "Ay ih, iffun-nay!"

"That's right," Henry said, and began to cry. "Same shit, different day."

"I know why you're here," she said, "but don't. Please, Henry. I'm begging you. Don't take my boy away from me. He's dying."

9

Kurtz was about to ask Perlmutter for an update on Underhill and his new friend—Henry was the new friend's name, Henry Devlin—when Pearly let out a long, ululating scream, his face turned up to the roof of the Humvee. Kurtz had helped a woman have a baby in Nicaragua (*and they always call us the bad guys,* he thought sentimentally), and this scream reminded him of hers, heard on the shores of the beautiful La Juvena River.

"Hold on, Pearly!" Kurtz cried. "Hold on, buck! Deep breaths, now!"

"Fuck you!" Pearly screamed. *"Look what you got me into, you dirty cunt! FUCK YOU!"*

Kurtz did not hold this against him. Women said terrible things in childbirth, and while Pearly was definitely one of the fellas, Kurtz had an idea that he was going through something as close to childbirth as any man had ever experienced. He knew it might be wise to put Perlmutter out of his misery—

"You better not," Pearly groaned. Tears of pain were rolling down his red-bearded cheeks. "You better not, you lizard-skin old fuck."

"Don't you worry, laddie," Kurtz soothed, and patted Perlmutter's shivering shoulder. From ahead of them came the steady clanking rumble of the plow Kurtz had persuaded to break trail for them (as gray light began to creep back into the world, their speed had risen to a giddy thirty-five miles an hour). The plow's taillights glowed like dirty red stars.

Kurtz leaned forward, looking at Perlmutter with bright-eyed interest. It was very cold in the back seat of the Humvee because of the broken window, but for the moment Kurtz didn't notice this. The front of

Pearly's coat was swelling outward like a balloon, and Kurtz once more drew his nine-millimeter.

"Boss, if he pops—"

Before Freddy could finish, Perlmutter produced a deafening fart. The stench was immediate and enormous, but Pearly appeared not to notice. His head lolled back against the seat, his eyes half-lidded, his expression one of sublime relief.

"*Oh my fuckin GRANDMOTHER!*" Freddy cried, and cranked his window all the way down despite the draft already coursing through the vehicle.

Fascinated, Kurtz watched Perlmutter's distended belly deflate. Not yet, then. Not yet and probably just as well. It was possible that the thing growing inside Perlmutter's works might come in handy. Not likely, but possible. All things served the Lord, said the Scripture, and that might include the shit-weasels.

"Hold on, soldier," Kurtz said, patting Pearly's shoulder with one hand and putting the nine on the seat beside him with the other. "You just hold on and think about the Lord."

"Fuck the Lord," Perlmutter said sullenly, and Kurtz was mildly amazed. He never would have dreamed Perlmutter could have so much profanity in him.

Ahead of them, the plow's taillights flashed bright and pulled over to the right side of the road.

"Oh-oh," Kurtz said.

"What should I do, boss?"

"Pull right in behind him," Kurtz said. He spoke

cheerfully, but picked the nine-millimeter up off the seat again. "We'll see what our new friend wants." Although he believed he knew. "Freddy, what do you hear from our old friends? Are you picking them up?"

Very reluctantly, Freddy said, "Only Owen. Not the guy with him or the guys they're chasing. Owen's off the road. In a house. Talking with someone."

"A house in Derry?"

"Yeah."

And here came the plow's driver, striding through the snow in great green gumrubber boots and a hooded parka fit for an Eskimo. Wrapped around the lower part of his face was a vast woolen muffler, its ends flying out behind him in the wind, and Kurtz didn't have to be telepathic to know the man's wife or mother had made it for him.

The plowman leaned in the window and wrinkled his nose at the lingering aroma of sulfur and ethyl alcohol. He looked doubtfully at Freddy, at the only-half-conscious Perlmutter, then at Kurtz in the back seat, who was leaning forward and looking at him with bright-eyed interest. Kurtz thought it prudent to hold his weapon beneath his left knee, at least for the time being.

"Yes, Cap'n?" Kurtz asked.

"I've had a radio message from a fella says his name is Randall." The plowman raised his voice to be heard over the wind. His accent was pure downeast Yankee. "*Gen'rul* Randall. Claimed to be talkin to me by satellite relay straight from Cheyenne Mountain in Wyomin."

"Name means nothing to me, Cap," Kurtz said in

the same bright tone—absolutely ignoring Perlmutter, who groaned "You lie, you lie, you lie."

The plow driver's eyes flicked to him, then returned to Kurtz. "Fella gave me a code phrase. *Blue exit.* Mean anything to you?"

" 'The name is Bond, James Bond,' " Kurtz said, and laughed. "Someone's pulling your leg, Cap."

"Said to tell you that your part of the mission's over and your country thanks you."

"Did they mention anything about a gold watch, laddie-buck?" Kurtz asked, eyes sparkling.

The plowman licked his lips. It was interesting, Kurtz thought. He could see the exact moment the plowman decided he was dealing with a lunatic. The *exact moment.*

"Don't know nawthin bout no gold watch. Just wanted to tell you I can't take you any further. Not without authorization, that is."

Kurtz produced the nine from where it had been hiding under his knee and pointed it into the plowman's face. "Here's your authorization, buck, all signed and filed in triplicate. Will it suit?"

The plowman looked at the gun with his long Yankee eyes. He did not look particularly afraid. "Ayuh, that looks to be in order."

Kurtz laughed. "Good man! *Very* good man! Now let's get going. And you want to speed it up a little, God love you. There's someone in Derry I have to" Kurtz searched for *le mot juste,* and found it. "To debrief."

Perlmutter half-groaned, half-laughed. The plowman glanced at him.

"Don't mind him, he's pregnant," Kurtz said in a confiding tone. "Next thing you know, he'll be yelling for oysters and dill pickles."

"Pregnant," the plowman echoed. His voice was perfectly flat.

"Yes, but never mind that. Not your problem. The thing is, buck—" Kurtz leaned forward, speaking warmly and confidentially over the barrel of his nine-millimeter—"this fellow I have to catch is in Derry *now*. I expect he'll be back on the road again before too long, I'd guess he must know I'm coming for his ass—"

"He knows, all right," Freddy Johnson said. He scratched the side of his neck, then dropped his hand into his crotch and scratched there.

"—but in the meantime," Kurtz continued, "I think I can make up some ground. Now do you want to put your elderly ass in gear, or what?"

The plowman nodded and went walking back to the cab of his plow. The light was brighter now. *This light very likely belongs to the last day of my life,* Kurtz thought with mild wonder.

Perlmutter began uttering a low sound of pain. It growled along for a bit, then rose to a scream. Perlmutter clutched his stomach again.

"Jesus," Freddy said. "Lookit his gut, boss. Rising like a loaf of bread."

"Deep breaths," Kurtz said, and patted Pearly's shoulder with a benevolent hand. Ahead of them, the plow had begun to move again. "Deep breaths, laddie. Relax. You just relax and think good thoughts."

10

Forty miles to Derry. *Forty miles between me and Owen,* Kurtz thought. *Not bad at all. I'm coming for you, buck. Need to take you to school. Teach you what you forgot about crossing the Kurtz Line.*

Twenty miles later and they were still there—this according to both Freddy and Perlmutter, although Freddy seemed less sure of himself now. Pearly, however, said they were talking to the mother—Owen and the other one were talking to the mother. The mother didn't want to let him go.

"Let who go?" Kurtz asked. He hardly cared. The mother was holding them in Derry, allowing them to close the distance, so God bless the mother no matter who she was or what her motivations might be.

"I don't know," Pearly said. His guts had been relatively still ever since Kurtz's conversation with the plowman, but he sounded exhausted. "I can't see. There's someone, but it's like there's no mind there to look into."

"Freddy?"

Freddy shook his head. "Owen's gone for me. I can barely hear the plow guy. It's like . . . I dunno . . . like losing a radio signal."

Kurtz leaned forward over the seat and took a close look at the Ripley on Freddy's cheek. The stuff in the middle was still bright red-orange, but around the edges it appeared to be turning an ashy white.

It's dying, Kurtz thought. *Either Freddy's system is*

killing it or the environment is. Owen was right. I'll be damned.

Not that it changed anything. The line was still the line, and Owen had stepped over it.

"The plow guy," Perlmutter said in his tired voice.

"What about the plow guy, buck?"

Only there was no need for Perlmutter to answer. Up ahead, twinkling in the blowing snow, was a sign reading EXIT 32—GRANDVIEW/GRANDVIEW STATION. The plow suddenly sped up, raising its blade as it did so. All at once the Humvee was running in slippery powder again, better than a foot of it. The plowman didn't bother with his blinker, simply took the exit at fifty, yanking up a tall rooster-tail of snow in his wake.

"Follow him?" Freddy asked. "I can run him down, boss!"

Kurtz mastered a strong urge to tell Freddy to go ahead—they'd run the long-eyed Yankee son of a bitch to earth and teach him what happened to folks who crossed the line. Give him a little dose of Owen Underhill's medicine. Except the plow was bigger than the Hummer, a lot bigger, and who knew what might happen if they got into a game of bumper cars?

"Stay on the pike, laddie," Kurtz said, settling back. "Eyes on the prize." Still, he watched the plow angling off into the frigid, windy morning with real regret. He couldn't even hope the damn Yankee had caught a hot dose from Freddy and Archie Perlmutter, because the stuff didn't last.

They went on, speed dropping back to twenty in the drifts, but Kurtz guessed conditions would improve as they got farther south. The storm was almost over.

"And congratulations," he told Freddy.

"Huh?"

Kurtz patted him on the shoulder. "You appear to be getting better." He turned to Perlmutter. "I don't know about you, laddie-buck."

11

A hundred miles north of Kurtz's position and less than two miles from the junction of back roads where Henry had been taken, the new commander of the Imperial Valleys—a woman of severe good looks, in her late forties—stood beside a pine tree in a valley which had been code-named Clean Sweep One. Clean Sweep One was, quite literally, a valley of death. Piled along its length were heaps of tangled bodies, most wearing hunter orange. There were over a hundred in all. If the corpses had ID, it had been taped around their necks. The majority of the dead were wearing their driver's licenses, but there were also Visa and Discover cards, Blue Cross cards, and hunting licenses. One woman with a large black hole in her forehead had been tagged with her Blockbuster Video card.

Standing beside the largest pile of bodies, Kate Gallagher was finishing a rough tally before writing her second report. In one hand she held a PalmPilot computer, a tool that Adolf Eichmann, that famous accountant of the dead, would certainly have envied. The Pilots hadn't worked earlier, but now most of the cool electronics gear seemed to be back on-line.

Kate wore earphones and a mike suspended in front of her mouth-and-nose mask. Occasionally she would ask someone for clarification or give an order. Kurtz had chosen a successor who was both enthusiastic and efficient. Totting up the bodies here and elsewhere, Gallagher estimated that they had bagged at least sixty percent of the escapees. The John Q's had fought, which was certainly a surprise, but in the long run, most of them just weren't survivors. It was as simple as that.

"Yo, Katie-Kate."

Jocelyn McAvoy appeared through the trees at the south end of the valley, her hood pushed back, her short hair covered by a scarf of green silk, her burp-gun slung over her shoulder. There was a splash of blood across the front of her parka.

"Scared you, didn't I?" she asked the new OIC.

"You might have raised my blood pressure a point or two."

"Well, Quadrant Four is clear, maybe that'll lower it a little." McAvoy's eyes sparkled. "We got over forty. Jackson has got hard numbers for you, and speaking of hard, right about now I could really use a hard—"

"Excuse me? Ladies?"

They turned. Emerging from the snow-covered brush at the north end of the valley was a group of half a dozen men and two women. Most were wearing orange, but their leader was a squat tugboat of a man wearing a regulation Blue Group coverall under his parka. He was also still wearing his transparent face-mask, although below his mouth there was a Ripley soul-patch which was definitely non-reg. All of the newcomers had automatic weapons.

Gallagher and McAvoy had time to exchange a single wide-eyed, caught-with-our-pants-down look. Then Jocelyn McAvoy went for her burp-gun and Kate Gallagher went for the Browning she had propped against the tree. Neither of them made it. The thunder of the guns was deafening. McAvoy was thrown nearly twenty feet through the air. One of her boots came off.

"That's for Larry!" one of the orange-clad women was screaming. "That's for Larry, you bitches, that's for Larry!"

12

When the shooting was over, the squat man with the Ripley goatee assembled his group near the facedown corpse of Kate Gallagher, who had graduated ninth in her class at West Point before running afoul of the disease that was Kurtz. The squat man had appropriated her gun, which was better than his own.

"I'm a firm believer in democracy," he said, "and you folks can do what you want, but I'm heading north now. I don't know how long it'll take me to learn the words to 'O Canada,' but I'm going to find out."

"I'm going with you," one of the men said, and it quickly became apparent that they were all going with him. Before they left the clearing the leader bent down and plucked the PalmPilot out of a snowdrift.

"Always wanted one of these," said Emil "Dawg"

Brodsky. "I'm a sucker for the new technology."

They left the valley of death from the direction they'd entered it, heading north. From around them came isolated pops and bursts of gunfire, but for all practical purposes, Operation Clean Sweep was also over.

13

Mr. Gray had committed another murder and stolen another vehicle, this time a DPW plow. Jonesy didn't see it happen. Mr. Gray, having apparently decided he couldn't get Jonesy out of his office (not, at least, until he could devote all his time and energy to the problem), had decided to do the next best thing, which was to wall him off from the outside world. Jonesy now thought he knew how Fortunato must have felt when Montressor bricked him up in the wine-cellar.

It happened not long after Mr. Gray put the State Trooper's car back in the turnpike's southbound lane (there was just the one, at least for the time being, and that was treacherous). Jonesy was in a closet at the time, following up what seemed to him to be an absolutely brilliant idea.

Mr. Gray had cut off his telephone service? Okay, he would simply create a new form of communication, as he had created a thermostat to cool the place down when Mr. Gray tried to force him out by overloading him with heat. A fax machine would be just the thing, he decided. And why not? All the gadgets were symbolic, only visualizations to help him first focus and then exercise powers that had been in him for over twenty years. Mr. Gray had sensed those powers, and after his initial dismay had moved very efficiently to keep Jonesy from using them. The trick was to keep finding ways around Mr. Gray's roadblocks, just as Mr. Gray himself kept finding ways to move south.

Jonesy closed his eyes and visualized a fax like the one in the History Department office, only he put it in the closet of his new office. Then, feeling like Aladdin rubbing the magic lamp (only the number of wishes he was granted seemed infinite, as long as he didn't get carried away), he also visualized a stack of paper and a Berol Black Beauty pencil lying beside it. Then he went into the closet to see how he'd done.

Pretty well, it appeared at first glance . . . although the pencil was a tad eerie, brand-new and sharpened to a virgin point, but still gnawed all along the barrel. Yet that was as it should be, wasn't it? Beaver was the one who had used Black Beauty pencils, even way back in Witcham Street Grammar. The rest of them had carried the more standard yellow Eberhard Fabers.

The fax looked perfect, sitting there on the floor beneath a dangle of empty coathangers and one jacket (the bright orange parka his mother had bought him for his first hunting trip, then made him promise—with his hand over his heart—to wear *every single moment he was out of doors*), and it was humming in an encouraging way.

Disappointment set in when he knelt in front of it and read the message in the lighted window: GIVE UP JONESY COME OUT.

He picked up the phone on the side of the machine and heard Mr. Gray's recorded voice: "Give up, Jonesy, come out. Give up, Jonesy, come o—"

A series of violent bangs, almost as loud as thunderclaps, made him cry out and jump to his feet. His first thought was that Mr. Gray was using one of those SWAT squad door-busters, battering his way in.

It wasn't the door, though. It was the window, and in some ways that was even worse. Mr. Gray had put industrial gray shutters—steel, they looked like—across his window. Now he wasn't just imprisoned; he was blind, as well.

Written across the inside, easily readable through the glass: GIVE UP COME OUT. Jonesy had a brief memory of *The Wizard of Oz*—SURRENDER DOROTHY written across the sky—and wanted to laugh. He couldn't. Nothing was funny, nothing was ironic. This was horrible.

"No!" he shouted. "Take them down! Take them down, damn you!"

No answer. Jonesy raised his hands, meaning to shatter the glass and beat on the steel shutters beyond, then thought, *Are you crazy? That's what he wants! The minute you break the glass, those shutters disappear and Mr. Gray is in here. And you're gone, buddy.*

He was aware of movement—the heavy rumble of the plow. Where were they by now? Waterville? Augusta? Even farther south? Into the zone where the precip had fallen as rain? No, probably not, Mr. Gray would have switched the plow for something faster if they had gotten clear of the snow. But they *would* be clear of it, and soon. Because they were going south.

Going *where?*

I might as well be dead already, Jonesy thought, looking disconsolately at the closed shutter with its taunt of a message. *I might as well be dead right now.*

14

In the end it was Owen who took Roberta Cavell by the arms and—with one eye on the racing clock, all too aware that every minute and a half brought Kurtz a mile closer—told her why they had to take Duddits, no matter how ill he was. Even in these circumstances, Henry didn't know if he could have uttered the phrase *fate of the world may depend on it* with a straight face. Underhill, who had spent his life carrying a gun for his country, could and did.

Duddits stood with his arm around Henry, staring raptly down at him with his brilliant green eyes. Those eyes, at least, had not changed. Nor had the feeling they'd always had when around Duddits—that things were either perfectly all right or soon would be.

Roberta looked at Owen, her face seeming to grow older with every sentence he spoke. It was as if some malign time-lapse photography were at work.

"Yes," she said, "yes, I understand you want to find Jonesy—to catch him—but what does he want to do? And if he *came* here, why didn't he *do* it here?"

"Ma'am, I can't answer those questions—"

"War," Duddits said suddenly. "Onesy ont war."

War? Owen's mind asked Henry, alarmed. *What war?*

Never mind, Henry responded, and all at once the voice in Owen's head was faint, hard to hear. *We have to go.*

"Ma'am. Mrs. Cavell." Owen took her arms again, very gently. Henry loved this woman a lot, although he had ignored her quite cruelly over the last dozen years or so, and Owen knew why he'd loved her. It came off her like a sweet smoke. "We have to go."

"No. Oh please say no." The tears coming again. *Don't do that, lady,* Owen wanted to say. *Things are bad enough already. Please don't do that.*

"There's a man coming. A very bad man. We have to be gone when he gets here."

Roberta's distracted, sorrowing face filled with resolution. "All right, then. If you have to. But I'm coming with you."

"Roberta, no," Henry said.

"Yes! Yes, I can take care of him . . . give him his pills . . . his Prednisone . . . I'll make sure to bring his lemon swabs and—"

"Umma, oo ay ere."

"No, Duddie, no!'

"Umma, oo ay ere! Ayfe! Ayfe!" Safe, safe. Duddits growing agitated now.

"We really don't have any more time," Owen said.

"Roberta," Henry said. "Please."

"Let me come!" she cried. "He's all I have!"

"Umma," Duddits said. His voice was not a bit childish. *"Ooo . . . ay . . . ERE."*

She looked at him fixedly, and her face sagged. "All right," she said. "Just one more minute. I have to get something."

She went into Duddits's room and came back with a paper bag, which she handed to Henry.

"It's his pills," she said. "He has his Prednisone at nine o'clock. Don't forget or he gets wheezy and his chest hurts. He can have a Percocet if he asks, and he probably *will* ask, because being out in the cold hurts him."

She looked at Henry with sorrow but no reproach. He almost wished for reproach. God knew he'd never done anything which had made him feel this ashamed. It wasn't just that Duddits had leukemia; it was that he'd had it for so long and none of them had known.

"Also his lemon swabs, but only on his lips, because his gums bleed a lot now and the swabs sting him. There's cotton for his nose if it bleeds. Oh, and the catheter. See it there on his shoulder?"

Henry nodded. A plastic tube protruding from a packing of bandage. Looking at it gave him a weirdly strong feeling of *déjà vu*.

"If you're outside, keep it covered . . . Dr. Briscoe laughs at me, but I'm always afraid the cold will get down inside . . . a scarf will work . . . even a handkerchief . . ." She was crying again, the sobs breaking through.

"Roberta—" Henry began. Now he was looking at the clock, too.

"I'll take care of him," Owen said. "I saw my Pop

through to the end of it. I know about Prednisone and Percocet." And more: bigger steroids, better painkillers. At the end, marijuana, methadone, and finally pure morphine, so much better than heroin. Morphine, death's sleekest engine.

He felt her in his head, then, a strange, tickling sensation like bare feet so light they barely touched down. Tickly, but not unpleasant. She was trying to make out if what he'd said about his father was the truth or a lie. This was her little gift from her extraordinary son, Owen realized, and she had been using it so long she no longer even knew she was doing it . . . like Henry's friend Beaver chewing on his toothpicks. It wasn't as powerful as what Henry had, but it was there, and Owen had never in his life been so glad he had told the truth.

"Not leukemia, though," she said.

"Lung cancer. Mrs. Cavell, we really have to—"

"I need to get him one more thing."

"Roberta, we can't—" Henry began.

"In a flash, in a flash." She darted for the kitchen.

Owen felt really frightened for the first time. "Kurtz and Freddy and Perlmutter—Henry, I can't tell where they are! I've lost them!"

Henry had unrolled the top of the bag and looked inside. What he saw there, lying on top of the box of lemon-flavored glycerine swabs, transfixed him. He replied to Owen, but his voice seemed to be coming from the far end of some previously undisclosed— hell, *unsuspected*—valley. There *was* such a valley, he knew that now. A trough of years. He would not, could not, say he had never suspected that such geography existed, but how in God's name could he have suspected so *little*?

"They just passed Exit 29," he said. "Twenty miles behind us now. Maybe even closer."

"What's wrong with you?"

Henry reached into the brown bag and brought out the little creation of string, so like a cobweb, which had hung over Duddits's bed here, and over the bed at the Maple Lane house before Alfie had died.

"Duddits, where did you get this?" he asked, but of course he knew. This dreamcatcher was smaller than the one which had hung in the main room at Hole in the Wall, but was otherwise its twin.

"Eeeyer," Duddits said. He had never taken his eyes off Henry. It was as if he could still not entirely believe that Henry was here. "Eeeyer ent ooo eee. Or eye Issmuss ass-eek."

Although his mind-reading ability was fading rapidly as his body beat back the byrus, Owen understood this easily enough; *Beaver sent to me,* Duddits said. *For my Christmas last week.* Down's sufferers had difficulty expressing concepts of time past and time to come, and Owen suspected that to Duddits the past was always last week, the future always next week. It seemed to Owen that if everyone thought that way, there would be a lot less grief and rancor in the world.

Henry looked at the little string dreamcatcher a moment longer, then returned it to the brown bag just as Roberta bustled back in. Duddits broke into a huge grin when he saw what she'd gone for. "Oooby-Doo!" he cried. "Ooby-Doo unnox!" He took it and gave her a kiss on each cheek.

"Owen," Henry said. His eyes were bright. "I have some *extremely* good news."

"Tell me."

"The bastards just hit a detour—jackknifed tractor-trailer just shy of Exit 28. It's going to cost them ten, maybe twenty minutes."

"Thank Christ. Let's use them." He glanced at the coat-tree in the corner. Hanging from it was a huge blue duffel coat with RED SOX WINTER BALL printed on the back in bright scarlet. "That yours, Duddits?"

"Ine!" Duddits said, smiling and nodding. "I-acket." And, as Owen reached for it: "Ooo saw us ine Osie." He got that one, too, and it sent a chill up his back. *You saw us find Josie.*

So he had . . . and Duddits had seen him. Only last night, or had Duddits seen him on that day, nineteen years ago? Did Duddits's gift also involve a kind of time travel?

This wasn't the time to ask such questions, and Owen was almost glad.

"I said I wouldn't pack his lunchbox, but of course I did. In the end, I did."

Roberta looked at it—at Duddits holding it, shifting it from hand to hand as he struggled into the enormous parka, which had also been a gift from the Boston Red Sox. His face was unbelievably pale against the bright blue and even brighter yellow of the lunchbox. "I knew he was going. And that I wasn't." Her eyes searched Henry's face. "Please may I not go, Henry?"

"If you do, you could die in front of him," Henry said—hating the cruelty of it, also hating how well his life's work had prepared him to push the right buttons. "Would you want him to see that, Roberta?"

"No, of course not." And, as an afterthought, hurting him all the way to the center of his heart: "Damn you."

She went to Duddits, pushed Owen aside, and quickly ran up her son's zipper. Then she took him by the shoulders, pulled him down, and fixed him with her eyes. Tiny, fierce little bird of a woman. Tall, pale son, floating inside his parka. Roberta had stopped crying.

"You be good, Duddie."

"I eee ood, Umma."

"You mind Henry."

"I-ill, Umma. I ine Ennie."

"Stay bundled up."

"I-ill." Still obedient, but a little impatient now, wanting to be off, and how all this took Henry back: trips to get ice cream, trips to play minigolf (Duddits had been weirdly good at the game, only Pete had been able to beat him with any consistency), trips to the movies; always *you mind Henry* or *you mind Jonesy* or *you mind your friends;* always *you be good, Duddie* and *I eee oood, Umma.*

She looked him up and down.

"I love you, Douglas. You have always been a good

son to me, and I love you so very much. Give me a kiss, now."

He kissed her; her hand stole out and caressed his beard-sandy cheek. Henry could hardly bear to look, but he *did* look, was as helpless as any fly caught in any spiderweb. Every dreamcatcher was also a trap.

Duddits gave her another perfunctory kiss, but his brilliant green eyes shifted between Henry and the door. Duddits was anxious to be off. Because he knew the people after Henry and his friend were close? Because it was an adventure, like all the adventures the five of them had had in the old days? Both? Yes, probably both. Roberta let him go, her hands leaving her son for the last time.

"Roberta," Henry said. "Why didn't you tell any of us this was happening? Why didn't you call?"

"Why didn't you ever come?"

Henry might have asked another of his own—Why didn't *Duddits* call?—but the very question would have been a lie. Duddits had called repeatedly since March, when Jonesy had had his accident. He thought of Pete, sitting in the snow beside the overturned Scout, drinking beer and writing DUDDITS over and over again in the snow. Duddits, marooned in Never-Never Land and dying there, Duddits sending his messages and receiving back only silence. Finally one of them had come, but only to take him away with nothing but a bag of pills and his old yellow lunchbox. There was no kindness in the dreamcatcher. They had meant only good for Duddits, even on that first day; they had loved him honestly. Still, it came down to this.

"Take care of him, Henry." Her gaze shifted to Owen. "You too. Take care of my son."

Henry said, "We'll try."

15

There was no place to turn around on Dearborn Street; every driveway had been plowed under. In the strengthening morning light, the sleeping neighborhood looked like a town deep in the Alaskan tundra. Owen threw the Hummer in reverse and went flying backward down the street, the bulky vehicle's rear end wagging clumsily from side to side. Its high steel bumper smacked some snow-shrouded vehicle parked at the curb, there was a tinkle of breaking glass, and then they again burst through the frozen roadblock of snow at the intersection, swerving wildly back into Kansas Street, pointing toward the turnpike. During all this Duddits sat in the back seat, perfectly complacent, his lunchbox on his lap.

Henry, why did Duddits say Jonesy wants war? What war?

Henry tried to send the answer telepathically, but Owen could no longer hear him. The patches of byrus on Owen's face had all turned white, and when he scratched absently at his cheek, he pulled clumps of the stuff out with his nails. The skin beneath looked chapped and irritated, but not really hurt. *Like getting over a cold,* Henry marvelled. *Really not more serious than that.*

"He didn't say war, Owen."

"War," Duddits agreed from the back seat. He leaned forward to look at the big green sign reading 95 SOUTHBOUND. "Onesy ont *war.*"

Owen's brow wrinkled; a dust of dead byrus flakes sifted down like dandruff. "What—"

"*Water,*" Henry said, and reached back to pat Duddits's bony knee. "Jonesy wants *water* is what he was trying to say. Only it's not Jonesy who wants it. It's the other one. The one he calls Mr. Gray."

16

Roberta went into Duddits's room and began to pick up the litter of his clothes—the way he left them around drove her crazy, but she supposed she wouldn't have to worry about that anymore. She had been at it scarcely five minutes before a weakness overcame her legs, and she had to sit in his chair by the window. The sight of the bed, where he had come to spend more and more of his time, haunted her. The dull morning light on the pillow, which still bore the circular indentation of his head, was inexpressibly cruel.

Henry thought she'd let Duddits go because they believed the future of the whole world somehow hinged on finding Jonesy, and finding him fast. But that wasn't it. She had let him go because it was what Duddits wanted. The dying got signed baseball caps; the dying also got to go on trips with old friends.

But it was hard.

Losing him was so hard.

She put her handful of tee-shirts to her face in

order to blot out the sight of the bed and there was his smell: Johnson's shampoo, Dial soap, and most of all, *worst* of all, the arnica cream she put on his back and legs when his muscles hurt.

In her desperation she reached out to him, trying to find him with the two men who had come like the dead and taken him away, but his mind was gone.

He's blocked himself off from me, she thought. They had enjoyed (*mostly* enjoyed) their own ordinary telepathy over the years, perhaps only different in minor degree from the telepathy most mothers of special children experienced (she had heard the word *rapport* over and over again at the support-group meetings she and Alfie sometimes attended), but that was gone now. Duddits had blocked himself off, and that meant he knew something terrible was going to happen.

He knew.

Still holding the shirts to her face and inhaling his scent, Roberta began to cry again.

17

Kurtz had been okay (*mostly* okay) until they saw the road-flares and blue police lightbars flashing in the grim morning light, and beyond it, a huge semi lying on its side like a dead dinosaur. Standing out front, so bundled up his face was completely invisible, was a cop waving them toward an exit ramp.

"Fuck!" Kurtz spat. He had to fight an urge to draw the nine and just start spraying away. He knew that would be disaster—there were other cops milling around the stalled semi—but he felt the urge, all but ungovernable, just the same. They were so close! Closing in, by the hands of the nailed-up Christ! And then stopped like this! "Fuck, fuck, *fuck!*"

"What do you want me to do, boss?" Freddy had asked. Impassive behind the wheel, but he had drawn his own weapon—an automatic rifle—across his lap. "If I nail it, I think we can skate by on the right. Gone in sixty seconds."

Again Kurtz had to fight the urge to just say *Yeah, punch it, Freddy, and if one of those bluesuits gets in the way, bust his gut for him.* Freddy might get by . . . but he might not. He wasn't the driver he thought he was, that Kurtz had already ascertained. Like too many pilots, Freddy had the erroneous belief that his skills in the sky were mirrored by skills on the ground. And even if they did get by, they'd be marked. And that was not acceptable, not after General Yellow-Balls Randall had hollered Blue Exit. His Get-Out-of-Jail-Free card had been revoked. He was strictly a vigilante now.

Got to do the smart thing, he thought. *That's why they pay me the big bucks.*

"Be a good boy and just go the way he's pointing you," Kurtz said. "In fact, I want you to give him a wave and a big thumb's-up when you take the ramp. Then keep moving south and get back on the turnpike at your earliest opportunity." He sighed. "Lord love a duck." He leaned forward, close enough to Freddy to see the whitening fuzz of Ripley in his right ear. He whispered, ardent as a lover, "And if you ditch us, lad-die-buck, I'll put a round in the back of your neck." Kurtz touched the place where the soft nape joined the hard skull. "Right here."

Freddy's wooden-Indian face didn't change. "Yes, boss."

Next, Kurtz had gripped the now-nearly-comatose Perlmutter by the shoulder and had shaken him until Pearly's eyes at last fluttered open.

"Lea' me 'lone, boss. Need to sleep."

Kurtz placed the muzzle of his nine-millimeter against the back of his former aide's head. "Nope. Rise and shine, buck. Time for a little debriefing."

Pearly had groaned, but he had also sat up. When he opened his mouth to say something, a tooth had tumbled out onto the front of his parka. The tooth had looked perfect to Kurtz. Look, Ma, no cavities.

Pearly said that Owen and his new buddy were still stopped, still in Derry. Very good. Yummy. Not so good fifteen minutes later, as Freddy sent the Humvee trudging down another snow-covered entrance ramp and back onto the turnpike. This was Exit 28, only one interchange away from their target, but a miss was as good as a mile.

"They're on the move again," Perlmutter said. He sounded weak and washed out.

"Goddammit!" He was full of rage—sick and use-less rage at Owen Underhill, who now symbolized (at least to Abe Kurtz) the whole sorry, busted operation.

Pearly uttered a deep groan, a sound of utter, hol-low despair. His stomach had begun to rise again. He was clutching it, his cheeks wet with perspiration. His normally unremarkable face had become almost handsome in his pain.

Now he let another long and ghastly fart, a passage of wind which seemed to go on and on. The sound of it made Kurtz think of gadgets they'd constructed at summer camp a thousand or so years ago, noisemakers that consisted of tin cans and lengths of waxed string. Bullroarers, they'd called them.

The stench that filled the Humvee was the smell of the red cancer growing in Pearly's sewage-treatment plant, first feeding on his wastes, then getting to the good stuff. Pretty horrible. Still, there was an upside. Freddy was getting better and Kurtz had never caught the damned Ripley in the first place (perhaps he was immune; in any case, he had taken off the mask and tossed it indifferently in back fifteen minutes ago). And Pearly, although undoubtedly ill, was also valuable, a man with a really good radar jammed up his ass. So Kurtz patted Perlmutter on the shoulder, ignoring the stench. Sooner or later the thing inside him would get out, and that would likely mean an end to Pearly's usefulness, but Kurtz wouldn't worry about that until he had to.

"Hold on," Kurtz said tenderly. "Just tell it to go back to sleep again."

"You . . . fucking . . . idiot!" Perlmutter gasped.

"That's right," Kurtz agreed. "Whatever you say, buck." After all, he was a fucking idiot. Owen had turned out to be a cowardly coyote, and who had put him in the damn henhouse?

They were passing Exit 27 now. Kurtz looked up the ramp and fancied he could almost see the tracks of the Hummer Owen was driving. Somewhere up there, on one side of the overpass or the other, was the house to which Owen and his new friend had made their inexplicable detour. Why?

"They stopped to get Duddits," Perlmutter said. His belly was going down again and the worst of his pain seemed to have passed. For now, at least.

"Duddits? What kind of name is that?"

"I don't know. I'm picking this up from his mother. Him I can't see. He's different, boss. It's almost as if he's a grayboy instead of human."

Kurtz felt his back prickle at that.

"The mother thinks of this guy Duddits as both a boy and a man," Pearly said. This was the most unprompted communication from him Kurtz had gotten since they'd left Gosselin's. Perlmutter sounded almost interested, by God.

"Maybe he's retarded," Freddy said.

Perlmutter glanced over at Freddy. "That could be. Whatever he is, he's sick." Pearly sighed. "I know how he feels."

Kurtz patted Perlmutter's shoulder again. "Chin up, laddie. What about the fellows they're after? This Gary Jones and the supposed Mr. Gray?" He didn't much care, but there *was* the possibility that the course and progress of Jones—and Gray, if Gray existed outside of Owen Underhill's fevered imagination—would impact upon the course and progress of Underhill, Devlin, and . . . Duddits?

Perlmutter shook his head, then closed his eyes and leaned his head back against the seat again. His little spate of energy and interest seemed to have passed. "Nothing," he said. "Blocked off."

"Maybe not there at all?"

"Oh, something's there," Perlmutter said. "It's like a black hole." Dreamily, he said: "I hear so many voices. They're already sending in the reinforcements . . ."

As if Perlmutter had conjured it, the biggest convoy Kurtz had seen in twenty years appeared in the northbound lanes of I-95. First came two enormous plows, as big as elephants, running side by side with their clifflike blades spuming up snow on either side, baring both lanes all the way down to the pavement. Behind them, a pair of sand-trucks, also running in tandem. And behind the sand-trucks, a double line of Army vehicles and heavy ordnance. Kurtz saw shrouded shapes on flatbed haulers and knew they could only be missiles. Other flatbeds held radar dishes, range-finders, God knew what else. Interspersed among them were big canvasback troop-carriers, their headlamps glaring in the brightening daylight. Not hundreds of men but *thousands,* prepared for God knew what— World War Three, hand-to-hand combat with two-headed creatures or maybe the intelligent bugs from *Starship Troopers,* plague, madness, death, doomsday. If any of Katie Gallagher's Imperial Valleys were still operating up there, Kurtz hoped they would soon cease what they were doing and head for Canada. Raising their hands in the air and calling out *Il n'y a pas d'infec-*

tion ici wouldn't do them any good, certainly; that ploy had already been tried. And it was all so meaningless. In his heart of hearts, Kurtz knew Owen had been right about at least one thing: it was over up there. They could shut the barn door, praise God, but the horse had been stolen.

"They're going to close it down for good," Perlmutter said. "The Jefferson Tract just became the fifty-first state. And it's a police state."

"You can still key on Owen?"

"Yes," Perlmutter said absently. "But not for long. He's getting better, too. Losing the telepathy."

"Where is he, buck?"

"They just passed Exit 25. They might have fifteen miles on us. Not much more."

"Want me to punch it a little?" Freddy asked.

They had lost their chance to head Owen off because of the goddam semi. The last thing in the world Kurtz wanted was to lose another chance by skidding off the road.

"Negative," Kurtz said. "For the time being, I think we'll just lay back and let em run." He crossed his arms and looked out at the linen-white world passing by. But now the snow had stopped, and as they continued south, road conditions would doubtless improve.

It had been an eventful twenty-four hours. He had blown up an alien spacecraft, been betrayed by the man he had regarded as his logical successor, survived a mutiny and a civilian riot, and to top it all off, he had been relieved of his command by a sunshine soldier who had never heard a shot fired in anger. Kurtz's eyes slipped shut. After a few moments, he dozed.

18

Jonesy sat moodily behind his desk for quite awhile, sometimes looking at the phone which no longer worked, sometimes at the dreamcatcher which hung from the ceiling (it wafted in some barely felt air-current), sometimes at the new steel shutters with which that bastard Gray had blocked his vision. And always that low rumble, both in his ears and shivering his buttocks as he sat in his chair. It could have been a rather noisy furnace, one in need of servicing, but it wasn't. It was the plow, beating its way south and south and south. Mr. Gray behind the wheel, likely wearing a DPW cap stolen from his most recent victim, horsing the plow along, working the wheel with Jonesy's muscles, listening to developments on the plow's CB with Jonesy's ears.

So, Jonesy, how long you going to sit here feeling sorry for yourself?

Jonesy, who had been slumping in his seat—almost dozing, in fact—straightened up at that. Henry's voice. Not arriving telepathically—there were no voices now, Mr. Gray had blocked all but his own—but, rather, coming from his own mind. Nonetheless, it stung him.

I'm not feeling sorry for myself, I'm blocked off! Not liking the sulky, defensive quality of the thought; vocalized, it would no doubt have come out as a whine. *Can't call out, can't see out, can't go out. I don't know where you are, Henry, but I'm in a goddam isolation booth.*

Did he steal your brains?

"Shut up." Jonesy rubbed at his temple.

Did he take your memories?

No. Of course not. Even in here, with a double-locked door between him and those billions of labeled cartons, he could recall wiping a booger on the end of Bonnie Deal's braid in first grade (and then asking that same Bonnie to dance at the seventh-grade Harvest Hop six years later), watching carefully as Lamar Clarendon taught them to play the game (known as cribbage to the low and the uninitiated), seeing Rick McCarthy come out of the woods and thinking he was a deer. He could remember all those things. There might be an advantage in that, but Jonesy was damned if he knew what it was. Maybe because it was too big, too obvious.

To be stuck like this after all the mysteries you've read, his mind's version of Henry taunted him. *Not to mention all those science-fiction movies where the aliens arrive, everything from* The Day the Earth Stood Still *to* The Attack of the Killer Tomatoes. *All of that and you still can't figure this guy out? Can't follow his smoke down from the sky and see where he's camped?*

Jonesy rubbed harder at his temple. This wasn't ESP, it was his own mind, and why couldn't he shut it up? He was fucking *trapped,* so what difference did it make, anyway? He was a motor without a transmission, a cart without a horse; he was Donovan's Brain, kept alive in a tank of cloudy fluid and dreaming useless dreams.

What does he want? Start there.

Jonesy looked up at the dreamcatcher, dancing in the vague currents of warm air. Felt the rumble of the plow, strong enough to vibrate the pictures on the walls. Tina Jean Schlossinger, that had been her name, and supposedly there had been a picture of her in here, a picture of her holding her skirt up so you could see her pussy, and how many adolescent boys had been caught by such a dream?

Jonesy got up—almost leaped up—and began to pace around the office, limping only a little. The storm was over, and his hip hurt a bit less now.

Think like Hercule Poirot, he told himself. *Exercise those little gray cells. Never mind your memories for the time being, think about Mr. Gray. Think logically. What does he want?*

Jonesy stopped. What Gray wanted was obvious, really. He had gone to the Standpipe—where the Standpipe had been, anyway—because he wanted water. Not just any water; drinking water. But the Standpipe was gone, destroyed in the big blow of '85—ha, ha, Mr. Gray, gotcha last—and Derry's current water supply was north and east, probably not reachable because of the storm, and not concentrated in one place, anyway. So Mr. Gray had, after consulting Jonesy's available store of knowledge, turned south again. Toward—

Suddenly it was all clear. The strength ran out of his legs and he collapsed to the carpeted floor, ignoring the flare of pain in his hip.

The dog. Lad. Did he still have the dog?

"Of course he does," Jonesy whispered. "Of course the son of a bitch does, I can smell him even in here. Farting just like McCarthy."

This world was inimical to the byrus, and this world's inhabitants fought with a surprising vigor which arose from deep wells of emotion. Bad luck. But now the last surviving grayboy had had an unbroken chain of *good* luck; he was like some daffy in-the-zone Vegas crapshooter rolling a string of sevens: four, six, eight, oh goddam, a dozen in a row. He had found Jonesy, his Typhoid Mary, had invaded him and conquered him. He had found Pete, who had gotten him where he wanted to go after the flashlight—the kim—had given out. Next, Andy Janas, the Minnesota boy. He had been hauling the corpses of two deer killed by the Ripley. The deer had been useless to Mr. Gray . . . but Janas had also been hauling the decomposing body of one of the aliens.

Fruiting bodies, Jonesy thought randomly. *Fruiting bodies, what's that from?*

No matter. Because Mr. Gray's next seven had been the Dodge Ram, old Mr. I ♥ MY BORDER COLLIE. What had Gray done? Fed some of the gray's dead body to the dog? Put the dog's nose to the corpse and forced him to inhale of that fruiting body? No, eating was much more likely; c'mon, boy, chow time. Whatever process started the weasels, it began in the gut, not the lungs. Jonesy had a momentary image of McCarthy lost in the woods. Beaver had asked *What the hell have you been eating? Woodchuck turds?* And what had McCarthy replied? *Bushes . . . and things . . . I don't know just what . . . I was just so hungry, you know . . .*

Sure. Hungry. Lost, scared, and hungry. Not noticing the red splotches of byrus on the leaves of some of the bushes, the red speckles on the green moss he crammed into his mouth, gagging it down because somewhere back there in his tame oh-gosh oh-dear lawyer's life, he had read that you could eat moss if you were lost in the woods, that moss wouldn't hurt you. Did everyone who swallowed some of the byrus (grains of it, almost too small to be seen, floating in the air) incubate one of the vicious little monsters that had torn McCarthy apart and then killed the Beav? Probably not, no more than every woman who had unprotected sex got pregnant. But McCarthy had caught . . . and so had Lad.

"He knows about the cottage," Jonesy said.

Of course. The cottage in Ware, some sixty miles west of Boston. And he'd know the story of the Russian woman, everyone knew it; Jonesy had passed it on himself. It was too gruesomely good not to pass on. They knew it in Ware, in New Salem, in Cooleyville and Belchertown, Hardwick and Packardsville and Pelham. *All* the surrounding towns. And what, pray tell, did those towns surround?

Why, the Quabbin, that was what they surrounded. Quabbin Reservoir. The water supply for Boston and the adjacent metropolitan area. How many people drank their daily water from the Quabbin? Two million? Three? Jonesy didn't know for sure, but a lot more than had ever drunk from the supply stored in the Derry Standpipe. Mr. Gray, rolling seven after seven, a run for the ages and now only one away from breaking the bank.

Two or three million people. Mr. Gray wanted to introduce them to Lad the border collie, and to Lad's new friend.

And delivered in this new medium, the byrus would take.

CHAPTER TWENTY

THE CHASE ENDS

1

South and south and south.

By the time Mr. Gray passed the Gardiner exit, the first one below Augusta, the snow-cover on the ground was considerably less and the turnpike was slushy but two lanes wide again. It was time to trade the plow for something less conspicuous, partly because he no longer needed it, but also because Jonesy's arms were aching with the unaccustomed strain of controlling the oversized vehicle. Mr. Gray didn't care much for Jonesy's body (or so he told himself; in truth it was hard not to feel at least some affection for something capable of providing such unexpected pleasures as "bacon" and "murder"), but it *did* have to take him another couple of hundred miles. He suspected that Jonesy wasn't in very good shape for a man in the middle of his life. Part of that was the accident he'd been in, but it also had to do with his job. He was an "academic." As a result, he had pretty much ignored the more physical aspects of his life, which stunned Mr. Gray. These creatures were sixty percent emotion, thirty percent sensation, ten percent thought (and ten percent, Mr. Gray reflected, was probably on the generous side). To ignore the body the way Jonesy had seemed both willful and stupid to Mr. Gray. But, of course, that was not his problem. Nor Jonesy's, either. Not anymore. Now Jonesy was what he had apparently always wanted to be: nothing but mind. Judging from the way he'd reacted, he didn't actually care for that state much once he had attained it.

On the floor of the plow, where Lad lay in a litter of cigarette butts, cardboard coffee cups, and balled-up snack-wrappers, the dog whined in pain. Its body was grotesquely bloated, the torso the size of a water-barrel. Soon the dog would pass gas and its midsection would deflate again. Mr. Gray had established contact with the byrum growing inside the dog, and would hence regulate its gestation.

The dog would be his version of what his host thought of as "the Russian woman." And once the dog had been placed, his job would be done.

He reached behind him with his mind, feeling for the others. Henry and his friend Owen were entirely gone, like a radio station that has ceased to broadcast, and that was troubling. Farther behind (they were just passing the Newport exits, sixty or so miles north of Mr. Gray's current position), was a group of three with one clear contact: "Pearly." This Pearly, like the dog, was incubating a byrum, and Mr. Gray could receive him clearly.

He had also been receiving another of that group—
"Freddy"—but now "Freddy" was gone. The byrus on
him had died; "Pearly" said so.

Here was one of the green turnpike signs: REST AREA.
There was a Burger King here, which Jonesy's files
identified as both a "restaurant" and a "fast-food joint."
There would be bacon there, and his stomach gurgled
at the thought. Yes, it would be hard in many ways to
give this body up. It had its pleasures, definitely had its
pleasures. No time for bacon now, however; now it
was time to change vehicles. And he had to be fairly
unobtrusive about it.

This exit into the rest area split in two, with one
road for PASSENGER VEHICLES and one for TRUCKS AND
BUSES. Mr. Gray drove the big orange plow into the
parking lot for trucks (Jonesy's muscles trembling
with the strain of turning the big steering wheel), and
was delighted to see four other plows, practically
identical to his own, all parked together. He nosed
into a space at the end of the line and killed the
engine.

He felt for Jonesy. Jonesy was there, hunkered in
his perplexing safety zone. "What you up to, partner?" Mr. Gray murmured.

No answer . . . but he sensed Jonesy listening.

"What you doing?"

No answer still. And really, what *could* he be doing?
He was locked in and blind. Still, it would behoove him
not to forget Jonesy . . . Jonesy with his somehow
exciting suggestion that Mr. Gray forgo the imperative—the need to seed—and simply enjoy life on earth.

Every now and then a thought would occur to Mr. Gray, a letter pushed under the door from Jonesy's haven. This sort of thought, according to Jonesy's files, was a "slogan." Slogans were simple and to the point. The most recent said: BACON IS JUST THE BEGINNING. And Mr. Gray was sure that was true. Even in his hospital room (*what hospital room? what hospital? who is Marcy? who wants a shot?*), he understood that life here was very delicious. But the imperative was deep and unbreakable: he would seed this world and then die. And if he got to eat a little bacon along the way, why, so much the better.

"Who was Richie? Was he a Tiger? Why did you kill him?"

No answer. But Jonesy was listening. Very carefully. Mr. Gray *hated* having him in there. It was (the simile came from Jonesy's store) like having a tiny fishbone stuck in your throat. Not big enough to choke you, but plenty big enough to "bug" you.

"You annoy the shit out of me, Jonesy." Putting on his gloves now, the ones that had belonged to the owner of the Dodge Ram. The owner of Lad.

This time there was a reply. *The feeling is mutual, partner. So why don't you go someplace where you're wanted? Take your act and put it on the road?*

"Can't do that," Mr. Gray said. He extended a hand to the dog, and Lad sniffed gratefully at the scent of its master on the glove. Mr. Gray sent it a be-calm thought, then got out of the plow and began to walk toward the side of the restaurant. Around back would be the "employee's parking lot."

Henry and the other guy are right on top of you, asshole. Sniffing up your tailpipe. So relax. Spend as much time here as you want. Have a triple order of bacon.

"They can't feel me," Mr. Gray said, his breath puffing out in front of him (the sensation of the cold air in his mouth and throat and lungs was exquisite, invigorating—even the smells of gasoline and diesel fuel were wonderful). "If I can't feel them, they can't feel me."

Jonesy laughed—actually *laughed.* It stopped Mr. Gray in his tracks beside the Dumpster.

The rules have changed, my friend. They stopped for Duddits, and Duddits sees the line.

"I don't know what that means."

Of course you do, asshole.

"Stop calling me that!" Mr. Gray snapped.

If you stop insulting my intelligence, maybe I will.

Mr. Gray started walking again, and yes, here, around the corner, was a little clutch of cars, most of them old and battered.

Duddits sees the line.

He knew what it meant, all right; the one named Pete had possessed the same thing, the same *talent,* although likely not as strongly as this puzzling other, this Duddits.

Mr. Gray didn't like the idea of leaving a trail "Duddits" could see, but he knew something Jonesy didn't. "Pearly" believed that Henry, Owen, and Duddits were only fifteen miles south of Pearly's own position. If that was indeed the case, Henry and Owen were forty-five miles back, somewhere between Pittsfield and Waterville. Mr. Gray didn't believe that actually qualified as "sniffing up one's tailpipe."

Still, it would not do to linger here.

The back door of the restaurant opened. A young man in a uniform the Jonesy-files identified as "cook's whites" came out carrying two large bags of garbage, clearly bound for the Dumpsters. This young man's name was John, but his friends called him "Butch." Mr. Gray thought it would be enjoyable to kill him, but "Butch" looked a good deal stronger than Jonesy, not to mention younger and probably much quicker. Also, murder had annoying side effects, the worst being how quickly it rendered a stolen car useless.

Hey, Butch.

Butch stopped, looking at him alertly.

Which car is yours?

Actually, it wasn't his but his mother's, and that was good. Butch's own rustbucket was back home, victim of a dead battery. He had his Mom's unit, an all-wheel-drive Subaru. Mr. Gray, Jonesy would have said, had just rolled another seven.

Butch handed over the keys willingly enough. He still looked alert ("bright-eyed and bushy-tailed" was how Jonesy put it, although the young cook had no tail Mr. Gray could see), but his consciousness was gone. "Out on his feet," Jonesy thought.

You won't remember this, Mr. Gray said.

"No," Butch agreed.

Just back to work.

"You bet," Butch agreed. He picked up his bags of garbage and headed for the Dumpsters again. By the time his shift was over and he realized his mother's car was gone, all this would likely be over.

Mr. Gray unlocked the red Subaru and got in. There was half a bag of barbecue potato chips on the seat. Mr. Gray gobbled them greedily as he drove back to the plow. He finished by licking Jonesy's fingers. Greasy. Good. Like the bacon. He got the dog. Five minutes later he was on the turnpike again.

South and south and south.

2

The night roars with music and laughter and loud voices; the air is big with the smell of grilled hot dogs, chocolate, roasted peanuts; the sky blooms with colored fire. Binding it all together, identifying it, signing it like summer's own autograph, is an amplified rock-and-roll song from the speakers that have been set up in Strawford Park:

> *Hey pretty baby take a ride with me,*
> *We're goin down to Alabama on the C&C.*

And here comes the tallest cowboy in the world, a nine-foot Pecos Bill under the burning sky, towering over the crowd, little kids with their ice cream–smeared mouths dropped open in wonder, their eyes wide; laughing parents hold them up or put them on their shoulders so they can see better. In one hand Pecos Bill waves his hat; in the other a banner which reads DERRY DAYS 1981.

We're gonna walk the tracks, stay up all night,
If we get a little bored, then we'll have a little fight.

"Ow eee-oh all?" Duddits asks. He has a cone of blue cotton candy in one hand, but it is forgotten; as he watches the stilt-walking cowboy pass under the burning fireworks sky, his eyes are as wide as any three-year-old's. Standing on one side of Duddits are Pete and Jonesy; on the other are Henry and the Beav. Behind the cowboy comes a retinue of vestal virgins (surely *some* of them are still virgins, even in this year of grace 1981) in spangly cowboy skirts and white cowboy boots, tossing the batons that won the West.

"Don't know *how* he can be so tall, Duds," Pete says, laughing. He yanks a hank of blue floss from the cone in Duddits's hand and tucks it into Duddits's amazed mouth. "Must be magic."

They all laugh at how Duddits chews without even taking his eyes from the cowpoke on stilts. Duds is taller than all of them now, even taller than Henry. But he's still just a kid, and he makes them all happy. Magic is what he is; he won't find Josie Rinkenhauer for another year, but they know—he's fuckin magic. It was scary going up against Richie Grenadeau and his friends, but that was still the luckiest day of their lives—they all think so.

Don't say no, baby, come with me
We're gonna take a little ride on the C&C.

"Hey, Tex!" Beaver shouts, waving his own lid (a Derry Tigers baseball hat) up at the tall cowboy. "Kiss my bender, big boy! I mean, sit on it and *spin*!"

And they're all killing themselves laughing (it is a memory for the ages, all right, the night Beaver ranked on the stilt-walking cowboy in the Derry Days Parade beneath that burning gunpowder sky), all but Duddits, who is staring with that expression of stoned wonder, and Owen Underhill (*Owen!* Henry thinks, *how did you get here, buddy?*), who looks worried.

Owen is shaking him, Owen is once more telling him to wake up, Henry, wake up, wake

3

up, for God's sake!"

It was the fright in Owen's voice that finally roused Henry from his dream. For a moment he could still smell peanuts and Duddits's cotton candy. Then the world came back in: white sky, snow-covered turnpike lanes, a green sign reading AUGUSTA NEXT TWO EXITS. Also Owen shaking him, and from behind them a barking sound, hoarse and desperate. Duddits coughing.

"Wake up, Henry, he's *bleeding*! Will you please wake the fuck—"

"I'm awake, I'm awake."

He unbuckled his seatbelt, twisted around, got up on his knees. The overstrained muscles in his thighs shrieked in protest, but Henry paid no attention.

It was better than he expected. From the panic in

Owen's voice, he had expected some sort of hemorrhage, but it was just a trickle from one nostril and a fine spray of blood from Duddits's mouth when he coughed. Owen had probably thought poor old Duds was coughing up his lungs, when in fact he'd probably strained something in his throat. Not that this wasn't potentially serious. In Duddits's increasingly fragile condition, anything was potentially serious; a random cold-germ could kill him. From the moment he'd seen him, Henry had known Duds was coming out of the last turn and heading for home.

"Duds!" he called sharply. Something different. Something different in *him,* Henry. What? No time to think about it now. "Duddits, breathe in through your nose! Your *nose,* Duds! Like this!"

Henry demonstrated, taking big breaths through flared nostrils . . . and when he exhaled, little threads of white flew from his nostrils. Like the fluff in milkweed pods, or dandelions gone to seed. *Byrus,* Henry thought. *It was growing up my nose, but now it's dead. I'm sloughing it off, literally breath by breath.* And then he understood the difference: the itching had stopped, in his leg and in his mouth and in the thatch of his groin. His mouth still tasted as if it had been lined with someone's old carpet, but it didn't itch.

Duddits began to imitate him, breathing deep through his nose, and his coughing began to ease as soon as it did. Henry took his paper bag, found a bottle of harmless no-alcohol cough medicine, and poured Duddits a capful. "This'll take care of you," Henry said. Confidence in the thought as well as the words; with Duddits, how you sounded was only part of it.

Duddits drank the capful of Robitussin, grimaced, then smiled at Henry. The coughing had stopped, but blood was still trickling from one nostril . . . and from the corner of one eye as well, Henry saw. Not good. Nor was Duddits's extreme pallor, much more noticeable than it had been at the house back in Derry. The cold . . . his lost night's sleep . . . all this untoward excitement in someone who was an invalid . . . not good. He was getting sick, and in a late-stage ALL patient, even a nasal infection could be fatal.

"He all right?" Owen asked.

"Duds? Duds is iron. Right, Duddits?"

"I ion," Duddits agreed, and flexed one woefully skinny arm. The sight of his face—thin and tired but still trying to smile—made Henry feel like screaming. Life was unfair; that was something he supposed he'd known for years. But this went far beyond unfair. This was monstrous.

"Let's see what she put in here for good boys to drink." Henry took the yellow lunchbox.

"Oooby-Doo," Duddits said. He was smiling, but his voice sounded thin and exhausted.

"Yep, got some work to do now," Henry agreed, and opened the Thermos. He gave Duds his morning Prednisone tablet, although it hadn't yet gone eight, and then asked Duddits if he wanted a Percocet, as well. Duddits thought about it, then held up two fingers. Henry's heart sank.

"Pretty bad, huh?" he asked, passing Duddits a

couple of Percocet tablets over the seat between them. He hardly needed an answer—people like Duddits didn't ask for the extra pill so they could get high.

Duddits made a seesawing gesture with his hand—*comme ci, comme ça.* Henry remembered it well, that seesawing hand as much a part of Pete as the chewed pencils and toothpicks were of Beaver.

Roberta had filled Duddits's Thermos with chocolate milk, his favorite. Henry poured him a cup, held it a moment as the Humvee skidded on a slick patch, then handed it over. Duddits took his pills.

"Where does it hurt, Duds?"

"Here." Hand to the throat. "More here." Hand to the chest. Hesitating, coloring a little, then a hand to his crotch. "Here, ooo."

A urinary-tract infection, Henry thought. *Oh, goody.*

"Ills ake ee etter?"

Henry nodded. "Pills'll make you better. Just give em a chance to work. Are we still on the line, Duddits?"

Duddits nodded emphatically and pointed through the windshield. Henry wondered (not for the first time) just what he saw. Once he'd asked Pete, who told him it was something like a thread, often faint and hard to see. *It's best when it's yellow,* Pete had said. *Yellow's always easier to pick up. I don't know why.* And if Pete saw a yellow thread, perhaps Duddits saw something like a broad yellow stripe, perhaps even Dorothy's yellow brick road.

"If it goes off on another road, you tell us, okay?"

"I tell."

"Not going to go to sleep, are you?"

Duddits shook his head. In fact he had never looked more alive and awake, his eyes glowing in his exhausted face. Henry thought of how lightbulbs would sometimes go mysteriously bright before burning out for good.

"If you *do* start to get sleepy, you tell me and we'll pull over. Get you some coffee. We need you awake."

"O-ay."

Henry started to turn around, moving his aching body with as much care as he could muster, when Duddits said something else.

"Isser Ay ont aykin."

"Does he, now?" Henry said thoughtfully.

"What?" Owen asked. "I didn't get that one."

"He says Mr. Gray wants bacon."

"Is that important?"

"I don't know. Is there a regular radio in this heap, Owen? I'd like to get some news."

The regular radio was hanging under the dash, and looked freshly installed. Not part of the original equipment. Owen reached for it, then hit the brakes as a Pontiac sedan—two-wheel drive and no snow-tires—cut in front of them. The Pontiac slued from side to side, finally decided to stay on the road a little longer, and squirted ahead. Soon it was doing at least sixty, Henry estimated, and was pulling away. Owen was frowning after it.

"You driver, me passenger," Henry said, "but if that guy can do it with no snows, why can't we? It might be a good idea to make up some ground."

"Hummers are better in mud than snow. Take my word for it."

"Still—"

"Also, we're going to pass that guy in the next ten minutes. I'll bet you a quart of good Scotch. He'll either be through the guardrails and down the embankment or spun out on the median. If he's lucky, he'll be right-side up. Plus—this is just a technicality—we're fugitives running from duly constituted authority, and we can't save the world if we're locked up in some County . . . *Jesus!*"

A Ford Explorer—four-wheel drive but moving far too fast for the conditions, maybe seventy miles an hour—roared past them, pulling a rooster-tail of snow. The roof-rack had been piled high and covered with a blue tarp. This had been indifferently lashed down, and Henry could see what was beneath: luggage. He guessed that much of it would soon be in the road.

With Duddits seen to, Henry took a clear-eyed look at the highway. What he saw did not exactly surprise him. Although the turnpike's northern barrel was still all but deserted, the southbound lanes were now filling up fast . . . and yes, there were cars off it everywhere.

Owen turned on the radio as a Mercedes hurried past him, throwing up fans of slush. He hit SEEK, found classical music, hit it again, found Kenny G tootling away, hit it a third time . . . and happened on a voice.

". . . great big fucking bomber joint," the voice

said, and Henry exchanged a glance with Owen.

"He say uck onna rayo," Duddits observed from the back seat.

"That's right," Henry said, and, as the owner of the voice inhaled audibly into the mike: "Also, I'd say he's smoking a fatty."

"I doubt if the FCC'd be in favor," the deejay said after a long and noisy exhale, "but if half of what I'm hearin is true, the FCC is the least of my worries. Interstellar plague on the loose, brothers and sisters, that's the word. Call it the Hot Zone, the Dead Zone, or the Twilight Zone, you want to cancel your trip up north."

Another long and noisy inhale.

"Marvin the Martian's on the march, brothers and sisters, that's the word from Somerset County and Castle County. Plague, deathrays, the living will envy the dead. I got a spot here for Century Tire, but fuck that shit." Sound of something breaking. Plastic, from the sound. Henry listened, fascinated. Here it was once more, here was darkness his old friend, not in his head but on the goddam *radio*. "Brethren and sistern, if you're north of Augusta right now, here's a little tip from your pal Lonesome Dave at WWVE: relocate south. Like, *immediately*. And here's a little relocation music."

Lonesome Dave at WWVE spun The Doors, of course. Jim Morrison droning "The End." Owen switched to the AM band.

Eventually he found a newscast. The fellow giving it didn't sound wrecked, which was a step forward, and he said there was no need to panic, which was another step forward. He then played sound-bites from both the

President and Maine's Governor, both saying essentially the same thing: take it easy, people, chill. It's all under control. Nice soothing stuff, Robitussin for the body politic. The President was scheduled to make a complete report to the American people at eleven A.M., EST.

"It'll be the speech Kurtz told me about," Owen said. "Just moved up a day or so."

"What speech is—"

"Shhh." Owen pointed to the radio.

Having soothed, the newscaster next proceeded to stir his listeners up again by repeating many of the rumors they had already heard from the stoned FM jock, only in politer language: plague, non-human invaders from space, deathrays. Then the weather: snow showers, followed by rain and gusty winds as a warm front (not to mention the killer Martians) moved in. There was a *meee-eep,* and then the newscast they'd just heard began playing again.

"Ook!" Duddits said. "Ey ent eye us, ember?" He was pointing through the dirty window. The pointing finger, like Duddits's voice, wouldn't hold steady. He was shivering now, his teeth clittering together.

Owen glanced briefly at the Pontiac—it had indeed ended up on the snowy median strip between the northbound and southbound barrels, and although it hadn't rolled all the way over, it was on its side with its disconsolate passengers standing around it—and then looked back at Duddits. Paler than ever now, shivering, a blood-streaked fluff of cotton protruding from one nostril.

"Henry, is he all right?"

"I don't know."

"Run out your tongue."

"Don't you think you better keep your eyes on—"

"I'm fine, so don't sass me. Run out your tongue."

Henry did. Owen looked at it and grimaced. "Looks worse, but it's probably better. All that crap has turned white."

"Same with the gash on my leg. Same with your face and eyebrows. We're just lucky we didn't get it in the lungs or the brain or the gut." He paused. "Perlmutter got it in the gut. He's growing one of those things."

"How far back are they, Henry?"

"I'd say twenty miles. Maybe a little less. So if you could goose it . . . even if just a little . . ."

Owen did, knowing that Kurtz would, as soon as he realized he was now part of a general exodus and much less likely to become a target of either the civilian or the military police.

"You're still in touch with Pearly," Owen said. "Even though the byrus is dying on you, you're still hooked up. Is it . . ." He lifted a thumb to the back seat, where Duddits was leaning back. His shakes had eased, at least for the time being.

"Sure," Henry said. "I had stuff from Duddits long before all this happened. Jonesy, Pete, and Beaver did, too. We hardly noticed. It was just a part of our lives." *Sure, that's right. Like all those thoughts about plastic bags and bridge abutments, and shotguns. Just a part of my life.* "Now it's stronger. Maybe in time it'll drop back, but for now . . ." He shrugged. "For now I hear voices."

"Pearly."

"For one," Henry agreed. "Others with the byrus in its active stage, too. Mostly behind us."

"Jonesy? Your friend Jonesy? Or Gray?"

Henry shook his head. "But *Pearly* hears something."

"Pearly—? How can *he*—"

"He's got more mental range than I do right now, because of the byrum—"

"The what?"

"The thing that's up his ass," Henry said. "The shit-weasel."

"Oh." Owen felt momentarily sick to his stomach.

"What he hears doesn't seem to be human. I don't think it's Mr. Gray, but I suppose it might be. Whatever it is, he's homing on it."

They drove in silence for awhile. The traffic was moderately heavy and some of the drivers were wild (they passed the Explorer just south of Augusta, ditched and apparently abandoned with its load of luggage spread around it), but Owen counted himself lucky. The storm had kept plenty of folks off the road, he guessed. They might decide to flee now that the storm had stopped, but he and Owen had gotten ahead of the worst of the wave. In many ways, the storm had been their friend.

"I want you to know something," Owen said finally.

"You don't need to say it. You're sitting right next to me—short range—and I'm still getting some of your thoughts."

What Owen was thinking was that he would pull

the Humvee over and get out, if he thought the pursuit would end once Kurtz had him. Owen did not, in fact, believe that. Owen Underhill was Kurtz's prime objective, but he understood that Owen wouldn't have committed such a monstrous act of treason had he not been coerced into it. No, he'd put a bullet in Owen's head, and then continue on. With Owen, Henry had at least some chance. Without him, he'd likely be a dead duck. And Duddits too.

"We stay together," Henry said. "Friends to the end, as the saying goes."

And, from the back seat: "Otsum urk ooo do now."

"That's right, Duds." Henry reached back and briefly squeezed Duddits's cold hand. "Got some work to do now."

4

Ten minutes later, Duddits came fully to life, pointing them into the first turnpike rest area below Augusta. They were almost to Lewiston now, in fact. "Ine! *Ine!*" he shouted, then began to cough again.

"Take it easy, Duddits," Henry said.

"They probably stopped for coffee and a Danish." Owen said. "Or maybe a bacon sandwich."

But Duddits directed them around back, to the employees' parking lot. Here they stopped, and Duddits got out. He stood quiet and muttering for a moment or so, looking frail under the cloudy sky and seemingly buffeted by every gust of wind.

"Henry," Owen said, "I don't know what bee he's

got in his bonnet, but if Kurtz is really close—"

But then Duddits nodded, got back in the Hummer, and pointed toward the exit sign. He looked more tired than ever, but he also looked satisfied.

"What in God's name was *that* all about?" Owen asked, mystified.

"I think he switched cars," Henry said. "Is that what he did, Duddits? Did he switch cars?"

Duddits nodded emphatically. "*Tole!* Tole! a car!"

"He'll be moving faster now," Henry said. "You've got to step it up, Owen. Never mind Kurtz—we've got to catch Mr. Gray."

Owen looked over at Henry . . . then looked again. "What's wrong with you? You've come over all pale."

"I've been very stupid—I should have known what the bastard was up to from the first. My only excuses are being tired and scared, and none of that will matter if . . . Owen, you *have* to catch him. He's headed for western Massachusetts, and you have to catch him before he can get there."

Now they were running in slush, and the going was messy but far less dangerous. Owen walked the Hummer up to sixty-five, all he dared for now.

"I'll try," he said. "But unless he has an accident or a breakdown . . ." Owen shook his head slowly back and forth. "I don't think so, pal. I really don't."

5

This was a dream he'd had often as a child (when his name had been Coonts), but only once or twice since the squirts and sweats of adolescence. In it, he was running through a field under a harvest moon and afraid to look behind him because it was after him, *it*. He ran as hard as he could but of course that wasn't good enough, in dreams your best never is. Then it was close enough for him to hear its dry breathing, and to smell its peculiar dry smell.

He came to the shore of a great still lake, although there had never been any lakes in the dry and miserable Kansas town of his childhood, and although it was very beautiful (the moon burned in its depths like a lamp), it terrified him because it blocked his way and he could not swim.

He fell on his knees at the shore of the lake—in that way this dream was exactly like those childhood dreams—but instead of seeing the reflection of *it* in the still water, the terrible scarecrow man with his stuffed burlap head and pudgy blue-gloved hands, this time he saw Owen Underhill, his face covered with splotches. In the moonlight, the byrus looked like great black moles, spongy and shapeless.

As a child he had always wakened at this point (often with his stiff wang wagging, although why such an awful dream would give a kid a stiffy God alone knew), but this time the *it*—Owen—actually *touched* him, the reflected eyes in the water reproachful. Maybe questioning.

Because you disobeyed orders, buck! Because you crossed the line!

He raised his hand to ward Owen off, to remove

that hand . . . and saw his own hand in the moon-glow. It was *gray.*

No, he told himself, *that's just the moonlight.*

Only three fingers, though—was *that* the moon-light?

Owen's hand on him, touching him, passing on his filthy disease . . . and still daring to call him

6

boss. Wake up, boss!"

Kurtz opened his eyes and sat up with a grunt, simultaneously pushing Freddy's hand away. On his knee instead of his shoulder, Freddy reaching back from his place behind the wheel and shaking his knee, but still intolerable.

"I'm awake, I'm awake." He held his own hands up in front of his face to prove it. Not baby-pink, they were a long way from that, but they weren't gray and each had the requisite five fingers.

"What time is it, Freddy?"

"Don't know, boss—still morning's all I can say for sure."

Of course. Clocks all fucked up. Even his pocket-watch had run down. As much a victim of modern times as anyone else, he had forgotten to wind it. To Kurtz, whose time sense had always been at least fairly sharp, it felt like about nine, which would mean he'd gotten about two hours of shuteye. Not much, but he didn't need much. He felt better. Well enough, cer-tainly, to hear the concern in Freddy's voice.

"What's up, bucko?"

"Pearly says he's lost contact with all of them now. He says Owen was the last, and now he's gone, too. He says Owen must have beat back the Ripley fungus, sir."

Kurtz caught sight of Perlmutter's sunken, I-fooled-you grin in the wide rearview mirror.

"What's the deal, Archie?"

"No deal," Pearly said, sounding considerably more lucid than before Kurtz's nap. "I . . . boss, I *could* use a drink of water. I'm not hungry, but—"

"We could stop for water, I guess," Kurtz allowed. "If we had a contact, that is. But if we've lost *all* of them—this guy Jones as well as Owen and Devlin—well, you know how I am, buck. I'll bite when I die, and it'll take two surgeons and a shotgun to get me to let go even then. You're going to have a long and thirsty day sitting there while Freddy and I course the southbound roads, looking for a trace of them . . . unless you can help out. You do that, Archie, and I'll order Freddy to pull off at the next exit. I will personally trot into the Stop n Go or Seven-Eleven and buy you the biggest bottle of Poland Spring water in the cooler. How does that sound?"

It sounded good, Kurtz could tell that just by the way Perlmutter first smacked his lips and then ran his tongue out to wet them (on Perlmutter's lips and cheeks the Ripley was still full and rich, most patches the color of strawberries, some as dark as burgundy wine), but that sly look had come back. His eyes, rimmed with crusts of Ripley, darted from side to side.

And all at once Kurtz understood the picture he was looking at. Pearly had gone crazy, God love him. Perhaps it took one to know one.

"I told him the God's truth. I'm out of touch with all of them now." But then Archie laid his finger alongside his nose and looked slyly up into the mirror again.

"We catch them, I think there's a good chance we can get you cured up, laddie." Kurtz said this in his driest just-making-my-report voice. "Now which of them are you still in touch with? Jonesy? Or is it the new one? Duddits?" What Kurtz actually said was "Dud-Duts."

"Not him. None of *them*." But still the finger by the nose, still the sly look.

"Tell me and you get water," Kurtz said. "Continue to yank my crank, soldier, and I will put a bullet in you and roll you out into the snow. Now you go on and read my mind and tell me that's not so."

Pearly looked at him sulkily in the rearview a moment longer and then said, "Jonesy and Mr. Gray are still on the turnpike. They're down around Portland, now. Jonesy told Mr. Gray how to go around the city on 295. Only it isn't like telling. Mr. Gray is in his head, and when he wants something, I think he just takes it."

Kurtz listened to this with mounting awe, all the time calculating.

"There's a dog," Pearly said. "They have a dog with them. His name is Lad. He's the one I'm in contact with. He's . . . like me." His eyes met Kurtz's again in the mirror, only this time the slyness was gone. In its place was a miserable half-sanity. "Do you think there's really a chance I could be . . . you know . . . myself again?"

Knowing that Perlmutter could see into his mind made Kurtz proceed cautiously. "I think there's a chance you could be delivered of your burden, at least. With a doctor in attendance who understands the situation? Yes, I think that could be. A big whiff of chloro, and when you wake up . . . poof." Kurtz kissed the ends of his fingers, then turned to Freddy. "If they're in Portland, what's their lead on us?"

"Maybe seventy miles, boss."

"Then step it up a little, praise Jesus. Don't put us in the ditch, but step it up." Seventy miles. And if Owen and Devlin and "Dud-Duts" knew what Archie Perlmutter knew, they were still on track.

"Let me get this straight, Archie. Mr. Gray is in Jonesy—"

"Yes—"

"And they have a dog with them that can read their minds?"

"The dog hears their thoughts, but he doesn't understand them. He's still only a dog. Boss, I'm thirsty."

He's listening to the dog like it's a fucking radio, Kurtz marvelled.

"Freddy, next exit. Drinks all around." He resented having to make a pit-stop—resented losing even a couple of miles on Owen—but he needed Perlmutter. Happy, if possible.

Up ahead was the rest area where Mr. Gray had traded his plow for the cook's Subaru, where Owen and Henry had also briefly pulled in because the line went in there. The parking lot was crammed, but among the three of them they had enough change for the vending machines out front.

Praise God.

7

Whatever the triumphs and failures of the so-called "Florida Presidency" (that record is in large part still unwritten), there will always be this: he put an end to the Space Scare with his speech that November morning.

There were differing views on why the speech worked ("It wasn't leadership, it was timing," one critic sniffed), but it *did* work. Hungry for hard information, people who were already on the run pulled off the highway to see the President speak. Appliance stores in malls filled up with crowds of silent, staring people. At the food-fuel stops along I-95, the counters shut down. TVs were placed beside the quiet cash-registers. Bars filled up. In many places, people threw their homes open to others who wanted to watch the speech. They could have listened on their car radios (as Jonesy and Mr. Gray did) and kept on trucking, but only a minority did. Most people wanted to see the leader's face. According to the President's detractors, the speech did nothing but break the momentum of the panic—"Porky Pig could have given a speech at that particular time and gotten that particular result," one of them opined. Another took a different view. "It was a pivotal moment in the crisis," this fellow said. "There were maybe six thousand people on the road. If the President had said the wrong thing, there would have been sixty thousand by two in the afternoon and maybe six hundred thousand by the time the wave hit New York—the biggest wave of DPs since the Dust Bowl. The American people, especially those in New England, came to their narrowly elected leader for help . . . for comfort and reassurance. He responded with what may have been the greatest my fellow-Americans speech of all time. Simple as that."

Simple or not, sociology or great leadership, the speech was about what Owen and Henry had expected . . . and Kurtz could have predicted every word and turn. At the center were two simple ideas, both presented as absolute facts and both calculated to soothe the terror which beat that morning in the ordinarily complacent American breast. The first idea was that, while they had not come waving olive branches and handing out free introductory gifts, the newcomers had evinced absolutely no signs of aggressive or hostile behavior. The second was that, while they had brought some sort of virus with them, it had been contained within the Jefferson Tract (the President pointed it out on a Chroma-Key green-screen as adeptly as any weatherman pointing out a low-pressure system). And even there it was dying, with absolutely no help from the scientists and military experts who were on the scene.

"While we cannot say for sure at this juncture," the President told his breathless watchers (those who found themselves at the New England end of the Northeast Corridor were, perhaps understandably, the most breathless of all), "we believe that our visitors brought this virus with them much as travelers from abroad may bring certain insects into their country of origin in their luggage or on the produce they've purchased. This is something customs officials look for, but of course"—big smile from Great White Father—"our recent visitors did not pass through a customs checkpoint."

Yes, a few people had succumbed to the virus. Most were military personnel. The great majority of those who contracted it ("a fungal growth not unlike athlete's foot," said the Great White Father) beat it quite easily on their own. A quarantine had been imposed around the area, but the people outside that zone were in no danger, repeat, no danger. "If you are in Maine and have left your homes," said the President, "I suggest you return. In the words of Franklin Delano Roosevelt, we have nothing to fear but fear itself."

Nothing about the slaughter of the grayboys, the blown ship, the interred hunters, the fire at Gosselin's, or the breakout. Nothing about the last of Gallagher's Imperial Valleys being hunted down like dogs (they *were* dogs, in the view of many; worse than dogs). Nothing about Kurtz and not a whisper about Typhoid Jonesy. The President gave them just enough to break the back of the panic before it surged out of control.

Most people followed his advice and went home.

For some, of course, this was impossible.

For some, home had been cancelled.

8

The little parade moved south under dark skies, led by the rusty red Subaru that Marie Turgeon of Litchfield would never see again. Henry, Owen, and Duddits were fifty-five miles, or about fifty minutes, behind. Pulling out of the Mile 81 rest area (Pearly was greedily glugging down his second bottle of Naya water by the time they rejoined the traffic flow), Kurtz and his men were roughly seventy-five miles behind Jonesy and Mr. Gray, twenty miles behind Kurtz's prime quarry.

If not for the cloud cover, a spotter in a low-flying plane might have been able to see all three at the same time, the Subaru and both Humvees, at 11:43 EST, when the President finished his speech by saying, "God bless you, my fellow Americans, and God bless America."

Jonesy and Mr. Gray were crossing the Kittery-Portsmouth bridge into New Hampshire; Henry, Owen, and Duddits were passing Exit 9, which gives access to the communities of Falmouth, Cumberland, and Jerusalem's Lot; Kurtz, Freddy, and Perlmutter (Perlmutter's belly was swelling again; he lay back groaning and passing noxious gas, perhaps a kind of critical comment on the Great White Father's speech) were near the Bowdoinham exit of 295, not far north of Brunswick. All three vehicles would have been easy enough to pick out because so many people had pulled in somewhere to watch the President give his soothing, Chroma-Key-aided lecture.

Drawing on Jonesy's admirably organized memories, Mr. Gray left 95 for 495 just after crossing over the New Hampshire–Massachusetts border . . . and directed by Duddits, who saw Jonesy's passage as a bright yellow line, the lead Humvee would follow. At the town of Marlborough, Mr. Gray would leave 495 for I-90, one of America's major east–west highways. In the Bay State this road is known as the Mass Pike. Exit 8, according to Jonesy, was marked Palmer, UMass, Amherst, and Ware. Six miles beyond Ware was the Quabbin.

Shaft 12 was what he wanted; Jonesy said so, and Jonesy couldn't lie, much as he might have liked to. There was a Massachusetts Water Authority office at the Winsor Dam, on the south end of the Quabbin Reservoir. Jonesy could get him that far, and then Mr. Gray would do the rest.

9

Jonesy couldn't sit behind the desk anymore—if he did, he'd start to blubber. From blubbering he would no doubt progress to gibbering, from gibbering to yammering, and once he started to yammer, he'd probably be out and rushing into Mr. Gray's arms, totally bonkers and ready to be extinguished.

Where are we now, anyway? he wondered. *Marlborough yet? Leaving 495 for 90? That sounds about right.*

Not that there was any way to tell for sure, with his window shuttered. Jonesy looked at the window . . . and grinned in spite of himself. Had to. GIVE UP COME OUT had been replaced with what he'd been thinking of: SURRENDER DOROTHY. .

I did that, he thought, *and I bet I could make the goddam shutters vanish, if I wanted to.*

And so what? Mr. Gray would put up another set, or maybe just slop some black paint on the glass. If he didn't want Jonesy looking out, Jonesy would stay blind. The point was, Mr. Gray controlled the outside part of him. Mr. Gray's head had exploded, he'd sporulated right in front of Jonesy's eyes—Dr. Jekyll turns into Mr. Byrus—and Jonesy had inhaled him. Now Mr. Gray was . . .

He's a pain, Jonesy thought. *Mr. Gray is the pain in my brain.*

Something tried to protest this view, and he actually had a coherent dissenting thought—*No, you've got it all backward, you were the one who got out, who escaped*—but he pushed it away. That was pseudo-intuitive bullshit, a cognitive hallucination, not much different than a thirsty man seeing a nonexistent oasis in the desert. He was locked in here. Mr. Gray was out there, eating bacon and ruling the roost. If Jonesy allowed himself to think differently, he'd be an April Fool in November.

Got to slow him down. If I can't stop him, is there a way I can at least throw a monkeywrench into the works?

He got up and began to walk around the edge of the office. It was thirty-four paces. Hell of a short roundtrip. Still, he supposed, it was bigger than your average jail cell; guys in Walpole or Danvers or Shawshank would think this was the cat's ass. In the middle of the room, the dreamcatcher danced and turned. One part of Jonesy's mind counted paces; the other wondered how close they were getting to Exit 8 of the Mass Pike.

Thirty-one, thirty-two, thirty-three, thirty-four. And here he was, back behind his chair again. Time for Round Two.

They'd be in Ware soon enough . . . not that they'd stop there. Unlike the Russian woman, Mr. Gray knew exactly where he wanted to go.

Thirty-two, thirty-three, thirty-four, thirty-five, thirty-six. Behind his chair again and ready for another spin.

He and Carla had had three children by the time they turned thirty (number four had come less than a year ago), and neither of them had expected to own a summer cottage, not even a modest one like the place on Osborne Road in North Ware, any time soon. Then there had been a seismic shift in Jonesy's department. A good friend had assumed the chairmanship, and Jonesy had found himself an associate professor at least three years earlier than his most optimistic expectations. The salary bump had been considerable.

Thirty-five, thirty-six, thirty-seven, thirty-eight, and behind his chair again. This was good. It was pacing the cell, no more than that, but it was calming him.

That same year, Carla's grandmother had passed away, and there had been a considerable estate, settled between Carla and her sister, as the close blood kin in the intervening generation had died. So they got the cottage, and that first summer they'd taken the kids up to the Winsor Dam. From there they'd gone on one of the regularly scheduled summer tours. Their guide, an MWA employee in a forest-green uniform, had told them the area around the Quabbin Reservoir was called "the accidental wilderness," and had become the major nesting area for eagles in Massachusetts. (John and Misha, the older kids, had hoped to see an eagle or two, but they had been disappointed.) The Reservoir had been formed in the thirties by flooding three farming communities, each with its own little market-town. At that time the land surrounding the new lake had been tame. In the sixty or so years since, it had returned to what all of New England must have been like before the tillage and industry began midway through the seventeenth century. A tangle of rutted, unpaved roads ran up the east side of the lake—one of the purest reservoirs in North America, their guide had told them—but that was it. If you wanted to go much beyond Shaft 12 on the East Branch, you'd need your hiking shoes. That was what the guide said. Lorrington, his name had been.

There had been maybe a dozen other people on the tour, and by then they had been about back to their starting place again. Standing on the edge of the road which ran across Winsor Dam, looking north at the Reservoir (the Quabbin bright blue in the sunlight, sparkling with a million points of light, Joey fast asleep in the Papoose carrier on Jonesy's back). Lorrington had been wrapping up his spiel, just about to wish them a nice day, when some guy in a Rutgers sweat-shirt had raised his hand like a school kid and said: *Shaft 12. Isn't that where the Russian woman . . . ?*

Thirty-eight, thirty-nine, forty, forty-one, and back to the desk chair. Counting without really thinking about the numbers, something he did all the time. Carla said it was a sign of obsessive-compulsive disor-der. Jonesy didn't know about that, but he knew that the counting was soothing him, and so he set off on another round.

Lorrington's mouth had tightened at the words "Russian woman." Not part of the lecture, appar-ently; not part of the good vibes the Water Authority wanted visitors to take with them. Depending upon which municipal pipes it flowed through during the last eight or ten miles of its journey, Boston tap water could be the purest, best tap water in the world: *that* was the gospel they wanted to spread.

I really don't know much about that, sir, Lorrington had said, and Jonesy had thought: *My goodness, I think our guide just told a wittle fibby-wibby.*

Forty-one, forty-two, forty-three, back behind the chair and ready to start around again. Walking a little faster now. Hands clasped behind his back like a ship's cap-tain pacing the foredeck . . . or pacing the brig after a successful mutiny. He supposed that was really more like it.

Jonesy had been a history teacher most of his life, and curiosity came as second nature. He had gone to the library one day later that week, had looked for the story in the local paper, and had eventually found it. It had been brief and dry—there were stories about lawn-parties inside that had more detail and color—but their postman had known more and had been happy to share. Old Mr. Beckwith. Jonesy still remembered his final words before he'd put his blue-and-white mail-truck back in gear and rolled on down Osborne Road to the next rural box; there was a lot of mail to be delivered on the south end of the lake in summertime. Jonesy had walked back to the cottage, their unex-pected gift, thinking it was no wonder Lorrington hadn't wanted to talk about the Russian woman.

Not good public relations at all.

10

Her name is either Ilena or Elaina Timarova—no one seems sure which. She turns up in Ware in the early fall of 1995 in a Ford Escort with a discreet yellow Hertz sticker on the windshield. The car turns out to be stolen, and a story makes the rounds—unsubstan-tiated but juicy—that she obtained it at Logan Air-port, swapping sex for a set of car keys. Who knows, it could have happened that way.

However it happens, she is clearly disoriented, not quite right in the head. Someone remembers the bruise on the side of her face, someone else the fact that her blouse is buttoned wrong. Her English is poor, but good enough for her to get across what she wants: directions to the Quabbin Reservoir. These she writes down (in Russian) on a slip of paper. That evening, when the road across the Winsor Dam is closed, the Escort is found, abandoned, in the picnic area at Goodnough Dike. When the car is still there the next morning, two Water Authority guys (who knows, perhaps Lorrington was one of them) and two Forest Service rangers start looking for her.

Two miles up East Street, they find her shoes. Two miles farther up, where East Street goes to dirt (it winds through the wilderness on the east shore of the Reservoir and is really not a street at all but a Massachusetts version of the Deep Cut Road) they find her shirt . . . oh-oh. Two miles beyond the abandoned shirt, East Street ends, and a rutty logging stripe—Fitzpatrick Road—leads away from the lake. The searchers are about to go this way when one of them sees something pink hanging from a tree-limb down by the water. It proves to be the lady's bra.

The ground here is damp—not quite marshy—and they can follow both her tracks and the broken branches through which she has pushed, doing damage they don't like to think of to her bare skin. Yet the evidence of the damage is there, and they must see it, like it or not—the blood on the branches and then on the rocks is part of her trail.

A mile from where East Street ends, they come to a stone building which stands on an outcropping. It looks across the East Branch at Mount Pomery. This building houses Shaft 12, and is accessible by car only from the north. Why Ilena or Elaina did not just *start* from the north is a question that will never be answered.

The water-bearing aqueduct which begins at the Quabbin runs sixty-five miles dead east to Boston, picking up more water from the Wachusett and Sudbury Reservoirs as it goes (the latter two sources are smaller and not quite so pure). There are no pumps; the aqueduct-pipe, thirteen feet high and eleven feet wide, needs none to do its job. Boston's water supply is provided by simple gravity feed, a technique used by the Egyptians thirty-five centuries before. Twelve vertical shafts run between the ground and the aqueduct. These serve as vents and pressure-regulation points. They also serve as points of access, should the aqueduct become clogged. Shaft 12, the one closest to the Reservoir, is also known as the Intake Shaft. Water purity is tested there, and female virtue has often been tested there, as well (the stone building isn't locked, and is a frequent stopping place for lovers in canoes).

On the lowest of the eight steps leading up to the door, they find the woman's jeans, neatly folded. On the top step is a pair of plain white cotton underpants. The door is open. The men look at each other, but no one speaks. They have a good idea of what they're going to find inside: one dead Russian lady, hold the clothes.

But they don't. The circular iron cover over the top of Shaft 12 has been moved just enough to create a crescent moon of darkness on the Reservoir side. Beyond it is the crowbar the woman used to shift the lid—it would have been leaning behind the door, where there are a few other tools. And beyond the crowbar is the Russian woman's purse. On top of it is her billfold, open to show her identification card. On top of the billfold—the apex of the pyramid, so to speak—is her passport. Poking out of it is a slip of paper, covered with chicken-scratches that have to be Russian, or Cyrillic, or whatever they call it. The men believe it is a suicide note, but upon translation it proves to be nothing but the Russian woman's directions. At the very bottom she has written *When road ends, walk along shore.* And so she did, disrobing as she went, unmindful of the branches which poked and the bushes which scratched.

The men stand around the partially covered shaft-head, scratching their heads and listening to the babble of the water as it starts on its way to the taps and faucets and fountains and backyard hoses of Boston. The sound is hollow, somehow dank, and there's good reason for that: Shaft 12 is a hundred and twenty-five feet deep. The men cannot understand why she chose to do it the way she did, but they can see *what* she did all too clearly, can see her sitting on the stone floor with her feet dangling; she looks like a nakedy version of the girl on the White Rock labels. She takes a final look over her shoulder, perhaps, to make sure her billfold and her passport are still where she put them. She wants someone to know who passed this way, and there is something hideously, unassuageably sad about that. One look back, and then she slips into the eclipse between the partially dislodged cover and the side of the shaft. Perhaps she held her nose, like a kid cannonballing into the community swimming pool. Perhaps not. Either way, she is gone in less than a second. Hello darkness my old friend.

11

Old Mr. Beckwith's final words on the subject before driving on down the road in his mail-truck had been these: *Way I heard it, the folks in Boston'll be drinking her in their morning coffee right around Valentine's Day.* Then he'd given Jonesy a grin. *I don't drink the water myself. I stick to beer.*

In Massachusetts, as in Australia, you say that *beah.*

12

Jonesy had paced around his office twelve or fourteen times now. He stopped for a moment behind his desk chair, absently rubbing his hip, then set off again, still counting, good old obsessive-compulsive Jonesy.

One . . . two . . . three . . .

The story of the Russian woman was certainly a fine one, a superior example of the Small Town Creepy Yarn (haunted houses where multiple murders had taken place and the sites of terrible roadside accidents were also good), and it certainly cast a clear light on Mr. Gray's plans for Lad, the unfortunate border collie, but what good did it do *him* to know where Mr. Gray was going? After all . . .

Back to the chair again, *forty-eight, forty-nine, fifty,* and *wait* a minute, just wait a goddam minute. The first time he'd gone around the room, he'd done it in just thirty-four paces, hadn't he? So how could it be fifty this time? He wasn't shuffling, taking baby steps, anything like that, so how—

You've been making it bigger. Walking around it and making it bigger. Because you were restless. It's your room, after all. I bet you could make it as big as the Waldorf-Astoria ballroom, if you wanted to . . . and Mr. Gray couldn't stop you.

"Is that possible?" Jonesy whispered. He stood by his desk chair, one hand on the back, like a man posing for a portrait. He didn't need an answer to his question; eyesight was enough. The room *was* bigger.

Henry was coming. If he had Duddits with him, following Mr. Gray would be easy enough no matter how many times Mr. Gray changed vehicles, because Duddits saw the line. He had led them to Richie Grenadeau in a dream, later he had led them to Josie Rinkenhauer in reality, and he could direct Henry now as easily as a keen-nosed hound leads a hunter to the fox's earth. The problem was the *lead,* the goddam *lead* that Mr. Gray had. An hour at least. Maybe more. And once Mr. Gray had chucked the dog down Shaft 12, there went your ballgame. There'd be time to shut off Boston's water supply—theoretically—but could Henry convince anyone to take such an enormous, disruptive step? Jonesy doubted it. And what about all the people along the way who would drink the water almost immediately? Sixty-five hundred in Ware, eleven thousand in Athol, over a hundred and fifty thousand in Worcester. Those people would have weeks instead of months. Only days in some cases.

Was there any way to slow the son of a bitch down? Give Henry a chance to catch up?

Jonesy looked up at the dreamcatcher, and as he did, something in the room changed—there was a sigh, almost, the sort of sound ghosts are reputed to make at séances. But this was no ghost, and Jonesy felt his arms prickle. At the same time his eyes filled with tears. A line from Thomas Wolfe occurred to him—*o lost, a stone, a leaf, an unfound door.* Thomas Wolfe, whose thesis had been that you can't go home again.

"Duddits?" he whispered. The hair on his neck had stiffened. "Duddie, is that you?"

No answer . . . but when he looked at the desk where the useless phone had stood, he saw that something new had been added. Not a stone or a leaf, not an unfound door, but a cribbage board and a deck of cards.

Someone wanted to play the game.

13

Hurt pretty much all the time now. Mumma know, he tell Mumma. Jesus know, he tell Jesus. He don't tell Henry, Henry hurts too, Henry tired and make sad. Beaver and Pete are in heaven where they sitteth at the right hand of God the Father all righty, maker of heaven and earth forever and ever, Jesus' sake, hey man. That makes him sad, they were good friends and played games but never made fun. Once they found osie and once they saw a tall guy, he a cowboy, and nce they play the game.

This a game too, only Pete used to say *Duddits it does- 't matter if you win or booze it's how you play the game* only his time it *does* matter, it *does,* Jonesy say it does, onesy hard of hearing but pretty soon it'll be better, retty soon. If only he don't hurt. Even his Perco don't elp. His throat make sore and his body shakes and his elly make hurty kind of like when he has to go poopoo, ind of like that, but he doesn't *have* to go poopoo, and vhen he cough sometimes make blood. He would like o sleep but there is Henry and his new friend Owen hat was there the day they found Josie and they say *If nly we could slow him down* and *If only we could catch up* nd he has to stay awake and help them but he has to lose his eyes to hear Jonesy and they think he's asleep, Owen says *Shouldn't we wake him up, what if the son of a itch turns off somewhere,* and Henry says *I tell you I know vhere he's going, but we'll wake him up at I-90 just to be sure. or now let him sleep, my God, he looks so tired.* And again, nly this time thinking it: *If only we could slow the son of bitch down.*

Eyes closed. Arms crossed over his aching chest. Breathing slow, Mumma say breathe slow when you ough. Jonesy's not dead, not in heaven with Beaver nd Pete, but Mr. Gray say Jonesy locked and Jonesy elieves him. Jonesy's in the office, no phone and no acts, hard to talk to because Mr. Gray is mean and Mr. Gray is scared. Scared Jonesy will find out which one is eally locked up.

When did they talk most?

When they played the game.

The game.

A shudder racks him. He has to make hard think and it hurts, he can feel it stealing away his strength, the last little bits of his strength, but this time it's more than just a game, this time it matters who wins and who boozes, so he gives his strength, he makes the board and he makes the cards, Jonesy is crying, Jonesy thinks *o lost* but Duddits Cavell isn't lost, Duddits sees the line, the line goes to the office, and this time he will do more than peg the pegs.

Don't cry Jonesy, he says, and the words are clear, in his mind they always are, it is only his stupid mouth that mushes them up. *Don't cry, I'm not lost.*

Eyes closed. Arms crossed.

In Jonesy's office, beneath the dreamcatcher, Duddits plays the game.

14

"I've got the dog," Henry said. He sounded exhausted. "The one Perlmutter's homed in on. I've got it. We're a little bit closer. Christ, if there was just a way to slow them down!"

It was raining now, and Owen could only hope they'd be south of the freeze-line if it went over to sleet. The wind was gusting hard enough to sway the Hummer on the road. It was noon, and they were between Saco and Biddeford. Owen glanced into the rearview mirror and saw Duddits in the back seat, eyes closed, head back, skinny arms crossed on his chest. His complexion was an alarming yellow, but a thin line of bright blood trickled from the corner of his mouth.

"Is there any way your friend can help?" Owen asked.

"I think he's trying."

"I thought you said he was asleep."

Henry turned, looked at Duddits, then looked at Owen. "I was wrong," he said.

15

Jonesy dealt the cards, threw two into the crib from his hand, then picked up the other hand and added two more.

"Don't cry, Jonesy. Don't cry, I'm not lost."

Jonesy glanced up at the dreamcatcher, quite sure the words had come from there. "I'm not crying, Duds. Fuckin allergies, that's all. Now I think you want to play—"

"Two," said the voice from the dreamcatcher.

Jonesy played the deuce from Duddits's hand— not a bad lead, actually—then played a seven from his own. That made nine. Duddits had a six in his hand; the question was whether or not—

"Six for fifteen," said the voice from the dream-catcher. "Fifteen for two. Kiss my bender!"

Jonesy laughed in spite of himself. It was Duddits, all right, but for a moment he had sounded just like the Beav. "Go on and peg it, then." And watched, fascinated, as one of the pegs on the board rose, floated, and settled back down in the second hole on First Street.

Suddenly he understood something.

"You could play all along, couldn't you, Duds? You used to peg all crazy just because it made us laugh." The idea brought fresh tears to his eyes. All those years they'd thought they were playing with Duddits, he had been playing with them. And on that day behind Tracker Brothers, who had found whom? Who had saved whom?

"Twenty-one," he said.

"Thirty-one for two." From the dreamcatcher. And once again the unseen hand lifted the peg and played it two holes farther on. "He's blocked to me, Jonesy."

"I know." Jonesy played a three. Duddits called thirteen, and Jonesy played it out of Duddits's hand.

"But you're not. You can talk to him."

Jonesy played his own deuce and pegged two. Duddits played, pegged one for last card, and Jonesy thought: *Outpegged by a retard—what do you know.* Except this Duddits *wasn't* retarded. Exhausted and dying, but not retarded.

They pegged their hands, and Duddits was far ahead even though it had been Jonesy's crib. Jonesy swept the cards together and began to shuffle them.

"What does he want, Jonesy? What does he want besides water?"

Murder, Jonesy thought. *He likes to kill people.* But no more of that. Please God, no more of that.

"Bacon," he said. "He does like bacon."

He began to shuffle the cards . . . then froze as

Duddits filled his mind. The real Duddits, young and strong and ready to fight.

16

Behind them, in the back seat, Duddits groaned loudly. Henry turned and saw fresh blood, red as byrus, running from his nostrils. His face was twisted in a terrible cramp of concentration. Beneath their closed lids, his eyeballs rolled rapidly back and forth.

"What's the matter with him?" Owen asked.

"I don't know."

Duddits began to cough: deep and racking bronchial sounds. Blood flew from between his lips in a fine spray.

"Wake him up, Henry! For Christ's sake, wake him up!"

Henry gave Owen Underhill a frightened look. They were approaching Kennebunkport now, no more than twenty miles from the New Hampshire border, a hundred and ten from the Quabbin Reservoir. Jonesy had a picture of the Quabbin on the wall of his office; Henry had seen it. And a cottage nearby, in Ware.

Duddits cried out: a single word repeated three times between bursts of coughing. The sprays of blood weren't heavy, not yet, the stuff was coming from his mouth and throat, but if his lungs began to rupture—

"Wake him up! He says he's aching! Can't you hear him—"

"He's not saying aykin."

"What, then? What?"

"He's saying *bacon*."

17

The entity which now thought of itself as Mr. Gray—who thought of *himself* as Mr. Gray—had a serious problem, but at least it (*he*) knew it.

Forewarned is forearmed was how Jonesy put it. There were hundreds of such sayings in Jonesy's storage cartons, perhaps thousands. Some of them Mr. Gray found utterly incomprehensible—*A nod's as good as a wink to a blind horse* was one such, *What goes around comes around* was another—but *forewarned is forearmed* was a good one.

His problem could be best summed up with how he felt about Jonesy . . . and of course that he felt at all was bad enough. He could think *Now Jonesy is cut off and I have solved my problem; I have quarantined him just as their military tried to quarantine us. I am being followed—chased, in fact—but barring engine trouble or a flat tire, neither group of followers has much chance of catching me. I have too great a lead.*

These things were facts—truth—but they had no savor. What had savor was the idea of going to the door behind which his reluctant host was imprisoned and yelling: *"I fixed you, didn't I? I fixed your little red wagon, didn't I?"* What a wagon, red or otherwise, had to do with any of this Mr. Gray didn't know, but it was an emotional bullet of fairly high caliber from Jonesy's armory—it had a deep and satisfying childhood resonance. And then he would stick Jonesy's tongue (*my tongue now,* Mr. Gray thought with undeniable satisfaction) between Jonesy's lips and "give him the old raspberry."

As for the followers, he wanted to drop Jonesy's pants and show them Jonesy's buttocks. This was as senseless as *What goes around comes around,* as senseless as *little red wagon,* but he wanted to do it. It was called "mooning the assholes" and he wanted to do it.

He was, Mr. Gray realized, infected with this world's byrus. It began with emotion, progressed to sensory awareness (the taste of food, the undeniable savage pleasure of making the State Trooper beat his head in against the tiled bathroom wall—the hollow *thud-thud* of it), and then progressed to what Jonesy called *higher thinking.* This was a joke, in Mr. Gray's view, not much different from calling shit reprocessed food or genocide ethnic cleansing. And yet *thinking* had its attractions for a being which had always existed as part of a vegetative mind, a sort of highly intelligent not-consciousness.

Before Mr. Gray had shut him up, Jonesy had suggested that he give over his mission and simply enjoy being human. Now he discovered that desire in himself as his previously harmonious mind, his *not-conscious* mind, began to fragment, to turn into a crowd of opposing voices, some wanting A, some wanting B, some wanting Q squared and divided by Z. He would have thought such babble would be horrible, the stuff of madness. Instead he found himself enjoying the wrangle.

There was bacon. There was "sex with Carla," which Jonesy's mind identified as a superlatively enjoyable act, involving both sensory and emotional input. There was fast driving and bumper pool in O'Leary's Bar near Fenway Park and beer and live bands that played loud and Patty Loveless singing "Blame it on your lyin cheatin cold deadbeatin two-timin double-dealin mean mistreatin lovin heart" (whatever *that* meant). There was the look of the land rising from the fog on a summer morning. And murder, of course. There was that.

His problem was that if he didn't finish this business quickly, he might never finish it at all. He was no longer byrum but Mr. Gray. How long before he left Mr. Gray behind and became Jonesy?

It's not going to happen, he thought. He pressed the accelerator down, and although it didn't have much, the Subaru gave him a little more. In the back seat the dog yipped . . . then howled in pain. Mr. Gray sent out his mind and touched the byrum growing inside the dog. It was growing fast. Almost too fast. And here was something else—there was no pleasure in meeting its mind, none of the warmth that comes when like encounters like. The mind of the byrum felt cold . . . rancid . . .

"Alien," he muttered.

Nevertheless, he quieted it. When the dog went into the water supply, the byrum should still be inside. It would need time to adapt. The dog would drown, but the byrum would live yet awhile, feeding on the dog's dead body, until it was time. But first he had to get there.

It wouldn't be long now.

As he drove west on I-90, past little towns (*shitsplats*, Jonesy thought them, but not without affection) like Westborough, Grafton, and Dorothy Pond (getting closer now, maybe forty miles to go), he looked for a place to put his new and uneasy consciousness where it wouldn't get him in trouble. He tried Jonesy's kids, then backed away—far too emotional. Tried Duddits again, but that was still a blank; Jonesy had stolen the memories. Finally he settled on Jonesy's work, which was teaching history, and his specialty, which was gruesomely fascinating. Between 1860 and 1865, it seemed, America had split in two, as byrus colonies did near the end of each growth cycle. There had been all sorts of causes, the chief of which had to do with "slavery," but again, this was like calling shit or vomit reprocessed food. "Slavery" meant nothing. "Right of secession" meant nothing. "Preserving the Union" meant nothing. Basically, they had just done what these creatures did best: they "got mad," which was really the same thing as "going mad" but more socially acceptable. Oh, but on such a scale!

Mr. Gray was investigating boxes and boxes of fascinating weaponry—grapeshot, chainshot, minié balls, cannonballs, bayonets, landmines—when a voice intruded.

bacon

He pushed the thought aside, although Jonesy's stomach gurgled. He'd *like* some bacon, yes, bacon was fleshy and greasy and slippery and satisfying in a primitive, physical way, but this was not the time.

Perhaps after he'd gotten rid of the dog. Then, if he had time before the others caught up, he could eat himself to death if he so chose. But this was not the time. As he passed Exit 10—only two to go, now— he turned his mind back to the Civil War, to blue men and gray men running through the smoke, screaming and stabbing each other in the guts, fixing little red wagons without number, pounding the stocks of their rifles into the skulls of their ene- mies, producing those intoxicating *thud-thud* sounds, and—

bacon

His stomach gurgled again. Saliva squirted into Jonesy's mouth and he remembered Dysart's, the brown and crispy strips on the blue plate, you picked it up with your fingers, the texture was hard, the tex- ture of dead and tasty flesh—

Can't think of this.

A horn honked irritably, making Mr. Gray jump, making Lad whine. He had wandered into the wrong lane, what Jonesy's mind identified as "the passing lane," and he pulled over to let one of the big trucks, going faster than the Subaru could go, sweep by. It splashed the small car's windshield with muddy water, momentarily blinding him, and Mr. Gray thought *Catch you kill you beat the brains out of your head you unsafe johnny reb of a driver you, thud-thud, fix your wagon your little red*

bacon sandwich

That one was like a gunshot in his head. He fought it but the strength of it was something entirely new.

Could that be Jonesy? Surely not, Jonesy wasn't that strong. But suddenly he seemed all stomach, and the stomach was hollow, hurting, craving. Surely he could stop long enough to assuage it. If he didn't he was apt to drive right off the

bacon sandwich!
with mayo!

Mr. Gray let out an inarticulate cry, unaware that he'd begun to drool helplessly.

18

"I hear him," Henry said suddenly. He put his fists to his temples, as if to contain a headache. "Christ, it hurts. He's so *hungry.*"

"Who?" Owen asked. They had just crossed the state line into Massachusetts. In front of the car, the rain fell in silver, wind-slanted lines. "The dog? Jonesy? Who?"

"*Him,*" Henry said. "Mr. Gray." He looked at Owen, a sudden wild hope in his eye. "I think he's pulling over. *I think he's stopping.*"

19

"Boss."

Kurtz was on the verge of dozing again when Perlmutter turned—not without effort—and spoke to him.

They had just gone through the New Hampshire tolls, Freddy Johnson being careful to use the automated exact-change lane (he was afraid a human toll-taker might notice the stench in the Humvee's cabin, the broken window in back, the weaponry . . . or all three).

Kurtz looked into Archie Perlmutter's sweat-streaked, haggard face with interest. With fascination, even. The colorless bean-counting bureaucrat, he of the briefcase on station and clipboard in the field, hair always neatly combed and parted ruler-straight on the left? The man who could not for the life of him train himself out of using the word *sir*? That man was gone. Thin though it was, he thought Pearly's countenance had somehow richened. *He's turning into Ma Joad,* Kurtz thought, and almost giggled.

"Boss, I'm still thirsty." Pearly cast longing eyes on Kurtz's Pepsi, then blew out another hideous fart. *Ma Joad on trumpet in hell* Kurtz thought and this time he *did* giggle. Freddy cursed, but not with his former shocked disgust; now he sounded resigned, almost bored.

"I'm afraid this is mine, buck," Kurtz said. "And I'm a wee parched myself."

Perlmutter began to speak, then winced as a fresh pain struck him. He farted again, the sound thinner this time, not a trumpet but an untalented child blowing over a piccolo. His eyes narrowed, became crafty. "Give me a drink and I'll tell you something you want to know." A pause. "Something you *need* to know."

Kurtz considered. Rain slapped the side of the car and came in through the busted window. The goddamned window was a pain in the ass, praise Jesus, the arm of his jacket was soaked right through, but he would have to bear up. Who was responsible, after all?

"*You* are," Pearly said, and Kurtz jumped. The mind-reading thing was just so *spooky*. You thought you were getting used to it and then realized that no, negative, you were not. "*You're* responsible. So give me a fucking drink. *Boss*."

"Watch your mouth, cheeseboy," Freddy rumbled.

"Tell me what you know and you can have the rest of this." Kurtz raised the Pepsi bottle, waggling it in front of Pearly's tortured gaze. Kurtz was not without humorous self-loathing as he did this. Once he had commanded whole units and had used them to alter entire geopolitical landscapes. Now his command was two men and a soft drink. He had fallen low. *Pride* had brought him low, praise God. He had the pride of Satan, and if it was a fault, it was a hard one to give up. Pride was the belt you could use to hold up your pants even after your pants were gone.

"Do you promise?" Pearly's red-fuzzed tongue came out and licked at his parched lips.

"If I'm lyin I'm dyin," Kurtz said solemnly. "Hell, buck, read my fucking mind!"

Pearly studied him for a moment and Kurtz could almost feel the man's creepy little fingers (mats of red stuff now growing under each nail) in his head. An awful sensation, but he bore it.

At last Perlmutter seemed satisfied. He nodded.

"I'm getting more now," he said, and then his voice lowered to a confidential, horrified whisper. "It's eating me, you know. It's eating my guts. I can feel it."

Kurtz patted him on the arm. Just now they were passing a sign which read WELCOME TO MASSACHU-SETTS. "I'm going to take care of you, laddie-buck; I promised, didn't I? Meantime, tell me what you're getting."

"Mr. Gray is stopping. He's hungry."

Kurtz had left his hand on Perlmutter's arm. Now he tightened his grip, turning his fingernails into talons. "Where?"

"Close to where he's going. It's a store." In a chanting, childish voice that made Kurtz's skin crawl, Archie Perlmutter said: " 'Best bait, why wait? Best bait, why wait?' " Then, resuming a more normal tone: "Jonesy knows Henry and Owen and Duddits are coming. That's why he made Mr. Gray stop."

The idea of Owen's catching Jonesy/Mr. Gray filled Kurtz with panic. "Archie, listen to me carefully."

"I'm thirsty," Perlmutter whined. "I'm *thirsty*, you son of a bitch."

Kurtz held the Pepsi bottle up in front of Perlmutter's eyes, then slapped away Perlmutter's hand when Pearly reached for it.

"Do Henry, Owen, and Dud-Duts know Jonesy and Mr. Gray have stopped?"

"Dud-*dits,* you old fool!" Perlmutter snarled, then groaned with pain and clutched at his stomach, which was on the rise again. "*Dits, dits,* Dud-*dits*! Yes, they know! Duddits helped make Mr. Gray hungry! He and Jonesy did it together!"

"I don't like this," Freddy said.

Join the club, Kurtz thought.

"Please, boss," Pearly said. "I'm so thirsty."

Kurtz gave him the bottle, watched with a jaundiced eye as Perlmutter drained it.

"495, boss," Freddy announced. "What do I do?"

"Take it," Perlmutter said. "Then 90 west." He burped. It was loud but blessedly odorless. "*It* wants another Pepsi. It likes the sugar. Also the caffeine."

Kurtz pondered. Owen knew their quarry had stopped, at least temporarily. Now Owen and Henry would sprint, trying to make up as much of that ninety- to a hundred-minute lag as they could. Consequently, they must sprint, as well.

Any cops who got in their way would have to die, God bless them. One way or the other, this was coming to a head.

"Freddy."

"Boss."

"Pedal to the metal. Make this bitch strut, God love you. Make her strut."

Freddy Johnson did as ordered.

20

There was no barn, no corral, no paddock, and instead of OUT-OF-STATE LICS the sign in the window showed a photograph of the Quabbin Reservoir over the legend BEST BAIT, WHY WAIT?, but otherwise the little store could have been Gosselin's all over again: same ratty siding, same mud-brown shingles, same crooked chimney dribbling smoke into the rainy sky, same rusty gas-pump out front. Another sign leaned against the pump, this one reading NO GAS BLAME THE RAGHEADS.

On that early afternoon in November the store was empty save for the proprietor, a gentleman named Deke McCaskell. Like most other folks, he had spent the morning glued to the TV. All the coverage (repetitive stuff, for the most part, and with that part of the North Woods cordoned off, no good pictures of anything but Army, Navy, and Air Force hardware) had led up to the President's speech. Deke called the President Mr. Okeefenokee, on account of the fucked-up way he'd been elected—couldn't anybody down there fucking count? Although he had not exercised his own option to vote since the Gipper (now *there* had been a President), Deke hated President Okeefenokee, thought he was an oily, untrustworthy motherfucker with big teeth (good-looking wife, though), and he thought the President's eleven o'clock speech had been the usual blah-dee-blah. Deke didn't believe a word old Okeefenokee said. In his view, the whole thing was probably a hoax, scare tactics calculated to make the American taxpayer more willing to hike defense spending and thus taxes. There was nobody out there in space, science had proved it. The only aliens in America (except for President Okeefenokee himself, that was) were the beaners who swam across the border from Mexico. But people were scared, sitting home and watching TV. A few would be in later for beer or bottles of wine, but for now the place was as dead as a cat run over in the highway.

Deke had turned off the TV half an hour ago—
enough was enough, by the Christ—and when the
bell over his door jangled at quarter past one, he was
studying a magazine from the rack at the back of the
store, where a sign proclaimed B 21 OR B GONE. This
particular periodical was titled *Lasses in Glasses,* a fair
title since all the lasses within *were* wearing spectacles. Nothing else, but glasses, *sí.*

He looked up at the newcomer, started to say
something like "How ya doin" or "Roads gettin slippery yet," and then didn't. He felt a bolt of unease,
followed by a sudden certainty that he was going to
be robbed . . . and if robbery was all, he'd be off
lucky. He never *had* been robbed, not in the twelve
years he'd owned the place—if a fellow wanted to
risk prison for a handful of cash, there were places in
the area where bigger handfuls could be had. A guy
would have to be . . .

Deke swallowed. *A guy would have to be crazy,* he'd
been thinking, and maybe this guy *was,* maybe he
was one of those maniacs who'd just offed his whole
family and then decided to ramble around a bit, kill a
few more folks before turning one of his guns on himself.

Deke wasn't paranoid by nature (he was *lumpish* by
nature, his ex-wife would have told you), but that
didn't change the fact that he felt suddenly menaced
by the afternoon's first customer. He didn't care very
much for the fellows who sometimes turned up and
loafed around the store, talking about the Patriots or
the Red Sox or telling stories about the whoppers

they'd caught up to the Reservoir, but he wished for a few of them now. A whole gang of them, actually.

The man just stood there inside the door at first, and yeah, there was something wrong with him. He was wearing an orange hunting coat and deer season hadn't started yet in Massachusetts, but that could have been nothing. What Deke didn't like were the scratches on the man's face, as if he had spent at least some of the last couple of days going cross-country through the woods, and the haunted, drawn quality of the features themselves. His mouth was moving, as though he was talking to himself. Something else, too. The gray afternoon light slanting in through the dusty front window glinted oddly on his lips and chin.

That sonofabitch is drooling, Deke thought. *Be god-damned if he ain't.*

The newcomer's head snapped around in quick little tics while his body remained perfectly still, reminding Deke of the way an owl remains perfectly still on its branch as it looks for prey. Deke thought briefly of sliding out of his chair and hiding under the counter, but before he could do more than begin to consider the pros and cons of such a move (not a particularly quick thinker, his ex-wife would have told you that, as well), the guy's head did another of those quick flicks and was pointing right at him.

The rational part of Deke's mind had been harboring the hope (it was not quite an articulated idea) that he was imagining the whole thing, just suffering the whimwhams from all the weird news and weirder rumors, each dutifully reported by the press, coming out of northern Maine. Maybe this was just a guy who wanted smokes or a six-pack or maybe a bottle of coffee brandy and a stroke-book, something to get him through a long, sleety night in a motel outside of Ware or Belchertown.

That hope died when the man's eyes met his.

It wasn't the gaze of a family-murdering maniac off on his own private cruise to nowhere; it almost would have been better if that had been the case. The newcomer's eyes, far from empty, were too full. A million thoughts and ideas seemed to be crossing them, like one of those big-city tickertapes being run at super-speed. They seemed almost to be hopping in their sockets.

And they were the *hungriest* eyes Deke McCaskell had seen in his entire life.

"We're closed," Deke said. The words came out in a croak that didn't sound like his voice at all. "Me and my partner—he's in the back—we closed for the day. On account of the goings-on up north. I—*we*, I mean—just forgot to flip over the sign. We—"

He might have run on for hours—days, even—but the man in the hunting coat interrupted him. "Bacon," he said. "Where is it?"

Deke knew, suddenly and absolutely, that if he didn't have bacon, this man would kill him. He might kill him anyway, but without bacon . . . yes, certainly. He *did* have bacon. Thank God, thank Christ, thank Okeefenokee and all the hopping ragheads, he *did* have bacon.

"Cooler in back," he said in his new, strange voice. The hand lying on top of his magazine felt as cold as a block of ice. In his head, he heard whispering voices that didn't seem to be his own. Red thoughts and black thoughts. *Hungry* thoughts.

An inhuman voice asked, *What's a cooler?* A tired voice, *very* human, responded: *Go on up the aisle, handsome. You'll see it.*

Hearing voices, Deke thought. *Aw, Jesus, no. That's what happens to people just before they flip out.*

The man moved past Deke and up the center aisle. He walked with a heavy limp.

There was a phone by the cash-register. Deke looked at it, then looked away. It was within reach, and he had 911 on the speed-dialer, but it might as well have been on the moon. Even if he was able to summon enough strength to reach for the phone—

I'll know, the inhuman voice said, and Deke let out a breathless little moan. It was inside his head, as if someone had planted a radio in his brain.

There was a convex mirror mounted over the door, a gadget that came in especially handy in the summer, when the store was full of kids headed up to the Reservoir with their parents—the Quabbin was only eighteen miles from here—for fishing or camping or just a picnic. Little bastards were always trying to kite stuff, particularly the candy and the girly magazines. Now Deke looked into it, watching with dread fascination as the man in the orange coat approached the cooler. He stood there a moment, gazing in, then grabbed not just one package of bacon but all four of them.

The man came back down the middle aisle with the bacon, limping along and scanning the shelves. He looked dangerous, he looked hungry, and he also looked dreadfully tired—like a marathon runner going into the last mile. Looking at him gave Deke the same sense of vertigo he felt when he looked down from a high place. It was like looking not at one person but at several, overlaid and shifting in and out of focus. Deke thought fleetingly of a movie he'd seen, some daffy cunt with about a hundred personalities.

The man stopped and got a jar of mayonnaise. At the foot of the aisle he stopped again and snagged a loaf of bread. Then he was at the counter again. Deke could almost smell the exhaustion coming out of his pores. And the craziness.

He set his purchases down and said, "Bacon sandwiches on white, with mayo. Those are the best." And smiled. It was a smile of such tired, heartbreaking sincerity that Deke forgot his fear for a moment.

Without thinking, he reached out. "Mister, are you all r—"

Deke's hand stopped as if it had run into a wall. It trembled for a moment over the counter, then flew up and slapped his own face—*crack!* It drew slowly away and stopped, floating like a Hovercraft. The third and fourth fingers folded slowly down against the palm.

Don't kill him!

Come out and stop me!

If you make me try, you might get a surprise.

These voices were in his head.

His Hovercraft hand floated forward and the first two fingers plunged into his nostrils, plugging them. For a moment they were still, and then oh dear Christ they began to dig. And while Deke McCaskell had many questionable habits, chewing his nails was not one of them. At first his fingers didn't want to move much up there—close quarters—but then, as the lubricating blood began to flow, they became positively frisky. They squirmed like worms. The dirty nails dug like fangs. They shoved up farther, burrowing brainward . . . he could feel cartilage tearing . . . could hear it . . .

Stop it, Mr. Gray, stop it!

And suddenly Deke's fingers belonged to him again. He pulled them free with a wet plop. Blood pattered down on the counter, on the rubber change-pad with the Skoal logo on it, also on the unclad lass in glasses whose anatomy he had been studying when this creature had come in.

"How much do I owe you, Deke?"

"Take it!" Still that crow-croak, but now it was a *nasal* croak, because his nostrils were plugged with blood. "Aw, man, just take it and go! The fuck outta here!"

"No, I insist. This is commerce, in which items of real worth are exchanged for currency plain."

"Three dollars!" Deke cried. Shock was setting in. His heart was beating wildly, his muscles thrumming with adrenaline. He believed the creature might be going, and this made everything infinitely worse: to be so close to a continued life and still know it could be snatched away at this fucking loony's least whim.

The loony brought out a battered old wallet, opened it, and rummaged for what seemed an age. Saliva drizzled steadily from his mouth as he bent over the wallet. At last he came out with three dollars. He put them on the counter. The wallet went back into his pocket. He rummaged in his nasty-looking jeans (*rode hard and put away wet,* Deke thought), came out with a fistful of change, and laid three coins on the Skoal pad. Two quarters and a dime.

"I tip twenty percent," his customer said with unmistakable pride. "Jonesy tips fifteen. This is better. This is more."

"Sure," Deke whispered. His nose was full of blood.

"Have a nice day."

"You . . . you take it easy."

The man in the orange coat stood with his head lowered. Deke could hear him sorting through possible responses. It made him feel like screaming. At last the man said, "I will take it any way I can get it." There was another pause. Then: "I don't want you to call anyone, partner."

"I won't."

"Swear to God?"

"Yeah. Swear to God."

"*I'm* like God," his customer remarked.

"Yeah, okay. Whatever you—"

"If you call someone, I'll know. I'll come back and fix your wagon."

"I won't!"

"Good idea." He opened the door. The bell jangled. He went out.

For a moment Deke stood where he was, as if frozen to the floor. Then he rushed around the counter, bumping his upper leg hard on the corner. By nightfall there would be a huge black bruise there, but for the moment he felt nothing. He turned the thumb-lock, shot the bolt, then stood there, peering out. Parked in front of the store was a little red shit-box Subaru, mudsplattered, also looking rode hard and put away wet. The man juggled his purchases into the crook of one arm, opened the door, and got in behind the wheel.

Drive away, Deke thought. *Please, mister, for the love of God just drive away.*

But he didn't. He picked something up instead—the loaf of bread—and pulled the tie off the end. He took out roughly a dozen slices. Next he opened the jar of mayonnaise, and, using his finger as a knife, began to slather the slices of bread with mayo. After finishing each slice, he licked his finger clean. Each time he did, his eyes slipped closed, his head tipped back, and an expression of ecstasy filled his features, radiating out from the mouth. When he had finished with the bread, he picked up one of the packages of meat and tore off the paper covering. He opened the plastic inner envelope with his teeth and shook out the pound of sliced bacon. He folded it and put it on a piece of bread, then put another piece on top. He tore into the sandwich as ravenously as a wolf. That expression of divine enjoyment never left his face; it was the look of a man enjoying the greatest gourmet meal of his life. His throat knotted as each huge bite went down. Three such bites and the sandwich was gone. As the man in the car reached for two more pieces of bread, a thought filled Deke McCaskell's brain, flashing there like a neon sign. *It's even better this way! Almost alive! Cold, but almost alive!*

Deke backed away from the door, moving slowly, as if underwater. The grayness of the day seemed to invade the store, dimming the lights. He felt his legs come unhinged, and before the dirty board floor tilted up to meet him, gray had gone to black.

21

When Deke came to, it was later—just how much later he couldn't tell, because the Budweiser digital clock over the beer cooler was flashing 88:88. Three of his teeth lay on the floor, knocked out when he fell down, he assumed. The blood around his nose and on his chin had dried to a spongy cake. He tried to get up, but his legs wouldn't support him. He crawled to the door instead, with his hair hanging in his face, praying.

His prayer was answered. The little red shitbox car was gone. Where it had been were four bacon packages, all empty, the mayonnaise jar, three-quarters empty, and half a loaf of Holsum white bread. Several crows—there were some almighty big ones around the Reservoir—had found the bread and were pecking slices out of the torn wrapper. At a distance—almost back to Route 32—two or three more were at work on a congealed mess of bacon and matted chunks of bread. *Monsieur*'s gourmet lunch had not agreed with him, it seemed.

God, Deke thought. *I hope you puked so hard you tore your plumbing loose, you—*

But then his own guts took a fantastical, skipping leap and he clapped his hand over his mouth. He had a hideously clear image of the man's teeth closing on the raw, fatty meat hanging out between the pieces of bread, gray flesh veined with brown like the severed tongue of a dead horse. Deke began to make muffled yurking sounds behind his hand.

A car turned in—just what he needed, a customer while he was on the verge of tossing his cookies. Not really a car at all, on second glance, nor a truck, either. Not even an SUV. It was one of those godawful Humvees, painted in smeary camouflage blobs of black and green. Two people in front and—Deke was almost sure of it—another in back.

He reached out, flipped the OPEN sign hanging in the door over to CLOSED, then backed away. He had gotten to his feet, had managed at least that much, but now he felt perilously close to collapsing again. *They saw me in here, just as sure as shit,* he thought. *They'll come in and ask where the other one went, because they're after him. They want him, they want the bacon sandwich man. And I'll tell. They'll make me tell. And then I'll—*

His hand rose in front of his eyes. The first two fingers, coated with dried blood up to the second knuckles, were poked out and hooked. They were trembling. To Deke, they almost looked like they were waving. *Hello, eyes, how you doing? Enjoy looking while you can, because we'll be coming for you soon.*

The person in the back of the Humvee leaned forward, seemed to say something to the driver, and the vehicle leaped backward, one rear wheel splashing through the puddle of vomit left by the store's last customer. It wheeled around on the road, paused for just a moment, then set off in the direction of Ware and the Quabbin.

When they disappeared over the first hill, Deke McCaskell began to weep. As he walked back toward the counter (staggering and weaving but still on his feet), his gaze fell on the teeth lying on the floor. Three teeth. His. A small price to pay. Oh yes, teeny dues. Then he stopped, gazing at the three dollar bills which still lay on the counter. They had grown a coating of pale red-orange fuzz.

22

"Oht ear! Eeep owen!"

Owen, that's me, Owen thought wearily, but he understood Duddits well enough (it wasn't that hard, once your ear had become attuned): *Not here! Keep going!*

Owen reversed the Humvee to Route 32 as Duddits sat back—collapsed back—and began to cough again.

"Look," Henry said, and pointed. "See that?"

Owen saw. A bunch of wrappers soaking into the ground under the force of the pelting downpour. And a jar of mayonnaise. He threw the Hummer back into drive and headed north. The rain hitting the windshield had a particularly fat quality that he recognized: soon it would turn back to sleet, and then—very likely—to snow. Close to exhausted now, and queerly sad in the wake of the telepathy's withdrawing wave, Owen found that his chief regret was having to die on such a dirty day.

"How far ahead is he now?" Owen asked, not daring to ask the real question, the only one that mattered: *Are we already too late?* He assumed that Henry would tell him, were that the case.

"He's there," Henry said absently. He had turned around in the seat and was wiping Duddits's face with a damp cloth. Duddits looked at him gratefully and tried to smile. His ashy cheeks were sweaty now, and the black patches under his eyes had spread, turning them into raccoon's eyes.

"If he's *there,* why did we have to come *here?*" Owen asked. He had the Hummer up to seventy, *very* dangerous on this slick stretch of two-lane blacktop, but now there was no choice.

"I didn't want to risk Duddits losing the line," Henry said. "If that happens . . ."

Duddits uttered a vast groan, wrapped his arms around his midsection, and doubled over them. Henry, still kneeling on the seat, stroked the slender column of his neck.

"Take it easy, Duds," Henry said. "You're all right."

But he wasn't. Owen knew it and so did Henry.

Feverish, crampy in spite of a second Prednisone pill and two more Percocets, now spraying blood every time he coughed, Duddits Cavell was several country miles from all right. The consolation prize was that the Jonesy-Gray combination was also a very long way from all right.

It was the bacon. All they'd hoped to do was to make Mr. Gray stop for awhile; none of them had guessed how prodigious his gluttony would turn out to be. The effect on Jonesy's digestion had been fairly predictable. Mr. Gray had vomited once in the parking lot of the little store, and had had to pull over twice more on the road to Ware, leaning out the window and offloading several pounds of raw bacon with almost convulsive force.

Diarrhea came next. He had stopped at the Mobil on Route 9, southeast of Ware, and had barely made it into the men's room. The sign outside the station read CHEAP GAS CLEAN TOILETS, but the CLEAN TOILETS part was certainly out of date by the time Mr. Gray left. He didn't kill anyone at the Mobil, which Henry counted as a plus.

Before turning onto the Quabbin access road, Mr. Gray had needed to stop twice more and dash into the sopping woods, where he tried to evacuate Jonesy's groaning bowels. By then the rain had changed over to huge flakes of wet snow. Jonesy's body had weakened considerably, and Henry was hoping for a faint. So far it hadn't happened.

Mr. Gray was furious with Jonesy, railing at him continuously by the time he slipped back behind the wheel of the car after his second trip into the woods. This was all Jonesy's fault, Jonesy had trapped him. He chose to ignore his own hunger and the compulsive greed with which he had eaten, pausing between bites only to lick the grease from his fingers. Henry had seen such selective arrangements of the facts—emphasizing some, ignoring others completely—many times before, in his patients. In some ways, Mr. Gray was Barry Newman all over again.

How human he's becoming, he thought. *How curiously human.*

"When you say he's there," Owen asked, "just how *there* do you mean?"

"I don't know. He's closed down again, at least pretty much. Duddits, do you hear Jonesy?"

Duddits looked at Henry wearily, then shook his head. "Isser Ay ookar cards," he said—*Mr. Gray took our cards*—but that was like a literal translation of a slang phrase. Duddits hadn't the vocabulary to express what had actually happened, but Henry could read it in his mind. Mr. Gray was unable to enter Jonesy's office stronghold and take the playing-cards, but he had somehow turned them all blank.

"Duddits, how are you making out?" Owen said, looking into the rearview mirror.

"I o-ay," Duddits said, and immediately began to shiver. On his lap was his yellow lunchbox and the brown bag with his medicines in it . . . his medicines and that odd little string thing. Surrounding him was the voluminous blue duffel coat, yet inside it, he still shivered.

He's going fast, Owen thought, as Henry began to swab his old friend's face again.

The Humvee skidded on a slick patch, danced on the edge of disaster—a crash at seventy miles an hour would probably kill them all, and even if it didn't, it would put paid to any final thin chance they might have of stopping Mr. Gray—and then came back under control again.

Owen found his eyes drifting back to the paper bag, his mind going again to that string-thing. *Beaver sent to me. For my Christmas last week.*

Trying to communicate now by telepathy was, Owen thought, like putting a message into a bottle and then tossing the bottle into the ocean. But he did it anyway, sending out a thought in what he hoped was Duddits's direction: *What do you call it, son?*

Suddenly and unexpectedly, he saw a large space, combination living room, dining room, and kitchen. The mellow pine boards glowed with varnish. There was a Navajo rug on the floor and a tapestry on one wall—tiny Indian hunters surrounding a gray figure, the archetypal alien of a thousand supermarket tabloids. There was a fireplace, a stone chimney, an oak dining table. But what riveted Owen's attention (it had to; it was at the center of the picture Duddits had sent him, and glowed with its own special light) was the string creation which hung from the center rafter. It was the Cadillac version of the one in Duddits's medicine bag, woven in bright colors instead of drab white string, but otherwise the same. Owen's eyes filled with tears. It was the most beautiful room in the world. He felt that way because Duddits felt that way. And Duddits felt that way because it was where his friends went, and he loved them.

"Dreamcatcher," said the dying man in the back seat, and he pronounced the word perfectly.

Owen nodded. Dreamcatcher, yes.

It's you, he sent, supposing that Henry was overhearing but not caring one way or the other. This message was for Duddits, strictly for Duddits. *You're the dreamcatcher, aren't you? Their dreamcatcher. You always were.*

In the mirror, Duddits smiled.

23

They passed a sign which read QUABBIN RESERVOIR 8 MILES NO FISHING NO SERVICES PICNIC AREA OPEN HIKING TRAILS OPEN PASS AT OWN RISK. There was more, but at eighty miles an hour, Henry had no time to read it.

"Any chance he'll park and walk in?" Owen asked.

"Don't even hope for it," Henry said. "He'll drive as far as he can. Maybe he'll get stuck. That's what you want to hope for. There's a good chance it might happen. And he's weak. He won't be able to move fast."

"What about you, Henry? Will you be able to move fast?"

Considering how stiff he was and how badly his legs ached, that was a fair question. "If there's a chance," he said, "I'll go as hard as I can. In any case, there's Duddits. I don't think he's going to be capable of a very strenuous hike."

Any hike at all, he didn't add.

"Kurtz and Freddy and Perlmutter, Henry. How far back are they?"

Henry considered this. He could feel Perlmutter clearly enough . . . and he could touch the ravening cannibal inside him, as well. It was like Mr. Gray, only the weasel was living in a world made of bacon. The bacon was Archibald Perlmutter, once a captain in the United States Army. Henry didn't like to go there. Too much pain. Too much hunger.

"Fifteen miles," he said. "Maybe only twelve. But it doesn't matter, Owen. We're going to beat them. The only question is whether or not we're going to catch Mr. Gray. We'll need some luck. Or some help."

"And if we catch him, Henry. Are we still going to be heroes?"

Henry gave him a tired smile. "I guess we'll have to try."

CHAPTER TWENTY-ONE

SHAFT 12

1

Mr. Gray drove the Subaru nearly three miles up East Street—muddy, rutted, and now covered with three inches of fresh snow—before crashing into a fault caused by a plugged culvert. The Subaru had fought its way gamely through several mires north of the Goodnough Dike, and had bottomed out in one place hard enough to tear off the muffler and most of the exhaust pipe, but this latest break in the road was too much. The car went forward nose-first into the crack and lodged on the pipe, unmuffled engine blatting stridently. Jonesy's body was thrown forward and the seatbelt locked. His diaphragm clenched and he vomited helplessly onto the dashboard: nothing solid now, only bilious strings of saliva. For a moment the color ran out of the world and the rackety roar of the engine faded. He fought viciously for consciousness, afraid that if he passed out for even a moment,

Jonesy might somehow be able to take control again.

The dog whined. Its eyes were still closed but its rear legs twitched spasmodically and its ears flicked. Its belly was distended, the skin rippling. Its moment was near.

A little at a time, color and reality began to return. Mr. Gray took several deep breaths, coaxing this sick and unhappy body back to something resembling calm. How far was there still to go? He didn't think it could be far now, but if the little car was really stuck, he would have to walk . . . and the dog couldn't. The dog must remain asleep, and it was already perilously close to waking again.

He caressed the sleep-centers of its rudimentary brain. He wiped at his slimy mouth as he did it. Part of his mind was aware of Jonesy, still in there, blind to the outside world but awaiting any chance to leap forward and sabotage his mission; and, incredibly, another part of his mind craved more food—craved bacon, the very stuff which had poisoned it.

Sleep, little friend. Speaking to the dog; speaking also to the byrum. And both listened. Lad ceased whining. His paws stopped twitching. The ripples running across the dog's belly slowed . . . slowed . . . stopped. This calm wouldn't last long, but for now all was well. As well as it could be.

Surrender, Dorothy.

"Shut up!" Mr. Gray said. "Kiss my bender!" He put the Subaru in reverse and floored the accelerator. The motor howled, scaring birds up from the trees, but it was no good. The front wheels were caught firmly, and the back wheels were up, spinning in the air.

"*Fuck!*" Mr. Gray cried, and slammed Jonesy's fist down on the steering wheel. "*Jesus-Christ-bananas! Fuck me Freddy!*"

He felt behind him for his pursuers and got nothing clear, only a sense of approach. Two groups of them, and the one that was closer had Duddits. Mr. Gray feared Duddits, sensed that he was the one most responsible for how absurdly, infuriatingly difficult this job had become. If he could stay ahead of Duddits, all would end well. It would help to know how close Duddits was, but they were blocking him—Duddits, Jonesy, and the one called Henry. The three of them together made a force Mr. Gray had never encountered before, and he was afraid.

"But I'm still enough ahead," he told Jonesy, getting out. He slipped, uttered a Beaver-curse, then slammed the door shut. It was snowing again, great white flakes that filled the air like confetti and splashed against Jonesy's cheeks. Mr. Gray slogged around the back of the car, boots sliding and smooching in the mud. He paused for a moment to examine the corrugated silver back of the pipe rising from the bottom of the ditch which had trapped his car (he had also fallen victim in some degree to his host's mostly useless but infernally sticky curiosity), then went on around to the passenger door. "I'm going to beat your asshole friends quite handily."

No answer to this goad, but he sensed Jonesy just as he sensed the others, Jonesy silent but still the bone in his throat.

Never mind him. Fuck him. The dog was the problem. The byrum was poised to come out. How to transport the dog?

Back into Jonesy's storage vault. For a moment there was nothing . . . and then an image from "Sunday School," where Jonesy had gone as a child to learn about "God" and "God's only begotten son," who appeared to be a byrum, creator of a byrus culture which Jonesy's mind identified simultaneously as "Christianity" and "bullshit." The image was very clear, from a book called "the Holy Bible." It showed "God's only begotten son" carrying a lamb—wearing it, almost. The lamb's front legs hung over one side of "begotten son's" chest, its rear legs over the other.

It would do.

Mr. Gray pulled out the sleeping dog and draped it around his neck. It was heavy already—Jonesy's muscles were stupidly, infuriatingly weak—and it would be much worse by the time he got where he was going . . . but he *would* get there.

He set off up East Street through the thickening snow, wearing the sleeping border collie like a fur stole.

2

The new snow was extremely slippery, and once they were on Route 32, Freddy was forced to drop his speed back to forty. Kurtz felt like howling with frustration. Worse, Perlmutter was slipping away from him, into something like a semi-coma. And this at a time, goddam him, when he had suddenly been able to read the one Owen and his new friends were after, the one they called Mr. Gray.

"He's too busy to hide," Pearly said. He spoke dreamily, like someone on the edge of sleep. "He's afraid. I don't know about Underhill, boss, but Jonesy . . . Henry . . . Duddits . . . he's afraid of them. And he's right to be afraid. They killed Richie."

"Who's Richie, buck?" Kurtz didn't give much of a squirt, but he wanted Perlmutter to stay awake. He sensed they were coming to a place where he wouldn't need Perlmutter anymore, but for now he still did.

"Don't . . . know . . ." The last word became a snore. The Humvee skidded almost sideways. Freddy cursed, fought the wheel, and managed to regain control just before the Hummer hit the ditch. Kurtz took no notice. He leaned over the seat and slapped Perlmutter on the side of the face, hard. As he did so, they passed the store with the sign reading BEST BAIT, WHY WAIT? in the window.

"Owwww!" Pearly's eyes fluttered open. The whites were now yellowish. Kurtz cared about this no more than he cared about Richie. "Dooon't, boss . . ."

"Where are they now?"

"The water," Pearly said. His voice was weak, that of a petulant invalid. The belly under his coat was a distended, occasionally twitching mountain. *Ma Joad in her ninth month, God bless and keep us,* Kurtz thought. "The waaaa . . ."

His eyes closed again. Kurtz drew his hand back to slap.

"Let him sleep," Freddy said.

Kurtz looked at him, eyebrows raised.

"It's got to be the Reservoir he means. And if it is, we don't need him anymore." He pointed through the windshield at the tracks of the few cars that had been out this afternoon ahead of them on Route 32. They were black and stark against the fall of fresh white snow. "There won't be anyone up there today but us, boss. Just us."

"Praise God." Kurtz sat back, picked his nine-millimeter up off the seat, looked at it, and put it back in its holster. "Tell me something, Freddy."

"I will if I can."

"When this is over, how does Mexico sound to you?"

"Good. As long as we don't drink the water."

Kurtz burst out laughing and patted Freddy on the shoulder. Beside Freddy, Archie Perlmutter slipped deeper into coma. Inside his lower intestine, in that rich dump of discarded food and worn-out dead cells, something for the first time opened its black eyes.

3

Two stone posts marked the entrance to the vast acreage surrounding the Quabbin Reservoir. Beyond them, the road closed down to what was essentially a single lane, and Henry had a sense of having come full circle. It wasn't Massachusetts, but Maine, and although the sign said Quabbin Access, it was really the Deep Cut Road all over again. He actually found himself looking up at the leaden sky, half-expecting to see the dancing lights. What he saw instead was a bald eagle, soaring almost close enough to touch. It landed on the lower branch of a pine tree and watched them go by.

Duddits raised his head from where it had lain against the cool glass and said, "Isser Ay walkin now."

Henry's heart leaped. "Owen, did you hear?"

"I heard," Owen said, and pressed the Humvee a little harder. The wet snow beneath them was as treacherous as ice, and with the state roads behind them, there was now only a single set of tracks leading north toward the Reservoir.

We'll be leaving our own set, Henry thought. *If Kurtz gets this far, he won't need telepathy.*

Duddits groaned, clutched his middle, and shivered all over. "Ennie, I sick. Duddits sick."

Henry brushed Duddits's hairless brow, not liking the heat of the skin. What came next? Seizures, probably. A big one might take Duds off in a hurry, given his weakened condition, and God knew that might be a mercy. The best thing. Still, it hurt to think of it. Henry Devlin, the potential suicide. And instead of him, the darkness had swallowed his friends, one by one.

"You hang in there, Duds. Almost done now." But he had an idea the toughest part might still be ahead.

Duddits's eyes opened again. "Isser Ay—ot *tuck.*"

"What?" Owen asked. "I didn't get that one."

"He says Mr. Gray got stuck," Henry said, still

brushing Duddits's brow. Wishing there was hair to brush, and remembering when there had been. Duddits's fine blond hair. His crying had hurt them, had chopped into their heads like a dull blade, but how happy his laughter had made them—you heard Duddits Cavell laugh and for a little while you believed the old lies again: that life was good, that the lives of boys and men, girls and women, had some purpose. That there was light as well as darkness.

"Why doesn't he just throw the goddam dog into the Reservoir?" Owen asked. His voice cracked with weariness. "Why does he feel he has to go all the way to this Shaft 12? Is it just because the Russian woman did?"

"I don't think the Reservoir is sure enough for him," Henry said. "The Standpipe would have been good, but the aqueduct is even better. It's an intestine sixty-five miles long. And Shaft 12 is the throat. Duddits, can we catch him?"

Duddits looked at him from his exhausted eyes, then shook his head. Owen pounded his own thigh in frustration. Duddits wet his lips. Spoke two words in a hoarse near-whisper. Owen heard them but couldn't make them out.

"What? What did he say?"

" 'Only Jonesy.' "

"What does that mean? Only Jonesy what?"

"Only Jonesy can stop him, I guess."

The Hummer skidded again and Henry grabbed hold of the seat. A cold hand closed over his. Duddits was looking at him with desperate intensity. He tried to speak and began coughing instead, gruesome wet hacking sounds. Some of the blood that came out of his mouth was markedly lighter, frothy and almost pink. Henry thought it was lung-blood. And even while the coughs shook him, Duddits's grip on Henry's hand didn't loosen.

"Think it to me," Henry said. "Can you think it to me, Duds?"

For a moment there was nothing but Duddits's cold hand closed over his, Duddits's eyes locked on his. Then Duddits and the khaki interior of the Humvee, with its faded scent of surreptitiously smoked cigarettes, was gone. In its place Henry sees a pay telephone—the old-fashioned kind with different-sized holes on top, one for quarters, one for dimes, one for nickels. The rumble of men's voices and a clack-clacking sound, hauntingly familiar. After a moment he realizes it's the sound of checkers on a checkerboard. He's looking at the pay phone in Gosselin's, the one from which they called Duddits after the death of Richie Grenadeau. Jonesy made the actual call, because he was the only one with a phone he could bill it to. The others gathered around, all of them still with their jackets on because it was so cold in the store, even living in the big woods with trees all around him, Old Man Gosselin wouldn't throw an extra log in the stove, what a fuckin pisser. There are two signs over the phone. One reads PLEASE LIMIT ALL CALLS TO 5 MINS. The other one—

There was a crunching bang. Duddits was thrown against the back of Henry's seat and Henry was thrown into the dashboard. Their hands parted. Owen had skidded off the road and into the ditch. Ahead of them, the Subaru's tracks, fading now under fresh cover, ran off into the thickening snow.

"Henry! You all right?"

"Yeah. Duds? Okay?"

Duddits nodded, but the cheek he had struck was turning black with amazing speed. Your Leukemia at Work for You.

Owen dropped the Humvee's transmission into low range and began to creep up the ditch. The Humvee was canted at a severe angle—maybe thirty degrees—but it rolled pretty well once Owen got it moving.

"Fasten your seatbelt. First fasten his, though."

"He was trying to tell me s—"

"I don't give a damn what he was trying to tell you. This time we were all right, next time we could roll three-sixty. Fasten his belt, then your own."

Henry did as he was told, thinking about the other sign over the pay phone. What had it said? Something about Jonesy. Only Jonesy could stop Mr. Gray now, that was the Gospel According to Duddits.

What had that other sign said?

4

Owen was forced to drop his speed to twenty. It made him crazy to creep like this, but the wet snow was falling furiously now and visibility was back to nearly zero.

Just before the Subaru's tracks disappeared entirely they came to the car itself, nose-down in a water-carved ditch running across the road, passenger door open, rear wheels in the air.

Owen stepped on the emergency brake, drew his Glock, opened his door. "Stay here, Henry," he said, and got out. He ran to the Subaru, bent low.

Henry unlatched his seatbelt and turned to Duddits, who was now sprawled against the back seat, gasping for breath, held in a sitting position only by the seatbelt. One cheek was a waxy yellow; the other had been engulfed by spreading blood under the skin. His nose was bleeding again, the wads of cotton sticking out of the nostrils soaked and dripping.

"Duds, I'm so sorry," Henry said. "This is a fuckarow."

Duddits nodded, then raised his arms. He could only hold them up for a few seconds, but to Henry his meaning seemed obvious enough. Henry opened his door and got out just as Owen came running back, his Glock now stuffed in his belt. The air was so thick with snow, the individual flakes so huge, that breathing had become difficult.

"I thought I told you to stay where you were," Owen said.

"I only want to get in the back with him."

"Why?"

Henry spoke calmly enough, although his voice trembled slightly. "Because he's dying," he said. "He's dying, but I think he has one more thing to tell me first."

5

Owen looked in the rearview mirror, saw Henry with his arms around Duddits, saw they were both wearing their seatbelts, and fastened his own.

"Hold him good," he said. "There's going to be a hell of a jounce."

He reversed a hundred feet, put the Hummer in low, and drove forward, aiming for the spot between the abandoned Subaru and the righthand ditch. The crack in the road looked a little narrower on that side.

There was indeed a hell of a jounce. Owen's seatbelt locked and he saw Duddits's body leap in Henry's arms. Duddits's bald head bounced against Henry's chest. Then they were over the crack and once more rolling up East Street. Owen could just make out the last phantom shapes of shoeprints on the now-white ribbon of the road. Mr. Gray was on foot and they were still rolling. If they could catch up before the bastard cut into the woods—

But they didn't.

6

With a final tremendous effort, Duddits raised his head. Now, Henry saw with dismay and horror, Duddits's eyes were also filling with blood.

Clack. Clack-clack. The dry chuckles of old men as someone accomplishes the fabled triple jump. The phone began to swim into his field of vision again. And the signs over it.

"No, Duddits," Henry whispered. "Don't try. Save your strength."

But for what? For what if not for this?

The sign on the left: PLEASE LIMIT ALL CALLS TO 5 MINS. Smells of tobacco, smells of woodsmoke, the old brine of pickles. His friend's arms around him.

And the sign on the right: CALL JONESY NOW.

"Duddits . . ." His voice floating in the darkness. Darkness, his old friend. "Duddits, I don't know *how.*"

Duddits's voice came to him a final time, very tired but calm: *Quick, Henry—I can only hold on a little longer—you need to talk to him.*

Henry picks the telephone's receiver out of its cradle. Thinks absurdly (but isn't the whole situation absurd?) that he doesn't have any change . . . not so much as a crying dime. Holds the phone to his ear.

Roberta Cavell's voice comes, impersonal and businesslike: "Massachusetts General Hospital, how may I direct your call?"

7

Mr. Gray flailed Jonesy's body along the path which ran up the east side of the Reservoir from the point where East Street ended, slipping, falling, grabbing branches, getting up again. Jonesy's knees were lacerated, the pants torn open and soaked with blood. His lungs were burning, his heart beating like a

steam-hammer. Yet the only thing that concerned
him was Jonesy's hip, the one he'd broken in the
accident. It was a hot and throbbing ball, shooting
pain all the way down the thigh to the knee, and up
to the middle of his back along the road of his spine.
The weight of the dog made things worse. It was
still asleep, but the thing inside was wide awake,
held in place only by Mr. Gray's will. Once, as he was
rising to his feet, the hip locked up entirely and Mr.
Gray had to beat it repeatedly with Jonesy's gloved
fist to make it let go again. How much farther? How
much farther through the cursed, stifling, blinding,
neverending snow? And what was Jonesy up to? Anything? Mr. Gray didn't dare let go of the byrum's
restless hunger—it had nothing even approaching a
mind—long enough to go to the door of the locked
room and listen.

A phantom shape appeared ahead in the snow. Mr.
Gray paused, gasping and peering at it, and then
fought his way forward again, holding the dog's limp
paws and dragging Jonesy's right foot.

Here was a sign nailed to the trunk of a tree:
ABSOLUTELY NO FISHING FROM SHAFT HOUSE. Fifty feet
beyond it, stone steps rose up from the path. Six of
them . . . no, eight. At the top was a stone building
on a stone foundation that jutted out into the snowy
gray nothing where the Reservoir lay—Jonesy's ears
could hear water lapping against stone even over the
rushing, labored beat of his heart.

He had come to the place.

Clutching the dog and using the last of Jonesy's

depleted strength, Mr. Gray began to totter up the snow-covered steps.

8

As they passed between the stone posts marking the entrance to the Reservoir, Kurtz said: "Pull over, Freddy. Side of the road."

Freddy did as he was asked without question.

"You got your auto, laddie?"

Freddy lifted it. The good old M-16, tried and true. Kurtz nodded.

"Sidearm?"

".44 Magnum, boss."

And Kurtz with the nine, which he liked for close work. He *wanted* this to be close work. He wanted to see the color of Owen Underhill's brains.

"Freddy?"

"Yes, boss."

"I just wanted you to know that this is my final mission, and I couldn't have hoped for a finer companion." He reached out and gave Freddy's shoulder a squeeze. Beside Freddy, Perlmutter snored with his Ma Joad face tipped up toward the roof. Five minutes or so before reaching the stone pillars he had passed several long, spectacularly odoriferous farts. After that, Pearly's distended gut had gone down again. Probably for the last time, Kurtz thought.

Freddy's eyes, meanwhile, had grown gratifyingly bright. Kurtz was delighted. He had not entirely lost his touch even now, it seemed.

"All right, buck," Kurtz said. "Full speed ahead and damn the torpedoes. Right?"

"Right, sir."

Kurtz guessed *sir* was okay again now. They could pretty well put the protocols of the mission behind them. They were Quantrill's boys, now; two final jayhawkers riding the western Massachusetts range.

With an unmistakable little grimace of distaste, Freddy jerked a thumb at Perlmutter. "Want me to try waking him up, sir? He may be too far gone, but—"

"Why bother?" Kurtz asked. Still gripping Freddy's shoulder, he pointed ahead, where the access road disappeared into a wall of white: the snow. The goddam snow that had chased them all this way, a grim fucking reaper dressed in white instead of black. The tracks of the Subaru were now entirely gone, but those of the Humvee Owen had stolen were still visible. If they moved along briskly, praise God, following these tracks would be a walk in the park. "I don't think we need him anymore, which I personally find a great relief. Go, Freddy. Go."

The Humvee flirted her tail and then steadied. Kurtz drew his nine and held it against his leg. *Coming for you, Owen. Coming for you, buck. And you better get your speech ready for God, because you're going to be making it just about an hour from now.*

9

The office which he had furnished so beautifully—furnished out of his mind and his memories—was now falling apart.

Jonesy limped restlessly back and forth, looking around the room, lips pressed so tightly together they were white, forehead beaded with sweat even though it had gotten damned cold in here.

This was The Fall of the Office of Jonesy instead of the House of Usher. The furnace was howling and clanking beneath him, making the floor shake. White stuff—frost crystals, maybe—puffed in through the vent and left a powdery triangular shape on the wall. Where it touched it went to work on the wood paneling, simultaneously rotting it and warping it. The pictures fell one by one, tumbling to the floor like suicides. The Eames chair—the one he'd always wanted, the very one—split in two as if it had been hacked by an invisible axe. The mahogany panels on the walls began to split and peel free like dead skin. The drawers juddered out of their places in the desk and clattered one by one to the floor. The shutters Mr. Gray had installed to block his view of the outside world were vibrating and shaking, producing a steady metallic squalling that set Jonesy's teeth on edge.

Crying out to Mr. Gray, demanding to know what was going on, would be useless . . . and besides, Jonesy had all the information he needed. He had slowed Mr. Gray down, but Mr. Gray had first risen to the chal-

lenge and then above it. *Viva* Mr. Gray, who had either
reached his goal or almost reached it. As the paneling
fell off the walls, he could see the dirty Sheetrock
beneath: the walls of the Tracker Brothers office as
four boys had seen it in 1978, lined up with their foreheads to the glass, their new chum standing behind
them as bidden, waiting for them to be done with
whatever it was they were doing, waiting for them to
take him home. Now another wood panel tore loose,
coming off the wall with a sound like tearing paper,
and beneath it was a bulletin board with a single
photo, a Polaroid, tacked to it. Not a beauty queen, not
Tina Jean Schlossinger, but just some woman with her
skirt hiked to the bottom of her panties, pretty stupid.
The nice rug on the floor suddenly shrivelled like skin,
revealing dirty Tracker Brothers tile beneath, and those
white tadpoles, scumbags left by couples who came in
here to screw beneath the disinterested gaze of the
Polaroid woman who was no one, really, just an artifact
of a hollow past.

He paced, lurching on his bad hip, which hadn't
hurt this badly since just after the accident, and he
understood all of this, oh yes indeed, you had better
believe it. His hip was full of splinters and ground
glass; his shoulders and neck ached with a fierce
tiredness. Mr. Gray was beating his body to death as
he made his final charge and there was nothing
Jonesy could do about it.

The dreamcatcher was still okay. Swaying back
and forth in great looping arcs, but still okay. Jonesy
fixed his eyes on it. He had thought himself ready to

die, but he didn't want to go like this, not in this stinking office. Outside of it, they had once done something good, something almost noble. To die in here, beneath the dusty, indifferent gaze of the woman pinned to the bulletin board . . . that didn't seem fair. Never mind the rest of the world; he, Gary Jones of Brookline, Massachusetts, once of Derry, Maine, lately of the Jefferson Tract, deserved better.

"Please, I deserve better than this!" he cried to the swaying cobweb shape in the air, and on the disintegrating desk behind him, the telephone rang.

Jonesy wheeled around, groaning at the fiery, complicated pain in his hip. The phone on which he'd called Henry earlier had been his office phone, the blue Trimline. The one on the cracked surface of the desk now was black and clunky, with a dial instead of buttons and a sticker on it reading MAY THE FORCE BE WITH YOU. It was the phone he'd had in his childhood room, the one his parents had given him for his birthday. 949-7784, the number to which he had charged the call to Duddits all those years ago.

He sprang for it, ignoring his hip, praying the line wouldn't disintegrate and disconnect before he could answer.

"Hello? Hello!" Swaying back and forth on the shaking, vibrating floor. The whole office now going up and down like a ship on a heavy sea.

Of all the voices he might have expected, Roberta's was the last. "Yes, Doctor, hold on for your call."

There was a click so loud it hurt his head, then

silence. Jonesy groaned and was about to put the phone down when there was another click.

"Jonesy?" It was Henry. Faint, but undoubtedly Henry.

"Where are you?" Jonesy shouted. "Christ, Henry, the place is falling apart! *I'm* falling apart!"

"I'm in Gosselin's," Henry said, "only I'm not. Wherever you are, you're not. We're in the hospital where they took you after you got hit . . ." A crackle on the line, a buzz, and then Henry came back, sounding closer and stronger. Sounding like a lifeline in all this disintegration. ". . . not there, either!"

"What?"

"We're in the dreamcatcher, Jonesy! *We're in the dreamcatcher and we always were!* Ever since '78! Duddits is the dreamcatcher, but he's dying! He's holding on, but I don't know how long . . ." Another click followed by another buzz, bitter and electric.

"Henry! *Henry!*"

". . . come out!" Faint again now. Henry sounded desperate. *"You have to come out, Jonesy!* Meet me! Run along the dreamcatcher and meet me! There's still time! We can take this son of a bitch! Do you hear me? We can—"

There was another click and the phone went dead. The body of his childhood phone cracked, split open, and vomited out a senseless tangle of wires. All of them were red-orange; all of them were contaminated with the byrus.

Jonesy dropped the phone and looked up at the swaying dreamcatcher, that ephemeral cobweb. He remembered a line they'd been fond of as kids, pulled out of some comedian's routine: *Wherever you are, there you are.* That had been right up there with *Same shit, different day,* had perhaps even taken over first place as they grew older and began to consider themselves sophisticated. *Wherever you are, there you are.* Only according to Henry's call just now, that wasn't true. Wherever they *thought* they were, they *weren't.*

They were in the dreamcatcher.

He noted that the one swaying in the air above the ruins of his desk had four central spokes radiating out from the center. Many connecting threads were held together by those spokes, but what held the spokes together was the center—the core where they merged.

Run along the dreamcatcher and meet me! There's still time!

Jonesy turned and sprinted for the door.

10

Mr. Gray was also at a door—the one into the shaft house. It was locked. Considering what had happened with the Russian woman, this didn't surprise him much. *Locking the barn door after the horse had been stolen* was Jonesy's phrase for it. If he'd had one of the kim, this would have been easy. As it was, he wasn't too perturbed. One of the interesting side effects of having emotions, he had discovered, was that they caused you to think ahead, *plan* ahead, so that you wouldn't trigger an all-out emotional attack if things went wrong. It might be one reason these creatures had survived as long as they had.

Jonesy's suggestion that he give in to all this—*go native* had been his phrase for it, one that struck Mr. Gray as both mysterious and exotic—wouldn't quite leave his mind, but Mr. Gray pushed it aside. He would accomplish his mission here, satisfy the imperative. After that, who knew? Bacon sandwiches, perhaps. And what Jonesy's mind identified as a "cocktail." This was a cool and refreshing drink, slightly intoxicating.

A gust of wind rolled off the Reservoir, slapping wet snow into his face, momentarily blinding him. It was like the snap of a wet towel, returning him to the here and now, where he had a job to finish.

He sidled to the left on the rectangular granite stoop, slipped, then dropped to his knees, ignoring the howl from Jonesy's hip. He hadn't come all this way—black light-years and white miles—either to fall back down the steps and break his neck or to tumble into the Quabbin and die of hypothermia in that chilly water.

The stoop had been placed atop a mound of crushed stone. Leaning over the left side of the stoop, he brushed snow away and began feeling for a loose chunk. There were windows flanking the locked door, narrow but not *too* narrow.

Sound was tamped down and flattened by the heavy fall of wet snow, but he could hear the sound of an approaching motor. There had been another, as well, but that one had already stopped, probably at the end of East Street. They were coming, but they were too late. It was a mile along the path, which was densely overgrown and slippery underfoot. By the time they got here the dog would be down the shaft, drowning and delivering the byrum into the aqueduct at the same time.

He found a loose rock and pulled it free, working carefully so as not to dislodge the pulsing body of the dog around his shoulders. He backed away from the edge on his knees, then tried to get to his feet. At first he couldn't. The ball of Jonesy's hip had swelled tight again. He finally lurched upright, although the pain was incredible, seeming to go all the way up to his teeth and his temples.

He stood for a moment, holding Jonesy's bad right leg a little off the ground like a horse with a stone in its hoof, bracing himself against the locked shaft-house door. When the pain had abated somewhat, he used the rock to beat the glass out of the window to the left of the door. He cut Jonesy's hand in several places, once deeply, and several cracked panes in the upper half of the window hung over the lower half like a cut-rate guillotine, but he paid no attention to these things. Nor did he sense that Jonesy had finally left his bolt-hole.

Mr. Gray squirmed in through the window, landed on the cold concrete floor, and looked around.

He was in a rectangular room about thirty feet long. At the far end, a window which no doubt would have given a spectacular view of the Reservoir on a clear day showed only white, as if a sheet had been tacked over it. To one side of it was what looked like a gigantic steel pail, its sides speckled with red—not byrus, but an oxide Jonesy identified as "rust." Mr. Gray didn't know for sure but guessed that men could be lowered down the shaft in the bucket, should some emergency require it.

The iron cover, four feet across, was in place, seated dead center in the middle of the floor. He could see the square notch on one side of it and looked around. A few tools leaned against the wall. One of them, in a scatter of glass from the broken window, was a crowbar. Quite possibly the same one the Russian woman had used as she prepared for her suicide.

Way I heard it, Mr. Gray thought, *the folks in Boston'll be drinking that last byrum in their morning coffee right around Valentine's Day.*

He seized the crowbar, limped painfully to the center of the room with his breath puffing cold and white before him, then seated the spatulate end of the tool in the slot of the cover.

The fit was perfect.

11

Henry racks the telephone, takes in a deep breath, holds it . . . and then runs for the door which is marked both OFFICE and PRIVATE.

"Hey!" old Reenie Gosselin squawks from her place at the cash-register. "Come back here, kid! You can't go in there!"

Henry doesn't stop, doesn't even slow, but as he goes through the door he realizes that yeah, he *is* a kid, at least a foot shy of his final height, and although he's wearing specs, they're nowhere near as heavy as they will be later on. He's a kid, but under all that flopping hair (which will have thinned a bit by the time he hits his thirties) there is an adult's brain. *I'm two, two, two mints in one,* he thinks, and as he bursts into Old Man Gosselin's office he is cackling madly—laughing like they did in the old days, when the strands of the dream-catcher were all close to the center and Duddits was running their pegs. *I almost busted a gut,* they used to say; *I almost busted a gut, what a fuckin pisser.*

Into the office he goes, but it's not Old Man Gosselin's office where a man named Owen Underhill once played a man whose name was not Abraham Kurtz a tape of the grayboys talking in famous voices; it is a corridor, a hospital corridor, and Henry is not in the least surprised. It's Mass General. He's made it.

The place is dank, colder than any hospital corridor should be, and the walls are splotched with byrus. Somewhere a voice is groaning *I don't want you, I don't want a shot, I want Jonesy. Jonesy knew Duddits, Jonesy died, died in the ambulance, Jonesy's the only one who will do. Stay away, kiss my bender, I want Jonesy.*

But he will not stay away. He is crafty old Mr. Death, and he will not stay away. He has business here.

He walks unseen down the corridor, where it's cold enough for him to see his breath puffing out in front

of him, a boy in an orange coat he will soon outgrow.
He wishes he had his rifle, the one Pete's Dad loaned
him, but that rifle is gone, left behind, buried in the
years along with Jonesy's phone with the *Star Wars*
sticker on it (how they had all envied that phone),
and Beaver's jacket of many zippers, and Pete's
sweater with the NASA logo on the breast. Buried in
the years. Some dreams die and fall free, that is
another of the world's bitter truths. How many bitter
truths there are.

He walks past a pair of laughing, talking nurses—
one of them is Josie Rinkenhauer, all grown up, and
the other is the woman in the Polaroid photograph
they saw that day through the Tracker Brothers office
window. They don't see him because he's not here for
them; he is in the dreamcatcher now, running back
along his strand, running toward the center. *I am the
eggman*, he thinks. *Time slowed, reality bent, on and on
the eggman went.*

Henry went on up the corridor toward the sound
of Mr. Gray's voice.

12

Kurtz heard it clearly enough through the shattered
window: the broken stutter of automatic-rifle fire. It
provoked an old sense of unease and impatience in
him: anger that the shooting had started without
him, and fear that it would be over before he got
there, nothing left but the wounded yelling *medic-
medic-medic*.

"Push it harder, Freddy." Directly in front of Kurtz, Perlmutter was snoring ever deeper into his coma.

"Pretty greasy underfoot, boss."

"Push it anyway. I've got a feeling we're almost—"

He saw a pink stain on the clean white curtain of the snow, as diffuse as blood from a facial cut seeping up through shaving cream, and then the ditched Subaru was right in front of them, nose-down and tail up. In the following moments Kurtz took back every unkind thought he'd had about Freddy's driving. His second in command simply twisted the steering wheel to the right and punched the gas when the Humvee started to skid. The big vehicle took hold and leaped at the break in the road. It hit with a tremendous jouncing crash. Kurtz flew upward, hitting the ceiling hard enough to produce a shower of stars in his field of vision. Perlmutter's arms flailed like those of a corpse; his head snapped backward and then forward. The Humvee passed close enough to the Subaru to tear the doorhandle off the car's passenger side. Then it was bucketing onward, now chasing a single pair of relatively fresh tire tracks.

Breathing down your neck now, Owen, Kurtz thought. *Right down your everloving neck, God rot your blue eyes.*

The only thing that worried him was that single burst of fire. What was that about? Whatever it was, it wasn't repeated.

Then, up ahead, another of those blotches in the snow. This one was olive-green. This one was the other Hummer. They were gone, probably gone, but—

"Lock and load," Kurtz said to Freddy. His voice

was just a trifle shrill. "It's time for someone to pay the piper."

13

By the time Owen got to the place where East Street ended (or turned into the northeast-meandering Fitz-patrick Road, depending on your interpretation), he could hear Kurtz behind him and guessed that Kurtz could probably hear him, as well—the Humvees weren't as loud as Harleys, but they were a long way from quiet.

Jonesy's footprints were entirely gone now, but Owen could see the path which led down from the road and along the shore of the Reservoir.

He killed the engine. "Henry, it looks like we're walking from h—"

Owen stopped. He had been concentrating too hard on his driving to look behind him or even check the rearview mirror, and he was unprepared for what he now saw. Unprepared and appalled.

Henry and Duddits were wrapped in what Owen first believed was a terminal embrace, their stubbly cheeks pressed together, their eyes closed, their faces and coats smeared with blood. He could see neither of them breathing and thought they had actually died together—Duddits of his leukemia, Henry per-haps of a heart attack brought on by exhaustion and the constant unrelieved stress of the last thirty hours or so—and then he saw the minute twitch of the eye-lids. Both sets.

Embracing. Splattered with blood. But not dead. Sleeping.

Dreaming.

Owen started to call Henry's name again and then reconsidered. Henry had refused to leave the compound back in Jefferson Tract without freeing the detainees, and although they'd gotten away with that once, it had only been through the sheerest luck . . . or providence, if you believed that was any more than a TV show. Nevertheless, they had gotten Kurtz on their tail, Kurtz had hung on like a booger, and now he was a lot closer than he would have been had Owen and Henry simply crept away into the storm.

Well, I wouldn't change that, Owen thought, opening the driver's door and getting out. From somewhere north, away in the white blank of the storm, came the scream of an eagle bitching about the weather. From behind, south, came the approaching racket of Kurtz, that annoying madman. It was impossible to tell how close because of the fucking snow. Coming down this fast and hard, it was like a sound-baffle. He could be two miles back; he could be a lot closer. Freddy would be with him, fucking Freddy, the perfect soldier, Dolph Lundgren from hell.

Owen went around to the back of the car, slipping and sliding in the snow, cursing it, and popped the Humvee's back gate, expecting automatic weapons, hoping for a portable rocket-launcher. No rocket-launcher, no grenades, either, but there were four MP5 auto-fire rifles, and a carton containing long banana-clips, the ones that held a hundred and twenty rounds.

He had played it Henry's way back at the compound, and Owen guessed that they had saved at least some lives, but he would not play it Henry's way this time—if he hadn't paid enough for the Rapeloews' goddam serving platter, he would simply have to live with the debt. Not for long, either, if Kurtz had his way.

Henry was either sleeping, unconscious, or joined to his dying childhood friend in some weird mind-meld. Let it be, then. Awake and by his side, Henry might balk at what needed to be done, especially if Henry was right in believing his other friend was still alive, hiding out in the mind the alien now controlled. Owen would not balk . . . and with the telepathy gone, he wouldn't hear Jonesy pleading for his life if he was still in there. The Glock was a good weapon, but not sure enough.

The MP5 would rip the body of Gary Jones apart.

Owen grabbed one, plus three extra clips which he stuffed into his coat pockets. Kurtz close now—close, close, close. He looked back at East Street, almost expecting to see the second Humvee materializing like a green-brown ghost, but as yet there was nothing. Praise Jesus, as Kurtz would say.

The Hummer's windows were already glazing over with snow, but he could see the dim shapes of the two men in the rear seat as he passed back along the body of the vehicle, trotting now. Still locked in each other's arms. "Goodbye, boys," he said. "Sleep well." And with any luck they would still be sleeping when Kurtz and Freddy arrived, putting an end to their lives before moving on after their main quarry.

Owen stopped suddenly, skidding in the snow and grabbing the Humvee's long hood to keep from falling. Duddits was clearly a lost cause, but he might be able to save Henry Devlin. It was just possible.

No! part of his mind screamed as he started back for the rear door. *No, there's no time!*

But Owen decided to gamble that there was—to gamble the whole world. Maybe to pay a little more on what he owed for the Rapeloews' plate; maybe for what he had done yesterday (those naked gray figures standing around their downed ship with their arms held up, as if in surrender); probably just for Henry, who had told him they would be heroes and who had tried splendidly to fulfill that promise.

No sympathy for the devil, he thought, wrenching open the rear door. *No sir, zero sympathy for that mother-fucker.*

Duddits was closer. Owen seized him by the collar of his big blue duffel coat and yanked. Duddits toppled sideways onto the seat. His hat fell off, revealing his shining bald skull. Henry, with his arms still around Duddits's shoulders, came with him, landing on top. His eyes didn't open but he groaned softly. Owen leaned forward and whispered fiercely into Henry's ear.

"Don't sit up. For the love of God, Henry, don't you sit up!"

Owen withdrew, slammed the door, backed off three steps, placed the butt of the rifle against his hip,

and fired a burst. The Humvee's windows turned to
milk, then fell in. Casings clinked around Owen's
feet. He stepped forward again and looked through
the shattered window into the rear seat. Henry and
Duddits still lay there, now covered with crumbles of
Saf-T-Glas as well as Duddits's blood, and to Owen
they looked like the two deadest people he had ever
seen. Owen hoped Kurtz would be in too much of a
hurry for a close examination. In any case, he had
done the best he could.

He heard a hard metallic jouncing sound and
grinned. That placed Kurtz, by God—they'd reached
the washout where the Subaru had finished up. He
wished mightily that Kurtz and Freddy had rear-
ended the fucking thing, but the sound had not,
unfortunately, been that loud. Still, it placed them. A
mile back, a mile back at least. Not as bad as he'd
thought.

"Plenty of time," he muttered, and that might be
true of Kurtz, but what about the other end? Where
was Mr. Gray now?

Holding the MP5 by the strap, Owen started
down the path that led to Shaft 12.

14

Mr. Gray had discovered another unlovely human emotion: panic. He had come all this way—light-years
through space, miles through the snow—to be balked
by Jonesy's muscles, which were weak and out of
shape, and the iron shaft cover, which was much heav-

ier than he had expected. He yanked down on the crowbar until Jonesy's back-muscles screamed in agonized protest . . . and was finally rewarded by a brief wink of darkness from beneath the edge of the rusty iron. And a grinding sound as it moved a bit—perhaps no more than an inch or two—on the concrete. Then Jonesy's lower back muscles locked up and Mr. Gray staggered away from the shaft, crying out through clenched teeth (thanks to his immunity, Jonesy still had a full set of them) and pressing his hands to the base of Jonesy's spine, as if to keep it from exploding.

Lad let out a series of yipping whines. Mr. Gray looked at him and saw that things had now reached the critical juncture. Although he was still asleep, Lad's abdomen was now so grotesquely swelled that one of his legs stuck stiffly up in the air. The skin of his lower belly had stretched to the point of splitting, and the veins there pulsed with clocklike rapidity. A trickle of bright blood spilled out from beneath his tail.

Mr. Gray looked balefully at the crowbar jutting from the slot in the iron cover. In Jonesy's imagination, the Russian woman had been a slim beauty with dark hair and dark tragic eyes. In reality, Mr. Gray thought, she must have been broad-shouldered and muscular. How else could she have—

There was a blast of gunfire, alarmingly close. Mr. Gray gasped and looked around. Thanks to Jonesy, the human corrosion of doubt was also part of his makeup now, and for the first time he realized that he might be balked—yes, even here, so close to his goal that he could *hear* it, the sound of rushing water starting on its sixty-mile underground journey. And all that stood between the byrum and this whole world was a circular iron plate weighing a hundred and twenty pounds.

Screaming a thin and desperate litany of Beaver-curses, Mr. Gray rushed forward, Jonesy's failing body jerking back and forth on the defective pivot-point of its right hip. One of them was coming, the one called Owen, and Mr. Gray dared not believe he could make this Owen turn his weapon on himself. Given time, given the element of surprise, maybe. Now he had neither. And this man who was coming had been trained to kill; it was his career.

Mr. Gray leaped into the air. There was a snap, quite audible, as Jonesy's overstressed hip broke free of the swollen socket which had held it. Mr. Gray landed on the crowbar with Jonesy's full weight. The edge lifted again, and this time the cover slid almost a foot across the concrete. The black crescent through which the Russian woman had slipped appeared again. Not much of a crescent, really no more than a delicate capital *C* drawn with a calligrapher's pen . . . but enough for the dog.

Jonesy's leg would no longer support Jonesy's weight (and where *was* Jonesy, anyway? Still not a murmur from his troublesome host), but that was all right. Crawling would do now.

Mr. Gray worked his way in such fashion across the cold cement floor to where the sleeping border collie lay, seized Lad by his collar, and began to drag him back to Shaft 12.

15

The Hall of Memories—that vast repository of boxes—is also on the verge of shaking itself apart. The floor shudders as if in the grip of an endless slow earthquake. Overhead, the fluorescents flicker on and off, giving the place a stuttery, hallucinatory look. In places tall stacks of cartons have fallen over, blocking some of the corridors.

Jonesy runs as best he can. He moves from corridor to corridor, threading his way through this maze purely on instinct. He tells himself repeatedly to ignore the goddam hip, he is nothing but mind now, anyway, but he might as well be an amputee trying to convince his missing limb to stop throbbing.

He runs past boxes marked AUSTRO-HUNGARIAN WAR and DEPARTMENTAL POLITICS and CHILDREN'S STORIES and CONTENTS OF UPSTAIRS CLOSET. He hurdles a pile of tumbled boxes marked CARLA, comes down on his bad leg, and screams at the pain. He clutches more boxes (these marked GETTYSBURG) in order to keep from falling, and at last sees the far side of the storage room. Thank God; it seems to him that he has run miles.

The door is marked ICU and QUIET PLEASE and NO VISITORS W/O PASS. And that is right; this is where they took him; this is where he had awakened and heard crafty old Mr. Death pretending to call for Marcy.

Jonesy bangs through the door and into another world, one he recognizes: the blue-over-white ICU

corridor where he took his first painful, tentative steps
four days after his surgery. He stumbles a dozen feet
down the tiled corridor, sees the splotches of byrus
growing on the walls, hears the Muzak, which is decidedly un-hospital-like; although it's turned low, it
appears to be the Rolling Stones singing "Sympathy for
the Devil."

He has no more than identified this song when his
hip suddenly goes nuclear. Jonesy utters a surprised
scream and falls to the black-and-red ICU tiles, clutching at himself. This is how it was just after he was hit:
an explosion of red agony. He rolls over and over, looking up at the glowing light-panels, at the circular
speakers from which the music (*"Anastasia screamed in
vain"*) is coming, music from another world, when the
pain is this bad *everything* is in another world, pain
makes a shadow of substance and a mockery even of
love, that is something he learned in March and must
learn again now. He rolls and he rolls, hands clutching
at his swollen hip, eyes bulging, mouth pulled back in
a vast rictus, and he knows what has happened, all
right: Mr. Gray. That son of a bitch Mr. Gray has re-
broken his hip.

Then, from far away in that other world, he hears a
voice he knows, a kid's voice.

Jonesy!

Echoing, distorted . . . but not that far away. Not
this corridor, but one of the adjacent ones. Whose
voice? One of his own kids? John, maybe? No—

*Jonesy, you have to hurry! He's coming to kill you! Owen
is coming to kill you!*

He doesn't know who Owen is, but he knows who that voice belongs to: Henry Devlin. But not as it is now, or as it was when he last saw Henry, going off to Gosselin's Market with Pete; this is the voice of the Henry he grew up with, the one who told Richie Grenadeau that they'd tell on him if he didn't stop, that Richie and his friends would never catch Pete because Pete ran like the fucking *wind*.

I can't! he calls back, still rolling on the floor. He is aware that something has changed, is still changing, but not what. *I can't, he broke my hip again, the son of a bitch broke—*

And then he realizes what is happening to him: *the pain is running backward*. It's like watching a video-tape as it rewinds—the milk flows up from the glass to the carton, the flower which should be blooming through the miracle of time-lapse photography closes up, instead.

The reason is obvious when he looks down at himself and sees the bright orange jacket he's wearing. It's the one his mother bought him in Sears for his first hunting trip to Hole in the Wall, the trip when Henry got his deer and they all killed Richie Grenadeau and his friends—killed them with a dream, maybe not meaning to but doing it just the same.

He has become a child again, a kid of fourteen, and there is no pain. Why would there be? His hip will not be broken for another twenty-three years. And then it all comes together with a crash in his mind: there was never any Mr. Gray, not really; Mr. Gray lives in the dreamcatcher and nowhere else. He is no more real than the pain in his hip. *I was immune,* he thinks, getting up. *I never got so much as a speck of the byrus. What's in my head isn't quite a memory, not that, but a true ghost in the machine. He's me. Dear God,* Mr. Gray is me.

Jonesy scrambles to his feet and begins to run, almost losing his feet as he swerves around a corner. He stays up, though; he is agile and quick as only a fourteen-year-old can be, and there is no pain, no pain.

The next corridor is one he knows. There is a parked gurney with a bedpan on it. Walking past it, moving delicately on tiny feet, is the deer he saw that day in Cambridge just before he was struck. There is a collar around its velvety neck and swinging from it like an oversized amulet is his Magic 8-Ball. Jonesy sprints past the deer, which looks at him with mild, surprised eyes.

Jonesy!

Close now. Very close.

Jonesy, hurry!

Jonesy redoubles his speed, feet flying, young lungs breathing easily, there is no byrus because he is immune, there is no Mr. Gray, not in *him,* at least, Mr. Gray is in the hospital and always was, Mr. Gray is the phantom limb you still feel, the one you could swear is still there, Mr. Gray is the ghost in the machine, the ghost on life support, and the life support is him.

He turns another corner. Here are three doors which are standing open. Beyond them, by the fourth door, the only one that is closed, Henry is standing. Henry is fourteen, as Jonesy is; Henry is wearing an orange coat, as Jonesy is. His glasses have slid down on his nose just as they always did, and he is beckoning urgently.

Hurry up! Hurry up, Jonesy! Duddits can't hold on much longer! If he dies before we kill Mr. Gray—

Jonesy joins Henry at the door. He wants to throw his arms around him, embrace him, but there's no time.

This is all my fault, he tells Henry, and his voice is higher in pitch than it has been in years.

Not true, Henry says. He's looking at Jonesy with the old impatience that awed Jonesy and Pete and Beaver as children—Henry always seemed farther ahead, always on the verge of sprinting into the future and leaving the rest of them behind. They always seemed to be holding him back.

But—

You might as well say that Duddits murdered Richie Grenadeau and that we were his accomplices. He was what he was, Jonesy, and he made us what we are . . . but not on purpose. It was all he could do to tie his shoes on purpose, don't you know that?

And Jonesy thinks: *Fit wha? Fit neek?*

Henry . . . is Duddits—

He's holding on for us, Jonesy, I told you. Holding us together.

In the dreamcatcher.

That's right. So are we going to stand out here arguing in the hall while the world goes down the chute, or are we going to—

We're going to kill the son of a bitch, Jonesy says, and reaches for the doorknob. Above it is a sign reading THERE IS NO INFECTION HERE, IL N'Y A PAS D'INFECTION ICI, and suddenly he sees both of that sign's bitter edges. It's like one of those Escher optical illusions. Look at it from one angle and it's true. Look at it from another and it's the most monstrous lie in the universe.

Dreamcatcher, Jonesy thinks, and turns the knob.

The room beyond the door is a byrus madhouse, a nightmare jungle overgrown with creepers and vines and lianas twisted together in blood-colored plaits. The air reeks of sulfur and chilly ethyl alcohol, the smell of starter fluid sprayed into a balky carb on a sub-zero January morning. At least they don't have the shit-weasel to worry about, not in here; that's on another strand of the dreamcatcher, in another place and time. The byrum is Lad's problem now; he's a border collie with a very dim future.

The television is on, and although the screen is over-grown with byrus, a ghostly black-and-white image comes straining through. A man is dragging the corpse of a dog across a concrete floor. Dusty and strewn with dead autumn leaves, it's like a tomb in one of the fifties horror flicks Jonesy still likes to watch on his VCR. But this isn't a tomb; it is filled with the hollow sound of rushing water.

In the center of the floor there is a rusty circular cover with MWRA stamped on it: Massachusetts Water Resources Authority. Even through the reddish scrum on the TV screen, these letters stand out. Of course they do. To Mr. Gray—who died as a physical being all the way back at Hole in the Wall—they mean everything.

They mean, quite literally, the world.

The shaft-lid has been partly pushed aside, revealing

a crescent shape of absolute darkness. The man dragging the dog is himself, Jonesy realizes, and the dog isn't quite dead. It is leaving a trail of frothy pink blood behind on the concrete, and its back legs are twitching. Almost paddling.

Never mind the movie, Henry almost snarls, and Jonesy turns his attention to the figure in the bed, the gray thing with the byrus-speckled sheet pulled up to its chest, which is a plain gray expanse of poreless, hairless, nippleless flesh. Although he can't see now because of the sheet, Jonesy knows there is no navel, either, because this thing was never born. It is a child's rendering of an alien, trolled directly from the subconscious minds of those who first came in contact with the byrum. They never existed as actual creatures, aliens, ETs. The grays as physical beings were always created out of the human imagination, out of the dreamcatcher, and knowing this affords Jonesy a measure of relief. He wasn't the only one who got fooled. At least there is that.

Something else pleases him: the look in those horrid black eyes. It's fear.

16

"I'm locked and loaded," Freddy said quietly, drawing to a stop behind the Humvee they had chased all these miles.

"Outstanding," Kurtz said. "Recon that HMW. I'll cover you."

"Right." Freddy looked at Perlmutter, whose belly

was swelling again, then at Owen's Hummer. The reason for the rifle-fire they'd heard earlier was clear now: the Hummer had been shot up pretty good. The only question left to be answered was who had been on the giving end and who on the receiving. Tracks led away from the Hummer, growing indistinct under the rapid snowfall, but for now clear enough to read. A single set. Boots. Probably Owen.

"Go on now, Freddy!"

Freddy got out into the snow. Kurtz slid out behind him and Freddy heard him rack the slide of his personal. Depending on the nine-millimeter. Well, maybe that was all right; he was good with it, no question of that.

Freddy felt a momentary coldness down his spine, as if Kurtz had the nine leveled there. Right there. But that was ridiculous, wasn't it? Owen, yes, but Owen was different. Owen had crossed the line.

Freddy hurried to the Hummer, bent low, carbine held at chest level. He didn't like having Kurtz behind him, that was undeniable. No, he didn't like that at all.

17

As the two boys advance on the overgrown bed, Mr. Gray begins to push the CALL button repeatedly, but nothing happens. *I think the works must be choked with byrus,* Jonesy thinks. *Too bad, Mr. Gray—too bad for you.* He glances up at the TV and sees that his film self has gotten the dog to the edge of the shaft.

Maybe they're too late after all; maybe not. There's no way to tell. The wheel is still spinning.

Hello, Mr. Gray, I've so much wanted to meet you, Henry says. As he speaks, he removes the byrus-splotched pillow from beneath Mr. Gray's narrow, earless head. Mr. Gray tries to wriggle toward the other side of the bed, but Jonesy holds him in place, grasping the alien's child-thin arms. The skin in his hands is neither hot nor cold. It doesn't feel like skin at all, not really. It feels like—

Like nothing, he thinks. *Like a dream.*

Mr. Gray? Henry asks. *This is how we say welcome to Planet Earth.* And he puts the pillow over Mr. Gray's face.

Beneath Jonesy's hands, Mr. Gray begins to struggle and thrash. Somewhere a monitor begins to beep frantically, as if this creature actually has a heart, and that it has now stopped beating.

Jonesy looks down at the dying monster and wishes only for this to be over.

18

Mr. Gray got the dog to the side of the shaft he had partially uncovered. Coming up through the narrow black semicircle was the steady hollow rush of running water and a waft of dank, cold air.

If it were done when 'tis done, then 'twere well it were done quickly—that from a box marked SHAKE-SPEARE. The dog's rear legs were bicycling rapidly, and Mr. Gray could hear the wet sound of tearing flesh as the byrum thrust with one end and chewed with the other, forcing itself out. Beneath the dog's tail, the chittering had started, a sound like an angry monkey. He had to get it into the shaft before it could emerge; it did not absolutely have to be born in the water, but its odds of survival would be much higher if it was.

Mr. Gray tried to shove the dog's head into the gap between the cover and the concrete and couldn't get it through. The neck bent and the dog's senselessly grinning snout twisted upward. Although still sleeping (or perhaps it was now unconscious) it began to utter a series of low, choked barks.

And it wouldn't go through the gap.

"*Fuck me Freddy!*" Mr. Gray screamed. He was barely aware of the snarling ache in Jonesy's hip now, certainly not aware that Jonesy's face was strained and pale, the hazel eyes wet with tears of effort and frustration. He *was* aware—terribly aware—that something was going on. *Going on behind my back,* Jonesy would have said. And who else could it be? Who else but Jonesy, his reluctant host?

"*Fuck YOU!*" he screamed at the damned, hateful, stubborn, just-a-little-too-big dog. "*You're going down, do you hear me? DO YOU—*"

The words stopped in his throat. All at once he couldn't yell anymore, although he dearly wanted to; how he loved to yell, and pound his fists on things (even a dying pregnant dog)! All at once he couldn't *breathe,* let alone yell. What was Jonesy doing to him?

He expected no answer, but one came—a stranger's voice, full of cold rage: *This is how we say welcome to Planet Earth.*

19

The flailing, three-fingered hands of the gray thing in the hospital bed come up and actually push the pillow aside for a moment. The black eyes starting from the otherwise featureless face are frantic with fear and rage. It gasps for breath. Considering that it doesn't really exist at all—not even in Jonesy's brain, at least as a physical artifact—it is fighting furiously for its life. Henry cannot sympathize, but he understands. It wants what Jonesy wants, what Duddits wants . . . what even Henry himself wants, for in spite of all his black thoughts, has his heart not gone on beating? Has his liver not gone on washing his blood? Has his body not gone on fighting its unseen wars against everything from the common cold to cancer to the byrus itself? The body is either stupid or infinitely wise, but in either case it is spared the terrible witchery of thought; it only knows how to stand its ground and fight until it can fight no more. If Mr. Gray was ever any different, he is different no longer. He wants to live.

But I don't think you will, Henry says in a voice that is calm, almost soothing. *I don't think so, my friend.* And once more puts the pillow over Mr. Gray's face.

20

Mr. Gray's airway opened. He got one breath of the cold shaft-house air . . . two . . . and then the airway closed up again. They were smothering him, stifling him, killing him.

No!! Kiss my bender! Kiss my fucking bender! YOU CAN'T DO THIS!

He yanked the dog back and turned it sideways; it was almost like watching a man already late for his plane trying to make one last bulky article fit into his suitcase.

It'll go through this way, he thought.

Yes. It would. Even if he had to collapse the dog's bulging middle with Jonesy's hands and allow the byrum to squirt free. One way or another, the damned thing *would* go through.

Face swelling, eyes bulging, breath stopped, a single fat vein swelling in the middle of Jonesy's forehead, Mr. Gray shoved Lad deeper into the crack and then began to thump the dog's chest with Jonesy's fists.

Go through, damn you, go through.

GO THROUGH!

21

Freddy Johnson pointed his carbine inside the abandoned Hummer while Kurtz, stationed shrewdly behind him (in that way it was like the attack on the grayboy ship all over again), waited to see what would develop.

"Two guys, boss. Looks like Owen decided to put out the trash before moving on."

"Dead?"

"They look pretty dead to me. Got to be Devlin and the other one, the one they stopped for."

Kurtz joined Freddy, took a brief glance in through the shattered window, and nodded. They looked pretty dead to him, too, a pair of white moles lying entwined in the back seat, covered with blood and shattered glass. He raised his nine-millimeter to make sure of them—one each in the head couldn't hurt—then lowered it again. Owen might not have heard their engine. The snow was amazingly heavy and wet, an acoustical blanket, and that was very possible. But he would hear gunshots. He turned toward the path instead.

"Lead the way, buck, and mind the footing—looks slippery. And we may still have the element of surprise. I think we should bear that in mind, don't you?"

Freddy nodded.

Kurtz smiled. It turned his face into a skull's face. "With any luck, buck, Owen Underhill will be in hell before he even knows he's dead."

22

The TV remote, a rectangle of black plastic covered with byrus, is lying on Mr. Gray's bedtable. Jonesy grabs it. In a voice that sounds eerily like Beaver's, he says "Fuck this shit" and slams it down as hard as he can on the table's edge, like a man cracking the shell of a hard-boiled egg. The controller shatters, spilling its batteries and leaving a jagged plastic wand in Jonesy's hand. He reaches below the pillow Henry is holding over the thrashing thing's face. He hesitates for just a moment, remembering his first meeting with Mr. Gray—his *only* meeting. The bathroom knob coming free in his hand as the rod snapped. The sense of darkness which was the creature's shadow falling over him. It had been real enough then, real as roses, real as raindrops. Jonesy had turned and seen him . . . it . . . whatever Mr. Gray had been before he was Mr. Gray . . . standing there in the big central room. The stuff of a hundred movies and "unexplained mysteries" documentaries, only old. Old and sick. Ready even then for this hospital bed in the Intensive Care Unit. *Marcy,* it had said, plucking the word straight out of Jonesy's brain. Pulling it like a cork. Making the hole through which it could enter. Then it had exploded like a noisemaker on New Year's Eve, spraying byrus instead of confetti, and . . .

. . . and I imagined the rest. That was it, wasn't it? Just another case of intergalactic schizophrenia. Basically, that was it.

Jonesy! Henry shouts. *If you're gonna do it, then do it!*

Here it comes, Mr. Gray, Jonesy thinks. *Get ready for it. Because payback's—*

23

Mr. Gray had gotten Lad's body halfway into the gap when Jonesy's voice filled his head.

Here it comes, Mr. Gray. Get ready for it. Because pay-
back's a bitch.

There was a ripping pain across the middle of
Jonesy's throat. Mr. Gray raised Jonesy's hands, making
a series of gagging grunts that would not quite attain
the status of screams. He didn't feel the beard-stubbled,
unbroken skin of Jonesy's throat but his own ragged
flesh. What he felt most strongly was shocked disbelief:
it was the last of Jonesy's emotions upon which he
drew. *This could not be happening.* They always came in
the ships of the old ones, those artifacts; they always
raised their hands in surrender; *they always won.* This
could not be happening.

And yet somehow it was.

The byrum's consciousness did not so much fade as
disintegrate. Dying, the entity once known as Mr.
Gray reverted to its former state. As *he* became *it*
(and just before *it* could become *nothing*), Mr. Gray
gave the dog's body a final vicious shove. It sank into
the gap . . . yet still not quite far enough to go
through.

The byrum's last Jonesy-tinged thought was *I*
should have taken him up on it. I should have gone na—

24

Jonesy slashes the jagged end of the TV controller across
Mr. Gray's naked wattled neck. Its throat peels open like
a mouth and a cloud of reddish-orange matter puffs
out, staining the air the color of blood before falling
back to the counterpane in a shower of dust and fluff.

Mr. Gray's body twitches once, galvanically, beneath Jonesy's and Henry's hands. Then it shrivels like the dream it always was and becomes something familiar. For a moment Jonesy can't make the connection and then it comes. Mr. Gray's remains look like one of the condoms they saw on the floor of the deserted office in the Tracker Brothers depot.

He's—

—*dead!* is how Jonesy means to finish, but then a terrible bolt of pain tears through him. Not his hip this time but his head. And his throat. All at once his throat is wearing a necklace of fire. And the whole room is transparent, damned if it isn't. He's looking through the wall and into the shaft house, where the dog stuck in the crack is giving birth to a vile red creature that looks like a weasel crossed with a huge, blood-soaked worm. He knows well enough what it is: one of the byrum.

Streaked with blood and shit and the remains of its own membranous placenta, its brainless black eyes staring (*they're his eyes,* Jonesy thinks, *Mr. Gray's eyes*), it is being born in front of him, stretching its body out, trying to pull free, wanting to drop into the darkness and fall toward the sound of running water.

Jonesy looks at Henry.

Henry looks back.

For just a moment their young and startled eyes meet . . . and then *they* are disappearing, as well.

Duddits, Henry says. His voice comes from far away. *Duddits is going. Jonesy . . .*

Goodbye. Perhaps Henry means to say goodbye. Before he can, they're both gone.

25

There was a moment of vertigo when Jonesy was exactly nowhere, a sense of utter disconnection. He thought it must be death, that he had killed himself as well as Mr. Gray—cut his own throat, as the saying went.

What brought him back was pain. Not in his throat, that was gone and he could breathe again—he could hear the air going in and out of him in great dry gasps. No, this pain was an old acquaintance. It was in his hip. It caught him and swung him back into the world around its swollen, howling axis, winding him up like a tether-ball on a post. There was concrete under his knees, his hands were full of fur, and he heard an inhuman chittering sound. *At least this part is real,* he thought. *This part is outside the dreamcatcher.*

That godawful chittering sound.

Jonesy saw the weasel-thing now dangling into the dark, held to the upper world only by its tail, which wasn't yet free of the dog. Jonesy lunged forward and clamped his hands around its slippery, shivering middle just as it did pull free.

He rocked backward, his bad hip throbbing, holding the writhing, yammering thing above his head like a carny performer with a boa constrictor. It whipped back and forth, teeth gnashing at the air, bending back on itself, trying to get at Jonesy's wrist and snagging the right sleeve of his parka instead, tearing it open and releasing near-weightless tangles of white down filling.

Jonesy pivoted on his howling hip and saw a man framed in the broken window through which Mr. Gray had wriggled. The newcomer, his face long with surprise, was dressed in a camouflage parka and holding a rifle.

Jonesy flung the wriggling weasel as hard as he could, which wasn't very hard. It flew perhaps ten feet, landed on the leaf-littered floor with a wet thump, and immediately began slithering back toward the shaft. The dog's body plugged part of it, but not enough. There was plenty of room.

"Shoot it!" Jonesy screamed at the man with the rifle. *"For God's sake shoot it before it can get into the water!"*

But the man in the window did nothing. The world's last hope only stood there with his mouth hanging open.

26

Owen simply couldn't believe what he was seeing. Some sort of red thing, a freakish weasel with no legs. To hear about such things was one matter; to actually *see* one was another. It squirmed toward the hole in the middle of the floor. A dog with its stiffening paws held up as if in surrender was wedged there.

The man—it had to be Typhoid Jonesy—was screaming at him to shoot the thing, but Owen's arms simply wouldn't come up. They seemed to be coated in lead. The thing was going to get away; after all that had happened, what he had hoped to prevent was going to happen right in front of him. It was like being in hell.

He watched it wriggle forward, making a godawful monkey-sound that he seemed to hear in the center of his head; he watched Jonesy lunging with desperate awkwardness, hoping to catch it or at least head it off. It wasn't going to work. The dog was in the way.

Owen again commanded his arms to raise the gun and point it, but nothing happened. The MP5 might as well have been in another universe. He was going to let it get away. He was going to stand here like a post and let it get away. God help him.

God help them all.

27

Henry sat up in the back seat of the Humvee, dazed. There was stuff in his hair. He brushed at it, still feeling caught in the dream of the hospital (*except that was no dream,* he thought), and then a sharp prick of pain restored him to something like reality. It was glass. His hair was filled with glass. More of it, Saf-T-Glas crumbles of it, covered the seat. And Duddits.

"Dud?"

Useless, of course. Duddits was dead. Must be dead. He had expended the last of his failing energy to bring Jonesy and Henry together in that hospital room.

But Duddits groaned. His eyes opened, and looking into them brought Henry all the way back to this snowy dead-end road. Duddits's eyes were red and bloody zeroes, the eyes of a sibyl.

"Ooby!" Duddits cried. His hands rose and made a weak aiming gesture, as if he held a rifle. *"Ooby-Doo! Ot-sum urk-ooo do now!"*

From somewhere up ahead in the woods, two rifle shots came in answer. A pause, then a third one.

"Dud?" Henry whispered. "Duddits?"

Duddits saw him. Even through his bloody eyes, Duddits saw him. Henry more than felt this; for a moment he actually saw *himself* through Duddits's eyes. It was like looking into a magic mirror. He saw the Henry who had been: a kid looking out at the world through horn-rimmed glasses that were too big for his face and always sliding down to the end of his nose. He felt Duddits's love for him, a simple and uncomplicated emotion untinctured by doubt or selfishness or even gratitude. Henry took Duddits in his arms, and when he felt the lightness of his old friend's body, Henry began to cry.

"You were the lucky one, buddy," he said, and wished Beaver were here. Beaver could have done what Henry could not; Beav could have sung Duddits to sleep. "You were always the lucky one, that's what I think."

"Ennie," Duddits said, and touched Henry's cheek with one hand. He was smiling, and his final words were perfectly clear. "I love you, Ennie."

28

Two shots rang out up ahead—carbine whipcracks. Not far up ahead, either. Kurtz stopped. Freddy was about twenty feet ahead of him, standing by a sign Kurtz could just make out: ABSOLUTELY NO FISHING FROM SHAFT HOUSE.

A third shot, then silence.

"Boss?" Freddy murmured. "Some kind of building up ahead."

"Can you see anyone?"

Freddy shook his head.

Kurtz joined him, amused even at this point at the slight jump Freddy gave when Kurtz put his hand on Freddy's shoulder. And he was right to jump. If Abe Kurtz survived the next fifteen or twenty minutes, he intended to go forward alone into whatever brave new world there might be. No one to slow him down; no witnesses to this final guerrilla action. And while he might suspect, Freddy couldn't know for sure. Too bad the telepathy was gone. Too bad for Freddy.

"Sounds like Owen found someone else to kill." Kurtz spoke low into Freddy's ear, which still sported a few curls of the Ripley, now white and dead.

"Do we go get him?"

"Goodness, no," Kurtz replied. "Perish the thought. I believe the time has come—regrettably, it comes in almost every life—when we must step off the path, buck. Mingle with the trees. See who stays and who comes back. If anyone does. We'll give it ten minutes, shall we? I think ten minutes should be more than enough."

29

The words which filled Owen Underhill's mind were nonsensical but unmistakable: *Scooby! Scooby-Doo! Got some work to do now!*

The carbine came up. He wasn't the one who did it, but when the force lifting the rifle left him, Owen was able to take over smoothly. He flicked the auto's selector-switch to single-shot fire, sighted, and squeezed the trigger twice. The first round missed, hitting the concrete in front of the weasel and ricocheting. Chips of concrete flew. The thing pulled back, turned, saw him, and bared its mouthful of needle teeth.

"That's right, beautiful," Owen said. "Smile for the camera."

His second shot went right through the weasel's humorless grin. It tumbled backward, struck the wall of the shaft house, then fell to the concrete. Yet even with its rudiment of a head blown off, its instincts remained. It began to crawl slowly forward again. Owen aimed, and as he centered the sight, he thought of the Rapeloews, Dick and Irene. Nice people. Good neighbors. If you needed a cup of sugar or a pint of milk (or a shoulder to cry on, for that matter), you could always go next door and get fixed up. *They said it was a stroke!* Mr. Rapeloew had called, only Owen had thought he was saying *stork.* Kids got everything wrong.

So this was for the Rapeloews. And for the kid who had kept getting it wrong.

Owen fired a third time. This slug caught the byrum amidships and tore it in two. The ragged pieces twitched . . . twitched . . . lay still.

With that done, Owen swung his carbine in a short arc. This time he settled the sight on the middle of Gary Jones's forehead.

Jonesy looked unblinkingly back at him. Owen was tired—almost to death, that was what it felt like—but this guy looked far past even that point. Jonesy raised his empty hands.

"You have no reason to believe this," he said, "but Mr. Gray is dead. I cut his throat while Henry held a pillow over his face—it was right out of *The Godfather.*"

"Really," Owen said. There was no inflection in his voice whatsoever. "And where, exactly, did you perform this execution?"

"In a Massachusetts General Hospital of the mind," Jonesy said. He then uttered the most joyless laugh Owen had ever heard in his life. "One where deer roam the halls and the only TV program is an old movie called *Sympathy for the Devil.*"

Owen jerked a little at that.

"Shoot me if you have to, soldier. I saved the world—with a little ninth-inning relief help from you, I freely admit. You might as well pay me for the service in the traditional manner. Also, the bastard broke my hip again. A little going-away present from the little man who wasn't there. The pain is . . ." Jonesy bared his teeth. "It's very large."

Owen held the gun where it was a moment longer,

then lowered it. "You can live with it," he said.

Jonesy fell backward on the points of his elbows, groaned, turned his weight as well as he could onto his unhurt side. "Duddits is dead. He was worth both of us put together—more—and he's dead." He covered his eyes for a moment, then dropped his arm. "Man, what a fuckarow this is. That's what Beaver would have called it, a total fuckarow. That is opposed to a fuckaree, you understand, which in Beaver-ese means a particularly fine time, possibly but not necessarily of a sexual nature."

Owen had no idea what the man was talking about; likely he was delirious. "Duddits may be dead, but Henry's not. There are some people after us, Jonesy. Bad people. Do you hear them? Know where they are?"

Lying on the cold, leaf-littered floor, Jonesy shook his head. "I'm back to the standard five senses, I'm afraid. ESP's all gone. The Greeks may come bearing gifts, but they're Indian givers." He laughed. "Jesus, I could lose my job for a crack like that. Sure you don't want to just shoot me?"

Owen paid no more attention to this than he had to the semantical differences between fuckarow and fuckaree. Kurtz was coming, that was the problem he had to deal with now. He hadn't heard him arrive, but he might not have done. The snow was falling heavily enough to damp all but loud sounds. Gunshots, for instance.

"I have to go back to the road," he said. "You hang in there."

"What choice?" Jonesy asked, and closed his eyes.

"Man, I wish I could go back to my nice warm office. I never thought I'd say that, but there it is."

Owen turned and went back down the steps, slipping and sliding but managing to keep his feet. He scanned the woods to either side of the path, but not closely. If Kurtz and Freddy were laid up, waiting someplace between here and the Hummer, he doubted he would see them in time to do anything. He might see tracks, but by then he'd be so close to them they'd likely be the *last* things he saw. He had to hope he was still ahead, that was all. Had to trust to plain old baldass luck, and why not? He'd been in plenty of tight places, and baldass luck had always pulled him through. Maybe it would do so ag—

The first bullet took him in the belly, knocking him backward and blowing the back of his coat out in a bell-shape. He pumped his feet, trying to stay upright, also trying to hang onto the MP5. There was no pain, just a feeling of having been sucker-punched by a large boxing glove on the fist of a mean opponent. The second round shaved the side of his head, producing a burn-and-sting like rubbing alcohol poured into an open wound. The third shot hit him high up on the right side of the chest and that was Katie bar the door; he lost both his feet and the carbine.

What had Jonesy said? Something about having saved the world and getting paid off in the traditional manner. And this wasn't so bad, really; it had taken Jesus six hours, they'd put a joke sign over His head, and come cocktail hour they'd given Him a stiff vinegar-and-water.

He lay half on and half off the snow-covered path, vaguely aware that something was screaming and it wasn't him. It sounded like an enormous pissed-off blue jay.

That's an eagle, Owen thought.

He managed to get a breath, and although the exhale was more blood than air, he was able to get up on his elbows. He saw two figures emerge from the tangle of birches and pines, bent low, very much in combat-advance mode. One was squat and broad-shouldered, the other slim and gray-haired and positively perky. Johnson and Kurtz. The bulldog and the greyhound. His luck had run out after all. In the end, luck always did.

Kurtz knelt beside him, eyes sparkling. In one hand he held a triangle of newspaper. It was battered and slightly curved from its long trip in Kurtz's rear pocket, but still recognizable. It was a cocked hat. A fool's hat. "Tough luck, buck," Kurtz said.

Owen nodded. It was. Very tough luck. "I see you found time to make me a little something."

"I did. Did you achieve your prime objective, at least?" Kurtz lifted his chin in the direction of the shaft house.

"Got him," Owen managed. His mouth was full of blood. He spat it out, tried to pull in another breath, and heard the good part of it wheeze out of some new hole instead.

"Well, then," Kurtz said benevolently, "all's well that ends well, wouldn't you say?" He put the newspaper hat tenderly on Owen's head. Blood soaked it immediately, spreading upward, turning the UFO story red.

There was another scream from somewhere out over the Reservoir, perhaps from one of the islands that were actually hills poking up from a purposely drowned landscape.

"That's an eagle," Kurtz said, and patted Owen's shoulder. "Count yourself lucky, laddie. God sent you a warbird to sing you to——"

Kurtz's head exploded in a spray of blood and brains and bone. Owen saw one final expression in the man's blue, white-lashed eyes: amazed disbelief. For a moment Kurtz remained on his knees, then toppled forward on what remained of his face. Behind him, Freddy Johnson stood with his carbine still raised and smoke drifting from the muzzle.

Freddy, Owen tried to say. No sound came out, but Freddy must have read his lips. He nodded.

"Didn't want to, but the bastard was going to do it to me. Didn't have to read his mind to know that. Not after all these years."

Finish it, Owen tried to say. Freddy nodded again. Perhaps there was a vestige of that goddam telepathy left inside Freddy, after all.

Owen was fading. Tired and fading. Goodnight, sweet ladies, goodnight, David, goodnight, Chet. Goodnight, sweet prince. He lay back on the snow and it was like falling back into a bed stuffed with the softest down. From somewhere, faint and far, he heard the eagle scream again. They had invaded its territory, disturbed its snowy autumn peace, but soon they would be gone. The eagle would have the Reservoir to itself again.

We were heroes, Owen thought. *Damned if we weren't. Fuck your hat, Kurtz, we were h—*

He never heard the final shot.

30

There had been more firing; now there was silence. Henry sat in the back seat of the Humvee beside his dead friend, trying to decide what to do next. The chances that they had all killed each other seemed slim. The chances that the good guys—correction, the good *guy*—had taken out the bad ones seemed slimmer still.

His first impulse following this conclusion was to vacate the Hummer posthaste and hide in the woods. Then he looked at the snow (*If I ever see snow again,* he thought, *it'll be too soon*) and rejected the idea. If Kurtz or whoever was with him came back in the next half hour, Henry's tracks would still be there. They would follow his trail, and at the end of it they'd shoot him like a rabid dog. Or a weasel.

Get a gun, then. Shoot them before they can shoot you.

A better idea. He was no Wyatt Earp, but he could shoot straight. Shooting men was a lot different from shooting deer, you didn't have to be a headshrinker to know that, but he believed, given a clear line of fire, he could shoot these guys with very little hesitation.

He was reaching for the doorhandle when he heard a surprised curse, a thump, yet another gunshot. This one was *very* close. Henry thought someone had lost his footing and gone down in the snow, discharging his weapon when he landed on his ass. Perhaps the son of a bitch had just shot himself? Was that too much to hope for? Wouldn't that just—

But no. No joy. Henry heard a low grunt as the person who'd fallen got up and came on again. There was only one option, and Henry took it. He lay back down on the seat, put Duddits's arms around him again (as best he could), and played dead. He didn't think there was much chance this hugger-mugger would work. The bad guys had passed by on their way in—obviously, as he was still alive—but on their way in they must have been in a pants-ripping hurry. Now they would be a lot less likely to be fooled by a few bullet holes, some broken glass, and the blood of poor old Duddits's final hemorrhages.

Henry heard soft, crunching footsteps in the snow. Only one set, by the sound. Probably the infamous Kurtz. Last man standing. Darkness approaching. Death in the afternoon. No longer his old friend— now he was only *playing* dead—but approaching, just the same.

Henry closed his eyes . . . waited . . .

The footsteps passed the Humvee without slowing.

31

Freddy Johnson's strategic goal was, for the time being, both extremely practical and extremely short-term:

he wanted to get the goddam Hummer turned around without getting stuck. If he managed that, he wanted to get past the break in East Street (where the Subaru Owen had been chasing had come to grief) without getting ditched himself. If he made it back to the access road, he might widen his horizons a trifle. The idea of the Mass Pike surfaced briefly in his mind as he swung open the door of the boss's Hummer and slid behind the wheel. There was a lot of western America down I-90. A lot of places to hide.

The stench of stale farts and chilly ethyl alcohol struck him like a slap as he swung the door closed. Pearly! Goddam Pearly! In the excitement, he had forgotten all about *that* little motherfucker.

Freddy turned, raising the carbine . . . but Pearly was still out cold. No need to use another bullet. He could just tip Perlmutter out into the snow. If he was lucky, Pearly would freeze to death without ever waking up. Him, and his little sideki—

Pearly wasn't sleeping, though. Nor out cold. Nor in a coma, not even that. Pearly was dead. And he was . . . *shrunken,* somehow. Almost mummified. His cheeks were drawn in, hollow, wrinkled. The sockets of his eyes were deep divots, as if behind the thin veils of his closed lids the eyeballs had fallen into what was now a hollow bucket. And he was tilted strangely against the passenger door, one leg raised, almost crossed over the other. It was as if he had died trying to perform the ever-popular one-cheek-sneak. His fatigue pants were now dark, the muted colors turned to mud, and the seat under him was wet. The fingers of the stain spreading toward Freddy were red. "What the f—"

From the back seat there arose an ear-splitting yammering; it was like listening to a powerful stereo turned rapidly up to full volume. Freddy caught movement from the corner of his right eye. A creature beyond belief appeared in the rearview mirror. It tore off Freddy's ear and then struck at his cheek, punched through into his mouth, and latched onto his jaw at the inner gumline. And then Archie Perlmutter's shit-weasel tore off the side of Freddy's face as a hungry man might tear a drumstick off a chicken.

Freddy shrieked and discharged his weapon into the passenger door of the Hummer. He got an arm up and tried to shove the thing off; his fingers slipped on its slick, newborn skin. The weasel withdrew, tossed its head back, and swallowed what it had torn off like a parrot with a piece of raw steak. Freddy flailed for the driver's-side doorhandle and found it, but before he could yank it up the thing struck again, this time burying its mouth in the muscular flesh where Freddy's neck and shoulder merged. There was a vast jet of blood as his jugular opened; it spurted up to the Humvee's roof, then began to drip back like red rain.

Freddy's feet jittered, bopping the Humvee's wide brake in a rapid tapdance. The creature in the back seat drew back again, seemed to consider, then slithered snakelike over Freddy's shoulder. It dropped into his lap.

Freddy screamed once as the weasel tore off his plumbing . . . and then he screamed no more.

32

Henry sat twisted around in the back seat of the other Humvee, watching as the figure in the vehicle parked behind him jerked back and forth behind the wheel. Henry was glad of the thickly falling snow, equally glad of the blood that sprayed up, striking the windshield of the other Humvee, partially obscuring the view.

He could see all too well as it was.

At last the figure behind the wheel stopped moving and fell sideways. A bulky shadow rose over it, seeming to hulk in triumph. Henry knew what it was; he'd seen one on Jonesy's bed, back at Hole in the Wall. One thing he *could* see was that there was a broken window in the Humvee which had been chasing them. He doubted if the thing had much in the way of intelligence, but how much would it need to register fresh air?

They don't like the cold. It kills them.

Yes, indeed it did. But Henry had no intention of leaving it at that, and not just because the Reservoir was so close he could hear the water lapping on the rocks. Something had run up an extremely high debt, and only he was left to present the bill. Payback's a bitch, as Jonesy had so often observed, and payback time had arrived.

He leaned over the seat. No weapons there. He leaned over farther and thumbed open the glove compartment. Nothing in there but a litter of invoices, gasoline receipts, and a tattered paperback titled *How to Be Your Own Best Friend*.

Henry opened the door, got out into the snow . . . and his feet immediately flew out from under him. He went on his butt with a thump and scraped his back on the Hummer's high splashboard. Fuck me Freddy. He got up, slipped again, grabbed the top of the open door, and managed to stay afoot this time. He shuffled his feet around to the back of the vehicle he'd come in, never taking his eyes from its twin, parked behind. He could still see the thing inside, thrashing and shuffling, dining on the driver.

"Stay where you are, beautiful," Henry said, and began to laugh. The laughter sounded crazy as hell, but that didn't stop him. "Lay a few eggs. I am the eggman, after all. Your friendly neighborhood eggman. Or how about a copy of *How to Be Your Own Best Friend*? I got one."

Laughing so hard now he could barely speak. Sliding in the wet and treacherous snow like a kid let out of school and on his way to the nearest sledding hill. Holding onto the flank of the Hummer as best he could, except there was really nothing to hold onto once you were south of the doors. Watching the thing shift and move . . . and then he couldn't see it anymore. Oh-oh. Where the hell had it gotten to? *In one of Jonesy's dopey movies, this is where the scary music would start,* Henry thought. *Attack of the Killer Shit-Weasels.* That got him laughing again.

He was around to the back of the vehicle now. There was a button you could push to unlatch the rear window

. . . unless, of course, it was locked. Probably wasn't, though. Hadn't Owen gotten into the back this way? Henry couldn't remember. Couldn't for the life of him. He was clearly not being his own best friend.

Still cackling, fresh tears gushing out of his eyes, he thumbed the button and the back window popped open. Henry yanked it wider and looked in. Guns, thank God. Army carbines like the kind that Owen had taken on his last patrol. Henry grabbed one and examined it. Safety, check. Fire-selection switch, check. Clip marked U.S. ARMY 5.56 CAL 120 RNDS, check.

"So simple even a byrum can do it," Henry said, and laughed some more. He bent over, holding his stomach and slipping around in the slop, trying not to fall again. His legs ached, his back ached, his heart ached most of all . . . and still he laughed. He was the eggman, he was the eggman, he was the laughing hyena.

He walked around to the driver's side of Kurtz's Humvee, gun raised (safety in what he devoutly hoped was the OFF position), spooky music playing in his head, but still laughing. There was the gasoline hatch; no mistaking that. But where was Gamera, The Terror from Beyond Space?

As if it had heard his thought—and, Henry realized, that was perfectly likely—the weasel smashed headfirst against the rear window. The one that was, thankfully, unbroken. Its head was smeared with blood, hair, and bits of flesh. Its dreadful sea-grape eyes stared into Henry's. Did it know it had a way out, an escape hatch? Perhaps. And perhaps it understood that using it would likely mean a quick death.

It bared its teeth.

Henry Devlin, who had once won the American Psychiatric Association's Compassionate Caring Award for a *New York Times* op-ed piece called "The End of Hate," bared his own in return. It felt good. Then he gave it the finger. For Beaver. And for Pete. That felt good, too.

When he raised the carbine, the weasel—stupid, perhaps, but not *utterly* stupid—dove out of sight. That was cool; Henry had never had the slightest intention of trying to shoot it through the window. He *did* like the idea of it down there on the floor, though. *Close to the gas as you want to get, darling,* he thought. He thumbed the carbine's selector-switch to full auto and fired a long burst into the gas tank.

The sound of the gun was deafening. A huge ragged hole appeared where the gasoline port had been, but for a moment there was nothing else. *So much for the Hollywood version of how shit like this works,* Henry thought, and then heard a hoarse whisper of sound, rising to a throaty hiss. He took two steps backward and his feet shot out from under him again. This time falling quite likely saved his eyesight and perhaps his life. The back of Kurtz's Humvee exploded only a second later, fire lashing out from underneath in big yellow petals. The rear tires jumped out of the snow. Glass sprayed through the snowy air, all of it going over Henry's head. Then the heat began to bake him and he crawled away rapidly, dragging the carbine by its strap and laughing wildly. There was a second explosion and the air was filled with whirling hooks of shrapnel.

Henry got to his feet like a man climbing a ladder, using the lower branches of a handy tree as rungs. He stood, panting and laughing, legs aching, back aching, neck with an odd *sprung* feeling. The entire back half of Kurtz's Humvee was engulfed in flames. He could hear the thing inside, chittering furiously as it burned.

He made a wide circle to the passenger side of the blazing Humvee and aimed the carbine at the broken window. He stood there for a moment, frowning, then realized why this seemed so stupid. *All* the windows in the Humvee were broken now; all the glass but the windshield. He began to laugh again. What a dork he was! What a total dork!

Through the hell of flames in the Humvee's cabin, he could still see the weasel lurching back and forth like a drunk. How many rounds did he have left in the clip if the fucking thing *did* come out? Fifty? Twenty? Five? However many rounds there were, it would have to be enough. He wouldn't risk retreating to Owen's Humvee for another clip.

But the thing never came out.

Henry stood guard for five minutes, then stretched it to ten. The snow fell and the Humvee burned, pouring black smoke into the white sky. Henry stood there thinking of the Derry Days Parade, Gary U.S. Bonds singing "New Orleans," and here comes a tall man on stilts, here comes the legendary cowboy, and how excited Duddits had been, jumping right up and down. Thinking of Pete, standing outside DJHS, hands cupped, pretending to smoke, waiting for the rest of them. Pete, whose plan had been to captain NASA's first manned Mars expedition. Thinking of Beaver and his Fonzie jacket, Beav and his toothpicks, Beav singing to Duddits, Baby's boat's a silver dream. Beav hugging Jonesy at Jonesy's wedding and saying Jonesy had to be happy, he had to be happy for all of them.

Jonesy.

When Henry was absolutely sure the weasel was dead—incinerated—he started up the path to see if Jonesy was still alive. He didn't hold out much hope of that . . . but he discovered he hadn't given up hope, either.

33

Only pain pinned Jonesy to the world, and at first he thought the haggard, sooty-cheeked man kneeling beside him had to be a dream, or a final figment of his imagination. Because the man appeared to be Henry.

"Jonesy? Hey, Jonesy, are you there?" Henry snapped his fingers in front of Jonesy's eyes. "Earth to Jonesy."

"Henry, is it you? Is it really?"

"It's me," Henry said. He glanced at the dog still partly stuck into the crack at the top of Shaft 12, then back at Jonesy. He brushed Jonesy's sweat-soaked hair off his forehead with infinite tenderness.

"Man, it took you . . ." Jonesy began, and then the world wavered. He closed his eyes, concentrated hard, then opened them again. ". . . took you long enough to get back from the store. Did you remember the bread?"

"Yeah, but I lost the hot dogs."

"What a fuckin pisser." Jonesy took a long and wavering breath. "I'll go myself, next time."

"Kiss my bender, pal," Henry said, and Jonesy slipped into darkness smiling.

LABOR DAY

The universe, she is a bitch.

NORMAN MACLEAN

Another summer down the tubes, Henry thought.

There was nothing sad about the thought, though; summer had been good, and fall would be good, too. No hunting this year, and there would undoubtedly be the occasional visit from his new military friends (his new military friends wanted to be sure above all things that he wasn't growing any red foliage on his skin), but fall would be good just the same. Cool air, bright days, long nights.

Sometimes, in the post-midnight hours of his nights, Henry's old friend still came to visit, but when it did, he simply sat up in his study with a book in his lap and waited for it to go again. Eventually it always did. Eventually the sun always came up. The sleep you didn't get one night sometimes came to you on the next, and then it came like a lover. This was something he'd learned since last November.

He was drinking a beer on the porch of Jonesy and Carla's cottage in Ware, the one on the shore of Pepper Pond. The south end of the Quabbin Reservoir was about four miles northwest of where he sat. And East Street, of course.

The hand holding the can of Coors only had three fingers. He'd lost the two on the end to frostbite, perhaps while skiing out the Deep Cut Road from Hole in the Wall, perhaps while dragging Jonesy back to the remaining Humvee on a lashed-together travois. Last fall had been his season to drag people through the snow, it seemed, and with mixed results.

Near the little scrape of beach, Carla Jones was tending a barbecue. Noel, the baby, was toddling around the picnic table to her left, diaper sagging. He was waving a charred hot dog cheerily in one hand. The other three Jones kids, ranging in ages from eleven to three, were in the water, splashing around and yelling at each other. Henry supposed there might be some value to that Biblical imperative about being fruitful and multiplying, but it seemed to him that Jonesy and Carla had taken it to absurd lengths.

Behind him, the screen door clapped. Jonesy came out, carrying a bucket filled with iced beers. His limp wasn't all that bad; this time the doc had just said fuck the original equipment and had replaced the whole thing with steel and Teflon. It would have come to that, anyway, the doc had told Jonesy, but if you'd been a little more careful, Chief, you could've gotten another five years out of the old one. He'd had the operation in February, shortly after Henry and Jonesy's six-week "vacation" with the military intelligence and PsyOps people had ended.

The military folks had offered to throw in the hip replacement courtesy of Uncle Sam—sort of a coda to their debriefing—but Jonesy had refused with thanks, saying he wouldn't want to deprive his own orthopedist of the work, or his insurance company of the bill.

By then, all the two of them had wanted was to get out of Wyoming. The apartments were nice (if you could get used to living underground, that was), the food was four-star (Jonesy put on ten pounds, Henry close to twenty), and the movies were always first-run. The atmosphere, however, was just a teensy bit on the Dr. Strangelove side. For Henry, those six weeks had been infinitely worse than they had been for Jonesy. Jonesy suffered, but mostly with his derailed hip; his memories of sharing a body with Mr. Gray had faded to the consistency of dreams in a remarkably short space of time.

Henry's memories, on the other hand, had only grown stronger. Those of the barn were the worst. The debriefers had been compassionate, not a Kurtz in the bunch, but Henry couldn't block his thoughts of Bill and Marsha and Darren Chiles, Mr. Bomber-Joint-from-Newton. They often came to visit in his dreams.

So did Owen Underhill.

"Reinforcements," Jonesy said, setting the bucket of beer down. He then lowered himself into the sagging cane-bottomed rocker beside Henry with a grunt and a grimace.

"One more and I'm done," Henry said. "I'm driving back to Portland in an hour or so, and an OUI I don't need."

"Stay the night," Jonesy said, watching Noel. The baby had plumped down on the grass beneath the picnic table and now seemed intent upon inserting the remains of his hot dog into his navel.

"With your kids squabbling their way toward midnight and maybe beyond?" Henry asked. "Getting my pick of Mario Bava horror movies?"

"I've pretty well signed off the fright flicks," Jonesy said. "We're having a Kevin Costner festival tonight, starting with *The Bodyguard*."

"I thought you said no horror movies."

"Smartass." Then he shrugged, grinned. "Whatever you feel."

Henry raised his beer can. "Here's to absent friends."

Jonesy raised his own. "Absent friends."

They clinked cans and drank.

"How's Roberta?" Jonesy asked.

Henry smiled. "Doing very well. I had my doubts at the funeral . . ."

Jonesy nodded. At Duddits's funeral they had flanked her, and that had been a good thing, because Roberta had hardly been able to stand on her own.

". . . but now she's coming on strong. Talking about opening a craft shop. I think it's a good idea. Of course she misses him. After Alfie died, Duds was her life."

"He was ours, too," Jonesy said.

"Yes. I suppose he was."

"I feel so bad about the way we left him on his own all those years. I mean, he had leukemia and we didn't even fucking *know.*"

"Sure we knew," Henry said.

Jonesy looked at him, eyebrows raised.

"Hey, Henry!" Carla called. "How do you want your burger?"

"Cooked!" he yelled back.

"I will make it so, sire. Would you be a love and get the baby? That hot dog's rapidly turning into a dirt-dog. Take it away from him and give him to his Dad."

Henry went down the steps, fished Noel out from under the table, and carried him back toward the porch.

"Ennie!" Noel cried brightly. He was now eighteen months old.

Henry stopped, feeling a chill spread up his back. It was as if he had been hailed by a ghost.

"Eee foo, Ennie! Eee *foo!*" Noel bopped Henry briskly on the nose with his dirt-dog to underline the thrust of his thesis.

"I'll wait for my burger, thanks," he said, and resumed walking.

"No eee my foo?"

"Ennie eee his own foo, honeybunch. But maybe I ought to have that nasty thing. You can have another one as soon as they're ready." He tweezed the dirt-dog out of Noel's little hand, then plumped him down in Jonesy's lap and resumed his seat. By the time Jonesy had finished swabbing mustard and ketchup out of his son's belly-button, the kid was almost asleep.

"What did you mean, 'Sure we knew'?" Jonesy asked.

"Ah, Jonesy, come on. Maybe we left him, or tried, but do you think Duddits ever left us? After all that happened, do you really believe that?"

Very slowly, Jonesy shook his head.

"Some of it was growing up—growing apart—but some of it was the Richie Grenadeau thing. That worked on us the way the business of the Rapeloews' serving platter worked on Owen Underhill."

Jonesy didn't need to ask what this meant; in Wyoming, they'd had all the time they needed to catch up on each other's story.

"There's an old poem about a man trying to outrun God," Henry said. " 'The Hound of Heaven,' it's called. Duddits wasn't God—God forbid—but he was our hound. We ran as fast and as far as we could, but—"

"We could never run off the dreamcatcher, could we?" Jonesy said. "None of us could do that. And then *they* came. The byrum. Stupid spores in space-ships built by some other race. Is that what they were? *All* they were?"

"I don't think we'll ever know. Only one question got answered last fall. For centuries we've looked up at the stars and asked ourselves if we're alone in the universe. Well, now we know we're not. Big whoop, huh? Gerritsen . . . do you remember Gerritsen?"

Jonesy nodded. Of course he remembered Terry Gerritsen. Navy psychologist, in charge of the

Wyoming debriefing team, always joking about how typical it was that Uncle Sammy would post him to a place where the nearest water was Lars Kilborn's cow-wallow. Gerritsen and Henry had become close—if not quite friends, only because the situation didn't quite allow it. Jonesy and Henry had been well-treated in Wyoming, but they hadn't been guests. Still, Henry Devlin and Terry Gerritsen were professional colleagues, and such things made a difference.

"Gerritsen started by assuming *two* questions had been answered: that we're not alone in the universe and that we're not the only intelligent beings in the universe. I labored hard to convince him that the second postulate was based on faulty logic, a house built on sand. I don't think I entirely succeeded in getting through, but I may have planted a seed of doubt, at least. Whatever else the byrum may be, they're not shipbuilders, and the race that built the ships may be gone. May in fact be byrum themselves by now."

"Mr. Gray wasn't stupid."

"Not once he got inside your head, that much I agree with. Mr. Gray was *you*, Jonesy. He stole your emotions, your memories, your taste for bacon—"

"I don't eat it anymore."

"I'm not surprised. He also stole your basic personality. That included the subconscious kinks. Whatever there is in you that liked the Mario Bava horror movies and the Sergio Leone westerns, whatever it is that got off on the fear and the violence . . . man, Mr. Gray *loved* that shit. And why wouldn't he? Those things are primitive survival tools. As the last of his kind in a hostile environment, he grabbed every damned tool he could lay his hands on."

"Bullshit." Jonesy's dislike of this idea was plain on his face.

"It's not. At Hole in the Wall, you saw what you expected to see, which was an *X-Files*–slash–*Close Encounters of the Third Kind* alien. You inhaled the byrus . . . I have no doubt there was at least that much physical contact . . . but you were completely immune to it. As, we now know, at least fifty percent of the human race seems to be. What you caught was an intention . . . a kind of blind imperative. Fuck, there's no word for it, because there's no word for *them*. But I think it got in because you *believed* it was there."

"You are telling me," Jonesy said, looking at Henry over the top of his sleeping son's head, "that I almost destroyed the human race because I had a hysterical pregnancy?"

"Oh, no," Henry said. "If that had been all, it would have passed off. Would have amounted to no more than a . . . a fugue. But in you, the idea of Mr. Gray stuck like a fly in a spiderweb."

"It stuck in the dreamcatcher."

"Yes."

They fell quiet. Soon Carla would call them and they would eat hot dogs and hamburgers, potato salad and watermelon, beneath the blue shield of the infinitely permeable sky.

"And will you say it was all coincidence?" Jonesy asked. "That they just happened to come down in the

Jefferson Tract and I just happened to be there? And not just me, either. You and Peter and Beav. Plus Duddits, just a couple of hundred miles to the south, don't forget that. Because it was Duddits who held us together."

"Duddits was always a sword with two edges," Henry said. "Josie Rinkenhauer on one—Duddits the finder, Duddits the savior. Richie Grenadeau on the other—Duddits the killer. Only Duddits needed us to help him kill. I'm sure of that. We were the ones with the deeper subconscious layer. We supplied the hate and the fear—the fear that Richie really *would* get us, the way he promised he would. We always had more of the dark stuff than Duds. His idea of being mean was counting your crib backward, and that was more in the spirit of fun than anything else. Still . . . do you remember the time Pete pulled Duddits's hat over his eyes and Duds walked into the wall?"

Jonesy did, vaguely. Out at the mall, that had been. When they had been young and the mall had been the place to go. Same shit, different day.

"For quite awhile after that, Pete lost whenever we played the Duddits game. Duddits *always* counted him backward, and none of us tipped to it. We probably thought it was just coincidence, but in light of everything I know now, I tend to doubt that."

"You think even Duddits knew payback's a bitch?"

"He learned it from us, Jonesy."

"Duddits gave Mr. Gray his foothold. His *mindhold*."

"Yeah, but he also gave *you* a stronghold—a place where you could hide from Mr. Gray. Don't forget that."

No, Jonesy thought, he would never forget that.

"All of it on our end started with Duddits," Henry said. "We've been odd, Jonesy, ever since we knew him. You know it's true. The things with Richie Grenadeau were only the big things, the ones that stood out. If you look back over your life, you'll see other things. I'm sure of it."

"Defuniak," Jonesy murmured.

"Who's that?"

"The kid I caught cheating just before my accident. I caught him even though I wasn't there on the day the test was given."

"You see? But in the end, it was Duddits who broke the little gray son of a bitch. I'll tell you something else: I think Duddits saved my life at the end of East Street. I think it's entirely possible that when Kurtz's sidekick looked into the back of the Humvee at us—the first time, I'm talking about—he had a little Duddits in his head saying 'Don't worry, old hoss, go on about your business, they dead.' "

But Jonesy had not left his earlier thought. "And are we supposed to believe that the byrum connecting with us—us, of all the people in the world—was just random coincidence? Because that's what Gerritsen believed. He never said it in so many words, but his take on it was clear enough."

"Why not? There are scientists, brilliant men like Stephen Jay Gould, who believe that our own species exists thanks to an even longer and more improbable chain of coincidences."

"Is that what you believe?"

Henry lifted his hands. He hardly knew how to reply without invoking God, who had crept back into his life over these last few months. By the back door, as it were, and in the dead of many sleepless nights. But did one have to invoke that old *deus ex machina* to make sense of this?

"What I believe is that Duddits is *us,* Jonesy. *L'enfant c'est moi . . . toi . . . tout le monde.* Race, species, genus; game, set, and match. We are, in our sum, Duddits, and all our noblest aspirations come down to no more than keeping track of the yellow lunchbox and learning to put our shoes on the right way—fit wha, fit neek. Our wickedest motions, in a cosmic sense, come down to no more than counting someone's crib, pegging it backward, then playing dumb about it."

Jonesy was regarding him with fascination. "That's either inspiring or horrible. I can't tell which."

"And it doesn't matter."

Jonesy thought about this, then asked: "If we're Duddits, who sings to us? Who sings the lullaby, helps us go to sleep when we're sad and scared?"

"Oh, God still does that," Henry said, and could have kicked himself. There it was, out in spite of all his intentions.

"And did God keep that last weasel out of Shaft 12? Because if that thing had gotten in the water, Henry—"

Technically, the weasel that had incubated inside of Perlmutter had actually been the last, but it was a fine point, a hair that needed no splitting.

"It would have caused trouble, I don't dispute that; for a couple of years, whether or not to tear down Fenway Park would have been the least of Boston's concerns. But destroy us? I don't think so. We were a new thing to them. Mr. Gray knew it; those tapes of you under hypnosis—"

"Don't talk about those." Jonesy had listened to two of them, and believed doing so had been the biggest mistake he'd made during his time in Wyoming. Listening to himself speak as Mr. Gray—under deep hypnosis to *become* Mr. Gray—had been like listening to a malevolent ghost. There were times when he thought he might be the only man on earth who truly understood what it was to be raped. Some things were better forgotten.

"Sorry."

Jonesy waved his hand to show it was okay—not a problem—but he had paled considerably.

"All I'm saying is that, to a greater or lesser degree, we are a *species* living in the dreamcatcher. I hate the way that sounds, phony transcendentalism, rings on the ear like pure tin, but we don't have the right words for this part of it, either. We may have to invent some eventually, but in the meantime, *dreamcatcher* will have to do."

Henry turned in his seat. Jonesy did the same, shifting Noel a little bit on his lap. A dreamcatcher hung over the door to the cabin. Henry had brought it as a house present, and Jonesy had put it up at once, like a Catholic peasant nailing a crucifix to the door of his cottage during a time of vampires.

"Maybe they were just drawn to you," Henry said. "To *us*. The way flowers turn to follow the sun, or the way iron filings line up when they feel the pull of a magnet. We can't tell for sure, because the byrum is so different from us."

"Will they be back?"

"Oh yes," Henry said. "Them or others."

He looked up at the blue sky of this late-summer day. Somewhere in the distance, toward the Quabbin Reservoir, an eagle screamed. "I think you can take that to the bank. But not today."

"Guys!" Carla shouted. "Lunch is ready!"

Henry took Noel from Jonesy. For a moment their hands touched, their eyes touched, and their minds touched—for a moment they saw the line. Henry smiled. Jonesy smiled back. Then they walked down the steps and across the lawn side by side, Jonesy limping, Henry with the sleeping child in his arms, and for that moment the only darkness was their shadows trailing behind them on the grass.

Lovell, Maine
May 29, 2000

AUTHOR'S NOTE

I was never so grateful to be writing as during my time of work (November 16, 1999–May 29, 2000) on *Dreamcatcher*. I was in a lot of physical discomfort during those six and a half months, and the book took me away. The reader will see that pieces of that physical discomfort followed me into the story, but what I remember most is the sublime release we find in vivid dreams.

A good many people helped me. One was my wife, Tabitha, who simply refused to call this novel by its original title, which was *Cancer*. She considered it both ugly and an invitation to bad luck and trouble. Eventually I came around to her way of thinking, and she no longer refers to it as "that book" or "the one about the shit-weasels."

I'm also indebted to Bill Pula, who took me four-wheeling at the Quabbin Reservoir, and to his cohorts, Peter Baldracci, Terry Campbell, and Joe McGinn. Another group of people, who would perhaps prefer not to be named, took me out behind the Air National Guard base in a Humvee, and foolishly let me drive, assuring me I couldn't get the beast stuck. I didn't, but it was close. I came back mudsplattered and happy. They would also want me to tell you that Hummers are better in mud than in snow; I have fictionalized their capabilities in that regard to suit the course of my fiction.

Thanks are also in order to Susan Moldow and Nan Graham at Scribner, to Chuck Verrill, who edited the book, and to Arthur Greene, who agented it. And I mustn't forget Ralph Vicinanza, my foreign rights agent, who found at least six ways to say "There is no infection here" in French.

One final note. This book was written with the world's finest word processor, a Waterman cartridge fountain pen. To write the first draft of such a long book by hand put me in touch with the language as I haven't been for years. I even wrote one night (during a power outage) by candlelight. One rarely finds such opportunities in the twenty-first century, and they are to be savored.

And to those of you who have come so far, thank you for reading my story.

Stephen King